# Building It All From Scraps

# Building It All From Scraps

To chase, to embrace, to savor the deepest passions of her heart, a quirky carpenter's daughter builds her social work career and captivates the love of her life, in this vibrant and comical celebration of Gay Pride! Set at the Jersey Shore in the 1970's and 1980's, this campy fiction revels in the clash of the Sexual Revolution, balancing disco community and true love, with family life and working class values. But no good deed goes unpunished, as Jordan Mathews' career evolves into an outrageous battle of office politics — and only the power of love survives! The result is a humorous and solidifying testimonial to all Gay people, an educational and informative book for all human service workers, and a great piece of philosophical entertainment for those who are neither.

A variety of social issues—and especially, issues affecting Gay people—are presented in the Appendix and Bibliography section of the book. These condensed, professional articles are easily read and readily understood by all. They form a great reference, and serve as a political history and social commentary for Gay people everywhere. But you don't have to use the Appendix to enjoy this wonderful story about human relationships. You just have to know about love.

A Gay Social Work Love Story

# Building It All From Scraps

Beverly Ann Kessler

Copyright © 2010 by Beverly Ann Kessler.

Library of Congress Control Number: 2010900837
ISBN: Hardcover 978-1-4500-3050-2
Softcover 978-1-4500-3049-6

All rights reserved. No part of this book may be reproduced or transmitted in any form or by any means, electronic or mechanical, including photocopying, recording, or by any information storage and retrieval system, without permission in writing from the copyright owner.

This is a work of fiction. Names, characters, places and incidents either are the product of the author's imagination or are used fictitiously, and any resemblance to any actual persons, living or dead, events, or locales is entirely coincidental.

This book was printed in the United States of America.

**To order additional copies of this book, contact:**
Xlibris Corporation
1-888-795-4274
www.Xlibris.com
Orders@Xlibris.com

68989

# CONTENTS

Building It All From Scraps ................................................................ 2
Acknowledgments ............................................................................. 9

Chapter 1 ......................................................................................... 13
Chapter 2 ......................................................................................... 45
Chapter 3 ......................................................................................... 84
Chapter 4 ....................................................................................... 142
Chapter 5 ....................................................................................... 191
Chapter 6 ....................................................................................... 215
Chapter 7 ....................................................................................... 242
Chapter 8 ....................................................................................... 304
Chapter 9 ....................................................................................... 360
Chapter 10 ..................................................................................... 426

Epilogue ........................................................................................ 478
Appendix and Bibliography ........................................................... 489
For Quick Reference:
    Article Listings in Appendix and Bibliography ......................... 561

This book is dedicated to

Deborah Elise Hill
June 11, 1953—May 4, 1974

Isabel Margarita Antonia Hernandez Cordero
a.k.a Elizabeth "Cord" Cordero
August 24, 1955—November 13, 1990

Robert J. Kessler
August 29, 1923—May 2, 1989

Whose love and laughter so enriched my life,
and whose cancers took them from me all too soon.

And to all gay people who strive for connection, love, and life,
despite the impossible obstacles put before them—and to their friends and
family who stand beside them as they weather the storm.

# Acknowledgments

As you stand before the mirror on the your 55th year, you peer through the wrinkles, the frown lines, those smiley crinkles, and take full stock of where you've been, and where you're going. You shake your head at the graying nap just above the brows, walk slowly to the kitchen, grab your third cup of coffee, and climb the creaky stairs (or was that your knees?) toward den and computer. You can't help but look back over the relationships you've shared, the people you've loved, the hopes at the start, the events that brought meaning to your life. And as you look across your life, your mind's eye catches full glimpse of your profession, the bread and butter that carried you to this point. After all, for almost 30 years you have dedicated to it nearly every cognitive moment not absorbed in family, friends, or chores. It's all so intertwined, the tapestry of life. But what does it all mean?

Loving Social Work is like having a bad relationship. No one respects you. No one thanks you. No one rewards or even acknowledges you . . . at least not usually. But you try to stick with it in the hope that things will get better. Sometimes it does get better, and you're thankful that you made the investment; sometimes it doesn't, and you're thankful that you moved on to something else. Who knows why you stay, or why you go? In relationships as in profession, you can only answer that question for yourself. For me, the answer came easily—I wanted to make a difference! And I am from a generation that believed that such things were possible. And I am from a minority who now believes that such things must happen.

So I found myself at my computer, a million ideas, and huge chunks of time now not being filled by service to others. And so I thought, if I could start over, what would I do differently? And how could I share what I've learned with social workers at the start of the arc that I am now completing. And how could I help young gay people, professional or not, meet the challenges of daily life here on earth—hence, the purposes of this book. Sure, it sounds idealistic, even grandiose! But you have to start with a goal, and the loftier, the better! That's the basis for the whole "a person's reach should exceed his grasp" thing! Besides, we all like that stuff—the high ideals, I mean. That's where we all start, really, but who knows at the start what the end piece will be?

Let me clarify that this is a literary fiction, and not an autobiography. My intent is both to entertain and to educate. Yes, this is a gay social work love story! Although the economic, social, and professional backgrounds are similar to my own, the similarities end there. I took what I had, I used what I knew, and I made use of those resources to construct a story. And I use the story to offer life affirmations and social work lessons not taught in class. But I also use this backdrop to emphasize that healthy gay relationships, committed relationships, exist all around us. We are everywhere, and in all walks of life. I hope that young gay people will find validation in living their lives as they were intended—with pride, with wholeness, with meaning, and with integrity. And I hope that non-gay persons and professionals will learn about Gay culture, so that fear, and prejudice, and myth will be healed. I chose the 1970's, because they were a growing time for Gay Pride and for Social Work. Much of the history of both is included here.

And so, I offer this book to you, in the hope that my observations might help further your careers and your relationships—and like that Social Work Everyman Jordan Mathews, you may push humanity forward with the sweat of your brow, the work of your hands, the creativity of your mind, and the love in your heart. I offer this to you, so that you may find the peace of knowing who you are, and loving yourself because of it.

I would like to thank the many friends in the profession and in the gay community who contributed stories, offered advice, and helped to edit this book. I caution that any resemblance of characters to any parties living or dead is purely coincidental. The characters are actually composites of personality traits, and no parody is intended. But, if you see a phrase, or catch a quirk, or find a hint of your own humor here, it is only because you have captured a place in my heart. Either that, or you're projecting . . . !

Special thanks to my clients, and especially, to the children whom I have had the privilege of working with throughout my career. Each of you is special in this world, and you should know that! Thanks to the many mentors who have guided me along my professional journey. And thanks, too, to my adversaries throughout the years, for you have been my strongest advocates. We all owe thanks to the many social advocates, who work tirelessly to improve the lives of all people every day. We are diversity, and we are the better for it. Because of their efforts, Gay people now share a place at this table.

If you thumb through the Appendix and Bibliography section of this book, you will find scraps of the wisdom of the profession. I do hope that you will use this section as a professional resource. But even if you aren't in Social Work, you can still enjoy it as a great source of information. The abridged articles can be understood by everyone! I wish to thank each author for the contributions that they have made not only to this book, but to society. You have truly helped guide a generation of new social workers toward its highest standards, and we are the better for it. You have helped Gay people find their place at the table, and humanity is the better for it. And thanks also to the staff at Ocean County Library for helping to bring these works to my—and now, to your—attention. I am the better for it.

Lastly, heartfelt thanks to my family, and especially to my life partner (and editor!) without whose patience, support, humor, and organization, this book would not have been possible. You have been my inspiration—but you already know that!

* * *

Post Script: While the movement for Marriage Equality has been dealt some horrendous blows in the past year, do not lose sight of the success of the Movement itself. We are continuously marching forward in acknowledgment of our healthy existence, in recognition of our every day contributions to society, and in acceptance of our right to exist on equal terms with all other human beings. We may have temporarily lost the battle, but overall, we are winning this war of respect and human dignity. We love you, Steve Goldstein and Garden State Equality. You have done us proud.

# Chapter 1

She was a helper, and had been one all of her life. You know the type—somebody trips and sprawls across the sidewalk, and everybody laughs their asses off! Everybody, that is, but her... She'd be the one to shoot caustic looks at the crowd, and then nearly genuflect as she helped the poor klutz to his feet! Or maybe the wind would snatch a $10 bill from a knurled and elderly hand. Now other feet might trounce on that bill in hopes of acquisition. But not her! She would leap a turnstile, plow through a line like a defensive tackle, practically throw herself right onto the tracks just to retrieve that cash—and then, only to return it to its rightful owner! Some kid was beaten out of his lunch money, or mocked out till he cried? She would rise as his champion, his shield from the hurt, keeping each and every lowlife jerk off the poor kid's back! A friend needed a ride to the bus? "Hey, no problem!" She'd drive them passed the bus stop and to their destination, even an hour away! She was mesmerized by her own goodness, but the world despised her for it! Yet she would remain true to this basic tenet, and the world, at least in her eyes, was the better for it. She would be the example, the bar by which all others should be measured. She would be the saving grace of her civilization, that proverbial barrier between humanity and cannibalism. She was, for all intents and purposes, the last safety net in the very fabric of society. She was prepared to be a martyr to that cause, and that would be the cause of her demise. But enough of that for now—she wanted to concentrate on life in the present.

She refused to stumble through life in sublime oblivion. No, she wanted to embrace life, to wrap her arms and legs around it, to fold her mind and body

13

through it, to drip heart and soul into it like some Dali painting! She wanted to drink from the fountain, to lap up the energies that all life could offer, and to chug it down fast and furious. She just didn't know how . . . And she was drawn to the Arts and Humanities. Maybe this was a kind of compensation for the frustration that she felt growing every day. She was a loner of sorts, never really feeling comfortable in the company of her peers, and yet never really feeling comfortable alone. Shy, yet drawn to connection, she struggled with this diametric opposition in the hopes that she would one day find the key to her life. She stood as the perpetual outsider, an observer, an analyzer, but never a participant. Life bounced off of her. She was not allowed, or would not allow, any direct contact with it. Books told her how to think; poets stenciled her soul; artists defined her sense of beauty. But she never really found these things out for herself. She was the frame on which her culture displayed itself. She was not the culture. Affected upon, and never effecting—that was her lot in life! Of course, she didn't know it then. She was too steeped in the quest to find true meaning! And ultimately, she decided that that meaning would come from service to others. As she stood back, she viewed herself, and the world around her, with an awe and a wonder—while the world laughed at her behind her back.

So, it shouldn't have been a surprise really, looking back on it now, that she would be drawn to Social Work. Here she would find her true calling, the canvas on which she could paint the meaning of her life, the avenue by which she would claim her place in the universe! She stood out like trouble whenever she walked through a door. But sometimes, the only thing you can do is stand back and let the forces of the universe manifest themselves through the one who sets herself apart. And yes, the world would do some serious ass kicking here.

Her name was Jordan Mathews—a rather strong sounding name for someone so secretly lacking. She often felt that she had to stretch herself in some way just to fit into it. Her parents believed in the destiny of a name, and thought that this strength might help guide her. There was no pattern to the name. No family connection, except, of course, to the father's lineage. Not that lineage really mattered. She was working class, but she didn't really know what that meant until years later. Her parents never really knew what that meant. They raised her on the premise that all opportunity would be open to her, within her grasp, and just ripe for the plucking! Why, even presidents could be made from the likes of her! So, of course, she had high expectations. She had a college degree from a non-Ivy League school, but she was the first in her family to have gotten so far. Yes, they all had great expectations of her. And this certainly weighed more heavily into the emptiness that she felt growing each day. Strive as she might, the world would not accept her. They would work her, they would pay her, but they would never let her play. You see, she was not one of them.

She stumbled onto her profession, really. In the early seventies, women were just emerging in numbers in the work force. And given the cultural lag, the best that could be expected of a girl like Jordan was that she would mature early, marry relatively young, birth some children, and wife her husband. But here, too, Jordan didn't seem to make the "right choices." She remained young, athletic, distant, and unresponsive to the advances of the young men in her neighborhood. Yet, she was not prepared to deal with the meaning or consequences of those decisions. She heard the silent voices of her heart, but she could not listen to them. She focused instead, on completing college. She had partial financial assistance in the form of loans. She worked part time as a cashier in a pharmacy her family had used since at least her birth. She had continuity, and she would not gamble on a relationship that would distract her from her goals. Her parents did not support her in this quest, and they swarmed on her like Jersey mosquitoes.

"Whadeya gonna do with a college degree when your kids are born?" her mother asked. "And who's gonna cook and clean? Bein' a wife and mother is hard enough, ya know, without addin' a full time job to it."

The poor woman—too much change way too fast for her to comprehend the real opportunities that might lie ahead.

"And how's your husband gonna handle your education? Ya don't want him to feel inferior. He'll still be the head of the house, ya know, regardless of your degree," her father chided.

He didn't want his oldest daughter living in some make-believe world, where women might actually have a say over their own lives.

Her parents wanted answers, and so did she! But her life, as it began revealing itself to her, would be far different from their own. And she would make no apologies, once she accepted the truth of her being. There would be no place for a husband or children in her plan. After all, her goal was to save the world, not to populate it. Yeah, she could hide behind that excuse.

She didn't share her goal with her family at first. She wanted to be a writer, but didn't have the confidence to pursue that goal. She often imagined, though, her million-and-two seller on the shelves of the local W.T. Grant store. A banner across the store front would feature "A new book by the most seriously acclaimed author of our time." And of course, there would be the portrait of the author posted on the window, glasses held in one hand, with glass frame held in mouth, a coy smile, and a caption simply reading "Jordan Mathews." That fantasy would remain in her mind, but she would ultimately gain acclaim by writing a different kind of book much later in her career.

No, she couldn't be a writer. She considered being a teacher, until she tried student teaching. But the very thought of standing and speaking in front of a huge group of kids generated such a panic that she had violent nausea and vomiting for days before. She tried to dismiss this as the flu, or maybe even food poisoning from the college cafeteria (not so unlikely), but inside, she knew the truth. She loved children, but she could not be open to them. You see, children have that uncanny ability to see, and to say, way too much. Besides, she couldn't handle being in front of a crowd of any age, any way. She realized that she would need to be a behind-the-scenes change agent. She would later learn that the world has a way of ferreting out such people.

And so it went. She experimented with Philosophy, Political Science, Sociology—but none offered that connection to other people that she so craved. She began panicking, as sophomore year came to a close, and still, no major selected. Her family continued their pressure to have her succeed on their terms, offering yet each and another neighborhood boy as a probable success candidate as husband and breadwinner. Her family did not understand her drive. And for the most part, neither did she. But silently, in the quietest moments of her thinking, she heard her destiny: she would be a helper to others. She believed this mission would allow no space for a husband, and in some ways she was right. But that decision might also have been a matter of some convenience. She could avoid intimacy. She liked men, but she never wanted to own one. Marital success ratios were not a factor in her plan.

She took several pre-Social Work classes at the county college before she shared her goal with her family. She knew they wouldn't really understand her choice. She was aware of her parents' social conscience. After all, she and her family had watched the evening news together each night after dinner. There would be the usual parade of robberies, cheats, murders, protests and general mayhem, to which her parents shook their heads in disgust.

"How could all this be happenin' here in our own country? Doesn't anyone believe in decency anymore? Don't the rules matter?" her mother asked.

Poor woman—the world was so different for her now.

"And where'd all those long-haired jerks come from in the first place? Damn hippies are ruinin' this country! The whole world gets more and more ridiculous... Things would be different if Patton was here," her father would comment.

Everything was changing so quickly! To him, the whole place had just gone damn crazy!

Then came the nightly treat, the global news, a synopsis of America and the true state of the world. Jordan held her breath with each headline, she cringed with each news story flashed on the screen. Vietnam was a favorite topic. Not that her folks were war mongers, but they did consider themselves patriots. Like all of their generation, they had fought the Big One. Her father was a decorated WWII veteran, the winner of two purple hearts. He often entertained neighbors, friends, relatives—even strangers on line in the A&P—with his stories of his march through Europe. He had a real knack for turning things like a two-for-one coupon sale into the Battle of the Bulge! By the time he hit the register, you'd swear you'd "hit the beach" with him on D-Day. Her mother had been a member of the Church League's Buy Bonds Program. They were just your typical, working class Americans. And Jordan loved them with all that she was.

These were two people who did not understand the anti-war movement at all. Of course, they were just Jordan's age, when they fought their own war. Then they went through Korea, and now, they were facing this one! And let's not forget—they started their lives during the Depression! Jordan actually had a hard time believing how her parents, just kids themselves then, could have accomplished so much, and in the face of such adversity. She envied them in some ways, for their unity of purpose, their oneness of spirit, with what would later be called the "Greatest Generation." She never felt such unity with her own peers. Yeah, she was one of the "Baby Boomers," but what was that supposed to mean? She never felt connection with them, not even at the few peace marches she secretly attended at the state capitol. But still, she'd hop in the van with Ban-the-Bomb Stan, and proudly, she'd take her place among the high school intellectual elite.

"What do we want?" the organizers barked.

"World Peace!" the protestors shouted.

"When do we want it?" they prompted again.

"NOW!" came the shouts, as fists darted skyward.

She screamed the slogans till her throat was raw, but somehow, the sentiment never really stuck in her brain or lodged in her heart. She supposed that peace was a good thing, though. So, she shouted the slogans, she held the picket signs, she held the hands of the Friends as they marched and sang against the war, but inside, she had no deep sense of commitment or connection to anything. She felt two dimensional, in a world where everyone else had three dimensions. Jordan was halfway through high school by then, and hoped that with age and maturity, she would evolve into that three dimensional being. But there was something that held her back from this growth of spirit, even for years beyond college.

The TV news brought other issues into her home, too. There were the marches for civil rights, the riots in Watts, Newark, and Detroit, and the assassinations of Martin Luther King Jr., Malcolm X, and Jack and Bobby Kennedy. There were space flights and moon walks, Black and Gray Panthers, student protests, Women's Rights, the UCLA sit-ins, the Democratic National Convention takeover, demonstrations, campaigns, campus riots, elections, George Wallace, the Summer Of Love—all a swirl in the mind of young Jordan, and a source of real controversy in the family.[1] Her parents took a peculiar stance of supporting civil rights in the cities, but they were less magnanimous in their own town. There were issues of mixed marriage, economics, property values, and crime, you see. Her father was a carpenter, and he had worked with many people of color. He respected a working man, regardless of his race. He did not believe that there were real issues of discrimination, because he had never knowingly witnessed such things. A man worked hard and was paid, simple as that. Her mother was raised in the city, and proudly stated that she had several Negro friends growing up, and that there were never any problems.

"Those girls could play ball better then some of the majors," her mother would say. "And could they cook, and sing, and dance!" Her mother genuinely envied these skills.

They took real offense, though, to the Kerner Commission. "Do ya believe that they're blamin' white people for the ghettos and the riots? There they are—lootin',

---

[1] Historical context for this chapter was accessed from: Braunstein, Peter, et.al. (2004). *The Sixties Chronicle*. Lincolnwood, Illinois: Legacy Publications, Publications International Ltd.

shootin', and killin' their own. I don't get it," her father commented. "Just like some people to blame everybody else for their own problems."

Jordan slowly bowed her head in silent disbelief.

Her mother was less judgmental, and could at least relate to the desperation of poverty.

"I don't know, Pete. After all," she would say, "look at all the winters we had trouble buyin' food an' oil, 'cause ya didn't have work."

Jordan silently nodded in response.

"Maybe, but I didn't go tear-assin' the neighborhood! . . . What's burnin' down your own place gonna do? Now there's really nothin' there for 'em! I think that they should just move outta the city, and get a job. There's your answer!"

Some answer—Jordan couldn't imagine any of the neighbors hiring the rioters, and they sure weren't going to let them live next door. So her father's plan was a puzzlement to her!

"How would that work, Dad? I mean, where would they go?" Jordan challenged.

"There's still plentya places around where people can build a house. You don't haveta worry about that!"

Jordan didn't press him on the practicalities. She knew that he would never believe that a person would treat another human being with such hatred and disrespect, just because of their color. He would never think that that happened . . . except maybe down south.

Her parents had even less tolerance for Mohammad Ali's refusal to be drafted, despite the fact that they had cheered him as Cassius Clay right up to his world heavyweight title—although they much preferred Saturday Night Wrestling.

Jordan would often participate in these debates among her family members. She welcomed the chance to preach and convert. For the most part, though, her sister Kelly and brother Jonathan were more interested in the commercials and nightly line-up. They were young enough, and lucky enough, to remain spectators in this daily contest between generations. Her father would usually lead off the challenge with a comment that seemed like a line drive to center field.

"Wouldya look at those troublemakers traipsin' across the screen? What is it that they want now?" He'd lean his body toward the right side of his recliner, look over his baggy jeans and orange-stained white socks, and look right into Jordan, as if she were the spokesman for her whole generation. She braced herself.

"Well, what is it that anyone wants, Dad? A decent job, for a decent wage, a decent home, and a decent place to raise their kids," she hit back. She knew she should have dodged the comment, but her father would only have rocketed another statement at her. Besides, she loved the man, and loved their conversations together.

"Is that what ya think, or what they're tellin' ya to think in that Humanities class at high school?" He had only limited respect for the Arts of any kind. If you couldn't build it from wood, keep it together with a nail, or cut it with a 7 $^{1/4}$" circular, it was of no use. Not that he expected Jordan to follow in the family business. But he did believe that her someday husband would. It had been that way for generations. At one point, the Mathews family could pull together a whole construction project, using uncles, cousins, in-laws, etc. for electrical, plumbing, framing, sheet rocking, masonry, and whatever else was needed. But at least her father knew that she was taking a Humanities class.

"It's very simple, Dad. Just look at what people need. If they have it, they're not riotin'. If they don't have it, they are. Look at you and Mom. Ya work, ya got a house, ya got at least one good kid, and are ya riotin'? No. So there ya have it. Proof positive!" Jordan replied with the smugness of the Sultan of Swat.

"Ya still didn't answer my question. Is that what ya think, or what they're tellin' ya to think?" He continued to drill her. He might have been a patriot, but he also had a healthy paranoia about governments of any kind. "My country love it or leave it" really only went so far with him. And he loved to challenge her. He would sometimes take the opposing view just to incite a riot in his own house!

He loved to hear her fire back the liberal position, knowing full well, that she understood only a fraction of what she said. Jordan was very good at mimicry.

"Of course it's what I think, she replied, "but we have been discussing such things in class, if that's your real question." She used her most uppity attitude. She knew he was monitoring all of their classes. He had not much education himself, having had to strike off early to help support his family as a child. So he valued an education, even if he didn't believe in the practicality of it for his daughters.

And so it would go—the conversations would run the gamut, from politics and social commentary, to religion and ethics, from racial equality and economic entrapment, to war atrocities and the strive to survive—whatever Cronkite would put before the public each night. And with each night, Jordan stepped closer to the formation of her own sense of political rightness, of moral judgment, and of her destiny in the universe. She would be a helper in every sense of the word! Yeah, she could hide herself behind that line, too!

So although the announcement came as quite a shock to her parents, it really should not have been so unexpected. A better educated couple would have surmised her direction, but Jordan's parents had little idea really of what a social worker was. Now a teacher . . . that was something you could assess from experience. Her parents had both attended school for at least 10 years. A teacher could marry a man of some stature, perhaps a master carpenter or electrician. She could have her babies and return to the job when they were grown. Both had known married teachers. And both believed Jordan was going to college to be a teacher. They could not understand her change in plan, and this underscored their belief that while schooling was positive, college was excessive. Jordan could already feel the stress of impending separation from her parents' world.

"No, I won't be goin' to college for four years to be a welfare worker."

Her mother cringed and her father shuttered at the very thought that any of their children would engage in activities that might support someone's lack of drive, as they called it.

"I may be goin' to college for four years to help develop programs that bring people back to the workforce," Jordan explained. She hoped they would not see as manipulative, her effort to tie her career goals to the WPA or other Roosevelt type program. Jordan had not intended the comment to manipulate, but rather, to help define her goals in terms that her parents might better understand.

"Maybe I'll help improve a neighborhood by coalition building, or create greater access to education and economic opportunity, by helping to remove barriers like hatred and prejudice."

Her parents remained incredulous.

"Or maybe I'll develop programs to improve the housing stock."

Ah, now she was talking in terms that they both understood! But for the most part, it all sounded like welfare work to them, and they were not pleased. Jordan remained steadfast . . . and puzzled! She often wondered how she could have been born from these two genetic contributors. She was convinced that she must somehow have lapped the gene pool! And they were both convinced that she had been switched at birth, a victim of some gypsy plot that spirited away their own baby, and left them with this oddball! But they loved her anyway, and she just looked so much like them, that they decided to keep her . . .

Carpentry is a seasonal employment. Jordan's father had not worked for much of that winter. In fact, he rarely worked during any of the winters, with the exception of the occasional kitchen or bath remodeling. "Can't build a house without a foundation," he would say, and in winter, the ground would be too frozen to pour concrete. No concrete, no foundation; no foundation, no work; no work, no money. The family lived on see-saw budgeting, a cyclic feast or famine. But they would sacrifice for Jordan. The family pooled their resources over the course of the summer, and focused on amassing a variety of items that the college recommended new dorm residents would require. While her parents did not agree with Jordan's choice of profession, and were very hesitant about sending their oldest daughter alone to a school three states away, they tried to remain supportive of her decision. Jordan had barely earned enough money for new shoes, a new coat, and a few new outfits. The remainder of her savings were earmarked for books and school supplies. Her parents bought a popcorn popper, blankets and bedding, a modest stereo, and a desk lamp. Jordan packed her belongings into a trunk that a family friend had given her for graduation, and left the home carrying the hopes of this newest generation riding squarely on her shoulders.

Her parents drove her to the campus in the family station wagon. Jordan was relieved that her father had decided against taking his pick up truck. He agreed that three in the cab over a five hour trip would be too cramped. It never occurred to him that other families arriving at campus might make negative assumptions about Jordan simply due to their vehicle! He was proud of his company, and the logo and family name emblazoned on the truck's doors. The pick up was an older vehicle, but it still ran well, and had only a few scratches, a testament to its use as a machine of labor. The wagon was a Chevy, also older, but at least it was still a car . . .

Jordan's parents helped carry her belongings to her dorm room, and her mom began helping her unpack. Her dad secretly worried that Jordan would one day feel that they were not good enough for her. But he shrugged this off, and busied himself by examining the room's structure. He found an insufficiently caulked window, and a heater in need of an air filter. He reported these deficits to the dorm rep. at the desk. He had proven his worth! He would always work to prove himself worthy of her love. After all, she was his first-born daughter, and they would share that special bond to eternity. He would not let her go far. And he knew that she would not want to stray.

The parents had one last meal with their daughter, and left her, amidst tears and hugs, to start her journey toward full adulthood.

\* \* \*

Jordan transferred to a small, out-of-state college that held a rising reputation in the social sciences. The school would be known as the political think tank for the majority conservative view in later years, and at a time when liberalism had really fallen out of favor. But at the time of Jordan's arrival, the college typified a kind of quiet, southern grace, protected from the whirlwind of a culture in evolution. The school was surrounded by the Appalachian Mountains, and was cradled in a valley on the leeward side of one of its more prominent ridges. There were farms, and pastures, and cattle—Holsteins, she would learn—and the aroma of fresh mowed grass. In the fall, especially, there was a cacophony of apples and smoke houses, and of forest earth laden with dew. And the wet, sweet smell of the river nearby—some nights, the campus was so still, she could hear the water rush through the cobbles and boulders and against the shore. In winter, the air was so cold and so clean that she would momentarily lose her breath as she stepped out of the dorm, and would have to retreat inside just to regain it. And the moon against the dark night sky—she had never seen so many stars near her own home, unless she went to the ocean. Too much light pollution to see all the stars there. But at the college, if you stood in the center of the football field, you could see the stars of half a universe. Jordan felt small against its magnificence. And for the first time in her life, she felt safe, comfortable, and, nearly, accepted.

That the town itself had failed to integrate was a source of much ridicule by the out-of-state student body. Somehow the nearly all white campus had escaped their attention, as did the all white northern suburbs from which many had come. Jordan observed that people so quickly adopted an elitist position when judging another culture, and too readily overlooked the flaws in their own. Still in all, the college was the figurehead for social stewardship in the area. The school often formed community coalitions among the local churches in effort to provide aid to the migrant workers. These poor working families traveled through the county in spring and fall, in search of work in the fields. Jordan helped distribute canned foods and clothing to them, as these families gleaned the fruits from tree and orchard with the speed and efficiency of an industrial vacuum. The town's resistance to integration seemed the last vestige of a community poised, and yet catapulted, into the next stage of man. This was an area rich in the history of struggle. The Civil

War unfolded not far from the dorm. A generation of townspeople one hundred and ten years prior had marched with Lee through the cornfields of Maryland and Virginia, had shed their southern blood in Pennsylvania, and had stayed loyally by the General's side to his surrender in Appomattox. Jordan felt a chill each time she considered the magnitude of their sacrifice, and their belief in the Cause, even if she did not support the Cause itself. She wished that she could find something to so strongly believe in. She hoped that she might find it in Social Work.

Suburbanization would change the face of the county, and the college would gradually move from left to right, like the pendulum of the antique clock that chimed in the foyer of the old Briggs Library. The college would more and more attract "C+" students from the privileged middle and upper classes. But when Jordan arrived on campus, she was electrified by the unlimited possibilities that presented themselves through the doors of each building. She believed that her life's mission would soon manifest itself under the tutelage of the young but experienced Department of Social Work.

Jordan had the names of several students attending the college who lived in or near her home town. The names were given to her by high school guidance counselor, who hoped that they each could be a source of support and transportation for the other. While Jordan did not know the other students, she did know that they were not registered in the social sciences. Two graduated a year after her, and some were from different high schools near her hometown. But certainly there would still be many things that the girls would have in common.

"If only Jordan wasn't so intense," the guidance counselor thought . . .

Jordan decorated her room in the Balmural Dormitory for Women, and settled into the pattern of daily student activity. She wanted friends, and quickly sought out the students from her hometown. They already had connections, because they had been at the campus since freshman year. These girls knew the routine. So although just starting out, Jordan already felt way behind. She put that thought aside, and sought the help of the upperclassmen to help arrange her schedule.

"No early morning classes, and no morning classes on Mondays—too disruptive to the weekend drinking regimen. No classes scheduled after Phys Ed. You'll need the time to fix your hair and make-up. Allow plenty of time for lunch, so that you can meet up with your friends and plan the evening's social calendar..."

And suddenly, she was looking into the most beautiful pair of dark brown eyes that she had ever seen! She felt that uncomfortable excitement, that jump deep inside herself, that happened only on rare occasion, but now, with more frequency, with more intensity, with more urgency. She fought off the feeling, felt the flush on her cheek, and struggled to recover.

Jordan nodded and smiled in agreement.

"And absolutely, no classes with Thompkins! Believe me, you walk into his class, and kick back into snooz-o-matic! Taking his class is like watching the soaps—you could miss three weeks, and when you come back, he's still droning on about the same topic! The man is incredible... I heard that Sominex once tried to sue him so they could cut out the competition! And the class is so noisy—you can never hear anything above all the snoring there! The man is so boring, that they tried to recruit him as coach of the Olympic Sleep Team! The college even nominated him as Chairman of the Bored—a title he has held without challenge for the last fifteen years! I could go on, but you've already caught the yawn... er, I mean 'yarn.' Well, I've said enough. Any questions?"

Well Jordan had a million questions, but she dare not speak. She was captivated in this single moment, a prisoner of the Goddess before her.

Karen had a knack for encapsulating the experience of three years of college into a single breath. She would use this communication style throughout most of her life. Karen was a senior who dated—and was now engaged to—Todd Sommers, a TKE, and a defensive lineman. At twenty years old, Karen was already well on her way to a life of success and fulfillment, Jordan could see that. After all, she had already maxed two milestones on the "Ann Mathews Barometer of Success."

"How far have you gotten in this academic entrapment, this educational rockpile, to which we are all chained?" Karen asked Jordan. The inquisition had begun. The voice of the Goddess floated on the warm currents of the sweet summer air.

"Well, I completed my sophomore year at the county college, but with the transfer and the change in majors, I should complete my degree in three years," Jordan replied.

"Oh, so you're here on the five year plan. Not bad, but with no man yet. You should milk it for all it's worth. What would you do at home anyway, but work in your father's store . . ."

"My father is a carpenter. And how would you know whether or not I have a man?" Jordan asked.

"Ah, a carpenter's daughter. I knew he wasn't a doctor. And about the man? It's how you dress . . . Nothing too tight, or too revealing, nothing really attractive at all, in the sexual sense. Actually, you seem a bit ambiguous. You're not one of those girls are you?" Karen asked.

"One of what," Jordan replied, and before she had finished, caught the implication. "Nope, I'm not one of anything. I pride myself on bein' a member of nothing. What you see is what you get. A life without pretense, some would say."

"And an intellectual, too. Never-the-less, you'll find this a pretty good place to hang out, until you find someone, find yourself, or find a job." Karen replied.

"A place to hang out . . . ?" Jordan was stunned. How could anyone so devalue a seat of higher learning! But she hoped that she would be so attuned by her senior year. Throughout their association, Jordan would rely on Karen's unique ability to cut the bullshit to its least common denominator. Karen would become the bridge for Jordan between the confined past and the unlimited future. She would also function as Jordan's social safety net—as Karen soon announced to her friends that another hometown girl had found her place in the South! And from that point forward, Jordan would hold her thoughts close, while her heart sang out to Karen in sonnets.

Jordan's first roommate was a sophomore named Joanne, who left in mid-semester due to pregnancy. Of course Jordan was the only person on campus who knew this truth, and she won the reputation as one who could be trusted, when the birth announcements arrived. Joanne had decided to keep the baby, and was staying with an aunt in upstate New York. Questions remained as to the identity of the father, but calculations brought the impregnation to about the time of the TKE kegger. That was one good thing, at least, that Joanne and her son could be proud of—papa was a TKE, and not a Phi Sig! This was a good gene pool for someone interested in athletics. Karen decided to room with Jordan when the space became available. The two had become close friends almost immediately. Karen called them kindred.

As for the sororities, Jordan would have none of it—too exclusionary, you know. But the truth was that Jordan had never been asked to pledge.

"Too awkward and insecure," the Alpha Deltas would proclaim.

"No polish, no money, no class," the Beta Phis would assess.

Jordan did, however, accept membership as a Phi Kap, the Social Work Honor Society—a group that, with the exception of the Social Work Department, no woman on campus would want to belong! Yet this membership would look good on a resume, and could be a rung in the ladder of her climb to success. Who knows what heights she might attain with the support of the Phi Kaps backing her? She never belonged to anything before. Maybe this was the missing "pull" that she always needed. But Jordan never attended a single membership meeting. Even with the lure of networking, the group could draw, at best, a handful of students. The professors tried to bolster attendance by using "extra credit" bribery, and with another elite group of high achievers this might have worked. But Social Work was almost exclusively a woman's profession, and the women would rather hang out with their men! And they did not want to damage their reputations! They wanted no "brown noser" remarks associated with their names. Such besmirching could diminish their chances with a B-man, and could ostracize them from their fellow classmates. Jordan did not understand this, but she succumbed to the advice of peer pressure. She made a mental pledge, though, that this would never happen again. She would never kowtow to the pressures of her peers. Never! It was this rigidity in the end that would lead to things inescapable.

The Mathews family made their return trip to the campus for Parents' Weekend. The event was a week before Homecoming, and was a gala in its own right. The college was alive with hope and expectation for the new academic year. Banners proclaiming "The Year of Excellence" flew from the rooftops of the dorms, as parents traipsed behind their would-be scholars—their not-yet-failing children—who still claimed a 4.0 GPA, and begged for an increase in allowance! Pete was glad that Jordan wasn't like that. He knew that she'd keep up her grades. And though unspoken, Jordan knew that she couldn't ask for money—she had learned early that there was never any left. But she was still glad that they had come.

Pete and Ann toured the campus like pilgrims going to Mecca! They were so proud that their daughter was now a member of this sacred institution—and they walked each step like it was hallowed ground! As he watched the student elite stroll through the footpaths and entrances to each building, Pete thought that there would have been no boundaries to detain him, if only he had been able to finish high school. Still, he had done well enough with his family, despite the lack of opportunity. He could not imagine how far Jordan would go, now that these doors had opened to her! And he thanked his God for all that they had, and he wished His blessings on her.

It was a circus atmosphere, that weekend at the college. Balmural Dorm was decorated with the photos of parents and their students as babies. Karen laughed at how much Jordan looked like her father! But Ann was a little hurt that no one had seen her own smile in Jordan's, and even Jordan held back that usual comment. Ann just shrugged this off, though, as she would learn to shrug off many things to come. The two families walked through campus together, and listened to the anecdotes that Karen and Jordan shared with them, sometimes with Jordan giving a bit more information than any of the parents wanted! And some of the professors were also available for light discussion.

"It has already become quite obvious that Jordan will be one of our honor students in the Social Work Department," her professors proclaimed.

Jordan's parents hugged their daughter with pride, as Karen's parents nodded in approval. Yes, the Mathews' had no doubt about Jordan's academic potential for success. It was the usefulness of that success that troubled them. Yet, they would support her emotionally, even if they couldn't help her financially. A dream fulfilled, a life of meaning—that was their wish for her.

They spent most of the weekend with Karen and her parents. Karen's father won a gift certificate at a dart toss game, and donated it back to the college. Jordan's father won a round of horseshoes, and got a ticket for a free pizza at the student center. Pete Mathews stood slim, tall, and muscular next to the puffy, bookishness of Dr. Docherty. And Karen's parents were all style and grace. The couples got along well, and the parents frequently commented on the close friendship that the girls had already formed. Karen and her parents joked with Jonathan, and by Saturday night, had him trusting enough to tease back.

Kelly vied for the full attention of the group, but that was still not enough for her. She used every unobserved moment to flirt with a student nearby, and despite Jordan's stare.

Whumph! A foot targeted Kelly's shin with the accuracy of a Green Bay field goal kicker! Kelly shot ten feet above her chair.

"Hey, what was that for! You better knock it off, Jordan!" Kelly was indignant.

"Oh, was that you? I'm sorry, I was just stretchin' my legs." Jordan gave an icy reply.

"Both of ya knock it off!" Pete cautioned them. Ann just shook her head at them.

Karen shot Jordan a glare, the kind that she had already learned to cringe from, while the Docherty's gave a nervous chuckle in response.

Thankfully, the dinner passed quickly, much to Jordan's relief. She could now see her parents' awkwardness glaring against the polish of Karen's family. For the first time, she felt strangely embarrassed by them, then overwhelmed with guilt for the feeling that she didn't quite understand. She stuffed the thought in the same way that she had seen Ann do so many times. She would think about that later. She was glad that her family was comfortable at the football game, though, as they shouted the Bobcats to their third win of the season. Karen's parents nodded in approval.

Sunday was more subdued, and Mass was followed by the exodus of parents from campus to their homes of origin. Jordan stood curbside and waived goodbye to her parents until the Chevy was no longer visible. She tried not to cry as they left, but tears streamed down her face, and she felt the pit of loneliness rise in her stomach. Some things even friends could not replace. Jordan would continue to write to them weekly, and would call home every Sunday for a five minute report of the week's events. Jordan began to feel that she was suspended between these two worlds, and could not find real comfort, a real belonging, in either one. She did find escape in her studies, however, and found real validation in her grades.

\* \* \*

Erikson was the "Big Man on Campus" when Jordan began her studies. While Freud's theories still prevailed, it was the Erikson Stages of Human Development[2] that captured the imaginations of the Social Work assembly. She tried to follow her own development along the continuum from birth to young adulthood, and determined that she had not yet resolved the issue of intimacy. Perhaps she had

---

[2] For a description of Erikson's Stages of Psychosocial Human Development, please refer to the Appendix and Bibliography for Chapter One.

not fully mastered the whole "trust vs. mistrust" thing, and could not therefore allow another human being to know the real Jordan that lay beneath the surface. This was probably due to some maternal lacking, she surmised, and she would often mentally assess the family stories to determine where her mom had gone so wrong. At other times, she was gripped by an intense anxiety, a terrible fear—that maybe there wasn't really anything there, beneath the surface! Yet, she pushed these thoughts aside, and devoured each textbook, held each theory as a truism, and drank each lecture as a fine wine.

Her notes were meticulous—an outline form containing every syllable that the professor uttered. Her classmates marveled at her detail, and felt confident missing a class, knowing that Jordan would copy her notes for them. Jordan was disturbed by their lack of commitment to the profession.

"How can they push humanity forward, if they have not even participated in a class discussion?" Jordan would whisper to her lunch pals, as she nodded toward the offenders.

"Listen Jordan," Karen would coach, "you've got to lighten up a bit. People are who they are. Just enjoy your lunch, and worry about a suffering humanity later!"

While Jordan accepted this advice, she could not stop her heart from its leap to her throat with each request for the day's notes. It was not that Jordan minded the inconvenience of going to Briggs Library to make a copy. She would freely share anything that she had, as any true helper would. But she was concerned for the state of her fellow man.

"How could these actions, this laxity in academic study and achievement, later impact on the field of Social Work, if these same classmates somehow rose to the top levels of Human Services?" Jordan could not live with herself, if she thought that she had contributed to the demise of her civilization. She set out to educate them by role modeling in class.

Jordan enjoyed class participation, and she often followed the pattern of discussion she had developed at home with her father. She would challenge each professor with a question of theory, and then would dissect their explanation. She did not see her behavior as rude. She was merely in pursuit of knowledge at its highest levels. She hoped that she could complement their lectures with points of fact. She wanted to share her observations with others, in the hopes that, together, they could formulate some major insight that might answer the world's most pressing problems. She liked discussions of poverty best, because she could readily draw on her Sociology background. And she knew what she was talking about! After all, she had read Cruel City Streets[3], so she knew about life in the ghetto. She had read Poor and Struggling[4], so she knew about rural poverty. She had seen West Side Story[5], so she knew about gangs and the struggle for assimilation. She had personally handed out clothing and food packages to migrant workers. Yes, she had even this first hand knowledge of a suffering humanity!

Some of her classmates grew to detest her, and they would secretly sabotage her in front of the group. If Jordan gave a class presentation, coughing would erupt that could rival a TB ward! Or, a student would detain her, pretending to seek clarification of the previous day's assignment. Jordan would, of course oblige, being the helper that she was. This would cause Jordan to be late for class, miss the assignment for the next day, and provide opportunity for other classmates to give her the wrong information. That this was occurring had never occurred to Jordan. After all, they were all there for the same reason, and were striving toward the same lofty goals—to make the world a better place, and to help each individual

---

[3] A reference to: A book I've made up, because the author of the book I had originally chosen has refused to allow use of his book's name in a gay story.

[4] A reference to: Another book I've made up, because the author of the original book I had chosen has refused to allow use of his book's name in a gay story. Yup, we're two for two here!

[5] A reference to: Wise, Robert (Producer/Director) (1961). *West Side Story*. [musical motion picture]. Hollywood: United Artists.

maximize his potential. She could not fathom such insidiousness in a helping profession. She was still too naïve to catch on!

Karen was instrumental in explaining the finer points of social pressure, but even with Karen's tact, Jordan felt the need to withdraw emotionally from them. Outwardly, Jordan became the class clown; inwardly, Jordan felt a slow crush in her strive for connection. She laughed behind an invisible wall, she lived inside an invisible bubble. She liked people, but she would not reach out to them. She liked people, but she would not let them reach in to her. She was emotionally available only to a select few—her Group—and that connection began with Karen. She did become known as a good sport, though, and would be elected as the Balmural Hall Rep. to the Student Council at the start of her junior year. Yes, Jordan was very good at mimicry. But she could never share the real stuff that was going on inside of her. She lived each day with dread of discovery. Yet she could not articulate what she most feared.

*   *   *

By the time that Karen had graduated and left the school for a life with her Todd, Jordan had formulated some very close relationships with Karen's friends (the other students from her home area), and with their men. None of the relationships had the deep sense of commitment that Karen and Todd had made, but each had its own rhythm, its own course. Like the ebb and flow of the tides from which they had come, the couples would distance and pursue. Oftentimes, the distance would become so great, that the partners would change places, reminding Jordan of the square dances she had seen in that college town. Other times, the couples would be so intense, that Jordan dare not speak, so as not to impinge on their urgency. They all shared meals together, and formed the nucleus of a larger group, with an ebb and flow of its own. Regardless of any other demands, the nucleus met sharply at 8:00, 12:30, and 5:30 for meals, conversation, and social commentary. Since the others were math and science majors, Jordan often chaired any discussion about the state of the world as it was that day. The others would nod in agreement, and gently toss Jell-O to the ceiling, where it would stick and remain till semester's end. Tyler especially believed in the power of permanence, and felt that a tribute in Jell-O most befitted his scholastic achievements there. In lieu of Jell-O, he could form an effigy of string beans, or a self portrait in mashed potatoes. He would ultimately change his major, and would become a culinary guru of some merit in the New York area.

Marge was somewhat more restrained, and would limit her dislike of the college cuisine to a single, pointed word. "Disgusting!" she would declare, as she lifted a slab of mystery meat. "Petrified!" she would assess, as she stabbed the alleged scrambled eggs. Jordan found this a strange characteristic for so brilliant a young chemist, and she suggested on more than one occasion, that Marge take the offending specimen to the lab for analysis.

"But if you really found out what all this stuff is, would you really want to eat it?" Well, they all saw Marge's point. To wit, Martin would offer ketchup as a remedy to all evils yet uneaten. Marge would avoid the truth about many things, and found much comfort in the denial. This included her own emerging drinking problem, and maybe Jordan's, as well.

Martin was more the pragmatist. "It is what it is," he would exclaim, as he trotted past the cafeteria serving aisle.

"But what is it?" Tyler would ask. The possibilities would extend beyond the meal hour, if the conversation was not directed toward some other interest. Martin was a math major. He extolled the value of numbers, the unwavering faithfulness that each held to its principles, and suggested that this was the true permanence that Tyler sought, something he could always count on.

"Take for example, the number 1. You can divide it, multiply it, subtract it or add it . . . It holds the same properties each time you need 1. The same properties each time! It's still the same old 1 you've come to love . . . Although 2 would be far better, but that's an identity of a different scope. If you would like a demonstration of these concepts, you may see me after class." He looked toward

Jordan. There were times when she might have accepted the offer, but he would always remain like a brother to her. There was simply no romance. In fact, Jordan had never really experienced romance with any man. She did occasionally pretend to have the obligatory crush, however, as social situations dictated.

"Thanks, but tonight I think I'll just split, due to a denominator of a different proportion," she replied.

"Did someone say 'split'?" Janice interrupted, as she joined the group at the table. She and Martin had been dating pretty regularly, but had an open relationship. They would casually date others, but would save the big events—special football or basketball games, concerts, holiday gatherings, formal and semi-formal dances—for each other. They did not want to get too intense so early in their careers. This did not dissuade Janice from rubbing Martin's leg under the table as the group shared dinners. They would occasionally kiss in public, but never lingering. Janice was a Physics major. She was very interested in the Space Program, but believed that she would more likely be a teacher than an astronaut. Besides, she was intent on raising a family. Martin viewed their chromosomal coupling as an inevitability, but he did not want to sacrifice his "manly freedoms" before age thirty. He never shared the significance of that number.

The peripheral members ("the shell orbitals" as Janice would designate them) were varied in academic interest and ability, but each contributed something to the whole; and as a result, the whole was greater than its parts.

"A true demonstration of Systems Theory," Jordan would lecture, as the group quaffed down a pitcher of 3.2 beer at the off-campus pub. "Take, for example, Sturgis here, a musician and an artist of some merit here on campus. Yet still able to chug a mug and burp the full alphabet!"

"He could give you the Greek alphabet, too, if you would follow that with a J.D.chaser," Karen interjected.

"And with an armpit serenade, if any of you fine ladies would hold my t-shirt," he slurred in reply.

"Now taken alone, would anyone but us so appreciate this man's true genius? Of course not, but add our twisted tribe, and he becomes the much sought after maestro of the all-loathed human sound, a virtuoso of the Uncouth. Ladies and Gentleman, this simple guitar picker and sometime portrait painter now becomes the focal point of our evening's entertainment, and we are the better for it. A toast to this fine American!"

Jordan raised a mug amidst the applause and shouts from all the group. She felt most confident, and felt most accepted, when she was drinking. It's amazing how slight inebriation can cause such great distortion.

They fell into a group gyration as Maggie May[6] blared over the speakers. The dance floor was vibrant with lights and sweat, and the throb, throb, throb of base speakers so loud you could feel them pounding through your chest. And still they danced. They danced to Led Zeppelin, and danced to the Doors. They stomped to the Who, and screeched to Janice Joplin. They drank a mug to the Beatles, they dedicated a pitcher to the Stones. They drank, and danced, and sang their way through three years of academic wonder every Friday and Saturday night. And still Jordan felt alone. It was the slow songs really, that drove the point home. Everyone would be a singular, united mass of non-stop movement, a ballet of youthful bliss expressed at 45 RPMs. But when the ballads came, only the couples remained, and the singles would light a smoke, or slink off to the restroom.

This night, she thought she would try something different. Jordan stood at the table and made eye contact with a guy several tables away. He was rather attractive, slightly overweight, acceptably clean, and still seemed sober in comparison to his friends. Jordan had seen him around campus, near the vicinity of the TKE dorm, but she had not seen him on any of the college teams. His friends first noted her interest and nudged the target to make contact.

---

[6] A reference to: Stewart, Roderick David, and Quittendon, M. (1971). "Maggie May" [as recorded by Rod Stewart and the Faces]. On *Every Picture Tells A Story* [audio album]. Chicago: Mercury Records.

"Hey," one of the less desirables shouted from the table with him. "Aren't you one of the 'Ball-Morals' girls? Meet my friend Jack here."

The talker had drool running from the corner of his mouth. Jordan now recognized him as the tobacco-spitter she had dodged in town. She had learned early in her academic life never to walk too closely behind such a man. Tobacco squirting to the curb could easily fly backward and coat the non-attentive girl walking behind, especially if the wind was just right. The northern girls referred to such creatures as "hoolies." Jordan realized that she could not extricate herself from this predicament, as Jack was already heading toward the seat next to her! He held out his hand and identified himself as Jack Dempsey. She knew she had heard the name before, and so, felt a little more at ease. She shook his hand, and invited him to sit with her.

Jack was initially formal, but became more casual as they spoke. He expressed great embarrassment, and dismissed his friend's crudeness as attributable to alcohol. Jack clarified that he himself only occasionally imbibed, and never to excess. He wanted to taste every part of the world, he said, and did not want his appetites, or his senses, dulled by chemical substances of any kind. Jordan was pleased that she had chosen someone not drug involved.

Jack had a soothing confidence that made a woman feel like she was in a snuggly robe. His slow southern speech and his welcoming manner gently seduced her. With each word, with each movement of his fingertips along her arm, he had somehow found a way around her otherwise cautious nature. And she was letting him reach her. And the night was moving to its completion. She and Jack were still at the pub at last call, but neither had a final drink. Jordan was pleasantly buzzed, though she stumbled somewhat as they headed to the door. She had only partial recollection of her friends leaving the pub, but did remember that she had accepted Jack's offer for a ride home. He suggested that they go down to the river, where they could continue their conversation. This was familiar ground for Jordan, so she felt relatively secure. The night was cool even for mid fall, and she kept her jacket draped over her shoulders. After a few faltering steps along the riverbank, Jack suggested they return to the car.

Jordan held his arm as he led her to the back seat. She was hesitant, but succumbed. It was not that she had never been in the back seat of a Nova before, she just had never gone there with someone she had only just met! The conversation was short, and the foreplay was focused toward a singular goal. Jack was not satisfied with deep kissing, the farthest that Jordan had been prepared to go. Yet she allowed him to rub her thigh under her miniskirt, and to feel her breasts over her bra. She could feel his penis swell as he rubbed himself against her leg, and as he tried to maneuver her to a recline. Suddenly, she realized that her bra had been undone with a singular pluck of his finger! And she thought that, perhaps, he had a bit more experience than she.

She found her hand being guided to the protuberance, a large, hard, erect organ now waiting for some form of release. She felt his pubic hair as his penis found the center of her palm. And she thought she heard the command to "Move faster, Move harder," as he guided her fingers along the shaft. She, too, could feel his fingers, first over her panties, and then inside of them. She had not worn pantyhose that night, thus allowing his quick access. Maybe this had been the plan all along . . .

She could feel the wetness between her legs, and the excitement in the pit of her stomach. She had masturbated before, and she was familiar with the mechanics of the process. But it was more intense with a partner. Her clitoris was swollen with the touch of his fingers, and she could feel him gently rubbing, then tapping her, as he breathed deeply into her ear. Her vagina began to pulse as his fingers slid inside of her, and she responded rhythmically with his touch. He stretched a condom over that phallic marauder before he actually entered her, but made no comment, as if they had done this a thousand times. Once dressed in his condom tuxedo, he sucked her breast softly, then moved to position. The full weight of his body momentarily lay crushing upon her, his arms then suspending his torso above her, like some parallel bars gymnast.

There was no conversation between them, except for Jack's slow, soft chant as he entered her.

"Easy . . . easy." After a few pokes in all the wrong places, Jordan guided him to the passageway, the portal to womanhood. She opened herself wide to him, and waited in silent anticipation, for confirmation of her gender. He settled into her, and buried his face in her neck.

The car windows were steamed, yet still she could see the moonlight, as she watched her legs bounce across the top of the seats, and her foot lightly tap, tap, tap the back window. She tried to give it her all, to really get into the dance, but there was no excitement, no connection, no interest, beyond the newness of it. She had never really seen a penis totally unclothed before. But once disappeared, there was nothing to hold her attention! Her mind kept drifting off, and the excitement only came when her thoughts fell upon . . . NO! She could not think about that! She would not think about her! And still his alcohol-tainted breath leaped from his throat to her ear.

"Easy . . . Easy . . ."

The scent of Canoe covered stale onion! Jordan glanced again out the back window, the seats now creaking to the beat. She waited for something to happen, but her body just would not get into it! And her mind kept drifting to the events of the day, to a song on the radio, to the assignments due on Monday . . . to another partner touched only in thought . . . to the occasional obligatory moan she would offer to her partner of the evening.

"Eeeesssyy . . ." he would moan in reply.

"What's that, the Little Dipper?" she thought, as she caught brief sight of the stars, and tried to name the tune that matched Jack's rhythm and the Nova seat accompaniment. Her knees now draped the top of the seats, and she thought she could probably knock off a hundred sit-ups from this position, if Jack would only move over! But he continued his slow gyration, his rapid popping, his undulating quiver of self sensuality. Most of the action was now at pelvis level. But still nothing, and even with concentration! Still nothing, even when she moved to meet his thrust! She thought back over the process. Maybe she was trying too hard. "There has to be more to it than this!" He did not hear her. He was lost in his own world.

"Excuse me . . . But I'm gonna leave my twat here and go out for a pizza. I'll be back later to pick up my parts. OK?" She was convinced that he would still be in that same prone position, gratifying himself on the back seat, immersed in his own bliss, unaware that she had even vacated. Her mind wandered back to the forbidden fruit. She shook herself back to this reality.

"Oh . . . it's good for you too!" He panted in reply. "EEEassy . . ." he began again, and his voice trailed off.

Jack was now the focus of his own action, pumping then halting, just before he might come. He sucked her breasts as an afterthought, as he coached himself, his hair falling into her face.

"EASY, EASY!" he said, as he slid back and forth within her. Finally, her vagina was seeing some real action, but still, there was nothing! Were they all lying to her? She was taking bets in her mind that they were!

At first she believed that he was trying to be careful with her. He did not realize that she was a virgin until she told him. This made the act even more special to him, and he wanted to make his rocking go the night. Even when she was no longer wet, even when she told him she was getting sore, he would continue his chant of "Easy, Easy!" and the rock would go on, as if she was not even there. And she could not find that elusive "O" no matter how hard she tried! All night long, and no orgasm in sight! She wondered what the payoff was. The only time she had gotten close, was when she started thinking about . . . QUIT IT! She could not allow that thought to enter her mind! Yet, she could not seem to keep it out!

By morning, her muscles were stiff, her body exhausted, and still, nothing to show for it! With all this effort—with this gentle, if selfish, pursuit of excellence that Jack demonstrated—she had not come herself. She had not even gotten close, once he started fucking her! She wondered what all the talk was about! She swore that the other girls didn't know either! This night hardly answered the question. In fact, it only complicated it!

Jack exploded in a finale of "EASY's!" and rhythmic contortions, and she joined in the chorus of "oohs and ahhs." She felt that she owed him that much.

Jordan cleaned herself with a napkin from a McDonald's bag that Jack had stowed in the glove compartment of his car. She collected her panties from the front seat, and managed to wiggle back into them, as Jack returned to the car after taking a leak. She also had to go, but could not squat in the presence of a man she had only just met! Jordan looked in the rearview mirror, and saw that her face was a smear of blush and eyeliner. And she had "bed-head"—the back of her hair was a tangled mess, a web formed by the rhythmic movement of her head from side to side as she feigned each orgasm. She had seen this technique used many times in the movies. And her mouth had the foul taste of stale beer! Jack appeared tired but satisfied. They talked little, smiled much, and made no comment about when they might see each other again. Jordan fixed hair and make-up as best she could, then headed back to her dorm. Jack drove her to the door, where she arrived just before dawn. She saw that he had acne—a fact lost in the froth of a good brew.

Jordan fumbled with the front door combination, but did gain access to the dorm on the third try. Jack was already gone by then.

"Not a good sign," she said, as she sauntered through the hallways lined with pictures of the "Cosmo Burt Reynolds." The faint aroma of last night's popcorn still lingered in the air, a testament to those women who stayed in at night, every night, and formed their own regiment of the Lonely Hearts Club. Jordan refused membership in that clique as well, and much preferred the love of the Group, her group, to any other relationships imaginable.

Karen was already dressed when Jordan arrived in their room. She did not immediately speak, adding to the eerie silence of the dorm on an early Sunday morning.

"Well, did you have a good time with Michael?" Karen asked, suddenly breaking the silence.

"I wasn't with Michael," Jordan replied, "I was with Jack Dempsey."

"Jordan, his name is Michael O'Keefe. His father owns the Pic-N-Pac store in town. His uncle owns the pub. He's there hitting on some northern girl nearly every weekend. Didn't you recognize him?"

Jordan stopped for a moment, then realized that she had confused her "Jack" with another man on campus—perhaps because "Jack" had gotten contacts, and was a little better dressed than usual. He was certainly better mannered, at least initially . . . that would explain though, the acne she had overlooked.

"You weren't with 'Jack Dempsey' . . . he was a fighter before you were born. I'm surprised you didn't remember that. You left with 'Jack Daniels' and you didn't even realize it. Are you o.k.? You were out with him all night."

"I'm o.k.," Jordan replied, offering only a grimace and rolled eyes in clarification.

"Well, how far did it go? I mean, did you do it with him?" Karen asked, sounding more like her mother than her friend.

"No . . . more like he did it TO me," Jordan responded.

"Are you o.k.? Is there anything I can do for you? Are you hurt . . . ," Karen's mind was racing toward the worst case scenario, again, just like her mother.

"I'm fine," Jordan replied, "just a bit more embarrassed—and a hell of a lot more disappointed—than I thought I would be." As she laughed, she could see the tension immediately leave Karen's body, and she gratefully accepted the hug and the laughter of her friend.

"Don't you ever do this to me again . . . I mean, to leave with a chunk of pond scum like Michael O'Keefe is bad enough, but not to let anyone know where you are going is just damned dangerous. And another thing, Jordan. Never, never let anyone use you like that again," Karen instructed.

"What makes you think he used me?" Jordan asked. "I used him."

# Chapter 2

Karen and Jordan spent the next few weekends studying for midterms and working on research papers. Karen was trying for anything that would bolster sobriety! They attended the college lecture series, met the Group regularly for meals, and saw a few campus-sponsored movies with Janice and Martin. Marge and Tyler would sometimes join them at the movies, but they still preferred the weekend pub trips. But Karen found other activities for Jordan until she felt more confident that Jordan's mind—and her liver—were back in fine working order. She was worried about her. She secretly monitored Jordan's drinking throughout the rest of their year together. Karen wanted to protect her, to stop her from falling into any of the life traps that might lay hidden in the path ahead. But she could not confront her. She knew that Jordan wouldn't read the signs until it was too late, and by then, she would already be a goner! Karen knew that Jordan could ace any college course. She had book knowledge. She just had no survival skills, no social sense—at least, not that Karen could see!

And as inept as Jordan was in other arenas, she was a killer with a research paper! She could accept any topic, find some obscure theory, and formulate a defense of preposterous proportions. But she would not stop there. She would then extrapolate the theory, and find practical application in some imagined social program that would cure the world of all ills. Karen respected her brilliance as a bull-shitter of the highest order. Yet, she knew that in some ways, Jordan was deadly serious. It was this competence of pen that gave Jordan a revered position in the pecking order of Balmural Dormitory. On more than one occasion, Karen would wait in the Student Center until Jordan finished "conferencing" with a student in their room.

"So you call these trysts 'tutoring'? No! No, Jordan, it's plagiarism! . . . That's what this is, you know—how else would you describe the act of having someone else write a term paper, and then turn the work in as your own?" Karen tried to convince her, but Jordan remained undaunted.

"Don't be ridiculous! It's not like I'm sitting in a class for 'em, or taking their tests . . ."

"Give It Time!" Karen snapped back.

"Look, this is just a reasonable attempt to help a friend pass a class and obtain a life's goal. Nothing more than that . . . Just simple tutoring!"

"Maybe that's how you see it, but believe me, there will be plenty of other opinions when the proverbial shit hits the fan! And that discovery could bring consequences that neither you nor I want to pay. It's OK to give a little help, but you've crossed the line into some completion thing, noble though it be. Jordan, face it—you're not helping, you're DOING . . . And it's just not worth the risk—to you, or to them! Forget about the writing . . . Don't you think they'll recognize your ideas? You do seem to see things a little out of the ordinary, you know . . ."

"Trust me. Nothin' is gonna happen. We're not doing anything wrong! And we won't get caught . . . Nobody ever pays attention, anyway . . . You give people way too much credit."

"Sometimes it's better to over-estimate a situation than to under-appreciate the dangers."

Jordan ignored this advice, and continued her daily "classes."

It was only when Dr. Giordano, her English Lit professor, noted the "probable coincidence" in the writing styles of the Balmural girls, that Jordan realized her own jeopardy. He made the comment in Jordan's class, and as he glared right at her! Jordan nearly fell out of her seat. Her own desk rattled her guilt! Her chair was hot as a fryer! Her mind raced with a thousand plausible reasons for the coincidence! She was pale but silent, as she tried to feign the best look of innocence that she could fake! Karen never saw her so unnerved! Yet Jordan held her breath and prayed that the challenge would pass. After a few moments that spent like hell's fire, the professor moved on. He had given them the benefit of the doubt. Jordan shot Karen the Wide-Eye, and got a Caution Eye Brow in response. The other girls stayed glued to their books, and dared not look up.

"Good for him! Now maybe she'll understand a little more about what I've been trying to tell her. Maybe now she'll listen to me." Karen wasn't usually smug, but when she was right, she knew it!

After that, Jordan became far less generous with her gift. And as that consequence, several women failed out and were forced to leave the college. Of course this decision caused Jordan a great deal of angst. On the one hand, she was helping someone to achieve their potential; but on the other hand, she had become their potential! Never-the-less, neither she nor Karen could dismiss the "power of the written word" that Jordan had already developed. Her pen was her sword, her weapon of "write," and she honed the blade on the cut and slash of illusion, and freed an opening for social justice. Neither could know then the implications that this could have.

But the Group quietly marveled at how close Jordan had come to discovery without being "picked off." They believed that she was truly born under some lucky sign, or that she had some watchful eye of anonymous protection. Jordan was just thankful that she had learned the lesson without having to pay the price of her education for it! Like so many things, she chose not to share this experience with her family—and she learned to rely on Karen's judgment.

The Holidays were now luring them, calling to them, tempting them just beyond the semester finals. Jordan was really looking forward to the time at home. She would be sharing a ride with Marge, Karen and Janice. George, an upperclassman, would drive the girls to the Stelton Mall, a central drop off point for the three. He would then continue on to his home in the next county. George was a likable guy, a 3.8 student, and a very cautious driver. The girls would often complain, though, about the extra forty-five minutes his trips would take. Jordan's mother could make the route in just under four hours and fifteen minutes. With George, they could count on at least five hours, and even without a stop! Yet the time passed quickly for them. The girls would spend the initial hours chatting about Martin, Tyler, Todd, or whoever else had attracted their womanly interests at that point in time. But George remained aloof, uninterested, a confirmed family man. His young wife lived with his parents, and he commuted home twice monthly. The couple already had a year-old son, the likely cause of these living arrangements. Yet he remained devoted to Sharon, and readily discussed the life he hoped to make for them. The girls secretly longed to find a man of his caliber. They privately joked that this would be quite the task, given the quality of men they had already seen on campus. This, of course, excepted Todd, Martin, and Tyler!

The discussion would lapse into a momentary silence, and one of the girls would crank up the radio. Together they would fall into a chorus of the Top Twenty Hits so crowned by Casey Kasem. In quieter moments, George would pop in an 8-track, and the girls would croon along.

They'd sing ballads with Karen and Richard Carpenter—maybe "Rainy Days and Mondays,"[7] or maybe even "Superstar."[8] While Marge would sing the lead, Janice, Karen, and Jordan would wait to belt out the chorus! Not a dry eye in the Fairlane . . .

---

[7] A reference to: Nichols, Roger S., and Williams, Paul H. (11971). "Rainy Days and Mondays" [recorded by Karen and Richard Carpenter]. On *Carpenters* [audio album]. New York: A&M Records

[8] A reference to: Russell, Leon, and Bramlett, Bonnie (1969). "Superstar" [re-recorded by Karen and Richard Carpenter]. On *Carpenters* [audio album]. New York: A&M Records (1971)

Or they'd take up the challenge of Don McLean to sing each and every verse of the 8 and ½ minute "American Pie,"[9] the anthem of their generation.

Or, Jordan would shout out the first lines, of the first song, on the first 8 track they always grabbed on the ride home.[10] And as Carole King would bang out the chords on the piano, the girls would bop and sing together.

Or they'd sing with Carly Simon the closing of Anticipation:

"And stay right here, 'cause these are the good ol' days,

these are the good ol' days . . .

these are the good ol' days . . .

these are the good ol' days . . .

these are, ARE . . . the good ol' days." [11]

And they'd drum the finale on the seats.

As landscapes skated passed the windows, the girls would sing through turnpike and countryside, and George would drive the slow creep back home. Twice each semester they would make the trip. And three years clipped by faster than the dotted lines on the Interstate.

If ever there was any singular force that united them all, it was music. Once, the Group hitch-hiked en mass to the next town, nearly twenty miles away, just to buy a communal copy of Carol King's Tapestry when that album was first released.

---

[9] A reference to McLean, Don ( 1971). "American Pie" [as recorded by Don McLean]. On *American Pie* [audio album]. New York: Mediarts/United Artists

[10] A reference to: King, Carole. (1971). "I Feel the Earth Move". On *Tapestry* [audio album]. New York: Ode/CBS

[11] A reference to: "Anticipation". Words and Music by Carly Simon. Copyright©1971Quakenbush Music Limited. Copyright Renewed.All Rights Reserved.Used by Permission. Reprinted by permission of Hal Leonard Corporation.

The album became a cultural icon almost immediately, and the Group pooled its money to buy the record. A combined total of nine college students of every size and dimension were picked up and packed into Volkswagen and pick-up truck, Mercedes and hay wagon, as they made their way to the record store, then back to campus. Music was the spirit that carried them through the ups and downs of academia, and webbed the connection in their lives. Music was the cultural arc that carried their generation to its own place in history. Music formed the backdrop, as the rides to and from college wove the threads of experience into the bonds that kept the Group together.

There would be many times in Jordan's life that she would wish that she was again traveling in George's car—traveling back to that same time and place, with that same musical backdrop, and with those same people. Those memories became the emotional keel that kept Jordan in balance, a psychological security blanket, even through the harshest times that lay ahead. Although the ride was over, the tunes would roll on forever, and with them, the memories in safe-keeping. In later years, she would visit them often. And they would reach out to her, across the decades, each time she heard one of their songs on the radio.

And once back home, life there seemed strange—the comfortable now viewed as commonplace. Though gone only a few months, Jordan began to notice the differences between the lives of her parents, and the lifestyles of her friends. This had not been obvious at college. Since she had not known the other girls prior to her admission there, she had nothing really to compare. She did occasionally react, as she listened to the cafeteria talk from distant tables. How they joked about the smell of the maintenance men, or the baggy jeans hung low on the hips of the groundskeepers there!

"Elitists!" Jordan declared, as she motioned toward the hecklers.

"SSHH!" The Group would quickly respond. They had no idea.

She often felt a sense of peace and comfort when one of the men would walk by, a day's sweat dried on his blue, cotton work shirt. She enjoyed this aromatic, soothing familiarity, and used it as a kind of antidote to her sometimes overwhelming homesickness. She had never been away from home or family before, and would never admit being homesick. She believed that such a flaw would further deny her status as an adult and as a woman. And she was not a kid anymore!

Her grades arrived during Winter Break, and her parents met her at the door with the good news. "A 4.0 once again!" her mom exclaimed.

"Hopefully, you'll be ableta turn that inta bread and butter some time," her dad chided. She could see the pride swell in them both, as they relayed her academic conquests to each member of the extended family who arrived for Holiday visits. Her mom had even posted the "report card" on the refrigerator, to which Jordan stealthfully slid past, bumped the card with her elbow, and whisked it off to her room. After all, she was not a kid anymore! Her brother and sister had a "big deal attitude" about her accomplishment, though, and took every chance to show that off. Jordan warned them both that she would not feign stupidity to cover for their underachievement.

Yet despite the obvious pressures that her grades brought, both Jonathan and Kelly were happy to have their sister home again. Kelly often phoned Jordan at college just for girl talk. They could have gone on for hours, had not their father been monitoring the bill.

"Ya wanna communicate, try the mail. Or maybe talk ta each other once in a while when you're home. I can't build money, ya know," he would yell.

Kelly was an active high school sophomore, usually a member of one of the girl's teams, or president of one club or another. She was never without a boyfriend, a source of additional pressure for Jordan. Kelly was the outgoing member of the family. She had a flashy smile, a build that wouldn't quit, and a fairly good personality. Jordan had to admit that. But she even heard her mother joke to an aunt once that Kelly "must be a hard act to precede," indicating that, though several years younger, Kelly was light years ahead of Jordan.

Jonathan was a lot more like Jordan. His shyness was a source of some consternation for his father, who believed that people were quick to attribute such characteristics to a "less manly" man. Although only in eighth grade, he preferred art to football. He occasionally sent some of his sketched landscapes to Jordan at college to decorate her room. Jonathan played baseball on the little league teams, but was usually stuck in left outfield. Like Jordan, he enjoyed most sports, but wasn't really good at any of them. Unlike Jordan, though, he was poor in academics, lacked motivation, and was not goal-focused. He reminded Jordan of a leaf blowing in the autumn winds—a child pushed here or there, depending on the strength of the breeze, the direction of the gust, just whipped up in a dirt devil, until a calmer air again deposited him on the ground. Jordan had already taken a substance abuse class, and she saw personality traits in Jonathan that would suggest a propensity toward addiction. She would be careful to monitor Jonathan for this as he grew older. She loved her brother, and she vowed forever to protect him especially.

The family spent the days before Christmas completing shopping and finishing decoration of home and tree. Jordan purchased most of the family gifts while at college, budgeting one gift every two weeks. She bought a sweater for her mother, a robe for her father, a macramé purse for Kelly, and a box of pastels for Jonathan. She received a silver I.D. bracelet from her parents, and an assortment of clothing and other necessities for school. Jonathan gave Jordan a seascape featuring sea gulls that he painted from a photo she had taken last summer. Kelly gave her a record album because she liked the music, and figured she'd borrow it from Jordan sometime. The Mathews family truly enjoyed this especially close, though typical, Holiday time in their lives.

Yet Jordan longed to see her friends (especially Karen), and she missed the sense of freedom that she enjoyed at college. She couldn't believe how quickly they had all become so close! She didn't want to remember how lonely life had been before them. Jordan met Marge and Janice several times for a movie or for a night out at a coffee house in town. She made a few private phone calls to Martin and Tyler, even though she knew she would have to face her father's wrath for the long distance calls. She couldn't help herself—she just missed them so!

And they missed her, phoning her, too, several times during the break, and with nothing in particular to say. Karen was less accessible, as she was in the throes of wedding preparation. Jordan had already been fitted for her bridesmaid gown, the first responsibility scheduled the day after they arrived home. And Todd lived in Virginia. He had already purchased a house near his parents' home for their own someday family. His parents had given a generous down payment, and he and his father were making necessary repairs for the couple's immediate occupancy, once wed. Jordan intentionally forced this thought from her mind. But without warning, the nagging vision would re-emerge. There would be a time, too soon, that Karen would leave the area, and probably, her life forever. Those thoughts filled Jordan with a monstrous anxiety that she could not share or accept.

But Jordan's parents were really impressed that Karen's life had already been so established! When they met Karen during Parents' Weekend, they commented to Jordan about her maturity and sophistication. They were even more impressed that she would soon have husband, home, and family—a Susie Homemaker Grand Slam, as the Mathews' saw it! Jordan's mother commented that she and her husband had worked and saved for ten years for the down payment on their own home. She secretly hoped that Jordan might find someone who could so adequately provide for her.

The days of Winter Break blew passed like a silent storm. Jordan continued to assert her adulthood while her parents struggled to maintain her role as a child. This tension lay just beneath the surface. Her mother made rude suggestions about her clothes, and complained about her late night hours. Her father was appalled by her casual use of foul language. Jordan often slept in late, and now, was disrupting the family's schedules. She could not believe how quickly they had all accommodated to life without her! In compromise, she began getting up just before dawn, and driving across the bridge to the ocean. There, she would sit among the sea gulls, have a coffee, and wait for the first signs of the day's new sun. The air was bitter cold so early at the shore, and it reminded her of the mornings on campus. Sometimes the sea breeze would be so harsh that it seemed to cut right through her jacket! She would sometimes jog along the shore, sending the gulls into an explosion of winged flight. She loved the sanderlings, especially, and likened them to groups of students running between class and dorm. She missed them now that winter was here. Her life was changing, and with each step, she felt she was moving farther away from the people who meant the most to her. Yet, she ran on—one foot before the next, frozen air filling her lungs, eyes focused on the beach ahead, and thoughts set miles away in time and space. She was running from the life that her parents so cherished, but she had no idea where she was going. She would graduate, of course, but beyond that, the path was dark and scary. The thoughts would race through her mind nearly as quickly as she could suppress them! She saw the hopes of her parents dissipate in the mist she exhaled in the early morning air. And with each breath, she feared that she would plunge headlong into the abyss.

\* \* \*

The Group met for breakfast promptly at 7:30 on the morning of their first day back at campus. Karen did not accompany George and the girls back to school. She was having problems finalizing the reception hall. Jordan expected her back later that evening. Breakfast conversation focused on the issues of re-assimilating into their respective families, which at least, gave the scrambled eggs a break for the day . . .

"The crimes were the same, but the names were changed to protect each dastardly culprit," Tyler commented, as they compared stories. He had had a brutal argument with his father about use of the car, late night hours, failure to help around the house, and, what Tyler called "breathing his air." He and his father had always had a difficult relationship, and he viewed college as an escape route to a brighter, happier life without him. His father and mother were divorced, and he had not had contact from his mother since he was quite young.

"Would you believe it . . . my mother complained because I slept until 9:00 o'clock. And I mean 9:00 in the morning! I told her that it wasn't like I had a job or something to go to, but that didn't seem to matter to her," Marge said. "She was also not very happy about that bottle of Sloe Gin she found under my bed. But what was she doing under my bed, anyway?"

"Yeah!" Janice exclaimed, with righteous indignation. 'What about your right to privacy!" Marge shrugged in reply.

"So, I also got popped for late night hours, late rising, and use of foul language," Jordan said. "Believe that?"

"Ouuhh," they all gave a hardy emphasis in reply.

"Yeah, that's right, I'm bad! I slept 'till 8:00 and I said the 'F' word once—Jordan 'The Rule-Breaker' Mathews, Public Enemy Number 1! Yeah, that's me alright!"

"Lucky if you'll be paroled by May, Rule-Breaker!" Tyler said.

"Really! And how did we all become so horrible, and all at once? You must be some very bad seeds that I'm hanging with! I have to find a better class of friends, and get away from this 'wrong crowd' that you all are!" Janice got popped too, but she wouldn't confess to her crimes. Her family was more private than that.

Jordan laughed herself to tears with the others. They were so different, and yet so much the same. Jordan realized then, that she really loved them all. Maybe she was finally beginning to make that elusive connection to other human beings. At least she hoped so, as she listened to the Group make the usual plans for the evening. They'd be going to a coffee house, an open mike/acoustic guitar thing, at the Student Center. The basketball season would resume with a home game on Thursday, and of course, the Group would attend. There would be a pre-game meeting behind the Student Center, a pep rally of sorts. It would be unofficial, and the cheers, and the booze, would flow freely. The team was already tagged as the likely winner of their Division that year. And so, the spirit was with them—the chants and applause during the games would be deafening, and the bleacher-stomping of 2000 feet seemed like an earthquake!

Karen arrived back at Balmural Dorm by dinner. Jordan had already begun the semester's readings, and was reviewing the outlines and requirements of each of her subjects. She had purchased her books well in advance. She wanted to ensure that she would have time to read every line of her assignments, as usual! The two talked as they strolled to join the others in the cafeteria. Karen shared the nightmare of arranging a wedding without a consultant, and was thankful that her mother was overseeing many of the details. She discussed the chore of selecting not only the right photographer, but also of formulating a written outline dictating the mandatory shots she wanted him to take. She and her mother had surveyed several possible locations for the photo shoot following the ceremony. They had mutually decided to use the gazebo along the boardwalk, with several additional poses taken on the beach. Since the wedding was in June, the weather should accommodate that plan. Although the reception would be at the Country Club, she and her mother had some difficulty agreeing on the place settings and tableware. This caused the delay in finalizing the hall, and resulted in Karen's mother having to drive her back to school. The ride was tense and quiet.

"Ya know, this really is all your fault," Jordan said. "You should'a listened to me and had the wedding catered at the firehouse, like we do . . . My uncle would've even brought his Polaroid for ya!"

"Yeah," Karen laughed. "I'm sure the Dr. and Mrs. Docherty would have gone for that arrangement."

\* \* \*

The team did win the Division championship that year, but lost the NCAA Regional title in the final seconds of the game. A pallor reverberated throughout the campus for weeks afterward, and despite the placards and banners that still declared the team "Number 1." Classes moved from indoor to outdoor settings, as winter melted into spring. The otherwise formal lectures took on a more casual feel on the lawns, and class participation seemed to rise a bit. Jordan had some difficulty concentrating when outside, though. The bird song called to her, or she would watch the other students, or their convertibles, move around campus. The new spring crocuses and daffodils sprouted to fulfillment, adding swatches of color to the dark dirt earth. The trees brought forth the leaves of their next cycle of life. And Jordan's A's continued to blossom, bringing to a close, yet another semester. She would need to plan carefully, if her life's mission was to be realized.

Jordan met with her assigned advisor at the Department of Social Work, and requested a field placement in an anti-poverty program. She longed for a position in a social action organization, and could see herself as leading a march, demanding fair treatment for the disadvantaged, and helping to effect legislation that would ban poverty in America! Yes, Jordan believed that she would be a soldier in that War on Poverty! She was furious when she was given a field placement as an income maintenance worker at the local welfare board. She let out a roll of expletives!

"Some people just don't realize when true talent presents itself to the world!"

Karen tried to calm her. "You're only going to be at the agency once or twice a week, right? And think of all the knowledge of government supported programs you're going to come away with! This is the perfect place to start!"

Jordan only partially accepted that explanation. She looked at them all with half-hearted optimism. Tyler and Martin tried to support Karen, and nodded to Jordan in agreement. Janice added a "Yeah, that's right!" nodding to Karen as she spoke.

"My father didn't start surgery while he was an intern. He was a resident in the E.R, and learned the functioning of the entire hospital before he met that goal. Same is probably true here," Karen encouraged. Martin and Tyler chimed in to help the process along. But Marge was not buying into it.

"Wait a minute—I smell conspiracy!" Marge challenged. "You know that the college is probably getting huge kick-backs by supplementing government jobs with the free labor of poor college interns. Who knows where the program funds are really going, and whose pockets are being lined by the sweat of your brow!"

The Group stifled the comment with a universal sneer launched in Marge's direction. She pushed back from the table in surprise.

"Wooow! Come on, guys . . . It's a joke! Lighten up! I think welfare is a great way to start a career . . ." The glares shot her in the face.

"Maybe I've said too much . . ." The glares continued. "Nope—I say 'fight 'em to the bitter end!" She raised a fist in defiance. "Show 'em that you know how the game is really played! Talk to my mother . . . She'll give you some pointers!" Crumpled napkins launched across the table and pelted Marge to silence. Marge gulped a breath.

"OK, OK, I get it. You do what you have to do . . ."

But Jordan already knew that she had very little choice in the matter. She decided to accept the placement without a fight. She worried, though, about how her parents might view this set-back. She wouldn't tell them right off. It was another decision she had to make for their own good.

And life went on, despite her objections. Karen had begun preparing for graduation, and was already starting to pack the less useful things in their room. Todd seemed to be with them constantly now, and the stress of the wedding was already taking its toll. The couple began arguing, but never in front of the others. But the Group knew instinctively about the tensions between them, just as they knew that Karen and Todd would work things out. They had always worked things out in their two years of romance. They knew that it was the thought of living so far from home that weighed on Karen's mind. It wasn't her life with Todd.

Karen started sharing these thoughts with Jordan in their room one day, after Todd had gone back to his dorm. There was a long silence before she spoke.

"I know that I can live independently of my parents, but I have never wanted to, you know? I've always imagined them being part of my married life . . . sharing things with me, sharing my happiness. We'll still have close phone contact, of course, but they can't actively participate in the rearing of their grandchildren. Our homes will be six hours apart! Todd's parents are warm, you know, welcoming, but they're no substitute for my own parents . . . I really hadn't bargained on this when I accepted Todd's proposal. Sometimes I think he intentionally hid that plan from me . . ."

Jordan was surprised that Karen was confiding such things to her, even though they were alone. She was typically the most reserved of the Group.

Jordan sat quietly as Karen discussed her feelings, being fully present with her as she spoke. Karen nearly cried several times as she relayed the conflict that she was experiencing—loving Todd, and wanting to spend her life with him, and in the world he would create for them; and wanting to stay close by her parents, so that she could share this world each day with them. Jordan was silent, knowing that Karen had already made her decision. She just needed a friend to help process the enormous change she was about to make. She needed support and validation.

Then things started to take a different turn, although Jordan was never really sure how this happened. But Jordan soon found herself answering in detail, Karen's questions about the night with Michael O'Keefe. Jordan shared her motives for allowing the encounter with him.

"Ya know, I never really had complete sex with anyone before. The farthest things ever went, well . . . just kissing and touching . . . I think this is why, maybe . . . why maybe I never really felt attracted to the guys I dated. I mean I liked them well enough, but just not in that way. Certainly nothing like what you and Todd have. Even though I love Martin and Tyler, and I even went to bed with each of them once since that Michael fiasco, I still don't feel attracted to them in that way. No matter how hard I try."

Jordan waited for a response, but Karen remained quiet, listening carefully, and only nodding to accent a point of agreement.

"I really envy you and Todd . . . how you two have found someone who you can so completely share your lives with . . . Ya know, I often wonder if I will ever find someone . . . But deep down, I wonder why I can't allow myself this same happiness."

After several moments, Karen rose calmly and quietly from her chair, and walked with deliberate intent, to the bedside where Jordan was sitting. She gently reached her hand to Jordan's chin, raised her face toward her, and passionately kissed her on the lips. Jordan sat silent and motionless, stunned, as Karen turned off the light, and returned to her.

Karen began slowly unbuttoning Jordan's blouse, while gently kissing her cheek, her hair, her lips. Jordan could hardly breathe, could barely swallow—she was so nervous about being discovered! But Jordan could feel the warmth of her breath, and each exhale sent chills though her body. She was acutely aware of the closeness she felt, of the longing now suddenly satisfied, and not at her own action! She closed her eyes and tasted the gentle lips of the woman she had fantasized a million times about. Karen gently caressed her breasts, and with each touch, Jordan felt herself pulling her more and more tightly against her. She was apprehensive with surprise of her touch, yet alive with an unquenchable excitement. She wanted to stroke her, but was too afraid to reach out to her, as if the action would somehow jolt reality. Yet, she continued to hold Karen tightly, nestling her body as a cherished piece.

As Karen began to undress, she gently and playfully unzipped Jordan's jeans, and began sliding her fingertips along Jordan's crotch, splitting her to a thousand delights. She slowly drew light circles on her stomach, and swirled her fingertips along her nipples, and to her lips. She watched her fingers play on Jordan's skin. Jordan could hear her own breath filling the room. She could hear herself calling softly to Karen. She felt herself opening to her, and felt her own wetness saturate her thighs. She lay back, and allowed herself to fall into the million deep secrets that she kept from Karen for all time. Then slowly, Karen joined her, her body lay warm against her own. Jordan glanced her tongue along Karen's body as she held her, allowing her lips to caress her shoulders, then breasts, until she once again tenderly, passionately, hungrily found her lips. As they kissed, Karen gently pressed Jordan back again on her bed, and lay naked beside her, allowing Jordan to explore, to reciprocate her touch. They knew without speaking, they acted without words. Jordan never felt so complete, so one in spirit, with another human being. She could never have imagined such a feeling, and could never have explained it to anyone. She savored the touch, the moment, the ecstasy. The two were intertwined, leg tenderly rubbing against leg, hands exploring the full length of their bodies, with deep, soul-blending kisses between their full, slow breathing, as they stroked each other to climax. Jordan wanted to hold the moment eternal, but Karen's movement signaled the end.

Jordan remained quiet and puzzled. Karen rose and stood near Jordan, who was now sitting again on the edge of the bed. She cupped Jordan's face in her hands, made full eye contact with her and kissed her again.

"I think that's why you aren't attracted to men. Hopefully you'll soon be able to move beyond your fear, Jordan, because you do deserve happiness."

The two never discussed, never mentioned, this experience again. Even at meals the next day, Karen's eyes never betrayed the wondrous moment they shared the night before. Jordan's eyes searched hers for some clue, some silent signal, that would confirm the love that they shared. Yet Karen remained stoic, unresponsive to Jordan's yearning. It was if Jordan had been seduced by some Karen doppelganger, while the real Karen remained unknowing. The truth cut Jordan like a saw. She wondered if the others had sensed the new intensity between them. Then she realized, she accepted, that the intensity was one-sided. Yet Jordan would replay that night a thousand times in her mind. She could not suppress the passion that flowed each time she was again near Karen. She could not hold her mind still from the hundred possible futures of their lives together. Jordan would never repress the softness, the gentleness of another woman's touch. And she would never again question an attraction that was as normal to her as the color of her eyes. She found her answer that night, but the proclamation would remain secret. She could know, but she could not articulate it. She had tasted, but she could not have.

Karen's graduation signaled the start of the next chapter in her life, and brought to a close, the daily mentoring that she had provided Jordan. That the two would remain close throughout their lives—despite the separation of nearly four hundred miles and lifestyles light-years apart—seemed lost in the whirlwind of pomp, circumstance, and ceremony.

\* \* \*

It was Marge's idea to give Karen an appropriate test toward marital vow, and she took full charge of the plan. She conspired with the other girls to give Karen a bachelorette party that she would always remember. Something raunchy and raucous, guaranteed to excite and to incite, an unrehearsed reaction from the one person in the Group not known for reaction. The girls knew the basics of the plan. Marge would pick them up at their homes, and together, they would kidnap Karen for a night of wanton pleasures! The girls loved the idea—especially when they learned that Todd's friends had already planned a night out for him. After all, they were women of the world now, and they would not be denied any experience that men had long squandered for themselves! Both parties were scheduled the night before the wedding—a singles bash for each half of the happy couple, a last chance to opt out before the big plunge! The girls knew that Karen had finalized all wedding arrangements weeks prior, as was her way. Her parents confirmed this, and agreed that a night out would be just the thing to calm her. And her friends secretly wanted to give Karen the one thing that she had never really had—an experience, an encounter, a memory of something that would not be in her control!

As the car pulled up to the home, Karen's parents played along and encouraged their daughter to enjoy an evening out with her friends. Karen reluctantly agreed, only when Marge produced her ticket to the Symphony! She was dressed and ready to go in less than half an hour, having just arrived home from the rehearsal dinner that her parents gave. Jordan, a member of the bridal party, was already at Karen's house. She was silently having immense separation issues, but intellectualized the wedding ceremony as a formal right of passage—not an end to their relationship.

She could not handle that possibility, and she could not let anyone else know how she felt about it! She would not admit the implication, but would not let go of the silent longing.

The girls talked, and joked, and sang, and laughed as they drove up the Parkway, and finally, rode off an exit ramp to a side route. Karen became suspicious with this "detour to the city," and began questioning Marge about the destination. The girls reveled and played in her rising discomfort. They loved to see her squirm! Marge gave uncharacteristic, serious response.

"Karen, don't you know us well enough to know that we would never do anything to harm you?"

"Yeah," added Janice, "We're just trying to have a little fun . . . at your expense . . ."

"Don't listen to them, Karen. Remember, there are some times in life when you have to lighten up, just a bit . . ." Jordan added.

"Oh, so I take it that we are NOT going to the concert? My, what a surprise . . . I should have guessed that, knowing you all as I do! I suppose we're going to some place jam-packed with booze and low class sex acts! I would expect nothing less from you . . . That would be your Symphony, all right!" Karen shook her head and cast a disapproving glance at them. She had suspected the event for weeks, but she would not spoil it for her friends. Those three could never keep a secret, and especially, not from her! She could read them as easily as any college textbook.

"Hey, what makes you say it's low class? You make symphonies wherever you can! And we all know that you could use a good tune! . . ." Marge laughed out loud.

"Yeah, what a prude! I thought that wouldn't start until after the wedding . . . ." Janice laughed in reply. Karen smirked back.

"You can bet ole Todd isn't worrying about anything! He's probably droolin' over some pole dance genie even as we speak. He's probably got those big Todd eyes glued to some pastie delights bouncing all over the place right now! Yup. He's smokin', and drinkin', and shoutin' after some shameless hussy, while you're here shorin' up the Moral Majority! Boring! I'm really worried about you, Karen!" Jordan shook her head in disapproval. She wanted to carry her away.

"OK—so maybe Todd is a little like that, but aren't they all? They have that pack mentality, you know. They think they smell a bitch in heat, and they lose all sense of propriety and judgment. Then they try to outdo each other just to get to her! Once they get that scent, it's all over for them, Poor Dears! Judgment goes right out the window, and they become slaves to that other head of theirs. Poor things! Can you imagine your lives being ruled by your crotch? And they run Big Business! Damn, they even run the country! . . . Well, believe me when I say that MY home won't be run that way!" Karen was emphatic.

"Our home would never be like that!" Jordan wanted to scream out to her. "I'd follow you like a puppy, and through our whole lives together. I'd protect and defend you like a wolverine, and I would never stray from your side! . . . Karen, don't go through with this!" She wanted to beg her, but her thoughts stayed bound in her mind, and her bark was silenced.

"But don't you worry, Karen. Trust us, relax, and have a good time. And remember, we're doing this for our own . . . I mean, your own good. There's more to life than the must-dos and the have-tos." Marge intended to carry them through a tradition spanning a hundred generations and a thousand different cultures. She would be the guide for Karen on this new twist to the female rite of passage.

The parking lot and facade of the building gave the club a classier appearance, but inside, it was all raunch, as Marge had promised. There were women packed at tables surrounding the dance floor; women standing along the walls; women standing in the foyer areas; and women standing at the bar. A smokey haze filled the club, and the lights were so dim that they could barely see before them. Only the crackling feeling of peanut shells under foot gave assurance that the structure had a floor. Strobe lights bounced off the walls and ceiling. Recessed lighting above the bar gave it the appearance of a runway—as if at any moment, Cheryl Tiegs, or some other famous model would strut onto the scene. Jordan gulped a

Vodka Collins so she wouldn't have to carry a conversation there. She just felt so out of place that night. Karen nodded to her in disbelief.

Suddenly, flood lights were focused on the bar, and well-built, barely clad young Chippendales stepped onstage amid the thunderous screams of a thousand lusty women shouting, "Take it off! Take it off!" and "Shake it, Don't Break it!" A crush of women suddenly pushed to the bar! Those vulnerable, brave young gods of sex and sensuality stood on the bar top amid the flash of lights, and the scent of sweat and perfume, while fruit juiced vodka drinks splashed among the crowd, and rum and coke flew through the air.

"Come on, Sweetheart, show me whatcha got!" The women began pounding on the bar top, demanding some man-slut action! The men danced in Speedos, they stripped from costumes, they jumped down from the bar top to bump and grind their tightly packaged piece of manhood before the faces of each and every female letch in the place! Karen secretly detested the bar, but would never have ruined it for her friends. They were trying so hard to show her a good time! She just hoped that she could somehow escape the night unnoticed. Jordan caught the message.

Marge was in her glory, though! "Hey Baby! Hey Baby!" She kept cat-calling and waving to the men, all the while shoving dollar bills inside their g-strings! And she really knew how to call them right to her—despite the hands and shouts of a hundred other women in the place! At one point, she signaled to "Athens," a swarthy, athletic, six foot hunk of man-magic, and nodded toward the unsuspecting Karen. Athens crouched on his toes and boogied his gorgeous, bronzed musculature right into her scarlet face. The women cheered and coaxed him to "let it all hang out!" Karen thought she would pass out, but before she could act, his tight buns bopped down the runway, his legs springing to the pound of the music! Marge stroked his calf as he managed to slip passed her, her friends all cheering her on.

"Go on, Karen, go after him!" Marge waved and yelled to her. Karen wanted to crawl under a table, but there were too many spiked heels and boots stomping to make it out alive! She suffered the embarrassment for the amusement of her friends, and counted the moments until she could make a hasty retreat from the club! Perspiration now ran down the sides of her cheeks, her face now a permanent crimson. And still, the women cheered them on.

"Come on, Honey, show me whatcha got! Don't be shy, Boy!" Arms flailed and waved in the air, and dollars swished back and forth across the path. The dancers smiled, licked their lips, and winked back to women of their choice!

The bar was wild, as women vied for the attention of each male stripper. But it was the loudest and the rowdiest that won their time—and that was Marge! She called to another dancer, a hard hat who had stripped to his white jockeys by the time he reached Jordan. She sat half-dazed, half-crazed, and totally intoxicated, her eyes as big as saucers. The Hard Hat wiggled his shaven and oiled chest toward her body as his arms surrounded but did not touch her shoulders, his hips a gyrating tool! Jordan glanced to Karen, then back to the stripper. But when she tried to touch his tight white beauties, the dancer playfully wagged his finger "NO, NO" and bounded on to the next group of screaming, lust-hungry women. Jordan tried to call him back, but the music stifled her voice.

"Hey, I was only checkin' for the brand name!" Her pleas were drowned out by the whoops and hollers of women in frenzy! More drinks, and the crowd grew rowdier! Women were launching themselves as sexual projectiles onto the stage and toward those dancing young men, those torrid specimens of male anatomy!

The girls held hands high, as Janice screamed to "Captain America," whose stars and stripes barely covered the bulge in his G-string.

"Hey, he's already standing at attention!" She joked to the others, amid their laughs and screams. She tried to salute him, her fingertips just glancing off of his chest, as she raised her hand to her forehead. She, too, was busy stuffing dollars into the front of any dancer that braved the stroll down the runway and bopped his stuff before her. It was the Captain who actually called Marge up onto the bar, and the two began a sensuous meld—accompanied by the chants and screams of the multitude—before the bartender finally flagged her down. She let her hands run along his sinew as she headed again to the floor. She was Woman Personified! Karen cringed and prayed that Marge would not want her to share in the conquest! And all the while, the friends cheered each other on!

The room became a blur of music, a dizzying array of colors and shouts, as Jordan stumbled to the restroom, and joined the line of women now nearly out to the foyer. By the time she had returned, Marge was being escorted out of the club, having refused to remove her hands from the muscled back of yet another male stripper!

"What the hell! I wasn't tasting. It was just a quick sample!" Marge screamed in indignation. She was trying to shrug off the bouncer's hand from her shoulder. The girls joined in her protests, but the manager refused to be swayed by the drunken begging of three women without pride or shame! Karen was mortified!

"Let's go Ladies . . ." He barked at them as they were promptly and firmly escorted out the door! The Group reluctantly accepted Karen's decision that she drive them home, and abandoned any thought of carrying the party to another club. Jordan immediately fell asleep in the back seat, and Janice, also drunk, slept with her head on Jordan's shoulder.

"Hey, I've been thrown out of better joints than this." Marge continued to protest, and she screamed at the bouncer one last time.

Karen's response was swift, "Quit it!" and Marge snapped to! Karen surveyed her friends from the rear view mirror, and silently shook her head. She had some real concerns about their futures without her.

\* \* \*

Jordan was still hung-over from the bachelorette party as she maneuvered into her bridesmaid gown. Her head pounded as she bent over to slip on her high heels. Although she had her hair done at the same salon with Karen, Marge, and Janice earlier that morning, she hardly remembered the meeting. Her headache was blinding, and her nausea unrelenting. She tried several strategies including drinking what seemed like a gallon of cold water. She tried a bit of the "hair of the dog," some pink stuff like Pepto, and even an egg concoction her mother prepared, but nothing could generate remedy. She would have to suffer through the wedding of the closest friend she had ever had! She vowed never to drink another Vodka Collins! Her head ached from the alcoholic numbing of the night before, but her heart broke now with each thought that Karen would soon be gone. She detested Todd for this, but she would suffer that thought in silence.

Tyler and Martin picked up Jordan, Janice, and Marge at Marge's home, and drove them to the Church. Jordan would ride in the limo with the other bridal party members following the ceremony. She was only briefly acquainted with the other members, and dreaded the thought of making small talk with them. She did not believe that she could talk above the pounding in her head, and did not believe that anyone would be able to hear her above it. Her friends assured her that this was not the case. She fought back panic and tears, as she pictured Karen exchanging vows for a lifetime with someone else. Yet, she would not acknowledge her resentment.

Jordan had only a minute alone with Karen before the ceremony. She took Karen's hand, pulled her to a shouldered hug, and wished her every happiness. But inside, her heart was screaming to Karen to leave with her, to tear off the veil, to dump the gown at curb side, to toss her white satin heels to the wind! "Fly with me to a thousand possible tomorrows!"

"Karen, you know that if you ever need anything, no matter what it is, no matter where you are, just call me, and I will be there for you. And another thing—Todd better treat you well. He's a dead man if he doesn't." She fought hard to hold back her tears, but she could still feel the words forming in her mouth. Her throat so ached that she could not speak. She wanted to beg Karen to leave with her. She wanted to run away with her, to drag her off, to be at her side forever. But she couldn't get out the words that would make it all happen. "He better be good to you, or else!"

"You've got that right! But I think . . . it'll be ok. So, you just lighten up a bit, and you'll be ok too." She then pulled a small angel pin from her purse, and pinned it to the shoulder of Jordan's gown.

"Just to get you through the next two years without me," she said. They cried together. Jordan could not imagine life without her, but Karen could not offer her more.

The Bridal party fell into line, and as the organist played The Wedding March from Figaro, Jordan completed the walk to the altar, being escorted by Todd's brother. She saw the Group sitting near the aisle, the bride's side of the Church, and felt tears streaming down her face. Todd stood confident at the altar, took the hand of his bride, and led her away from both parents and friends. As Jordan watched Karen run to the limo, with Todd pulling her into their next stage of life, she felt the deepest sense of loss.

\* \* \*

It was nearly a month before Jordan actually spoke with Karen again. She received post cards from the Riviera, where the couple had honeymooned, one of the wedding gifts Karen's parents had given. Jordan treasured these bits of Karen, and placed the cards in her special drawer. She held them close to her breast, when she was felt confident that no one would see her. At other times, she would slap herself for carrying on so about a friend. But the deepest recesses of her heart talked to her about the truth of their relationship. Jordan busied herself that summer working at the Shop-Rite as a cashier. She was preparing for return to college and the start of her official junior year. Her father referred to Jordan as the "Junior Senior," and joked that she might graduate with more credits than an MGM extravaganza! Jordan's mother continued to parade the names of eligible young men before her.

"Healthy, well-liked young men workin' in the buildin' trades," her mother stated, "who'd fit well into the family." Her mom had no clue.

Jordan knew most of the boys her mother named, and she did not understand her mother's rating system. In fact, Jordan did not understand her mother very well at all. What she found most puzzling was that a woman of her mother's intelligence could be satisfied with a life of servitude to a man and his offspring. She often questioned her mother, taunted her about this choice, and praised the women of her own generation, for finally finding the nerve to seek meaning on their own terms. No man would dictate to Jordan. She was amazed that her mother had accepted such behavior from her father. Jordan worshipped him, but he could be demanding. Her mother never viewed this as sacrifice, and noted that most of the other mothers in the area were living the same lifestyle. She could not understand Jordan's refusal to accept what had been commonplace for a thousand years.

"Man is the hunter and gatherer," her father said, "and women will rear the children, cook meals, and bring the occasional beer." That summarized her mother's life, alright, but it would not be hers!

The tensions between Jordan and her mother escalated if the two were together for more than a few hours at a time. Her mother felt indignation toward her, as if Jordan's feminist philosophy was a personal rejection of her value as a woman and as a human being. Jordan felt frustration with her mother, believing that advocacy for husband and family meant a lack of support for her career goals and sacrifice. The two would argue bitterly, never realizing that they were riding the crest of a generational discord, a cultural and social upheaval. Without Karen to act as sounding board, Jordan again felt lost and alone.

Although she worked long hours between the pharmacy, and now, the food store, Jordan found this a refuge from the tornado that was her home. And she was making the money she needed for the next semesters. And the jobs kept her occupied, kept her mind busy. She wouldn't have the time to fantasize about the life that she should be sharing, the life that Todd was now living, with the Love he had taken from her. But at night, in the quiet of her room, and as her family slept, she would replay again, the few moments they shared together, and the dream that she had built around Karen. Try as she might, she could not calm that tornado either.

Martin and Tyler each made their weekly phone calls to her, and Jordan was amazed at how easily they were able to pick up a conversation—just like they had only been talking at breakfast! And she ran to the mail tray each night in hopes of a letter or postcard from them. They sent her all sorts of things—gum wrapper chains, braided friendship bracelets, poolside photos showing their best muscle poses—anything that could maintain the close ties. Martin's calls were filled with large gaps of silence, usually filled only by taunts from his sister. He was just comfortable sharing space with Jordan. But Tyler's calls were more secretive, more troublesome, as he tried to hide all conversation from his father. One call in particular was quickly aborted, when his father's yelling showed that Tyler's call was discovered. Yet Tyler would never really talk about any of this. He, too, seemed to live a life alone, but for a very different reason.

Jordan managed some time with Marge and Janice as the summer passed, and the three would go to the boardwalk to pick up guys, or would go to the beach to work on their tans. They wanted to return to college with that St. Tropez' tan so often touted on the radio! Who would know that their vacationland was only ten minutes from home? And she would go to the beach alone in early morning or late evening, whenever she had the chance. She loved the beach, and often thought that this was the only thing in her life that had not changed. The shoreline might alter a bit, the dunes would rise and fall as the nor'easters dictated, but the sounds of the surf and the laughing gulls were forever constant. She found much peace there, sitting by the shore. She loved body surfing on the waves, or skipping clam shells across the tides. She loved breathing the fresh, brine, salt air, and feeling the sand mold around her ankles as the surf retreated. She loved the warmth of the sun on her body, and the smell of coconut oil smoothed over her skin. She loved the feeling of rejuvenation, and of renewal. The beach was a life source for her.

Although she was eager to return to school, Jordan felt the intense homesickness returning before her parents had even left the campus parking lot. There had been arguments that summer, the result of growing pains in the family. Jordan was establishing her independence. Kelly was not far behind. Her parents would still have time with Jonathan. But her mother commented about how sad it seemed, to mark their own advancing years, by subtracting the number of children still left at home. Even her father, the notorious "tough guy," had tears as he carried the last box to her room, and kissed her goodbye. She would be home again at Thanksgiving and Christmas, but she was changing so quickly! She hardly seemed like the same little girl who had tagged along with him to his jobs on Saturdays. Yet when she looked up into his eyes, he could still see that same tomboy smile that had so often charmed him out of an otherwise deserved punishment. She was his little girl. He tried to remember when he had first realized that his daughter had become a woman. He then dismissed the thought, and assured himself that she would always be his little girl! He knew that his family was moving toward the next stage of its cycle of life, and he was filled with a deep sadness. Some things, even he could not control or change.

Jordan had been attending her Fall '72 classes for only a week, before the first real pangs of the "Outside World" began to impinge on her piece of heaven. It was still summer, really, but given the southern climate and the area's reliance on farming, the school's schedules varied a bit from those up north. Classes started two weeks before Labor Day. The students were still enjoying the mix and blend of education and socializing, while the pressure of grades still lay in the future. The campus was alive with youthful competition, as the collegians shared the broadcasts of the XX Olympiad from Munich. The Group was playing Ultimate Frisbee on the back lawn of Balmoral Dorm during the commercials. Martin was showing off his newest moves.

"Go out for a long one!" he shouted to Janice, as he flipped the disk behind his back. Tyler and Jordan were racing her for the catch and the score. Tyler dove and snatched the disc just before it reached her hand. He ran the distance to the goal line.

"Touchdown! And once again, the cream rises to the top!" Tyler was prancing back to the dorm's day room, his arms held high in victory.

But suddenly, the hopeful promise of the world at play together collapsed with the news bulletins that interrupted the viewing. As the horrifying details of the hostage Israeli Wrestling Team broke into world consciousness, the dreams of a generation yearning for peace were again shattered. They exploded with a grenade in a helicopter, and with the gun fire of the PLO's Black September faction.

Jordan and the other students sat motionless, speechless, as the accounts were reported by a stunned Jim McKay. Violence now dominated even the games that human beings played together! From then on, all sporting events would be tainted by some international connotation, some political contamination. The Cold War shadows of China and Russia were joined by a new enemy, and the dorms and classrooms were filled with speculation of a renewed war in the Middle East. Jordan abhorred politics, and became increasingly verbal in her condemnation of the political elite—both foreign and American—who so readily and casually wagered human life and suffering for the accomplishment of their own interests. Jordan was not a communist; she was not a socialist; she was not an anarchist. Jordan was a humanist. But as she became more politically aware and more confident in her verbalizations, these lines became increasingly blurred.

Her friends were concerned for her safety—both figuratively and literally—as she soap-boxed her way through her remaining college years. Each new international crisis brought renewed vehemence and public oratory. She did not hold public speaking engagements, as such. She only held conversations with other students, whenever the opportunity would arise. And she seemed more and more to make that happen. The unsuspecting audience found it near impossible to extricate themselves from this verbal foray, unless they shared Jordan's "enlightenment." Each national issue generated a new political lecture, and she seemed to move farther and farther to the left. And there were many comment-worthy events that year—the Nixon visit to China; the shooting of George Wallace; the re-election of Nixon-Agnew over McGovern-Shriver, and the subsequent fall of the executive office the next year—the resignation of Agnew (his nolo contend ere statement, and Jordan's pride as a self anointed Pointy Headed Liberal); the appointment of Gerald Ford as Vice-President (and his unfortunate golfing); the rise of the IRA, and the British seizure of control of Northern Ireland; the bombing of North Vietnam; the Third World famine; Roe vs. Wade; the Watergate break-in and the loss of integrity; the rise of Kissinger, the fall of Haldeman, Ehrlichman, Kleindienst, Dean—and later, in 1974, of Nixon himself!

Her friends found it difficult to contain her "righteous indignation." They would try to balance these conversations with cultural points of interest, in the hopes of swinging the topics away from Jordan's fervor. They talked of Picasso's death; Mark Spitz; Apollo 17's walk on the moon; Pioneer 10's view of Jupiter; Jonathan Livingston Seagull; Fiddler On the Roof; Mary Tyler Moore; All In The Family; Carlos Castaneda; Neil Young; Neil Simon; Carly Simon; The Godfather; Dirty Harry; Mohammad Ali; the Miami Dolphins; The Oakland A's—but Jordan would remain undaunted. She was becoming a political preacher as well as a social worker. She preached the word of love for all humanity, due them just by virtue of their membership in the species! She could not tolerate man's inhumanity to man, regardless of political boundaries or geographic dictates. Jordan was finding her connection to the Universal Other, and to humanity itself. She especially liked this emerging part of herself, and thought that, maybe, this would become the core of her missing third dimension. But what she was also missing was that she had now come to the attention of both the Student Council, and the Executive Board of the college.

\* \* \*

Jordan was rooming with Marge that year. The two got along well, although, at times, Marge's housekeeping could be somewhat below par. Marge's philosophy was that if you could at least enter a room, the place was clean. If you did not trip over the dust clumps and food chunks, vacuuming was unnecessary. Laundry was especially problematic. On more than one occasion, Jordan would use a hanger to prod the pile of debris in search of decayed matter. But Marge explained that she had a system.

"I use my desk chair as a pile-on for those outfits too dirty to hang up, but too clean to wash. These are your "once-worn" blouses or blue jeans. As a rule, clothing can be worn at least twice, as long as there are no food spills present, and the wrinkles can be easily explained. Now, your freshly laundered jeans—you have to be wear them just before they dry completely, so that you can fit back into them. Otherwise, you're not going to be able to breathe, let alone sit! Got it? So you see, there is a plan in place!" Her laundry cycle would thus repeat twice monthly.

Jordan couldn't respond, although it did seem rather odd to her, that someone so hell-bent on rejecting authority would develop a set of rules for a simple chore! Jordan often had visions, though, that one day she would find Marge buried under a pile of her "once-worn" clothing!

Although Marge's family was well-to-do by Jordan's standards, Marge spent large parts of her psyche rejecting her family's values, her family's affluence, and her family's status in the community. She had a rebellious nature, a wild heart. And while she and Jordan may have shared some of the same behaviors and behavioral deficits, they were operating from very different places. Marge was assailing what she considered the middle class rigidity of mind. Jordan's behaviors were more of exploration and the strive for experience. Jordan often thought that Marge's parents were too tolerant of her dissident behaviors, too indulgent of her antisocial ways. But they loved their only daughter, and showered her with nurturing, with support, and with a trust sometimes undeserved. Her father was a mid-level corporate executive with a pharmaceutical company. Marge described him as brilliant, and attributed her genetic propensity for chemistry to his side of the gene pool. Marge's mother volunteered at various civic organizations and at the town's local food bank. In recognition of her mother's accomplishments, Marge had a food bank poster taped to her wall, across which she had written "Eat the Rich." Her mother thought that was hysterical.

Tyler and Martin spent part of their summer biking together along the Virginia and Maryland shores. They even brought their bikes back to college with them. They were rooming together in Hill Hall that year, although Janice was skeptical that they could maintain their grades under this arrangement. Like the girls, they could feed on each other, and be either a very positive influence, or a very negative one. Jordan wondered how the Group would fair without Karen helping and holding them all together. She had been the enforcer, coaching them to meet research assignments and term paper deadlines. She tutored, or arranged for tutoring, if one or another began to fall below an "A" average. She scheduled study sessions into their nightly social calendars. She had really been their leader. Although Janice was best suited to fill this void, it would be some time before she could develop the charisma or the insight to pull it off.[12] Even if just a friend, Jordan missed Karen horribly, but could not share this with anyone.

She observed this same sense of loss as an undercurrent moving among all of her friends. The Group was now moving through its own cycle of life, she thought, and was struggling to re-establish its balance, its equilibrium. Jordan could clearly see the affects that occur when group membership changes. She drew correlations in these dynamics, to the changes occurring in her own family. And these changes in her family and in the Group filled her with even more anxiety. She feared that she would lose herself, if she lost either! Karen maintained phone contact at least twice monthly, and sent the appropriate card as the situation warranted. Jordan's parents sent biweekly care packages of Scooter Pies and Twinkies. Jordan drew a strong sense of comfort from these tangible connections to the people that she loved. She held each contact, each item, as if it was a cherished jewel.[13]

---

[12] A brief discussion of Systems Theory can be found in the Appendix and Bibliography for Chapter Two.

[13] A brief discussion of the life cycles of a family can be found in the Appendix and Bibliography for Chapter Two.

Jordan's classes moved much as they had during her first year. But the number of research papers nearly doubled, as the Social Work Department began its simulation of the typical paperwork requirements in the field. She was instructed to "examine her feelings" so much, that she began mentally narrating even simple tasks throughout her day. She was identifying her personal values, so that she would not inadvertently impose her own value system onto her clients. She was analyzing her feelings and belief systems, so that her own prejudices would not jeopardize the rights of her clients. She was developing a tolerance and respect for the rights of all people. She was now formulating a Social Work value system.

She assumed a new speech pattern with the Group, and open-ended statements like, "But how did you feel when this occurred" became her catch phrase. Martin teased her to annoyance. Janice suggested that there might still be time to transfer to the Physics Department. At one point, Jordan left the table, and returned only after he apologized.

"How did that comment make me feel?" Jordan repeated, as she stood at tableside in indignation. "Pretty dammed pissed off!" she exclaimed.

"Now let me see if Ah have this raght," Martin teased in his exaggerated Southern drawl. "Ah hear you sayin' that you have become increasin'ly agitated with the childish jocularity of your moronic friends, and that you would really lahke to tell them all to fuck off. Is that what Ahm hearin' you say, Jordan?"

Jordan, exasperated, promptly flipped Martin the finger, and stormed off to the dorm. He sent her flowers the next day, with a card that said simply, "But Jordan, you know we all love you." Maybe she did.

Back at the dorm, Marge was having her own share of problems with her coursework. She tried to explain the concepts that were giving her the most trouble. Although Jordan listened intently to Marge's remarks, she had no idea what Marge was talking about. She found herself drifting off momentarily in thought, making Marge's explanation even less accessible. When Marge realized that Jordan was not following their conversation, she suggested that they take Tyler and Martin's bikes, and ride along the tow path by the river. They hadn't been far along the path when Marge stopped by the side of the trail and lit a joint. At first Jordan thought that Marge had started smoking, but then caught a whiff of the weed, and realized that Marge was now smoking pot.

"When did this all start?" Jordan asked. "I thought you were into booze."

"When I couldn't get booze, of course," Marge stated, and passed the joint to Jordan. Being the aspiring social worker that she was, Jordan decided to partake. How else would she understand what her drug-addicted clients might experience? But the reality was that Jordan was using experiences like this to dismantle the walls that seemed to separate her from everyone but Karen.

"Ak-hoowa!" The first draw caught Jordan by surprise, and she choked and coughed a bit. But once beyond that barrier, Jordan enjoyed the calming effects of the drug. She became hysterical with the nonsensical statements Marge quoted as chemical theory.

"Now I've got it!" Marge finally exclaimed, and she drew several formulas in the dirt. Jordan punctuated the equations by turning the formulas into happy faces and stick figures! She had diagrammed an entire family before Marge's equation was done!

"A melding of art and science—technology gives birth to emotion! Man has, at last, found his place in the universe! Quantum physics simplified by the mere toke of a weed!"

The two continued their ride on the tow path. Jordan's mind raced as her legs pedaled along the dirt trail. She loved the freedom that she was feeling, and loved the wind blowing through her hair. And she loved the thoughts that kept flowing to her, like the sun filtering through the branches of trees.

"First, a carbon atom, and then one of hydrogen. Meld their organic compounds, and life emerges! First a zygote, then an embryo. Next a fetus, and then a human. Then a person, and onto a family. Next a neighborhood, and then a community. Now a state, and then a nation. Next the countries, and then the world. From a single atom, the universe flows, doubling and duplicating, connecting and uniting! We are a part of the whole of life—and this is the connection that we have with each other. This is the thread of shared existence that holds us as one. At last, I have found the secret peace that I crave!"

"Wow!" was all that Marge could add, as Jordan followed close behind her.

Jordan was amazed that she had finally reached the secret that lay just beyond her grasp. And she was amazed that she could feel so elated in one way, and yet, still feel so much in control in another. But she knew other things about herself, even if she could not readily admit it. She realized that she could enjoy these feelings way too much.

"This is one pattern that we can definitely not get into." She made the proclamation with authority.

"Not to worry, Jordan. I only bought a dime bag. And by the way, it's hidden in the heater in our room! So be careful when you turn on the juice, or you'll have the whole dorm tokin' it up! It's right next to the pint of Seagrams." Marge felt that Jordan should know. They both agreed not to share this secret with the others.

The girls returned to the dorm and scoffed down a few scooter pies, then joined a group of students in the day room. Sturgis was playing guitar accompanied by a group of the "peripherals" who were singing along with him. They had just finished "Peace Train"[14] when Tyler challenged Sturgis to a duel, a musical "Can you top this?" With the intro chords played out on the piano, Tyler led the group through an Elton John medley, beginning with "Tiny Dancer."[15] The friends sang and played point/counter-point for several songs. But it was Tyler's version of

---

[14] A reference to: Stevens, Cat (1971). "Peace Train". [as recorded by Cat Stevens]. On *Teaser and the Firecat* [audio album]. Santa Monica, Ca.: A&M Records

[15] A reference to: John, Elton, and Taupin, Bernie (1971). "Tiny Dancer" [as recorded by Elton John]. On *Madman Across The Water* [audio album]. Universal City, Ca.: Uni Records

"Burn Down the Mission"[16] that finally won him acclaim as the victor. A small group of Betas were playing cards in the corner, but even they stopped to watch Tyler bang out the chorus. The chords brought the crowd to a standing ovation, and brought Sturgis to his knees, as he held up his guitar, and bowed to the master!

"So much for eight years of classical piano . . ." Tyler said, to which the crowd screamed "Fix!" in reply. They all finished the night with a rousing discussion about Nixon, Lenin, Lincoln, Jesus, and the political implications and influences each had exerted on economics, philosophy, and plight of the common man.

The next few days went along normally, and Jordan noted no ill effects from her encounter with drugs. There were no hallucinations, no irresistible urges to use again, no problems with memory or perception. The Group, however, suspected that she and Marge were holding some kind of secret! They had even seen them whispering and giggling together! Although both denied that there was anything happening, Jordan was a notoriously bad liar—a fact that would haunt her throughout her life—and this gave little credence to their statements.

Later, Jordan sat smugly in class listening to a heated discussion about the politics of drugs, and the movement for legalization of marijuana.[17] She contributed to the discussion in support of legalization. She saw it as a means to avoid the unnecessary imprisonment of those who occasionally chose to use. After all, she thought, she had smoked a joint once—she had been there, and she knew! She didn't share this experience with the class, but several of her colleagues were overheard to suggest that Jordan had been drug involved! The rumor grew and spread that Jordan had even completed a rehab. program once, and that she

---

[16] A reference to: John, Elton, and Taupin, Bernie (1970). "Burn Down The Mission" [as recorded by Elton John]. On *Tumbleweed Connection* [audio album]. Universal City, Ca.: Uni Records

[17] For a brief discussion of social policy formation as a function of social work, please refer to Appendix and Bibliography for Chapter Two.

had a recent "slip!" This drew the interest of fellow Social Work students far and wide, as each vied to be the support to their wayward counterpart, and perhaps, take credit for her recovery!

Jordan tried to extricate herself from this center of attention. But her efforts to refute these rumors became the fodder for theories of denial,[18] and each adamant statement she made seemed to cement rumor to fact. She was amazed that such distortions could result from simple assumption based on a single discussion. She paid close attention to her appearance, her behaviors, even her mannerisms and conversations over the next week. Marge and Janice openly joked to hysterics about the rumors, while Tyler and Martin ran interference. They formed a united front in defense of Jordan, an effort to quell the nonsense.

Several evenings later, other rumors were rampant—"There's gonna be a raid in the dorm!" Jordan spread the word. "They were tipped off about the pot!" A rash of toilet flushings could be heard throughout the building! Marge was panicked, and carried her stash to the bathroom by hiding it in her bra. She was almost back, when a group of ski-masked men pushed through the hallways and forced themselves into each room.

"Panty raid!" some girl screamed, and began pummeling the intruders with pillows. The marauders pushed through the women's lines of defense, and started ransacking the rooms at will! Drawers were left askew, and underwear of every style, color, and proportion were tossed irreverently along the hallways. Nearly every woman's lingerie had been captured and kidnapped. Every room had been desecrated, every panty had been mauled—everyone's, but Jordan's. Her drawers were left opened, but her underwear remained intact.

As they surveyed the damage, Janice chided, "You're so lucky—I guess there isn't much of a fantasy in white, cotton, grannies . . ."

"That's so very funny," came the reply.

---

[18] What's denial? See the Appendix and Bibliography for Chapter Two.

Marge skulked into the hallway from their room. She somberly gathered up her red lace bra and panties, now devalued by lack of surprise, and that now lay against the wall. Those items had somehow been dropped when the intruders were attacked themselves. She looked at the underwear, and then to her friends, in dismay.

"For this, we lost the hooch! How many good times have just been flushed away as a result of this childishness! Probably pounds of the stuff have disappeared, now irretrievable, in the septic system of our beloved college! Is no one to be accountable for this waste? And what was the point? Nothing at all! If they had just waited till Saturday, they could probably have gotten things like this filled with 'girl!' . . . Well that's men for you—what simpletons!"

The next morning every male dorm displayed the mark of conquest—a flag of women's lingerie! The men coyly smiled at the women on line in the cafeteria, each imagining the owner's build, each trying to match face to bra cup size! The girls faked ownership of the crimson lace that boasted tales of frequent visits, as they smiled back at boys who were as yet sexually untested.

And so went life in this quiet collegiate corner of the country.

*  *  *

Jordan continued her devoted study to the art and science of Social Work. She committed to memory the author and basic tenets of each of its major theories. She researched the origins of these theories, and often drew outlines for posting on the bulletin board above her desk. She found herself studying more, and spending more time alone, since Karen had gone. The Group was becoming less cohesive, but still had all of their meals together. New members were being added to the periphery. Old members, like Marge and Tyler, were spending more time alone as their relationships progressed. Jordan continued the pub schedules with them every weekend, and cherished this time with her friends. When they felt that their drinking was escalating, they simply chose to sit out a weekend. They also cut down on the amount consumed at the pub, as the glamour of a predictable hang-over, and a sure date at the rim of a toilet, had begun to wear thin.[19]

Marge now used their room heater as her personal bar, often hiding small bottles of sloe gin, vodka, or other alcohol-based contraband there. While this was a source of some concern to Jordan, she did not object. On the more difficult evenings, the girls would lock their door and toast off the day. Jordan still only casually dated. She excused this as necessity in the face of a demanding course of study. Secretly, however, she was beginning to recognize the inescapable truth that Karen brought to her attention—and she was very afraid. This probably contributed to Jordan's own escalating drinking at the time. Yet, she focused, instead, on her chosen vocation.

---

[19] A definition of binge drinking can be found in Appendix and Bibliography for Chapter Two.

# Chapter 3

It was just after sunrise, and she was already at her desk, plugging away at a term paper:

"The history of Social Work has paralleled the needs of man, and was inspired by one of his highest sensitivities. That is compassion, an awareness of the suffering of others, and a desire to reduce and to eradicate that suffering. The concept of Social Work is nearly as old as man himself. Yet, this concept has morphed in response to the values of any given time. It's a noble idea, really, the idea that man holds some responsibility for his fellow man. It's been around probably since he first tribed and shared the results of the hunt. There were divisions of labor, assignment of tasks, and allocation of resources according to tribal custom. There were children to be fed, clothed, and tended. There were the tribe's elderly, who were also dependent. The clan either made provision for its vulnerable members, or found a means to discharge themselves from that responsibility. Their actions were governed by their tribal value system, their customs, their rules for life in the tribe. At a later time, feudal lords cared for the community and doled out shelter, protection, and status according to the contributions made by their serfs, who paid with traded goods, later substituted as taxes. The poor were shunned then, and begging became the basis for a kind of welfare of that time.

Moving along the social evolutionary chain, individual farm families in the American wilderness shared their scarce food stuffs with other members of the community when needed. A similar kind of sharing can be found in most cultures and throughout history. This stands as a further testament to the universal nature of compassion that exists in all men. This sharing came with the expectation, of course, that such assistance would be reciprocated, and the concept became a primary survival tool for the group. This mutual aid later evolved into a belief system of philanthropy (call it charity) that grew from the local churches, and later, through helping organizations dedicated to specific tasks. These groups became known as mutual aid societies. These societies augmented the austere help given by almshouses (a.k.a. "poorhouses") provided by towns and counties in America since pre-revolutionary times. And the poorhouse concept found its basis back in England . . ."

"Hummm!" Jordan said to herself as she read the opening paragraphs to her term paper. "A little rough here and there, but not a bad start." She'd write and re-write the thing until the paper found the perfect rhythm.

"Due to the severe depressions of the mid nineteenth century, and the rise of the Industrial Revolution, the mutual aid societies could not keep pace with the monumental needs of the growing poor! A new strategy gave rise to the settlement house movement as a way to address those pressures. Toynbee Hall, the first settlement house, was started in London in the mid 1800's. It rose in response to the disparity between classes, and the lack of basic resources, like food, clothing, and shelter. The settlement houses provided tangible assistance to the folks at society's lowest economic levels. These people faced their unfortunate predicaments largely due to changes forced by the Industrial Revolution, and when humanity began its migration from farm to city. These situations were not caused by individual failures. Instead, they were caused by factors (a.k.a. social environmental factors) that were out of a person's control!

The Industrial Revolution in America, the Civil War, and the Reconstruction also resulted in a movement from the rural southern farms to the northern cities. Farmers, field hands, and families, now urban and without work, were also without life's necessities. The immigration movements from Europe to America compounded these problems. Charity Organization Societies (COS), churches, and private citizens struggled to meet these burgeoning demands. Government had not yet considered the need for the large scale assistance programs that would become commonplace in the next century. But the Freedman's Bureau did provide limited assistance to the country's newly freed slaves, and it is considered the first federally funded social welfare program in the United States.

Jayne Addams (considered a founder of Social Work), and Ellen Gates Starr began Hull House in Chicago in the 1890's, establishing the Settlement House Movement here in America. Addams patterned this on the Neighborhood Guild of New York, the first U.S. settlement house. Not only did she provide help in meeting basic needs, but she also taught skills that were needed for survival in the city. It was the whole "give a fish vs. teach to fish" idea. These included classes in morality, hygiene, English, parenting, and work ethic. She used the threefold strategy of casework, education, and advocacy to meet the needs of her clients, and to help improve their lives. She was among the first community organizers, as she established "voting blocs" to impact on elected officials. She recognized that she could use knowledge, values, and beliefs to impact the power structure, and thereby, affect the distribution of resources. Simply said, Addams used voters in numbers to convince politicians to provide help where it was needed. As a result, she was instrumental in establishing a juvenile court system, widows' pension programs, public health concepts, and child labor laws. She also opposed US involvement in WWI. Jane Addams was awarded the Nobel Peace Prize in 1931. She stands as an example of the role of advocacy in the profession of Social Work . . ."

Jordan worshipped Jane Addams as her idol, and kept a framed photocopy of her picture above her bed, and next to her photo of Mother Theresa. She looked up at the photos for a moment, as if to gain inspiration from their mere sight. After a moment's reflection, she returned to her task.

"Mary Richmond was another philanthropist of the 1890's intent on improving the plight of the immigrant masses. Mary established the Friendly Visitors Movement, a formulation of untrained, upper class men and women in religious organizations who worked with the poor. They used morality and personal example as a method to encourage economic improvement. They also assisted in placing poor immigrant children on farms in the mid-west to ensure that these children had the basic necessities. They helped establish such organizations as the Children's Aid Society, and the Association for the Improvement of the Condition of the Poor. These paraprofessionals became the forerunners of the professional Social Workers of today.

Medical Social Work evolved in the 1920's in response to the needs of soldiers returning from WWI. These social workers were largely responsible for discharge planning and public education regarding disease. In the 1930's to 1940's, the country was in the throes of The Great Depression. Frances Perkins, a social worker, rose as a key figure in FDR's New Deal. Through a variety of social programs that she helped to devise, Americans received food stuffs, financial assistance, and work assistance, as showcased in the Social Security Act of 1935. This social worker helped Americans survive, and kept their dignity and their hopes alive, by helping to create programs that met this national need. This is an example of social work as an instrument in the formation of government sponsored programs that help to shape society. In other words, Social Work impacts on Social Policy.[20] . . ."

As Jordan's typewriter droned on, the words wrapped her mind like an intoxicant. She loved playing the intellectual. She loved rolling the words off of her tongue. She loved spinning an insight and forming a connection. She loved seeing her thoughts dance across the page. She loved the power that such words

---

[20] For a reference list of materials on the impact of social values on social policy, please refer to the Appendix and Bibliography for Chapter Three.

could bring. And she loved these exercises that built her persuasive muscle. She turned herself back to her task so that the romance with her own mind could continue.

"Peace also brought change. During the late 1940's and into the 1950's, America experienced the impact of the Post-WWII Baby Boom. This change in national demographics also brought about changes in society. Women who worked in factories while their men served in war were now forced to return to the home, as the men returned to their jobs. This caused role changes and subsequent conflicts in the family, and in response, the family therapy movement was born.

These societal changes continued to impact America as it moved into the 1960's and 1970's. The Civil Rights Movement, the Women's Movement, and the Gay Rights Movement were all born during this period. These movements further resulted in change in both home and society. They pushed humanity forward in its own evolution, as disenfranchised groups demanded the equal protections of the law. Social upheaval resulted in the mandated respect and dignity for the basic rights of others. Social workers helped organize voting blocs; contributed their knowledge base; participated in public education; and impacted on elected officials! These elected officials brought forth the legislation that guaranteed equal protections, and allowed equal access, to the American way of life. Yet despite this progress, some groups have continued to struggle for acceptance . . ."

Of course, Jordan had not yet accepted that she belonged to one such minority—or at least, she hadn't verbalized that fact. Instead, she focused her desires on a single person, and honed her mind on her work.

"Although the first school of Social Work was started in conjunction with New York's COS and Columbia University in 1898, such schools soon became established in conjunction with the schools of Urban Planning and Administration. These schools typically focused on casework practice. Social Work as a profession was solidified with the establishment of the Council of Social Work Education in 1952, with a unification of minimum course curriculum, and with the formation of the National Association of Social Workers in 1955. [21] Through these organizations, Social Work will continue to advance its own knowledge base, as it strives to advance the causes of humanity itself. And man will be the better because of it."

"Ta-daa!" she proclaimed. "Finished!"

Jordan joined NASW as a student when she was first enrolled in the curriculum. She clearly saw no benefit in putting off membership until graduation, and she nudged her classmates to do the same. She always wanted to be affiliated with a powerful professional organization.

Reviewing the history of the Social Work profession inspired Jordan to feel that she, too, could contribute to meaningful change in America. Perhaps her name would one day be written among its pages. She was too young yet to see the changes that would come in the field as the result of Reaganomics, nor could she envision the changing country some thirty years ahead. She could however, see the imaginary banner at the W.T. Grant store changing already!

"Jordan Mathews, foremost leading authority on Social Policy in America, lectures tonight on her newly released book, Social Policy, Not Social Politics."

She laughed and shook her head as she dismissed this delusion, and then caught herself thinking, "But, you never know. Hey, why not me?"

Clearly, she had not yet gotten the picture! But at least she was well on her way to writing her term papers. In her heart, she knew that she had chosen the right career. She believed that she would make a significant contribution to the field of

---

[21] For a reference on the history of Social Work, please refer to the Appendix and Bibliography for Chapter Three. Special thanks to the University of Michigan Department of Social Work: www.ssw.umich.edu/ongoing/fall2001

Social Work and to humanity as a whole. Her degree would be the stepping stone for her gift to mankind.

"Now on to paper two . . ."

* * *

"The profession of Social Work is people-focused. The purpose of Social Work is to enhance the problem-solving and coping capabilities of individuals; to link people with systems that provide needed services or resources; to promote the humane functioning of these systems; and to contribute to the development and improvement of social programs and social policy . . ."

Jordan found the quote in "Social Work Practice: Model and Method[22] (a.k.a. the 'Pincus and Manahan')," her new bible. She used the book as a guide to her second paper. She moved quickly through the paper and built up her logic for the "Big Finish."

"The values of the Social Work profession include the belief that the individual is the primary concern of society; and that society recognizes the interdependence that exists between the individual and his society. In other words, society should function to help man, and man should function to contribute to society. This is to the advantage of both. Although people share common basic needs, each person is uniquely different. As a democratic society, people are recognized as having the right to maximize their individual potential, or, the right to 'be the best that they can be.' This, so they can better contribute. Society is therefore charged with the responsibility to remove any barriers that would prevent this self actualization from occurring. When people are able to contribute their best, society operates at

---

[22] Pincus, Alan, and Minahan, Anne (1973; 8th ed.1977) *Social Work Practice: Model and Method.* Itasca, Illinois: F.E. Peacock Publishers, Inc.

its best. Social Work becomes the tool, then, by which these barriers are removed. For example, social workers may form linkages between a homeless family and permanent housing. They may offer counseling and treatment services that help a person beat his addiction and resume employment. Social workers may provide protections to individuals who are mentally, physically, intellectually, or economically challenged, so that they can enjoy safety and quality of life.[23] The list of needs and possibilities is endless, when one considers the plight of humanity. Social Work is, therefore, a helping profession, and as such, it is a noble one."

Thus concluded Jordan's second paper! By noon, she was free for the weekend! But Jordan clung tightly to this belief system, as it formed the basis of the profession that would catapult her to success! These tenets would guide her efforts as the consummate helper. She copied pages 38 and 39 from her Pincus and Minahan, posted them in a frame, and gave them a prominent place on her desk. She was anxious to put these words into a practice that would help others, that would give her own life its direction and meaning. Jordan would devote herself as the tool by which humanity would manifest its self-actualization! She would save, and be saved, while still making a decent living. She felt that was a pretty good deal.

Jordan accepted the field placement at the county welfare department, but was nervous as she walked to the door on her first day there. She arrived fifteen minutes early, and found a line of clients already waiting for entry. She noted only limited commonalities among the clients, with the exception that they all looked a bit disheveled, wearing clothes that appeared too old, and wearing faces that seemed too worn. She tried not to stare, but rather, to survey. Their ages varied as much as their hygiene. A few young girls, perhaps younger than Jordan, sat on a

---

[23] These concepts form the theoretic basis for the Social Work profession, as presented by Allen Pincus and Anne Minahan (1973; 8th ed. 1977). *Social Work Practice: Model and Method.* Itasca, Illinois: F.E. Peacock Publishers, Inc. Pp. 26; 9-10; 15; 38-39

bench with a child or two and talked with each other. An older man sat huddled by the corner of the building, and was probably drinking before he arrived. Jordan detected the smell of urine and alcohol on his clothing. He momentarily made eye contact with her, and then looked away. Jordan felt fearful and hopeful with this exchange, but stepped closer to the street. She had seen poverty on the TV, but she had never experienced what poverty actually smelled like! She was glad that a security guard sat in his car a few feet from the entrance.

As the doors opened, Jordan dutifully took her place on line before the receptionist, a middle-aged woman who directed each of the clients to a table in the back office. By the time Jordan arrived at the receptionist's desk, the reception area was nearly full. She felt a great discomfort as the "downtrodden masses" pressed against her back.

Jordan quietly announced her arrival. The receptionist called to the office clerk, who escorted Jordan to Donna Bromley, the unit manager, Jordan's field supervisor. Donna smiled, shook Jordan's hand, gave her a stack of manuals, and led her to a seat at a desk on the opposite wall. She did not see Donna for the remainder of the day. There were at least eight other social workers that Jordan could see, and who shared the same room. They did not acknowledge her. The room was dingy, and in need of paint. On one corner of the ceiling, there was a large water stain, the remnants of a roof job gone bad. The desks were bulky, steel monstrosities in colors of green or brown, and with no pattern to their arrangement. Narrow trails separated these spaces stacked with files, piles of papers, a few office supplies, and a personal photo or two. The file cabinets were also steel greens or browns, with several obvious dents and scratches, and with drawers left askew. The phones were black desk rotary models, and they rang incessantly. Only occasionally, a social worker would answer the phone, and only between the trail of clients. Although sounds were muffled, Jordan could hear the strain in the voices of her new co-workers. Jordan sat and observed several of the workers interview clients to complete AFDC applications. She was otherwise invisible, a nonentity for the remainder of her first day. She did not share this experience with either the Group or with the other Social Work Students. She was too proud for that.

Jordan was determined that the second week of field placement would not go as had the first. She gathered more spirit, and feigned confidence as she strode to her desk. She used the initial moments of the morning to introduce herself to the other social workers. They were friendly but hurried, and gave no indication that they could be available for her. Jordan spent the remainder of that day typing and filing at the request of the clerk. She reluctantly accepted the assignment in the hopes that she might use this as the inroad to the others. By the third week, she realized the error of this strategy, as the clerk now had firm claim to her time there! Frustrated, Jordan discussed these problems with the Group. Tyler advised her to "ride it out," and take the grade. But Janice thought that she should speak with her field supervisor and negotiate her work assignments. Jordan opted for Janice's plan. She left a message for Donna Bromley requesting a meeting with her for the next week. The message was not returned.

At mid-day of the fourth week, Donna met with Jordan briefly and reviewed Jordan's "progress" at the agency.

"I'm concerned that you have not completed a single application, have not interviewed a single client, and have not opened a single file. Perhaps this isn't the right setting for you, or the right career." Donna threw down the gauntlet.

"But I haven't received an orientation or a job assignment yet. Didn't you get my message?" Jordan's reply sounded more like a plea, more like begging, than she would ever have admitted.

"If you're going to wait until someone hands this all to you, you will be idle for the remainder of your time here. This is a very busy department. We are limited by time constraints and staff shortages, and we do not have the time or the desire to baby-sit anyone! If you want to be a professional, you have to start acting like one. Take the initiative, and do the job!"

Donna challenged Jordan to be more proactive, and told her that she better advocate for the things she needed.

"If you can't champion your own cause, how will you advocate for your clients?"

Jordan was speechless, feeling the full sting of that personal criticism. Donna paired Jordan with Tillie, a social worker in her early forties, and she warned that Jordan's need for direction would be monitored from that point forward. Tillie allowed Jordan to observe her interviews with the clients scheduled that afternoon.

"Nothing too difficult, just verification for re-eligibility," Tillie said. Tillie droned on from client to client, limiting answers to the specific questions asked, often interrupting and redirecting to hurry the interview forward. At the close of the day, Donna gave Jordan a copy of the welfare regulations, and told her to become familiar with them by the next week. The volumes were so bulky that she could barely carry them back to the dorm. For the first time in her life, Jordan was worried that she might not pass.

Jordan joined Martin, Janice, and Tyler in the Balmural day room, where they were sharing a pizza, finishing their studies, and waiting to watch Night Gallery[24]. The show was always a big draw, and it was hard to find an empty chair. Jordan sat on the floor next to her friends, and tried to hide her upset. They tried to press her, but she deferred to a later point, and at the insistence of the others in the room. Marge also arrived by the time the Group decided to take Jordan for a walk. They strolled along the river towpath by moonlight, and patiently allowed Jordan to discuss the problems at her field placement. She shared her fear that she would not pass, and would not graduate. And she was deadly serious.

"You're just facing the fears of your first taste of failure," Tyler explained. "Take it from me, it's a meal much easier to swallow once you've acquired the taste."

"Spoken like a true underachiever," Martin responded.

---

[24] A reference to: Serling, Rod (1970-1973). *Night Gallery* [television program]. New York: National Broadcasting Company

"Not so," Tyler replied. "Under-achievement is the one thing I really excel at! . . . Just ask my old man . . ."

"Come on guys, this is really serious—this woman has the power to ruin my career before it's even started. It's not like somethin' I can study for, it's not somethin' I can memorize. This woman will crush me, if she thinks I don't meet her standards. Or if she decides that she just doesn't like me . . . or if she just finds the whole power trip a source for her personal entertainment. You know how some people are . . ."

"Jordan, who could not like you . . ." Martin asked.

"How about someone who has already made that judgment without knowin' me," Jordan replied.

"But don't you think you're a little early on the panic button? Don't you think your fears are a little unfounded, at least for now? You just got there! Think about how many times a boss came at you like gangbusters, setting down the law, making demands, making sure you'll tow the line. Once you show them subservience, things usually get better, right?" Janice asked.

Yeah, maybe that's what she wants . . . a little subservience," Martin said, tossing a rock into the river.

"It's pretty hard to be subservient to someone who's not there . . . and how do you do that and still be proactive? That's what she said she wants . . . Maybe I should just change placements . . ."

"Now you get the idea . . . " Tyler shot back.

"Wait . . . she gave you the key. She hooked you up with a social worker there, right? Just stick with that woman, Tillie is it? Just stick with her, charm her, work for her, and use her," Janice coached.

And again, Jordan thought that Janice's plan offered the best possibility of success. She thought about this strategy as the Group continued their walk along the river, with moonlight and the rush of water leading them along the towpath. They went through a discussion about Joni Mitchell and somehow, back onto Tyler's father.

When she had finally heard enough, Jordan turned to Tyler as if she had been struck by some earth-shattering revelation. "Ya know, Tyler, your father is a real asshole . . . The problem isn't that you're into under-achievement. The problem is that he's into under-appreciation."

"You've got that right!" Marge concurred.

"Here, here!" added Martin and Janice in unison.

"Finally, someone who sees things my way! Any possibility that any of you would like to confront that asshole on my behalf? . . . Just as I thought . . . Sentiment without the real muscle to back it up! Doesn't matter. He wouldn't get the message if you drew it out for him on a billboard! Now, if you could really make money talk, that he'd probably listen to. Anything else is just a simple waste of time. So you see? Once again I've come up with the perfect strategy! No money, no father! . . . Believe me, I much prefer the peace . . ."

"You can have my father," Marge smiled in reply.

"That's just what I'm afraid of!" Tyler kidded back.

The rest of the conversation was easy, comfortable, playful. Jordan couldn't recall later what else they had discussed. Probably some talk about who's dating who now in the dorms, or what concert or game was coming up. Jordan loved the security and support of her friends, and felt that she could talk to them about anything. Well, almost anything. She also knew that they would allow her to distance when necessary. She didn't feel this same confidence in the Social Work students, and so, didn't share her field placement problems with them. She couldn't admit the possibility of failure to anyone but her friends. And again, she would not be sharing this information with her family, unless it became necessary.

Jordan's networking with the other Social Work students became more pronounced near the middle of the semester. It was more a survival tactic really. She needed professional connections within the campus community—someone to help her sort through the demands of her major. She needed a resource chain that she could call upon when working in the larger community. She wasn't quite good at making those connections.

Karen was the bridge between Jordan and the Group. They were really Karen's friends, and she paved the way for Jordan's access to them. And Jordan spent most of her free time with the Group, while the other Social Work students morphed into their own study cliques. Jordan occasionally worked with them because there were so many social work group assignments. But she had not partied with them—the real source of meaningful networking there! Now that she was interning, Jordan realized this deficit. Although she offered her writing and logic as passport to these cliques, she was still viewed as second class, as a hanger-on, not a real player. She could not find her way around being the "new guy" until that drug rumor. That coupled with the potential field placement issues made life very uncomfortable for her.

Jordan discussed these issues with Karen whenever she called, and would write pages-long letters detailing the incidents and reporting her responses. Although Karen offered good advice, the real comfort came in just speaking to her. She had never before had a friend that she could trust so explicitly. With each new trial, Karen remained her source of comfort and coping. Karen helped to interpret this new world to Jordan. And Jordan's feelings toward her only grew more intense. She loved her deeply, and could not keep her out of her mind. She loved her deeply, and could not get completely into her life.

And the professional politics—Jordan was determined to work that relationship with Tillie. She also used her newly elected title as Balmural Dorm Rep. to the Student Council as a bargaining chip among the Social Work students. She was amazed at how quickly title and position can breed acceptance. She became again a welcome and sought-after member of the Social Work Department, and frequently shared her emerging political savvy and observation during class discussion. Yet, she still felt like an outsider, for reasons that she could not ascertain, despite her soul searching and hours of mandatory journaling. And then there was the matter of that internship . . .

The next week at field placement would be the deciding one. Although Jordan had not read the complete Welfare regulations posted in the Federal Register, she at least made efforts to familiarize herself with the agency policies and guidelines for eligibility. She had read the table of contents, and felt she could quickly access information as needed. Her plan was to approach Tillie that next field day, observe her with the clients that morning, and ask that Tillie observe her interviewing a client in the afternoon. Jordan spent the remainder of the week completing two short term papers (one on the history of Social Welfare Policy; one on Systems Theory). She had not even selected the topic of her major paper for the semester, although the other Social Work students were already completing their papers!

Jordan decided to incorporate her Welfare regulations readings into a paper on the politics of Welfare. She hoped to use this topic as a bonding strategy with Tillie. The Group thought that that strategy had real possibility. They even offered several opening lines for introduction of the idea. Jordan was determined to make her move, although this did not actually occur until the sixth week. Groveling and ass-kissing never really came easily for her, no matter what the possible benefit might be!

Jordan brought Tillie a coffee at the start of her field day, a gesture that received a mere grunt of acknowledgment, as Tillie continued to review several client files. Watching her, Jordan could think of only a handful of times that Tillie had ever made eye contact with her. She never spoke socially to Jordan, and only occasionally had they shared lunch. Tillie would use these ½ hour breaks to further clarify a welfare regulation or to answer a procedural question. There was no time to discuss these issues at any other point during the day, and certainly no time to socialize at all. Tillie was not a college educated social worker, but she had qualified by Civil Service, and had a great knowledge of her job. Jordan relied on Tillie's knowledge, if not her style, and she had already developed a respect for her.

That day, Tillie also gave Jordan several case files for review. Tillie confronted that Jordan spent far too much time perusing, commenting, and suggesting possible scenarios for each client's history. Jordan was sure that each file represented a wealth of human suffering in need of repair! The morning went on as each of the previous weeks—a collection of old cases for re-evaluation, a mix of new cases for General Assistance or AFDC, a few Food Stamp reviews. At lunch, Jordan decided that she would make her move. She suggested that Tillie observe her as she completed the applications for the afternoon. Tillie was skeptical that Jordan was ready for such a step, but she reluctantly agreed.

The first few applicants of the afternoon were pretty standard—single mothers renting a room or an apartment in town. Jordan could barely contain her excitement as each new client stepped to the desk. Although she was calm, she heard her own voice waiver occasionally as she spoke. She was careful to make good eye contact with each woman, smiled as they sat at her desk, and addressed each client as "Ms." So-and-So. She was a true conduit of human dignity! At various points, Jordan observed Tillie rolling her eyes following a question; or glancing at her watch if the interview took too long; or closing her eyes if Jordan delved too deeply into the interview; or shaking her head if Jordan began sharing personal information. Only once did Jordan get a nod of approval; and only once did she get kicked under the desk!

There was one client that got upset during the interview—and was nearly refused welfare assistance—when she refused to the name the father of her baby or to provide other relevant information. Jordan tried to use her best Social Work interventions to reassure the client, but before she could do so, Tillie interceded.

"Don't yah realize that by withholdin' infamation, you ah preventin' us from completin' your application? You are jeopardizin' any payments that you would lahkly be entitled to! Is he really worth it? Don't hafta look very fahr to see that ansar! Before she had even finished her sentence, the woman was spilling out all of the information amid a crush of tears and apologies! Jordan handed the woman a tissue.

"Poor girl, involved with a married man." Jordan was trying to think of some service or resource that she could suggest to the woman, but her thoughts were interrupted by Tillie's call of "Next" and the woman's scurry out the door.

"If yah want ta be a therapist, find a mental health office. We don't have time for that heah!" Tillie stated.

The next client was a periodic General Assistance client, who reported monthly due to his alcoholism, and his partial attempts at recovery. Although Jordan had not seen him before, the other workers were acquainted with him, and an uneasiness fell as he entered the room. Tillie immediately took the lead.

"Hi George, how'va yah bin?"

"Ah've had mah troubles, as usual, but I'm tryin' to make some changes," replied the man, who appeared much older than his forty years. His speech was deliberate and distinctly southern, with a faint odor of alcohol. His face was red-veined and weathered. Tillie minced no words.

"Have yah been drinkin' today?" she asked the man, who now assumed a posture of indignation.

"No I have not, and I have not had a drink in three days." He spit his reply. "I'm stayin' at mah brother's raght now, but he won't help no more 'less he gets paid. This time I'm goin' ta do it. Cin yah help me out heah?" He appeared deserving, sincere, and afflicted, and Jordan believed she could reach him. She began taking information for completion of his application. Jordan noted a slight tremor in his hands as he moved to sign his paperwork.

"Have you ever tried a 12 step program?" Jordan asked, and leaned toward the man. He grimaced at her briefly, as she handed him a list of local AA meetings in the area. She began explaining the A.A. concept to him, but he seemed preoccupied.

Then suddenly, the man lurched forward. "Blehh!"—and the foulest bile was brought forth!

"Look out!" Tillie commanded, as she pushed Jordan back with her arm.

The client vomited on the corner of the desk, on his application, and on the new pantyhose and shoes that Jordan was wearing! Jordan immediately joined him in this mutual vomit volley, heaving in response to his heaving, chumming as he chummed! But she was at least able to reach the waste paper basket! Jordan screamed and fled the scene!

Tillie and another social worker interceded, helping the man to the restroom, and coaxing him to clean up. The man refused medical treatment, and called his brother, who arrived in an old pick up truck and carted him home or to detox. No one was sure.

Jordan felt like she was going to faint, but managed to get to the women's room. She took off her pantyhose, wrapped them in paper towels, and shoved them into the garbage.

"Oh My God! Disgus . . ." she managed a whisper, as she wiped her shoes with wet paper towels, gagging with each movement. She splashed water on her face, her legs, and her feet. She considered crawling into the sink, and letting the cleansing water rush over her body, but the sink was too small, and she was still retching too hard.

"Breathe, breathe!" she commanded, as she took several deep breaths in an effort to clear her mind, and her nose, of the event. But the stench clung like the vomit itself. As she exited the restroom, she saw Tillie cleaning the desk, and another worker spraying Lysol throughout the building. Both laughed at Jordan as she grabbed her purse, and walked to the door.

"Are yah alraght, Ms. Mathews?" Tillie bellowed, as she held the paper towels far away from her body. She scowled at the stench.

"I'm goin' back to the dorm," she tried to answer, but each time she opened her mouth, the gag reflex would activate, and the retching would begin again. The receptionist offered Jordan a plastic bag, which she gratefully accepted.

Jordan heaved and gagged for the almost mile walk back to the dorm. The cold, dark night air of the mountains did little to revive her. She could not expel the odor of vomit from her nostrils, and could not dismiss the mental image of what seemed like gallons of emesis projectiling in her direction! And she could not silence Tillie's scream. As if in slow motion, her mind's eye replayed the scene of Tillie jumping to a stand, and in a single shout, trying to protect her new protégé.

"LLLLLOOOKKKKOOOUUUUTTTT!" The shout reverberated a thousandfold in her mind, an echo chamber of warning!

She could see Tillie pushing her backward, as buckets of green yellow bile flowed toward them, like the eruption of a great putrid volcano! She could not erase the mile-high bounce of each drop of goo as it splattered on her! She could not help but think that something in the universe did not want her in Social Work, and she began to question the price she would pay to raise humanity from his basest levels. She could not share these doubts with anyone. She was too close to quitting herself.

Marge was in the dorm room preparing for dinner when Jordan arrived. She was aghast at the sight, as Jordan stumbled, pale and shivering, into the room. Jordan waved her off, immediately stripped, and tossed her clothes into a paper bag. At her instruction, Marge took the bag to the dumpster outside, while Jordan ran to the bathroom. She stood there in the shower, letting the hot water roll over her head, down her breasts and back, and then into the drain. She cried with disgust at the incident, cried with shame at her response, and cried with annoyance at the response of her co-workers. She wondered how many times in her career she would be hit by someone else's puke! And again, the walls of her stomach tensed to spasm, pushed up and out, and she vomited.

The water carried the fluids down the drain and away from her body. The warmth of the water felt like the soothing arms of her mother around her. She wrapped herself in this blanket of heated calmness, and was filled with the deepest sense of self-doubt and despair. She was overwhelmed with homesickness. Marge came to the shower stall to check on her, and Jordan very briefly told her what happened. She refused dinner with the Group that night, the first time she had ever done so, and opted instead, just to go to sleep. She told herself that she would call Karen in the morning, but promised herself that she would never tell her parents about this incident.

Rumor had already informed the Social Work Department, and several students came by that evening to see her. Jordan declined all visitors, and buried her head under her pillows. She could not stop the swimming thoughts in her mind. She could not quiet the vision of human goop running down her legs and dripping off of her new shoes. And with each thought, the retching would begin anew. She broke into the heater-bar, found a pint of Smirnoff's, and repeatedly rinsed, swallowed, and drank herself to sleep.

Marge offered to bring breakfast back for Jordan the next morning, but Jordan still did not think she could eat without gagging. She cut classes that day and skipped lunch. She spent most of her time listening to music under the headphones, and attending to the voice of her heart. She did not believe that lectures on the plight of humanity were enough to carry her through this experience. She tried to focus on the Vomitter, a poor soul trapped in the throes of addiction! She tried to put herself in his position, to let herself "walk in his shoes," but her mind's eye kept returning to glimpses of her own! She tried to find empathy for him, but she lacked that connected sense to the universal man. She knew that she should have a connectedness, a commonality, with all beings. She could articulate how she should feel (she had read articles on the subject), but she did not feel that way! She felt helpless, embarrassed, frustrated, humiliated, and alone—as if she had done something to conjure up the evil fluids that erupted from the Vomitter's mouth and into her lap! She could not find peace or humor in it, and could not find the connection to the client that she hoped would foster growth of that elusive third dimension.

When she felt sufficiently calm, Jordan phoned Karen, and the discussion began. She told Karen about the few clients that she had interviewed without difficulty. She shared with Karen the quality of her relationship with Tillie, and the expectations she had made for herself. She expressed her hope that once "seen in action" she would win the respect, and the time, of the other staff at her field placement.

Although this was not a new discussion, Karen sat quietly and supportively, and let Jordan vent. Jordan had some difficulty discussing her interview with the Vomitter, and when she described the actual "fluid assault," as it came to be known, Karen nearly gagged, herself—the only time that she had ever reacted to something that Jordan had discussed with her. Yet, Karen tried to put things into perspective.

"What about this incident upsets you the most?" Karen asked. Jordan considered the issues before responding.

"That I did not anticipate that he would throw up, that I left myself open to that . . . that I did not stop myself from throwing up, too . . . that I was embarrassed about this, and that I ran to the bathroom . . . that the staff laughed. And most . . . that when I tried to feel, to understand, to appreciate what my client was going through, I was serenaded with a rendition of Barf River!"

After several moments, Karen responded.

"First of all, you could not have anticipated that the man would barf. He was calm, he was stating his needs, he was focused, right? Did he say that he was feeling poorly? Did he say he was going to be ill? Did he say he was going to barf? Even a doctor may not have seen that coming."

"True," Jordan replied, "but as a Social Worker, I should have recognized that the man was going through alcohol withdrawal. I did see his hands shaking. He said he hadn't had a drink in three days . . ."

"Not to be confrontational, but how many times did you end a Saturday night out, with a visit to the rim of the toilet? He could have been drinking that day, for all you know. And would it really have mattered? He barfed, and that was not in your control . . . nothing you could have done about it."

"But I barfed, too, and in front of everyone . . ."

"That would rank up there with the autonomic processes. Again, nothing you had control over. Maybe the staff didn't barf with you, because they had been through that before . . . You said they knew the man . . . Or, maybe they just have a higher level of tolerance. Did anyone criticize you while you were barfing? No. They tried to help him, and you."

"They laughed about it . . . They thought it was a scream . . . Let's face it—I was trying out my best Social Work technique, and he gave me an overwhelming review, so to speak . . ."

"Ah, so now you're beginning to see the humor in this . . . So next week when you go back to the agency, just keep that in mind. There's probably a thousand other good lines that you can come up with and hurl at them. No pun intended."

"I'm sure I'll be terrific . . . but there's something else—I don't know that I want to go back. Besides the humiliation of this, the fact is, that I cannot find empathy for the man. I thought it would be different once I was actually in the field, but the truth is, I still don't feel a connection to my clients. I don't feel a connection to anyone."

"That'll probably take a little more time," Karen replied.

The conversation went on to the more mundane topics. Karen and Todd were decorating their home with the help of one of Todd's cousins, an interior decorator. Todd's job was going well. Karen had registered for the MBA program at University of Virginia, a nearby campus. Karen did not know when they would be back to see everyone at college, but she hoped that they might spend a weekend there near the Holidays.

At the close of the conversation, Karen said goodbye, and asked Jordan to tell everyone to keep in touch. As she hung up the receiver, Jordan looked at the phone, stopped a moment, and then said to herself, "I love and miss you so very much." Jordan did have connection to one human being, at least, not counting her family. But she could not have her, and could not even tell her about it.

Jordan joined Marge and the others for dinner promptly at 5:30. They were unusually gentle with her, getting her soda, sharing extra rolls, returning her tray. Tyler even made a monument heart with his potatoes and dedicated it to Jordan. As they walked back to the dorm, they made plans for the home football game that Saturday. This would be the one of the last home games of the season, and the last real chance to party before the push to midterms. This celebration would have to last at least two weeks! Martin and Tyler would meet them in the Balmural Day Room, and they would join the peripherals at the bonfire along the river. TKE was hosting another party, and their pledges were in charge of entertainment and drinks. As the Group discussed the final details, Jordan seemed to step outside herself a bit, and became once again, the observer. As the others chatted and joked, she realized that she did have a strong connection to these four people. She found comfort in the fact that she loved them, too.

Jordan dressed especially well for the next day's classes, suspecting that her fellow students and professors might turn conversation toward her encounter with the Vomitter. As she anticipated, "Difficult Field Situations" was the lecture given during Field Practicum class, with class discussion following. Several students shared embarrassing incidents that occurred to them while in the field. One student talked about her failure to remember the client's name, even after she had written it down. The client then questioned her competence, and asked for a supervisor. Another student discussed a teenager who became verbally abusive toward her during a juvenile probation interview. A third student discussed an active alcoholic who came to a Food Bank intoxicated, and who was escorted out by police.

Given the line-up, Jordan did not feel that her situation was that uncommon. Without being graphic, Jordan discussed the "fluid assault" and her feelings of helplessness and humiliation. Several of the students expressed their own feelings of incompetence in the face of such great human need. All expressed a fear that they would be in situations that they could not handle, or would face a statement to which they could not reply.

The professor replied, "Let your heart talk to your client's heart, and all the rest will come easily." She then turned to Jordan, and said, "So, you got a vomit Christening—well, you're halfway there. Wait until you get your first good case of lice, and then you'll know that you are a real Social Worker."

\* \* \*

Karen and Todd made a surprise visit to the football game, more out of concern for Jordan than from their support of the team. Jordan was ecstatic to see them, and she nearly tackled Karen when she saw her! But Karen was suddenly engulfed by a barrage of arms-to-shouldered hugs from the Group, as Jordan was nudged out of the way. She reached for her with her eyes. Karen could hardly carry a conversation with Jordan, the Group was so excited to have her and Todd with them again! There was no pattern to their comments, no blending of topics. They would just blurt out whatever information or updates would come to mind! Karen's mind was spinning, she was so overwhelmed by them all. Jordan was wild with frustration.

Jordan, too, was anxious to talk, and all of her feelings surged at the sight of her Love. She casually, intentionally, kept bumping into Karen's arm, enjoying at least that level of contact. Each minor nudge cascaded into a wave of chills that she savored but would not acknowledge. Karen was there now, and Jordan basked in her aura. Todd hung out more with Martin and Tyler, and talked about his father's company. He accepted a position there, and was already making his mark in the polymer industry. He had a maturity they had not seen before. He had even started smoking a pipe! He held Karen's hand as they talked with the others, and the couple was a solid image of contentment, a fortress against the pressures of the outside world. Jordan envied him in ways she would not allow herself to consider. "I would hold you close forever," she screamed in the silence of her heart.

The Group walked to the TKE party at the river, where the main course was hot dogs and burgers, and the main drinks were Green Goblins (vodka and something green), or Purple People Eaters (vodka and something purple), as served from large garbage cans. Rumors that the pledges had used grain alcohol to mix the drinks were vehemently denied, but the taste of the brews raised question. Although not nearly dark, the bonfire was ablaze when the Group arrived, and many of the party-goers were already drunk. The event was a fund-raiser of sorts—the pledges were being auctioned off to help a children's hospital in the area. The auctioneer hawked that any one of these fine young men could be purchased at a small cost, and for a written summary of the dirty deeds following their release! Those men unsold would tend the fire while the crowd watched the game. Partying would resume immediately following the victory! The Group had another round. They all agreed that the stuff was horrible regardless of color, and that both batches had a kick! One of the young pledges bragged that his stuff was better than anything from his Daddy's still, or from his carburetor!

The bonfire stood nearly a story high, a compilation of old dorm furniture, used clothing, flotsam from the river, broken benches and bleacher seats, used books, and trunks and branches of fallen trees. As the flames rose, the spectators would ooh and ahh, as if they were watching a boardwalk fireworks display! As the embers tumbled, the crowd would chide the pledges to add more fuel to the fire, "More wood!" they would scream. The pledges would accommodate to the roar of the crowd!

When the auctioning began, the crowd became barbaric, and women—normally mild-mannered and cultured—shouted a barrage of vulgarities, masqueraded as questions, about the virility of each the young studs for hire.

"He's got big hands, how 'bout the rest of him?" a young princess shouted.

"He's a TKE! Ever'thang's goin'a be big 'nough to please yah!" The Auctioneer shouted back. He hawked the crowd that each of the pledges was "large enough to make 'em smile, and strong 'nough to carry 'em the distance."

"Is he all over muscular? Take off your pants and let's see you flex," coaxed another young lady from Balmural.

"Sorry Ladies," the Auctioneer replied, "no free sample, but I guarantee yeh, he's ample." He pulled the young pledge toward him, and smacked him on the shoulder. "He's got good teeth, a good disposition, and he's good in dis' position!" added the Auctioneer, as he pushed the pledge to his knees!

Cheers roared after each of the comments, and the half naked men stood proud, arms flexed, and stomachs sucked flat against their backs. One man strutted out in only a pair of very high cut-off blue jeans. He posed, and then sent his musculature into a rippled frenzy across his body—and sent the women into pandemonium! He brought top dollar that night, and was a one-man harem for the Alpha Deltas!

Martin and Tyler pooled their money in the hopes of buying a young stud for Jordan. She emphatically declined their offer, stating that they were both nearly more man than she could handle. She would consider, however, meeting them both after the game, and with the good blessings of Janice and Marge. Her chidings went unnoticed. When John Meredith came up for sale, Tyler found himself in a bidding war with one of the Alpha Deltas. Like the other pledges, John strutted the stage with his shirt off, but even when he struck a pose, he still seemed too thin, like a xylophone on toothpicks! Each rib made a ravenous statement, and any musculature barely covered his bones. "So unlike the curve, the symmetry, the natural beauty of a woman," Jordan thought.

"He's skinny, but he's wiry," taunted the Auctioneer, "and he'll bend any way yeh lahk, Ladies." After a barrage of offers and counter-offers, John was purchased for Jordan at the price of $44.00.

"Not a bad sum for a prospective TKE," the Auctioneer said.

Jordan gave Tyler a glare that went unnoticed by the crowd. He cringed, but then smiled back at her, sending her the love and humor he reserved for only a select few. Jordan climbed the stage, claimed and grabbed her bondaged man about the waist, and pulled him down, shivering, into the Group. He was all smiles, but a little light on conversation. "Just as well," Jordan thought. His accent was so heavy she could hardly understand him. He kept asking her to say things like "dog" or "coffee" and laughed about her "Yankee" verbage. They had very little in common—after all, she was a Social Work major, and he was a TKE! But John was caught in the web of a physical attraction, and he seemed mesmerized in the glow of bonfire flames and Jordan's blue eyes.

As the night progressed, Jordan became increasingly annoyed with John's intrusions on her time with Karen. He seemed nice enough, but he often interrupted the conversation with unrelated discussion or comments. When he failed to win the conversation, he would return to discussion about sports, trying to navigate the dialogue back to points that felt most comfortable to him. No matter how hard he tried, he could not maintain his share of any conversation! Jordan realized that it must have been difficult for him to break into the Group. She respected his effort, even if she minimized the outcome. John was all smiles though, the whole night, and Jordan could not imagine what life with him would be like.

"Some people are just too happy for their own good," she thought. Tyler sensed her frustration, and asked John to join him and Martin for another drink. They would be leaving soon for the game.

While the men were gone, the women chatted in their old familiar way, as if not a day had separated them. Karen wanted to share her plans. "I think I can manage studying and motherhood. Balancing a career and a family should be a piece of cake after all the juggling I've done here. Don't you think? But my family will always come first." Karen had registered for Masters level classes at the University of Virginia. Jordan started to discuss the Social Work Department's responses to her "fluid assault," but Todd returned too early. Again, he had taken Karen away! He gave Karen a hug.

"I know she'll be an excellent mother, because she's already so good at mothering me. And as for the masters degree, well, I know she can do it all! She always has. And I'll be there for her." He hugged her again, and held her close to his side. Again, he had pulled Karen away from her! Jordan felt the pangs of jealousy, but she reframed this instead, as a wish that she had someone who would be so supportive to her. She looked at John, and theorized that this would be unlikely.

The men returned with additional drinks as the TKE Color Guard gathered on stage. They carried the American Flag, the navy blue and gold of the college, and their Greek Flag in colors of grey and red. A surge of pride united the crowd as they viewed, with solemn dignity, the banners that flew before them. Several of the men carried base drums and beat a slow, steady rhythm, as two bagpipers played a marching tune that Jordan recognized but could not name. As the crowd assembled behind them, the men led the procession to the football field. As they neared the bleachers, the pipers played the college anthem, and the assemblage sang along. A tear came to Jordan's eye as she wallowed in sentiment and swallowed more alcohol. She was feeling a bit dizzy from the drink, and the cool of the open field helped revive her. A brief stumble and she momentarily took John's arm, but once she regained balance, she let the arm drop. The appendage hit his side with a thud, a sound strangely similar to the beating drums. John was all smiles. He had made contact!

The Group sat in a circular formation in the bleachers, so that they could converse easily, share food, and scream in unison at the refs. The crowd followed the cheerleaders, and throats were raw by halftime. Although behind, the Bobcats had tied with a field goal as the teams left the field. The excitement in the stands was near frenzy, and John used this opportunity to make his move. As the crowd jumped to its feet for the three pointer, John grabbed Jordan, hugged her, and placed his arm around her. She discretely bent down to pick up her purse, and his arm was dislodged from her shoulder. And still, John was smiling.

Jordan joined Janice, Karen, and Marge in the trek to the line at the Ladies Restroom. At least she would have these few moments with Karen free of any competition from the men.

"Never enough seats for everyone," someone called from the front.

"If you don't hurry up in there, I swear to Gawd I'm gonna pee in the grass," someone else shouted back.

The girls ignored the usual comments and accepted the line as part of the feminine lot in life. The situation worsened with the stoppage of one of the available commodes. Jordan was thankful that, for a change, she did not have her period during a party. Not that she wanted to use her womanly apparatus, and especially not with John, but just to enjoy the freedom of not having to worry about cramps or leakage—or of finding an available bathroom when the moment required! Marge wanted to stage a take-over of the men's room! Janice suggested that this was the only time she had ever considered a sex change.

"Not for pleasure, but just for the convenience of it," she said, in her usual pragmatic style. The other girls, including several strangers still "holding" in line, agreed with the statement. It was well into the third quarter when Marge and Jordan had cleared their respective stalls. They joined Karen and Janice, and walked passed the mile-long line of women still waiting to enjoy urinary release.

"Men would not tolerate this," Jordan proclaimed. The others agreed, but were skeptical of any meaningful change.

"Women will forever be forced to endure this public humiliation, this immense waste of time—perhaps adding up to five years over the course of their lives—while men stroll freely to the urinals of their choice," Marge replied.

"It's the same way in the workforce," Janice stated, "so you'd better get used to it. Think of this as an exercise in patience. Meditation and toileting . . . You can increase your Wah, as you wait to pee. You can even start a mantra to the high god of discharge . . . something like this . . . OOOOOHHHHMMMANDOIHAVETOGOOOOO . . ." The girls laughed as they concluded that life was not fair, and especially, not for women!

The men were used to waiting for the women (since they were not urinally oppressed), and used the time to analyze coaching strategy and team play. They bought hot chocolates for everyone, although the thought of mixing that drink with the previous alcohol had little attraction. Martin pulled a pocket bottle from his coat, and added a shot of rye to each of the cups. This increased the interest, if not the taste, and helped to invigorate the lull of the third quarter. John again tried to make a move, but his arm around Jordan's shoulder held the appeal of a 2x4! And still he smiled, presumably unknowing. The teams jostled back and forth on the field, the chants continued, and the Bobcats kicked, passed, ran, and tackled their way to a 17-10 victory. John used this opportunity to hug Jordan, and he gave her a quick kiss on the lips. His aim was bad, though and the kiss erroneously landed to the left upper lip. Jordan could not help but wonder if he was always such a bad aim, and to what other body parts this disability might apply! Perhaps she could draw a target for him! Jordan than cringed at the thought that she could possibly be intimate with him. The date did not go well—perhaps because Jordan's attention was constantly trained on Karen! Maybe John sensed this, because he did not ask Jordan out at the conclusion of the game, and did not join the Group at the Victory Party. He did, however, leave them smiling.

The Group returned to the TKE party, but found it too raucous to stay. The pledges were now drunken servants to their inebriated masters. The bonfire burned toward the night sky, and reminded Jordan of a scene from some primitive tribal rite, maybe a photo she had seen about Margaret Meade. The dancing had now become lewd, sexual advances crass, and vulgarity flowed as freely as the Green Goblins. Todd nearly punched out a young pledge who tripped over Martin's foot and stumbled into Karen's breast. The pledge's master interceded, apologized, and led the young man off to a less populated place near the river. The pledge collapsed there unbothered by noise or mayhem. Martin and Marge were almost knocked to the ground by a college anthem-singing conga line gone astray! Jordan, Tyler, and Janice were beginning to feel the physical effects of a party gone too far. Sometimes there could be just too much frivolity! They all agreed to go back to the dorm, and walked along the riverbank to escape detection from the riotous throng. They reached the bridge as several young pledges dove off and into the mid-October river at the singular command of their masters.

"What some people won't do to belong," Jordan said to the others. Suddenly, her membership in nothing took on a more positive meaning.

Back at the day room, the Group chatted quietly until nearly 3:00 a.m. Karen and Todd left hours before, and stayed at a small motel in town. The Group talked about the closeness between Todd and Karen now. It was as if each had lost their individual self, so that the other might live. They were now a combined entity, not the worse for the loss, but somehow, strangely different. They hadn't been so fused at college. They concluded that life struggle in the real world had altered them in some way. Perhaps this was the mystery found in relationships destined to last a lifetime. Jordan was in sorrow with the thought, then mentally slapped herself back into reality. She knew the difference between wanting and having.

\* \* \*

Jordan could not sleep the night before her next field day. Although she had used several assigned readings as a means of diverting her attention, the strategy had not worked. She tried to work on her class presentation about family interactions, but could barely get beyond the first page. She found herself drifting off into potential conversations with Tillie and the others. She saw herself as the target of every stupid vomit comment imaginable. She dramatized various scenarios in her mind, and then tried to think up—and rehearse—a snappy comeback. This would be difficult, since the others rarely spoke with her, and since Tillie was all business. She looked at her shoes, and began the script:

"Hey, new loafers?" Her response would be, "Yeah, easier to kick off in an emergency."

"Nice stockings . . ." She would reply, "Thanks, it's a much better look than the last pair . . ."

"Slacks today?" She would retort, "Yes, my toxic waste suit is still at the cleaners."

"You brought an umbrella . . ." Her response: "Well, you never know what the weather may hurl at you."

"Your desk is so clean." She would state, "More room for whatever comes up."

And the challenges and responses went on "ad nauseam" in her mind.

She decided to go with her blue pants suit, hoping that legs unseen would lessen any triggers for comment. At Marge's request, Jordan turned off her desk light, but still could not sleep, and tossed in bed for most of the night. At several points, Marge went out of the room in search of a quiet couch to crash on. These offered even less relief, and she would ultimately return to the room, and to the rumble of sheets and feet being thrown from one side of a bed to the other. By morning, Jordan looked haggard, and was mentally exhausted. She considered calling out of field placement that day, but Marge convinced her that she would only be putting off the inevitable. She recommended that it might be better to go there quickly and without thought, swallow her pride, take the ribbing, and be done with it.

"This is not the kind of thing that you want worrying you for another week," she said. Jordan agreed, and walked with Marge to the cafeteria—and then, to her destiny.

Upon arrival at the Welfare office, Jordan noted the usual line waiting for entry into the building. She quickly scanned the faces of all who had arrived, and was relieved that the Vomitter was no where in sight. Upon entering, she was greeted by the receptionist, who smiled and continued her work. There seemed to be no memory, no remnant, of last week's fiasco! She felt relieved, and intended to move the day along as if nothing had ever happened. It was not until she entered the office proper, that she saw the effects. Her desk had now been moved next to Tillie's, and the file cabinets were rearranged to prevent any barrier between them. On her desk was a lovely bouquet of fresh-cut flowers neatly arranged in an emesis basin! A stack of new files was at desk center.

Tillie instructed her to begin calling the applicants now waiting in the reception area. Jordan graciously accepted the assignment. She felt that she had somehow gained acceptance as a co-worker. She even had lunch with Tillie and the other women that day. And no comment about that dreadful incident was ever made. Not a word, not a breath, nothing! The rest of the semester, and the rest of her field placement, went smoothly, and without further incident.

*   *   *

Jordan breathed a sigh of relief as she typed the concluding sentence to her major term paper for the semester:

> "Truly, welfare policy has shaped the American psyche, and will continue as both a means of assistance and as a means of social control."

She was pleased with the poignancy of the statement, and marveled at her ability to sound brilliant, even if she didn't feel very insightful. She had, after all, paraphrased these opinions from various articles, and just drew correlations to the specific welfare policies they cited. She found the Welfare regulations really too cumbersome to be understood, "a mix of dribble-babble drawn out in bullshit," she thought to herself.

"How could someone actually make a living writing this stuff and still maintain sanity?" She marveled at the extravagance of the educated, as she packed her Brother typewriter back into its carrying case and gently blew it a kiss. She slid the machine under her desk for winter break. Her clothes were packed. She was ready to leave at the conclusion of her last class for the day, a brief gathering, in which she would turn in her paper, and complete a course evaluation. Janice and Marge were already at the dorm when she returned, and together they waited, in silent anticipation, for the stead George to carry them back to their Northern homeland. As they made the slow, winding way back to their homes of origin, the music of James Taylor transported them through three states, and into the loving arms of their families.

Jordan's father was waiting at the Stelton Mall as his eldest child arrived. He spoke briefly with the parents of Janice and Marge, helped carry suitcases to their respective cars, slipped George a $10 bill, and hugged his favorite daughter. For the first time, Jordan no longer felt like a child. She believed that she had ascended into an adult status, but she could not determine at what point the transformation had actually occurred. She was hugging this man, her father, but felt now almost like a peer to him. She was becoming wise in the ways of the world, she thought. She realized that her father was getting older, too. She had a momentary panic with the thought that he would someday pass from this world, and from her. She shook her mind from that thought immediately, but held his hand as they drove home together in the pick up truck. She thought of all the times they had traveled like this in her childhood. The scent of sawdust and stale coffee—and the crackle of several sets of plans under foot on the floor of the cab—filled her with an intense feeling of home.

The Christmas lights were strung neatly across the front of the home, and Jordan's father had placed sprigs of evergreen and holly along the fascia of their house. The Christmas tree was placed in its stand in the rear corner of the living room, but the tree had not yet been decorated.

"We've been waitin' for ya to come home and help us with it," her mom said.

The home was filled with the fragrance of pine, and the aroma of freshly baked peanut butter and sugar cookies, two of Jordan's favorites. She could smell a pot roast on the stove, and her glasses fogged with the heat of the house. Neither Kelly nor Jonathan was home when Jordan arrived. They were out finishing their last shopping for the Holiday. Jordan walked to her mother, gave her a hug, and let her mother hold her for some time. She wanted to record the feeling of her mother's arms around her, so that she could draw on this memory in the difficult times of the future. She had done the same thing in the pick-up with her father—she had mentally recorded the sight of his large, rough, callused hand gently cradling her much smaller one. She loved her parents, and despite their different life paths, she respected them. She hoped that they would be with her forever. Jordan became teary, as she carried her suitcase to her room. There were several boxes and a small desk present there, and she realized that her room was now dedicated to other purposes. This rude awakening helped bump Jordan again back into the reality that not only could life go on without her, but that it had. At least the picture of Karen and her parents was still on her bookcase. She touched Karen's face with her fingertips.

Her mother made pot roast in her honor, and with mashed potatoes and plenty of gravy. She was holding dinner for Jordan's arrival, and expected Jonathan and Kelly home at any moment. Jordan used this time to lay down briefly on her bed. She had been up most of the night completing her paper, and just couldn't seem to nap on the ride home. She fell asleep almost immediately, and had a dream about her and Kelly as small children. It was a Christmas Eve, perhaps when they were about five or six. Kelly was so excited, that she could not sleep, and she kept sneaking down the hall to see if Santa brought her a Betsy Wetsy. Kelly was about to open the wrapped gift box, when suddenly, Jordan was shaken to awakening by Jonathan. He had made several statements before she was able to focus on his presence.

She assumed that he was saying that he was glad to see her, that their shopping was done, that dinner was ready, etc. She hugged him, too, but briefly, as he squirmed away.

"People'll talk if they see that kinda thing! I'm not a kid anymore, ya know." Jordan was shocked to see that her brother had also matured to a new level of behavior and understanding.

"Everything changes," she said.

Dinner was a bit noisier than usual, due to the excitement of the upcoming Holiday, the return of Jordan to the family's table, and due to the meal itself. Their manners were unchanged, though, with each member grabbing, hording, and reaching over the competitors in culinary frenzy. The pot roast went quickly, and mashed potatoes nearly overflowed from Jonathan's plate. At several points, his mother had to remind him that there were others who needed to eat. The green beans were accessorized with chopped almonds to add an even more special touch to the meal.

Kelly had begun applying to schools, and stated that she wanted to try the community college first. Jonathan was already looking into the Art Institute for possible training as an artist. Their dad told him that he would take him out on a job, if he wanted to learn how to paint! Apparently, he was equally lacking in support of his son's choice of careers. Kelly had escaped this scrutiny, because she had no career choice in mind. Jordan held her breath as her dad asked how her Welfare job was going. Jordan told him that things were great. She told him that she was learning quite a lot from Tillie about how the government works, and about the services they offer.

"Humph," her dad said, as he reached for the coffee, and accepted a piece of cake from his wife. Her mom immediately jumped in.

"Now Pete, don't go gettin' her upset. We haven't even finished eatin' yet, and already you're drillin' her."

"It's alright, Mom. I wouldn't feel like I was really at home without an inquest," Jordan smiled. "But the internship is goin' well. I don't think that I'd like to make a career of the place, but I am gettin' to see how it could fit into my overall career goals . . . And I'm already interviewin' clients, completin' applications for benefits, and counselin' people about how they can improve their lives. I think I already helped quite a few. It's a great feeling to think that you can impact positively on the life of another human being. Don'tcha think?" Jordan asked her father.

"Lookin' at my children . . . I wouldn't know. The only impact I've had on 'em is to turn 'em toward some other direction. Well, I guess carpentry isn't for everyone. But talk about your impact—you know yourself. I can drive anywhere in the county and see the things that I built, and see the impact that I've made with my life. And I look at my wife and kids, and I know the impact that I've made there. I wonder if you'll be able to look back at the end of it all, and feel the same satisfaction that I feel."

"I hope I do, Dad. That's really what this is all about. I want to make a difference. I want things to be better than they were before I got there. I want to help people find their way. I want to improve the lives of the people around me . . . I want to decrease the suffering and the poverty and the sadness that I see everywhere. I just want to help make people happy again . . . and stop all the hatred and anger that I see everywhere . . . I want to use my life to make a difference."

Jordan's family sat silent as she discussed her feelings and life goals. They had never seen her serious or passionate about anything before. Sure, they had seen her regurgitate some class assignment or repeat some editorial she heard on T.V., but they had never actually heard her express her own feelings or beliefs. And they were speechless. She looked to each of them, silent, but puzzled that they had not understood this about her. She wondered how they could have all lived together for so long, without recognizing this singular atom of her personality, the most basic sense of her being. Then she realized how little she really knew about each of them as people. And she wondered if all families operated like this—to be there, but to be so unaware. She realized, too, that she was finding her own way, and perhaps in the course of things, she was discovering that third dimension, that part of her world that separated her as uniquely different from all other beings, but then united her to them. She was finding herself, and she was beginning to express this person in her own voice.

Her father looked at Jordan, shook his head, and said in reply, "Do you have any questions now about the impact that my life'll make? Look what my daughter is tryin' to do already."

Then after a moment, her mother said, "So who's ready for Cronkite?" and the family followed her into the living room, took their respective seats, and began anew the nightly debates of politics, social upheaval, economics, and religion.

Christmas Eve was celebrated with a duck dinner at the home of Jordan's aunt, and was followed by attendance at Midnight Mass. This had not become tradition until the children were older, and with the fading belief in Santa. The Mass was followed by pies and hot chocolate when the family returned home. They would tune in the Yule Log/Holiday music on Channel 5, and each would open a present or two before bed. Kelly still could not sleep on Christmas Eve, despite her age. Her anticipation and enthusiasm charged the whole family. Jonathan tried to play cool to this, but his excitement was sometimes uncontained. He was hoping for a pool table that Christmas, a gift to both him and his father. While he was skeptical about getting the gift, he thought that the restriction from the basement was pretty encouraging. Still, money was tight, so he could not be certain. History was on his side, though. Despite any financial problems that the family may have had during the course of the year, Christmas was always a special time. And the children would receive most of what they had written Santa for—even if the electric and oil bills would be a month or two behind. The Mathews children were just as good as any other children.

"They may not get anything else during the year, but they will always have a good Christmas," their mother said. She would not let the birth of Our Lord Jesus go unnoticed, or uncelebrated.

The morning came quickly and to the cheers of Jonathan, who was already racking balls and shooting corner pockets when his parents awoke. The pool table was a used model his father had purchased from a local game dealer. There were a few nicks in the green felt that lined the table, but the balls could easily make their way from cue to pocket undeterred. There was a triangle, a box of fresh chalk, four cues, and a scoreboard that hung from the wall. One of the cues was personalized with Jonathan's name lightly carved by the hands of his father. The table came with an attachment ping pong table top, and with netting and paddles.

"This should pretty much cover the whole family," Pete Mathews said. He felt proud that he was able to provide this entertainment for them. They thought, too, that this would be one way to keep Jonathan out of trouble, or at least, in association with the more manly boys in the neighborhood. Pete planned to finish the basement with the trash wood and paneling from a job he was finishing. They planned to use the old rug in Jordan's room for the flooring. Her room would now have a single area rug. Jordan was a little upset that she had not been included in this decision, but she did not comment on it.

For the most part, the girls received clothing, a few pieces of jewelry, new purses, and several books. Jordan also received a camera, and Kelly received a watch. Ann Mathews received a new vacuum cleaner from her husband, and she gave him an electric shaving kit, the kind with the floating heads. She hummed the tune to the commercial as she waited in the line at Two Guys with her coupons and purchases. Following the exchange of gifts, the family assembled in the station wagon and drove to the home of Ann's mother. There they would join the extended family in celebration.

These gatherings could get tense at times. Although both sides of the family were known to drink, Ann's side of the family became the rowdier when the alcohol was poured. This Holiday would be no exception. The turkey dinner finished, the men adjourned to the living room to watch football. Jordan helped clear the table and wash dishes, and was joking with her cousins about some of the boys she had dated on campus. She exaggerated their drawls, mocked their clothing, laughed about their opening lines—basically, just girl talk. Suddenly, her Uncle Pat came up to her, stogie in fist, and with smoke-filled, alcohol-tainted breath, began talking to her about her Welfare work. At first, Jordan was pleased that he was so interested in her schooling. But before long, she realized that her uncle was more drunk than he realized. She could not think otherwise of the exchange.

"So I hear that you're workin' Welfare now. That's what they're sendin' you to school for?" He poured himself another scotch.

"Well, not exactly. I'm in school for Social Work, but I'm an intern in a local Welfare office," she replied. "Part of the requirements for graduation."

"So . . . are you happy with the job? Whadeya workin' with mostly coloreds and white trash?" he asked. If he wasn't so ignorant, and so intoxicated, she might have gotten mad. Instead, she tried to diffuse the conversation.

"No, mostly I'm trying to help migrant workers and women with young children. You know, everyone needs help every now and again," she replied, and was surprised that she had subconsciously adopted a Southern turn of phrase.

"That may be," he stated, "but don't most people usually try to get more work when they have ta? I would never take a charity handout from anyone. That's the start of the end, my friend . . . when a man has to grovel for his food and home. I'd rather be dead than have to ask the Government for help, regardless . . . How can ya work there? That's not the way you were brought up. I mean, your father is a hard-workin' man. Maybe ya should become a teacher, like your parents wanted . . ." He became louder—and more vehement—with each statement.

"Well, I'll consider that." Jordan did not want further confrontation. Pat Jr. came to her rescue, and escorted his father back to the T.V, with the enticement that the teams were about to tie.

Jordan was stunned that her uncle had spoken to her in such a way, but she was even more shocked that he held those views. She had never been exposed to such thinking in her own home. She was startled with the abruptness of the exchange, but was more concerned that the other family members in the room seemed unmoved by his statements. She began to understand how different she was becoming from the rest of her family—if not her immediate family, then at least, from her extended one. She knew that they would not respect her work. Jordan would replay the exchange several more times before she dismissed the incident as the drunken statements of an uneducated man. She would allow no other explanation. She remained aloof from her uncle, though, for the remainder of the Holiday season. Her parents never discussed the incident with her either, and she began to fear that maybe they also shared these views. She couldn't wait to get back to everybody, and to leave this hidiousness behind her.

The Winter Break drew quickly to a close, and it seemed that she had barely unpacked before she was traveling again, with George and friends, through the Appalachian Mountains to her college home. But the ride seemed vacant now, without Karen sharing this time with her. Jordan would have three more semesters until she graduated, and with the general requirements completed, her coursework focused exclusively on Social Work. Even if she had wanted to, she had gone too far now to change majors. Jordan could not afford more student loans, and had already dedicated herself to the profession. She would not allow the misunderstandings, the prejudices, or the pressures of her family to deter her from attaining this life's goal. With this new commitment to Social Work, Jordan firmly strode through the aisles of the college bookstore, and purchased the books on her designated course lists. She got pelted with a T shirt tossed over the aisle by Martin. She was home again.

Classes for the semester included Human Behavior and the Social Environment, Family Therapy, Group Work, and Field Practicum. She retained the placement with Tillie at the Welfare office, and was quite proficient now both in focused interviewing and in crisis counseling. By the middle of the Spring semester, she was carrying her own caseload. Even Donna Bromley commented on her ability to adapt to the demands of the agency; she praised her ability to maintain a professional posture! She even suggested that Jordan apply for a job at the agency when she graduated. Jordan was tasting her first success. Not so for Tyler, however . . .

Tyler continued to struggle with his coursework, and with each "C+" grade, his father became more demeaning toward him. At one point, he had even threatened to discontinue Tyler's college supports if his grades did not improve. But worse, he assailed his personal character and his sense of self-worth. Tyler was holding a solid "C" average, and felt that his father placed too much emphasis on "the perfection thing." He was confident that his culinary instincts would carry him to places where his grade point average had no meaning. He mistakenly made this statement to his father, maybe a bit flippantly, during Winter Break. The ensuing altercation resulted in a black eye for Tyler, and a cracked tooth for his father.

Tyler vowed that he would not go back to his home, and he returned early from break to campus. He did not seek help from the authorities, and his father did not file charges. He did, however, discontinue all college supports, and this move now jeopardized Tyler's graduation and degree. Jordan tried to counsel Tyler about the fight and the dangers that each posed to the other. Before she had finished, Tyler thanked her for the information, but refused to discuss the situation further. There were some things he could not share with his friends. He decided to take a job working at the grill at the Student Center. Marge was furious, but was otherwise unable to help him. Her parents offered to give him a loan, but he declined. He felt that he was on his own now, completely alone, and that he would make his own way without his father's help. He liked it much better that way—and in some ways, it came as a relief to him.

Tyler later accepted a loan from Marge's father for car repairs only, but he paid the loan back in full. They believed that he had the integrity and good nature to be a good husband to their daughter, and they wanted to invest in that relationship. Marge was beginning to see her life probably going in that direction. Her own behavior became more settled, less wild. She was finding contentment. Jordan began to envy her. But Jordan found no attraction to the men that she dated. She still struggled with issues of intimacy, and she often teased about having the Man of the Week. Marge suggested that it was more like the Man of the Hour! Marge was probably the more right—Jordan could not handle romantic relationships with men. She could work with them, she could talk with them, she could hang out with them, she could befriend them, but she could not love them. She just couldn't. There was simply no attraction. She more and more let her mind sneak back to the night with Karen, the infinite pleasure of her touch, the passions of her desires spelled out in the evening light, and her heart was sustained.

\* \* \*

Spring came early that year, and with spring came an intense restlessness that settled through the campus. Jordan was still holding a firm 4.0 average despite her continued, and sometimes escalated, drinking. Martin and Janice were nearly inseparable now, and they had begun talk of possible marriage. Tyler was less available, but he joined the group for meals on his days off. He was now a short order cook at the Student Center. Although this was not the kind of cooking he aspired to, it did provide a little immediate money until he could square his finances. He applied for student loans to help pay for his fourth, final year at school. He had no contact with his father since the altercation, and never made statement about planning to see him again. He was afraid that his father might somehow break his will. His father had so often undermined his confidence in the past! He believed that there would always be a risk of another altercation, now that that barrier had been breached. Their past history confirmed this, and that fight gave good insight into the things that might come in the future. He viewed as his choice the separation from his father, and believed it to be a matter of emotional and physical necessity. He found a kind of liberation in the decision, and that thought made the independence much less threatening to him. He viewed their relationship as "something lost, something gained," and he was even more determined to succeed. His father had not attempted to reach out to him. This was not an abnormal pattern for him. In fact, his father had never reached out to him.

Jordan was again engrossed in one of her class presentations. She was about to begin her third page of this analysis, when a gust of the warm spring air filtered through her window and broke her concentration. She could hear students playing Frisbee on the back lawns of the dorm, as their stereos blared their favorite albums from the windows. She saw the morning light cast shadows across her room, the breeze through the curtains calling her toward them. As she looked out the window, she saw lovers sharing a blanket and a kiss, while the pages of their books gently turned with the breeze. She inhaled the faint aroma of the dogwoods, as their blossoms lifted toward the sun. Bicyclists were peddling off to the trails along the river. Professors were chatting with students as they strolled through the campus. A kite floated against the clear, crisp morning sky. And suddenly, being indoors became a prison that she could not bear! Jordan woke Marge from her usual Friday morning nap, and convinced her to cut her afternoon class. They would be hiking the Appalachian Trail—or at least part of it—that afternoon!

Marge was hesitant, but Jordan continued to rationalize. "A love of nature, and an association with it, are all part of the well-rounded education that made this college great!"

"Oh please!" Marge remarked, and rolled her eyes in feigned disgust. "Anything to dodge that stupid assignment!"

"Think of it! This simple extracurricular activity will broaden our wealth of knowledge, and thereby increase our professional marketability. We cannot afford NOT to go!"

"Nice spin! Ok, you forced me into it!" Marge jumped at the chance! There usually wasn't too much that would stand between her and fun. She would never apologize for that part of her personality, for something that was just her nature. She accepted fun as a part of her worldly entitlement.

"Hey, just remember that I was not the one who tore you away from your project," she added. "I will not be pegged as the bad influence this time out!"

The girls quickly found Janice and Martin, and the twosome again grew into the Group! The outing had also morphed from an afternoon hike, to a combo hike/weekend camping retreat with the use of Tyler's gear. Tyler would join them after work on Saturday night.

Although the Group planned to wander off into the wilderness Thoreau-style, and set up camp along a quiet lake somewhere, there were no open lands nearby. They chose, instead, to camp at an established KOA campground that abutted the Appalachian Trail. So early in spring, they would have privacy and seclusion, and could still enjoy the amenities of a real toilet and hot shower! They loved nature, but they were not woodsmen. They all agreed that they would take a tiled bathroom over an outhouse any day! The site also offered the luxury of a camp store where they purchased provisions—specifically, hot dogs, eggs and bacon, orange juice, paper plates, cups, napkins, and plastic utensils. Martin and Marge both brought bottles of their favorites, slow gin and vodka. Sturgis decided to join them, and he brought the beer and his guitar.

Once at the campsite, the girls collected kindling and small branches. Martin used a hatchet from Tyler's camping gear to split some of the wood he bought at the camp store. The men set up two tents and opened two sleeping bags for communal use. The girls also brought bed rolls made from the sheets and blankets they had grabbed from the dorm. All in all, the place had most of the comforts of home, and all of the excitement of the newness of experience.

When the campsite seemed secure and adequately comfortable, the Group struck out for their first hike along the Appalachian Trail. The Trail was well worn near the campground, and there was little possibility that they would become lost. Still, Martin made rock pilings at various intervals, so that they could easily find their way back. The clean mountain air was so refreshing, and the climb up rock and down gully so invigorating, that there were many periods of silence. The Group seemed to meditate on each singular step. Jordan could not help but feel the awesome wonder that surrounded her! One of the Group would occasionally break out a few lines of a song, usually with some contorted connection to the conversation at hand. The sky was a bright blue, with a few puffs of white stratus hovering in the distance. The freshly budded trees stood juxtaposed against the harsh cold of rock, boulder, and the dark, brown earth.

Jordan found that she watched them all from a much closer distance now. Like vines in the garden, they each were meshed, inseparable now, and part of the same root. They were family. There was a comfort, a unity, an acceptance—call it an understanding—a simple pleasure in the company of people who, too, were struggling to grow into their own lives. She tried to freeze their images, their mannerisms, the sounds of their laughter, even their individual scents, forever in her memory. She knew that there would come a time when they, too, would all part. Life was like that—a series of intense, emotional bondings starting at birth, and if lucky, would foster new relationships, as one moved their way from birth to death. Another cycle of life. Maybe she could not be with them all of her life, but she would try to surround herself with people who were just like them. To her, there were none better.

They took a break from the trail along a ridge, and Sturgis began tossing rocks into the ravine. They were sharing water from a canteen, and a small rill ran down Janice's blouse. She welcomed the coolness of the water. Janice was the least athletic, and the climb had been difficult for her. Martin stood beside her and pulled her under the protection of his arm. She placed her head on his shoulder, and someone commented that they looked like a college version of American Gothic! At Sturgis' direction, the Group started watching a cooper hawk riding the thermals of the ravine. The hawk was joined by several crows and other birds, but without his binoculars, Sturgis could not properly identify them. The hawk was at full wing span, as it glided passed them, unbothered by the less aggressive birds. He took little note of the group enthralled by his presence. Jordan felt that she could stretch out, climb upon his back, and fly with him through the valleys to the highest perches of the Appalachian Ridge. The afternoon was that dreamlike.

"There once was a young girl named Jayne, who hiked herself damn near lame, amid the high mountain hills of Scotland . . ." The Group laughed as Sturgis started singing a shanty limerick. He was of Eastern European descent, but his step mother was Scottish, and he felt an affinity for her people. Not to be outdone, Janice intercepted the moment.

"Five hundred bottles of beer on the wall, five hundred bottles of beer . . ." Janice followed Sturgis with her old favorite, but mercifully got no further than 490, before being overtaken by Jordan's "Yellow Submarine.[25]" The Group hiked and sang and joked its way back to camp, amid the laughter and the voices of youth untested.

They prepared the evening meal by dusk. The warmth of the campfire lit the site, and lent a romantic aura to the aroma of hot dogs and baked beans. As the sun set behind a stand of spruce and oaks, the evening sky was awash with pinks, golds, and oranges. The girls cleaned the pans and cooking utensils, while the men cleaned the area, piled more wood, and arranged more comfortable seating for the evening. The mood was calm and relaxed, as Sturgis plucked instrumentals on his 12 string guitar, and the Group toked several joints that Marge passed around the circle. With beer in hand and his campfire shadow projecting over them, Martin began telling a story, while Sturgis played riffs on his guitar to accent the mood.

"Seems there was this small group of college students who were stranded in the Outback. They were out there on a mineral exploration for one of their

---

[25] A reference to: Lennon, John and McCartney, Paul (1966). "Yellow Submarine" [recorded by the Beatles]. On *Revolver* [audio album]. UK: Capitol Records

classes. Mixing work with pleasure, laughing and joking it up. Just like we do. Until their truck broke down . . . ."

Sturgis strummed his guitar boldly to accent the statement.

"The group was stranded out there for several days . . . No water and no provisions. They had nothing . . . ."

An ominous pluck belched from the guitar.

"A week, they were like this. They were so weak that they could barely stand! They were seeing mirages and stuff, too, and they just couldn't find their way out! Every place looked the same to them. So finally, they decided to stay put and wait for help. The nights were cold and dark. And they couldn't see anything, in the middle of nowhere like that. Just using blankets and jackets for shelter. Everything was quiet, ghostlike there, too." The guitar strum continued.

"Then suddenly, there was a rattle in the brush . . . They only had time to catch a flash of paws, a glimpse of fur, some white fanged teeth . . . and they were attacked by dingoes!" Martin stated slowly, then deliberately. He looked around at the group who only half believed him.

"They were attacked by DINGOES! Surrounded by the viscous beasts! And only one of the guys was still strong enough to try to fight them off . . ."

A chorus of discordant chords filled the air!

"There he was, watching his friends scream as they got chewed and eaten! And all he could do was to swing a thick cut branch at that hungry pack of wild animals . . . But the bastards kept coming at him!" Martin was flailing his arm back and forth, while Sturgis pounded on the guitar strings.

A moment of stillness, and Martin continued.

"Well . . . none of the group survived . . . And afterward, the only things the search party could find were bits and pieces of clothing, chips of bone, chunks of human flesh . . . It was horrible!"

Heavy chords of finality leaped from the instrument.

"Ouhh," they gasped in feigned fear, the girls gathering a blanket around them.

"I swear to you . . . I'm not lying. I read it in a National Geographic! The dingoes tore those guys apart!" Martin held his right hand to his heart, and raised his left hand as a pledge.

"Hey Buddy, you'd have to tell something like 'Night of the Living Dead'[26] before you'll get a rise out of these folks! You know, they want some serious people-munchin!" Sturgis teased.

But then the wind rose suddenly, and several of the trees rustled, causing spontaneous screams and masculine reassurances that there were no dingoes or dead-corpse zombies roaming the area! They did not share that there were bears, bobcats, wild dogs, wolves, and a sundry of night creatures—animal and human—that might still threaten their safety! They huddled close. A collection of ghost stories appeared, then dissipated among the dying embers of the fire, and the strumming of chords in harmony with the evening.

As the last flames faded into ash, the Group converged into a singular tent, quite cramped but comfortably warm, and talked till each fell off to sleep. Jordan was not sure what happened to cause the midnight awakening, but she accepted the newly lit joint as it passed from hand to hand, and accepted the open invitation to cuddle with the closest body. She believed it was male, likely Martin, but knew that Sturgis was also awake and available. Janice and Marge were partially dressed, as she assessed by the light of the joint as she dragged on it. She had no idea how the scene had evolved, or how this had happened without waking her before now. She was usually a pretty light sleeper. She felt tense but exhilarated by the hormones floating about the tent, and the excitement in the laughter and playfulness of her friends. She caught on quickly.

"Oh," she exclaimed in her most official voice, "Did somebody schedule an orgy and fail to notify me? I am deeply hurt."

---

[26] A reference to: Romero, George (1968). *Night of the Living Dead* [motion picture]. New York: Walter Reade Organization

"No, Janice replied, "It's a serendipity of sorts, with Martin and I starting a little quiet intimacy, and suddenly, this group of voyeurs joining in! So I guess at this point, it's a free for all . . ."

Jordan realized that the body she was clinging to was Sturgis, and that he was now turning his attention toward the more available Marge. Jordan's posture spoke volumes even if her voice mouthed agreement. Marge saw this as a purely physical expression, and without a real commitment from Tyler, she was free to enjoy the experience. Women's Equality!

All the girls were on birth control pills of one sort or another. This was a rite of passage for college girls since their development in the mid 1960's. They were free women now, and available to experience, just as their male counterparts had done for centuries! And they were cashing in! Bodies disappeared under piles of sleeping bags and blankets, and the outlines of the bundled associations resembled the shadowy contours of the Appalachian Ridge—except for the undulating movement, and the sighs and gasps of genuine, unadulterated, youthful lust! Jordan did not have intercourse, but she did deep kiss both Martin and Sturgis, and touched, fondled, and messaged them. She allowed herself to be touched by them, and was secretly amazed at how gently both Sturgis and Martin were with her. They both seemed more masculine than their movements would suggest. She had chills as each entered her with his fingers, and she thrust her hips toward their touch. But before more response, the body, the finger, the tongue, the person, was gone to someone else, and she was joined by another! Maybe even more than one other, she couldn't be sure. Lust and laughter were co-mingled with human bodies enjoying the pleasures of pure sensuality. It was an astonishing experience of shear physical delights and without emotional restriction. There were no moral dilemmas, no judgments. It was boundaries vs. pleasure—and pure, base, lecherous pleasure had won! Jordan would reconcile the morality issue later.

Marge mounted each man during the foray, and was in total control! Jordan was amazed at her sexual confidence, her prowess, and her appetite. She was

Woman, The Goddess! She dismounted Martin only after she sensed a jealousy from Janice, who watched them while Sturgis entered her. Both men came to climax, although their breaths were muffled and postures subdued, given the audience of women analyzing their responses.

Jordan thought about calling out scores like she had seen during the Olympics Gymnastics events: "8.9; 8.7; 9.0 . . ." but she dismissed the thought when Marge started masturbating. Jordan was stunned and shook her head. "No secrets here," she thought.

The Group gradually fell back to sleep, until they were awakened by robin song, and the shrill of blue jays. The crisp mountain air rattled the flaps of the tent. Martin was already up, had dressed in the pup tent, and had started the morning fire. The smell of coffee brewing sent waves of beckoning to the remaining members, and each toppled out of the tent with mug in hand. Sweatshirts and hoods were crimped to the neck, an odd sight given the evening's entertainment. Bacon was sizzling alongside the eggs when Jordan emerged from the tent.

"Some night," Sturgis said, and each agreed, smiling. "Whose big idea was that, anyway?"

Marge answered, "Well, if we're talking big ideas, you have the idea I had in mind."

"Yeah, only you didn't have it in mind . . ." Janice replied.

"Don't, you'll embarrass the woman!" Martin said.

Jordan responded, "And you're not embarrassed?"

"Of course I'm embarrassed . . . the day after is always uncomfortable at first, but I'm not sorry, and I'm not ashamed. I had a beautiful experience . . . In fact, I had several beautiful experiences . . ."

"Ditto!" said Marge.

"Oh, so that's what you call it—Ditto?" Janice asked. "Well don't get too comfortable with that! Martin is mine, and I'm not interested in sharing him beyond the occasional fluke camping trip."

"I, however, am always available, and will do what I can to help out a friend. If you ever need, I am your steed. That goes for all of you," Sturgis added grinning, as he nodded to Jordan.

"I'll keep THAT in mind . . ." Jordan responded, but they all knew that she just wasn't interested. Sturgis accepted this, and was content with the friendship he found with them.

The Group woofed down breakfast and were in the midst of cleanup, when the sound of a car, and the dust of the dirt road, rose in the distance. It was maybe 9:30 by then.

"That sounds like Tyler's car!" Marge exclaimed, as the engine echoed off of the mountains surrounding them. The sun was just above the ridge, and the morning fog lay across the mountains like swirls of purple blue veil. Startled, everyone came to a standstill and watched the road before them. Tyler's mustang could be seen between the breaks in forest and outcropping.

"Tyler!" Marge screamed, and she ran down the road, excited to see him. The car stopped well away from her. Tyler emerged, silent and hesitant. He appeared near tears.

"Tyler, Tyler, what is it?" Marge asked, as she stopped abruptly and stared at him.

He looked down, then into her eyes. "Is Janice here with you now?" Marge nodded in agreement. He looked down again, and then toward the Group. He could see Janice sitting on a log next to Martin. They were all laughing and joking together as Tyler stepped from the car. Now all eyes were fixed on him. After a moment, Tyler went on.

"It's her brother . . . there was an accident . . . he was killed near Saigon."

"Stephen? Oh my God . . ." Marge fell into him with the words. Tyler held her for a moment. Then together, they gathered their composure and walked slowly toward the others. Motionless, the Group watched silently, dreadfully, as the couple made their way toward them. Each face read the message and waited for confirmation. Something horrible had happened. Tyler left Marge, and held his hand out toward Janice. She took several short gasps, as Tyler looked quietly into her eyes. He believed that he could feel her soul searching his own in disbelief.

Tyler's voice was slow but steady. "Janice, I got a call from your father. He's on his way down to pick you up. A Marine came to the house, to tell him . . . to tell them . . . that your brother was killed yesterday. They will be flying his body home . . . I don't have any other information. I . . . I am so sorry . . ." Tyler's voice faltered amid the shrill sound of anguish.

"NO! God, Please, NO!" Janice clutched her mouth as she fell to the ground. Startled, a pheasant flew from a nearby trail. Her scream reverberated in the minds of her friends, a lasting scar gashed into the peace and innocence of their youth. Then suddenly, Janice looked up into the faces of each of her friends, in hopeful disbelief.

"But the cease fire . . . That can't be . . . How can that be?" She looked hysterically from face to face for the answer. "That just can't be!" She was on her knees now, crying, groping toward her friends for the answer. But they could not reply, even when she tugged at them frantically for response. Jordan would never forget the wildness in her eyes, the look that only comes from raw human sorrow. Janice collapsed against the ground, sobbing.

The Group stood as silent witness, suddenly thrust into the horror of current events that had only been headlines—had only been film clips on the evening news, or made-up stories on some hour-long army show—until now. These things didn't happen to them or to their friends. They had a weird kind of immunity from grief—nothing painful could ever touch them. These things only happened to the nameless images that shot across the TV screen each night, or to those captured on the front pages of the New York Times. These things simply could not happen to them! A sense of the surreal overwhelmed them like a cold, dark, wave that crashed upon the shore, insidious and inescapable. Time stood motionless. They were suddenly pulled from the familiar and bumped onto another plane of consciousness, where tragedy now delighted, and anguish reveled in its own power.

Marge stood with hand cupping her mouth, as tears rolled silently down her cheeks. Jordan bent down to Janice, and cradled her sobbing body against her own. She did not know how to comfort her friend. Janice cried wholly, but without further outburst, without further demand, without further questioning. Jordan wept quietly with Janice, as she held her for what seemed an eternity. Even the birds and the winds grew silent in the mourning of this older brother—now passed—and in the respect for his family. Janice's scream echoed through the mountains, and the pangs of grief cloaked them all in the darkness of intense loss.

Janice was shivering now, and Marge brought a blanket to cover her. She cried herself from hysterics to sleep, before Jordan attempted to move her from the ground. Sturgis and Martin helped them to their feet. Tyler remained distant, silent, but wept for his friend. He and Marge helped Janice to the car. It would be hours before Janice's father would arrive, but she would need time for a shower, for packing, and to arrange for class assignments. Her mind was flying through the list of preparations, as she avoided all thought of the cause. Jordan would help her in that process.

As the three drove off, Sturgis led the others in breaking camp, packing their cars, and heading back to campus. Except for an occasional statement of false doubt, there was little talk. Sturgis agreed to drive Jordan and Marge back home to attend the funeral. Tyler would also be driving. The men would stay at Marge's home, since they were not from that area. They would be there for Janice—they would stand by her side, and help her garner the strength to support her parents. She was like that, always caring for her family first. There were only two children, but now, just one. The Group would be there for Janice, and for her grief. They waited back at the dorm for the arrival of Janice's father, and for the arrangements made for the parting of his only son. Jordan helped Janice pack, and offered comfort to her as best she could. Janice regained her composure, and moved through the day robot-like in efficiency, wholly focused on task. She could not allow herself to think about what she was actually doing.

News traveled quickly through Balmural first, then through the campus. Many friends from the college and from the Physics Department stopped by to offer help or condolences, but Jordan diverted them at Janice's request. She could not handle their sympathy. She had not fully accepted the truth that now faced her. Her only brother was dead—as immediate, and as permanent as that. She could not comprehend it. There was no bargaining. There was only denial, and the hope that the information was somehow incorrect. She would not comprehend this. She would only go through the day until her father arrived. Jordan did not know how Janice was functioning at all.

After she finished packing, Janice lay down for a nap. Jordan used this time to contact Karen, and to call her own parents. Karen and Todd would be attending the funeral, but could not attend the viewing. They would stay at a motel in town, and would call Jordan when they arrived. Jordan phoned her own family and advised them of Stephen's death, but she could not provide further details until she spoke with Janice's family.

It was well before dusk when Janice's father and her uncle arrived at the dorm. Both appeared haggard and tear-worn. Mr. Guilford introduced his brother Paul, and asked him to relate information to the Group, while he joined his daughter in her room. Paul Guilford sat hunched in the chair next to Tyler as he spoke. Martin wanted to go with Mr. Guilford and to be with Janice, but Paul stopped him.

"They need time alone together as a family." Martin stood silent, knowing that he was the family that Janice needed most. Paul continued.

"There was an accident outside of Saigon . . . Stephen was coming back to camp. I guess he was trying hard to beat the night. He took a short cut through a field, and he hit a land mine . . . His jeep overturned. I don't know how long he was there before he was found." Paul took a breath and continued.

"He could have been buried at Arlington . . . but his mother wanted him home near them. He's going to be buried in the cemetery at their church. I think it would mean a lot to Janice, if you could all be there for her."

Jordan shook her head. "We'll be there for her." Tyler and Martin nodded in agreement.

"Stephen will be at rest in the good company of Guilfords of the last several generations. He's finally come home to us." As he choked out these last words, Janice and her father joined them in the day room. They were stoic and dignified, a family united in mourning.

As Janice and her family left the campus, the Group stood in the doorway of Balmural Hall, and watched the family drive off. Tyler first broke the silence. "I never worried about the draft because my lottery number is 302. Stephen's was above 200. I don't get why he enlisted in that mess."

"He told Janice that he wanted to be there when it all ended. He wanted to be a part of it. He even told her that he felt safer over there than at home. But to go through everything over there, and to have it end like this? It doesn't make any sense, "Martin said.

"It's so fucking weird . . . Janice prayed every night that he wouldn't get killed in the line of fire. She thought he was safe now . . . It's almost like he wasn't supposed to come home," Marge whispered.

"He wanted a career in the military," Martin replied. "But with the cease fire in place, he should have been coming home. Why would he have signed up for another tour?"

"Almost like he wasn't supposed to come home," Marge whispered back.

As Janice sat in her room, she could hear the controlled sobs of grief from her mother, while her father tried to comfort her. Janice searched a photo of her brother for the answers. Stephen wanted to be a Marine almost from the time that he could walk. As she looked in his eyes, she could still the boy who always defended her by shooting "Commies" or "taking out Krauts or Japs" in the neighborhood. He'd wave her to stay down, while he'd slink around the corners of the house, crawl along the floors and under the windows, and toss imaginary hand grenades into the garden, or near the dog house. He would "machine gun" any intruders, like the postman or the occasional salesman who ventured onto the property. In each scenario, he had always been the hero. He never died in any of these play battles. He was never even wounded in any of the real fire fights in country. How could she believe that he could die now? There might have been an almost morbid draw to the situation, if it had not been someone she so loved. She wanted to pull Martin around her like a blanket, to hide within him from the storm. She tried to hear Stephen's voice, but the muffled silence was shattered by the screaming of her own mind.

The next few days moved slowly and with a stillness, as if the campus itself was mourning the loss of one of its family. Everyone felt sympathy for Janice and her family, but no one knew quite how to express it. No one knew how to make things better for them. No one knew how to deal with it. Certainly the home town would honor Stephen with a plaque at Veterans Park, and there would be the Military Honors given during the funeral ceremony. Jordan wondered what would go beyond that. A man's life should account for more than a day's ceremony—no matter how solemn. Could all of this ritual ease the loss of a son, or of a brother? Was the flag enough to cling to, when all else has been taken from you?

She wanted to be a patriot, like her parents, but realized that it was a lot easier to be patriotic when strangers were dying. It was a lot harder to hold close to God and country, when your loved one had to sacrifice his life in some odd country somewhere. Maybe she was wrong—maybe it was easier to hold close to the flag when your brother had given his life for it. Maybe that was the only way you could derive any sense or meaning from his death. She could not be sure, and could not sort out the confusion of her thoughts. She only knew for certain that she hurt for her friend, and that her friend was hurting beyond comprehension.

\* \* \*

The sun shone brightly on the morning of Stephen Guilford's funeral. This came as some relief, since it had rained bitterly during his wake. His casket was draped with the American Flag, and there were several pictures of Stephen and his family on display at a table nearby. A young Marine also stood by the casket. The room had the sickening odor of gladiolas, a favorite flower of Jordan's until that day. She now vowed never to plant such flowers in her own garden. There were wreathes and floral arrangements, baskets and live plants surrounding Stephen's coffin. Janice commented that Stephen would have liked that—that he always liked being outdoors or in the woods, and that all the plants and flowers made the parlor look just like a meadow. Janice stayed with her parents, greeting visitors, and occasionally holding her mother's hand when she became teary. Martin stood by her side. Jordan stayed with Tyler, Sturgis, and Marge. The Group spoke quietly, superficially, together. They occasionally tried to match the persona with the stories Janice told them about some of her relatives. The visitors broke off into smaller groups, some laughing and reminiscing, and seemed to use the wake as a social affair. Although Jordan had attended a wake once for an uncle, she was still uncomfortable with the seeming cheerfulness of such events. Her mother told her this was Irish custom, and that she should be happy that the departed was now free of his veil of tears—but what could a twenty-five year old possibly feel tearful about? Stephen's wake otherwise passed more easily than Jordan would have guessed.

Yes, the sun shone brightly on the morning of Stephen Guilford's funeral. Its beams seemed to reach down and kiss the earth where his cold body would be laid to rest. The ground was still saturated from the pounding rain of the day before, but the warmth of the spring air lent promise that better times were coming. Jordan's parents accompanied her to Smith Funeral Home, where the Marine Military Guard was already posted. Unlike the day before, there was the solemnity of ceremony that guided the participants in their communal mourning. Janice's minister stood at the pulpit, while the Marine Guard stood at full attention, hats stowed under arm, and in prayer for their fallen comrade. Jordan could not recall much of the minister's sermon. She had hoped he could give insight into why such tragedies occur. Apparently, there were mysteries in the Episcopal faith as well, because the minister could only offer that no one but God could know God's will; and no one but the faithful could fully accept it. Jordan did not begin to cry until she tried to sing "How Great Thou Art." She loved the old hymn as much as she loved nature itself, and she believed in her heart that its verses had been whispered by God's own lips.

Karen and Todd joined Marge, Tyler, and Marge's parents, and were seated near the back of the room. Jordan smiled and nodded when she spotted them. Karen had obviously been crying. Jordan wanted to hold her, to comfort her, but Todd was now tending her, his arm supporting and protecting her, as Jordan could only look on. She turned her attention back to the casket. As the minister gave the signal, the Marines took their positions, and gently wheeled Stephen Guilford to the hearse that would transport him to his eternity. A police car led the procession, and flags throughout the town were displayed at half mast in his honor. It would have been a spectacular tribute, if he had been alive to enjoy it himself. As the funeral procession made its way through the cemetery of the First Episcopal Church, and to the tent covering the plot, Jordan caught views of tombstones bearing the family name. Stephen would be comfortable there, she thought, and probably so would Janice, in time. They would fit in there, cradled among their relatives, for all eternity.

As the minister concluded his prayers, and with the consecration of the ground complete, the Marine Guard played Taps, and fired off a salute. With each shot, Jordan imagined the blast that stole his life's light, and snuffed his flame of happiness from his family. Stephen's parents remained stoic and silent throughout the ceremony. It was only when Mrs. Guilford was handed the folded flag—the flag that had blanketed her son to the afterlife—that she began sobbing. As she clutched the flag tightly to her motherly breast, Jordan realized her answer. For the Guilford's, the flag would be the silent, profound justification for their son's short life. He had died for America. [27]

---

[27] For a discussion on differential diagnosis in bereavement issues, please see the Appendix and Bibliography Section for Chapter Three.

# Chapter 4

Summer passed slowly following the death of Stephen Guilford, and the close of the semester. Although Janice missed nearly two weeks' classes, she was able to make up most of the work while she was at home. She returned to college for the last week of the semester, and just for finals. Janice kept busy and spent much of her free time alone. Jordan noticed that her normally clear, alert eyes now appeared dull and sullen. She was having difficulty sleeping. She maintained the meal routines with the Group, but mostly, she seemed barely there beyond the initial smile in greeting, or the occasional one word comment. At other times, Janice was so animated, that it seemed like she was pretending to be someone else, and in full denial that anything had ever happened. It was her labile mood, as the texts would describe, that had her friends so concerned. Jordan was worried that Janice was now in a place from which there was no recovery, a realm from which there was no return. She hoped that Janice's mood swings were due to the newness of her grief, and that, in time, she would learn to cope with the loss. She was worried that Stephen's death was having a more profound effect, though, because they could not console her. And she was isolating herself from everyone. Since she had never experienced such loss, Jordan did not know what "normal" should look like. She only knew that her friend was very different now, and she ached silently for her. She had very little contact from Janice during that summer, and she rarely returned Jordan's calls. When she did call, she always had other plans, and never had time to talk. She was the same with Marge. Clearly, she needed time to heal. Martin was tending to her as best as their long distance relationship could allow.

He was worried about her too, but like the others, he just didn't know what to do.

The rhythm of summer soon fell into its familiar cadence. Jordan started a summer job at the Shop Rite, and was working well over 40 hours a week. She hoped to make college tuition and books for her final two semesters. Her loans were in place, but they usually covered only 2/3 of the cost. While her parents supported her emotionally, they could not assist her financially. They were just barely making the household bills. Jordan was acutely conscious of her monetary limitations. She was especially uncomfortable on outings with Marge, who laughed at the emphasis "most people" placed on costs. In her world, you purchased what you liked, or what you wanted, or what thought you might like, or what you thought you might want in the future. Or, you just purchased! She commented frequently on Jordan's self-control, perhaps never realizing that finances were the true restraint. If she did realize this, she never let on to Jordan or to the others. Money was Marge's greatest inconsistency. While she mocked her parents and their quest for a dollar bill, she often held hand open, as these same bills would flood her palm, and then fly off from hand to cash register! And she bought quality, too! No Greens or Two Guys stuff for her! She was strictly a Macy's and Bamberger's woman! Boutiques throughout the state knew her on a first name basis! Jordan often wondered what it would be like to buy something and not feel guilty about it.

Marge was bored with the summer since her two closest friends were not usually available. She decided to take a job as a camp counselor at the local YMCA, so that she could devote her talents toward helping disadvantaged children. Her mother helped her get the position, and even suggested that she join some of the women's groups in the community. Marge thought that was a hoot! Years later, Marge Jorgenson would be the president of the County League of Women Voters, and Recording Secretary to the board of the local hospital. Had she lived longer, her mother would have thought that that was a hoot! Tyler was staying with Marge and her family for the summer, and was working as an assistant to Marge's father. He and Mr. Jorgenson spent several weeks traveling between corporate offices in preparation for the start of the new fiscal year. Tyler was at Marge's home exclusively in late July and August. Marge's father was also able to secure a job for him as a chef's assistant at the Country Club, where Mr. Jorgensen played golf with the community elite, and had wet dreams about corporate mergers—or so Marge said.

Jordan's parents spent the summer as usual, working hard, building a life, cutting monetary corners, and enjoying the occasional family picnic or trip to the beach. Summer was the busy time for carpenters. Her father had to make a year's earnings in five months! There would be no summer vacation, no family get-aways to Block Island or Martha's Vineyard. There might, however, be the occasional family fun night—usually Pokeno or Uno with the neighbors—or a jaunt together through one of the area parks. Jordan could never recall a time that her parents had gone on vacation, and even asked her father about this once.

"With a family like this, isn't every day a vacation?" Pete Mathews sarcastically replied.

Her mother had always dreamed of touring Europe. But her father said that he had already been there once, and that he did not want to return. He did agree, however, that the tour might possibly be more pleasant going in peacetime with his wife, than in wartime with Patton! At other times, he said that he might hardly have known the difference! Ann Mathews would scowl back in feigned disgust. Jordan's Uncle Pat and family were taking a vacation in Florida that included several days at Miami Beach and at Disney World. They would bring back plenty of slides for screening at Christmas. Jonathan was working part time with his father, and was also working at his own lawn business. Kelly was busy doing whatever Kelly had to do to maintain her popularity. This included working part time at an exclusive boutique, a job that Marge had arranged for her.

Karen and Todd Sommers spent this time preparing for the birth of their first child. Todd was now working long hours, while Karen single-handedly painted and decorated the nursery. Although she had enrolled in UV for the fall, she withdrew from classes in anticipation of motherhood. She was still quite healthy and had plenty of time until the birth, scheduled for late December. Karen just wanted to be sure that everything would go well. She registered for parenting and child development classes at their community adult school in preparation. Karen was elated whenever she and Jordan talked. Jordan could not imagine how one person could have earned the right to so much happiness! Certainly Karen and Todd deserved it. But it did help that their parents were both well off. Jordan envied that part of their lives, and thought about how much easier her own life could be, if only her parents were able to help a little more. At other times, she would imagine herself as Todd, caring for Karen and their family. She consciously had to fight off a jealousy of him whenever she thought of them together.

"That should be us . . ." The voice echoed through Jordan's mind whenever she thought about them. The thought nagged at her constantly.

Tillie gave Jordan the highest possible rating for an internship, and that, with the reference from Donna Bromley, her Field Placement Supervisor, helped Jordan arrange her senior internship at the Merton Mental Health Clinic. This was a real step up from the mundane completion of eligibility paperwork. She would now be interviewing, assessing, and counseling patients in real mental anguish. She could not fathom the opportunity that she would now have to minister to others, to help people pull their lives together, to help them live again. She could hardly wait to contribute her talents in that direction! Maybe that was her true calling. She was a good listener, she had empathy, she could be goal-focused, she could advocate—she could be a success—and in an area that her family might feel more comfortable about! Sure, there would still be welfare clients, but these were the truly deserving, the mentally ill, who had no other choice but to accept government assistance. Their little Jordan would be moving people to emotional recovery! She would be the veritable doctor in the family! How could they complain about that? But they did . . . And now that Jordan was home for the summer, her mother stepped up the pressure for marriage and family. Maybe that's what drove Jordan to accept a night out with two older women that she met at the supermarket where she worked.

There were rumors about those two. Nothing really concrete, but whenever women work together, the conversation invariably turns to discussion about who is fucking who. These women never really participated in the talk. They were friends, but they were somehow aloof from the others. They were cordial enough, but they just didn't divulge. They were in their late twenties and not an engagement ring—not even a steady man—in sight! But Jordan liked them both. The fact that they were part of the socially disadvantaged, the less desirable, the clique-less, made them even more appealing to her. Marge often commented on Jordan's penchant for the "low man" as a kind of social underachievement. She was wrong! Jordan felt most comfortable with people who were outsiders, who didn't quite fit in. They understood each other, and Jordan understood them. Maybe that was the greatest strength that she would bring to Social Work. She understood not fitting in.

So when the women casually said that they were going to a club in the city, and without a better offer for the evening, Jordan accepted their invitation to go along. She never consciously considered that they would be going to a gay bar. That fact had been left out of the conversation. The women mentioned the name of the bar, and Jordan pretended that she had heard of it. Maybe she had, but she had never heard of it in quite that context. In more honest moments, and in the silence of her heart, Jordan knew what she was doing. She had positioned herself for that invitation! She had taken both Social Deviance and Social Change as part of her Sociology minor. She told herself that she wanted the chance to experience an underground—a counter-culture—first-hand. And maybe there was more to it than that—but she was not going to think about that, just then. On a Saturday night, the Path would be safe, the plans were in place, and she was going!

Jordan and her two new friends finished their shift at the supermarket by 2:00 p.m., and agreed to meet back at the parking lot by 3:30. They would be in Newark by 5:00, on the Path by 5:15, in Grand Central Station by 6:00, and would jump the subway to Bleeker Street. They'd have dinner at Clyde's, in Greenwich Village. They told Jordan that they usually had brunch there on Sunday mornings, for what the place was really known. The rest of the evening was open. Since all three had to be back at work in the morning, it would be an early night. The women had planned to stay over in the city, but could not get anyone to take their shifts at the food store. So, they would catch the 1:00 a.m. Path back to Newark, and would be home by 3:30. On a Saturday night, the Path would be busy, and the ride would be safe. The plan sounded solid.

Jordan told her parents that she was going to the city and that she would be home by 4:00 a.m. After loud objections, her parents realized that she would not be dissuaded. They bit their lips and prayed that the foundation they had laid in rearing her would keep her safe. They could not protect her from all dangers, or from all of the traps of the world. They had to have faith that her own good judgment could do that for them. They would be a safety net if Jordan had problems, but they realized that they could not stop her. She was a woman, and she was asserting her independence. They reviewed the safety plan that included phone calls home before and after use of the trains. She gave the names and numbers of her friends, and agreed that she would not leave them to go alone with anyone. Her parents would have nailed shut the door to her room if they had known Jordan's real intention! They just knew that she was going to one of the clubs in the city. Her cousins had already done this before, and even on New Year's Eve! They could not refute the point, and they knew that they could not stop her.

Jordan showered, fixed her hair, and squirted some Charlie on the nape of her neck. She was wearing tight jeans, a sleeveless top, and a light blazer. She could have been going to any club in the city! Her father was thankful that she was not a provocative type—never a plunging neckline, and rarely a mini skirt. He believed that she was a sensible dresser, although Kelly said that she dressed "functionally unfashionable." Jordan still seemed sexually ambiguous, and maybe that was the look she was going for. If so, she had succeeded! She realized that her two friends had opted for a similar style. Jordan thought this coincidental, that they were all just being collegiate, wearing one style among many. She said that Kelly was wrong, as usual.

Jordan and her new friends chatted throughout the ride to the train station. Most of their conversation focused on the Women's Liberation Movement, a relatively safe topic. They never indicated that they were gay, never apologized for being lesbians. They simply reveled in who they were as human beings. Jordan thought this to be the real joy of being on the verge of thirty! She could not wait to be so settled herself as a woman. Her curiosity—and to some extent, her discomfort—became obvious, though, at several points during the night. Jordan had been to the city only three times that she could remember—once, with the Girl Scouts to see the 1964 World's Fair; another time with the Girl Scouts to see the Rockettes at Radio City Music Hall; and once, with her 8th grade class to tour the Museum of Natural History. Other than that, she knew only of life in her quiet, shore community, and in the controlled existence of her small college. So she tried hard to hide her surprise as she stepped off the subway and onto Bleeker Street. She found herself half talking to her friends, half gawking at the people she passed as they walked by. She could not keep her eyes from following the cross dressers! Her mind kept wandering from the conversation as she tried to decipher the real gender of the people she surveyed.

"Jordan," Betty said, "Don't be so perplexed. People are what they are. Just accept what you see."

"Is it that obvious?" She didn't want to offend anyone, and definitely did not want an order of "knuckle sandwich" for dinner! Betty and Jan were treating her more like a kid sister than like a friend. They were half taunting her, enjoying her embarrassment.

"I've never known a lady yet, that would ruin a gown to punch out an admirer," Jan replied, "But I hope this won't be another first for the evening . . . Are ya sure this is gonna' help ya in Social Work . . . A single night out in the Big City? What is it that you're really looking for, anyway?"

"Who said I'm looking for anything? I'm here to have a good time with my friends..."

"Oh, I see," Jan replied. "Well, let's see what we can do... There's plenty of leather bars around... Are ya up for a little bondage/discipline stuff? Maybe some dominance/submission action? Wanna see what your average sadomasochist looks for in a date? How 'bout water sports? Are ya into degradation, humiliation, that kind of thing?"

"What!?" Jordan said, shocked and afraid of what she might have gotten herself into.

"Well that ain't us! Stop it, Jan!" Betty said. "You'll scare the hell out of her. In fact, you're scarin' the hell outta me! Listen, women don't usually go to leather bars, unless they're fag-haggin', and they're still not usually welcome there... That's kinda changin' though. Anyway, the whole leather scene is a male macho thing, ya know, like the bikers. Except now, they're drawin' people who go for that other stuff. I'm not saying that gay people don't ever get into that. I'm saying that as many gay people as straight people get into it. Do you know anybody who really does get into that stuff? I mean beyond the joking around about it?"

Jordan shook her head.

"Neither do we! Look, man, I don't know what you expect to see, but we will definitely try to show you a good time, with the little time that we have here... So, who's up for Clyde's?"[28]

The restaurant was full when they arrived, and this allowed for a drink at the bar before the meal. The atmosphere was definitively gay, the clientele eclectic, but subdued. The place looked rather upscale , and was better known for its Sunday brunches. Joni Mitchell was playing over the speakers. The bartender was slender and attractive, and she had short, well styled black hair. She wore a lose tie and vest, a possible precursor to Annie Hall. Jordan liked the look. The conversation

---

[28] For information on the function of gay bars in the Gay Community in the 1970's, please refer to Appendix and Bibliography for Chapter Four.

was pretty light, and focused on some of the clubs the women enjoyed. Jan and Betty had been going to a place called the Sanctuary on West 43rd, until it closed the year before. It was a deconsecrated church, and the music blared from a DJ set up on the altar. The crowd was mixed, but primarily gay. The place could be wild! Then they tried the Lib, an exclusively women's club on 3rd Avenue, but they felt that the place was too dykey. They liked the mixed clubs better. So if they had more time, they'd stop by the Oscar Wilde Bookstore on Christopher Street, then go over to the Ninth Circle on West 10th. Jordan was up for the plans.

Dinner was delayed further, and by the time Jordan finished her steak, it was nearly 10:00! The waiter suggested that they try the Limelight, a new club that opened on 7th. They walked to the Oscar Wilde, a fairly long walk, but in her excitement, Jordan hardly noticed. She liked the window shopping, and darting in and out of the shops with her friends. She liked the art galleries and boutiques, the head shops and the street corner poets. She liked the jugglers and street performers near Sheridan Park. The place was all so alive, even for the late evening. Jan even pointed out the Stonewall Inn. Jordan recognized the name of the bar from her classes. [29] She thought back to the discussions at college:

The Stonewall Inn was a mixed gay bar, rather nondescript, and like the other gay bars, allegedly owned by the Mafia. They had a relationship with the police, who reportedly accepted pay-offs (known as "gayola," a twist on "payola") for overlooking certain illegal indiscretions, like the lack of a liquor license. Police periodically raided gay bars throughout the city based on the morals statutes. It was illegal for men to dance with men, or for anyone to dress in clothing inappropriate to one's sex. But the bars had developed a system since the 1950's to warn patrons: when a raid was imminent, they'd flash the white lights! On the early morning of June 28, 1969, there was no raid warning call to the Stonewall Inn.

---

[29] For a resource list of gay bars/descriptions in Greenwich Village in the 1970's, please refer to Appendix and Bibliography for Chapter Four.

Police raided the bar, arrested several drag queens and employees, and generally harassed the clientele before they let the nearly 200 people leave. During the raid, a cop reportedly hit a cross-dressing dyke named Stormie' De Larverie (although many have challenged this identity), and she punched him back. Pandemonium ensued. Police were pelted with pennies and dimes, significant of "gayola," and were barraged with a variety of insults. Dave Van Ronk, a straight folk singer performing at a club nearby, was severely beaten by the police when he came to investigate the ruckus. Gay people from throughout the surrounding area came to join the Stonewall Inn protestors. Police barricaded themselves inside the Stonewall and called for back up. The crowd used a broken parking meter as a battering ram, while someone else sprayed lighter fluid and tossed a lit match through a broken window.

The Tactical Police Force arrived and helped disperse the crowd, who had now started fires in trash cans, and were throwing bottles at police. Crowds of demonstrators gathered outside the Stonewall for the next five nights. The typically docile gay community had taken the lead of the Civil Rights Movement, and like other oppressed peoples, began demanding their own treatment with dignity and respect. The Gay Rights Movement was born just twelve hours after Judy Garland's public viewing and funeral in New York City. Maybe it was the weather (a hot night), maybe it was the social climate at the time, maybe it was years of pent up frustration, or maybe it was the loss of Judy and their shared mourning that finally gave the community the strength to stand up and shout that it would take no more.[30]

"The Stonewall Riots are a hot topic in my class discussions," Jordan said.
"Is that right!" Jan chided.

---

[30] For resources on the accounts of the Stonewall Riots, please refer to Appendix and Bibliography for Chapter Four.

"My professors have been discussing that event with an eye on the future . . ." No response from either of her friends.

"They're monitoring social change, like a kind of history in the making . . . They said that there have been other incidents, other demonstrations, after the Stonewall Riots. This indicates that it's a social movement now and not just an isolated episode. They believe that they're witnessing a pivotal event that will have national and worldwide implications . . . . Even though there are no elegant, charismatic leaders, like a Martin Luther King, Jr. or a Caesar Chavez . . ."

"Nope! Just throngs of drag queens, bull daggers, and closeted business people—male and female—who refuse to be bullied or intimidated anymore," Jan declared, while Betty laughed at that comment.

"Your professors said that? I'm sure the Gay Community will be pleased to hear that one!" Betty replied.

"Mr. Rawlings, my Social Deviance professor, discussed deviance as a part of culture, a socially defined quality. He said that as people are labeled deviant, their deviant behavior escalates in response, a kind of self-fulfilling prophesy. My professors believe that as the Gay Rights Movement pushes more into the mainstream, the need for deviant-like—meaning "different than"—behaviors will subside, and gay people themselves will move toward the mainstream." Jordan looked to them both, and realized that neither Jan nor Betty understood what she said. And she also knew that she had somehow insulted them. They looked to each other in silence, and continued their walk to the club. Jordan didn't say any more about the subject.

Years later, they could all look back on that night, and think again about her comments. Her professors would probably be patting themselves on the back at the end of the century, if they could see the decline of the leather bars, the growing emphasis on long term committed relationships, and the movement for gay marriage. But the effects of the AIDS epidemic of the 1980s probably contributed to much of that change . . .

At any rate, AIDS would decimate much of the community that Jordan met that night—well over half of the men there would be dead from the disease within the next decade—and most of them would die within just a few years of the first identification of the disease itself.[31] But no one could have seen that coming that night . . .

The trio arrived at the Oscar Wilde just before closing, but Jordan was able to peruse at least several rows of books before exiting the shop. She made a mental note of the address so that she could return one day on her own, and buy books of interest on the lifestyle. She rationalized this as a good professional resource. The women now headed back toward 7th Avenue, and to the Limelight.

"The Gay Community can be a pretty tight knit group," Jan explained. "Most of the people here know each other, and maybe have even been lovers at some point. It's kinda incestuous that way."

"But in all fairness, how many other places are you gonna meet someone who'll come out to you immediately, and accept you for who you are? Already, ya have a lot in common!" Betty added. "So you date who you know. Simple as that! If the community was bigger, there'd be more opportunity to meet someone. It's just like any club scene, straight or gay, really. Ya date who ya meet. Things don't work out, and you move on to the next partner . . ."

"And ya get tired of this bar or that scene, ya go to the next favorite place. Somebody's always there that ya know, and they introduce ya around . . . People here usually move between the bars in the city and at the shore." Jan and Betty knew many of the people that night at the Limelight, most of them from the Ninth Circle, or from M and K's in Asbury

There were a lot of tables still free in the bar when they first arrived. The clubs usually didn't start to gather a crowd much before 11:30. The Limelight

---

[31] For a resource list on AIDS and its impact, please refer to Appendix and Bibliography for Chapter Four.

closed at 3:00. On a good night out, they would follow a club with a trip to the Loft, an after-hours, members-only place, also with a mixed crowd. But once at the Limelight, Jordan felt more comfortable. The music was blaring, despite the absence of couples on the dance floor. She could relate to that from the straight clubs. The music was loud, but pounding a rhythm different than the rock clubs where she usually partied. Several women came by to greet Jan and Betty and each was introduced to Jordan. She was thankful that she did not have to carry a conversation with any of these strangers. And when the music faded between songs once, she distinctly heard Betty say that Jordan was a straight friend, not a lesbian. The other woman shook her hand, and moved to her friends at the next table. Many other friends came momentarily to their table and left as whim or opportunity dictated.

Jordan was up at the bar ordering her usual Vodka Collins, when Betty and Jan surrounded her there. They had been talking to a cross dresser (or so Jordan surmised), who hugged both emphatically, and followed them to the thirsty Jordan. Jan introduced the "woman" as Rose, a dear and old friend of theirs. Rose took immediate offense.

"Wait a minute, I'm not THAT old," Rose replied, moving her bejeweled arm up and around her head with the grace of a Balanchine dancer. "I'm certainly no older than either of you . . . And I look quite a bit foxier this evening, if I do say so myself."

The women all agreed. Rose said that she was waiting for her man James to arrive. He was a waiter at one of the restaurants nearby. Jordan surmised that they were leaders of sorts, since Rose had a steady crowd around her. Betty then introduced Jordan.

"Oh, so you're queer-touring! Just checking things out in homoburbia, are you? Good Lord, just what we need . . . another fag-hag to mess with a boy's mind," Rose commented as she gave Jordan the once-over. Betty interceded.

"It's really not like that, Rose. Jordan is a little unsure about who she is as a person. So she just wanted a little more information. That's all," Betty clarified.

Both could see Jordan stiffen with the comment. Jordan would have run out of that place, right then and there—nothing but a cloud of cocktail napkins and mixer straws in her wake—if she thought that she could have found her way back to the subway! But curiosity, and now compulsively, she was drawn to the woman before her. Instead of running, she focused on Rose, a pretty flashy white male probably about early thirties, and with a platinum blonde wig. She wore a sleek black dress three quarter length, with a side slit, and a low cut back. Her black heels looked to be about a size 13. Jordan could not remember ever seeing heels that big! She wondered where she bought her clothes! Her shoes, her feet, did not mesh with the slenderness of her body. Her legs were shaved, as was her chest! Jordan also noted that Rose was bustier than she was. That wasn't unusual—everyone she knew was bustier than she was! She just hated the thought that even a transvestite[32] would be better endowed than she. Jordan smiled at Rose, as she surveyed, with critical eye, Jordan's total ensemble.

"Humph . . . a little light on style . . . You dykes just don't know how to dress . . . Well, not to worry. Your secret is safe with me. I'm not the type to gossip, at least not without someone to listen," she laughed. "Never you mind, Honey. Any friend of Betty and Jan's is a friend of mine." Rose then shoulder hugged and kissed Jordan on the cheek.

"Thanks! I couldn't help but admire your dress," Jordan said, smiling at Rose. "Where did you buy it?"

"There's plenty of places here in the city who can fix you up right, if you're a woman conscious of real style," she replied. "But I bet I know what you're thinking. You're wondering how I can wrap all of this lusciousness into such a well fitting package . . . Well, here's the trick . . ."

Rose leaned in toward Jordan, hiked up the front of her dress, and showed a blue velvet g-string type garment that seemed to pull Rose's penis—in fact, the

---

[32] For a discussion of the terms: transvestite, cross dresser, transsexual, and transgender, please see Appendix and Bibliography for Chapter Four.

whole package—down and under! Jordan was aghast with this brief disclosure! She quickly grabbed her Vodka Collins, and sipped away as she cast her eyes on the velvety tuft hidden under purple laced panties! Again, the slow motion mental cameras surveyed the sight, but like an accident on the Parkway, Jordan could not seem to look away!

"Hey," shouted the bartender. "This is a respectable joint. How many times do I have to tell you that if you want to play show and tell, go to the bathroom . . . Or see me after my shift!" He then winked at Rose.

Rose chided back, "Now Sherman, I belong to James, as everyone knows. And I am far too classy for a bathroom show-down!" She fluffed up her stuff, and pulled down her dress, the secret again safe under black silk and nylon.

Panic overtook Jordan! She had a flash mental vision of the front page of the morning's papers. There would be a large headline and a black and white photo of Jordan and the others being THROWN OUT OF A GAY BAR, the purple-tufted Rose tumbling behind them! Jordan would die if that ever happened!

Turning to Jordan, Rose commented, "If you think that's something, you should see my tiger print! Some ladies buy their stuff from a catalogue, but I prefer to sew my own . . . so much more personal. More intimate, don't you agree?"

Jordan, dumbfounded, could only reply, "I don't know . . . I can't really sew."

"Somehow I knew that," Rose replied. Then in the same breath, she screamed "James!" and made a dramatic bolt to the door, commanding the attention of half the club. She dragged James, a well dressed, well groomed, and well built man of his mid-forties to the bar where Jordan and the others were standing.

"I want you to meet a new friend of mine. Jordan, this is my man James. James, this is my new friend Jordan."

Jordan reached out to shake his hand, but James smiled, pushed her hand aside, and gave her a hug. He then acknowledged Betty and Jan. They all discussed the next Gay Activist Alliance meeting, and their plan to challenge the NYPD for poor follow up on several recent gay bashings near the subway. They'd probably get together again at the M and K down at the shore. Then holding hands, they joined the crowd on the dance floor. Another male couple had taken the center, and the crowds parted for their exhibition. They were followed by couples, male and female, cross dressers and bull daggers, all who joined in the dance. Jordan was amazed at the seeming ease and free movement of couples rubbing body against body! She had never seen dancing so erotic or provocative in the straight clubs!

Some of the dancers were inhaling a substance from small canisters. Betty said that these were "poppers," amyl nitrate. She cautioned against using it.

"Anything that gets you that high that fast can't be good for ya! And the effects fade quick." Jordan readily accepted that advice.

The other drugs Jordan had seen in the straight clubs. She refused hits of acid that were making their way around the room. Marijuana was the only drug Jordan had ever tried, and she had no interest in exploring that realm any further. Betty and Jan had also smoked pot occasionally, and told Jordan that they had tried cocaine. They really didn't feel much for it. Jordan was glad that they were only drinking that night, and that they had limited their alcohol to just a few bottles of Bud. Jordan had only two drinks the whole evening, not counting the glass of wine she had with dinner. This was one night that she wanted to be in full control of her faculties. Years later, she would join a generation's decry against "chemical experimentation" of any kind. But tonight, she continued to watch the crowd as she sipped her drink.

As McCartney sang "My Love"[33] from the speakers above the bar, couples throughout the place let out a low sigh and moved back onto the dance floor. They clutched each other tightly, gazed into the eyes of their beloveds, and closed out all interference from the outside world. They had found love, at least for the evening, and hoped that the comfort they drew from it might help nurture the

---

[33] A reference to: McCartney, Paul (1973). "My Love" [as recorded by Paul McCartney and Wings]. On *Red Rose Speedway* [audio album]. UK: Apple Records

relationship of a lifetime. Jan signaled that it was time for them to leave. They needed to be on the subway, so they could make the connection with the 1:00 a.m. Path. Jordan said goodbye to her new friends at the club, and formulated questions for Jan and Betty, as they road the Path back to Newark. Once in the car, the barrage started.

"I don't get the whole cross dressing scene," Jordan said, waiting for a reply. When one did not immediately emerge, Jordan asked, "Is it that they just want to be women?"[34]

"That's a tough question, because it all depends on the PERSON that you're talking about," Betty replied. "You met some gay cross dressers here tonight. But most cross dressers are straight men, and many are even happily married! . . . I think the biggest problem that anyone has, is that their minds have been programmed to think in a certain way, right from birth. Think about yourself. You were defined as a girl the moment ya slipped out of your mother's womb, right? They looked at the parts, and they made their proclamation: This is a girl. As such, she will like dolls, play house, wear dresses, and marry a man who is anatomically much different than she is. Am I right?" Betty asked. Jordan agreed.

"But there's the catch! While everyone is caught up on the anatomy thing, no one is focusin' on the spirit of the person. Sometimes the two don't mesh—spirit and physique, I mean. For Rose, her dominating spirit is clearly feminine. She feels comfortable, womanly, when she dresses consistent with that spirit. And it's erotic for her! James would probably love her no matter how she dressed. He loves the person. The fact that Rose is a male at night's end is just an added bonus. See, James has male characteristics in mind and behavior, but his sexual desires are toward other men . . . At least that's how I see it . . ."

"Huh!" Jordan responded. She understood what Betty meant.

---

[34] For discussion on cross dressing and treatment implications, please see Appendix and Bibliography for Chapter Four.

"They been together now for nearly four years. In the gay community, with all the pressures to force couples to break up, that's really something! That's why they get so much respect. They're succeedin' at being who they truly are! And they would do anything to help out a friend. You can really depend on them." Jan added.

"As for the straight cross dressers, I don't really know any . . . But they say it's a form of anxiety release, a form of erotic behavior, just a different type of sexual behavior, simple as that."[35]

Jordan had never even seen a cross dresser, except on TV. She was fascinated.

"They say that the boss is a cross-dresser! Guess only Mrs. Moore knows for sure . . . Just goes to show ya, you never really know!" Jan snapped out the comment with a shrug.

"Ignore her! . . . But like I was sayin', the dichotomy you've been taught to believe really doesn't exist," Betty added. "It's never just one way or the other, black or white, male or female—like that. Sexuality is a combination of factors, and how these all play out depends on who ya are as an individual. Sure, you can try to suppress, you can try to hide one facet or another of your personality, but in the end, all of you comes screamin' out for recognition! Your integrity as a person rests on your ability to negotiate, kinda, among these factors, so that you can become the total person that you were intended to be."[36]

"But neither of ya look or act like some of the women I saw tonight. You both seem pretty regular, like anybody I'd know at school . . ."

"Well that's the point! We are like anyone you'd know at school! Only our sexual being, our spirit, is toward other women. I'm sure that you've met many women at school, at work, wherever, who are also gay. You just never realized it,

---

[35] A resource tool for the discussion of sexuality and gender can be found in Appendix and Bibliography for Chapter Four.

[36] For a discussion of integrity issues as they relate to gay identity, please see Appendix and Bibliography for Chapter Four.

and they never told ya. Some people say that bein' gay is by choice. But I say that it's by nature. This is how our gift, our sexuality, manifests itself in us. Just like your gift, your sexuality, manifests toward men. Otherwise, we're the same!" Betty shrugged to emphasize her point. Jordan did know several girls that she thought might have been . . .

"Check it out! We even have the same tastes in clothes, like the same books, even like the same people at work. It's just one facet of many that makes us who we are as individual people," Betty added.

"But think of this—how many dykey women do ya know, who hang all over guys? Think about Jennie in the Meat Department. Did ya ever meet a tougher cookie than that one? Look at her hands. Look at her shoes. But she's the mother of six, and her husband is a tough-guy biker type! It's a confusing world, isn't it?" Jan laughed as she shook her head. Jordan had to agree, and laughed back as she watched cars fly passed them on the Parkway. There was a lot of traffic for 3:00 a.m.

"But you gotta be careful! No matter what they teach you in class, the real world is not like that! Your professors are seein' the birth of a social movement. Good for them! But there are many other people who are very threatened by that change, and they will target you, make you pay for it, in ways that you could not imagine! I'm not tryin' to scare ya . . . I'm only tryin' to share with you the realities of the world we all live in . . . If you read the Village Voice, you'll often see reports of gay men or women bein' beaten, victimized, and even killed! In the regular papers, this violence goes unreported, or it's buried near the end of the paper . . . People have more concern over the loss of a Yankees game, than over the beating death of a dyke, or the bludgeoning of a queen. That's why all the secrecy! That's what the underground is all about. It's the need for protection! Violence and discrimination will continue for decades ahead, regardless of how successful the Gay Rights Movement is now . . . Don't let them kid you." Betty was serious and emphatic. She looked toward Jordan, then back to the road. Jordan listened but did not comment.

"Change takes time, and we recognize that, but we don't like it. For our safety, we're not out when we're out of the gay community. This is just simple coping . . . Ya know, adapting to the situations at hand! If ya have any questions, don't ask us at work. I'll be glad to answer 'em for ya, but we'll have to make a special time and place for that to happen. This is as much for your safety as for ours." Jordan nodded to Jan that she understood.

"So, if anyone asks where we all went tonight, the answer is always, The Electric Circus. Are you familiar with that place? It's a straight club. Got it?" Betty asked Jordan. She shook her head. She had been there before. Jordan appreciated the warning. She had never considered the real dangers of being different. She hoped that they were exaggerating, but she didn't think so. The world was a confusing place.

"And another thing—we introduced you to our friends tonight. But remember that gay people live in a very hostile world. And that hostility, that abject hatred, can affect people in very different ways at different times in their lives. Gay, Black, Jewish, Chinese, fat, ugly, whatever . . . If you're considered different in any way, sooner or later, you will be targeted! Gay people are barraged with this hostility every day, and from every source—sometimes, even from their own families! Without the support of healthy people, this hostility can have an extreme effect on a person's mental health. Ya met some basically sound people this evening, who have come through their crisis of gay identity. They have found healthy ways to pull together all of the facets of their personality. But this is not so for everyone! Real members in the gay community seem to do the best. They have developed the strong friendships and support they need to survive the hatred they encounter every day. That's another good thing about the Gay Activist Alliance! . . . Humans are always in the process of change. Some people are further along than others . . . but there are crazy people everywhere! You just have to learn to spot them early, and to give them a wide berth. You never want that karma spillin' off onto you."

Jordan understood what Betty meant, just by her experience at the Welfare Department. She had met "crazy people" in all manner and form. She had much to consider. But before she realized it, the ride was over. Her other questions would have to wait until she could talk to them again in private.

Jordan got home about 4:15 a.m., and much to the consternation of her father, who waited up for her. She used the safety measures he designed, but he still got no comfort from this until she was again safe at home. Jordan went immediately to bed, but found it difficult to sleep. She had a lot to think about. There was so much yet to process. She lay in bed, and allowed her thoughts to race through the evening, until finally, sleep broke through chaos. She nearly snored her way to a late punch-in at work. Jan and Betty were there already. They nodded to her and went about their cashiering and shelf stocking. The experience solidified their friendships. The rest of the summer passed by as quickly as the summer winds, but with the inner emotional turbulence of a hurricane. Jordan did have much to consider.

* * *

Marge had already claimed her side of the room and was nearly unpacked, when Jordan arrived at the dorm with her family. Jordan surveyed the hallway as she entered. The walls were newly painted, and the rugs freshly vacuumed. The odor of burnt popcorn was missing, and the confusion of a dozen different perfumes and hair sprays was gone. The medaled Mark Spitz or the bare-chested Joe Namath now covered the doors once hidden by the "Cosmo Burt Reynolds." Only half of the available stereos were blaring. Other than that, things were pretty much the same. Jordan's father helped carry her things, while her mother surveyed the cleanliness of the wing's kitchenette. Balmural Hall had the same floor plan on each level. The degree of cleanliness did not change regardless of floor or wing. The place would be sparkling at semester's start, but would be a mess by mid-terms! This was the price to be paid for forty women living together on a single floor! Jordan hated most the mornings in the bathroom. There was nothing more disgusting first thing in the morning than seeing eight women lined up spitting toothpaste! Yet she loved living in the dorm. She felt that there was an automatic camaraderie among the women sharing this singular experience. She felt like she belonged there, and she was glad to be back. Pete and Ann Mathews left the dorm—and their daughter—with an ease and a readiness that made Jordan feel uncomfortable. They were probably glad that she was back, too. They seemed to much prefer "not knowing" to "knowing" any day!

With parents now gone, Marge and Jordan continued decorating their room, and caught up on the gossip among friends. Marge had a perfect summer with Tyler, and she thought that they could become engaged by Christmas, if she could maneuver him right. He was not a man to be pushed, she knew, but he did respond to mild coaxing—as long as she was careful enough not to cross the line into "naggery." She didn't share this plan with Jordan during the summer. She was afraid that Jordan might somehow tip Tyler off, before she had positioned him to broach the subject. Marge said that Tyler even talked about them marrying sometime (actually, living together), as they were preparing to return to college that morning. Well, that was all the lead-in that Marge needed! She could be a real take-charge kind of a woman, when she thought that this approach might help meet her goals. Jordan really admired this about her—when she knew what she wanted, she went for it like a barracuda! There was no awkwardness. There was no hesitancy. There was no apology.

Believe it or not, though, Marge had actually fallen in love with Tyler! She confided that this was no girly crush, no mere physical attraction—she could actually see herself making a real life with this man. She respected him more with each day that she lived with him. She saw his drive to succeed, she envied his independence, and she loved his humor. But what she liked most was that Tyler was a person of some good, of some real integrity, in a world that she perceived as markedly phony. To Marge, that was a commodity of real value, and one that she would not easily let go.

The conversation then turned to Jordan's love life. Marge tried to probe her about her summer romances, but Jordan was evasive, as usual. She had not yet met the ultimate match, and the rest weren't worth the time it took to talk about them. Marge accepted this, knowing that Jordan would settle for nothing less than sheer perfection. This was their anchor in all circumstance. Jordan would never settle for anything. The fact that perfection usually takes some time helped keep them both out of trouble. They did not go to the Phi Ep's Frat party, for example, because Jordan was not satisfied with her term paper on the culture of poverty. She used the weekend writing and rewriting her concluding thesis, while Marge read several chapters of the Physics assignment that she had only planned to skim. And so, they avoided the mass haul-in by local police who were tipped off about the frat party's marijuana stash! Marge could think of countless incidents like this one: refusing a date with a less desirable someone who turned out later to be a real loser; missing a ride home in search of the perfect blouse, only to find out that the friend's car had been totaled in an accident; going to the Pic-N-Pac for the perfect pork sandwich, and missing the floor-wide cat fight at the dorm!

Jordan told Marge about the ongoing problems with her mother, and her parents' marginal support of her goals. They each received many phone calls and letters from Martin, but neither had heard much from Janice. Marge believed that Janice was now on valium. She said that Martin sent Tyler a few letters telling him that Janice had a prescription. Marge thought that this was probably why Janice kept canceling nights out with them. Jordan had a few phone calls from Karen, but they had not really talked since the funeral. Marge was surprised by the huge disappointment she heard in Jordan's voice, and she shot Jordan a puzzled look. Jordan quickly corrected, by saying that Janice and her parents were in therapy. No sooner had they finished this part of the conversation, than Janice knocked on their door.

"Who's ready for dinner?" Janice asked. The door flew open and both ran to Janice and hugged her. Shrieks filled the hallway.

"What the hell—you'd think you guys haven't seen me in a year . . . it does feel that way . . . Well, I'm here now, and I'm hungry, and it's nearly 5:30. So what's the hold-up? Let's go."

"Ok, Ok! We're with ya! Just let us get our meal cards, and we're gone!" Jordan said, as she tried to make eye contact. Janice looked away, not welcoming the intrusion.

Jordan sensed the feigned happiness. Neither the laughter, nor the valium, was strong enough to mask her pain. Janice looked like a shadow person, a shell of the woman she had known only a few months ago. She still did not know how to comfort her. She could not avoid staring at her, and shook herself to break the morbid compulsion that drew her eyes to Janice's. She kept scolding herself silently to give Janice space, to give her privacy, and to let Janice come to her. She hoped that once this initial contact was over, Janice would be much more comfortable back with her friends. Janice hadn't seen them together since the funeral. Jordan was certain that she was having trouble because of this mental connection. She just seemed so uncomfortable with them now. Jordan sensed this, and decided not to try so hard to connect with her friend. Instead, she would hold back, and let Janice come to her when she was ready.

Martin and Tyler were already en route to Balmural Hall when the girls emerged from the dorm. They were rooming together again at Hill Hall. Their conversations were always light, and this helped Janice get back into the mealtime regimen. That was the amazing thing about them all—if one was hurting, the unique combination of the others in the Group smoothed the way back to balance. They collectively were a kind of psychic valium, given in the proper dosages. Martin launched into the usual tirade about the tomato-covered, non-vegetable, non-edible main course. Tyler talked about seeing the movie Billy Jack,[37] as he molded another self portrait in potatoes and green beans.

"This is a more mature work of the artist," Marge stated, as she added a chef's hat with a piece of lettuce. She liked the movie, too.

---

[37] A reference to: Frank, T.C. (1971). *Billy Jack* [motion picture]. Hollywood: Warner Brothers

Janice added a diploma made from a piece of bread, and nearly laughed herself to tears. They all joined in the Color-Forms food portrait now, with pasta doubling as a sports car, and pudding smeared as the "road to success." Bits of carrot and celery were attached to hunks of the mystery meat that made the restaurant, and then, the frame. As Jordan looked up from this culinary free-for-all, she caught a glance from Janice and smiled back at her. For a moment, at least, Janice was with them again. Jordan hoped that the worst was over, and that she would now more easily find her way back to them. But Jordan knew that even under the best of circumstances, this healing would take much time. As Janice fell back into the shadow woman she had become, Jordan choked back the lump in her throat. She wondered if Janice would ever really make it back.

The Group plowed into another semester's academics. Jordan's summer readings paid off with a decreased pressure in both class and at field placement. She hated working under stress. For this reason, she liked the low keyed harmony of staying in the middle of the pack. The trouble was that the pack often moved too slowly for her! Before she knew it, she was leading them again, dragging them to new heights of excellence by virtue of her own striving. She broke the bell curve, and they hated her for it! Yet, they could not dismiss that she brought them to a higher level of being, a greater awareness of the profession, and of the people that they vowed to assist. Even when she consciously tried not to be, she was a leader! So it came as no surprise that as her tenure as Balmural Dorm Rep. drew to a close, that she would be called upon to save the butt of a less fortunate, less wise, underclassman.

This was a new challenge for Jordan, and one that she quickly sopped up. She was intrigued by the prospect of defending the underdog. Her year as dorm rep. had been pretty unassuming until then: she sat on the Homecoming Committee; she brought back input for the next year's student-sponsored concerts and lectures; and she helped defeat a college president-inspired movement to bring back the dress code. And that was it! Jordan had never been part of the Ethics Committee.

Now she was being asked to defend the accused! She basked in the idea that she could successfully and positively impact on the life of a fellow student. She accepted the assignment without concern that the student was innocent or guilty. That question was not difficult for Jordan. There was no agonizing moment of truth here. As her lawyer, the student was clearly innocent! She put on her best Perry Mason persona and dug in hard to the task.

Patty Spenser was accused of cheating. She denied the charge, and asked that her Dorm Rep. defend her before the Student Council. Jordan successfully pulled together a defense and a closing statement that not only saved the butts of both Patty Spenser and codefendant Alice Watkins, but that also established new procedural guidelines, in situations when a student's integrity is questioned.

"And against all odds, she had won!" Jordan mused. She basked in the success, and in the celebrity that comes from such victory. She believed that the two girls had been sanctioned because they did not have the class, the style, the hygiene, the friends, or the clique memberships to avoid being targeted by the college hierarchy. The girls hung out together, and in their own isolated world, they stood back to back—they stood together—as they were teased, cajoled, or ignored every day of their college lives. Now, these social pariahs had some respect. Jordan took pride in being a champion of the downtrodden, the righter of wrongs. For the first—but not the last—time in her life, Jordan had seen the makings of a railroad job. Several of the Committee members scowled at Jordan in disgust.

"Thank you, God. Oh thank you, God!" The girls were ecstatic when they learned that they had been vindicated! Patty began crying and hugged Jordan several times. Jordan ignored a combination of tears and snot that now mixed on the shoulder of her new sweater. She felt elated that she had made such a difference in the life of another human being. She could not wait until she was impacting on people like this on a daily basis. She could not imagine what that sensation would be like. She could not wait to graduate, and to begin to practice her craft full time. But the celebration was short-lived. Jordan caught the glares from several of the Ethics Committee members, and she felt a quick chill run down her spine. She moved the girls out of the admin building and beyond the psychic reach of those few who now claimed an unsettled score. She dismissed her own concern as just imagination.

But this question of integrity really railed at Jordan. She thought of her own integrity, compromised so many times a day by the lie that she knew she was living. She imagined a hearing of her own one day:

"Isn't it true, Jordan Mathews, that you are in love with Karen Docherty Sommers, a married woman and an expectant mother, and that you would risk reputation, status, economic security, professional standing—in fact, ALL THAT LIFE HAS BECOME—for a few simple moments of pleasure with her?" Jordan would stand uncomfortably as the accusations were read.

"And isn't it true that you have hidden this fact from both friends and family for the full time of your relationship with her—that you have carried on this facade, this masquerade, to avoid detection, while you have secretly longed for the knowledge of that woman in the Biblical sense? . . . And isn't it true that by doing so, you have LIED to them all?" Jordan would not look up.

"And isn't it true that you have feigned interest in men, so that you can pursue your interests with this woman, and all other women around you—even at a cost of life or limb, scaling whatever obstacles lay in your path, come hell or high water?" Jordan would continue her stare at the floor.

"Isn't it also true that you have sacrificed honesty and personal integrity to avoid the consequences of your baser instincts? . . . And in fact, weren't there MANY other women before Karen that you were secretly attracted to!" Jordan would cringe with the statement.

"Well then isn't it also true, Jordan Mathews, that you are a homosexual of the female persuasion, a lesbian hiding in a straight woman's life?"

"Yes! Yes, it's all true!" Jordan would hear herself scream to the court of her own imagination, as she crumbled in the chair behind her! The truth came crashing through her thoughts, but she still could not say the words to anyone. That was her reality. That was her integrity. That was her honesty. And she would live in secret because of it!

Word soon spread throughout the dorms that Jordan won the case for Alice and Patty. She was treated as a hero, at least for the next several days, and garnered acclaim whenever she entered the cafeteria. Jordan wanted to use this experience as a topic in the advocacy part of her Social Change II class. Her professor would have none of it! She could see that it would not have been wise to become further embroiled in the "campus-wide cheating controversy." Jordan equated this to the witch hunts of the McCarthy Era, or so she proclaimed during a dinner tirade in the cafeteria. The Group interrupted her with discussion about the college Jazz ensemble, and with a critique on a scheduled campus movie. That night, they would be showing Frankenstein.[38] They pointed out the combo Oktoberfest/Halloween theme in the cafeteria—beer mugs and spider webs, barrels and black cats, witches and sausages—the Group would use anything to distract Jordan from political conversation on any level! She only partially accepted their redirection. But what the Group found even more interesting that evening was the obvious attempt by Patty and Alice to be more "Jordan-like."

Janice noticed it first. The girls had changed their meal times to coincide with the schedules of the Group. They did not sit near the Group, they did not intrude. But they did seem to go out of their way to talk with Jordan when they saw her around campus, or in the cafeteria. In the three days since their hearing, the girls had also changed their hairstyles to something more like Jordan's—straight, long, and parted in the middle. They had begun wearing jeans exclusively, and wore

---

[38] A reference to: Whales, James (1931). *Frankenstein* [motion picture]. Hollywood, Ca.: Universal Pictures

either tennis sneakers or Charlie Browns. They both ditched their too short mini skirts and knee highs! At first Jordan felt flattered, but she left that quickly, and moved through annoyance to real concern. Janice told her to lighten up, and to let the girls experience their new found confidence. Jordan agreed, but she thought about them during most of the movie. For all she knew, the girls might be some kind of stalkers! Martin convinced her that that probably wasn't true. He thought, instead, that they had adopted Jordan as their role model, their idol! Jordan began cautiously watching them from afar. With a sense of someone finally on their side, the girls experienced a growth spurt in confidence and self-esteem. And with their additional bathing and breath mints, they had even begun dating awkward, smelly men on campus by semester's end!

* * *

Jordan was also experiencing much success at her new field placement. Her Field Supervisor was Dean Benning, an MSW who had been in counseling agencies for the last ten years. He wanted a student with both counseling and advocacy background. And Jordan's skills best matched these needs. Dean worked at the Merton Mental Health Clinic, a private, non-profit agency with a reputation as a frontrunner in the field of community mental health services. Dean worked in a state mental institution after his Masters degree. He vowed then that he would work to establish supportive services that would circumvent the need for commitment to such places. His mother was a schizophrenic, and she spent large amounts of his childhood in and out of such facilities. He was raised primarily by his father, a mechanic, who operated a repair shop from a garage on their property. Dean held fast to his Southern accent and custom, even though he had been college-educated in Massachusetts. He was proud of his roots, and felt that these aspects of his personality formed the touchstones that kept him grounded in a world full of crazy people—and then, he would say, you have to deal with the patients!

Jordan liked Dean, and felt immediately comfortable sharing her concerns and her aspirations with him. He often gazed at the pictures of his wife and children placed along the window sill, as they met for weekly conferencing. Jordan's caseload was split between individual/family counseling, and a self-help advocacy group Dean was forming among his higher functioning patients. Dean was striving to establish a job bank with the local merchants and businessmen, who had agreed to accept his patients for potential employment. The majority of these patients were recovering depressives, most with average or better intelligence, and many with viable job skills and experience prior to their psychotic break. Most of the businessmen knew the patients being referred, or knew their families. Although a college town, the number of resident families in the area was relatively small and very stable, as you would expect in most farm communities. Jordan found it easy to dial a number and refer a patient for employment. She found it a lot tougher to help maintain those jobs. But just a quick phone call from Dean, and the placements would be salvaged! The patients were monitored monthly for medication adjustment by the staff psychiatrist for the first three months following job placement. If they remained stable, the medication monitoring was extended to three month intervals. While some patients may have lost their jobs, Dean was proud that he had never lost a patient. He frequently reviewed with Jordan the key indicators of suicidal risk.[39] She felt that, learning-wise, she had the best of all possible worlds.

Jordan liked the patients on her caseload. Dean was careful to assign only those patients who were moderately depressed. He also allowed her to sit in on sessions with his psychotic or schizophrenic patients. She was amazed at how docile, how calm, most of the patients were. She thought about the many violent mental health patients she had seen portrayed in the movies. She thought about how damaging stereotypes can be! She believed that these stereotypes may have

---

[39] For a sample list of questions used to assess suicidal risk, please refer to Appendix and Bibliography for Chapter Four.

worsened the mental illness, and thought again, about her conversation with Betty and Jan. Employment placement was the first step back to normalcy for her patients, and it was important that the experience would be positive for them. Jordan was becoming entrenched in this helping environment, and she was proud to be a part of the contribution. She pledged herself to the mission that lay before her.

Besides her employment advocacy work, Jordan carried a caseload of four patients that she counseled weekly. These included Mrs. Thomson, a mother of three with a history of post-partum depression[40] following the birth of her second child; John, a twenty-one year old male with a history of depression[41] since age fifteen; Martha, a thirty-seven year old widow and mother of two, who came for bereavement counseling; and Teresa, a nineteen year old female recovering from a psychotic break.[42] Jordan was assuming a caseload from a previous student intern who graduated last spring. Jordan knew the student only slightly, as she lived at home with her family and commuted to the college. She had been working part time for Dean, until he could secure another student. Apparently, though a noble profession, Social Work did not pay well, and its programs were funded at notoriously meager levels.

Jordan made it a point to call Karen at the end of her fourth week of field placement, so that she could share her good fortune. But Karen was getting ready for the delivery of her baby, now perhaps somewhat earlier than the last week of December.

---

[40] For DSM-IV Criteria for Postpartum Onset Specifier, please refer to Appendix and Bibliography for Chapter Four.

[41] For DSM-IV Criteria for Dysthymic Disorder, and for Major Depressive Disorder, please refer to Appendix and Bibliography for Chapter Four.

[42] The DSM-IV criteria for Brief Psychotic Disorder can be found in Appendix and Bibliography for Chapter Four.

"Since this is my first, we don't really know for sure when the baby will arrive. Todd is so excited. Every night he comes home and listens to my stomach, listens to his baby. He even sings to him sometimes, and the baby kicks back! Jordan, I can't tell you how happy we are! We're going to be a family soon!"

Again, Jordan felt the pangs of jealousy, but she was powerless to act.

"Todd's spending a lot more time at home now as we get closer to the baby's birth. He's already packed a bag for the delivery. We're going to try natural child birth, and we've just started Lamaze classes . . . I'm still a little skeptical of the idea, especially given the thought that I'm the one actually doing the delivering! Todd left the choice to me, but he shares articles on natural child birth whenever he finds them."

Jordan wanted to scream, but there was only silence.

"Our coach is very positive, and she counseled us that this is a healthy, rewarding alternative to the usual epidural given with assisted birth. I've read articles about birthing by midwives, birthing in bath water, birthing in quiet musical surroundings, birthing in nature—women have so many options now!"

Jordan stifled her comment: "But the end result will still be the same. You'll be pushing an object the size of a basketball through a hoop the size of a bracelet!" Jordan shuttered at the thought, but could not share this mental image with her.

Jordan's only comment was, "Go with as much medication as you need to pop that little sweetheart out as quickly and as safely as possible. Let Todd worry about being trendy." Karen actually thought that Jordan made good sense.

"What was it that you wanted to talk about?" Karen asked.

"I just wanted to wish you luck," Jordan responded. She knew now that her dreams of a life with Karen would forever be fantasy. She mourned the dream; she held close the love.

The Group planned their usual Saturday night at the Pub, but dedicated the celebration to Jordan's victory. Martin even suggested that Jordan consider changing her major to Law. Jordan half believed that that might be the better option, given the salaries of most social workers at the time. But Jordan was not interested in working with criminals. She was not interested in verbal fencing for a living. Jordan wanted to be in the "nuts and bolts" of making things better for everyone. She wanted to use her talent in all its facets, to make the world a better place. She did not want to be a puppet for some large law firm somewhere. She did not want to be in the pocket of some political big wig somewhere. She wanted to work in the trenches with the common man, so that she could raise him up to uncommon heights. That was her dream, her life vision, and she would follow it.

Martin called the attention of the Pub to the noble Jordan, Defender of the Downtrodden. He led a toast and a cheer, and helped her to the top of the bar. She humbly and graciously thanked all who had made that victory possible—her mother, who constantly argued with her; her fourth grade teacher, who taught her how to write complete sentences; Hawthorne's Subs, who made late night munching possible; and Pope John XXIII and the Fathers Brannigan, role models who championed the rights of the less fortunate. With Chicago blaring through the speakers, Jordan made her exit that night with her usual flair—half carried out by Martin and Tyler, half dragging the tops of her shoes on the concrete. But she had not been drunk for a while.

* * *

Jordan enjoyed working at the mental health clinic so much, that she found herself pushing through her term papers and readings so that she could spend extra hours there. In fact, Jordan had been doing so well at the clinic, that she had now begun covering the reception desk during lunch hour two days per week. Dean was very pleased that he had drawn Jordan in the lottery, as he called it. He felt that she had good raw skills, and that with a little honing, she could become an excellent therapist. Jordan was not ready to make that kind of professional commitment, but she was very ready to learn as much as she could, as quickly as possible.

It was on the Tuesday of the eighth week of field placement that things really took a turn for Jordan. She had counseled both Teresa and John that morning, and was feeling especially pleased with some of the comments that she made during treatment session. Dean told her once that you could never be totally sure whether your comments had effect. Jordan had not suggested specific courses of action in either case, but instead, had offered questions that helped each patient clarify his issues and set goals. Dean praised this as quite an accomplishment, given the confusion and hopelessness that can accompany depression. With that pat on the back, Jordan assumed her place behind the reception desk, and answered phones during the lunch hour.

About halfway through the shift, an older black woman, perhaps in her early sixties, came into the agency and asked to meet with Dean. Jordan did not recognize her, but the woman had obviously been a former patient. She presented as calm and pleasant, but was insistent that she needed to speak with a counselor immediately. Jordan decided to break protocol, and agreed to meet briefly with her. She led the woman to a small counseling room located not far from the reception desk, so that she could still tend her responsibilities there.

Once settled in, the woman closed the door to the office, so that she and Jordan could speak privately. Jordan respected this need and did not correct her. The woman also pulled up a chair from the side of the room, rather than taking the usual seat opposite the desk where Jordan was sitting. She was now seated squarely to Jordan's right. Jordan's back was toward the wall, with the woman now blocking her exit. Although this was of some minor concern to Jordan, she did not react, but allowed the woman to continue her discussion of needs. She strove to be attentive to her.

The woman called herself Josie, and spoke with a slow, drawled dialect not from that area.

"Mah husbin' an' Ah moved here from Mizzippi a feew yeahrs back. We come fo' work. Mah husbin' Willis is a day lab'er on a fahrm neahr bah. Raght now, we got no money an' no food fo' da baby. See mah breast don't give no mo' milk, an' da baby's too yung fo' grains or beef."

Jordan nodded as she listened, and fumbled with some papers on the desk before she found the intake forms. Nothing ever seemed to be where it should be there.

"So, are you caring for your grandchild then?" Jordan asked. She knew the woman was too old to have a baby of her own. That much she could surmise just from appearance.

"No, No . . . I jus gave birph dis maurnin.' Da baby's wif Willis, 'till Ah could see what food Ah could git."

Jordan paused, not knowing what to make of the situation. She moved the rolodex of resources closer to her, as she tried to think of the next question she should ask. Before she could respond, the woman began again.

"Ah cinnot go back to da 'partment raght now, 'cause Willis an' me had a faght this maurnin.' Wez fussin' o're money. So Willis . . . then he starts drankin,' and Ah toll him ta quit it, dat dat don't hep nuphin.' So den, he starts beatin' on me! . . . So Ah tossed da baby on da bed!"

Jordan sat quietly, nodding in recognition of the woman's upset.

"So Willis starts yellin,' 'Yah gonna hirt da baby,' an' now he's poundin' me wif dem fists! It was hor'ble what he done, an' all the whahl, da baby is cryin' fo' breast milk . . ."

Her speech was rapid and pressured, and her posture was rigid and tense. Her gaze seemed fixed, and at other moments, almost wild.

Jordan pressed the panic button on the bottom of her desk, and then realized that there was no one in the reception area, or even in the office.

"Willis, Willis," Josie started calling as she began sobbing. Jordan handed her a tissue, and sat quiet, motionless, hoping they both would regain composure. She prayed that Dean and the others would return. After a moment, Josie smiled and spoke calmly again.

"Ah know da baby's ahlwraght, 'cause Willis is 'dere wif her now. He's takin' care a' huh . . . Ah got ta go ta da ma'kit' soon as da bills is done . . ."

Jordan was struggling to understand her through her accent, and through the veil of confused images she presented.

"Da bougainvillea's beautiful now in summah. Ah cut some ta put in mah haihr." Josie reached into her purse and pulled out a mirror. She started placing imaginary flowers in her tight curls. She offered some to Jordan, which she politely refused.

Josie immediately returned to the discussion about Willis and the baby.

"She has da prittiest brown ahes . . ." She smiled as if she was gazing into them. She then reached her finger out as if to take the baby's hand, and let out a screech in anguish.

"Willis! Yah beat da baby ta deph! Yah beat da baby ta deph!" She cried as she rocked herself back and forth in the chair, with arms tightly held to chest. "Why could yah do sech a thang? Willis, Why, Why! Please God, don't let it be so . . . Please God, don't let it be so. Willis, why could yah do sech a thang! Beat me! Don't beat da baby . . . Why beat da baby? Willis, please!"

Her screams trailed off, but her sobbing continued. Her heavy frame heaved with each sob, and her arms flailed toward the heavens, as if she was begging the intercession of some distant Deity. Jordan could not respond. She was frightened to immobility, to unreality, to denial. After some moments, she made an effort to soothe her.

"Josie," Jordan spoke softly and calmly to her. "You have been through a terrible ordeal. Just try to relax now, and we'll try to make a plan together . . . Just take a few deep breaths, and relax a bit . . . that's it . . . that's better." Jordan's heart was pounding so loudly she could hear it in her head.

"Thank yah, thank yah . . . fo' bein' so kind . . . So yah see, Ah don't really know what ta do now . . . wif Willis an' da baby, Ah mean. Ah hafta think . . . Ah hafta thaink." She clutched her face in her hands, then shook her head. She began smiling again at Jordan, then let out an exclamation.

"Ah know what ta do . . . Ah know how ta make dis' raght . . . Ah have a gif' fo' Willis."

She then slowly leaned over, and took up her bag. She reached inside, pulled out a butcher knife, and stabbed it into the desktop! Jordan saw only the silver flash of the blade as it pierced into the wooden desk. She could not react. She could only sit in her stillness, and await whatever fate Josie held for her! Josie again reached toward her canvas bag.

"An' dis' is fo' mah landlord, who 'victed us dis' maurnin'." Josie quickly pulled an ice pick from her bag and stabbed it into the desktop! Jordan sat frozen-like as she watched the two weapons standing erect in the desk, and just inches from her own chest! Josie sat blankly, breathing heavily, seemingly not there. She had killed the beasts within her, and she was calming again. Jordan knew that she had to act fast; that she had to take control!

Jordan stood slowly, reached out her palm toward Josie's face, and gave a gentle touch, one that a mother might give to an injured child.

"Josie, your face is swollen . . . I think you need medical attention. Please let me call an ambulance for you." As she considered this offer, Jordan slowly removed the knife and the ice pick from the desktop, and shoved them into a lower drawer.

"Ah'm so tired . . . Ah'm so tired." She said, as she slowly, rhythmically, rocked herself in the chair. She shook her head slowly, unbelieving, back and forth. Her breathing was labored, tortured, and fraught with sigh. Her body was limp now, the result of her emotional exhaustion.

"Can I call an ambulance for you now?" Jordan asked, still speaking softly and gently to her.

"Yeah, yah cin caul me an amb'lance," she said without missing a singular movement of her rocking.

Jordan picked up the receiver of the phone as she stood next to Josie. She asked the operator to contact County Hospital, and asked that they send an ambulance to the Merton Mental Health Clinic.

"Is this an emergency?" the operator asked.

"Yes" Jordan replied tersely.

"Is this a mental health emergency?"

"Yes, and I believe that the patient may also have a fractured jaw."

"We'll ask the hospital to send someone over immediately."

"Thank you," Jordan replied.

Jordan returned to her desk, opened the lower drawer, placed the weapons in a paper bag she found there, and carried them out of the room. Jordan was gasping for air, but still, she could not breathe. She felt a dizziness, as a surreal pallor fell over the images in her mind. She felt like she was walking sort of out of time, or out of sync, with the rest of the Universe—like she and Josie were on some bizarre plain of consciousness somewhere together, and that no one else could reach them. Josie sat quietly rocking, and did not prevent Jordan from leaving the room. She hardly seemed to notice that Jordan was gone. Once out of the room, Jordan contacted County Hospital, spoke with the ambulance crew, and advised them what had happened. They would request police assistance.[43]

Dean, the other two therapists, and the secretary arrived back at the office just as police arrived. Jordan was shaking and could barely speak. She told them about her encounter with Josie and the weapons, and about Willis beating Josie and their baby. Dean clarified that this incident had actually happened when Josie was sixteen years old. Willis was killed by a group of vigilante neighbors who chose not to wait for the police. They had grown tired of the beatings,[44] and became outraged when they found the baby dead. Dean said that this had happened in Mississippi according to Josie's relatives. She'd been living in this area for almost

---

[43] A discussion of DSM-IV Criteria for the patient "Josie" can be found in Appendix and Bibliography for Chapter Four.

[44] Resource articles regarding domestic violence can be found in Appendix and Bibliography for Chapter Four.

forty years, and had been in and out of institutions most of her adult life. She had not been in treatment with Dean for nearly two years.

Contrary to Jordan's belief, Josie went easily and readily with the ambulance crew. She did not speak a word. She did not look to anyone for help or clarification. She just slid onto the gurney, and let the crew carry her away from the pain of that day. She would soon be medicated into a blissful oblivion, with the tragedy far off and in some distant place. She would finally find peace, at least for a few hours. Jordan stood silent, and watched the crew carry Josie off in their rig, with Dean and the others tending to their client. She then gathered her things, and quietly left the office. It was nearly ten minutes before Dean and the others realized that she had gone. Jordan took a cab back to the dorm, trembling as they rode through the town. She replayed a thousand times the knife's flash of steel and heard the crack of wood. In her mind's eye, she could see the knife plunging into her chest! She could feel the ice pick puncturing her lung! She heard the nagging voice within her say over and over, that there was something in the Universe that did not want her in Social Work. And she now believed it. Still early in the afternoon, Marge and the others had not yet come back to the dorm. Jordan had several drinks, and used the hours to quiet her mind and to make her decisions. Although Dean left several messages for her, Jordan did not return his calls. She did, however, arrange an appointment with her Field Placement Advisor at the college. She would not be returning to the clinic, and would not accept another mental health placement. She would not continue in Social Work.[45]

\* \* \*

Jordan was drunk and lay half asleep on her bed when Marge and Janice came to the room to prepare for dinner. At first they thought she had been celebrating

---

[45] For information regarding client violence against social workers, please see Appendix and Bibliography for Chapter Four

another win at the clinic, and they teased her about her outrageous infallibility. They teased her about being the child genius of the Social Work profession. They bowed to her as Goddess of World Change and as Hero of the Hopeless. When they did not face a single biting remark in reply, Janice sat next to her and shook her gently by the shoulder.

"Hey, what's wrong? What's going on?" She asked.

Jordan gave a heavy sigh, and clumsily turned over on the bed and toward them both. They could see that she had been crying.

"Don't tell me you're having another crying jag," Marge said. "You really shouldn't drink so much . . . and you shouldn't drink alone—you're not good at it! . . . So tell Aunt Marge and Aunt Janice what set you off this time . . . But I swear to God, if you tell me that you're this upset for getting a B on a term paper, I swear I'll smother you with my C+ exams, and then I'll beat you to death with my encyclopedia." Jordan did not respond.

"Hey Jordan, what is it? What happened?" Janice asked. She and Marge awaited the response in silence.

"I almost got killed today at the clinic. I was so stupid . . . I wanted so much to help. I thought I could handle it. I had to be someone special there . . . And I almost got myself killed because of it . . ."

"Oh come on, Jordan. You're exaggerating. I'm sure it wasn't as bad as all that," Marge said.

"What didn't you get about what I just said, Marge? You're so sure of yourself—ALWAYS sure of yourself! Did it ever cross your mind that something terrible could really happen to you? Just once . . . did it ever cross your mind that you would be in a situation where your luck, and your family name, and your status, couldn't carry you? You think you're fucking indestructible . . . that you're somehow immune from any hardship . . . that somehow nothing horrible can happen, because you're Marge Jorgensen. Guess what, Marge—terrible things happen to people every day. So you just better wake up and wise up to it . . . And another thing—"

"Woow there, my friend—let's not push this any farther. There's plenty I could say to you right now. But for the sake of friendship, I'll just let it all slide and figure you're drunk out of your fucking head."

"That's the answer, right Marge? Someone says something you don't like, and right away they must be drunk . . . Maybe I have been drinking, but that doesn't change the fact that I almost got myself stabbed today . . . And just that fast. And everything's over. I'll never go back there again . . . I was so stupid."

"Jordan," Janice replied, "I DO know that terrible things can happen to anyone . . . and just that fast. If you want to tell me about it, I'm here to listen to you. And Marge is here for you, too. You know that."

Jordan, crying and gasping for air, began to relate the day's events.

"I was at the clinic, doing my usual lunchtime reception duty . . . and this older woman came into the office. She wanted to speak to a therapist right away. There was no one else there, so I took her into an interview room to meet with her alone. God, I was so stupid—I never saw it coming . . . She was so calm, and so polite, and so friendly, and I thought, what would be the harm of me handling this situation? Dean would be happy that I had taken the initiative. We could conference the case when he got back. I thought she was looking for a referral of some sort. You know, we have the Resource Bank lists right there . . . So what harm would it have done, to meet with her . . . and to give her a few referrals?"

Janice and Marge sat with Jordan on her bed, and gave her full attention. Marge was mentally kicking herself for being so taunting and skeptical at first discussion. She should have known better. She should have realized something was wrong as soon as she saw her on the bed. She would be a better friend to her from now on. She would be a better person to everyone.

Jordan continued. "We were sitting in the office together, things going pretty smoothly at first. Then she started talking about having a baby that morning. But I thought, she's too old to have a baby . . . I should have stopped right then, but I didn't. Then she talked about being beaten by her husband, and saying that he beat their baby to death! . . . She was so hopped up at that moment. You know, excited, kind of wild . . . I kept pressing the panic button on the desk, but there was nobody there to help me! I kept pressing and pressing, I was so scared. When she pulled out the knife, I just froze—I couldn't even defend myself, I was so scared . . . And then the ice pick! Both of them there, stuck in the desk. And me, too frightened to move! All I could think of . . . was that she was going to stab me next! All I could think of . . . was that blade landing in my chest! And still, I couldn't move . . . I was so afraid." Jordan had stopped crying, but was still struggling for breath. She blew her nose and wiped her tears. She pulled the blankets up around her neck. After a few moments, she began again.

"Then she just seemed to like . . . collapse in the chair, she was so exhausted. And I thought, if I'm going to come out of this alive, I've got to think fast; I've got to act fast . . . So I told her that I thought her face was swollen, and that she needed medical attention. All the while, I'm pulling the knife and ice pick out of the desk! And I'm thinking, if she comes at me, I'm gonna havta use this! . . . But she didn't come at me . . . She just let me call an ambulance for her. Dean got back just as they were taking her away."

"Well what did he say?" Marge asked. She and Janice were incredulous with what they had just heard. Jordan could see their genuine concern, and she took comfort and strength from her friends.

"He didn't say anything really . . . just that she was a former patient, and that she was talking about an incident that happened to her when she was sixteen . . . I didn't give him a chance to say anything else. I just got my stuff and left. I've been here ever since. I picked up two messages from him at the desk, but I don't think I'll be calling him back . . . It's over."

The girls sat silently, thoroughly horrified, as Jordan finished her story. Janice started lightly stroking her back.

"Thank God you're all right!" Marge said.

That was the first time that Jordan had ever heard Marge say "God" without some kind of curse attached to it. Marge was not vulgar. She was not a blasphemer. She just liked the shock effect, and saw this as a sort of sophistication. This time, though, her appreciation to the God of her choosing was genuine. She was truly relieved that her friend was home safe and unharmed.

Janice phoned Martin and told him and Tyler only that they would not be going to dinner that night. The girls ordered a pizza and ate together in the room. For Jordan's sake and at her request, they pledged secrecy. Jordan would meet with her Social Work Advisor, and would tell him that she intended to withdraw from the program. She had no idea what she would tell her parents. Maybe her Advisor could suggest a related curriculum that she could transfer into, another major, so that she could still graduate in the spring. She thought that she already had enough credits for a major in Sociology and a minor in English. She could take a B.A. instead of the BSW degree. From there, maybe she'd find some work in industry. She just didn't know.

The girls had never seen Jordan's confidence so shaken. She always seemed so strong, so focused toward that singular goal. Without that goal, there was no driving force. She lost her spirit. She lost her enthusiasm. She lost her idealism. All of it gone in a few moment's time. She was actually seeking advice now from someone other than Karen. She was turning to her friends and to her college advisor. This was her surrender. She could not see a way to proceed in any direction. She did not have the will to go on, even if someone pointed her toward the path.

Janice suggested that Jordan give it some time, and that she just reserve her decisions for the morning. No one would have to know what happened. They had already promised her that. She could take the time she needed to sort things out. Maybe she should take the day off from classes, and spend some time walking along the path by the river. The girls both knew that Jordan drew strength from nature, and convinced her that with some fresh air and sunshine, she would see everything more clearly. Jordan agreed that she might try that. She then fell off to sleep, while Marge sat up to read, and Janice went back to her room. Marge would be caring for Jordan that night. Marge would be watching over her.

The morning light came too quickly for her. Yet she was still hidden under her covers when Marge left for class. Jordan took her friends' advice and decided to skip her own classes that day. In fact, she skipped the next several days' classes, and missed most meals. She decided that she had some serious thinking—and drinking—to do. Although she did not drink to total intoxication, she was drinking daily, and throughout the days. She was drinking at least to the point that she missed her scheduled appointment with her advisor. Several Social Work students came to the room to speak with Jordan, but Marge would not let them in.

"Jordan's got the flu . . . an early case. She's afraid she'll infect someone and take down the whole college! You know how the flu—and especially that diarrhea—can travel through a dorm. You know, you don't want that happening . . ."

"A nice touch," Jordan thought.

Though skeptical, they allowed Jordan her distance. Jordan would occasionally give the obligatory cough and sniff to confirm the alibi. Janice dropped an apology note off to Professor Lambert, and requested a rescheduling of Jordan's appointment. The Group had now taken charge, and they would not allow Jordan to falter, even if she was hell-bent on it!

When several additional messages went unanswered, Dean decided to go to the campus to talk to Jordan. He genuinely liked his protégé, and he felt responsible for what had happened to her. Marge was initially resistant to the visit. But when Jordan heard that Dean was downstairs waiting to speak with her—and with Janice coaxing her on—she agreed to meet with him. They took one of the small visiting parlors located between the dorm reception area and the day room. Dean suspected that Jordan was a binge drinker from their conversations during their conferencing sessions. He initially dismissed this as misguided college youth, and thought about how much he drank at school. But he could smell the alcohol on her breath—mid-day, mid-week, and without a party! Jordan had been drinking alone for the last several days, he surmised. He was immediately concerned with what he saw, and he intended to address this with her at the proper moment. Jordan shyly and cautiously entered the room to meet him. She closed the door behind her.

"Hi Dean, what a surprise to see you," she said. "Are you here on some sort of college business?"

"Yeah, Jordan, I am. I've come to talk with you, since you didn't seem to want to discuss things over the phone."

"Oh, I'm sorry about that . . . I really intended to call you when I decided what I was going to do. I haven't decided yet, so no call." Jordan knew Dean could see through the answer.

"Listen Jordan, I'm so very sorry about what happened the other day. I feel like I failed you. I should have been more clear about the protocol, about the safety measures. You know, you always plan for the worst, but hope for the best . . . I should not have left you alone in the agency. But you were doing so well, that I lost sight of the fact that you had been there for only sixteen days, really. You fit in so well there, that I lost sight of the fact that you are still a student . . . I let you down, and I'm sorry for that. I'm just so thankful that you had the presence of mind to get out of that situation without anyone getting hurt."

Jordan looked at Dean, and then at the floor. She took her time as she spoke, perhaps fearful of hearing herself say out loud, the real truth of the situation.

"I'm so sorry . . . I was so stupid . . . I thought I could handle the situation, but I couldn't. She just didn't give any indication that she was unstable until we were in the room together . . . You're wrong, Dean. You were clear on the protocol. I was the one who ignored it, and I nearly got myself, and maybe even a patient, killed—and all to feed my stupid ego. I thought I could handle the situation, but I couldn't . . ."

"You know, Jordan, sometimes you really are too hard on yourself. You broke protocol, and you nearly died because of it. OK, if that's what you want to focus on, that one piece of the whole puzzle, I'll give you that. That was stupid on both of our parts . . . And I can't dismiss the role I played in that situation—but what about the rest of it? I can't take credit for what you did from that point forward . . . Yeah, I've been teaching you. Yeah, we've been conferencing. But what you did that day . . . that came from sheer instinct, not from something I taught you.

As he looked at Jordan, he could see the skepticism through her veil of feigned hope.

"You made a mistake, but you managed to get yourself and your patient out of it, without either of you being hurt. She was able to get the treatment she needed, because your gut instincts spoke to you in ways that all the book learning and mentoring could not . . . You knew in your heart that she needed help, and you got her the help that she needed. I would say that that was a pretty special thing for anyone to do for another human being."

"I can't go back, Dean. I'm so frightened now, that I can't even see myself in Social Work any more. Whenever I meet with a patient from this point forward, I'll always be fearful that this is the one who ends my life. I'll always be fearful of making that emotional contact with them, and then, having them use that to harm me in some way. How can I help anyone, if I'm afraid of them?" Jordan half asked, half stated the answer to her dilemma.

"I cannot go back to Social Work."

"Look, even the best of us have been assaulted or near assaulted at least once in their careers. It is life altering, to see the possibility of your life suddenly pass from you. But we take the same risks when we climb in a car, or walk on the sidewalk, or even sit down to a steak sandwich . . . There are no guarantees that your life will always be safe. In fact, the only guarantee that we ever have, is that one day, our lives will end. The fact being, though, that your life did not end that day. And it did not end, perhaps, because it was not your time. Or, perhaps, because you are better at the job than you really believe . . . I can't convince you to come back, and I wouldn't want you to come back, unless you felt comfortable there. But I hope I can convince you to stay in the field, because I believe that you belong there. I believe that you could make quite a contribution in the years ahead. And I know that that's what you really want to do. You have some amazing gifts. I hope that you continue to use those gifts, and that you make the world a better place . . ."

"But where do I go from here? I'm too afraid right now to do anything . . ."

"Jordan, I know that you're upset. You have every right to be. But I can't help but wonder how much the alcohol is affecting your judgment right now."

Jordan was stunned to silence.

"Leave it to a therapist to pin the blame on a substance, rather than on an incident."

"Well it is a lot easier to treat at this point . . . I mean, helping you to stop drinking, rather than trying to do the whole counseling thing to process an assault . . . Although I think that would be pretty helpful, too. Do you think that your drinking is affecting your judgment?"

"Honestly, I think that drinking is the only thing right now getting me through this. I admit . . . I have been drinking a lot lately. But who wouldn't?"

"But there has to come a time, when you can muster the energy to push this aside, and resume your life. Or do you plan to spend the rest of the semester drunk here at the dorm?"

"Dean, tell me how to get out of this, and I will do it gladly."

Jordan knew she needed counseling help, and perhaps otherwise. She was not willing to concede that she was developing an alcohol problem. Or that she had one.

"Up until the other day, I was maintaining a 4.0 average, meeting all of my course work and other responsibilities, never missing a class—and knowing exactly where I was going in my career, and in my life. So I get drunk on weekends, and maybe even for the last three years. Everyone in college drinks like that."

"Well, since the other day, have you attended a single class? Have you prepared a single assignment? Have you even eaten meals regularly?" Dean was trying to help Jordan see the differences now in her drinking patterns, and to help her see how this was affecting her life.

Jordan knew the truth, and she gave a resounding and resentful, "No."

"Do you have a plan in mind, a time limit set, for when you will return to class?" Dean was moving Jordan toward a commitment for recovery. She looked at him, and shrugged.

"Well, if you're going to survive the semester, you're going to have to move pretty quickly, or else you'll be too far behind to catch up. Let me suggest this timetable. Can you commit to not drinking from here on, and that you resume classes tomorrow? I'll stop by on Friday around 6:30p.m. I'm going to an open speakers meeting with AA. I like to keep a good contact with the groups in the area. Maybe you'd like to come along. You can even use the experience for one of your research papers. No pressure, just information. What do you say?"

Jordan looked at Dean for a moment, shook her head, and agreed to go with him. She wanted to save the friendship even if she could not salvage the placement. Besides, she could probably use the AA information to help people in the future. That need for knowledge seemed pretty much universal, no matter where she worked, even if not in Social Work. Alcoholics, and their need for treatment, were everywhere.

Jordan attended classes the next day as promised, but she did not participate in discussion. There were no term paper deadlines that week, so her professors hardly noticed her absence. Classes just seemed a bit quieter for the days that she stayed back at the dorm. And as promised, she didn't have a single drink. Dean arrived at the dorm on Friday evening to take Jordan to an open speakers meeting.[46] The meeting was held in the basement of an old Methodist Church in the next town. Jordan didn't recognize any of the participants. Professor Allen, an adjunct professor, was a scheduled speaker. He discussed his eight years of sobriety following a near fatal car accident. He told stories of the loss of his relationships with his wife and children, and said that he had at least been able to re-establish his relationship with his children, since he established his sobriety.

Professor Allen then introduced a young man he was sponsoring.

"Hi everyone. My name is Bob, and I'm an alcoholic."

"Hi Bob," the crowd welcomed in reply.

---

[46] For A brief history of Alcoholics Anonymous, and a list of the Twelve Steps, please refer to Appendix and Bibliography for Chapter Four.

Jordan was taken aback by the response. She had heard of this greeting, but she had never actually seen it in practice.

Bob was celebrating his own ninety days of sobriety. He shared his story of recovery—with his drinking starting in high school, and becoming serious now in college. He said that he realized that if he did not stop drinking, he would lose everything he was working for. When he found that he could not stop on his own, he turned to AA at the suggestion of a friend. He was amazed at how well his life was going, since he made the commitment to put his sobriety first.

Jordan saw the similarities in their drinking habits, at least in college. But unlike Bob, she was able to stop drinking when Dean suggested this. She felt that she was still ok, still in control. Yet, she thought from time to time about Bob's admission and his greeting from the crowd, and she drew comfort from it. Jordan didn't know it then, but she would be hearing her own admission—and receiving her own AA greeting in reply—at several points in her life ahead.[47]

---

[47] For a brief discussion of the Differential Diagnoses between Substance Abuse and Substance Dependence, please refer to the Appendix and Bibliography for Chapter Four.

# Chapter 5

Jordan continued to see Dean weekly at the clinic, but he was counseling her now as a victim of an assault. Each week they would review in painful detail the events and decisions leading up to, and through, the assault. These included the clothes that she and Josie were both wearing; the type of day that it was; the colors in the room that she could remember; the way they both smelled; the sounds in the room; the cadence of their breathing; the heaving of Josie's heavy frame; the look of her tight curls as her head bobbed back and forth; the sound of the chair as she rocked; the flash of the knife blade as it moved from bag to desk; the skinny awl of the ice pick, as it darted into the desk; the sounds of the cracking wood as each pierced the desktop; the racing thoughts that rushed through Jordan's mind; the feel of her finger on the panic button; the fear that overwhelmed her when she knew that she was alone; the belief that she had to respond quickly and calmly; the sound of her own voice calling to an operator for help; the thought that she might have to stab Josie to save herself; the removal of the weapons from the desktop, and their placement in the bottom drawer; her exit from the room, and the securing of the weapons; the second call to the ambulance crew; the safe transport of Josie for treatment; the arrival of Dean and the others; and the development of a potential safety plan if ever she found herself in a life-threatening situation.[48]

---

[48] For DSM-IV-TR Criteria for Posttraumatic Stress Disorder, please refer to Appendix and Bibliography for Chapter Five.

This was an experimental technique at the time, and one that would not come into popular use for perhaps two decades. But it was a technique that Dean had found some success with, and from which, Jordan found some comfort. Each week they would review together this series of events, and with each week, Jordan felt the fears of that day lessening. Dean was desensitizing her to the triggers that might act as a gateway for her paralyzing fear. Jordan even practiced this drill mentally when she was alone. And with each week, she felt herself slowly rising back to health.[49] Yet her confidence had been altered in inexplicable ways. She trembled each week as she approached the clinic. She used a side entrance now to avoid the reception area. She looked haggard and weary from the lack of sleep—and she was having much difficulty sleeping, the flash of the blade like a bright light searing through her dreams. She did not like being alone at any time. She was irritable. She could not make decisions, and she second-guessed herself whenever she did make them. For the first time in her academic life, Jordan received Bs in all of her classes. She just couldn't pull it together.

Dean continued to encourage Jordan and remained a mentor to her. He advocated for her with Mrs. Murphy, the Field Placement Advisor. Together they were able to arrange an immediate position for Jordan at the adoption center of the state's child protective service agency. Dean convinced Jordan to accept the position as the next phase of her treatment. Jordan would function primarily as an administrative intern, and would assist in compiling reports and statistical data needed by the Feds. She would also be involved in the funding process of the agency. Dean convinced Jordan to accept the position. But secretly, Jordan accepted the placement because she thought that she could more easily transition into the business sector. It was an escape hatch for her, an ejector seat into a safer, gentler career, where she still might be able to support herself, and turn a blind eye to human suffering.

---

[49] For Resources regarding the use of Exposure therapy in the treatment of Posttraumatic Stress Disorder, please refer to Appendix and Bibliography for Chapter Five.

The Group mounted their support and care of both Janice and Jordan from that point. Marge kept close watch on Jordan's drinking, and did not restock the heater/bar when the bottles there were empty. Martin stayed close to Janice, although her need for valium had already begun to decrease when Jordan plummeted. Janice seemed to muster emotional energy now that her friend needed her, and she showered Jordan with huge portions of it whenever she had the chance. Strangely, Jordan's issues seemed to divert attention away from her own. Janice finally tossed her valium down the toilet, and vowed never to rely on medications like that again. Karen stepped up her phone calls, but the contacts only made Jordan feel more alone in the world. Like Janice, Jordan, too, now lived in a separate consciousness, where she could see her friends, but could not reach out to them. Even if she touched them, she could not connect. Jordan and Janice seemed both tethered to, yet set separately adrift, from the safe haven of their friendships of the Group.

Jordan's field placement at the adoption center went cautiously at first. She was involved in quality assurance tasks, a re-review of applications for adoption. Jordan believed that her new field placement supervisor, Allison Hartz, gave her "make work" assignments to gauge how she was functioning. Jordan welcomed that change. In time, Allison gained her trust and respect, and by semester's end, Jordan was half-trying again to contribute to humanity in meaningful ways. But there always seemed a shadow, an overcast, a pallor, that colored her perceptions now and robbed her of the joy of her work. And despite her efforts— her conscious attempts to slay the fear, and at the oddest moments— she could see the knurled, shaky, Josie hand reaching out to snatch anything positive that she might get from her from her work. She maintained the outward facade and pushed for her grades, but her spirit was gone.

Her dad noticed the changes first. Jordan was more restrained, less animated, less enthused about her future. Her mom attributed this to the normal fear of having to make a life on her own, and with graduation looming in the too near future. But Pete Mathews knew his children, and he believed it was more than that. He didn't buy his wife's notion that Jordan was beginning to feel her biological clock, and that she was worried because she had not yet found a suitable mate. Pete Mathews would find out what was worrying his oldest daughter, although he doubted that it had anything to do with men. He quickly dodged that implication. So, when Saturday morning came, he made pancakes for the family, and then took Jordan with him to a job that he had been working for the last several weeks—just like they used to.

"So whadeya think of this place, huh? What a monster of a house! It's over 3,500 square feet, and so close to the Island! A young doctor owns it. He might be here today. He likes to pop in and check things out. Sometimes he brings his little girl, too."

Pete smiled at Jordan, as he helped her out of the truck's cab. He then grabbed a set of plans, and laid them over the hood of the truck.

"Ya see that place over there? That'll be the conservatory. That's a beefed-up den, so his wife can play her piano there." He pointed to a half circular room framed on the right side of the building.

"The main entrance of the house'll have two supportin' columns on each side of the door, and a wrap-around porch! They can take advantage of the sunrise and sunsets without leavin' the place . . . A real nice lay out! And wait 'til ya see the kitchen . . . it's about the size of our whole basement!"

Jordan surveyed the structure, a skeleton of 2x4s, rafters, and floor joists. Her cousins were nailing the exterior sheathing. The sub flooring was already in place. Her Uncle Pat and Pat Jr. were nailing down shingles on the roof. They got a lumber delivery that morning, and had to get everything nailed in place by nightfall. If not, scavengers would swarm on the materials under the cloak of night, and like a colony of ants, they would carry off whatever had not been secured to the supports and studs. Jordan walked through the structure and picked up steel punch-outs from the electrical boxes Billy Thornton was installing. She and Kelly used them as coins in their "store" when they were kids. Billy always had a crush on Jordan, but he was almost seven years older than her. Now that she was entering her twenties, though, age differences seemed less a factor. Billy smiled at Jordan, gave her the look-over, and continued his work. He did not want to incur the wrath of Pete Mathews. He did not want to lose the prospects of future jobs because Pete might think that he goofed off. He had a reputation to uphold, a career of his own to protect! When Pete wasn't looking, though, he winked at Jordan. She winked back at him in exaggerated, comedic display.

Her father gave several instructions to her cousins. They were to leave the job for the day after they finished those tasks. Pete arranged for a window delivery on Monday morning, and they would likely have to work late that night. He needed to save the overtime till then. The conservancy had large picture windows, and they would need all hands to fit them into place. He also hired a small crane to help swing the windows into position. Once back in the truck, though, Pete tried to swing the conversation back to Jordan's life. They talked as they traveled to their favorite donut shop—a place that had been around since the late 1940's, and was renowned for their homemade donuts. Jordan's old scout leader still owned the shop. Jordan spent many a rainy Girl Scout meeting filling donuts and working on her cooking and baking badges there. She loved her scout leader, and hoped to be like her one day. So what if they were the fattest troop in the county?

"Is everything ok with ya, Jordan?" Pete Mathews asked, never smooth enough to conceal his motives.

"Yeah, Dad. Whydeya ask?"

"Well, your mother seems to think that you're not yourself this time out. Ya know, a little quieter than she's used to. I haveta say, I noticed it, too. So what's up?"

"Does anything have to be up?" She could hear the harshness of her tone, and hoped that her father would again attribute her mood to her period. He always attributed any changes in his daughters to their periods. Men were simple like that.

"Ya haven't really talked about school . . . ya haven't called Marge or Janice much since ya been home . . . your grades have lowered. Is it a guy thing?" Her father was hopeful, but doubtful.

"No Dad. It's not a guy thing . . . It's my grades," she said, knowing that he would accept that explanation, regardless of the truth.

"Classes were really rough this semester, and I'm wonderin' if I can keep up next semester . . . And ya know . . . I'm wonderin' if I'm really cut out for Social Work . . ."

"Is that all? . . . Sometimes in life ya haveta accept the fact that things are gonna be a B, no matter how hard ya push for that A . . . But ya just keep goin' and work for the things ya really want in life. Maybe this has shook your confidence, or your desire to be a Social Worker . . . But don't let that stop ya. There'll be plenty a' other opportunities to come in your life. With your brains, and your drive, and your character, you will never fail! Ya haveta believe that. It's what makes life worthwhile . . . it's what keeps the world turnin' . . . A faith that no matter where we are, things will get better."

Jordan smiled at her father, took his hand, and gave it a squeeze.

"Thanks Dad. I'll be ok."

She never considered telling him the truth, because she knew that he could not comprehend what was happening to her. Even with his war experience, he had never been so near to death as she had been herself—at least, he never shared such stories with her. She sucked the jelly out of one end of her donut, and followed it with a gulp of coffee.

"Is there anything in the world that can't be solved by a trip to this place?" she asked.

Her father did not believe her explanation, but he had learned long ago never to press her, if he wanted the truth. She knew now that he was concerned, and that he was available to her. Pete Mathews could think of nothing more that he could do for his daughter. The ball was in her court. They drove back home with lighthearted conversation that centered on the Christmas Holiday. They'd be having dinner with Uncle Pat and his family at her grandmother's. Afterward, they'd go to Midnight Mass. Jordan especially liked the Choir Concert before the Mass, and she felt that a congregation offering song and music to the Baby

Jesus was among the greatest gifts to Him. She liked the Carole of the Bells best, and hoped that they would play again, as they had in years past. She could not imagine life without music.

As they arrived home, Jordan's mother greeted her at the door.

"I've got some news . . . Todd just called. Doris Theresa Sommers was born at 8:30 a.m. on December 20th! Both mother and baby are doing well! Daddy Todd is also doin' ok, although too excited to give all the particulars! Maybe you should give'em a call!"

Jordan raced to the phone, dialed the number to the maternity ward in Charlottesville, and spoke with Karen. Although she was still groggy from the nearly fourteen hours of labor, she brightened at the sound of Jordan's voice.

"Jordan! . . . She's finally here! We didn't call anyone before now, because I've already twice been to the hospital for false labor. I didn't believe that the baby was coming until we were halfway through the ordeal! And Todd was right there, coaching comfortably and painlessly, from bedside! . . . I swear, he'd recommend natural childbirth to anyone! But I wonder how quick he'd be to opt for that, if he was the one delivering . . . I saw him cringing the whole time! At one point, I thought he was going to lose it! But when he held his daughter, nothing else mattered."

"So tell me about her!" Jordan commanded.

"Well, Doris is 7 lbs.10 oz, and 19 inches long . . . Cute as a button, too!"

"So who does she look like? I hope not your mother-in-law . . ."

Karen laughed. "Oddly enough, Todd and I both think that she looks like Janice! You know how her nose wrinkles when she laughs? And how she moves her lips a few times before she actually says something? . . . But DO NOT tell her that we said that!"

"Of course not . . . Janice? . . . I won't ask . . ." Jordan laughed, but her heart was breaking. Some dreams die hard.

Jordan and Karen made plans for a visit on the first weekend that they were all back at college. This would give some time for mother and baby to adjust.

Todd would be back at work on Monday. After all, he had a family to support now! Todd's mother would be staying with them until Doris was on a proper schedule . . .

As she hung up the phone, Jordan whispered to herself, "And so goes my life . . . and again, without you. Why didn't you ever see how it could have been with us?"

She could not stop inserting herself into the position now taken by Todd, even though she loathed herself for this mental adultery. She could not wait to see Karen again, and to take up the life that she had planned for them, at least in her mind. Hell be damned! But in quieter moments, she knew the reality separate from the fantasy. She would have to accept watching Karen's life unfold from afar, knowing that she would never be the center of it. She sometimes hated Karen for that, too, though she could never admit that to herself. It was just easier to blame Todd, and she did that whenever her "better self" was out to lunch somewhere.

"But I know what love is . . ." Jordan whispered to herself, as she looked down again at the picture of the Group displayed on her nightstand. She focused her attention solely on Karen, and wondered how she could not have felt, even today, how Jordan felt.

The Holidays passed as they had in all previous years, or at least, in all the years that Jordan could remember. Uncle Pat and the usual family members got drunk and got loud. Kelly got another piece of jewelry, and had another man hanging on her arm to garner all attention. She used them both as fine accessories. Jonathan got a telescope, but found a quiet corner. He was never comfortable in crowds of any kind, even if they were family. Like Jordan, he would always feel as if he was watching things from afar. As Jordan took a mental step back from the scene, she realized, with great clarity, how different she was becoming from the rest of her family. She was changing by quantum leaps, and with each jump, she seemed to move farther and farther from their center. Although this thought scared her, she couldn't stop this change any more than she could stop the rising voice of her own sexuality—an inner voice that now screamed louder and louder for recognition. But she could not acknowledge it. She could not allow herself to hear that voice. Its tones frightened her, its implications devastated her. So, she clung to the old ways as best she could—hanging out with her cousins, and telling stories about the men that she had been dating on campus—a combination half of imagination, and half stories she had heard in the dorms. She remained the heroine—the Feminine Triumphant—in the eyes of her younger cousins! They loved hearing the stories, and she loved telling them. And she loved her family. And she loved being with her family. But she felt herself stretching more and more to reach them, as her new world pulled her farther and farther away. She struggled to find the common ground that tied them together as family. Nothing seemed right for her now. She had lost her balance in all ways.

Not long through the process, she began to feel more like herself—as if she found herself in the memories of the others. She began to appreciate the real benefit of this annual ritual. Yet, looking in another direction, she could almost hear the happiness that would abound in the Sommers household that Christmas morning. She wished her life could be different, that it could be with Karen, or more like Karen's, but she did not see her own life heading in those directions at all.

\* \* \*

Despite the Oil Embargo and the gas shortages, Tyler drove the Group to their visit with Todd, Karen, and baby Doris. The car was alive with political conversation focused on the Senate appointment of the new President Gerald Ford. Jordan led the talk, against attempts by the Group to discuss the upcoming Super Bowl VII—and bets from the men that the Dolphins would crush the Redskins and take the game! The girls could have cared less for either topic! They were imagining the privileged future that awaited this new young Duchess, Doris Sommers. Jordan fought off the horrendous jealousy that she felt each time she thought about Todd and Karen together. She knew that she should feel guilty about this, but her resentment overrode any sense of remorse. She only hoped that she could continue the charade, and that her true love would go undetected by all but Karen. She must have known that her feelings would continue despite the boundaries now building to keep them apart.

The trip took nearly three hours. As they drove to the front of the home, they could see signs neatly printed, and pointing the way to the new baby. The wooden stork was still present on the lawn with a banner that proudly proclaimed, "It's a girl!" Jordan could not help but remember the conversation with Jan and Betty, and the social and psychological implications that the young Duchess would face as the result of her anatomy. She believed that Karen would rear her well in the wisdom and philosophy of the Women's' Rights Movement, but with Todd's mother providing day care, the girls were skeptical that her negative traditional influences could be thwarted!

The men challenged that there was nothing wrong with a good ole' fashioned girl—the type that cooked, cleaned, shopped, child-reared, laundered, cut the grass, dusted the furniture, polished the silverware, arranged parties for family, friends and business associates, tended sick family members, washed and waxed floors, did the windows, did the vacuuming, did the ironing, planted gardens and landscaped the manor, and now, worked full time, too! The men championed this as the best of all possible worlds! They felt confident in the future success of the young Miss Doris Sommers.

Named for her paternal grandmother, Little Doris had stark blue eyes, and an ear-to-ear grin that did look a lot like Janice's! The baby was nearly bald, with the exception of a singular tuft of hair that mother Karen had twirled to the top of her head. She wore a pink hair ribbon, and was dressed in a dainty pink jumper with white knit booties, a handmade present from her namesake. Todd was holding the baby when the Group arrived, and he seemed a natural at fathering. He reminded Jordan of her own father, and she felt confident in the belief that the human race would continue. Karen made a chocolate layer cake, a favorite of the men. The dining room table was neatly set with a silver tea service that Karen had inherited from Todd's mother's family.

Todd's family was well known throughout the Charlottesville area, having lived there for nearly four generations. Although originally horse breeders, they had long ago split the farm, and were now involved in various merchant businesses in the Charlottesville area. Only Todd's father had turned to the chemical industry, and he was instrumental in establishing a plastics company almost a decade prior. Todd had visions that the corporation would one day be an international competitor. Jordan could not help but see how different Todd and Karen were now from the rest of the Group. She felt like a child amid these two "grown-ups." For the first time, she was self-conscious about the topics of conversation she chose with Karen. Yet, she could still feel their closeness.

Marge was the first to scoop up the unsuspecting baby Doris. She let out a singular whelp in protest.

"Come right up here to your Aunt Marge!" she said. "Don't let those others tell you any stories about me. I'm your favorite aunt, even if you haven't realized that yet." Within an instant, the child quieted and nestled contentedly against Marge's neck and bosom.

"Geez Marge, I never pegged you to be the mothering type!" Jordan exclaimed.

"Don't let this raucous exterior fool you. Underneath all this voluptuousness, there lies a heart just yearning to love and to mother . . . See how good I would be at this?" She addressed the question to Tyler.

"Humph" he replied, as he munched down another piece of cake. He smiled at Marge, but remained noncommittal. He knew where the conversation was heading, as it had been there so many times over the Winter Break. Marge was sporting a pre-engagement ring, if not the engagement ring that she desired. Tyler told her that all available cash was designated for his schooling. When he was financially set, then they could plan further. But he often silently compared the disparity between himself and Todd. And he despised himself for feeling that way. Yet he refused any help from Marge's family. She loved him all the more because of it.

With some nagging, Marge passed the baby first to Martin, who held her only briefly, then to Tyler, who passed her to Janice. She cuddled the child as if Doris had been her own. They all felt that way, really. They were laying claim to this child as her life sponsors. Jordan was the last to hold Doris before her next feeding. As she reached her hands out to take the baby, Jordan suddenly saw Josie's knurled fingers stretching out to take the hand of her dead child! Jordan jumped with shock, then excused herself, and went to the bathroom. No one made a comment. With a few deep, targeted breaths, Jordan focused on the present and struggled to regain her composure. She splashed some cold water on her face, and let the water run over her hands. The coolness helped anchor her in the present. She washed her hands with warm water, and when she had calmed, she returned to the waiting child.

She took Doris calmly, gently into her arms, and held her close to her heart. She knew the preciousness of life, and saw the life force manifest in this beautiful infant. She held Doris closely, securely, as she held onto life itself. Karen watched Jordan as if she could read her soul. She hoped now that Jordan would move forward, that she would survive. She wasn't sure about her emotional stability lately. None of them were.

It was nearly nightfall before the Group began the trek back to the campus, and to their dorms. They spoke volumes about the beauty and grace of their new goddaughter. Each shared their plans for her future. Each hoped to play a role in her life. Each hoped to share in her successes and to shield her from all adversity. Marge even projected that she would provide the son that would captivate the heart of the young Doris, and that the Sommers-Jorgensen Dynasty would monopolize Southern culture and gentility. The Group was less conversational about Karen and Todd—perhaps because they, too, felt the distances that develop when people grow.

Jordan didn't participate much in the conversation on the ride home. She was trying to reconcile the last vestiges of hope that she and Karen could enjoy a life together. The obvious reality now came crashing down. She had witnessed the truth all day. Their lives together would never be more than a fantasy, a glimpse of heaven in Jordan's own mind. Karen and Todd were raising a family now. Karen made her decision—she was gone from her. Jordan had to accept that fact so that she could move on. Although she had always known that truth, she couldn't stop the pain of seeing that truth flashed before her very eyes. And for a fleeting moment, she detested them both.

\* \* \*

As the semester resumed its usual harried pace, Jordan struggled to find her niche at the adoption center. She still couldn't concentrate, really. She read maybe three dozen files since she arrived there, and had already realized the demand for infant children. Yet, the agency had an over-supply of older kids, usually minority and bi-racial children. These children remained under the supervision of a state agency, and awaited a family willing to take a chance on them. She thought about the Humane Society where her dad once got an older dog for the family. Posie may have had her quirks, but you could never have found a more loving or protective dog. Jordan could not imagine her childhood without the woof of the old German shepherd trailing behind her. But children are not like dogs. And adoptive families have their own priorities. So the children would wait until an extraordinary family might come along and take a chance on them. Maybe the family was a little quirky, too, but that didn't seem to matter much to the children. They just wanted to be loved and to be cared for. They wanted roots. They wanted a place where they could grow in peace. They really just wanted a family of their own.

Maybe it was this childhood recollection, or maybe it was the kindred feeling of not belonging that actually touched Jordan the most. She viewed this rising feeling as one of life's miracles, a guiding force that led her gradually back to center, to an enthusiasm about her profession; to an enthusiasm about her life; to an enthusiasm about her goals. She felt a strange commonality with these less sought after children, even though she had never met them. She had read their files, though. She had seen their photographs. She knew their struggles. She adopted their cause as her own. Besides, if she plowed into her work, she could rake out the past. Her life could begin again. And it was also a good diversion from things, or people, who would always remain just outside of her reach.

Jordan arranged speaking engagements to actively recruit families for these children. She submitted articles in the local papers. She outreached to the churches, and to the graduate schools, to the business sector, and to the professional sectors. Children needed a family who could care for and nurture them, and she would find a place for them in the world. Jordan found renewed vigor from this new mission. Allison repeatedly redirected Jordan toward statistical analysis and government reporting.

Jordan was also becoming a folk hero among the other students in the Social Work Department. She had successfully defended a fellow student against the college administration, and now, she was using the campus paper to impact on the community-at-large! She was placing children for adoption! Truly, Jordan Mathews would one day rise to a prominent position in social welfare, in politics, or perhaps, in both. Maybe she would direct a large government agency, like Health and Human Services, or Housing and Urban Development. They were sure that there would be no limit to her professional potential! The other students tried to position themselves into the group assignments that Jordan was working. They tried to seek her advice in matters of public policy, and used her thoughts for position papers. Mostly, they just wanted to be able to say in the future that they were friends in college. They hoped she would remember them, and that she would pull them along on her ride to the top. They felt certain that she was headed that way. They didn't see, or wouldn't see, the struggle that she faced daily, as she dodged all reminders of that one day in her life. And she shared that fight with no one.

Martin and Janice teased Jordan to no end.

"Oh, let me touch you," Janice said. She was tugging at Jordan's arm as they walked from dorm to lecture hall. Martin begged for her autograph on a napkin in the cafeteria. Even Marge kidded that she could hardly get to their room, what with all the groupies standing outside. Tyler had her photo posted on the student center bulletin board with a label that said, "Top Contender for Who's Who In American Colleges." Jordan was really upset when she learned that he had posted the photo as a joke. But her confidence was rising. They were just happy that she was smiling again.

The success facade was getting to her, though. Jordan needed a cold blast of fresh air to ground her back into reality. She needed to clear her mind of false conceit. She needed to commune again with the natural world. She struck out on a night walk through the campus, and under the light of the full winter moon. Its light shown a pale blue hue across the snow, as her boots crunched against the crispness of the ice on the sidewalk. She was deep breathing the frozen mountain air, allowing it to fill her lungs and to clear her mind.

She knew the truth—that it was the manic rush of success from the "cheating hearing" that led her to disregard protocol at the clinic. She knew that it was her pride that placed her in such jeopardy. She would not listen to that Siren again! She kept telling herself that she was just plain Jordan Mathews, and with hard work, she might enjoy some modicum of success. Grandiose plans had no place in her world. She would touch the lives of those who entered her small realm of influence. There would be nothing beyond that. This was the most that anyone could expect. She focused her contentments on those simple things in life, and dismissed any thoughts that she would be rewarded with anything more than that.

As she turned the corner to return to her dorm, she saw a gathering crowd on the front lawn. At first, she believed that one of the sororities was pushing a pledge week there. But she noticed that the attendees were too tall, too broad, to be any of the women on campus. As she entered the dorm by its side door, she heard the chiding of women from the open windows above, and the cat calls of men now thronged together in the new snowfall. Suddenly, the men lined up shoulder to shoulder, and awaited the next command.

"About face!" the ring leader barked. And with the split-second precision of a drill team, the men dropped their pants, giving a full moon salute to the ladies of "Ball Morals Hall."

"Never in the history of the college have so many jockey shorts been unfurled in salute! Gentlemen, a new campus record!"

With the flip of a wrist, each pair rode down to the ground, and lay lifeless, inviting, at the ankles. The men's cheers rode well above the taunts of the ladies now hanging and gawking out of every dorm window that faced the front entrance. The women dowsed the male chorus line with an array of light beams from flash lights, emergency flood lights, and Polaroid instamatics! With a click and a flash, the butts of half the men of Hill Hall were captured for all posterity!

"Turn around and face us, Fellas! Don't be shy! Let's see what you got! Share that special delivery!"

"Eat your hearts out!" The guys bent over again, and cracked back to the girls.

"There really isn't much of a market for 'frozen twizzlers', so why dontcha just bring those cute, little kiesters up here to Momma!" Marge answered their call.

Suddenly, she saw Martin and Tyler standing prominently in the center of the line! That was one ass, at least, that she would recognize anywhere!

"Oh my God!" Marge shrieked at the sight.

She ducked back from the window and into the room. She prayed for anonymity! But she had been coaxing the men from the dorm window for most of the evening—and she was later sold out as the instigator! To the women of the dorm, Marge was now a folk hero in her own right. To the men on the lawn, she was a pretty likely date for a Saturday night!

Tyler took some offense to the new reputation of the woman destined to be his bride! Martin tried to calm him. "Even you made some pretty raunchy remarks about Marge before you two started dating . . ."

And it didn't help that she had a set of boobs that drew the immediate attention of half the men on campus. Some of the women, too, as Jordan could attest! And with the humor of a Mae West, she could be quite the cock-teaser, as such girls were known.

"In the circles of the campus male elite, Marge is being paid quite a compliment! And you have now risen in that hierarchy as a result!" Martin concluded.

Tyler really didn't appreciate the comments, though, and delivered a punch to Martin's shoulder! The two began a playful wrestling in the day room, and were promptly escorted out of the dorm. But Tyler spoke with Marge privately several days later, and warned her that he would not accept this behavior from her again. This incident may have been a precursor of trouble in paradise, but that would not manifest until the couple had been married for at least several years.

Jordan accepted her first speaking engagement at the Holiness Pentacostal Church. Jordan was raised as a strict Catholic, and prior to college, she attended Mass every Sunday with her family. But like most Catholic women her age, she took offense to the Church's thwarting of a more pronounced women's role in the religion. She resented the Church's doctrine of excluding women from the priesthood, and felt that she could not fully accept a church that did not fully accept her. Not that she wanted to be a priest—far from it! But she could not condone the Church's snubbing of those other women devout enough to want to serve God in that way. So, she removed herself from the arms of the Church as she accepted the welcome of the college. She still attended Mass with her family when she was home, though. She and her mother just had a silent truce that they would avoid any discussion on Catholic Doctrine.

Jordan was taken quite aback, when she entered the Pentecostal Church, and was immediately scooped into the congregational fervor. She loved the church choir. She loved the enthusiasm of the congregation. She loved the minister preaching himself into a sweat, and calling for an "Amen" to cement the deal! She was not prepared for the 2 ½ hour service though, and felt that this would be a sizeable detriment to her own conversion! She was a firm believer that anything you needed to say to Jesus could be said solidly within the confines of an hour, as long as it was framed with an Our Father or a Hail Mary! Since she talked to Jesus regularly during the week, she saw the 2 ½ hour service as intrusive and excessive.

"Give the Lord a little time to himself," she thought.

The minister preached on the evils of alcohol, and Jordan momentarily thought that she was set up. But as she looked around the church, she could see each face welded to the presence of the minister, and each heart open to his teachings. She saw their devoted eyes reaching to him from under their beautiful bonnets, and from their bodies clothed in Sunday best.

He quoted Proverbs, 20:1 and called out "wine a mocker and strong drink is raging."

"Amen! Tell them, Brother!" came the congregational response.

He quoted Romans, 14:21, and cautioned that "it is good neither to eat flesh nor to drink wine, nor any thing whereby thy brother stumbleth, or is offended, or is made weak."

"Umm Humm! Say it out!" agreed the congregation.

He returned to Proverbs, now citing Chapter 23, verses 20-21, and warned his congregation, "Be not among winebibbers; among riotous eaters of flesh; For the drunkard and the glutton shall come to poverty; and drowsiness shall clothe a man with rags."

"Yessah! We hear the truth!" The congregation cheered him on. He continued his rise to Glory.

"Woe to the crown of pride, to the drunkards of Ephraim, whose glorious beauty is a fading flower, which are on the head of the fat valleys of them that are overcome with wine!—Take a lesson from Isaiah 28:1"

"Tell them, Lord" and "Yessah"—the congregation answered their spiritual leader to highlight the point. All the while, they nodded to him, and to each other. "Hear us, Jesus!"

The minister concluded, "If you doubt my counsel, you should review 1 Corinthians, Chapter 6 verse 10: where it says clearly, 'Nor thieves, nor covetous, nor drunkards, nor revilers, nor extortioners, shall inherit the Kingdom of God.'"

"Yessah! We hear you, Lord," the congregation affirmed.

"And I now turn to Psalm 9, and ask that you join me in a final praise to Lord God, the King of All Glory." The Bibles flew open to Psalm and verse, as they followed the cheers of the Reverend. With heads bowed, the bonnets looked like a well tended garden.

"I will praise thee, O Lord, with my whole heart; I will shew forth all thy marvelous works. I will be glad and rejoice in thee: I will sing praise to thy name, O thou most High. When mine enemies are turned back, they shall fall and perish at thy presence. For thou hast maintained my right and my cause; thou satest in the throne judging right."

"Alleluia! Amen!" The congregation flew to its feet with the rising chants of the minister, raised hands toward heaven, swayed with hands held high, and gave themselves to the Spirit. The choir again joined in the worship and began singing "Go Tell It on the Mountain." The minister kept time with his fist, accenting each syllable, as he strutted up and own the aisles. Church members begged that he touch them, so as to bring the Spirit personally to their hearts. The minister bounded the aisles, placing hands on the heads of his repentant followers. Several members cried out that they had been saved. Jordan was enthralled by the shear spectacle, by the power of a people in faith. She had never seen anything like that before, not even at the Folk Mass!

After several more hymns, the congregation was directed to take their seats for the weekly announcements. Mrs. Johnson, age 82, was again sick, and the congregation was being called upon to offer help as they could.

"You have always been very good about sharing a meal with those of us who need it. Who can help us out today?" the minister questioned.

"I have a nice meat stew that I can bring over to her today, and with some corn bread," said a woman from the rear of the church.

"Hallelujah!" said the Preacher. "Who else can help?"

"I can bring a roast chicken tomorrow with some greens," said another woman from the back.

"UMM, sounds so good I might be eating there myself," he replied. "And who else?" The pledges covered the full week!

The Minister then turned attention to Jordan, introduced her as an employee of the adoption center, and asked that the congregation hear the young woman out. Jordan ascended the pulpit, placed her collage on an easel nearby, and began her talk. Her stomach flipped as she surveyed the crowd. She had never addressed such a large audience before.

"I want to thank you for allowing me to share in your worship here this morning, and for giving me this opportunity to talk about another aspect of alcohol abuse—the hundreds of children here in the state who have lost both parents and home life due to alcoholism, and who are awaiting a loving family to take them in. I'm not talking about caring for them for a few hours here and there. I'm talking about making a full fledged commitment to love and care for these children as your own. I'm looking for a few good families . . ."

Jordan was amazed at the ease in which she addressed the congregation, and the genuine support she felt there. She felt a strange connectedness to the people in the church that day, and believed that the Spirit had descended upon them all.

Following her speech, several members stopped by to meet with her and to take home a brochure. She did not believe that she had cultivated any adoptive homes that morning, but she did believe that she had cultivated some friends in the community. She even accepted the minister's offer, and volunteered at the church's Help Center whenever she had a free day.

* * *

Graduation day, and Jordan still didn't have a plan beyond getting A's. She always thought that she would eagerly leave campus to return home. Now, she wasn't so sure. She felt like a guest in her own house. There were always tensions between her and her mother. And she would miss her friends, even though Janice and Marge would still live nearby. Martin would be several hours away. His relationship with Janice had been interrupted by the death of her brother. They still weren't able to move toward that long term commitment. Tyler had an offer from the Continental, an upscale restaurant in the D.C. area. Marge's father thought that he could do better in New York, and he was already making some calls for him. Tyler resented the help, but knew that the best way into any position was through the door of a friend. But he was concerned that his future father-in-law was already involving himself in his business affairs. He wanted to make it on his own, so that he could shove this accomplishment at his father if ever they met again. They had not had contact in over a year, and he was not likely to attend Tyler's graduation. He probably didn't even realize that Tyler had made it that far without him! Tyler was no longer bothered by that thought, and had also not bothered to invite him.

Marge and Janice were both anxious to leave the campus and to start their adult lives. Janice would be teaching physics and chemistry at the Regional High School. Marge was still working out a plan. Her parents convinced her to take the summer off, so that she could more clearly decide what direction her Chemistry career should take. She was leaning toward cosmetics. Her mother was more hopeful that she would accept a research position at the Cancer Institute. Her parents had been contributors there, and her father was a personal friend of the

Director. Unlike Tyler, Marge graciously accepted their offer. She had become accustomed to the helping hand of her parents. How different that was for him!

The Jorgensen's rented a small banquet room at a conference center within a half hour of the campus to celebrate Marge's graduation, but insisted that the affair was "nothing fancy." They were saving "fancy" for the surprise bash they had planned for Marge at home. Many of the hospital board and country club elite would be in attendance there. Jordan would have ducked that invitation, even if she had been invited!

But she did accept the graduation dinner invitation for herself and her family. She knew that both Kelly and Jonathan would be attending the graduation with her parents. This was Pete Mathews' way of reinforcing their possibility of success, if they would just follow the path blazed by Jordan! She was always the pathfinder in the family. That was the price one paid for being the oldest child, she presumed. Her parents were lucky that she had not chosen to be a burn-out of one kind or another. Tyler, Martin and his family, and Janice and her parents would also be attending the dinner. They liked the bonding among families. The Jorgensen's believed that all of the world's business decisions were made in such environments. They were offering a step up, a boost for success in the future. This thought would never have occurred to Pete and Ann Mathews. Pete bid on a job, and he either got it, or he didn't. Politics never entered into the equation—at least not that he knew.

With exams now completed, the Group spent the weekend much as they had the weekends of the past. They nurtured a drunken stupor at the Pub, danced their college-educated asses off, and clung for dear life, to the rim of their respective toilets. Jordan rationalized this as the last major blow-out of her life. She was wrong. She felt the pangs of separation already setting in. Even living nearby, the Group would not maintain the closeness they had shared at the college. She looked at her relationship with Karen as example. Karen and Todd had each other now. They were a family, a unit in and of itself. They did not need the same closeness from those outside this realm. They had found that comfort in each other now, and in the family they were creating together. Anything else was the proverbial icing on the cake.

And Jordan knew that she had to let go—Karen would never be with her. She would never find with Jordan the kind of contentment that she found with Todd. She would never leave him, or the world he created for her. No matter how much she loved Jordan, she would never settle for a life with her. Karen could never handle the pressures! And beyond that one night that they shared together, she had been silently, but painfully, honest with her. Karen's life, her future, her love, was with Todd. Jordan had to come to terms with that fact. You would have thought that seeing baby Doris would have driven the point home! But instead, it only made Jordan ache more for the life she believed they could have made together. Karen was gone from her now. She had to accept that reality and move on. Yet she held the love close, and clung to every sensation, ever micro-second memory of that night to sustain her. She forgave Todd, but she envied him still. And she still cherished every accidental bump into Karen's hand, or into her body. The truth could not be denied—Karen was there to witness Jordan's accomplishment.

Graduation was held on the warmest May day in a decade. Jordan's dress was already sweaty and plastered to her back, as she slipped her arms into the gold gown, and zippered it closed. Her mother helped place the cap on her head, and made last minute adjustments to her hair and make-up. Her eye liner had begun to run a bit with the combination of sweat and tears. She dreaded the walk to the stage, and was afraid that she wouldn't maintain balance in her never-worn-before high heels. She was used to the thick, high soled shoes that clumped along the floor as she walked. These new heels were sleek, nearly three inches high, and almost pencil point at contact with the floor. She would not have purchased them, had it not been for the color—they matched perfectly with her dress—and had she not been with Marge! Her tassel hung smartly to the side of her cap. Her mom hugged her, kissed her on the cheek, and told her how proud she was of her. For the first time in this five year ordeal, Jordan felt that her mother understood and appreciated her drive to succeed. Jordan had accomplished this feat against some impossible odds. She doubted that either of her parents had fully grasped that.

With Pomp and Circumstance, the graduation march began. They stepped off in time to the music. They were taking the first big steps of their adult lives—leaving the comfort and security of harmony and academia, and heading into the harsh world of employment, politics, and rigid demand. Stepping again, they were moving from the contrived to the real, from the dream to the factual, from the ideal to the concrete. Another step, and now, in the celebration of a life goal achieved. Jordan felt the bitter sweetness of the day, and she rode her emotions like a boardwalk Wild Mouse! It was only with the glimpse of Tyler and Martin that she could lighten enough to taste the true magnitude of her achievement. She savored her success with the ardor of a wine connoisseur.

With each step in the march, Jordan could feel herself moving more and more distant from the closest friends that she had ever had. But she felt herself moving more and more distant from her family, as well. She smiled to the crowds as her name was called, but she felt an intense loneliness as she ascended the stage to accept her degree. She was now caught between two worlds—one, the world of carpenters, traditional homelife, and the working class ethic; and the other, the world of professionals, multiple choice lifestyles, and the middle class experience. She did not belong to either. As she reached out her hand to receive her diploma, she was shocked suddenly back into the moment, as she saw again Josie's hand reaching out to grasp her degree! Yes, Jordan could appreciate her accomplishments, and she cherished her diploma as a badge of courage. As she descended the stage to rejoin the line of also-accomplished scholars, she thought of the standard, comic-book, super-hero finish.

"And against all odds," she murmured, "she had won." [50]

---

[50] For a great resource on the struggles of blue collar people in a white collar world, please see Appendix and Bibliography for Chapter Five.

# Chapter 6

Contrary to student prophesy, success did not immediately embrace Jordan Mathews, who was now among the most recent recipients of the honored B.S.W. Although she tried to wait out the tide of her own discovery, finances forced her hand, and within a month's time, she had returned to her cashier booth at the Shop Rite. Marge chided that she would starve before she'd take such a step backward. Of course, it was easy for her to take that position, since her parents had paid 100% of her education, and they were totally supporting her at the moment. Not so for Jordan—she had student loan payments that were soon coming due, and a set of parents who would not allow her to sit idly at home. Besides, Jordan had been schooled in the fine art of real life survival. Her parents had been giving those classes for years! Maybe they didn't realize that, but Jordan did. She didn't respect Marge's privilege. She often thought that she would not want it, even if it had been given to her on her own engraved silver platter.

"Too much pretense," she rationalized, as she prepared for a potentially long bout of under-employment.

So she swallowed her pride, donned her smock, and went faithfully each day to man the register at the Express Aisle. All the while, she planned her escape. With each subtotal that flashed across the register, with each Green Stamp or savings coupon that she processed, she counted herself closer and closer to her job of a lifetime. She had to believe that it was so! She held this belief close to her heart, and remained confident in her ultimate success. She was, however, occasionally unnerved by those people who had graduated from high school with her—especially the ones who took the opportunity to waive a $20 bill, and brag about their new office. Then, as if to accent insult, they would invariably ask, "So Jordan, whatcha been up to?"

Was it not obvious enough? Still, she would answer as best she could.

"Well, I'm waiting for the go-ahead call from the Governor to head the Department of Urban Affairs. It's a pricey salary, but the real lure is the challenge of holding together so many smaller social programs in a way that is both efficient and effective. A lot of responsibility, too, providing affordable housing, community development, and meaningful employment opportunities . . . And the POLITICS! Now that has me a little concerned . . . But he thinks that I can do it, and he's offering his help and support . . . so I said I'd give it a try. Just waiting for the start date!"

She spoke this in such a serious and straight-forward manner, that they almost always believed her! In quieter moments, she cautiously surveyed the women who chose her register. She saw this as a way to distance from Karen. And sometimes, they were checking her back! She wasn't going to initiate anything, but she was going to admire in anonymity. There were plenty of other women out there who could appreciate a life with her. If only she could just get herself to the point of taking that next step! But there would be time for that. She would know when, or if, this was really the right path for her. So far, it had only been about Karen—or at least, any thought of a life beyond the shear physical attraction, anyway.

Jan and Betty still worked at the store, although Betty had been transferred to the night shift. Jordan surmised that the rumors were becoming more flagrant, and that management had taken the measure to prevent a possible romantic interlude, perhaps in the frozen food aisle, or in the seasonal section! The whole thing was so ridiculous! But neither woman ever commented about it. They just accepted this as the price one paid for merely being different. Jordan could not understand their docility. She would never have accepted such treatment quietly! She found herself more and more coming to their defense during breaks in the lunch room.

She scolded her co-workers for becoming part of a management plot, perhaps to turn employee against employee. "Who among us will be targeted next?"

Being a union shop, the women respected Jordan's perspective. The degradations toward Betty and Jan ceased. After all, they were all part of the Food Handlers Brotherhood! And they would stand together!

Jordan combed the want adds faithfully each day, and she took nearly a half-dozen civil service tests, but she had not received a single job offer by August. She was becoming depressed, and Marge's imminent success made Jordan resentful. She tried to discuss this feeling with Janice, but she was busy writing class plans and preparing coursework for her first teaching job. She had little time to socialize. None of the Group had heard from Martin in several months, although Janice maintained regular phone contacts with him. Tyler was settling into his job as a Prep Chef at the Cellar, in New York City. He worked long hours, and spent all his free time with Marge and her family. Jordan couldn't talk to Tyler anyway, even if she had wanted to. She was afraid that he might share some of their discussion with Marge. That could really crush their friendship. And she truly loved Marge, despite her obvious shortcomings. No, Jordan was the only one whose career had stalled, and she would have to suffer this professional degradation without the support of her friends.

So she took refuge one day in the confidence of another woman near her age, who was assigned the same break schedule at the store. Carolyn was also a struggling young professional, a certified teacher who had not been appointed to a job for the Fall Semester. She was a step better than Jordan, though, in that she took substitute teaching jobs on her days off. She was making contacts in the hope that she would be culled for the next year's secondary ed. staff. Still, there was a certain kindred spiritedness to their relationship, and they began spending more and more time together. They sat with each other during breaks and even began planning shared lunches days in advance. Jordan loved talking with Carolyn and felt that she was the only intellectual challenge in an otherwise mind-numbing day. When Carolyn wasn't scheduled for work, the time at the store seemed to drag on to infinity. Together, they saw the comedy of their plight, and joked that even though their careers were a disaster, they at least had each other. Their friendship was the only thing that made the situation bearable.

Jordan really liked Carolyn. She found herself looking forward to the time at work just so she could see her. Carolyn was an English major, and she could just as easily quote Tennyson as Asimov, Frost as Heinlein. She loved science fiction, but felt equally comfortable reading Castaneda and discussing philosophy. And she shared the same love of music. Carolyn would really belt out the songs on the radio, and often, she would be nearly hoarse by the time she reached the store! Jordan thought this an odd trait for a woman so heady. But she had a great sense of humor, and a real gift for making Jordan laugh at the most inappropriate moments. They seemed to know each other's thoughts early on. She was at least as articulate as Jordan, and they could spend an hour in a discourse on the true genius of a simple ketchup bottle. Their relationship actually started around such a treasure, poised delicately on the breakroom table. And the one-liners they bounced off of each other about the job, the bosses, the customers, the cash drawers, the produce, the shelf stocking, the canned goods, the spillage, the coupons—anything to distract them from the frustration and monotony of the job at hand. They had to laugh. How else could they live with their huge investments of time, money, and energy—and with nothing more than minimum wage to show for it? They were each other's tightrope above a canyon of canned vegetables and boxed cereals, poised precariously above a frozen food aisle of abject failure. They had each become the other's emotional salvation in no time at all.

Their friendship grew quickly, and it was able to sustain the move from the work place to the world at large. They were soon going to the movies or to the new mall, catching a quick dinner, or just basically hanging out together for the summer. Jordan found Carolyn a good substitute for the relationships she had had with the Group, although she knew that they could not be replaced by her or by anyone else. But she did recognize that she and Carolyn had become good friends—they defended each other, they confided in each other, and they trusted each other. They each were a diversion for the other, as they both waited for their professional lives to take flight.

Jordan found herself more and more thinking about Carolyn at the oddest moments—seeing a commercial on TV, looking for her in a crowd as she drove passed the boardwalk, in quiet moments as she walked along the bay. She found herself anticipating the next time that she would see her, so that she could share an observation, or make a joke. She caught herself checking Carolyn out when she thought she wasn't looking. She found herself wanting to share her thoughts, and wanting to share her company. She found herself thinking about Carolyn all the time! And she thought that she could see this same preoccupation now blossoming in her friend. She tried to dodge the idea, though, thinking that this was more likely a desire for a relationship, than an invitation to one. Jordan had to admit that she was lonely in ways that her friends could never understand. She just didn't know what to do about it. So she settled for the trips to the museum for a local lecture series, and enjoyed the hikes they took in the Pine Barrens around their hometown.

Carolyn, too, seemed a bit alone. She knew Betty and Jan as she had known other employees at the store. She just didn't seem to hang out with anyone else but Jordan. They had been friends for several months before Carolyn invited Jordan over to her apartment to watch a movie. Since neither had any spare cash, this seemed like a standard night out. Jordan accepted the offer and brought a large bottle of Mateus. She had been to her apartment briefly before, and knew that Carolyn decorated her living room with empty, candled wine bottles. The Mateus bottle was a college favorite in such décor, and Jordan thought she was showing a little sophistication. She even brought a large, white candle as a topper for the bottle, when finished. She recognized later, that she went to Carolyn's with the intention of finishing the bottle that night! She dismissed her momentary concern, and rationalized that she really had not had a good drunk since she left college—almost three months ago! She patted herself on the back, and thought about how proud Dean would be at yet this newest accomplishment. She felt she had again proven his suspicions wrong. She was just going to have a night out, and a few drinks, with a friend.

Carolyn made a fondue for the movie, and they settled down to watch The African Queen,[51] the feature on channel nine that night. Both had seen the movie before, but feminists throughout the country were craving anything Hepburn. And they were no exception. They sat close, as the Germans ransacked the African village and killed her missionary brother. They laughed at Bogart, as he mimicked the hippos in the river. They watched intently, as the two plotted to blow up the Luisa. And as Humphrey Bogart dragged the boat through the deepest swamps of Africa, Carolyn began dragging her fingers through Jordan's hair! Jordan had previously dismissed the occasional bumped hand as they shared the fondue. She tensely ignored the heat of Carolyn's thigh against her own, as they sat on the couch together. But she felt that this latest move was unmistakable—Carolyn was making advances! Jordan grabbed the Mateus, and poured another round of drinks. She needed time to think things through. She had fantasized about Carolyn several times in the past. In fact, she had fantasized about most of her friends. She suspected that they had probably fantasized about her, too, occasionally. It all just seemed quite natural to her. But she had never shared these thoughts with anyone, and she never had conscious intention of living out the fantasy, unless you counted Karen. Besides, she had no real experience. She did not know what to do even if she chose to accept the offer. So she took the same course of action that she had taken in all moments of indecision in her life—she took another swig, and waited for whatever came next!

And it all came quite quickly. Carolyn sensed Jordan's awkwardness, smiled broadly, then kissed Jordan on the lips. It was a full lipped, but brief kiss, planted squarely and unmistakably dead center! There was no sloppiness to it.

---

[51] A reference to: Huston, John (Director), and Spiegel, Sam (Producer). 1951. *The African Queen* [film]. (Horizon Pictures and Romulus Films). Hollywood, Ca: United Artists

There was no intense passion. But that singular kiss sent such a charge through Jordan, that she found herself fumbling a hug, and squarely, passionately, kissing her back. Within seconds, the two were entangled, intertwined on the couch. With each new kiss, a new sensation flooded her body, a new flow of wetness saturated Jordan's pants. She was amazed about how inadequate men can be – she cringed at the mere thought! And there was a gentle intensity to the touch of one woman to another, as lust turned to passion, and passion to unrivaled craving. Humor was now overcome by want, by a desire to stroke and to feel—not a purely physical touch, but a deeply emotional connection. Jordan wanted to share her soul, even if only for the moment—and only if Carolyn wanted her.

Carolyn felt Jordan's urgency. She held her closely, tightly, as Jordan kissed the nape of her neck. She reveled in the contact, her hair brushing softly across Jordan's cheek. She moved Jordan's face toward her own, and kissed her deeply, sensitively, as if she tasted her very essence. She grasped Jordan's hands in her own and began slowly kissing her palms, letting her tongue slide between each finger. She could feel the heaviness of Jordan's breath as she again held her tightly.

Finally, when she thought that she could stand it no longer, she looked into Jordan's eyes, and with a calm confidence, she asked. "Will you be folding your clothes, or should I?"

"Maybe we can fold together . . ." Jordan stood slowly from the sofa, took Carolyn's hand, and led her to the bedroom.

She carefully, playfully, intently unbuttoned each button of Carolyn's blouse, then slipped the garment off of her shoulders. She kissed her again, as she maneuvered her bra straps down the sides of her arms. She traced her lips carefully, briefly, perhaps a dozen times with her own, as she unfastened Carolyn's bra, and let it fall to the floor. Jordan, kneeling now, lightly kissed her abdomen, then slid her tongue over her nipples, and gently sucked her breasts. Carolyn was breathing deep, rhythmic breaths and continued playing with Jordan's hair. She then stood, and slowly removed her slacks. Jordan, fully clothed, stood at bedside, as she watched the beauty of her lover unfold before her. It did not matter to Jordan that Carolyn was slightly overweight. She loved the look of her tan skin as it blended with the silky whiteness of her bosom. Carolyn began undressing Jordan, until she, too, stood naked. They clasped hands as each admired the magnificence of the other. They smiled to each other in joking approval, but their moods soon shifted, as want now transcended fear. They melded into each other tightly, naked and standing, with each part of their body pressing against the other's. Jordan felt her hands slide down the curves of Carolyn's body, and, cupping her buttocks in her palms, she deep-kissed Carolyn into the bed. She lit a candle that rested atop the nightstand, and turned off the light.

Carolyn was exploring every part of her lover with the same gentle touch that had led them to the bedroom. Jordan could barely contain the ecstasy of the moment, and with each slide across her genitals, she let out a soft moan. It was a sound that erupted from genuine, deep feeling, from an intense pleasure, and not from obligation. She felt the rippling of sensations throughout her body, and the chill-like response that emanated from her clitoris to the tips of her fingers and toes. She felt herself moving in the rhythm of Carolyn's touch, and felt her own fingers dancing across the swollen wetness of her partner. Carolyn, too, was moaning now, and in soft, subtle sounds that heightened Jordan's arousal. They were communicating on a thousand different levels, the depths of their souls, the desires of their bodies, the hunger of their hearts. Jordan could feel Carolyn's fingers penetrating her, parting her gently like the petals of a rose. With each rise and fall of her hips, she was captivated by the full tingling of limitless perception. Jordan wanted deeply to share these feelings with her, and mirrored each of her movements. Their lovemaking spanned the night. Jordan's mind was a swirl of color, sound, texture, sensation. She could feel the heat of Carolyn's body deep within the soul of her own. Jordan allowed her fingers to slide up and down the length of her body, each touch a worship of the woman. She allowed her fingertips to caress her thighs, and her palms to embrace her pubis. Carolyn, too, was gliding on Jordan's movements. They were the tuned instruments now of their own orchestra, a couple in harmonic delight. They kissed each other passionately, profoundly, and clung to each other, as they trembled together in climax. Each tender form pressed against the other, and as body moved against body, each part fondled and nurtured the other to a calm stillness. At first, only their breathing could be heard, as Jordan lay nestled in Carolyn's arms. Then, she heard the beat of her heart, and watched her breasts rise and fall with each breath. For the second time in her life, Jordan found a unique closeness, a merging, an intimacy, in the arms of another human being. And she loved being loved. Carolyn kissed her gently on her head, as the two lay silently together. She, too, loved the profound comfort of a genuine caress, and of a kiss born in love.

Jordan accepted Carolyn's offer to stay the night, and she called home so that her parents would not worry about her. Jordan reached her father, and told him that she thought she was too drunk to drive home. Having heard the excuse, he agreed that she had probably made a good decision, but Jordan could still hear the suspicion in his voice. This unnerved her, and she began mentally questioning the rightness of her relationship with Carolyn. Of course, she did not share this feeling. But she could feel herself pulling away from her, with the afterglow now dissipating. Carolyn did not sense the hesitancy, and she pulled Jordan back down into the bed with her, and into her arms. Jordan dismissed her thoughts and allowed her mind to drink the peace, as she lay cuddled on Carolyn's shoulder. Her cheek pressed against Carolyn's breast. Jordan turned, blew out the candle, and snuggled again into sleep.

Carolyn prepared a scrambled egg breakfast, toast, and coffee as the dawn's first rays colored the kitchen. She plucked a single daisy from the vase of flowers in the center of her kitchen table, and placed it in a water glass. She positioned the flower on the right corner of the breakfast tray, and carried the morning's gift to the awakening Jordan. Jordan thought that she must have looked a sight without fresh make-up and a toothbrush. But how the eyes of love dismiss such petty shortcomings! Carolyn pushed Jordan's messed hair from her face, and kissed her gently.

"Good morning, Sleepy Head! It's time to greet the new day. I have a nice breakfast here to help get you started. I have a new spare toothbrush waiting for you in the bathroom. I left out a fresh towel and wash cloth. The shampoo and conditioner are in the shower. And of course, you are free to use any of my make up. You're even welcome to borrow any of my clothes, if you think anything will fit . . ."

"Well, you sure know how to make a girl feel welcome! I admire that in a . . ." She was afraid that she was going too far, too fast.

"And you're so efficient! Why, I'd recommend this place to anyone! . . . No, on second thought, I think I'll keep this gem all to myself . . ."

"A wise decision! . . . Why, Jordan Mathews, what kind of a girl do you think I am?" Carolyn feigned a prudish indignation, then playfully flashed her top, revealing a breast. She bopped her eyebrows in mocked seduction.

Jordan raised her coffee and toasted Carolyn.

"Ummm . . . All this, and the aroma of fresh brewed coffee!" She held the cup for a moment and inhaled the sweet fragrance. "Nectar of the gods . . . or I should say, Another nectar of the gods!" Jordan was stumbling over her thoughts, maybe trying too hard. She was never good first thing in the morning.

"I think I detect a bit of discomfort! Are you uncomfortable, Jordan? Perhaps a little shy this morning? My, how some things can change with a moment in time . . . !" Carolyn was playful as usual.

"Even love can't smooth the morning after, at first . . ." Jordan quipped.

"Oh, so you're in love with me, Jordan? Do I sense a potential commitment here?" Carolyn continued the challenge. "I was hoping to capitalize on your baser instincts until I could get you to that point! Great, that cuts the work in half!"

"Who can discern between lust and love at 6:30 in the morning! But whatever it is, I do hope that we can explore these things a bit further . . . you know, for clarification. There were a few things that I really wasn't sure of . . . Maybe with a little more practice, I might just get them right! I wouldn't want to jump to any conclusions right off..."

"A good point... Ok, we'll have to schedule another test drive some time.... Say listen, I hate to rush you like this, but I have a full day planned—you know, shopping, laundry, dry cleaning, library... Maybe we can get together again next weekend. And we'll be seeing each other at work, too, right?... You do want to see me again, don't you? Or am I being too presumptuous?"

"Well, I'd have to check my calendar... let me see..." Jordan thumbed through an imaginary calendar, and then smiled at Carolyn. "Yup, I'm free next weekend. What did you have in mind?"

"You have to ask...?"

\* \* \*

The next few months were a confusing blitz of commitments, self-doubts, work schedules, and weekends with Carolyn. They stole alone-time together whenever they could, and continued the facade of friendship at work. They were nearly together almost all of their free waking moments! Still, it never seemed enough. There was always something else to say, always something left unsaid, or left undone. Even the separations of a few hours drove Jordan to deep depressions, she missed Carolyn so much. And even though she was very independent, Carolyn could not stand the time away from her. Jordan did not share her new relationship with any of the Group, not even with Karen when she called. But given the excitement in her voice, and the happiness of her conversation, Karen surmised that she had found someone. Jordan remained non-committal, leading Karen to conclude that, 1) the other person was not aware of Jordan's interest, or 2) Karen's previous suspicions had been accurate. In either case, Karen was happy for Jordan, and knew silently that Jordan would share her secret, when she felt comfortable.

And that was the issue—she did not feel comfortable. Jordan could barely contain her excitement whenever she thought about Carolyn, and she acted like a woman possessed, whenever Carolyn stood near her. Yet, she was not prepared emotionally to accept the meaning or the consequences that such relationships can bring. Worse, she believed that her father suspected that she was romantically involved with Carolyn! She could tell by some of the general comments that he made when he and Jordan were alone together. The statements were never specific, but they were usually a kind of indirect, sarcastic, questioning.

"Haven't heard much from Marge or Janice lately, have you?" Or,

"Carolyn seems like a nice girl. Who's she dating; anyone we know?" Or,

"We're going over to the beach on Saturday. Why don't you come with us, or do you have more plans with Carolyn?" Or, . . . and so it went on.

Jordan's heart would jump with each inquisition. She truly loved Carolyn, but she loved her family, too—and she could not live without either. She thought that her parents would never accept them as a couple, no matter how much Jordan loved her. But she hoped that in time they might accept Carolyn, maybe as they came to know her, and as they better understood the love that they felt for each other. But such things take real time! And then, there was the larger issue of a society so hell-bent on a singular choice that it would resort even to violence—and maybe, even to murder—to crush such a love! She had already seen this with Jan and Betty! Jordan wanted respect, too, but she knew that the course that she was now taking would deny her that right. She wanted permanence, but she knew the toll that such pressures can take on the happiest of relationships. She wanted spirituality, but she heard the Church condemn such relationships and condone only the traditional family. She thought back to her disclosure in confession once, when she told the priest that she thought that she was gay. The priest told her not to tell anyone about it, and instructed her to say five Hail Mary's each night. He quickly corrected this to Our Fathers, instead, as if that would make a difference! She felt the guilt of her love, and she had no one really to talk to about the most important relationship of her life. How could anyone object to the perfect, pure love that they felt for each other? But she knew that they would! She had no one she trusted enough to really talk about any of it! She was deeply conflicted—happy and yet horrified—and her stress was beginning to pollute her relationship with Carolyn. She had begun living a double life.[52]

Yet, she knew from near birth that she was somehow different from the others. She could remember even in kindergarten, the crushes she had on her female classmates. While her girlfriends were busy kicking the shins of the boys they liked in school, she was busy mapping out sleep-rug arrangements, so that she could lie near her favorite girl during nap time! She volunteered as hall monitor, thinking that the power and prestige of that position might impress the girl of her dreams. She was acutely conscious of her behaviors in the locker room, fearing that a misplaced glance might lead to her detection. And then there was the incident with Karen! Yet all the while, she felt comfortable in the fantasy, if not in the reality that now presented itself. She wished that she could have been different, but she knew in her heart that she was gay. She could either live life alone, as a celibate, perhaps crammed into the full body straight jacket of a nun's habit at some cloistered convent somewhere, or she could accept the reality of who she was as a person, and live her life as she had been intended to live it!

She found herself being pulled in a million different directions, and at times, believed that she was near losing her sanity because of the pressures.[53] Her inner life had become a tornado of wants, of needs, of demands propelled against the turmoil of musts, and shoulds, and have-tos. She felt a splitting inside—self-esteem sacrificed for family acceptance; a façade of belonging juxtaposed against an innate longing. She found herself engaged in long-winded internal conversations debating what seemed so natural a choice for her, against the angry, imaginary voices of her parents, her Church, her community defining what must be natural for all! The ecstasy of her relationship was being drowned in her own self-loathing,

---

[52] For issues regarding "coming out," the acceptance of one's gay identity, please see the Appendix and Bibliography for Chapter Six.

[53] For issues regarding coping abilities and the "coming out process," please refer to Appendix and Bibliography for Chapter Six.

and she could not mediate a balance. She could not find the moral middle ground that would recognize her innate right as a human being to love and to be loved. She was suffocating at the hand of a cookie cutter morality that recognized only one choice as the correct choice. This one facet of her life overshadowed all other opinion of her own innate goodness. She even thought about committing suicide as the only available solution, the only acceptable resolution, to the quandary that had become her life. Mass murderers would have faired better!

Jordan's ambivalence overshadowed their relationship like a cold, dark cloud over a bright summer's day. Carolyn tried hard to help her work through this process. She knew that Jordan truly loved her, and she truly loved Jordan. There was no question in that. It hurt her to see Jordan torture herself in this way. But self acceptance is not an easy commodity to acquire in the face of such adversity! And Jordan had only risen to this level of self awareness, she had only begun to acknowledge her gay identity, a year prior to their meeting. So, no manner of love could quiet her soul. The tensions demanded answer.

Carolyn thought back on her own coming out, and she fully understood the struggle. She had been disowned by her family, at first. She was still working to re-establish her relationship with her parents, now that they had time to process her disclosure to them. She understood that no parent really wanted to hear that their child was queer, and that she would be living a life far different from their own. They would probably be denied the joy of grandchildren, and the continuation of their own genetics, their family lineage. They would lose the dream of daughter and family. They knew the true joys of family, and they wanted that same kind of happiness for her. But Carolyn also knew that in time, the truly good parents, the truly supportive parents, would accept their child's normal life drives, and would help them to establish a healthy, though different, life path. She had seen her parents accept that she could still find a family happiness of her own. She felt this for herself, and she hoped this for Jordan and her parents.

But the pressures were mounting daily, and the stress was near unbearable. When Carolyn could take the strain no longer, she confided their difficulties to Jan, while she and Jan were having coffee together at a diner one night after work. They met under the pretense that Jan's brother, a teacher in the area, could arrange an interview for Carolyn with the local school system.

"I don't know how to help her anymore . . . one minute she's all over me, the next minute she's pushing me away with her eyes . . . and with her attitude. And she just takes fits out of nowhere, and for no reason . . . and it all has to do with her family! They're really starting to suspect our relationship, and they're putting on the pressure. They don't want me over there anymore, and they give her a rough time whenever she leaves. And if she's out all night . . . Forget it! They don't want her to have any kind of life at all, and especially not if it includes me! But she doesn't hang out with any one else, and certainly, with no one that's gay . . . She has nobody else to talk to . . ."

"Ya know, Jordan might do better, if we started with a double date . . . maybe a night out at the Key West, a woman's bar in Asbury. She could use a little community support to balance off all of this negativity . . ." Jan offered some hope.

"And now they're piling on all this religious stuff! How do you compete with God and damnation! No wonder Jordan's falling apart . . . They don't care about her. They only care about what everyone will think about them! And she has no survival skills to combat them in all of this . . . I try to talk to her about the loving God that I know, but she keeps coming at me with the Pope! I tell her that he's just a man, and statistics would favor that there have even been gay popes before, but she just looks at me and says that I don't get it . . . Maybe I don't, but I'm not giving her up to satisfy the Pontiff!"

"Don't give her up for anyone! If your love is as strong as you believe it to be, she'll make the adjustment . . . and so will her family, in time. We'll stand by you both, you know that. Let the community be the family, until her family can make the adjustment that it needs to make, for her to survive there."

Carolyn accepted the advice. She knew that Jan made good sense. And she had the experience that Carolyn lacked. Jan had been through the fire, and she had survived the flames. Her relationship with Betty was living proof of that! So the next evening, she offered the double date to Jordan, who reluctantly agreed.

"What if we're seen there by somebody we know?" Jordan was afraid that her secret would be world news again.

"Did it ever occur to you that that "someone" might likely be at the bar for the same reasons you are? My guess is, if they're in the same gay bar as you are, they are probably just as gay as you are! I doubt that that will result in anything but friendship."

"OK, but I'm still wearing my sunglasses . . ."

"What, and leave the fake nose and mustache at home?"

And so they accepted the offer. Carolyn made plans with Jan and Betty, while Jordan tried to fabricate another excuse for the evening. As she exited her home that Friday night, Pete Mathews looked at Jordan, then down at the floor.

"Spending another weekend at Carolyn's?" Jordan nearly cried as she heard the disappointment, the condemnation, in his voice. But still, she stepped out the door, and walked toward the life more in keeping with her being.

The Key West was an older bar in the Asbury area, and like most gay bars, it was situated in the least desirable section of the city. Yet the parking lot was full of cars, and several of the tougher looking women "patrolled" the lot to insure the safety of their friends. Inside, the bar was full of women of all types, all ages, all races, all interests—yet united in the singular common factor of their homosexuality. The more militant women referred to themselves as lesbians. The word made Jordan cringe! She could think of a million derogatory jokes associated with it! She was more in keeping with the tones of the Gay Activist Alliance, adopting Gay as the unifying identifier of men and women. That, too, would undergo its own change, as politics, sentiment, and need would dictate. That night, though, Jordan was Gay. It was the only word describing her orientation that she did not stammer over. Jan and Betty tried a humorous approach in the car on the way to the bar. They wanted to help Jordan adjust to this new world.

"Now, repeat after me, Jordan. I am a lezzy. I'm a full fledged bulldyke of the highest order. I'm a bulldagger. I'm a muff diver. I'm a butch . . . Anyone got anything else to add?"

Jan was in reply. "You forgot: I'm a homo. I'm a queer. And yes, I'm gay, and I'm proud . . . Go ahead Jordan. Let's hear the chant . . . Come on . . . Remember, that which does not kill us makes us stronger."

Jordan took a breath, and then, in rapid fire succession, she repeated, "I'm a lezzy. I'm a full fledged bulldyke of the highest order. I'm a bulldagger. I'm a butch. I'm a homo. I'm a queer. And yes, I'm gay, and I'm proud."

"You forgot muff diver . . . and ya haveta say it with REAL conviction." Betty noted.

"I'm not gonna say that," Jordan replied, "And you can't make me."

"OK, but remember, Jordan, somewhere along the line someone is gonna say that to you, and you're not gonna know how to react. Then you'll be thinking, I shoulda listened to my dear friends who only had my best interests at heart. I shoulda said that I was a muff diver so many times that the word would bounce impenetrably off of me. But no—I'm gonna pretend that that word will never be hurled at me, and I will die a thousand deaths when it's finally tossed." Betty made her point.

"And another thing," Jan stated. "It's always better to be proud when you're among people who are like you!"

"And I think it's also a lot safer!" Carolyn added.

Jan and Betty introduced Carolyn and Jordan to some of the friends they saw at the bar, much as they had introduced Jordan to the New York City community the summer before. Jordan even recognized a few of the women, although she could not remember their names. She took comfort in being among women who were much like her. She enjoyed the freedom of holding Carolyn's hand or kissing her on the lips in this public place. Here, she was not ashamed. Here, she was not fearful. Here, they could be the couple that they were. They danced, and sang, and partied the night away with careless abandon!

But like Cinderella at the Ball, when the clock struck time to leave, and the pumpkin coach was gone, Jordan found herself in the same miserable reality. She could not freely express her love for Carolyn, and she was finding it difficult to even feel love for herself. She would be devastated if her family rejected her. She could intensely feel their pressures on her already! She could not handle the thought of her parents thinking that she was some kind of pervert—but she believed that they would know no different. She had even heard her mother make jokes about a gay man that worked at the dry cleaner's. She did not want them to talk—or to feel—the same way about her! She was caught in the web of self-loathing, and it was slowly tangling her in a netting of abject depression. She thought about seeking counseling, and even medication, but she did not feel comfortable disclosing her plight to anyone. When Carolyn suggested that a good therapist might help develop a healthy coping, Jordan still refused. She did not want the Social Work community to know her secret. She did not realize that she had begun advertising it in huge proportions—through her mannerisms, through her dress, through her interests, and through her lifestyle. She clung to Carolyn, and to their love, as her only support.

They had begun arguing by the middle of the fourth month, mostly because Carolyn could no longer handle Jordan's extremes of emotion. She was pursuing her and distancing from her at the same time! She often felt that Jordan was picking arguments with her, maybe in hopes of ending their relationship. Although Jordan denied this, her patterns remained unchanged. Carolyn felt like she had stepped onto a roller coaster, hands held above head, and screaming inside with each plunge! Yet, when they made love, there was never any question. Carolyn concluded that it was the idea of the relationship, and its social implications, that were really destroying them. They never once felt—neither of them—that they had stopped loving each other. But such dynamics take their toll in untoward ways, and Carolyn felt less and less able to emotionally care for herself. So it came as no surprise, really, that she decided to accept a fellowship at the University of Vermont, and to study for her Masters Degree in Education Counseling there.

Jordan was crushed when she heard the news, and she tapped Carolyn with her fists, as she cried in her arms.

"I can't believe that you're doin' this to me, and that you're doin' this to me now."

"Jordan, I've tried to help you . . . I've tried to help us as much as I could . . . But you still act like you have to ask their permission . . . to exist! Let me tell you, my friend, you have a right to be here. We have a right to be! . . . You know the biggest problem that you have? You let your parents' prejudice turn into a self-hate. You may want to spend your life in self-loathing, but I can't do it. I love who I am, and I love you for being you. To hell with THEIR small minded ideas of what your life should be. Learn to live YOUR life as it should be! Don't be afraid to take hold of the things that are rightfully yours by the matter of your birth! You're letting your fears crush what we have . . ."

Carolyn let Jordan cry, and continued to hold her and to rock her. She was crying herself. "You know I love you, Jordan, but I can't keep going on like this. We're fighting more and more . . . you're not happy unless we're alone, and even then, you're not really with me. I can't keep doing this . . . I can't. Maybe in time, things can be different. But right now, it's just not working for either of us . . ."

"Don't leave me, Carolyn. Please . . . I'll try to get things together. I'll find a counselor. Just don't leave. You know how much I love you . . ."

"I can't stay, Jordan . . . You know that, too. It's what you've been saying for weeks. I just didn't want to hear it . . . And I can't put my life on hold, waiting for you to get things together . . . Please, Jordan, understand that."

"All I understand right now is that you don't love me enough to try to work things out. So go ahead—go to Burlington, go to Mars, go to hell!"

"Jordan, please! Don't be this way . . . you know that I love you! I won't stop loving you just because I've moved. I'm hoping that you'll come along with me. Maybe away from here, things can be different for us . . ."

"Don't make me have to choose between you and my family!"

"I'm not making you choose—they are!"

"You know that I can't do that!"

"I know that they seem to be giving you less and less of a choice. You may want to stick around and watch this all go to the bitter end, but I can't. I love you, and I can't watch this happening to us any more . . . I can't be a part of this any more. Maybe I'm wrong to think that you could make up your mind so suddenly. I can accept that. Jordan, come with me . . . be with me . . . Believe me, they will make the adjustment in time, if they care about you as much as you say."

"Look, Carolyn, maybe you can handle things that way, but I can't. Maybe you're right, and in time that will all change. But I have to work things out now, in the present. I can't go with you . . . I can't leave them like this . . . I can't have them thinking that I'm some kind of creep, some kind of pervert . . . Please stay with me. Maybe we can get a place together, here, when I get a better job. And then when they can get to know you better . . ."

"Do you think you'll be any better able to stand up to your parents then? They are killing you . . . They are killing us! I won't die for them or for anyone. I won't let you die for them . . . You'd be better off coming with me until they adjust . . . until they can accept you as the wonderful woman that you are—without contingencies, without compromises, without question!"

It was the worst Christmas Jordan had ever spent. Both she and Carolyn knew that she would never get to that point, that she could never walk away from her family. And she doubted that her family would ever accept her for the person that she was. Jordan would not even talk with anyone but Jan and Betty about the conflicts raging inside of her. But her parents breathed a sigh of relief. They had seen a change. They believed that their daughter had come home. Jordan took comfort again in the warmth and familiarity of anything alcohol based, at least through the Holidays.[54] She continued to see Carolyn each weekend until

---

[54] For information regarding substance abuse and homosexuality, please refer to Appendix and Bibliography for Chapter 6.

late January, when she reported for her new job in Vermont. Jordan made plans to visit her there within the month.

* * *

It was New Years Eve morning, when the postman left a certified letter addressed to Jordan Mathews in the mailbox at the end of the driveway. Pete Mathews brought in the envelop with the rest of the mail, and placed it on the countertop in the kitchen. He hoped that this was the break that his daughter had been waiting for. He knew that Carolyn would be gone in a month, and he realized that Jordan had not been seeing as her regularly for the last two weeks. He surmised this as the cause of the empty wine bottles he found in the garbage. He knew his daughter was drinking, probably alone, and he was becoming concerned. But there were some questions that even Pete Mathews did not want answers to—so he just let it be for a time. After all, she was going to work every day, she was keeping up appearances, she was basically still "answering the bell." Maybe a new job would bring Jordan back to center.

Jordan's hands trembled as she held the envelop addressed from the state Department of Personnel. She was ranked seventh on the state's Social Worker II list. She immediately wrote a letter back expressing interest in a position. In mid-January, she was contacted by the state's child protective service agency. Jordan accepted an interview scheduled ten days later, and used the interim period to learn all she could about the child abuse and neglect. She would not lose this opportunity for anything! She also thought that this progress might entice Carolyn to change her mind and to stay with her. She was crushed again, when she found that it didn't. She also refused Carolyn's offer to go to Burlington with her. Yet, they both hungrily anticipated Jordan's visit there, once Carolyn was settled in. They agreed to phone each other every night.

Jordan took a full day picking out the standard navy blue interview suit. She bought a pair of low heeled navy pumps and a matching bag. She also arranged an appointment for a hair cut and styling. She looked every bit the professional, as she took her seat for a group interview at the county welfare office. Once seated, a thin, wiry-mustached man in his mid-forties stood at front of the group. He wore a grey suit, slightly wrinkled, a white pressed shirt, and a thin, green paisley tie. He introduced himself as Mr. Wilmer, Human Resources. He explained the general duties of the job, and advised about the salary and benefit package. If hired, Jordan would have full medical benefits, a pension plan, and a starting salary of $15,000 per year—more than her father had ever made in that time! She hoped that she would be among the chosen. She prayed that Mr. Wilmer would open the door that could lead her back to meaning, to mission, and to prosperity, albeit, at the suffering of the abused, and the abuser!

Jordan was the first candidate called from the group for her individual interview. Although the job assignment had not been fixed, the agency would attempt to place candidates in district offices near their homes. They hoped that the candidates would come with a good working knowledge of the communities in which they would serve. Jordan discussed her interest in the field of child abuse, and emphasized her background in the adoption center. The three member hiring board was impressed that Jordan was familiar with current issues in the field, but they were even more impressed with her ability to articulate these issues. They hired her immediately, and with a start date within a month.

The proud parents anxiously awaited Jordan's return from the interview, and all eyes of the family were focused upon her as she entered the home. With a singular screech and arms held high in "touchdown mode," Jordan signaled that she had been victorious! She would now assume the persona of "Jordan Mathews, Child Abuse Investigator!" The family was ecstatic for her! Pete was a little more than relieved that he would not have to assume her student loan payments. He had already helped repair her VW Beetle, and he still had Kelly and Jonathan to consider! He was amazed at the salary and benefit package. He used this as further incentive for Kelly to transfer to a four year college when she graduated from county college in the spring. She would receive an Associates Degree in Fine Arts, but she was still no further along in selecting a career. In Jordan's opinion, she was majoring in men! She seemed to be getting A's there, and would likely graduate with her "MRS." Degree. They were so different!

"It's like I'm sayin'—if ya study hard, if ya work hard, if ya pray hard, good things'll happen for ya! And here's the proof . . . A daughter half my age makin' just as much money as I do! Now that's an accomplishment! That's what an education'll buy ya!" Pete Mathews was convinced. It pained him to think how far he might have gotten, if he had just finished high school! But then, maybe he would have chosen another profession.

"And with that kind 'a background, ya never know what circles you'll be travelin' in. Ya never know who you'll be meetin'. Before ya know it, you'll be sittin' around your own table, lecturin' your own kids . . . And your own husband will ignore your own thoughts, as they have for countless generations!" Her mother was beginning to speak up! Maybe Jordan was impacting on her after all, even if she still had not abandoned the fantasy family dream of husband and kids for her oldest daughter.

Jordan noticed an odd tension between her parents lately. At first she believed that this had something to do with her relationship with Carolyn. But the fact was that Jordan thought that anything that happened was due to her relationship with Carolyn! Not volcanoes, not war, not famine, not pestilence, but certainly, anything that rocked the family! Stress had obviously affected her judgment. No, there was something else at work here, although she couldn't quite decipher the cause. Her parents never discussed adult issues with their children, and would shield them from even the smallest arguments between them. Then she suspected that the answer might lay within the confines of the envelope her mother received that day—Ann had signed up for a classes at the county college! She wanted to work toward an LPN, now that her children were grown. Pete Mathews even supported this plan. But Ann was dealing with her own lack of confidence. She was stepping out of the home on her own, for the first time in their 25 years of marriage. Jordan realized that hers was not the only life experiencing change, and that contrary to her own belief, she was not the center of the family. Such revelations can have a profound effect on moving one toward adulthood!

Following dinner, Jordan and Jonathan took his telescope and headed over to the ocean. The beach was one of the best places nearby where they could practice astronomy and talk privately together. They understood each other much better than either understood Kelly. Maybe it was jealousy, maybe it was personality, maybe it was popularity, but they both seemed more distant from her than from each other. Jordan theorized that Kelly was suffering the Middle Child Syndrome, and that being popular was merely her way of overcompensating for the natural lack of attention. Jonathan thought that she was just stuck up. He thought her friends were stuck up, too, once they thwarted his attempts for a date.

"Ya think anyone's lookin' down on us right now . . . I mean, if we're lookin' up at them, whadeya think the possibility is, that they're lookin' back at us?"

"There's prob'bly a pretty good chance that someone else is out there. Maybe in time, with space travel bein' what it is, you'll get that answer . . . Whether they're lookin' back at us right now . . . well, I guess it all depends on whether they finished their dinner, and homework, and chores, and whatever else they have to do on such planets to keep their parents off their backs! Or, maybe it's the parents who are watchin' . . . God, I hope they're not lookin' at us for any advice! . . . I do believe that there is intelligent life out there. I just don't understand why they would want to come here!"

"Ahh, I get it—the whole Star Trek[55] parallel universe thing . . . Hey Jordan, wait a minute! I see something here!" Jonathan quickly stepped from the scope, and pulled her to the sight. As she looked in, he put his fingers across the opposite lens.

"All I see is dark . . ."

---

[55] A reference to: Roddenberry, Gene (1966). *Star Trek* [television series]. New York: NBC

"That's the point, when I looked in, I could see Gemini. Then, nothin'. Whadeya make of it?" Jonathan feigned excitement.

"Humph—could be anything . . . a black hole eatin' through the galaxy, a time warp throwin' us into another dimension, a fusion of ion particles flooding the light refraction, a 17 year old thumb coverin' the lens . . ." Jordan stepped from the scope and shook her brother's arm. "Ya still think ya can fool me with that crap? Well, you're wrong. Ya see, when you're a college graduate, ya know far more about the world than ya did as a mere high school senior . . . that's what an education 'll buy ya . . . an opportunity to show up your smart ass little brother! . . . Let's get goin'. It's bitter cold out here!"

Jonathan packed the scope, and the two headed back to the car. The boardwalk was empty, and with the awnings pulled down tight and sealing the stands closed, the place had an eerie presence about it. They both stepped up the pace to get to the car.

"Nothin' out here tonight but stray cats and old drunks," Jonathan surmised.

"Don't let this happen to you!" Jordan replied, with the sound of authority used in the films they had often seen in health class.

They took seats on a bench to empty sand from their shoes, then got into the car and headed back home.

"Can I interest you in a cup of coffee?" Jordan asked.

"Don't mind if I do," Jonathan replied. "I'm frozen. Let's shoot over to Friendly's. Maybe I can tap ya for a burger, too, now that you're a paid agent of the state."

They had just crossed the bridge, when Jonathan spotted a young couple hitchhiking. Jordan decided to pick up the couple, when she saw that the woman was clearly six months pregnant. It wasn't until she had pulled to a stop, that she recognized the man as Michael Perkins. He and Jordan had gone to high school together, and knew each from several classes. He was an area football great, but he was strictly the Vo-tech type. Jordan often shared homework with him, so that he could stay on the team. That was her contribution to the Fish Hawk nation!

"Mike . . . Mike Perkins, it's me, Jordan Mathews . . . and this is my brother Jonathan. How are ya, man? Can I give ya a lift somewhere?"

"Hey Pal, thanks a lot for stoppin.' Damn car quit on us again. We're tryin' to get over to my mother's. It's her birthday. She lives over near the Parkway. This is my wife, Marta. We met in Germany when I was stationed over there. We're due in April. It's our first."

"Hi Marta, congratulations! It's nice to meet you. Mike and I went to school together."

"Zo nice to meet choo! Zo calt out tonight, ya? Mike keeps fixink da car, but still, ist kaput! Money and money and money, and still ist kaput, you know? I told him we shoult buy a Volkswagen like yours. Dey run alvays . . ."

"Ya know how it is when you're just startin' out . . . but I keep tellin' her that business 'll get better once the winter is over. I'm a roofer now, but I was clammin' on the side. Just too damn cold on the bay now to be out there. I can't think about buyin' a new car wit' the baby on'a way. Too many other things we need. Ya know how that goes . . ."

After several miles and a few moments of silence, Mike announced, "Hey listen, Jordan, here's our stop. We can walk a block in from here. Thanks, again. It was great seein' ya. Ya know what they say, a friend in need . . . Call me!"

Mike clicked his tongue, pointed his finger at her, and the two were gone. Jordan thanked all major Deities that she had not accepted his offer for a date sophomore year! She also thanked all Deities that she had not married anyone, that she was not popping out a baby, and that she was not moving toward a life not meant for her! She looked up again at the night sky now beaming down at her through the windshield, and she wondered if Carolyn had seen those same stars that night.

As they entered the Friendly's, Jordan heard her named called from a booth at the rear of the restaurant. She spotted Janice, Marge, and Tyler waving to her to join them. She was a little taken aback that she had not been invited to the diner.

"Hey, Lady, how've you been? Haven't heard from you in weeks . . ."

"Hey Everybody . . . You remember my brother Jonathan . . . Anyway, I've been busy getting a job with the state! How've you been?"

"Oh my God, congratulations! But surely you're not going to give up your job at the Shop Rite . . ." Marge teased.

"Of course not . . . I'm too near owning the place! And when that happens, I'm going to have my smock bronzed and placed right next to my baby shoes in the front office."

"Tyler and I were just out furniture shopping, and we ran into Janice in the mall. We thought we'd come here for a bite to eat, you know, for old time's sake," Marge said.

"And we just said that it was too bad that you weren't here, like a little reunion . . . and in you walk!" Janice added.

They were all so happy to see her, that Jordan immediately dismissed the thought that she was being snubbed by the Group. She stifled the fear that they were avoiding her because of Carolyn. She spent most of the time talking about her new job. Janice told them that Martin had gotten a job in a research facility near Gaithersburg, and that he was working to develop some form of alternate power. He planned to visit her in March. She thought that they might be rekindling their relationship. She certainly hoped that it was so. As they talked, Tyler made a portrait of the Group in sesame seed bun and french fries. His artwork won rave reviews!

Jordan then turned to him and said, "Tyler, that's a beautiful thing. But if you start chucking Jello on the ceiling, I swear to ya that I'm out'a here!"

# Chapter 7

"Good morning, Ladies and Gentlemen. I'm Dr. Edmund Rogers, a Forensics Specialist with the state Medical Examiners Office. I've been asked to discuss some of my work with you today, as an introduction to your training for the Bureau of Children's Services. I have previously worked in county coroner's offices of three different states. Yet, I am always amazed at the new things people can seem to do to children, who are among our most vulnerable citizens. While many of the slides I will show you today are quite graphic, I want to assure you that they cover the bulk of my career. Thankfully, you will likely not be encountering this level of abuse very often. But you must always be vigilant. It is my goal here today to educate you, so that you can quickly identify the signs and symptoms of abuse and neglect, and take appropriate measures to secure the safety of the children under your supervision. Please take notes if you wish, but be advised that other instructors will be reviewing these indicators again during the next three weeks of your training. Lights, please . . ."

The room gasped then fell to a shocked stillness as the first slide appeared on the screen—an infant of perhaps three months, with brown to purple bruising on her head and face, buttocks and legs, and with severely blackened eyes.

"As you can see, this child has been severely beaten, and has died. Note the different colorings of the bruises as they appear on the body. This is indicative of several different beatings over a course of perhaps a week. Note that there are three primary shapes to the bruises seen here. On the head and face, you can see distinct hand prints where the child was hit with an open palm. These also appear on the child's legs and buttocks. Also on the buttocks, you see the very distinct, straight lines of a wooden spoon. Since these bruises are darker in color, they were likely the result of the second beating. If you look closely to the right side of the skull, and on the right side of the abdomen, you will see two semi-circular marks that clearly match a human fist. These blows were the likely cause of death to this infant. The autopsy found a ruptured spleen, broken ribs, and a fractured skull. The black eyes were the result of the pooling of blood in the nasal cavities as a result of the skull fracture. These beatings were administered by the child's mother, a single parent, who had undiagnosed post-partum depression and psychosis. She believed that the child was evil, and that she could drive this evilness from her. With appropriate reporting and intervention, this child could have been spared this brutality, and her life could have been saved. Even though they heard the mother repeatedly screaming at the child, the neighbors did not want to get involved. They did not call in their concerns. The mother had not been referred for any supportive services. There was no follow up when she failed to keep her six week post natal appointment."

Dr. Rogers clicked the next photo into place on the screen—a pair of severely burned feet belonging to a three year old male.

"This father stated that he was preparing a bath for his son, but that the son jumped into the tub, before the father had a chance to check the temperature of the water. This story seems plausible, right? But take a closer look at the injuries. See the distinct water level marks on the child's legs? These are called "stocking burns" because of their resemblance to a pair of stockings or socks. Notice, too, that there are limited splash mark burns on the child's legs. If you jumped into a tub of hot water, you'd jump pretty frantically until you got out, right? So, there should be many more splash burns than those you see here. And look at the soles of the child's feet—the burns appear almost circular, with the inner part of the circle less severely burned then the outer edges. The story does not fit the injury. This father intentionally filled the tub with steaming hot water, and then forcibly held the child down in the tub. Why? The child had not been fully toilet-trained, and he wet his pants. You will see these burns quite commonly associated with toilet training."

"Since we are discussing burns, take a look at this next slide—a four year old child with second and third degree burns over 50 % of her body. Second degree burns are the blisters you see present on this child. The third degree burns have actually removed the first layers of epithelial tissue. As you can see by the burn patterns, the liquid, in this case boiling water, flowed from the head to the feet. This child was helping her mother cook spaghetti. In the one moment it took her mother to use the bathroom, the child was able to climb onto a pot, and then to pull the pot of boiling water down over her. She was lucky. She has had three different skin graph surgeries, and will have lifelong scarring. But she is alive. All it takes is a moment of non-attendance in most cases. This story fits the injury. By the way, in burn cases, secondary infection is usually the cause of death."

"This is my last burn slide for you—an eight year old male with cigarette burns over his entire body. These burns, too, are in various stages of healing, and are indicative of numerous different incidents of abuse over a three month period. Notice if you will, the symmetry, the patterns of the burns themselves."

He pulled up another slide for clarification.

"Notice that the burn on the right palm is almost identically located to the one on the left palm." He pulled up an accompanying slide of the child's back.

"Look at the circular pattern of cigarette burns on the right and left sides of the child's spine. He was being branded a little at a time by his mother's boyfriend. He also began sexually abusing him. Note again, the symmetrical burn pattern on the right and left buttocks, and the right and left rear thighs. There seems to be a correlation between burns like this and sexual abuse. It was the palm burns that alerted this child's teacher to a possible problem. She made an anonymous report, and helped to save this child."

"These twin ten year olds were having quite a happy time on a Saturday morning, until their mother came home, and found that they had been wrestling and had broken the living room lamp. She had been working the night shift and couldn't afford a sitter. They had been left alone all night. She was exhausted, she was frustrated, and she needed to teach them a lesson. What do you suppose caused these long, thin, loop-like marks across the children's backs and buttocks? If you said that they had been beaten with a looped electrical cord, you win the prize! Notice how the bruises reflect the objects used to cause them."

And another slide of a different child—"This twelve year old child also needed a lesson, but for sneaking out at night. So his father took him into the garage, and hit him over thirty times on the buttocks and upper thighs with a piece of wood he had hidden away there. He was ashamed about what he had done later, so he kept his son locked in his bedroom so that no one would find out. The trouble was that the son was listless and semi-conscious within two days of the beating. By the time the father actually took him to the hospital, the child was already in renal failure. This boy didn't make it. Autopsy revealed that he had been so severely beaten that he suffered muscular breakdown, forcing high amounts of protein into the bloodstream, and causing his kidney failure and death. Again, notice that the patterns of the individual bruises match perfectly with the wood used to beat him. You have to look closely though, because the bruises seem to blend together, a sign of the force used, and number of hits he received."

"This nine year old girl was brought to County Hospital with uncontrolled vaginal bleeding. The child's mother stated that she believed the child had started menstruating. She had no explanation for the bruising on the child's inner thighs, or for the vaginal and anal tearing so obvious here. Perhaps she had not looked closely enough, but not likely. This child had been bleeding for nearly ten hours without medical treatment. She nearly died from blood loss and subsequent infection. This child was sexually abused by her mother and her mother's boyfriend. They had been having relations when the child entered the bedroom unannounced. The mother and boyfriend were under the influence of a controlled substance, and in their impaired states, they assessed that the child was ready for lessons in sexuality. The mother initiated the sexual contact with her child, and then invited her boyfriend to help teach her daughter about sex. These are similar to injuries you would see in adult rape victims. Estimates state that nearly 70 % of child abuse and neglect cases are substance-related."

And another slide—"This sixteen year old retarded boy was found tied in his basement. His mother decided to take a five day vacation with a friend. Yes, that's right—she left her son at home, and locked him in the basement, tied to a support pole. She placed bowls of water and boxes of dried cereals, cookies, and some apples within reach. The child had a cot and had a large bucket near him for use as a chamber pot. The child became frightened when left in the dark, managed to break his tether, and cried to a passerby through a boarded window. He was brought to the hospital malnourished and dehydrated. He had not eaten regularly in several weeks."

With a click and a motion, another infant was on the screen for review. The child was being treated in a pediatric intensive care unit, and had a variety of tubes attached to him.

"This six month old child had been crying for several days as the result of the flu. The mother had gone shopping, leaving the fourteen year old neighbor to baby-sit. When the mother came home, the child appeared listless. She believed that the child's flu had worsened, and she called an ambulance. Upon examination, the attending pediatrician diagnosed detached retina in both eyes, and noted cerebral swelling associated with a subdural hematoma. This child has Shaken Baby Syndrome, a condition caused by a severe shaking of the child by a caretaker. Although again, the condition can be caused by a momentary loss of control, the impact can be lifelong, and may even result in death. The damage is caused because the brain sloshes to the front and then to the back of the skull as the child is shaken. This impact actually causes the brain damage, as well as the retinal damage. With luck, this child may fully recover. What is more likely, though, is that the child may have cerebral palsy, and will likely be blind. This is our most recent case, and the investigators still have not confirmed the perpetrator.

Another click, and another dead infant appeared on the screen—"This child was two months old when she died from septicemia and dehydration. The child's mother was a schizophrenic who recently moved to the apartment with the baby, and stopped taking her medication. The family could not locate mother and child, who were supposed to be living with an aunt, and under her care and supervision. They did not report this family missing. The mother became psychotic, and stopped all care of the baby. The child had severe diaper rash and oozing bug bites in addition to her malnourishment. The mother stated that the baby seldom cried, so she did not realize that the child needed to be fed or changed. The child had been dead four days before the mother's boyfriend tried to bury her on one of the barrier islands. He was spotted by a clammer. These white things you see over the child's diaper rash and body sores are maggots."

"This concludes my presentation. I hope that you will remember the key points that I have made here today. I will also be available during your lunch break for any questions that you may have. I wish you much success in this challenging and rewarding field . . . Lights?" [56]

A few of the social workers used morbid fascination to distance themselves from the horrors they saw that morning. They jumped right up to the screen in hopes of getting a closer look. But Jordan, like most others, let out a deep, guttural sigh, and looked around the room. They were shaking their heads in disbelief. They were looking to each other for reaction and support. Some of them went out alone for a cigarette. A few more glanced toward the door, as if contemplating a speedy exit to a less "challenging and rewarding field." Most passed on the offer for lunch. Their emotions seemed a mix of anger and hopelessness. They had all seen death and murder on television. But the screen would fade to black before the real gore was visible. They had not been spared that courtesy that morning. They could not turn away from the harsh reality of their new job assignments. They could not cover their eyes and wish it away. If they accepted the job, they

---

[56] For information regarding child abuse investigation and issues, please refer to Appendix and Bibliography for Chapter Seven.

would each be right in the thick of this nightmare. And they would be called upon to stop these incidents before they happened! They would be expected to intervene, in some Godlike way, before children came of harm. Although this seemed an insurmountable task, Jordan accepted this mission with a crusader-like urgency. She had again found her purpose. She couldn't wait to phone Carolyn about it that night.

The afternoon concluded with a history of the field of child protective services. Children have been victimized throughout history and culture, and society's response to this abuse is usually tied to cultural trend. Jordan was surprised to learn, though, that the first U.S. intervention in a child abuse case came in 1874, and was initiated by the American Society for the Prevention of Cruelty to Animals. The agency sought protection of an adopted child who was regularly beaten, was mistreated, and was malnourished. The Society was successful in winning legal protections for her under the claim that she was a member of the animal kingdom. In 1962, C. Henry Kempe coined the phrase "battered child syndrome" after analysis of surveys on child maltreatment. Within the next decade, most states had formulated a codified set of indicators of child abuse and neglect, had adopted laws protecting such children, and had established amnesty for any person who reported suspicions of abuse. The Bureau of Children's Services became the state's designated investigation and remediation unit. Jordan Mathews proudly accepted the identifying badge that gave her authority to intervene in such matters.

The following weeks were packed with information about the identification and investigation of abused and neglected children. A state pediatrician and expert in the field of child abuse gave a three hour presentation on bone injuries and their routine causes. With x-ray screen located at front of the room, and students crowded together before him like matches in a book, this Orthopedic Guru led them through each of the films. They saw simple non-displaced, and compound fractures on the arms and legs of infants and toddlers. They saw chip avulsion metaphyseal fractures, and spiral fractures on children under age five.

They saw multiple epiphyseal fractures and skull fractures on older children. They saw fractures at different stages of healing, and learned to identify mature callus on bones recently healed. With each example, the physician would demonstrate how the bone had been broken, and provided both the stated and the proven causes of the injuries.

Jordan was intrigued by the bulk of medical knowledge being thrown at her in such large doses, but she was most interested in interventions involving substance abuse. While this medical stuff could help her interpret reports, the physicians would actually be making those assessments. She would be out in the field investigating and addressing the potential causes of these injuries. She was now aware of the huge number of alcohol and drug dependent parents she would be supervising. She wanted to turn full attention to the reams of information given on that subject. She was only secondarily interested in mental health issues. Perhaps this had been the result of her experiences back at the Merton Clinic. At any rate, she was relieved to learn that only about 1% of child abuse cases were the result of a pathological abuse. By far, the majority of abuse cases were the result of impulse and poor judgment, with substance abuse playing a key role. And substance abuse was an area that she had some experience with—even if she did not readily admit to that flaw in herself.

Despite the many hours of training and role playing, Jordan still felt ill prepared to assume a full caseload. Yet, she drove to the district office to which she had been assigned, parked her car, and took a deep breath. She then ascended the stairs to the Bureau of Children's Services, the gateway now leading to her destiny. She was guided by a clerk to her place at the green, scratched, metal desk that bore her name neatly printed on a piece of cardboard. She assessed her work environment. She spied the décor, and concluded that the agency must have used Donna Bromley as their interior decorator! Had she not been in a different state, Jordan would have sworn that they were even using the same furniture! Still, she sat down on her swivel chair with an air of authority, and placed her briefcase squarely at her feet. She took a few more moments to survey the terrain. She was amazed at the similarities she saw now, as she compared her new space to the office where she had interned.

Certainly, the sights, the sounds, the disorganization were the same! There were columns of files stacked on each desk, and social workers of every variety hanging over a phone or a typewriter. The tall green, grey, or brown file cabinets stood like worshipped monoliths, offering canyons of privacy for the more experienced workers. The smell of mildew mixed well with the cigarette smoke, as ashtrays at several desks billowed their grey clouds into the air. There were full, large garbage bags present at a few of the desks, and several children seated beside them, waiting for another foster placement. Somewhere in the distance there had to be a coffee pot, because Jordan could smell the familiar stale aroma of the burnt brew. A few of the workers nodded to her as she took her desk, but it seemed that most didn't have the time for conversation. She didn't realize that, to them, she was just another "social work entrée." Secretly, the old-timers were already making bets on how long it would take before the system would suck her up, and expel her in chewed bits and pieces. The job was just like that. The majority vote was that she wouldn't last more than a year there. They gave her that much time because she seemed a little more at ease than the previous new workers. And they were already gone!

Jordan spent most of the first day with Head Clerk Vivian Johnson. She ran that clerical office, she ran the clerks, she maneuvered information, she awarded special favors, she lorded it over the car keys, and she sabotaged any social worker that did not pay her and her underlings the appropriate respect due them. One false move and you would be denied office supplies for a month! Snub a clerk in the hallway, and you'd be taking your own messages. Make the wrong comment, and you'd be getting the worst car in the lot. Make a complaint about a typo, and you'd be typing your own reports forever! Vivian knew the true value of real power, and she knew how to use it! Jordan completed the appropriate processing and paperwork, and collated her own copy of the office procedural manual. All the while, her eyes were keenly attuned to Vivian's interactions with staff and clients. She felt that she was being tutored by Machiavelli himself! She made a mental note to bring her a thank you card in the morning.

Jordan ate lunch alone that day, and quickly realized that most of the workers spent their time in the field. She introduced herself to District Office Manager Marsha McMillan as they passed in a hallway. Jordan made an appointment for a brief meeting with her in the late afternoon. She used the rest of the day to acclimate. She cleaned her desk, made a list of personal items she planned to bring in, and reviewed the twenty case files piled neatly on her desk. She took copious notes on each family, listing the presenting problem, the potential resources, and the case goals. She used a time log to plot the scheduled home visits she planned for the week. She would be meeting with her supervisor Jane Morrison in the morning, and she wanted to be prepared. Jane was returning from a two week sick leave, the result of a fall in the ice covered parking lot. In her absence, the unit was paired with supervisor Ted Thomas. He had scheduled case conferences that day, but did stop by Jordan's desk to welcome her to the office. Beyond that, she was on her own.

She wondered if she would always be on her own. The thought was frightening and exhilarating at the same time. She had so much to give, if given the right set of circumstances. And that usually could be done with minimal interference. She could never function well with someone hovering over her shoulder calling out commands, and pulling her cognitive strings like a grand puppeteer. She needed independence, she needed freedom, she needed room to work her professional magic! She could already see that this agency could provide the forum to merge her knowledge base, her personal skills, and her unique personality traits to really do some good. All she needed was a little experience, a little more confidence, and the appropriate amounts of supervisory space! She felt that the agency had the potential to be a Social Work Heaven for her!

Most of the workers were returning from the field at 4:00pm, the time scheduled for Jordan's meeting with the D.O. Manager. Yet each time she stepped to her office, another worker would step up and introduce herself. It would be a month before she could correctly identify all names and faces. So she focused on the one face that earned her attention at the moment. She was going to meet with the boss! Although she stepped to the door several times, the D.O. Manager was involved in phone conferences, and waived her away. Ultimately, she closed the door, indicating to Jordan at least, that the meeting had been cancelled. Jordan dutifully waited until nearly 5:30—and well after most workers had left the building—before she ventured again to the now open door.

"I thought we had an appointment at 4:00," the D.O. Manager said. "Don't ever keep me waiting like this again." She was already standing up to put on her coat. "So you're our new social worker. Welcome," she said, as she extended her hand. Jordan found the shake cold and limp, and without real feeling.

"I hope you'll find this a good place to work. I know that you haven't had much direction today, but Jane Morrison will be in tomorrow. She'll acquaint you with your work assignments, and with our expectations of you."

"Thank you," Jordan replied. "I did spend part of the day reviewing my caseload, and . . ."

"That will be all, thank you. I'm glad we had this opportunity to meet." The D.O. Manager gathered her purse and briefcase, and walked toward the door of her office, pushing Jordan invisibly with her steel blue glare. Jordan noted the rising full moon outside the office window, just as the door was closed and locked behind her. The D.O. Manager sailed through the agency and out the door without further detection by the others. For the first time in her professional life, Jordan felt like a prostitute.

"Except that they get kissed, instead of kissed off," she thought. It was a feeling that she would learn to tolerate over time.

As she drove home from her first full day as a bona fide helper of the downtrodden, Jordan considered the lives of the families she had read about. There were several repeat neglect cases in families with children between the ages of four and ten years old. It was a combination of a chronic lack of care and poor judgment. The families had not improved, even after they completed parenting skills classes. Most of the parents were described as low income, low educated, and low functioning. There were also several cases of substantiated abuse perpetrated against children under age five. These were high risk cases, although the bruising itself was not serious. But there had also been abuse on the older children in these homes in the past. Jordan would have to monitor these children closely! She was concerned because of the age of the child victims in these families. She was also worried about the continued use of physical punishments by these parents, despite previous agency interventions. And she would have to assess any cognitive deficits in these incidents. She wondered if the abuse was due to poor impulse control—maybe the result of an uncontrolled anger, or maybe the parents lacked an understanding of the child's developmental issues. She questioned whether the parents were under the influence of alcohol or drugs when these incidents occurred. She wondered why others in the home had not interceded to prevent the abuse. Most of all, she wondered what she could do to help these families, and especially, to help these children. There had to be a way to keep these families safely together. She barely heard "American Pie"[57] as it blared on the radio, but as she sang the end verse, she thought back to her nights at the Pub at college. She missed those days already.

As Jordan drove on, she imagined her entrance into her home as the conquering hero, and saw herself walking into the welcoming arms of her loving family—at least that's what she thought! But her parents displayed a cool disinterest, and this presented a puzzlement to her, at least until she entered her bedroom! Neatly poised on her dresser were two floral arrangements. A beautiful winter basket of flowers had arrived from Marge and Tyler. Their attached card congratulated Jordan on her "First Full Day of Paid Philanthropy." The second was an arrangement of red roses with a card from Carolyn. The note simply wished her much success and happiness in her career ahead. Jordan took in the floral scent of each rose,

---

[57] A reference to: McLean, Don. (1971). "American Pie". On *American Pie* [audio album]. New York: Mediarts/United Artists

and held the card tightly to her chest. She surmised that it was not Marge and Tyler's gift that had so unnerved her parents! She shivered with dread, but played it cool.

Jordan took her place at the dinner table, and was crushed by the strained silence. Her father barely acknowledged her, her mother made no eye contact. It was the quietest meal the Mathews family had ever had. Jonathan glanced toward Jordan, as Kelly tried to break the ice.

"So how was your first day as a social worker? Did ya bust anyone yet?" Kelly asked.

"Actually, it was pretty quiet for me . . . just the usual first day stuff, like any job . . . Ya know, fillin' out paperwork, cleanin' your desk, figurin' out where the bathroom and the lunch rooms are . . . Only difference is, now I'll be doin' these things for big bucks! Good bye, Shop-Rite minimum wage!"

"Well at least I'll have a financial resource to tap into now . . . ya know, when I start datin' your co-workers. Any hot prospects?" Jonathan chimed in.

"Couldn't tell ya. Haven't met anyone yet, really. Not even my supervisor!"

"So what's it like there? The responsibilities, I mean . . . Ya know, I'm thinkin' that I might like to work with kids myself someday. Whadeya think?" Kelly was still trying to pull her parents into the conversation.

"Well, I've only reviewed a small portion of my cases, but I think that there's some rewardin' work ahead. I believe that there's a real opportunity to make a difference here . . ." Jordan looked around the table to all family members, hoping that her parents would respond.

Her father half glanced at her, and then coolly replied, "Please pass the potatas." His detachment was obvious. Jordan's mother ate without comment.

"Most of my families are repeat referrals, and it'll be a real challenge to develop a strategy that'll keep everyone safe and together. Ya never realize how lucky ya have it, until ya start lookin' into the families that live around ya . . ."

"Is that so, Jordan? I guess we'll find that out soon enough." Pete Mathews left the table. He said enough to make an impact on his oldest girl.

Jordan was deeply hurt, but she tried to make conversation with her family as best she could. Her parents were obviously applying pressure, and she could feel the heat already! Jordan was afraid about what her parents would do when they learned about the planned visit to Carolyn in a few weeks. She thought she'd better put off sharing that plan for awhile. She slept that night dreaming of the life she and Carolyn could share together, now that her career had taken form. Yet her parents' disapproval still caused shivers of fear, and she worried about what might come next. Much like the dreaded childhood monsters she feared that once lurked under her bed, then as now, she was merely waiting for the pounce!

The next day at BCS was much different than the first. It was a cold, wet, wintry day, and the rain fell half frozen from sky to ground. The sidewalks were slippery, and clients and staff of every proportion trudged to the door, gliding half balanced, a foot skid here, an arm flung there, as they made their way into the building. Most of the social workers were already at their desks, and they would remain there for the day. It had not occurred to Jordan that the cars would be grounded. Jane Morrison left a note on Jordan's desk asking that she join her in her office when she arrived. Jordan took off her coat and boots, folded her umbrella, grabbed a pad and pencil, and made her way to the office of her supervisor.

While en route, she passed Marsha McMillan in the hallway.

"Good Morning!" Jordan smiled and cheerfully bellowed out the greeting. She got a grunt and a nod in reply. She could see that she was already making headway with the boss . . .

Jane Morrison was not what Jordan had imagined. She was a quiet, discerning older woman, aunt-like, motherly, in some ways. She could be either shy or assertive as the situation warranted. Of course, Jordan could not yet appreciate this, having only just met her. But she would come to rely on both her judgment and her fairness in matters involving the human lives under their care. Jordan would not know any agency supervisors in the future that so closely shared their unique idealistic perspective. Jordan would later think of them as two ends of the professional arc that brought them together. They represented the alpha and the omega, the beginning of one career, and the fading of another.

Jane carried her balance in her name. She was never just "Jane." From the point of her marriage, she would eternally be called "Jane Morrison"—without a break or a breath between the first and the last names. She had somehow absorbed this singular identity. She sat gracefully poised with casted leg propped on top of the garbage can as Jordan entered the room. She quickly covered her leg with a blanket that she brought from her home. Jordan knocked on the door before entering the office.

"Hello. I'm Jordan Mathews, your new social worker. I found your note at my desk. Would you like to meet now?"

"Of course, Jordan, and welcome! Would you like some coffee? . . . And would you get me a cup? This leg is really holding me back. Hopefully shouldn't be too much longer. A mere four weeks if you can believe the doctors . . ." Jane Morrison held out an empty mug with the finesse of a Times Square beggar.

"Not a problem. But where's the coffee?"

"Oh, you haven't had the office tour yet." Jane Morrison dialed a four digit number on her phone, and within seconds, Tina Murdock arrived at office doorway.

"Tina, this is our new unit member Jordan. Will you please show her the file room . . . and to the coffee pot."

"Sure! Come right with me." Tina made lighthearted conversation as they walked. "So, how long are you in for, and what was your charge?"

"Hopefully I'm here to retirement . . . although they're still trying to discredit anything I've done to get into this place."

"Very funny . . . But be careful what you wish for—you might just get stuck here till then! I see Jane Morrison is already breaking you in. Yes, coffee is always the first order of the day. After that, you're up for grabs, literally and figuratively! If you're going to survive here, you must learn the fine art of the "office dodge." Jordan looked puzzled.

"You know . . . how to avoid being everybody's everything. You're new, so they'll expect you to jump for them. Don't do it—the more you jump, the farther they'll expect you to land! Before you know it, you'll be the one-man BCS . . . But alas, I have said too much . . . Here's the coffee pot. Last one out at night rinses it out and shuts it down . . . The older files are kept in these cabinets. You know, cases closed more than eighteen months, but not longer than three years. The three year olds are shipped off to the central office to prop up desks, serve as coffee tables, step ladders, whatever is needed . . . Maybe we can tag up together for a few home visits."

"Sounds great! But I have my meeting with Jane Morrison now. Maybe she'll let me go a little later."

"OK then . . . but remember, don't tell anyone we had this conversation."

"What conversation?" But before Jordan could finish her comment, Tina had disappeared to a brown, scratched metal desk of unknown origin.

Jane Morrison advised Jordan that she would be a generic caseworker for her first year there, and then would likely be transferred to one of the intake units. She reviewed workflow. The initial abuse reports were assigned to the Intake Units, where investigations were completed and dispositions were made. As a generic caseworker, Jordan's caseload was already established. These were the families who had been investigated and were assessed as needing more services. Jordan would be assuming an uncovered caseload from the previous new worker who left over two months ago. The unit had only covered emergences on the caseload, so Jordan would need to make tracks to meet these families and to provide updated assessments. Jane Morrison and Jordan would be conferencing weekly, and would also conference any emergencies as needed. Jordan shared her perspective on the half caseload she had already reviewed. Jane Morrison approved her tentative case plans for these families, and then called Tina back into her office. She instructed Tina to pair with Jordan over the next week. They would be making home visits together on both caseloads.

Jordan spent the day reviewing her remaining cases and plotting home visit priorities. She and Tina arranged to meet late in the day, so they could plan these visits according to location. Tina was trying to teach Jordan office efficiency. They ordered a pizza with several other staff, and ate lunch together that day. Tina spent the bulk of the afternoon phone counseling a parent and child in distress, and was not able to meet with Jordan, as they had planned. Tina looked calmly at Jordan, and shrugged her shoulders as she covered the phone receiver with her hand.

"You just have to get used to this. It happens all the time."

By the next morning the storm had broken, and the sun shone brightly on the ice glazed streets and sidewalks. The community was already out plowing and sanding, and BCS cars were authorized for use at noon. Tina made a mad scramble to Vivian Johnson's desk, so that she could claim a car with a working heater. She was an experienced worker, and she had already paid her pound of flesh to the Goddess of Clerical. She received a good set of car keys and a bright smile from Vivian as she signed for possession. Vivian nodded to Jordan, as if directing her to follow Tina's example if she wanted to survive there. The lesson had not gone unnoticed. Jordan nodded and smiled back. Obviously, Vivian had appreciated her thank you card! "Manners can really go a long way toward building a relationship," she thought.

The first stop they would make would be at the McDonald's, for a drive-thru Big Mac, small fries, and small soda. Jordan juggled her meal on her lap, while Tina drove to her first appointment, nearly forty minutes away. She helped stuff sandwich, drink, or French fry into Tina's mouth as they traveled. They were heading toward a more rural area of the county, a place typically inhabited by clammers, day laborers, cranberry bog workers, blueberry pickers, and welfare recipients. Most of the residents were seasonal employees—something about which Jordan was pretty familiar.

"Now don't get me wrong, but you can always tell a client's house before you even pull up! Usually, the place is a wreck—broken toys, old furniture, old dogs, sometimes garbage, whatever, strewn about the yard. Now maybe this is due to depression, to a lack of supervision of the kids, to an inherent disorganization in the thought processes, to a tenant/landlord thing, who knows? But guaranteed, the place is always going to be a mess! Maybe that's why we got the call in the first place. The neighbor's fed up with the look of someone's house . . . you know, bringing down property values and so forth, so he looks at the kids, and makes the call . . . Doesn't really matter what the case is about, or who the family is . . . guaranteed, the yard, and even the house sometimes, is going to be a real mess. Tomorrow, wear flats and slacks . . . maybe even jeans and sneakers, if you've got them."

Tina gave Jordan the case history as she parked the car. This was a married couple with three kids, and two substantiated abuse incidents in the past year. In each case, the father was the perp, and was drinking at the time. Both times, the oldest son had bruises on his face. As they waded through a sea of plastic bottles, broken toys, torn blankets, a child's hooded coat, and an old shoe, Jordan spied a pile of used wood stacked against the house. She thought about how the father could easily use the 2x4 to fix the two lower steps of the porch. Tina knocked on the door, held her agency card for review, and waited for a response. They could hear the TV playing inside, and heard the sounds of children calling to their father. After several moments, a man about mid thirties, unshaven, and with greasy hair and greasy blue jeans answered the door. A blast of heat and cigarette smoke engulfed the two social workers.

"Hi, Mr. O'Brien, you remember me . . . I'm Tina Murdock from BCS, and this is my co-worker Jordan Mathews. May we speak with you for a few moments?"

"I suppose . . . Jeanine, we got company . . . BCS is here . . ."

After a few moments, a chunky woman also about mid-thirties appeared in a robe. Her hair was webbed in a towel.

"Oh hi, Tina . . . I forgot you were comin' today . . . Don't mind me, we just got our heat back, and I was takin' a shower. Danny worked most of the night on the furnace, but he got it workin' again."

The two younger kids and the teenager sat unresponsive on the torn couch, with eyes glued to television.

"Make a place for the girls to sit down," the mother barked, but without response.

"Now!" Danny O'Brien boomed, as he pointed to the kids.

Jordan jumped at the sound. The oldest boy turned toward his father, let out a sigh, and slowly trudged off to his room.

Dan O'Brien looked to Tina and spouted off, "Damn kids never listen! As you can see, things still haven't changed here, even wit' the school counselor bein' involved."

"Well, at least he moved after only one scream . . . When we first started, you said you had to beat him to get him to listen, right?" Tina was calm and personable with the parents.

"I guess if ya look at it that way, then things have made some improvement. Ya look at my kids, not a mark on 'em . . . I been goin' to counselin', too . . . So when are ya gonna close the case?" Dan O'Brien asked.

"I can't really say just yet . . . You know, everything has to go through the supervisor. You know how that is . . ." Tina shook her head and smiled.

"Yeah, I got a boss, too," he replied.

"Ah, so you're working again?" Tina asked. He nodded. Tina continued, "Pretty lucky . . . the way the weather's been, a lot of people are out of work right now. Good for you! Is there any thing you need? You o.k. on food?"

"Well, we could always use a little food, when you're down this way again. We are a little behind in the gas bill, but we should be caught up by next month. It's the weather," Mrs. O'Brien explained.

"Did you get a shut off notice for the gas? Maybe I could make a call . . . you know, talk to the company for you."

"Thanks, Tina, but we're o.k. for now," Mrs. O'Brien replied. She then looked to Jordan, and then back to Tina. "Are you transferrin' our case?"

"No! Jordan is just a new worker, and I'm breaking her in." Tina replied.

"I was gonna say, why transfer us now, when we're so close to bein' closed . . . Glad to hear that's not what this is about it."

"Nope, it's just a routine visit." Tina surveyed the house as she spoke. Everything seemed surprisingly in place. The kids were still in pajamas, and from what she could see, there was not a bruise on them! Jordan could see that Tina was pleased and relieved. Because of the heating crisis, Mrs. O'Brien had allowed the children to stay home from school. They hadn't yet bathed.

Tina asked the mother how the other two boys were doing.

"Good. Matty's on the Honor Roll again . . . This is the first day any of 'em has even missed school! . . . If ya wanna talk to 'em, you can speak to 'em in the other room. But they won't answer ya if the TV's still on . . . Or, I can shut it off." Mrs. O'Brien waited for direction.

"I'd like to speak with Steven, if that's o.k." Tina waited as Mrs. O'Brien called her oldest son. She and Jordan followed Steven to the dining room, and out of earshot of his parents. The boy looked toward the living room at several points, to insure that they were speaking privately.

"Hey Steven, how are things going?" Tina waited for a response.

Steven shrugged, and said, "OK I guess. I got two A's and three B's. Hopefully I'll get into VoTech by Junior year. I'd like to be an electrician. I think I can keep my grades up."

"That's a good plan. Last time we spoke, you really didn't know what you were going to do. Has Mr. Blaine been helping you with that?"

"Yeah, I been seein' him at school every week. My father's been goin' too. It wouldn't matter though. No matter how much counselin' he had, he'd still be an asshole, as far as I'm concerned . . ."

"So that hasn't gotten better?" Tina was assessing for potential renewed abuse.

"Well, he hasn't hit any of us in a while, but he still yells all the time. He can never just talk. And he always thinks he's right. And if ya prove he's wrong, then he yells even more. It's like some kind 'a power thing with him. So, I just stay out of his way, and he stays out of my life. We both like it better that way. Mom's a lot better than that. When he yells at me, she yells at him . . . I don't know why she ever married that asshole."

"Does he yell at the other kids too?"

"No, he mostly yells at me. He's not my real father, ya know. But he is theirs . . . That's alright. I'm glad he's not my father. I just keep thinkin' that in a few years, I'll be out on my own, and we won't have to play this game any more."

"What game do you mean?" Tina was concerned about what might be happening.

"You know, the game where we pretend we're a happy family, with everyone carin' about each other. It makes me sick . . . Everybody that knows him, knows he's an asshole. So, when it gets too bad, I just go over to my friend's house. He's got a cool family, and they like me a lot . . . Everybody's happy."

"Do you feel safe here? Is there something I can do to help you?"

"Like I said, we just stay outta each other's way. When I need to, I leave. I already told my mother that. Maybe my friend's family can take me in. But I don't need that right now . . . I still want to live here. This is my home. This is my mother, and these are my brothers, even if he isn't my father."

"You'd tell me, if you didn't feel safe here, right?" Steven nodded to her that he would. "You still have my card?"

"I keep it in my wallet. And my friend also has your number."

"Good! I hope that you call me whenever you think you need to. OK? Promise?"

Steven smiled and agreed that he would. The two ended their discussion, and Jordan followed them back to the living room and to the other waiting family members. The younger children were still watching Scooby-Doo.[58] Tina announced that she would be leaving.

---

[58] A reference to: Ruby, Joe, and Spears, Ken (1969). *Scooby-Doo* [CBS animated television series]. Studio City, Ca: Hanna-Barbara. "Rutt-Ro!" I should have referenced this on the next page as well.

Jordan then spoke. "Ya know Mr. O'Brien, I couldn't help but notice the wood on the side of the house. You could probably take that 2x4 and replace the two lower stairs up to the porch . . ."

"Whadeya, the fuckin' Buildin' Department now? . . . Maybe I will, when the weather breaks. It's too cold right now to worry about it. Besides, everybody knows just to hop over them stairs, except for the visitors, and they learn quick enough . . ." He looked at Jordan and laughed. "I'm gonna go in and get cleaned up now," he said to his wife.

"Well, we've got to be going. I'll probably be out to see you again next month. Just keep up the good work."

As they walked to the car, they both heard Dan O'Brien scream.

"Steven, when I tell ya somethin', I expect ya ta do it! Don't ever embarrass me in front of BCS or anyone ever again!"

Tina started the car and drove off, thankful that the engine responded to the key.

"Rutt-Ro!" Tina exclaimed to Jordan. "Better keep an eye on this one! Things are o.k. for the moment, but give it another year. Steven's going to be old enough, and big enough, to really challenge his step-father. That's when there'll be real trouble, unless the counseling works now." She knew that this wasn't a "Brady Bunch" kind of family, but she also knew that there had not been another physical abuse incident since she became involved. The father's drinking had diminished, though it had not stopped. There was a safety plan in place. It was not perfection, but it was enough to feel that the children were safe for the moment, despite the yelling. Sometimes that was the most they could hope for. She and Jordan discussed the visit as they traveled to their next stop, a family on Jordan's caseload, just several streets away.

As they waded through a sea of tied newspapers and old auto parts, and stepped over a broken ice skate and a sour mop, Jordan took out her BCS card, and prepared to knock on the door. Tina had worked with the family in the past, and was aware of the mother's drinking problem. But she had completed a detox.

three months ago, and had rejoined her children and her mother in the home. Tina quickly glanced into the garbage can now present at the curb. She noted no beer bottles or other alcohol related items apparent in the can.

"Hi, Mrs. Butler. I'm Jordan Mathews from BCS, and this is my co-worker Tina Murdock. May we speak with you for a few moments?"

"Sure, come on in. Cheryl has just went to the food store, but she should be back any minute. The kids should be home from school pretty soon, too. Is there somethin' I can help ya with?"

"Yes Ma'am . . . Well . . . howdeya think things are goin' here?" Jordan asked, using the same familiarity that she had seen Tina use, except that in Jordan's case, the vernacular was genuine.

"Oh, things have been goin' alright, I guess. Sue is givin' her mother quite a run, but she's at that age where she will do that. Timothy is doin' good. Cheryl is doin' good, too. Not a single problem, ya know, like before. She's not seein' that fella anymore either. Maybe that's why everything's goin' so well."

Cheryl Butler then entered the home. "Oh, I didn't realize that you'd be here so early . . . The kids aren't home yet."

"That's o.k. This gives us a little time to talk without them. I'm Jordan Mathews, your new social worker. You probably remember Tina Murdock. We were just speaking with your mother . . ."

"I hope that she told you that everything was goin' great here . . . I have been goin' to meetings every night, and I haven't had a drink in ninety-eight days. Look right here . . . it's my ninety day key chain."

Jordan took the AA key chain, smiled as she examined it, and then handed it to Tina for review. They both praised Cheryl Butler for her accomplishment.

"Jim is out of the picture now for good. Ya know who he is, right? He's the man I got into all the trouble with . . . my boyfriend. We broke up as soon as I came outta detox. I knew it was either him or the kids. I couldn't stay sober with him drinking like that all the time . . . and he just didn't wanna stop. He didn't even wanna try, not even for the kids . . . My kids 'll tell ya the same thing . . . I've been working my program."

"I know it must have been very tough for you, but you've made the right decisions. Keep working your program, and, ya know, stay away from people, places, and things that helped ya to drink in the first place . . . Sounds like you're doing that." Jordan provided this praise.

"I am. My sponsor is the greatest . . . always there when I need to talk. Sometimes she even gives me a lift to a meeting. Maybe when I have a little more sober time, I'll be able to return the gift, by sponsorin' someone myself. I'd try to be just like she is to me."

As Cheryl spoke, the kids arrived home from school. Susan was a thirteen year old, well developed girl, with short styled brown hair, a low cut blouse, and tight black jeans. She kissed her mother and grandmother as she came into the house. Rob was an eleven year old boy, with longer, unkempt hair, long sleeve sweat shirt, and blue jeans. He followed Susan in doling out his share of family affection. The two then said hello to the caseworkers, as their mother introduced them both. Jordan interviewed the children in the presence of their caretakers. Both children confirmed the statements made by their mother and grandmother. Cheryl's drinking stopped when Jim left the home. They confirmed that he had not been back.

The grandmother interrupted when Jordan and Tina announced that they would be leaving. "What about the problems with Sue? Don't ya think ya should be checkin' into that? That girl needs help . . ."

Before Jordan could respond, Cheryl interceded. "I'll handle this myself, Mother. I don't need outsiders tellin' me how to raise my kids . . ." She looked to Jordan and Tina. "It's just a boy thing . . . She's really a good girl. She's just at that age. She's just a little boy-crazy . . . nothin' to involve the state about . . ."

"But maybe there's something I can do to help you . . . We have a lot of resources . . . like counseling." Jordan waited for a response.

"It's not that serious yet, that I can't handle this on my own. She's already agreed not to see the boy again, without tellin' me first."

"So ya think that ya pretty much have everything under control . . ." Jordan then looked to Tina, who interceded.

"Well, if you don't need help, that's o.k. But if you ever do, you can always call Jordan, and she'll help you set up services for you and your daughter."

Without further issue, the two left the home and moved on to Tina's next scheduled visit. Tina explained to Jordan that she felt comfortable with the Butler situation, because of the presence of a protective adult. She believed that the grandmother would make a call at the first sign of trouble. She didn't want to undermine the mother's role as parent.

The next visit was a termination visit required for the case closing—a single abuse incident that resulted in facial bruising on an eight year old. The abuse occurred just three months prior, but there had been no other issues. Tina's last visit was a court ordered monitoring of a custody case. Mom and the twin six old girls were available for interview. The mother expressed her concern about the girls acting out following their weekend visits with Dad. The children denied any incidents with either parent. Tina advised that most children do have behavioral breaks following visits with a parent. She counseled that this was largely due to loyalty issues, feelings of ambivalence, and to the dynamics of the divorce.[59]

Tina later advised Jordan that when the parents worked together for the benefit of the children, despite their own relationship problems, the children did much better. Those families were never referred to BCS for monitoring and intervention. BCS received referrals only on divorcing parents who attempted to use their children as pawns in their marital war. Tina continued her instruction as they drove on. The afternoon passed quickly and uneventfully, and before she realized it, they were en route back to the office.

---

[59] For information regarding the psychological impact of divorce on children, please refer to Appendix and Bibliography for Chapter Seven.

"We got lucky today. Don't think for a minute that every day will be like this one. The gods just took mercy on us, because they saw that you were new at this. Believe me, there won't be a day that goes by here that something won't happen to somebody somewhere. And they will find some way to make you responsible for it all."

Jordan and Tina spent the remainder of the week meeting Jordan's assigned families, and honing her interviewing and observation skills. Even when appointments were scheduled, Jordan was amazed at how frequently families were not home when she arrived. She was astonished at how often the parents had not bothered to clean their houses, or to clean their children, even when they knew she was coming! She was perplexed at how often children would be beaten, despite state involvement and intervention. She was aghast at the parents who routinely and uncontrollably yelled at the kids in her presence. But what she found most disturbing was the way that some children seemed immune to the treatment! She soon identified a handful of kids on her caseload who could be beaten to a bloody pulp, and still would not adhere to the demands of their parents!

She was shocked by the remorselessness of some parents, who justified their abuse by the lessons, they believed, such inflicted pain "taught." She could not understand the parents who would swear that they were clean and sober, right through another "dirty" urine test! She could not understand the sex perps, who described their child victims the way one might describe an experienced street walker. She could not understand the women who protected such men at the cost of their daughters. And she could not understand how, in the midst of all this incivility, she could rehabilitate these families! But she did understand that the state would hold her exclusively accountable when she failed to do so. Tina and the other caseworkers made that abundantly clear. "CYA" was not just a catch phrase, it was not just an agency philosophy, it had become the agency mantra! And she had learned early in the process to cover her ass at all times.

But she had also seen a lot of good when she was out in the field. She attributed this mostly to the resilience of the human spirit. She saw battered women find the courage to leave their abusers, and to start new lives for themselves and their children. She saw single mothers choose their children over the men who had sexually used them. She saw alcoholics and drug addicts maintain their sobriety motivated only by their love and care for their families. She saw parents genuinely benefiting from the counseling and parenting skills programs, and she saw positive changes in their children as a result. She saw some foster children still reaching out for connectedness even after a series of failed foster placements. She saw a way that she could make a difference in the lives of other people—children and adults—and she believed that she could find a way to make it all work. By the end of her second week, she was already exhausted from the long hours at the job, but it was a productive, rewarding kind of fatigue.

Yet nothing would deter her from her scheduled weekend with Carolyn. It was the second week in March, and the weather was not cooperating. Carolyn called the night before and warned Jordan that they were expecting another snowfall over the weekend. But Jordan still wanted to take the chance. How many times had the weatherman predicted a hurricane, and all they got was a shower? How many times had they predicted a blizzard, and they got less than an inch of snow? If the road conditions were bad, she would turn around and go back home. Her car was gassed, the snow tires were on, her clothes were packed, and she was going! She told her parents that she had the afternoon off, and that she would be leaving right from work. She expected to be in Burlington by 8:00 pm. Maybe it was the authority that she used in relaying the plan to her parents, maybe it was the feeling that they could no longer control her life, maybe they had already surmised that she would be going that weekend—Jordan did not know. But for whatever reason, neither her mother nor her father made comment about the plan. They only asked that she call them when she arrived there, and that she call them again when she was leaving to come home. Jordan left the directions and Carolyn's phone number conspicuously displayed on her desk, in the event that her parents might need to contact her.

She thought about the children now in her care, as she made the trip through New York, Connecticut, and on to Vermont. The roads were plowed, salted, sanded, and clear for most of the trip. It was only as she left the Interstates and drove through the small towns leading to Burlington, that she had any skidding at all. All the while, she thought about three of the foster children on her caseload.[60] She was not concerned about the two toddlers in foster care. She had already been advised that they had been placed in pre-adoptive homes and were doing well. In both cases, their natural mothers were drug addicted, and had used throughout their pregnancies. The infants tested positive for opiates at birth—cocaine or heroin—and had obvious neurological issues. They each went through withdrawal following their births. They were cranky, colicky, difficult to feed or to soothe, and rejecting of touch. The withdrawal lasted a week, but the neurological impact would be life-long. These were the children who required close medical monitoring and supports, and who would fill the classrooms of Special Ed. programs. But these two children had great adoptive families, and they would be well cared for throughout their lives.

Jordan was more concerned about the three foster children who would grow up in the system.[61] There was John, a nine year old boy whose parents died from a drug overdose. He sabotaged his placements whenever he could, and insisted that he would not be adopted by anyone. There was Sarah, a twelve year old girl who was mildly retarded. She had six foster homes before she stabilized at her present one, but this older couple was not interested in adopting her.[62] And there was Mary, a fifteen year old girl with a history of acting out, both

---

[60] For information regarding annual foster placement figures nationally, please see Appendix and Bibliography for Chapter Seven.

[61] For information regarding adolescent foster placement, and aging out of the system, please refer to Appendix and Bibliography for Chapter Seven.

[62] For information regarding the instability of foster placements, please refer to Appendix and Bibliography for Chapter Seven.

behaviorally and sexually. With the number of other kids needing placement, there were few foster parents who would tolerate Mary's mouth or her attitude. She had been moving from foster home to foster home on an average of every eight weeks, and was nearly ready to restart the list of homes willing to take a teenager.

Jordan was making mental notes of the approaches she thought might work with these children, when she reached Burlington. She liked the quaintness of this university town, this settlement on Lake Champlain. She admired the architecture of the turn of the century homes now housing fraternities or apartments. She could feel her heart pounding as she turned onto Maple Street where Carolyn now lived. As Jordan pulled into the driveway parking lot of the two story home now holding her partner, she looked up to the second floor, and could see Carolyn's flickering silhouette waiting at the window. Jordan grabbed her suitcase and bounded the stairs to Carolyn's apartment. As she reached the top of the stairs, Carolyn opened the door and pulled her inside. There by the light of a half dozen candles, Jordan saw Carolyn clad only in a silk robe. She watched her lover's body unfurl before her, as the robe dropped to the floor. She could see the glimmer in Carolyn's eyes as the candles burned behind her. Jordan dropped her suitcase, and gently pulled Carolyn into her arms. With a long, deep kiss she greeted the love of her life. She dropped her coat to the floor, and led Carolyn passed the row of lit candled bottles and wisps of sandalwood incense. As they entered the bedroom, Jordan felt like she had finally come home.

\* \* \*

"Jordan, Jordan, wake up!" Carolyn shouted as she shook her by the arm. "I've never seen so much fucking snow in my life!" Carolyn still lay naked beside Jordan, and was peering out the window just above the bed.

"I don't believe it!" Jordan said, as she sat up and looked through blinds and frost. "Well, that's one for Uncle Weather Bee! Wouldn't you just know it! I hope we didn't have any plans for the day, because it doesn't look like anybody's going anywhere . . ."

They both continued their vigil out the window. They watched the dancing flakes of snow fall silently to the ground, and watched the wisps of wind turn snow flake to whirligig, a spiral white mist that blew across the yard and drifted against fence and doorway. The village was a dead silence, and only the squirrels dared venture into the white wonder. Carolyn stopped at the thermometer attached to the kitchen window as she traveled back from bathroom to bed.

"It's minus ten degrees out! Nice and snug in here though . . . Let's hide out!" She lay back down on Jordan's shoulder, and pulled the covers up and nearly over their heads. When she sat up again, she pulled a strawberry body lotion from her nightstand. She began massaging Jordan's back, as she lay quietly beside her. There was no reason to hurry. They couldn't have gone anywhere, even if they had wanted to! Jordan basked in the pampering, and when finished, she gave Carolyn a full body massage. She poured the lotion into the palm of her hand, then clasped her hands together in effort to warm the gel. She made light swirls with her fingertips across Carolyn's shoulders and back, and used her full palms to cup her buttocks and thighs. She smoothed the lotion down her calves, and worked the strawberry cream into the heels and soles of her feet. She used each stroke as a proclamation of her love, and each caress as a cherishing of her lover.

Carolyn made a pancake breakfast, and they ate together as Carole King played on the stereo. Jordan could not remember when she had ever felt more deeply in love. She would be content never to emerge from this wintry cocoon. It was Carolyn who finally suggested that they shower and ready themselves for the day. They showered together, and used the same gentle touch to cleanse, to love, to adore the sublime passions of the other. They spent the afternoon on the couch, with the wind now whipping across the home and rattling the window panes. Carolyn sat on the couch, with Jordan lying beside her, her head neatly tucked onto Carolyn's lap. They passed the afternoon sipping a chardonnay, while Carolyn read aloud poems by Pablo Neruda, and slowly twirled Jordan's hair between her fingers. They cooked a steak dinner together, ate by candlelight, and made love again that night. They slept in the joyful peace and comfort of one heart beating to another.

Carolyn was anxious to enjoy the new fallen snow, and woke Jordan with the news that temperatures had risen to minus five degrees. The early morning sun took its eight o'clock position, as the two showered, dried and styled their hair, ate bowls of hot oatmeal, and ventured out for provisions. Jordan borrowed an extra wool cap and wool mittens that Carolyn had hanging on the radiator by the apartment door. She wore her own boots, ski pants, and down jacket. She told Carolyn that she had forgotten her hat and gloves, but actually, she just wanted to wear Carolyn's things, so that she could feel closer to her. Carolyn took an empty backpack, and the two trudged off to the food store five blocks away. The wind had subsided, but the cold caught Jordan's breath, and she momentarily retreated back into the building to prepare herself. She thought about the cold Appalachian mountain mornings and missed again, the time that she spent with her friends there.

Most of the streets were already plowed, and the two walked along the roadway together. Several of the neighbors were already out shoveling their sidewalks and driveways. The snow clung like ice kittens to the branches of the trees, and even with the winds, the trees stood as white giants against the dark blue skies. Carolyn was especially playful that morning, making jokes, tossing snowballs, holding Jordan's humor like a treasured jewel. She, too, believed that they were meant to be together. She believed it would be only a matter of time and logistics before this would happen—but she knew in her heart that it would. Once in the store, they were amazed at the scarcity of items for sale there. Most of the staples were gone, leaving empty shelves and distraught shoppers.

"Must be some kind of national emergency again!" she said, as she grabbed a quart of skim milk, and a loaf of Italian bread. "Get a bag of carrots and some celery. I'll scrounge around for whatever is left."

Jordan snapped at the command, and tooled through the Produce Section like she was Mr. Green Jeans. Carolyn settled on a chocolate cake mix, a box of bisquick, and some Swiss steak. She had intended to make a ham, but hadn't realized that Jordan was not fond of the meat. So she chose instead, to make her "award winning" crock pot beef stew and dumplings. She liked coming into the warmth and aroma of a good stew cooking all day. As they walked back to the apartment, they met Bill and Marcus, the two men who lived in the apartment below Carolyn's. She introduced them both to Jordan.

"Oh, finally we meet! So this is Ms. Wonderful! Well how do you do! We've heard so much about you," Marcus said, as he kissed Jordan on the cheek. "Hey, we're getting ready to go tobogganing over at Ridgeway. Why don't you two come along?"

Carolyn looked at Jordan, who raised her eyebrows in reply. "Well, I have to throw this stew together, and then we have to dig out the cars . . ."

"Not a problem, "Marcus said. "We'll help you dig out the cars if you share dinner with us. We'll take my car . . . you know, four wheel drive, and we'll go spend a few hours playing outside in the snow . . . Then we'll dig out your cars, and have some dinner together. You did buy enough for four, didn't you?" Marcus looked pleadingly at Carolyn. They may have been gay men, but that never guaranteed that they could cook! Another stereotype bites the dust!

"I think I could make it stretch, if you load up on bread . . ."

"Great! It's a done deal then. We'll meet you out front here in an hour. Sound good?" The couples agreed, tended to their assigned tasks, and met out front of the building, as promised.

Jordan hadn't sledded since high school, although she occasionally slid down the hill behind Balmural Hall seated on a cafeteria tray. The men graciously shared their toboggan, and various assemblies of two's shot down the hill behind the Ridgeway School, where Carolyn worked part time as an art therapist intern. The University had arranged the placement as part of Carolyn's fellowship there. The hill was actually located in a Vermont state forest area, and even though before noon, the place was already crowded. Jordan estimated that she had traveled down the hill at least twenty times, with only a few topples off the toboggan. Her thighs burned from the climbs back up the hill, and by 3:00 p.m., they had all finished for the day. The group piled back into the car, frozen and stiff, and drove back to the apartment. Carolyn went inside to prepare an early dinner, while Jordan and the men shoveled snow from around the cars. They used a hammer to break apart the large, snow plow ice boulders that now blocked the driveway entrance, and drank shots of peppermint schnapps for warmth. The men had earlier shoveled their driveway. They chatted with Jordan as if they had been lifelong friends. She loved their familiarity, a sense of emerging family.

Jordan was unaccustomed to sharing her time with Carolyn, but the men were funny and so entertaining, that she hardly minded the intrusion. In fact, she could see all the more clearly, what their own lives together could be like. She could see a normalcy in their relationship now. She could see a settled permanence that allowed for time shared with others, like most straight couples enjoyed. She was feeling less threatened by her sexual orientation, and believed that she was making the necessary adjustments that her life called out for her. She was becoming aware that gay people exist everywhere, and in every walk of life. She was feeling less lonely and isolated. For the first time, she was feeling that she was living the life that had been intended for her—and that made all of the difference.

After the last spoonful of broth had been sopped with the last slice of bread, and after the last bit of dumpling slipped from his spoon to his mouth, Marcus feigned a stretch and a yawn. He finally caught on to Carolyn's cues.

"Will you just look at the time! Jordan and Carolyn, it's been great, but we have to be going." He nodded toward the door as he looked at Bill.

"But we didn't have dessert yet," Bill pleaded, until he caught the exaggerated wink from his partner. "Oh, I guess we can get it to go. Can't we?" he looked to Carolyn.

"You can get it, IF you go!" Carolyn gave an exaggerated wink back.

Bill and Marcus had lived apart for most of their relationship, and they appreciated the value of time alone. So they departed without fanfare or pretense, but with chocolate cake precariously balanced on two saucers. They could make their own coffee.

"Have a safe trip home, and a speedier trip back to Carolyn," Bill called, as Marcus pulled him out the door. Jordan liked them immensely, and hoped that they would become friends. She knew that Carolyn spent huge amounts of time in their company, and she was relieved that she had won their approval. She and Carolyn enjoyed a hot shower and went to bed early that night. Jordan would be leaving the next day. They were so tired, that they fell off to sleep almost as soon as they settled in next to each other, and with body molding against body. Jordan tried to freeze the images, the sensations, in her mind so that she could call them up on those nights she'd spend without her. She had finally found connection to another human being, the soul sharing that she had so longed for. She could already feel this connection beginning to extend to all of humanity. She found genuine contentment, a completion, in the arms of her beloved. And she could no longer imagine life without her.

They woke again to another snow storm. When the snow hadn't stopped by 4:00 p.m., Jordan decided that she would spend an additional night at Carolyn's. She didn't believe that she could safely travel in such weather, and especially not over a six hour drive. Jordan called home and spoke with Kelly, giving her the updated plan. She would phone Jane Morrison in the morning. The couple spent the afternoon playing Monopoly, building their respective financial empires, and rehearsing for their lives in the future. Of this, Jordan had no doubt. The roads were clear by 11:00 a.m. the next morning, and Jordan anticipated a slow trip back home. Carolyn packed lunch and snacks for her, and gave her a half dozen books she had read, so they could share even that time together. Jordan agreed to call her at various stops along the route. They made plans for another visit next month, as work schedules would permit. Jordan planned to volunteer for overtime, so that she could gain another three day weekend by then. In fact, she would do whatever was needed, if she could spend another weekend there soon. They both cried and held each other tenderly, as Jordan prepared to leave. When it was apparent that she could no longer postpone the inevitable, Jordan grabbed her suitcase and her jacket, and headed off, destination: Parkway. Carolyn waited at the window until Jordan's car disappeared behind the hills and two story federals, farmhouses, and Victorians that lined the streets leading to the Interstates.

The ride home was a mix of traffic jams, fender benders, slush covered windshields, and phone calls back to Carolyn. Jordan missed her terribly already, and she toyed with the idea of moving in with her. She thought that with more experience, she might secure a similar job in Vermont. She then dismissed the thought, realizing that Carolyn would be moving back when her fellowship ended next year. They would have to make due with the weekend visits that they could arrange whenever possible. She believed that their love could survive that, even though the wait seemed unbearable. She relived the weekend in her mind, again and again, as she monitored the endless line of taillights. Jordan arrived home just after midnight. Her father was waiting for her in the living room.

"Jordan, we haveta talk . . ." he said, as he made full eye contact with her.

"O.K. Dad, but can this wait until morning? I been drivin' for twelve hours, and I'm exhausted." She was hoping that her father would follow her lead, that he would cut her the leeway he had always given her in the past. But this time, her luck had run out. No amount of charm or pleading would deter Pete Mathews from his intended conversation.

"What's this all about? . . . Ya drive six hours away to be with a woman, and even put your career on the line to do it . . . I don't get this at all." He shook his head, and looked pleadingly but sternly at his daughter. He was afraid of the answer that he would get, but he could not put off the problem any longer. He couldn't do this to himself and his wife, and he wouldn't let his daughter ruin her life in this way.

"I didn't put my career on the line . . . I called out! I spoke with my supervisor and explained the situation. It was too dangerous to drive home." Jordan was flippant in her response. She did not believe that her father would pursue the matter further. But he did.

"So ya called your supervisor . . . you been workin' at that office two weeks, and already you're callin' out? What does that tell her about you? And what does that tell me, knowin' that you did this to be with another woman?"

Jordan did not respond. She did not want to confirm her father's thoughts. But she realized that she was now in the midst of the showdown that she had long feared.

"I'm very lonely, Dad . . . in ways that you could not understand. Do you really want me to go on with this? . . . I've tried it your way, but it doesn't work for me. You can't live my life for me. I can't live my life for you. That doesn't mean that I don't love you and Mom, or that I don't respect you both. It has nothing to do with that. It has to do with me, and living my life the way I was intended to live it."

"So it's all true . . . You wanna be a lesbian, a homosexual? . . . Then you'll do it without this family!" Her father looked down at the floor and maintained a momentary silence.

"I don't want to be a lesbian . . . like it's some choice I'm makin' today . . . like it's some club I wanna belong to . . . like it's some career I've chosen! I am WHO I am, and I've been who I am since I was born. I've only come to accept that fact now, and to strive for some semblance of happiness. You can't live my life for me, and I can't live my life any other way!"

"Maybe I can't live your life for ya. But I can say what kind of life you'll be livin', as long as you're livin' under my roof . . . So make your choices as you see fit, and do what ya have to do to make us all happy here."

"It's not a choice! I didn't choose to be gay—it's what I am, it's who I am, it's who I was intended to be from the point of my birth! The only choice that I have is . . . is the same choice that everyone else has—Do I spend my life alone, or can I share my life with someone. I'm choosing to share my life with someone. Don't you get that? . . . You think that by threatening me, that I will just stop being who I am . . . Well, you're wrong! You think it's so simple, because you don't understand. You're not telling me to stop being gay . . . you're telling me to stop "Being!" And I won't do that for anyone . . . So you have your choices to make, too!"

For the first time in his child's life, Pete Mathews left the room without kissing his daughter good night.[63]

Jordan cried herself to sleep that night. She cried herself to sleep for the next several nights. She used the job as a distraction, and threw herself wholeheartedly into the lives of her clients. She had made her decision, or rather, her father and her nature had made her decision for her. She called Janice and made arrangements to visit her at home. She couldn't say what the real problems were between her and her parents. Janice supposed that Jordan's relationship with her mother had taken another nose dive! She wanted to help. Jordan remembered that her uncle, Paul Guilford, was a realtor in the area. She hoped that he might be able to help locate an apartment for her. Janice agreed to speak with her uncle, and would call her within the week. Jordan was surprised to receive a message from Paul Guilford the next day at work. She contacted him and made an appointment to meet with him that evening. After viewing several apartments at various rent levels, Jordan selected a small, one bedroom flat. She chose the apartment because of its cost and location. The apartment was within two blocks of the ocean, but also within sight of the boardwalk. She rationalized that she could run on the beach before or after work, and in summer, she could ignore the noise and exuberance of young vacationers pretending that they had hooked a spot in Ft. Lauderdale!

Jordan signed a yearly rental agreement with Paul Guilford. Although the apartment was considered a winter rental, Paul balanced the monthly rents over the full year, so that Jordan could afford it. He knew that Janice was fond of Jordan, and that she had helped Janice after the death of her brother. He liked Jordan, too, and wanted to help her establish her first place. The apartment was only partially furnished, and contained an old but comfortable red couch, a double bed with new mattress, and a small dinette set. The kitchen was a galley type, and with a window perched over the sink. Jordan would have a small but clear view of

---

[63] For discussion regarding the loss of key supports due to a gay identity, please refer to Appendix and Bibliography for Chapter Seven.

the bay from this vantage point. She could have dinner as she watched the sunset through that window. The other windows were bright, but offered only views of the other buildings on any side of hers. Jordan would live on the second floor of a three story home on Porter Avenue. She was well acquainted with the area. The neighborhood was quiet in winter, but ungodly noisy in the summer. Spring and fall were a mixed bag, depending on the weather. The Police Department was located only several blocks away. The building was the only one in the area that still had off street parking. Most of the stores and shops in the neighborhood were closed for the winter, but would re-open by mid-May. Jordan arranged to take possession of the apartment on March 31st.

Jordan and Carolyn had been phoning daily since Jordan got back from their weekend together. She told Carolyn that she would be moving to her own apartment at month's end. Carolyn made arrangements to come down that weekend to help her move. Jordan didn't know if her parents would offer any assistance. They had been cold and distant since her return from Vermont. But she had to tell them. Following dinner the next evening, Jordan announced her plan to move. Her father gave a terse and hard, "Fine." Her mother left the room without comment, but Jordan could hear her crying in their bedroom for most of the night. She had anticipated a horrendous scene, and was thankful that both Jonathan and Kelly had unwittingly derailed this possibility by their mere presence.

\* \* \*

The office was especially busy over the next two weeks. In some ways, this was a good thing, because Jordan spent less time at home, and under the censure of her parents. Jordan responded to four abuse allegations on her own caseload in that time. Luckily, only two could be substantiated: welts from a bare-butt belt beating on a 10 year old; and in another family, an open hand slap with bruising on the face of an 11 year old. Both families agreed to return to counseling and to refrain from use of physical discipline. Jordan demonstrated how a facial slap could cause permanent injury if the child moved, or if the parent missed and hit the eye, nose, or throat. The mother realized that the potential risk of the slap outweighed the benefit of its use, even if teaching her child not to talk back. The mother indicated that she would rethink her discipline strategy. In yet another family, an allegation of a lack of supervision was unsubstantiated, when it was ascertained that a neighbor was actually watching the seven year old after school.

The fourth allegation was made by Mary against her foster parents. Mary reported that her foster mother threatened to "smack her face in," after she told the foster mother to "kiss her ass." Jordan spent most of the next two days locating another foster home, taking Mary for a physical at the hospital, moving Mary first to the shelter, and then to another foster home, transferring her to yet another school, and helping foster family and child make this newest adjustment. Jordan tried to counsel Mary, but without benefit.

"So, here we are again! But how did we get here? Tell me what you think brought on this newest change in foster homes." Jordan started to confront Mary about her behavior.

"Kiss my ass!" Mary responded with a curt demand.

"Oh come on now—I know you can do better that. You're a smart kid, and I know you have a better answer than that one." Jordan prodded in reply.

"OK, kiss my fucking ass!" Mary snorted back.

The afternoon was a three hour barrage of Mary's insults, and Jordan's striving for calm and patience with her. Somehow in the commotion to move, Mary lost a garbage bag full of her own clothes. Jordan had to take her clothes-shopping before the new foster mother would accept her into placement. They went to Donnelly's Department Store, and while Mary was supposedly trying on clothes, she tried to give Jordan the slip! Her plan was only foiled when she attempted to leave the store with several tapes and a bracelet stuffed under her blouse. The security alarm blared through the store as Mary was grabbed by a guard. She poured on the tears!

Store Security hauled Mary into their office and threatened to charge her with shoplifting. Jordan's name was suddenly paged over the store's loudspeaker, and she reported to the Security office. When she arrived there, Mary was now crying hysterically that she was a ward of the state, a poor foster child, and that her foster parents would make her go to an institution! Jordan presented I.D., validated Mary's statements, and accepted possession of her. The store agreed to forgo the charges. They did, however, place Mary's name on a shoplifter list, and warned that she was no longer welcome there. Jordan purchased the clothing that Mary left on the floor of the dressing room, much to her protests. She deposited Mary that evening in the care of her newest foster family, but she knew that she would be back within a month to start the process again. She almost felt guilty leaving the family within this child's reach.

And so it would go—Jordan and Mary seemed locked in this dance together, each an unwitting partner of the other. It seemed the more time Jordan devoted to the wayward girl, the more she acted out! Yet Jordan was beginning to genuinely like her, despite the protests and exasperations of the co-workers who went before her. She liked the wildness of her heart, and the creative processes of her thinking. Jordan marveled at how Mary strove for such individuality, for a uniqueness of thought, while she herself struggled so hard to be like others. She found Mary to be a wonderment in a culture of straight-jacket boxes! In a world where everyone else's thinking was already programmed by grade school, young Mary was ripe with thoughts outside the established possibility. Jordan started to guide her toward the humanities. With Mary's ability to conclude a full conversation with the simple flip of a middle finger, or the command of a single foul word, Jordan assessed that she would more likely enjoy Hemmingway than Faulkner! It would be some time, and several more foster homes, before Jordan realized that she would like neither. But she did like art—specifically, sketching and pastels. Her school books, her notepads, her clothing, her arms were covered in her own artwork! Jordan gleaned whatever supplies she could scrounge from Jonathan and Carolyn, and gave them to Mary each time that she saw her.

But she didn't really make progress with the girl, until she had moved her for the sixth time. They were having their usual placement discussions.

"Any thoughts about why you're having to go through this again?" Jordan asked.

"Yeah, you keep placing me with fucking assholes!" Mary replied.

"How do you think your behavior may have contributed to this whole placement problem?" Jordan was trying to help Mary examine her own role in the upheavals that now came every three weeks.

"Look, Jordan, I'm really not in the mood for your bullshit today," she snapped in reply. She then took out a notebook and started drawing a portrait of a mother and child seated at opposite end of the hospital waiting room. The child was obviously ill, coughing and whining, as his mother cradled him in her arms. Mary sat with her back to Jordan, but occasionally spewed out a line of vileness toward her that just bounced off Jordan's back.

"Fuckin' caseworkers think they know everything. You have no idea what it's like . . ." Then later, as if accenting her statement, she said, "Why don't you go fuck yourself?"

Throughout this time, Jordan sat quietly watching the waiting room TV, watching the emerging artwork, and listening to Mary's thought processes. She was amazed at the sensitivity that Mary captured between mother and child. Yet all the while, she launched her tirade of insults. Jordan did not try to set limits with Mary that day. She did not strive to redirect or to calm her. She did not try to ignore her, or to distance from her. She did not defend herself from the onslaught. She just sat quietly, patiently, and searched for a key to understanding her, as the child spewed forth her venom.

When she was without reaction, Mary said, "You make me sick!" and moved to another part of the room. Jordan allowed her the space. Mary was coolly cooperative with the pre-placement physical, and the nurse and attending physician hurried the ordeal along, so as not to incite a fist fight!

Not surprisingly, Mary had a sinus infection. Illness was common in foster children, particularly those subject to frequent re-placements. Jordan theorized that it was the result of the severe stress the children were under. At any rate, she needed an antibiotic, and Jordan and Mary went into the pharmacy to get the prescription filled. While standing in line to pay, Mary asked Jordan to buy her a candy bar. Jordan was taken aback, as Mary had never asked anyone for anything before. Jordan looked at Mary, and instructed her to pick out the candy bar of her choice.

"I'm buying you this candy, not because of the two hours of shear misery you have just put me through, but that despite those two hours of sheer misery, you remain a human being who is worthy of love."

For the first time in her life, Mary thanked someone for something she had been given. While there would be numerous confrontations and challenges as this young lady inched her way to adulthood, and as Jordan moved toward retirement, the two had established a groundwork that would move their relationship forward. This was Mary's breakthrough, and her life slowly began to turn for the better. Jordan held the memory of that day in her heart, as she struggled with perhaps the hundred other teenagers to come, who would also tell her to "kiss off" in unnatural, improbable, unspeakable, ways.[64]

\* \* \*

Carolyn actually came down the night before Jordan was to move, but stayed in a motel, and well away from the Mathews home. She and Jordan had dinner at a cafe nearby, but Jordan spent the night in her own bedroom. She did not want to taunt her parents. This was not about her relationship with them. She hoped that in time, they would accept and respect her as the person that she was, and not as the illusion that they wanted her to be. Surprisingly to Jordan, Pete Mathews and his pick up truck were available to help move her belongings from home to apartment. He even helped carry some of the heavier items, and brought

---

[64] For discussion on behavioral and psychological issues of adolescents in foster care, please refer to Appendix and Bibliography for Chapter Seven.

a small, used living room set from one of his friends. Jordan's mother stayed in her bedroom for most of the day, and was not present when the two drove the eight miles to the new apartment. Although Jordan mentioned that Carolyn was also down to help with the relocation, Pete Mathews was still taken aback, as she entered the apartment with a pizza. He and Jordan had just finished carrying the second chair of the living room set into the apartment. Jordan was downstairs re-parking her own car.

"Oh . . . Mr. Mathews . . . how nice to see you again. I'm Carolyn, Jordan's friend. Would you care for some pizza?"

"No thanks." He looked imploringly in her eyes, half threatening, half begging her. "Look, no small talk . . . You have taken my daughter from me . . ."

Before he could finish, Carolyn interjected, "I haven't taken Jordan from you, Mr. Mathews. She's right here for you whenever you want her. All you have to do is reach out to her . . . You know that. She loves you both so much . . ."

"Don't even start that with me. You know what I mean . . ."

Jordan then entered the apartment and the two fell silent. She feigned warmth and pleasantry, and tried to ignore the negative energy that she could see between the two. The tension was heightened by Pete Mathews' resolve. Carolyn was visibly shaken. Yet, she maintained her calm, and was gentle and polite to her would be father-in-law.

"Dad, why not stay and have something to eat?" Jordan asked her father.

"Nah, I haveta go!" Pete Mathews dismissed himself and walked toward the door.

"Dad, please! Don't go!" Jordan begged him again.

Pete Mathews looked at Carolyn, then kissed his daughter on the forehead, and left the apartment. He did not look back. Jordan cried for a bit, and allowed Carolyn to soothe her.

"Well, that was a good start. At least he talked to me . . . I think I read somewhere that a gay lover of a prince was tossed out the castle window by an English King, like, way back, when he met his father-in-law! Well, I'm still here...." Carolyn said. Jordan did not respond.

"Believe me, once they have the time to adjust, things will get better. Maybe we won't be invited over for a Sunday get-together, but you will be, in time... Just give them the time that they need. And no matter what, keep the lines of communication open to them."

Carolyn cradled Jordan in her arms, much as Jordan had seen the hospital mother caring for her child. Carolyn had now assumed the role of protector and nurturer as well as lover. Jordan took comfort from their deepening relationship, and from the genuine commitment they had made to each other. Still, she could not calm the fear that she had lost her father forever. She had to trust that Carolyn was right.

They spent the remainder of the day "playing house" as they called it—hanging curtains, washing and stacking dishes in the cupboard, cleaning and stocking the refrigerator and pantry, unpacking and hanging Jordan's clothes. By midnight, most of the essentials were in place. Jordan arranged a framed photo of her and Carolyn on the nightstand beside their bed. Bill had taken the photo when Jordan visited Carolyn in Vermont. Jordan also placed a framed photo of her family on the end table in the living room. She flipped the picture down in defiance of her father's behavior. Carolyn was making the bed when Jordan picked up a pillow from the couch, and pelted her with it.

Carolyn was exhausted. She just looked at Jordan, shook her head, and chided, "Must you..."

"Obviously, I must, or I would not have done it," Jordan replied. She smiled at her partner, then reached out to take her in her arms. As their bodies made contact, Carolyn pelted Jordan with the pillow she had thrown at her.

"Must you..." Jordan asked.

"Obviously, I must, or I would not have done it," Carolyn replied, mimicking Jordan's voice. Jordan kissed Carolyn, then tapping her on the chin, added, "Very

Funny." They kissed again, helped undress the other for a shower together, toweled off, and went to bed.

"Do you really think that they will ever make the adjustment?" Jordan asked. Carolyn's nakedness rolled against Jordan's own body.

"I do . . . just as I believed that you would resolve your issues and make the adjustment. But it takes time, and you have to be patient . . . and you have to be forgiving, and you have to bite your tongue sometimes . . . and most of all, you have to remember that you love them . . . that makes all the rest of it possible. In the meantime, you have your friends, and you have me, to help keep you on the right side of things . . . You know, it's too easy to let this destroy you . . . to rob you of your self esteem, your feelings of self worth. You have to remember that you are a good person who is worthy of love."

Jordan remembered Karen also once saying that to her.

"How do you know all of this stuff? I mean, how did you get to that point?"

"Therapy, much therapy," Carolyn replied.

They made slow, desperate love for most of the early morning hours, each surrendering to the touch of the other. Jordan let the waves of sensation wash through her body, as images of the ocean surf washed through her mind. Carolyn's mind danced with snowflakes and wisps of wind, as her body danced to the touch of her love. They watched together the rising sun move across the floor. The sunbeams made a rainbow of color against the wall, as the couple drank tea and perused the morning paper. They had to speed through the rest of the morning's tasks, so that Carolyn could get back to Vermont by early evening. She still had class preparations that needed tending before she could sleep again. Their partings were becoming more and more difficult, as each tried to find some reason to stay together just a few moments longer. They would likely not see each other again until mid-June. Carolyn planned to spend the first week following semester's close with Jordan at their "place at the shore," as she now referred to Jordan's apartment. But even the kidding about having both a shore and a mountain home failed to make the distance any less bitter.

With the expense of the new apartment, Jordan could only phone Carolyn on Saturdays, but she would write daily. Carolyn also wrote daily, and called her on Wednesdays. They had to save for the future. It was not the life that they would have preferred, but it was the only arrangement that could work for them both at that point in time. They clung to the belief that they would soon be together for the rest of their lives. It was this sole thought that carried them through this separation.

As Jordan watched the car speed off toward the parkway, she looked down at the stone chess set near the window overlooking the street below. Bill sent the chess game as a housewarming gift for Jordan. They played a game together when Jordan last visited Carolyn, and Bill clobbered her! Now, she saw that Carolyn had taken an interest.

"Opening with the same knight that Bill does! . . ." Jordan made a counter-move, and let the game stand until Carolyn's next visit. It was almost like she was just waiting for Carolyn to come back into the living room, and not like Jordan was living until Carolyn could come back home again.

And then, of course, there was the job. She was thankful for that. At least it kept her mind busy until she could be with Carolyn again. She was often so exhausted after a day in the field that she could barely cook and eat dinner before she would fall asleep on the couch. She spent so much time talking on the office phone that she grew to enjoy writing letters to Carolyn as the preferable release. She thought that she was getting "phone ear," and often heard her desk phone ringing in her mind well into REM sleep. Her co-workers were a great distraction, too, when they had the time to talk, usually at the start or the end of the day. She liked her unit members, and felt that they worked pretty well together. They had each taken her on home visits, as she assumed her caseload responsibilities there. They each shared their unique perspective on the job and the agency. Jordan assessed their individual styles, talents, and skills, and she learned to trust their opinions. She would often turn to them—use them as a sounding board—when a particularly difficult case was assigned to her. And they learned to trust and to seek advice from her, too. At least, most of them did.

Besides Tina, there was Michelle Higgins, Barbara Schmidt, Jennifer Malcolm, and John Crittenden. John assumed an unofficial leadership role on the unit whenever Jane Morrison was out. He actually had seniority over only half of the other unit members—Michelle and Jordan. He had no special training for the role, and no other outstanding characteristics, except that he was a male, and therefore, women naturally deferred to him. This partly caused the rising tension between John and Jordan, and became more obvious after Jordan had been there about six months. John feared her competence, and Jordan resented his de facto privilege! She could not say why it was so, but she did not trust him. Perhaps it was his eagerness to assume command without having received designation, or having proven his skills. For whatever the reason, Jordan tried hard to avoid him in the office, and would privately consult with other unit members when Jane Morrison was not available.

She would think back, much later in her career, to these dynamics of near sibling rivalry. She would imagine how much differently her career might have gone, had she not, back then, raised the ire of so formidable a foe. But she was young, and eager, and enthusiastic, and dedicated—and a ladder-climber like John Crittenden naturally took her in his sights! She found herself dodging his verbal bullets, and countering with professional proselytizing after just months on the unit. The women marveled at her aptitude, if not her balls! Jordan took in the office politics. She knew that she would never be in John's realm of power or protection there. John had identified Jordan early as one of the enemy!

But on the positive side, Jane Morrison praised Jordan to the D.O. Manager whenever she had the chance. She was impressed by Jordan's keen instincts, and her skills at assessing a family and engaging them in treatment. She thought that Jordan's persuasive discussions with her client families really moved them forward, and readied them for counseling interventions. She marveled at her patience in dealing with families in crisis. She believed that Jordan had a unique gift of relating to her clients, and that she used that gift to truly reach them. She encouraged Jordan to take specialized courses whenever BCS offered them. She mentored Jordan in her contacts with the community, and coached her in matters of court documentation, or in issues involving child placement. She was helping Jordan climb ladders of her own.

Jordan was quickly building an office-wide reputation! Although her approaches may have been somewhat unorthodox, she managed to bring families to their needed destinations, their appropriate case goals. She began to receive more complex case assignments. She tapped deeply into her knowledge base and personality reserves, as she searched for the appropriate words, the motivating ideas, that would bring families to a heightened awareness. She made good use of self. She dressed in jeans and flats, and wore casual blouses and coats. She used her natural vernacular, and discovered that she was raised in the language—the working class dialect—of most of her clients. Although she had not realized this, she used working class attitudes and beliefs as the framework for her interventions. She acknowledged the parents' rights and responsibilities to discipline their kids. She emphasized their love of their children, while she challenged their disciplining methods. She defined these inappropriate punishments as the "real culprits," the real cause of harm to the children, while praising the strengths in each family. She made herself available to her clients in the late afternoon and early evening hours, so that they would not miss work. She knew that they needed every cent possible to make ends meet! And she was keenly aware of financial struggle—after all, she had been raised in it! She viewed her interventions as a remedy, and not as a sentence. She saw that her families could accept state intervention on those terms.

Jordan soon found herself being called into case conferences with her supervisor and the D.O. Manager. She believed that she was being used as a consultant, and that she was being assigned the most difficult cases due to her expertise and her sensitivity. It never occurred to Jordan that she had been chosen because she was expendable! Yet with each new case, she and her assigned family met the designated case goals. She even testified on a few cases, and received praise from the Superior Court Judges. Jordan seemed poised for a long, successful career with the agency. She wished that she could share her success with her own parents, but her Dad and Mom limited their contacts with Jordan to brief conversations that she initiated over the phone. Jordan found this all a strange irony.

She was thinking about her parents as she pulled into the dirt road that led to her next client family, the Palinsky's. They were a "single mother" family, with a preteen son, and a teenaged daughter. James, a depressive uncle, also resided with them on their old chicken farm. Ms. Palinsky had inherited the resident rights from her parents, but her only brother held the deed to the place, and he charged her rent. The chickens had been gone for generations, but the faint odor of manure still rode the air on the wet, warm days of spring. Like most of Jordan's parents, Ms. Palinsky was a recovering alcoholic who had a recent slip. She completed a three day detox. and was again attending meetings. Jordan decided to make an unannounced visit to the Palinsky's, when the Branford's skipped out of their scheduled appointment. But she also felt an unexplainable and compelling need to visit the Palinsky's on that day. As she turned from the road to the field where the house was located, she could see several police cars and a sheriff's sedan parked along side of the house. Ms. Palinsky and the children were crying and pleading with the officers, who had apparently just removed them from the home! The family ran to Jordan's state car when they spotted it.

"Ms. Mathews! . . . We're bein' evicted, and the cops won't listen . . ." Jordan gleaned that much information from the competing screams, chaos, and distress of the family members.

Jordan parked the car near the house, and spoke with the family out of earshot of the police. She could smell alcohol, but she noted that Ms. Palinsky did not appear intoxicated. She did vomit once during the conversation, but said it was due to her nerves. Janet, the teenaged daughter, led the conversation. She was used to filling in whenever her mother wasn't able to parent or to make a logical decision.

"Uncle John and Mom have been arguin' for weeks over stupid stuff. We just found out this mornin' that he's tryin' to sell the property right out from under us! That's against Grandma's will, and he knows it! But somehow, he went to court behind Mom's back and got an eviction order. Look, the first papers are even dated when she was in the hospital! The police don't wanna hear anything. They said they have a court order, and that's what they have to go by. We didn't even know this was happenin' until the cops banged on the door this mornin'..." Janet pulled at Jordan's arm.

Young James added, "And we don't have no place to go. I said we should just go and plop ourselves down right in the middle of Uncle John's livin' room, but the police said that he has a court order, and that we're not allowed over there. I even tried to call him, but he's not answerin' the phone . . . How can he do this to his own kin like that!"

"It's disgusting," the girl added. "And all our stuff is in there, and they won't let us get anything."

Jordan was trying hard to think of something to say. The words would not seem to come.

"And Mr. Peepers is in there, too! John don't have the right!" Young James shouted, in part, echoing his mother's comments.

Jordan took the papers from Young James' hand and reviewed them. She had never seen an eviction notice before, and was not clear as to procedural issues. She tried to advocate for the family as best she could, and in her most official but cooperative voice, she introduced herself to the responding officers. They were cordial, yet firm.

"I'm Officer Loengren, and this is Sheriff's Deputy Scott Halpern. As you can see, the paperwork is in order, and the family is being evicted today at the request of the owner, and at the order of the court."

"Is it possible to delay the eviction?" Jordan asked. "Ms. Palinsky was in the hospital during the initial court proceedings, and this is only coming to my attention now. The family has no place to go . . . Can they lodge an appeal and stay here until the court reviews the matter? Don't the courts usually give thirty days following a court order before an eviction occurs?" She thought she had read something like that in her BCS Training Manual.

"Ma'am, the occupant was given official notice five days ago and failed to lodge an appeal with the Court within the prescribed time. We have no recourse but to enforce the eviction."

Jordan looked toward Ms. Palinsky, who looked to her, then down at the ground. "Were you advised that you could make an appeal?"

The mother shook her head, but gave no statement about why she failed to do so. She then sobbed, "I never thought he would do this to me. I never thought he would do this to us, his own flesh and blood . . ."

She began crying his name, as if he might finally hear her pleas and change his mind. The children started crying with her, stroking her back and telling her not to worry, in comforting ways. It was clear to them that they would again be taking care of her. Jordan knew she couldn't out-trump the cops, but she did convince them to wait with the family until she spoke with her supervisor.

Jane Morrison concurred that Ms. Palinsky missed her appeal deadline, and that the family had no recourse. She agreed to contact the County Welfare Board so that they could arrange emergency housing for the family. Jordan would assist with the family's transport to the assigned motel. And, by the way, Jordan would also have to investigate a neglect referral on another family on her caseload that evening! That father was chronically unemployed, and the family now had no food or working utilities.

As Jordan drove back to the Palinsky home, she wondered about how she could help the family through this crisis. They had only known life in that house. Jordan herself had only moved out of her parent's place a month ago! And some things they just didn't teach in school! Ms. Palinsky had no savings or other resources, and probably wouldn't receive any money when the house was sold.

Even if she did, the family had been living on welfare, and that agency would claim a repayment! They would be no better off.

With Ms. Palinsky's permission, Jordan tried to contact John Palinsky to ask that he rescind the eviction. He didn't return her call. Jordan also learned that the property was sold well before the eviction. Even with an appeal, the most the family could have hoped for was just a few more weeks to find a place! Jordan concluded that they would have to do that from a motel room. Since Uncle James Palinsky received General Assistance, he would be housed with the family at Welfare's expense. They were already helping him to reapply for SSI and Social Security Disability because of his mental illness. He was working odd jobs until recently. Uncle James Palinsky was calm and quiet throughout the whole ordeal. He was watching silently for a solution that he knew would never come.

Jordan again parked along side of the house, but the children could see from her stride that she wasn't successful in saving their home. These kids learned early to read body language. It was a primary survival technique in the family! They began crying almost immediately, as Mrs. Palinsky again wailed the name of her brother.

"John, John, what have ya done? What have ya done to us, your own family?"

She cried and rocked herself in the front seat of the state car, as the children cried in the back seat, each rubbing a child's hand across the shoulder and back of their mother. The anger now displaced by fear and despair, the family turned to Jordan Mathews as their only hope and hero of the future. It was probably best that they didn't know that she had only just gotten her own apartment! But she knew it. And she was afraid for them.

Jordan was able to negotiate with the police, and they allowed the family to pack whatever belongings they could cram into suitcases and garbage bags. The police transported these items to the motel room, while Jordan tried to console the family with whatever reassurance and cliché she could muster. She took the family and Mr. Peepers, their cat, to the home of a friend, who agreed to keep the calico until the family had housing again. The family cried at the separation from Mr. Peepers, as they would have mourned the separation from any other member of their family.

The motel was located in the north county, and was comprised of a series of small cabins. The family was placed in a duplex cabin, with an adjoining door that they could leave open. Like most of the welfare motels, the place had a worn appearance, and loitering drunks and drug addicts of every type lounged on the property. Jordan worried for the safety of the girl, knowing that she, too, was in the age of experimentation. She saw that Janet was parentified—that there was an inappropriate adultness and responsibility to her thinking and behaviors, the result of caring for her mother, as her mother should have cared for them. Maybe the kids should have been removed when they were young, but Jordan guessed that things probably hadn't deteriorated there until the grandmother died. The kids were older by then. The family bonding was strong, though—maybe too strong, even bordering on enmeshment—yet enough to sustain the children to adulthood. In the meantime, counseling could address and maybe resolve that enmeshment, so that the kids could grow into more healthy adult relationships. The mother was still working toward sobriety. Family supervision seemed shared between mother and uncle. When one slipped into depression or drunkenness, the other would rouse to assume control and responsibility—a kind of see-saw parenting, with Janet actually taking care of her younger brother.

Jordan thought about the alternatives—place the kids with John Palinsky, the only known relative, who himself was supervised periodically by BCS for alcoholism? Or, place them into foster homes until they aged out of the system? They probably wouldn't be placed together, and as Jordan had already seen, they would likely bounce from foster home to foster home until they reached eighteen. And then what? Think of the damage that strategy could cause! So she looked again at Ms. Palinsky and her Uncle James—a mother with periodic slips, and an uncle stabilized on medication. Maybe she could patch the family until the kids had grown, or at least, until a better situation could materialize. It was not perfection, but it seemed the best alternative for these kids—and for their family—at that point in time. Jordan would continue to monitor them, and possibly, she could develop other placement resources for them. She would provide interventive counseling and other services to ensure the safety of the children, as situation and circumstance warranted. Jordan called Ms. Palinsky out into the parking lot to speak with her privately.

"I know that you've had a very rough time today, and from what I've come to know about you, you've always had a pretty rough time of it. But you've always done best when you've been sober. Am I right here?" Jordan asked, as she looked into Ms. Palinsky's eyes. She nodded that she believed that this was true.

"It's especially important then, that you maintain your sobriety, now more than ever! If you keep drinkin', you will not be able to get out of this housing emergency, and you will lose your children to foster care. You won't be able to think rationally, or to problem solve any other way . . . Your kids can't do this for you. They're countin' on you to do this for them. I am here to help you get back on your feet. I am countin' on you to do this for them, and for yourself . . . I know that you were drinkin' today. You only got out of detox. five weeks ago! So I don't think that the AA meetings are enough to help you right now. So, I'm gonna refer you to a partial day treatment program in town. You'll be attending sessions three and a half hours every morning. That'll still leave plenty of time to look for a place in the afternoons. You might even be able to latch onto a housing grant if you maintain sobriety. You won't be able to latch onto anything but insanity, if you don't. I'm bankin' on your past success to help you through this. I know that you've been sober for long periods before. I don't know what's goin' on now, but the drinking has to stop NOW! Are you with me on this?"

"I wasn't drinkin'! I already told you that I got sick because I was upset. I was not drinkin'! I know what'll happen if I pick up again! You don't haveta tell me anything that I already know!"

"Don't tell me that! When you deny like that, the only one you're foolin' is yourself. Don't ya think I could smell the liquor on your breath? Don't ya think

I can see a difference in you, when you've been drinkin'? You're not the same person. It's that's obvious . . . Don't try to fool everybody so you can keep drinkin'. Just get the help ya need so that ya can maintain your sobriety. Without it, you will fail. And you will lose your kids."

After a few moments, the response came softly. "It was scotch. I know I gotta stop! I can't go on like this . . ."

"Then try the partial day treatment, OK? But make a pact with me now that you will not drink from this point out. I can make the referral in the morning, and if we're lucky, you could start the next day there." Jordan was praying that Ms. Palinsky would buy into the program. She saw this as her only hope for the family. And she didn't have a better line to convince her, if Ms. Palinsky started to challenge the logic!

"I can try . . . There's no booze in the room right now. Everything's back at the house . . . So, I guess that I'll be hearin' from ya tomorrow then? But how am I gonna find another place? There's no other place that I can afford . . ."

"The motel should have a newspaper, and the Welfare Department usually keeps a list of low income rentals. There's a few realtors in the area that may give ya a lead. Ya haveta start makin' calls to see what ya can find. I want you ta keep a list of all the places that ya contact, so that we can review them together . . . ya know, and figure out from there what to do next. But the important thing is not to get frustrated . . . Keep workin' your program, and take it one day at a time."

She heard the hollowness in her voice, as she tried to smooth out the enormous tasks that lay ahead for this woman. Jordan knew that she was telling her to do the near impossible! Mrs. Palinsky shook her head slowly and imploringly at Jordan. She could not answer.

"Maybe Uncle James can make some calls and help ferret out an apartment. Start with the garden apartments over on Palmer Avenue. And don't forget the duplexes and storefronts along Main Street. Some of the shopkeepers might know of a place that's open. They usually rent cheaper than the single family homes. Good luck, get some sleep, and we'll talk again tomorrow."

Jordan left the woman standing just outside of her motel room. She saw the woman's hopelessness seep through her body, as she stared at Jordan through the eyes of despair. Jordan shuddered with the thought that she was the last hope for this woman and her family. She felt herself shrink behind catch phrases and shell-game resources. She was no hero—she wasn't made of that stuff! And yet, she had to be everybody's hero! That familiar, sickening feeling of self-doubt again formed in the pit of her stomach. But she did have an epiphany about what it meant to "speak in tongues"—Jordan otherwise had no idea where her counseling statements came from, unless from the Holy Spirit!

"Well, maybe she could also hook up an apartment for them . . ." Jordan thought.

It was now 6:00 p.m. and already dark, as Jordan drove to her next investigation. The Bronson family should have been home several hours ago. Yet, the house was dark as Jordan drove up to the home. She usually parked slightly down the street from the homes of her clients, so that she would not attract the attention of the neighbors to her visits. She felt her families deserved that level of respect and privacy. She stepped over the broken cyclone gate, and knocked through the missing-screen storm door, her knuckles tapping loudly against the faded and peeling paint of front door. After several more knocks, she circled the home to ascertain if the family was present in one of the back rooms. She surmised then that no one was home.

"The Bronsons' ain't home," called a voice from the window next door. It was too dark to see the face connected with the flow of information. "They left early today to visit their relatives in Georgia. Don't know when they'll be back."

"Do you know why they decided to go? Is there some kind'a problem?" Jordan was fishing for information. She didn't expect to get answers, but sometimes she got lucky. She had several families in this neighborhood, and she had a pretty good reputation among the people there already. Sometimes they would give her information, if they thought it would help a family. She worked hard to establish and maintain this level of trust in the community.

"Didn't say, but I know they been havin' money problems. Marriage problems, too. Can't tell ya any more dan 'at."

"Thanks, you've been a great help already. Maybe I'll stop by later in the week to talk with them. Maybe they'll be back by then." Jordan left a card in the front door, with a note asking that Mrs. Bronson contact her. She knew that her husband would never call.

"OK, Ms. Mathews" the voice called back, and the window slammed to a shut. She didn't know the identity of the neighbor, and was taken aback that the woman knew her name! She felt confident, though, that she now had at least one member of the community that was looking out for her. Before long, there wasn't a part of the county that people wouldn't take up a baseball bat in her defense!

"Now that's a rapport with the community!" Jordan thought proudly, as she ministered to her clients. She thought again about the Holiness Pentecostal Church, and the relationships she had developed there as a volunteer in their outreach center.

It was almost 7:00 p.m. when she left the agency parking lot and headed over the bridge to her apartment. The driveway would be lit, but her staircase was always too dark to climb comfortably. She kept a flashlight in her car for just such occasions. As she unlocked her door, she heard the ringing of her phone and flew through the kitchen to answer it. The call was from Marge. She and Janice were getting together on Saturday for a day trip to the city to shop and have dinner at Tyler's restaurant. Jordan jumped at the chance to spend the day with her friends! She felt a great relief knowing that the recent separation from them was due to work schedules and not her lifestyle. She toyed with the idea of telling them about Carolyn but decided against it. Jordan already tasted how hard her life could be, and she did not want to add any more flavorings to the mixture!

Jordan gazed at Carolyn's picture as she jotted off the day's letter to her. She promised her, as she held the letter tight to her heart, that it wouldn't always have to be this way. She sealed the envelop with a kiss, and settled down for sleep in the hopes of sharing a dream with her.

\* \* \*

Saturday came before she realized it, and Jordan had to hustle to get an outfit together for the big jaunt to the city. It wasn't that she didn't have appropriate clothing—it was that she didn't have any appropriate clean clothing! She was so busy at work that week, that she didn't have time or inclination to do laundry! She thought about Marge's laundry strategy. She pulled out her hamper, and began smelling arm pits for a relatively acceptable blouse. When none could be located, she decided on a turtleneck sweater and a pair of faded blue jeans. She would try for the Village look! She accessorized with a large necklace, and placed bangles on her right wrist. She wore a matching pair of hoop earrings, and her brown leather boots. She chose a jean jacket, and gave thanks for the unusually warm spring day. Luckily, the sun was shining and the winds were quiet. She would not have to face the typically chilling breezes that notoriously whipped around skyscraper and storefront.

As she pulled into the driveway of the Jorgensen home, Janice and Marge ran out the door to greet her. The girls screamed and hugged each other, happy that they were finally together again! It was nearly three months since they had all been together, although Jordan had visited with each of them at least a few times. They had both been to her apartment, but work schedules kept blocking any possibility of a reunion before now. Marge commented that she and Tyler never had a weekend alone because of the restaurant. She guarded their days off like a vulture protecting carrion! And Janice had been traveling down to see Martin on the weekends at least twice a month. She liked the Gaithersburg area, and thought that they might settle there if they ever married, and after her parents were gone. She knew that her parents would never move from their family home. Life there kept them close to Stephen. And they were too old now to make the change.

The girls each continued their own contacts with Karen and Todd. It was as if Karen had tailored her relationships to meet the needs of each of her friends. Maybe this had been the real basis of their love all along. It saddened

Jordan when she realized that the dynamics of the Group had so changed over the last year. They no longer saw themselves as that single entity. They were individuals again, now living their lives in the adult world of job and family. The webs of connection, the threads of the tapestry, were still there, but they were less tightly interwoven. It saddened her more when she decided that she could not share with them the one relationship that gave her such a sense of completeness.

Janice drove them to the city. They parked in a day lot in Greenwich Village, and near the Cellar where Tyler worked as associate chef. The girls spent the afternoon perusing old bookstores and rummaging through the boutiques and antique shops that stood shoulder to shoulder along the avenues there. After a break at a coffeehouse, they lounged around Washington Square Park, watching the street performers and assessing the fashion of the local elite. Despite her attempts, Jordan seemed blatantly conservative by comparison, a source of real disappointment to her! Secretly, she wanted to blend with the Gay Community, but now, she looked just like any other straight college chick touring the Big Apple! She did get a few nods from some of the gay couples as they walked by, and she managed to sneak the "Hey Baby flirt-eye" to a few women who stared an interest in her. She thought that she must have tripped off their gayometer, the mythical though relevant internal barometer of all things homosexual! She loved Carolyn, but she was still a young, healthy, sexually alert lesbian (although she still choked on the word!). Marge and Janice were oblivious to it, as they basked in the sun, and watched the asses of the young men that trotted by. Jordan thought that this was just as well. She believed that she was now part of a sisterhood, whose members knew each other by instinct alone.

They arrived at the restaurant just before 6:00 p.m., and were immediately seated at a reserved table near the door of the kitchen. They occasionally caught sight of Tyler at work as the waiters and waitresses carted off his newest creations to a hungry and adoring public. He winked to Jordan when he caught her eye, and blew a kiss to his devoted Marge, as the swinging door again flopped to a close. He liked the job immensely, but the commuting sapped any possibility of free time or energy beyond sex.

Before they knew it, the group was surrounded by wait staff holding large circular serving trays bedecked with watercress salads adorned with almonds and splashed with a light raspberry vinaigrette. Fresh baked bread with a chewy crust and a dollop of butter melting in the center of the loaf accented the main course—duck papaya with a pineapple stuffing, baked potatoes, and julienne carrots and parsnips. They were served a blushing champagne just before dessert. Tyler joined them briefly, raised a toast to the girls, and made the announcement.

"Your attention please! I dedicate this meal, this day, this celebration to my lovely Marge, who has graciously accepted my invitation to share my life, to bare my children, to share apartment expenses starting next month in Montclair, and to join me in wedded bliss next June! To you, my Beloved!"

The girls let out a shriek, as Marge grabbed the center of attention.

"That's right, Ladies. All that cool handed calculation has finally paid off. The man has realized that he cannot go on through life without me! Of course there's the added benefit of more time for sex, and more energy for it, too, now that he won't have nearly the commute."

As Jordan silently guessed and secretly resented, Marge's father promised them a house as a wedding gift! He was already researching properties in the Nutley area. The couple would still be close enough to visit Marge's parents on a day off, and Marge presumed that any house purchased would accommodate overnight visits by them. It seemed that their lives were already fixed, and that neither objected now to the assistance or intrusions of her parents. Tyler made the adjustment as needs dictated—a sure sign that Marge had penetrated his psyche!

Discussion of the upcoming nuptials monopolized their ride, as Janice drove the three from the Village to Marge's home that night. The couple had not yet picked out wedding rings, and the engagement ring was still being sized. Tyler wanted Marge to put off the announcement until she actually had the engagement ring in her possession, but schedules and excitement dictated otherwise. So again,

Tyler submitted to Marge's demands. Jordan and Janice would be among the four bridesmaids, with Marge's cousin serving as Matron of Honor. The couple planned to have their wedding reception at the Country Club, where Karen and Todd's had been. They hoped this would bring them luck! The celebration would be huge and elaborate (Jordan could bet), and the Country Club was one of the few places classy enough, and expensive enough, to accommodate them! Marge's father was already in negotiations with the Club's director, and they were working out a date. The couple would be married at the First Presbyterian Church, where Marge's mother had attended for years. At Marge's insistence, Tyler agreed to send a wedding invitation to his father, but he hoped that he wouldn't accept it. He hadn't heard from his father since that fight. The couple hadn't yet told Martin, or Karen and Todd about their plans. Marge laughed, though, that the advance notice should give Jordan plenty of time to pick up a guy for the day! Jordan cringed at that prospect. Perhaps she could use a rent-a-date service . . . She knew that Carolyn wouldn't be invited, and certainly, not as her date! She toyed with the idea of a male disguise for her—maybe a mustache and a tailored suite—like she had seen once in an old sitcom she watched as a kid, when she stayed home sick from school one day. But with Carolyn's bust size, she gave up that idea almost immediately!

The wedding plans had finalized as the car entered Marge's driveway. The girls said their good-byes in their usual manner, and promised to get together again as schedules allowed. Jordan looked back at her friends as she exited the driveway. She could see their faces by the glow of the taillights. As she drove off, she realized that she was now moving farther and farther away from them, and from the lives that they had once shared. It seemed her life would always be that way—that she would always be driving off from the people that she most loved. She hoped that she could find a bridge that would still connect their lives despite their differences. She remained pessimistically optimistic, as she drew parallels to the bridge that she was trying to create with her own family. But there were some ravines that even the Army Corps of Engineers could not weld, span, and cross!

Yet, she hoped that love and friendship would transcend prejudice, and that they would maintain their half of the relationships that she so treasured. She believed that she could already do this with Karen, at least. In fact, she counted on it.

She phoned Carolyn that night to tell her the news.

"So, another of my friends now bites the dust! Marge and Tyler are sharing vows in June! It's gonna be a pretty uptight ceremony, too, as you could well imagine! My guess is that her parents are going to dictate the whole affair . . ."

"So what should I wear . . . the strapless pink gown with my spiked heels? Or are you going to wear the dress in this family?"

"Actually, I'll be a bridesmaid . . . another fashion decision sloughed off to those with more power and class! . . . Seriously though, you know that I can't take you . . ."

"Seriously though . . . . you know that you can't hide me forever! . . . OK, Jordan Mathews, I'll play the backstreet girl for another day. But some day, you and I will be exchanging vows. I wonder who you'll be inviting then? And I wonder how you'll tell them . . . Good night, My Love!" Carolyn kissed Jordan through the phone as she abruptly hung up.

Jordan did not fight the matter. She slept that night with thoughts of the old days, and with dreams of Carolyn neatly woven into them.

# Chapter 8

Despite issues in other areas, Jordan was developing some good relationships in the office. She quickly made friends among the staff there, and she had lunch with them whenever schedules permitted or weather dictated. Now that winter was over and spring was nearly at its close, there would be no more car groundings or other unplanned interruptions of her field days. This worked against her, because Jordan used this free time to help catch up on her phone conferences, and to organize her desk. She usually did her paperwork as she watched TV at home each night. Most of the staff did, actually, although they would never admit it! There was just no way around it! Once she set foot in the office, she was caught in a spider's web of competing demands and prioritized emergencies. There were no extrications until the job was done! She dared not report for a half day's work. If she had a doctor's appointment or maybe a night out with friends, she was smart to take the full day off. Otherwise, she would have to cancel her plans, because she'd just be stuck there at the job!

She learned to put her own life on hold, so that other families might survive. She learned to live for the weekends. And she looked forward, with great anticipation, to the weeklong vacation that Carolyn had planned with her. It shouldn't have been a surprise that Jordan was given only part of that time off. She had least seniority on the unit, and was scheduled to testify on a case. She accepted these decisions stoically, knowing that she would at least be going home each night to the woman that she loved. But even so, she could not share her objections with the other staff! She only told them that a friend was vacationing at her home for the week. They could not possibly know what that really meant to her.

She felt badly about it. Yet, she could not share—even with the other social workers—the deepest, the most loving relationship that anyone could hold and treasure. She accepted this as part of the work culture. No one really shared their personal lives with their co-workers. They learned to leave their personal stuff at home! It sort of came with the diploma. But for Jordan, it was different. She was leaving more than her personal life there—she was leaving a whole part of her personality at home! There could be no compromise. There were other gay people in the office. She could sense them, but she would never approach them. She was not prepared to reveal herself to anyone! She rationalized this as a survival tactic, a strategy validated by Jan and Betty on more than one occasion! Yet she often felt ghostlike as she sauntered through the office. She had dimensions of time and space, but she had no person—at least not one that she could share. The other staff members were intrigued by her! Jordan saw herself as a paper doll that she and Kelly used to play with as kids—only now, Jordan was the cardboard cut out, and the staff would attach the fitting characteristics to her, just like she had once attached a ball gown or a pair of pumps to a paper doll to complete a fantasy. They weren't ready to deal with the real life matters of it. And neither was she!

Maybe that was the real connection between Jordan and Marsha McMillan, if you could call it that. She intrigued Jordan. She, too, moved ghostlike through the office. She, too, seemed two dimensional. The staff had a number of perfect scenarios for her: a rich girl stuck in a government job until politics would allow her to progress further; the wife of a well-to-do businessman who entertained her attempts at philanthropy; a struggling ne'er-do-well, who was sentenced to the district office as atonement; a recovering alcoholic and drug addict, who was hiding in the D.O. to escape detection; a former stripper or a dominatrix too old now to cruise the shadier parts of town—the list of possibilities was endless, and Marsha was least willing to provide a clue. Maybe it was this aura of secrecy that drew them together, but Jordan hoped it was more due to a professional respect that she had earned with each successful case closing.

She and Marsha had a chance encounter in the Ladies Room once. Not much to speak of in the eyes of the other staff, Jordan was sure, although she would never have shared the incident with them. But she was also sensitive enough to appreciate the woman's drive for privacy on all levels. It was odd how the whole event took place really, and even more odd that a few seconds would have registered a lifetime recollection.

Marsha was already in a stall when Jordan entered the Ladies Room. Another staff member left the bathroom as Jordan entered, so she went undetected by the D.O. Manager. When that woman exited, Marsha started speaking.

"So how are we doing? Do you think you'll be able to survive here another day before they bring down the ax?"

Jordan was taken aback! For a quick moment, she thought that Marsha was speaking to her! Then she realized that she was actually talking to herself! Jordan cleared her throat to alert Marsha of her presence, flushed her commode, washed her hands, and left the Ladies Room. She felt like she had seen the boss naked! She thought that Marsha had accidentally exposed a piece of her soul! It was an odd feeling, almost an intimate discomfort. That was a turning point, because Marsha always presented as cold and as tough as nails. Jordan now saw her real vulnerability, and she somehow connected with it. But neither she nor Marsha McMillan ever spoke about the incident, and Jordan never shared the story with anyone.

A more public encounter came with a call from Mary, her notorious teenaged foster child. Mary was furious with her foster mother, because she wouldn't let her go to a friend's house after school. But the foster mother was older and wiser to the tricks of kids like her! She would not grant permission unless she spoke with the other girl's parents first! Mary called Jordan from school promptly at 9:02 a.m., and just as the office officially opened for the day. "Look Jordan, you gotta call Irene and tell her I can go! This is not fair, and you know it! She's just pullin' some power trip on me, so that she can prove that she's the boss. I'm sick of it! I mean it!" Jordan held the phone away so as not to burst an eardrum!

"I'm sure she has a good reason . . . She's been a foster mother for a long time."

"So? What does that have to do with me not bein' allowed to go to a friend's house? I haven't had detention for two weeks, I haven't missed a curfew, I haven't been in any kind of trouble! She's just being' a bitch to me, as usual! You have to call her and tell her it's OK!" Mary was barking out the orders.

"Nope, I can't get involved with that . . . That's something that you and Irene have to work out between you. I can't undermine her authority, especially when I think she's doing a good job for you! Maybe if you talk to her again, make some rules, you can negotiate this out with her . . ."

"Fine then, Jordan. You can fuck off . . . !" Jordan could hear the line of curses continuing as Mary slammed down the phone. Jordan hung up, slowly shook her head, and counted the hours till lunch.

Several minutes later, Mary phoned Jordan again. Jordan was amazed, and with all the humor she could muster on a Monday morning, she took the call.

"Oh, Mary, it's you. I'm sorry, but I'm too busy fucking off to talk to you on the phone!" Jordan then hung up on her!

As Jordan looked up from the call, she saw Marsha McMillan standing beside her. Jordan, embarrassed, made eye contact with Marsha, who smiled and apologized for the interruption. She said that she could speak with Jordan later. Marsha obviously appreciated the humor, even if she quietly detested the coarseness of the tactic! At least, she never called Jordan down about it! Mary called again later that day, but this time to apologize. She said that her friend's parents had spoken to her foster mother, and that they would be home to supervise the girls. Mary would be having dinner at her friend's house that night! She had tasted her first victory! All in all, Jordan thought that she had won the day. At least, she had won Mary and Marsha McMillan! Mary would still be the proverbial thorn in her side, but Jordan made her point. And Marsha McMillan would become a formidable ally! Relationships were the commodities that tied politics together. Jordan liked the relationships; she hated the politics!

It was the personal relationships that brought Jordan to life. She genuinely liked her clients, and believed that this facet, more than anything else, helped them to progress. That gave her professional life some meaning, and gave her clients motivation to utilize her interventions. It was her friendships in the office that made the stress there bearable. It was her friendships outside the office that gave her life zest. But it was her love relationship that gave her spirit energy, that really made her feel alive! Her love of Carolyn carried her through all other strife and struggle. And she knew that her love was returned in huge sums! Jordan could see it in the flowers that she received every month. She read it in the letters that came daily to her home. She heard it in Carolyn's voice as they chatted on the phone. She tasted it as they kissed whenever they were alone together.

As if in a time warp, Carolyn's visit was upon Jordan almost before she realized it! It was the one benefit of hard, fast-paced work—one day would naturally meld into the next, and time passed oh so quickly there! She tried to stop time whenever she and Carolyn were together, and she would freeze frame their moments in her mind, like some Polaroid reality. She would visit them again and again, long after Carolyn had gone. But for this moment, her attention was fixed on the clock and tuned to the sounds of Carolyn's car in the driveway. And suddenly, there it was! Jordan flew down the stairs and to the car now being parked beside her own. She flung the car door open, and pulled Carolyn out and into a hug.

"Wait, wait! You'll knock us both to the ground! Give a girl a chance to catch her breath . . . The way you act, you'd think that you never had company before . . . You have had company, haven't you?"

Carolyn held her at arm's length, as if surveying to see if anything had changed. With the exception of a fresh hairstyle and the start of a tan, everything was as she remembered it. She was thankful that Jordan was just as she left her. Nothing had changed!

Jordan looked at her in amazement. "You're so calm! Must be all those Parkway fumes—they've gone right to your head! Why, a girl would think that you come here every day! . . . Here, let me help you with that." She was grinning ear-to-ear. Jordan grabbed her suitcase and overnight bag, and they walked together up the stairs and into her apartment.

Once there, Carolyn gave Jordan a long and tender kiss. As she held her close, she whispered, "I do . . . I do come here every day . . . At least in my mind, I do . . . Can't you feel that?" Jordan nodded and held her close for a few moments before Carolyn broke free and moved to the window.

"So, you're going to move THAT pawn?" Jordan asked incredulously, as Carolyn edged her hand over the chess board. It was the first thing that Carolyn went for, as if she had been thinking that singular move for two months.

"Yup, Partner, I'm gonna move ya to a quick showdown! Now let's see whatcha got!" Carolyn had been practicing the Mathews vernacular as well as her chess game!

Jordan countered with the rook, her eyes on Carolyn's queen! Carolyn held off her next move.

They chatted for hours about their clients, about their jobs, about the friends they met, about the news, both national and local. Yet even with letters each day and phone calls twice a week, it seemed that they would never run out of topics for discussion. At other moments, they were so attuned that they needn't say a word. They were just happy to be in the same room together, and to be sharing the same world.

Jordan decided to take a quick run on the beach before they had dinner. Carolyn snacked all along the drive down, and really, neither was hungry. Carolyn walked with Jordan to the ocean, and waited on the beach for her as she ran. It was just past dusk, and the tide was moving toward its lowest point, as the sun began its descent above the bay. The seagulls were calling to each other, as they scavenged for bits of clam or soft shelled crab left by the fishermen, or presented to them by the waves. Carolyn plied the sand between her fingers, and felt the cool of the beach against her legs as she sat. She took deep, long breaths of the crisp, clean air, letting each breath roll through her mouth to her lungs, and then through her bloodstream. She missed being home, even though there were some aspects of the Vermont Mountains that she had already grown to love. But here was the anchor of her life. She could not wait to be back for good. She could not wait to really, finally, start her life with Jordan.

They grilled steaks for dinner, and cooked corn on the cob and baked potatoes in the coals. Carolyn bought a loaf of fresh bread from a bakery nearby, and the warmth and aroma of the baked dough blended with the cool salt air. They grilled their dinner in the driveway, but out of sight of the throngs of passing vacationers. They toasted with a chardonnay as they watched the sun set. And they watched the nightly news before bed. Carolyn had always objected to this ritual, believing that Jordan was welcoming the worst auras just before sleep. She condemned this as a morbid curiosity with the outside world, until she realized that Jordan was using the ritual to maintain a sense of closeness with her family. She knew that Jordan had grown up watching the news with them, and that she had not seen her parents since she moved out. Carolyn never made another derogatory comment about this practice, and she always waited for Jordan to give updates about the progress with her folks. She never wanted to intrude into such areas, and always waited for Jordan to invite her there.

Carolyn had long ago crossed that bridge with her own family. She scheduled a dinner visit with them for the next evening. Her parents also invited Jordan. Carolyn was eager for her family to meet Jordan, and she believed that they would love her nearly as much as she did. She never brought anyone home to meet them before, so her parents knew that this relationship was special. It was not perfection—they would have much preferred a husband and children for their daughter—but this was the relationship that made their daughter happy. They would never have wanted her tied to a miserable marriage, nor would they have wanted her to spend her life alone. They decided years ago that they would support her, and that they would help her in her relationships as best they could. Carolyn was their daughter, and Jordan was now her partner. There was no hesitancy in their commitment to them both!

Jordan was quite nervous as they walked the path to the front porch of the Berringer home. They lived in a middle class, bi-level house with a neatly landscaped yard, and a flower garden surrounding the front porch. Carolyn was the youngest of four girls, and there was a seven year gap between the third born sister Judy, and Carolyn. Her sisters were married and had families of their own. Only Toby and Judy still lived in the area. Barbara and her family lived in San Francisco, and visited once a year for the Christmas holiday. But Jordan could still sense a strong family presence.

The home reminded Jordan of the families she had seen on TV. Mrs. Berringer answered the door. She wore a deep blue dress that matched the hues of her garden, and an apron tied around her waist. Her gray hair was neatly coifed in a bun. Mr. Berringer was seated in a chair, and he laid his newspaper on the coffee table as he rose to greet them. He wore dress slacks, and a light blue sweater—a color coordinated marital pairing, if Jordan had ever seen one! She thought that this boded well for potential marital success with their daughter. But there was not a tool, not a pair of over-alls or work-jeans, not a set of work boots in sight! She thought that that was quite odd! Although she had seen pictures of the couple, Jordan had not realized how much older they were than her own parents. Mrs. Berringer made a pot roast, one of Jordan's favorite meals, and the aroma welcomed her into the home. She was already feeling a sense of warmth and acceptance there as they took their places at the table.

Both of Carolyn's parents were retired teachers, and they were very proud that Carolyn had selected their chosen profession. Mr. Berringer was a history teacher, but he really loved the arts. He and his wife shared a makeshift studio that they set up in the garage when they retired. He enjoyed oils and watercolors, and he gave Jordan a miniature seascape that she admired. Mrs. Berringer was a potter and sculptor. Their home was an art exhibit in progress! They belonged to the Artists Guild in town, and periodically displayed their work at exhibitions in the center, or at various fairs in the state. Jordan was at a distinct disadvantage whenever the conversation turned to art. She had no talent in the area, and joked that she could barely draw stick men! Yet even this, Carolyn's parents turned to the positive.

"Oh, so you're a primitivist, are you? You know, Grandma Moses is loved worldwide, and she didn't start painting seriously until she was in her 60's, I believe . . ." Mr. Berringer commented.

"That's right. And who knows when your true value as an artist will emerge and take the world by storm! I only started sculpting in my 50's. I actually started with pottery first, as a remedy for my arthritis. Using your hands is good, you know . . . but once I felt the cool wet clay in my fingers, I knew that I had found the right medium. If you look at my pastels and my charcoals, you'll see that I'm only mediocre. Now Ben has some real talent there! . . . But that's alright with me . . . I have found my own way to express myself now, through this medium. You see? All it takes is the right formula to make things happen. So much so in life, too. Don't you agree?" Mrs. Berringer turned the conversation to Jordan.

"I've never really thought about it in quite those terms," Jordan replied. "My family is not really artsy, as you would say. But I do think that I've found a medium to express myself, in a way . . . it's through the people that I try to help each day . . . through the lives that I touch as I work with them . . . to help pull them out of despair. Maybe I'm not really creating anything unique . . . I mean, the people are already there. They own their potential. But I do think that who I am as a person has affected them, and has helped them as people, to move forward. So in that sense, I guess, I am creating something . . . maybe it's hope, maybe it's opportunity, maybe it's just sheer will . . . But I do believe that in some small way, I have helped create that for them. That to me is beautiful. That is the only art that I have a talent for, I believe." Jordan looked to each of the parents, and then to Carolyn. They looked thoughtfully to her, and nodded in understanding.

The rest of the evening went smoothly and calmly. The Berringer's had genuine warmth of personality, and it was easy for Jordan to see how Carolyn had developed these characteristics. They shared family photos and shots of Carolyn from birth, to birthday parties, through communions, to proms and graduations. They told stories about her as best they could glean them from their memories. They showed the ribbons she won as a child artist, and brought out the ballet slippers she wore in her first recital. Jordan soaked up every piece of information. That she adored Carolyn was obvious. And that Carolyn adored her was a source of comfort to her parents. They seemed to like Jordan, but mostly, they liked that Carolyn had finally found someone that she loved, and who loved her in return. As the night ended, Mr. and Mrs. Berringer hugged and kissed them both, and made certain that Jordan would come regularly to visit them, even if Carolyn was not home to accompany her. Jordan breathed a sigh of relief as the two left the home and drove back to her apartment.

"That was a pretty esoteric comment you made at dinner. I'm impressed! I didn't know that you had it in you!" Carolyn joked as they drove.

"You'd be surprised what's really lurkin' inside 'a me—the depth, the intelligence, the insights, the profound! . . . Wanna spend a lifetime findin' out?"

"Maybe I will, if there's still some corner of your mind yet that I haven't scanned or scoured!" Carolyn replied.

"Oh, trust me, there's plenty more of that stuff just waitin' for the right moment to gush itself out . . ."

"My parents liked you!" Carolyn said, as she squeezed Jordan's hand. She spoke this with a pride that comes from real conviction! Although she felt confident that they would, she was concerned that both families might reject the most important relationship of her life. She had not shared that fear with Jordan.

"Thank God they did like me! I don't think I can handle another negative reaction right now. I'm still trying to figure out what to do about my own parents." Jordan again breathed a sigh of relief. She knew of several relationships that ended because of friction from their families. At least she and Carolyn could count on the support and experience of one successfully married couple, when life's problems tried their own.

Carolyn was station-hopping and lunged again toward the radio as a Springsteen pulse filled the car. Jordan beat her to the knob and cranked up the volume! The sound waves bounced around the car as the stereo blared. Carolyn caught Jordan's hand and raised it above their heads as they sang out together,

"I wanna die with you Wendy on the streets tonight

in an everlasting kiss"[65]

They sang all of the rest of that song—and all the other bits of the songs that they snagged as they bounced from station to station on the way back to their apartment. And they had lengthy debates about the unidentifiable lyrics, as they tended to the mediocre household chores.

The rest of their week together went at lightning pace. Carolyn took them sailing on a sunfish she rented from a bait shop on the cove. Jordan had often sailed with her father and Uncle Pat in his 17 foot Ventura. Her cousin Pat Jr. had even taught her how to sail when they were younger. But the sunfish was a bit trickier—a lot easier to tip, but at lot easier to upright. They sailed close to the wind as they tacked from shore to shore to exit the cove and to enter the Barnegat Bay. The moderate winds carried the boat quickly across the cove as the waves danced along topside, and the rills caressed Jordan's hand. She often slipped her hand over the side to feel the rush of bay water press against her fingers. The two moved in tandem, ducking boom and sail, with each tack across the inlet. Despite the near constant splash across the bow, they successfully defended against a capsizing!

And on night paddles around the cove, Carolyn would recite poetry, as they watched the bioluminescent trail that followed both boat and oar. Sometimes in

---

[65] A reference to: "Born To Run" by Bruce Springsteen. Copyright © 1975, Bruce Springsteen, renewed © 2003 Bruce Springsteen (ASCAP). Reprinted by permission. International copyright secured. All rights reserved.

the dawn, they would paddle into Cranberry Bog and chase turtle heads as they popped up to peek at the disruption of the glass calm water there. The girls spent most of their mornings sun bathing on the beach and body surfing in the ocean. Carolyn had now begun reading the newspaper to Jordan as they sat on the shore. She wanted to be a part of that family ritual. Sometimes they would crab off of a local dock, and Carolyn would cringe with the sight of uncooked chicken wings crowded with blue claws. Jordan had to let them go! Carolyn couldn't stand the thought of cooking something still alive!

The evenings were filled with visits—either to Carolyn's home, or to the homes of her sister or friends. They strolled on the Boardwalk and played the stands, as they gorged themselves on pizzas and zeppolis. One night they even joined Betty and Jan for a trip to the Key West. They danced to Donna Summer, and to the Village People, to Gloria Gaynor, and to the O'Jays . . . the dance list was as endless as the passions of their love! They danced with the new friends they met there, and made plans to see them again. They chatted about the Gay Activist Alliance, and discussed the politics of coming out. And they made love most nights before sleep, and held each other most mornings before they rose. Their lives seemed as near to perfect as could be, as content as any happy couple they had ever known. And then just as suddenly, she was gone. Their time together was over. Carolyn was following the Interstates back to Vermont, and Jordan was again entwined in the webs of her chosen profession. The chess pieces remained silently in place, a state of suspended animation, awaiting Carolyn's next maneuver.

* * *

Jordan threw herself back into her work. And each night ended with the regimen of daily letter writing. She waited impatiently for the phone calls on Wednesdays and Saturdays. Occasionally, she went with Jan and Betty to the Key West just to spend time. Most of the women there knew that Jordan was taken, and they respected her relationship. Jordan knew, too, that six hours away, Carolyn was probably doing the same scene with Marcus and Bill. Neither doubted the faithfulness of the other. In fact, neither could imagine their lives with anyone else! They would wait out the year, see each other as they could, and plan for their future together. Jordan pinned that future on the flowers and care packages that she received from Carolyn each week, and she shipped off bits of herself and boxes of candy in the hopes of further entrapping the woman she loved. Photos of Carolyn, and of the happy couple, were displayed throughout the apartment. Only occasionally would Jordan dump over the photos of her own family, and only when she thought about their refusal to accept what was so obvious: Carolyn made her happy!

Jordan also saw Marge, Tyler, and Janice whenever she could, but their lives were distancing as much as their interests. Yet despite their differences, there was a familiarity that thwarted time and space. Jordan fought hard to maintain these friendships. She loved them all, as she had loved no other friends in the world. And although they had been to Jordan's place many times, they never questioned the presence of Carolyn's things there. They also hadn't asked to meet her. They may have suspected their relationship, but they were not willing or comfortable enough to question it.

Jordan was also making friends in the office. She and Tina Murdock had become especially close co-workers, both as allies and as comrades united together in the fight against John Crittenden. They mimicked John behind his back, mocked his amateurish attempts at supervision, and criticized his casework. Not only was he notoriously conservative, but he was also quite outspoken. Jordan estimated that his mentality set the profession back forty years! Tina believed that Jordan was being far too generous.

Tina said that John was once rumored to be an advocate of some Nazi cause in the mid-west. He jokingly denied the allegation, offering instead, that he had once supported the KKK in a matter of free speech. He belonged to the John Birch Society at the time, and he was proud of it! But it was his strong religious convictions that Jordan and Tina found most troubling. He could wrap any issue in a Bible verse, and make it seem like the morally right path. Jordan feared for the families under his care, knowing that he could just as easily weave a supposition into a web of seeming truth. He might also utilize a net of bias to shade a case plan against a client family! And worse, he was a zealot in his own cause! He was certainly arrogant enough to believe that he was above reproach.

Jordan soon realized, well before Tina, that John Crittenden had the potential to be someone quite dangerous. They treated him more cautiously after that, but always with an eye on his actions. Jane Morrison was above believing that anyone would be so insidious. Jane was the truly decent force among a chaos of competing needs and conflicting belief systems. She focused instead, on maximizing unity in the office and enforcing the agency guidelines. Although close to the edge, John's work was always just within the bounds of the agency's procedures. Jordan knew that he would be pretty hard to catch. But Jordan also knew that she had attracted his attention, and now, she was developing a healthy fear of him. He looked at her with "predator eyes" whenever no one else was watching.

This first became obvious when John took interest in her case of a single mother and a two year old child. Sarah was young, just barely nineteen years old, when she decided to leave home with her baby. The case was periodically opened over the last several years, and under the suspicion that Sarah was being sexually abused. Although she was questioned numerous times about this possibility, Sarah always denied these allegations. Yet, her acting out—and her family's dynamics—spoke volumes in confirming that this belief had some real truth to it.

Sarah and her child Maria were now living in an efficiency apartment near the Boardwalk, and under the supports of the county Welfare office. Sarah had a history of alcohol and drug abuse as a much younger teen, but she completed a residential substance abuse program, and later, a group home, before she became pregnant and left her family. But she still had occasional slips. In each instance, Sarah placed her daughter with her older, more successful sister, Terry. Sarah was a binge drinker really, and had almost planned drinking episodes. Her "slips" would often grow into a binge of perhaps a few days. She would then seclude herself, usually with the help of a recovering friend, resume meetings, and bring Maria back home only when she stabilized. There were two such incidents in the last year. If Sarah had care of the baby while she was drinking, there would be no question. Maria would be removed and placed in either foster care or with Terry. The sister could even assume legal custody of Maria later, if she chose. But the agency would not remove a child whose physical safety had been assured, and whose mother was still trying to work her program! Slips were a known part of the recovery process. And Sarah's care of Maria otherwise met agency standards. Besides, Terry was raising her own family, and she really didn't want to overstep bounds with her sister. Jordan was working with Terry to further develop this potential resource for Maria if needed. The situation was not perfect, but it was adequate for the child at that point in time. Jordan believed that Sarah was chosen for Maria's life, and she did not want to disrupt that cosmic plan unless it became absolutely necessary! In fact, Jordan viewed all her client families that way.

Crittenden saw it differently, and used an "overheard" conference as opportunity to bring his own perspective to the case plan. He had been walking passed the open door to Jane Morrison's office on a Monday morning, and just as she had received the weekend report that Sarah had been drinking. The Emergency Response Unit (ERU) had investigated an anonymous charge phoned in by a neighbor. The ERU worker confirmed that although Sarah was intoxicated, the child spent the weekend with Sarah's sister Terry. She agreed to keep the child until the assigned worker could respond. Jane Morrison and Jordan were conferencing Sarah's case plan as John walked into Jane's office.

"Oh, Jordan, I didn't realize that you were conferencing with Jane Morrison now. I just wanted to ask a question about the Layton case, and I'll be on my way, if you don't mind." Crittenden was looking to Jane Morrison, who always acquiesced to any intrusion.

"Is something happening with the Layton's?" Jane Morrison asked. "I thought they were doing so well . . ."

"And they are, but they need help with food again, and I wanted your permission to refer them for a food basket. They had an increase in their rent."

"You don't need my permission for that, John" Jane said in reply. "Just contact the Emergency Food Bank, and document the referral in the case record. OK?"

"Will do," Crittenden replied, but he did not leave her office. Instead, he stood lingering over his mail tray as Jordan and Jane Morrison continued to conference the Sarah situation. He waited for the right moment, and then pounced on them both.

"I'm not sure why you're continuing to waste time with that woman. You know that she has a horrendous history of abuse as a child, and the likelihood of her maintaining sobriety is minimal. If I was the caseworker, I'd pull the child, and force the sister to make a decision—either she accepts care and custody of the child, or the agency places her for adoption. The child deserves the right to a stable home, and not a life with some mother who places partying above her responsibilities to parent!" He made this proclamation with a distinct authority that startled Jordan.[66]

"Thank you, John," Jane Morrison responded. "Please make the arrangements for the Layton's food basket." She then waited for him to leave her office.

Jane Morrison knew that most of the families that they were supervising could well meet those same criteria. If their families were not struggling, they would not have been open cases with the agency. If the agency—and society—had not valued the rights of parents and families to raise their own children, they would not have given the funding to make remedy possible. And children had a right to live with their own families! Maybe this funding would never have been available, if all children did well in out-of-home placements. But such placements too often brought a whole new set of problems for these kids, and years later, they would still be paying the price! If rehabilitation was not a genuine and possible goal, funding

---

[66] For discussion regarding the philosophy and controversy about when foster placement is necessary, please refer to Appendix and Bibliography for Chapter Eight.

for these services would have been terminated long ago! Jordan held close this philosophy as her standard of social work practice. This philosophy of impacting for positive change formed the very basis of the Social Work profession!

Yes, Sarah had a horrendous history as an abused child, but she was not an abuser herself. Should she be penalized because she was a victim? Because she had occasional slips, did that mean that sobriety was not an attainable goal for her? Surely, the nine million recovering alcoholics—in every walk of life and at every economic level—would have disagreed. And there was a safety plan in place. Terry provided good care of the child, and she was a solid resource for them. Sarah sought treatment when these episodes occurred, and she remained involved with AA and with her sponsor long after these drinking events were over. Sarah was recovering. That was her goal. And that was her case plan, whether Crittenden liked it or not!

Jordan would convince Sarah to start counseling. She hoped that Sarah could resolve the abuse issues that underlie her depression and her drinking. Now that she was over eighteen, she could feel reasonably comfortable that her therapist would not have to report any abuse that she disclosed to her. The fear of therapist reporting—and of the potential consequences to her father and her family—held Sarah's silence for so long! Maybe now, she could begin to lift the veil of secrecy, and to find a real peace in the acknowledgment of the truth, even if the only other person to hear that truth was a paid therapist. Jordan would continue to encourage her to reach out to her sponsor and to AA.

But Jordan feared that because Crittenden now identified an alternate plan for the family, Maria would be targeted for removal! After all, he had sown the seeds of doubt with Jordan's supervisor! Jordan was concerned for the future of this struggling mother and child. She had seen Crittenden's "smirk-eye" as he left Jane Morrison's office. It was a look half challenging, half threatening. She was already sorry that she had so many times joked about him behind his back. She now believed that he might use his influence to save his pride—that he would use his power to sabotage her, and to destroy that family! She was careful from that point, never to leave information on any of her clients within access of his grasp, either literally or figuratively. Jordan, too, had now seen the enemy!

The summer moved swiftly through the office. With caseworkers taking vacations, and with children now home full time, there was an endless barrage of child abuse allegations that required investigation and attention. Like the other social workers, Jordan responded to incidents on her own caseload, as well as to investigations about families on other caseloads—and often, without any prior conferencing or background information. There was simply no time to plan for real social work intervention! She was applying band aid solutions until the assigned caseworkers were back again and available. At one point, she was directed to complete three investigations in one day! The temperature had reached nearly 100 degrees, and in her haste to complete these assignments, she skipped lunch. By the third investigation, Jordan was dizzy and slightly confused. Perhaps that's why she missed a defensive bruise on a ten year old's right forearm.

She had not substantiated the physical abuse allegation in that instance. But late that afternoon, the child's grandmother also reported that Tony had bruises on his legs and buttocks. Jordan was alarmed when she received this additional information. She had not even thought to question the boy about it! She returned to the home, and in the presence of the child's grandmother, re-interviewed him. Although Tony again denied that he had been beaten, his younger brother confronted that the ten year old was hit "all the time." Tony then admitted that he was hit maybe three times a week, for things like not taking out the garbage, not cleaning his room, or just not listening. In the presence of the grandmother, Jordan had Tony undress. She used a blanket to cover the child during her observation. She was appalled by what she saw!

Jordan contacted the child's mother at work, and asked her to meet them at the hospital. The grandmother consented to the physical by the attending physician there, the only pediatrician available in the evening. The physician examined the child, confirmed and documented the abuse, and medically cleared him. Jordan contacted the Prosecutor's office, who could not immediately respond. She took photos of Tony's injuries using the hospital's Polaroid. The photos, along with the medical report, would be furnished to the Prosecutor for possible use in court.

Jordan interviewed the mother privately when she arrived at the hospital.

"What's he done now?" the mother challenged, upset that her evening had been ruined by this "unnecessary" trip.

"As you can see, we became concerned when we spoke with Tony earlier today, and found these bruises on his back and thighs. Do you know what may have caused them?" Jordan waited for her response.

"Tony caused 'em—by not listenin' as usual! He hasta learn that he's not gonna have things his own way. The world's not gonna cater to him . . . And he has a smart mouth that he flaps all the time! So his father hit 'um. Big deal! Did he learn anything from it? 'Course not . . . 'cause here we are the next night, and there's Tony, doin' the same things all over again . . . So my husband hit him again. One way or the other, he's gotta learn . . . He's been this way from the day he was born." His mother looked at him in disgust. Tony shot back a glance.

"But did you see how hard he was beaten? And how often? I mean, these bruises say a lot, too, about what's been happening . . ."

Jordan was unable to finish before the mother interrupted, "So take 'um then, if ya think ya can do any better . . . I'm tellin' ya, the boy's no good! And we've had it with 'um!"

Jordan tried to engage the mother. "I know how hard it can be to raise children these days, and-"

"Oh really? And how many kids do you have?" the mother tested, near screaming.

"I have no children, but I work with families everyday and all over the county, who are having the same problems that your family is having now. And together, we sometimes find solutions that work for everyone. But one solution cannot be that you will beat him into compliance . . . because that situation will only cause more serious physical injuries, and more disruptive behavior for Tony. And it will also cause legal issues, and maybe even incarceration for your husband! I want us to be very clear on that last point."

Tony's mother stepped back from her verbal position, and began to excuse their parental behaviors. "I don't get involved, 'cause I think Tony deserves to be beat, and 'cause I don't wanna undermine my husband as the other parent and head of the house . . . What's he done that's so wrong, anyway? So Tony's got a couple'a bruises . . . Big Deal! Paul was disciplinin' him, for God Sake! That's not against the law!"

"It's not against the state laws to spank a child with an open hand, but it is against the law if that spanking causes injuries—like the bruises so obvious on this child. Look at these things! These bruises show that Tony was even beaten with a belt! And on different days! And look at these bruises along his whole hip and leg, like he was dragged and beaten! And this one here looks like a punch! In fact, there's several marks like that!"

"No, that's not right—Paul would never 'a punched Tony no matter how mad he was! Maybe Tony was fightin' at school again . . . If he would just behave, none'a this woulda happened! But he's always gotta do what he wants ta do, and that's what that'll getcha!"

Jordan saw that this mother would not protect her child. She convinced her to allow Tony to stay with his grandmother until further assessment was completed.

Jordan later interviewed Tony's father at the hospital. Paul defended his actions and refused any counseling programs. He called the boy "a bad seed, like some of the others in his wife's family."

"There's no way I'm gonna let any'a my kids turn out that way! They don't work, they're havin' babies all over the place, half the time they're in jail or hopped up on drugs . . . I'd rather go ta jail myself then face that possibility . . . Nope, that boy's gonna behave . . . The kid won't do anything we ask 'um . . . and forget about homework, he doesn't even try . . . The kid can't even read yet! Believe that? . . . Nope, I'm gonna do what I haveta do until he listens! State or Not!"

"Ya know, Tony might have a learning disability, and with special help, special classes, a different approach—maybe you'd get the kind of results you're looking for." Jordan maintained an air of authority, the only posture that a man like Paul would respect.

"I know kids who are dumb as dirt and still listen to their parents! I'm tellin' ya, it's not like that wit' this kid. He thrives on causin' trouble, and then walks away an' laughs about it! . . . An' he's a pathological liar! If anything, that kid thinks he's smarter then the rest'a us, and now with you along, he'll get over that way, too . . . So you do whacha haveta do, an' I'll do what I haveta do!"

Jordan saw the hopelessness of the situation, the impenetrability of the parents' beliefs. With some mild coaxing, both Paul and his wife agreed that Tony could remain in the care and custody of his grandmother. The father was not prosecuted. Because the younger child, "the good son'" was never targeted, he was allowed to remain in the home.

Jordan thanked God that the father had not killed this boy! She blamed herself for not picking up the signs more quickly, and questioned whether she had just chosen to ignore what later became so obvious. Maybe it was the heat, or the missed lunch, or the lack of time between investigations, the overwork, or a thousand other excuses—but she vowed never again to allow any distraction to interfere with her investigations! It was the grandmother who saved that child from more pain and injury, and maybe, had even saved his life! Jordan was just a tool in the process. But she would remember Tony's face forever, as a caution to pay close attention to the responsibilities at hand!

Jordan called Carolyn that night for a little confidence boosting.

"Hi Sweetheart! A phone call on a Tuesday? What a surprise! I was just reading your letter again . . . Is there something wrong?" Carolyn was apprehensive.

"No no! I just needed to hear your voice. Terrible day at work, and nobody to unload on!" Jordan tried to downplay the impact of the incident.

"Well what happened? Tell me about it!"

"Not really anything in particular . . ." Jordan couldn't bring herself to admit to Carolyn that she had failed. "Just one of those situations that can really get to you. You know what I mean? And the parents were such assholes! . . . But enough about that. I called to see how your day was." Jordan applied a full dodge.

"My day was pretty good! The kids I saw today, they were such a hoot! You never really know what they're trying to say with their drawings until they start explaining it all to you. I've got one boy in particular, that drew Martians . . . at least I thought so! Turns out that his room has ants! He even made up little stories about the ant families there. But Jordan, I swear to you, those things looked alien! Although they did seem to get along well, by all accounts! . . . If only he could heed the lesson, and get along better with the other kids here. We'll be using this picture as a good starting point for that conversation, I guess . . ."

"Sounds like a good place to start . . ."

"Hey, did you start the book I sent you last week? It's really a super novel . . . and there's some history in it, too, about the Great Depression and the War. But it's the philosophy that I think you'll like the most . . . . especially since one of the main characters is from Nepal . . ." Carolyn started to critique the book. No matter how hard she tried, she couldn't seem to work the conversation back to Jordan's day. Jordan kept blocking the topic, derailing the subject at every turn.

"You really don't want to tell me about it, do you?" Carolyn asked after a silence.

"Not really. Just keep talking so that I can hear your voice. That's really all that I need for now. And about the book . . . I'll jump on it as soon as I get the chance . . . I promise!"

Carolyn chatted on about her coursework, her students, and even her plans to redecorate her apartment. Jordan listened and gave the occasional grunts at all the right moments.

"Well, guess I've gotta go now . . . You know that this call doesn't cancel out the Wednesday evening call you are scheduled to make to me tomorrow . . ." Jordan said.

"Are you kidding me? I can hardly wait to dial your number! You can't believe how lonely things can get up here sometimes . . . even with Bill and Marcus. They're good friends, but they're just not you."

"Same here, Baby. I'll talk to you tomorrow. Sleep well, and miss me like anything!"

"You know I always do." They kissed each other through the phone, and Jordan held the receiver to her ear until the line went dead.

Jordan couldn't dislodge from her mind the bruising on Tony's back, no matter how hard she tried to mask it with Carolyn's voice. She couldn't sleep, no matter how hard she tried to replay her nights with her. She put on her headphones and listened to Phoebe Snow, but still, she could not find peace or distraction. The bruises were a haunting condemnation of her failure to protect a child under her care.

Jordan conferenced with Jane Morrison by phone at various points in the investigation, but she could not confide to anyone, the guilt and inadequacy that engulfed her. She tried to talk with Tina about this, and just shortly after the incident. But Tina was always so full of confidence—and they both had so little time—that Jordan felt too embarrassed to discuss the situation with her. Jordan even called Janice one night to tell her about the boy. But Janice shared so many positive stories about her own students, that Jordan didn't feel comfortable discussing the incident with her, either. So she chose instead, to unburden her soul in the form of an anonymous letter to the District Office Manager.

In a scathing letter, Jordan advised Marsha McMillan that she had closely averted a near child tragedy. She expressed her belief that her judgment had been severely affected by overwork, the result of improper assignment of cases. She theorized that this was an office-wide problem, and that children were being left at risk as a result. She even suggested some remedy! She ended the letter with the hope that Marsha would review office policies and procedures, and that she would remove any factors that would deter solid investigation in the future. At the last possible moment, though, Jordan mailed the letter to Carolyn instead.

Carolyn was thankful that Jordan sent her the letter. She thought that a complaint to a district office manager would only cause Jordan more trouble! Still, she had to marvel at the brilliance of Jordan's statement! She was moved by her sincerity, and was touched by her perceptions. And her suggestions really made sense! So Carolyn decided to save the letter for a scrapbook that she was creating for Jordan for their anniversary. But this incident would become the portal for numerous letters from Jordan Mathews to Marsha McMillan in the future—most of which, Marsha would receive.

\* \* \*

Labor Day, and their plans had been in place for two months—Carolyn, Marcus, and Bill were coming down for a four day weekend! It really wasn't a long weekend, when you factored in the driving, but it was the visit that Jordan had been waiting all summer for! Marcus and Bill planned to share the driving with Carolyn, and they would be leaving Vermont very early Friday morning to beat the traffic. Of course, traffic also meant that they would be leaving very early Tuesday morning for their return trip. Carolyn's classes were starting again on Wednesday, and she would need time for last minute preparations. Besides, she wasn't convinced that she and the guys could be together for that long! But they begged to come and promised her that they would spend time on the beach, so that she and Jordan could have some "alone time." Carolyn just couldn't say no to them! They were all excited but exhausted when they finally arrived at the apartment, their place at the shore!

The guys staked their claim to the sofa bed in the living room, and had barely placed their luggage in the corner, before they were peeling off shirts and heading out the door! Bill paused briefly at the chess game, and laughed as he saw again Carolyn's foible.

"No coaching from the audience!" Jordan exclaimed.

"Not anything I haven't seen a half dozen times before . . . and for which she has been duly beaten!" Bill shook his head. "Tisk, tisk, tisk . . . You're a goner, my friend!" Carolyn gave a grimace in reply.

The apartment was small, but it had a great location. Bill and Marcus could already see the Boardwalk from the landing, and the cool salt breeze drew them out to play! Carolyn told them that she and Jordan would meet them later on the Sumner Avenue Beach. She gave them a nod and a wave as they disappeared down the stairs. She swore that she could still hear them laughing over a block away! She loved to see them out on some new adventure. Their feelings were always right at the surface. They each reminded her of Jordan, in a way, and her belief in life without pretense. To Bill and Marcus, every day was a new adventure, because they shared every day together. To Carolyn, sharing every day with Jordan had become her life's goal.

"I think they should be OK for a while, don't you?"

She turned to Jordan, held her closely, and gently kissed her again, her tongue tracing Jordan's lips. Jordan inhaled her kiss as if she was breathing in her soul. They smiled at each other, and then, so keenly and comically attuned, raced to the bedroom! With door flying closed, and clothes flying off, they met each other in center of the bed, and became reacquainted with the body, and with the being, that was their lover. They were playful at first, reveling in the sheer existence of the other, tracing each fold and curve, and breathing in each scent. They wrapped themselves in the presence of the other. They marveled at the familiar touch, and the gifts, the wants of the other. They moved in tandem, as if joined by some sacred connection. They tasted the nature of the other. They wanted to pleasure, they wanted to enthrall, they wanted to be, in all ways possible, the divine madness in the other. They held each other tightly, as passion brought collapse from the intensity of the coupling. Sweat rolled down the sides of their bodies, as they lay against each other in silent, profound release. For a brief moment in time, they were one being. This was the joining that they had so longed for! Jordan could not imagine sharing her life with such magnificence, and she cherished each moment they had together. She smiled as she watched Carolyn nod off in her arms. She drank in the smell of her hair, the scent of her perfume, the musk of her body, as they lay beside each other. Soon, she too, fell off to sleep.

Knocking broke the stillness.

"Hello, Ladies, it's us! We're back from the beach and looking for some friends for dinner! Anyone interested in there? Hello!" The voice was distinctly Marcus even if the sentiment was distinctly Bill. "We have two dozen cooked crabs, a loaf of Italian bread, and two six-packs of cold beer. Sound good?"

"And don't forget the fresh blueberries and vanilla ice cream for dessert," Bill added. "Is anyone interested? Hello . . ."

Carolyn heard the calls faintly through the haze of sleep. She looked around the room, and to Jordan beside her, before she could re-acclimate to the present.

"Just a minute, Guys . . ." She woke Jordan and pulled the covers over them both. She noticed their garments and under-things strewn in every direction of the room. She would have been embarrassed, if she had not seen a frequent and similar décor in the men's apartment! Finally she called, "Come on in."

"Well, well, well, what have we here?" Marcus called as he surveyed the room. He kicked a pair of panties to the side of the bed, and stepped over Carolyn's bra.

"Don't answer that, it's probably illegal! Anything you say, can and will be used against you in a court of law," Marcus added, using the MP voice he developed in the Army. He still had such presence.

"Oh come on, in this state, what isn't legal?" Bill said. "It's none of our business, anyway! Besides we have these beautiful blue claws just waiting to be eaten, and we have a volley ball game scheduled at 5:30 a few beaches down. A lovely gathering, I believe, and a mixed crowd—You know, some straight, some gay, a few "I don't knows," and a possible "whatever" or two—a nice group of people we met on the beach! And later, we want you to take us all to a good gay bar!"

"It's nice that you've already made so many friends, and so many plans! Maybe that'll help me get down here more often," Carolyn said. With the exception of Thanksgiving and Christmas, there were no other planned visits.

"We could go to the M and K. I'll call Jan and Betty. They know plenty of guys in the area to make you feel welcome here." Jordan wanted them to cultivate some friendships. She wanted them to feel comfortable there. Maybe they would be down more often. And she really liked having the men around. She needed gay friends and a connection with the community. It was a source of sanity for her, a touchstone of her own reality.

The men stepped out of the apartment while Carolyn and Jordan made their way to the shower and prepared for the night's activities. The cold, cooked crabs offered a nice balance to the bread and beer, but they saved dessert. The volleyball game was actually held on the property of a private beach club in the area, and where the vacationing group from New York was staying. Marcus had quite a serve, being able to lob the ball just over the net, or just inside the foul line. Sand flew as wrists pounded against the sphere, and sweaty physiques welcomed the cool of the beach as they made contact with it. Couples not yet paired clumsily but skillfully bounced into each other, while bathing suit-clad bodies dove and spiked the Marcus Team to victory! Marcus took a huge bow at center court amid shouts of "Fix!" He graciously accepted the six pack of Miller, a beer for each player on his team, and used the opportunity to invite the group to the bar. He didn't know that the place was almost an hour away! The distance didn't matter, though—the crowd had already been drawn into the Marcus mystique, and they all agreed to meet later at the club. So they showered, primped, and otherwise prepared, and drove off to the M and K for the night's amusement!

As the couples piled into the Asbury bar, there was a momentary lapse in play on the first floor—and they were overtaken by the sounds of Donna Summer's "Love to Love You, Baby"[67] beckoning them to the second! They had not even stopped to survey the crowd, before Marcus took Bill's hand and lunged toward

---

[67] Summer, Donna, Modorer, Giorgio, and Bellotte, Pete: (1975). "Love To Love You, Baby" [recorded by Donna Summer].On *Love To Love You Baby* [audio album] New York: Casablanca Records

the stairs leading them to the disco diva! Bill threw his stuff on the nearest table before Marcus dragged him out on the dance floor, and into the throng of dancing lesbians! But the girls just made room, while the men stepped together in sublime sensuality. The crowd was soon mixed, and the mix of party-goers took up several large tables in the club! Marcus had already attracted a following that continued to grow with the night! Although the gay men usually gravitated on the first floor, while the lesbians grouped on the second, this night it would be different—the crowds following the prompts, and the laughter, and the charm that was Marcus, this Gay Pied Piper! And they partied the night away—Marcus shouting:

> "Do a little dance, Make a little love,
> Get down tonight, Get down tonight . . .
>
> Baby, Get down, Get down, Get down, Get down, Get down
> Tonight Babe,
> ouh, ouh,ouh, ouh, ouh, ouh, ouh,ouh . . ."[68]

with his fist held high and pumping to the beat, his hips leading the crowd in the pounding rhythm of K.C. and the Sunshine Band! He made dance-sandwiches on a "Love Roller Coaster,"[69] arms above head, sweat rolling down cheeks, hips in thrust with each step, whooping and calling a beat, whistling and clapping in syncopation—as the DJ tantalized the crowd with waves of sound madness! The dancers shouted and cheered to each other, as the crowd of hips and feet stepped

---

[68] "Get Down Tonight". Words and Music by Harry Wayne Casey and Richard Finch. Copyright©1975 (Renewed 2003) EMI LONGITUDE MUSIC. All Rights Reserved. International Copyright Secured. Used by Permission. Reprinted with permission of Hal Leonard Corporation.

[69] Beck, Billy, et al (1975). "Love Rollercoaster" [recorded by the Ohio Players]. On *Honey* [audio album]. Chicago: Mercury Records

in pulsating strides across the floor! The strobe lights shot across the walls like fish across the bay, and the neon lights accented tee shirts and sandals, tans and snow white teeth, as they bopped, and pranced, and laughed, and flirted harmlessly. They drank Stoli shots, smoked a little weed, and inhaled some poppers that were making their way around the room. Jordan and Carolyn drank Coors, and took a hit from an occasional joint that made its way to their table. They laughed with their old friends, and bought rounds for the new ones. They danced tight and slow, or joined the throngs of partiers in center floor, as the pulse of the rhythms centrifuged into one mighty, united force of the body electric! They were tired, and perspired, and totally astounded with the feeling of community and belonging. They were now one with the Gay Universe!

Suddenly, a hand clasped her wrist, and Jordan was gently pulled from chair to dance floor, a salsa disco beat moving her body, spinning and spinning her in and out of the arms of the grinning Bill! Marcus, too, had Carolyn, and they were trotting in rhythm and steps they had practiced at the gay bars in Vermont!

"Meda, Meda! Que Pasa!" Bill chanted in rhythm to those still seated, his spirit energizing the room, as the piano, and the trumpets, and the drums melded them in a Latin fury! Then, just as quickly, Carolyn and Jordan were propelled back to each other, as Bill and Marcus now clasped hands, then changed partners with other men on the dance floor. The Latino chorus repeated the refrain, accented by the blare of the trumpets and the rhythm of the congas, as the piano led the melody. Another song, a change in tempo, and another change in partners—Carolyn and Jordan were now dancing with women they had only just met! Then suddenly spun together again, they locked eyes as they pulled each other close, and danced as if no one could ever pull them apart!

"Hey Carolyn, there's a Labor Day Gay Unity Beach Party up here tomorrow. Want to go?" Bill yelled as he spun his dance partner to another, and again caught Marcus, this time for keeps.

"Yeah? . . . Maybe . . . We'll see . . ." She was calculating the time that she would have to share Jordan with the others. They had so little time alone as it was! But they were so enjoying their time with their friends! It was hard to cram a lifetime into a single weekend!

Then the centrifuged dancers each busted a solo under the silver globe in the center of the dance floor, as the room encased them in the sweat and applause of sexuality released. But the Universe came to a standing ovation, as the young, well dressed, well endowed, Nubian Princess began a slow and sensuous strip, while the DJ blared Hot Chocolate:

> "I believe in miracles . . .
> Where you from . . .
> You sexy thing, you sexy thing you . . . . [70]"

She had their full attention, the crowd now becoming an arena focused on this singular prize! Seductively, she pulled off her scarf, and allowed the tips to glide ever so lightly along the length of her body. The crowd called out a moan of approval! In reward, the Onyx Enchantress then slid her jacket down the length of her arms and let the fabric drape between her legs, before she tossed it aside.

"All right!" the partiers responded their shouts, nearly drowning out the applause.

The crowds howled for the Ebony Beauty as she enchanted them with each article of clothing tossed from body to floor! Jan and Betty moved to the front of the crowd, leading Jordan, Carolyn, Marcus, and Bill to the front row of spectators.

---

[70] "You Sexy Thing". Words and Music by E. Brown. Copyright@1975 by Finchley Music Corp. Copyright Renewed. Administered in the USA and Canada by Music & Media International,Inc. Administered for the World excluding the USA and Canada by RAK Music Publishing Ltd. International. Copyright Secured. All Rights Reserved. Reprinted by permission of Hal Leonard Corporation.

"Oh Baby, Oh Baby!" Jordan whispered as the Raven Temptress now unbuttoned her blouse, and the mounds of breast burst out just above the bra line! She then caught Carolyn's glare, and said innocently, "What?"

"Let's get out of here before the place gets raided!" Carolyn was getting edgy! She shouted the command to Bill and Marcus.

"No way!" Marcus shouted back. "You see anybody else leaving? They're not going to call anyone, for a little entertainment like this!"

"Come on, Carolyn, we'll be OK!" Bill added. Then, addressing his attention back to the Goddess, he beckoned her.

"Oh yeah, My Lady. Do it now!" The Sable Diety proudly strutted by, then looked over her shoulder and back to Jordan and Carolyn. She smiled and tipped her breasts toward them.

"Um, Um, Um!" Jan replied to a blonde woman nodding next to her, as the crowd continued to cheer the dancer on!

The bartender, a rather rough looking woman called Lady Holliday moved slowly at first to stop the dancer, perhaps hoping as the rest, to catch a full glimpse of the Black Goddess. But when this Dusky Jewel began to stroke her thighs and move slowly toward breast and crotch, Lady Holliday bolted to the floor, clothed the young woman in her jacket, and quickly whisked her off to either restroom or backroom. Neither was to be seen again that evening! The crowds booed the bartender, hating to see such an end! But the dancing from that point—that night—was near frenzy to the finish.

> "Touch me, you sexy thing . . .
> Kiss me, you sexy thing . . .
> I love the way you touch me,
> You sexy thing you . . ."[71]

---

[71] ibid

The drivers stopped drinking by midnight, so that they could cart their drunken friends home at the 2:00 a.m. closing. Jordan hadn't had a date like that since she left college, and she and Carolyn had never had one together! And the frivolity at closing followed the group outside! As a final Diana Ross mix of "Ain't No Mountain High Enough"[72] faded to "Touch Me In The Morning,"[73] the crowds filed off to the line of waiting cars and drivers. It would still be several more years before Diana Ross, Thelma Houston, and Gloria Gaynor would be ousted by Donna Summer as THE Queen of Disco, and before every gay bar in the country would close the night with Summer's "Last Dance.[74]"

As Jordan stepped outside the club, she saw several couples making out just beyond the shadows, and a few more were steaming up the windows of their parked cars. It probably wasn't the best idea to close the place that night, but such assessments are always made in hindsight. Crowds of gay people could be a real target! But Jordan had never experienced such hatred, so the possibility of harm never occurred to her. That would be the only excuse she could offer later for the events that next took place.

She had gone to the parking lot alone and had driven the car to the front door of the club to pick up Carolyn, Marcus and Bill. She ignored the car waiting on the opposite side of the street. She thought that they were probably just another couple too poor or too shy to rent a motel room. No sooner had Carolyn and the

---

[72] Ashford, Nicholas, and Simpson, Valerie (1966). "Ain't No Mountain High Enough" [re-recorded by Diana Ross]. On *Diana Ross* [audio album]. Detroit: Motown Records (1970)

[73] Masser, Michael, and Miller, Ron (1973). "Touch Me In The Morning" [recorded by Diana Ross]. Released as a single record [audio record]. Detroit: Motown Records

[74] Jabara, Paul. (1978) "Last Dance" [recorded by Donna Summer for the motion picture *Thank God It's Friday*]. Released on *Live and More* [audio album]. New York: Casablanca Records

others emerged with the crowd of gay partiers, than that car squealed wheels, and headed toward the throng now crossing the street!

"Hey watch it, asshole!" someone shouted from the crowd. "You'll kill somebody!"

"That's the point, you fuckin' perverts! Get outa our town, you freakin' faggots, you lezzie whores, or you'll end up under the tires!"

The car kept revving its engine, while the driver kept his foot on the clutch. The wheels were screeching in the night! Suddenly, from the opposite end of the lot, a small group of men with bats and clubs started running toward the crowd! Carolyn and the others were already in the car, and were shouting to Jordan to floor it out of there. She was stunned.

"We can't just leave people here like this!"

She floored the gas pedal, and the car lurched toward the group of bat wielding freaks! They scattered like vermin in the night! In the confusion, most of the partiers had either reached the safety of their cars, or had retreated back into the bar. But it was not over! As Jordan sped away from the commotion, the screechy black car flew off after them! The passengers were screaming obscenities at her, hanging out of their car windows, as the black car tagged her bumper! She drove even faster through the tight, back city streets, running stop signs and dodging parked cars, moving back and forth between main streets and side streets, as Bill and Marcus shouted out commands!

"Turn here!" Marcus shouted, and Jordan whipped the steering wheel at his order. They were nearly broadsided by a sedan coming from a side street, as they fishtailed around a corner and back onto Cookman! But the black car stayed right with them, menacing them, pushing them off the road! A passenger hung out the window, blowing kisses, gesturing a hand-job, shaking his bat, while his buddies laughed and shouted obscenities. A beer bottle bounced off the trunk of Jordan's car, and nearly broke through the back window! She flew down Bangs Avenue, but the black tank kept pace.

"Fuck off, Assholes!" Jordan screamed out her window, and the car nearly tagged her bumper again! She skidded onto another side street, then raced again through the city streets, through parking lots, to back alleys, and back onto main streets! All the while, the black car kept pace, menacing them, taunting them through every section of town!

"Gun it, Jordan!" Bill shouted out at her. She floored the pedal, and the car hit the railroad tracks so hard, that the four flew into the air as the car bolted down Corlies Avenue, and again, back onto side streets. And still, the black car stayed with them, right at their trunk! She could see the grill work out the back window!

"Bastards! I can't see!" Jordan yelled, as she flipped the mirror so that she could drive without their headlights, or their faces, in her eyes! She slammed on her breaks, and the black car quickly swerved to miss her. The car again fell behind her and tagged the bumper! Carolyn screamed, and Marcus yelled, "Hold on!" The street lights and store fronts were a blur, the line of parked cars a wall from which they could not escape!

"Gun it! Go!" Bill shouted, and Jordan raced again down Corlies Avenue, as if she was heading toward the Parkway. They were running now to beat the maze of back streets and back alleys that nearly blocked them in.

"Turn here now!" Marcus shouted at the last possible moment. Jordan forced the car into the hospital parking lot, while the black car shot passed the entrance. The passengers screamed more vicious threats and obscenities as their car sped away. Jordan could hear the sound of police sirens in the distance. She hoped they were responding to their friends. They waited in the hospital parking lot for half an hour before they ventured onto the streets again.

"So . . . what the fuck! Real nice neighbors you have in this town! Remind me never to visit again without my helmet and riot gear! . . . Oh that's right, I forgot to pack it. Next time I'll have to remember . . . a night at Jordan's—OK, body armor goes right here in my overnight bag, and right next to my numchucks! You people sure have a strange way of making a gay man feel welcome!" Marcus tried to calm everyone with his humor.

"And you drive like an old fart! It's a wonder we're still alive! Go see a Bond[75] movie or something! You need to pick up some tips on the finer points of moron dodging . . ." Bill was tense. No joking about it.

"Excuse me, but I didn't think that stunt driving was a prerequisite for the evening! I might have done a lot better if I wasn't so afraid . . . and so afraid of wetting my pants! You know, it's pretty hard to snap a turn when you're clasping your thighs together! . . . By the way, I'm going in to use the Ladies Room. Care to join me?" She had now pulled into the lot of an all night diner. She parked the car toward the back of the lot, and out of the view of the highway. Her legs felt wobbly as she stood up from the car seat.

"Why not," Bill replied. "Gay bashers make me hungry."

As they looked over the menu and waited for the waitress, they continued their discussion about the incident. They spoke softly, so as not to arouse the ire of the other patrons there. After all, they had already met the welcome wagon!

"I can't believe that anyone could be so vicious toward us, just because we're gay. We weren't bothering anyone." Carolyn was incredulous. As Jordan looked toward the table, she could see Carolyn's hands still trembling.

"So, you still think that they did that to us because we're gay? Is that what you really think?" Bill was probing the girls for an answer. There were no takers.

"Believe me, some people don't need any excuse! They are so full of hatred, that any target, any victim, will suffice as long as it's vulnerable enough, and scared enough, not to fight back! . . . It's anger morphed into a fist, screaming for a release that will only be satisfied with the pound, pound, pounding on something weaker than they are! . . . So today, it's a group of faggots and

---

[75] A reference to the fictional British spy James Bond, as created by Ian Fleming, whose movie series was first produced by Albert Broccoli and Harry Saltzman in 1962 for EON Productions.

lesbians . . . Maybe tomorrow, it'll be a group of poor black kids. They can hurl a name, burn a cross, shake a rope—whatever it takes to scare the hell out of them, and to make themselves feel better. Oh, no black kids around? Hey, no problem . . . let's paint a couple of swastikas on that Jew's house over there, or toss a couple of bricks through that window while they're at temple. Oh, the synagogue's too far away? OK, we can hit that gay bar tonight . . . or, how about that group home for the retarded . . . or . . . No, let's torch that homeless guy that lives under the Boardwalk! . . . Or, let's terrorize that old lady who lives alone—she's half nuts anyway! . . . Anything, just so I'm not a target myself! . . . . What, no people we can torment? No problem! We can torture that kitten! We can bludgeon that swan! Hey, don't swerve! Run that animal down, I dare you. Double it, if you kill her chicks, too! Go ahead, just hit 'em, hit 'em, hit 'em, and it'll all be alright! . . . Except that it never is . . . and the fist goes on, silent but lurking, just waiting for the next opportunity for release . . . And so it goes . . . You see? Their choices are endless, there's plenty to go around! There is no end to the revelry!"

Bill shook his head and held his arms extended as if he were the Master of Ceremonies at some Circus of the Grotesque. He shook his head as if trying to understand, and then realizing that with some actions, there could be no understanding.

"I don't feel safe anymore," Jordan whispered. She looked to each of her friends, and then down again to the table.

"Don't be ridiculous!" Bill said "You were never safe in the first place! Only, you just didn't realize it! . . . None of us is safe really. We take our lives in our hands from the moment of conception. For the rest of the time, we exist in a world of false security—Mommy and Daddy will protect us . . . the teacher will protect us . . . the police will protect us . . . But at the end of it all, it just comes down to dumb luck! It's a wonder any of us makes it to adulthood, and then, to retirement! You just have to learn to keep your head down and your butt covered . . . The rest is up to the Lord . . ."

"Praying already? Oh, come on, our food's not that bad!" The waitress was smiling to them as she prepared to take their orders.

"I'll have a burger and a coffee," Marcus said.

"Sounds good to me too, only make my coffee a coke," Bill replied.

"Just coffee for me," Jordan ordered, "and maybe a piece of that pecan pie."

"I'll just have a tea," Carolyn said.

As they were waiting for their food, two cops emerged from a black and white cruiser and took stools at the counter. They each ordered cake and coffee.

"Hi Fellas! Anything exciting happening tonight?" the counter girl asked them.

"No, just a riot over at the M and K. I swear to God, I'll never understand those people! It's a shame we have to put our own lives on the line for the likes of them. And I have a family, you know . . ."

"So next time, we'll just get there a little slower." His partner was now lifting a forkful of chocolate cake as he eyed the ass of the waitress walking back to the cook.

Bill looked to Carolyn, Jordan, and Marcus, and said simply, "And there you have it . . ."

They stayed close to home for the rest of the holiday weekend, spending time basking in the sun, body surfing in the ocean, making sand castles with soap opera scripts, and grilling in the driveway. They had not seen again, the New York group of partiers that shared with them the terrifying night at the bar. They spent the first cool night of early September on the Boardwalk, playing the stands, riding the Wild Mouse and the Himalaya, eating treats from one end of the pier to the other, and just people-watching. They stood among the throngs as the fireworks burst overhead. As she looked among the crowd, Jordan saw very little difference between themselves and the straight couples that stood nearby. She thought again about the conversation she once had with her father.

"What is it that they want, now?" he challenged her.

"Well, what is it that anyone wants, Dad? A decent job, for a decent wage, a decent home, and a decent place to raise their kids . . ."

* * *

Thanksgiving was only a week away, and the office was crazy with new abuse and neglect referrals. The late fall was especially cold, and families were already having heating emergencies. Teenagers from all over the county were bad-mouthing their parents, and they were being beaten for it! Some of the usual culprits ran away, only to go back home when they saw that the juvenile shelter was full. Those kids would never accept a foster placement! Young children were left unsupervised. An assortment of bruises, bumps or other injuries flooded the custody cases. A broken bone and welts of every dimension on the arms and legs of kids of every size were reported for investigation! Sex perps. were celebrating their own kind of holiday. Foster kids needed re-placement. The Prosecutor's Office barked for reports or medical records. The Superior Courts were ordering caseworkers for testimony. On some days, the roster of caseworker coverage flipped twice through the ranks, and still there seemed no end to the mayhem!

Jordan was working hours of overtime nearly every night just to meet the agency timelines! She used the drive to the homes of her clients as a moment of peaceful reflection, a time to gather her thoughts. She was preparing to see her parents for the first time since she moved out eights months ago. The invitation to Thanksgiving dinner came by way of Kelly and Jonathan. Now that Kelly could drive, she and her brother often stopped by the apartment in the evenings to hang out, watch some TV, pig out on snacks, and to otherwise visit with their "exiled" sister. They got along much better now that they had some distance. Maybe it was true that absence made the heart grow fonder! Jordan verified the Thanksgiving invitation with a phone call to her mom. She wanted to use it as a chance to break the ice.

Ann was clear that they all just wanted to celebrate the holiday, and that Jordan wouldn't have any pressures there. The Mathews' just wanted to share time together again as a family! But as Jordan thought, the invitation did not extend to Carolyn. The next phone call went to her.

"She doesn't get it, my mother! She doesn't see that by not inviting you, she is applying pressure!"

"Of course she gets it!" Carolyn replied. "But are you going to abandon the first invitation from your family since you let them in on the news? Sounds counter-productive to me, since your goal is to win them back! Right?"

"Humph! All this time I've been waiting for them to accept me—to accept us—to understand, and to bless! What a waste of time! I'm telling you—if I was a drug slut whore, I'd be more welcome there! Anything but a lesbian! . . . I can hear them already! I could be Mother Theresa herself, and they still wouldn't accept me as their daughter unless I was cocked out under some man somewhere! Talk about your skewed priorities! . . . And that's the only thing about me that they can see anymore! Can you imagine your whole life—No, your total existence—being defined solely by who you love and bed? That's where they're at, ya know! I'm not a human being anymore, I'm not a woman . . . I'm just a twat . . . And a non-conforming twat at that! A twat with a mind of its own! How threatening must that be!"

"The twat that ate New Jersey!" Carolyn laughed in reply.

That's how they've calculated the sum total of my existence! How ridiculous!"

"You're probably right there, Partner! You are what you lay, or so it would seem . . . ! So what? They're your family, and you need them in your life. They'll get through this."

"Sure! But at what price to me? . . . Well, let's flip that idea a bit! Mom's a good daughter to my grandmother, she's the mother of three, she's the faithful wife of Pete, she's a God-fearing', American patriot who believes in works of charity, she helps the neighbors . . . But from now on, all I will ever see is that she's the twat Pete is screwing!"

"Oh! Now there's a mental image we don't want to see . . . What a thought! You think your parents really have sex?" Carolyn was trying to calm her.

"Be serious! What does that say about your existence, Mom! . . . How juvenile! I feel like I'm looking at my 5th grade teacher the day she told us she was pregnant, and all thoughts fell on the night in question! . . . Except that for my family, my whole life will be just that image! We'll be just that image!"

"It'll be their loss if it is! . . . But here we go again! Back on that counter-productive, think-tank ride to hell!"

"You know why I got invited? She just doesn't want to handle that embarrassing question: 'So where's Jordan on this fine Thanksgiving?' They don't want to say that I was home alone eating a TV dinner, because they have their own ideas about who I should fuck, and how I should do it! They don't even consider how I should live MY life! Like one life fits all! Like their way is the only way! They can't accept that I don't come in that size! I never have!"

"You wouldn't be home alone eating a TV dinner! You'd be accompanying your adoring partner to the home of your in-laws for a Holiday dinner with all of the fixins' and none of the trappings! . . . Now that I think about it, maybe that's how you should approach this—You've taken time out of your schedule for them, but you still have somewhere else to go. You go in, you say hello, you have dinner, and you're out of there, and on your way to my folks' home. And before anything intense develops! Married couples do that all the time!"

"That still doesn't make the point! I haven't changed! I'm the same person I've always been! This is who I am! My parents can't see what has been so obvious! Where have they been all my life, anyway? Who have they been raising? . . . I really don't get it!"

"Just another of life's mysteries that will work itself out in time . . . . I think . . ." Carolyn replied.

Jordan wanted to push it, but Carolyn told her not to argue. She planned to spend the day with her own parents anyway. Besides, they would still have time together at their apartment. Jordan knew that Carolyn was right, if she wanted to get back with her family, but that still didn't make her happy about it! So she agreed that she would leave early and join Carolyn at the Berringer's for Thanksgiving dessert, and without further comment to her parents. She felt that that was a pretty strong statement. And she tried hard to see the Holiday as a start with them.

And they would still be together at their apartment! Jordan was not certain when, but somewhere, their singular possessions had now become joint property. There was a oneness to them now! They were seen as a couple, each defined in terms of the other, the yin and her yang, melded in unity, spinning opposites that pulled together tightly. There was no "your-stuff and my-stuff" anymore—it was all "our stuff" now! They planned to exchange rings at Christmas, their first anniversary, and just before Midnight Mass. They were taking the next step in their relationship. They were committing themselves to each other for a lifetime! Jordan was already writing the vows she would be making to Carolyn, polishing every line so that the words would sing out her feelings. That she had found such love in so beautiful a companion made her the most thankful! And she would celebrate that love every day!

The office received its final delivery of donated turkeys and food for needy families on Thanksgiving Eve. Jordan had blocked out the day so that she could make the deliveries and still be home by night fall. She knew that Carolyn would already have arrived at their apartment by then. A bruise on the jaw of a seven year old disrupted Jordan's schedule, and by the time she had concluded that investigation, it was already late afternoon. And still, she had eight turkey stops to make in the south county! She shot a phone call to Carolyn and told her that she would be home late. She sped along the Parkway to save time. It was already dark at the point that she arrived at the last home on her list. It was an old farm, rundown, but still working. Mrs. Davidson lived there with her four kids, a few cats, several geese, two roosters, about two dozen chickens, a pig, three goats, an old cow, and a nasty old dog. The farmhouse was located at the end of a worn, graveled road that ran along side their field. Mrs. Davidson never cared much for intruders, so she staked Jake, the old bulldog, on a chain between the driveway and the porch. Jordan had been to the home about a dozen times before. She had learned that if she parked her car just to the right of the abandoned washing machine in the front yard, Jake was not able to reach her.

She beeped the horn a few times as she parked the car in its designated safety zone. Jake growled, but sat motionless, tethered to his tree stump. Jordan got out of the car, and opened its back door. As she bent down to pick up the turkey and the box of foodstuffs stored there, she felt a searing pain, and then a numbness, that emanated from her left buttock! She quickly turned to see Jake's jaw firmly clenched to her body! Either she had misjudged her parking job, or someone had lengthened his chain! She instinctively popped the dog across the snout with the back of her fist, and Jake's whelps brought the family running to his aid.

"What did ya do to my dog, Ms. Mathews? If ya hurt him, you're really gonna be sorry! I'm gonna call your supervisor! I'll sue you and the state, if ya hurt my Jake . . ." Mrs. Davidson stood on the porch flailing her fist as the ashes fell off of the cigarette she held tightly in her mouth. Her sweatshirt and jeans were full of the day's chores. The children ran to comfort their dog. Jordan thrust the box of food toward the oldest son.

"Happy Thanksgiving," she said, as she barely limped back to the car. She raised herself onto the opposite buttock, and attempted the drive to the local hospital. The pain shot through her each time she applied the brakes. She was at the hospital emergency room within fifteen minutes.

"What did you say happened to you?" the nurse at the admitting desk asked. She was grinning as she helped Jordan complete the triage paperwork. "And you say that you're a BCS worker, and that you were bitten on the job?"

"Yes, that's right. I was bending over to get a food basket out of the back seat of my car, and the family's dog bit me. I think he bit me twice, actually, but the pain is so bad, I can't really say where it's coming from."

"It's just coming from your behind somewhere?"

"Exactly."

"Arlene, take Ms. Mathews to exam room four and give her a gown. The doctor will have to do a full body exam for dog bites. I'll call the police. They'll have Animal Control pick up the dog."

"I don't want the dog harmed!" Jordan exclaimed.

"Of course not! But he will have to be quarantined for a week, to make sure that he's alright . . . not rabid. You follow me?"

Jordan shook her head and accompanied the volunteer Arlene to the exam room. She stood patiently and nakedly in her hospital gown, and waited for the doctor. The pain had now become a dull throb that wracked her body.

"Hello Ms. Mathews. I'm Dr. Kelleher . . . So you were delivering food for Thanksgiving, and the family sicked their dog on you?"

"No, no . . . it was strictly an interaction between me and the dog. If the family had come out, I'm sure he wouldn't have bothered me. I've never had a problem with him before tonight."

"And the injury is on your left buttock . . . I'll have to have you lay across this proctology table so that I can have a good angle to clean and dress the wounds. I'll also be applying an antibiotic . . . Did the dog have his shots?"

"Please . . . the kids haven't had their shots, so I doubt very seriously that the dog did! But he looks pretty healthy . . ."

The doctor left the room and returned with an intern and a resident, as Jordan lay across the table, her bare ass pointed to the ceiling, and her head facing the floor.

"I wanted to show these injuries to our other covering physicians. We don't often get multiple dog bites on a BCS worker." The doctors introduced themselves and left the room.

"It'll be a pleasure working with you in the future," one of the physicians laughed, and he pulled the drape to the room closed as he exited.

Jordan was mortified, but she was in no position to argue! The wounds did not require stitches, and as she suspected, they occurred only along the left flank of her body. And she was right—there were actually two bites. The doctor instructed that she stay off of her left backside for a few days to allow the healing, and he gave her a prescription for percodan for the pain. She drove herself back to the office, still propped up on her right cheek, got into her own car, and drove herself home the same way. Carolyn helped her from the car, parked her on the couch, and examined her wounds.

"Yikes, Almighty! Why didn'tcha just give him the turkey instead of your butt?" Carolyn had to feign concern to hide her laughter.

"Like I had some kind of choice? . . . Obviously, that dog knows good quality meat when he sees it! Sunk his teeth into me quicker than a shark in a feeding frenzy! I had to beat him off of me before he took my whole ass!"

"Ahh . . . escaped by the seat of your pants, I see . . . ! So what did you say to the family?"

"Ya mean after they threatened to sue me? And the State? And the Bureau? . . . I did what any dedicated public servant would do . . . . I wished them a Happy Thanksgiving, and limped back to my car!" Jordan was laughing so hard by this point that she was nearly choking out the words.

Carolyn nursed her heiny and pampered her with a robe and a hot tea. Jordan then called Jane Morrison and reported the on-the-job injury. Jane would complete the Workman's Comp paperwork to cover the costs of hospital treatment. It would be nearly six months, and three similar submits, before the account with the hospital was actually cleared! Jordan never received the promised compensation for her torn blue jeans, the office staff joked that Jordan would always be the first to put her butt on the line for her clients, and the Davidson's never thanked her for the turkey!

\* \* \*

The aroma of turkey and turnips overwhelmed Jordan as she opened the door to her family's home. Kelly was the first to greet her, and yelled the announcement of her arrival as she hugged her sister. Ann Mathews ran to the door, her apron hanging from around her neck, and neatly tied at the waist.

As she hugged her daughter and kissed her on the cheek, Ann said, "I'm so glad you've come home for Thanksgiving. It just wouldn't be the same without you. Have a glass of wine. Dinner will be ready in an hour, so we still have plenty of time . . . Pete, Jordan's here!"

Jordan knew that her father was already aware of her arrival. They each had a kind of radar for the other. She also knew that he was lingering a bit before he made his entrance and acknowledged her.

"Jordan" he said rather coolly," I'm so glad you're finally here!" She tried to ignore the seeming lack of warmth, and rationalized that she had been reading too much into the exchange. She was amazed at how much her parents had aged. She had never noted the passage of time before, but saw it now, marching across their faces.

"Hi Dad, I've missed you all so much! It feels so great to be here with you all again!"

She was using Carolyn's strategy of magnanimity. Carolyn had convinced her to focus on the goal of reuniting with her family, and not on any detracting objective that might frustrate that goal. In other words, sometimes she would have to eat a little crow, if she wanted to stay for the turkey! She truly missed her family, and she wanted them back. She saw this invitation as an important first step. She believed that ultimately, they, too, would welcome Carolyn, just as the Berringer's had welcomed her. It was as one of life's pleasant inevitabilities. It had to be! No one mentioned Carolyn's name that day, until Jordan was preparing to leave. No one alluded to their relationship. And no one tried to suggest a male prospect for Jordan. Yes, she viewed this as real progress.

Jordan helped set the table, prayed Grace with the family, and grabbed at the food just as they had done for a generation! Uncle Pat, Aunt Joy, and Pat Jr. arrived with her grandmother just after Jordan. This helped diffuse some of the initial awkwardness, especially since they still didn't know the family's "sordid secret!" Jordan shared stories of her new career, focusing on her client's struggles and on their successes. Her family sat spellbound. They howled as she relayed the account of her injury, and teased that she should be given a purple heart-seat. They commented on her accomplishments, and praised her for her dedication. In this, it was a much different kind of family gathering. Jordan had grown up.

As she left the home early that evening and said her good-byes, her father last hugged and kissed her. Then, he held her slightly apart from him, looked in her eyes, and said, "Jordan, don't stay gone so long. We all love and miss ya here."

She felt a glimpse of the past, and nearly cried. So did he.

Jordan waived to her family one last time as she pulled out of the driveway and headed for Carolyn and the Berringer's. As she drove through the familiar and frozen streets of her hometown, that one thought reverberated through her consciousness—"And against all odds, she had won."

And victories seemed to come in multiples that season—while she and Carolyn were out doing some holiday shopping at the new mall in town, they ran into Marge and Tyler, who were combing Bamberger's for a few gifts for Marge's parents. It was only by luck that Tyler was off on Black Friday. The restaurant had an electrical problem and was closed for the day. And Marge would never miss a good sale! So, it came as no surprise—awkward though it was—that the two couples would collide near the entrance to the store.

"Hey, look at you!" Marge screamed to Jordan as they nearly walked into each other. The two hugged, as Tyler and Carolyn each surveyed the scene, and each other.

"Whatcha been up to?"

"Work stuff, you know . . . making the world safe for all humanity . . ." Jordan replied.

"And really putting her heart and soul into it, too, if I might add . . . Not to mention her backside!" Carolyn laughed, trying to smooth her way into the conversation.

"She's alluding to my pending Workman's Comp case! Do you think I limp enough to score a cool million?"

"Well, that depends on what happened . . . and how rich the perpetrator is!" Tyler commented.

"Or, if there's insurance involved . . ." Marge added.

"Nope, the people are dirt poor, and the perp. is a dog!" Jordan replied with feigned sadness.

"Tough luck, Buddy . . . I think you're in for another huge disappointment. . . . So, maybe Workman's Comp is the way to go . . . Not much money in that though. Not even your full salary! I'm in management now. I know!" Tyler said.

"Oh, a management stiff! Who'd ever have thought that, way back then, huh?" Jordan kidded.

"So, are you going to tell us what happened?" Marge asked, as she tried to catch a glimpse of the wounded butt in question.

"Naturally! . . . Would I ever hide anything from you?" Jordan answered.

Carolyn took full advantage of the lead-in, and cleared her throat, hinting at introduction.

"Oh, you haven't met my friend yet . . . Tyler and Marge, this is Carolyn!"

"I think we might have met before . . . No, I think I saw your picture . . . at Jordan's apartment." Marge showed some momentary uneasiness, but no disrespect. She did not probe further into that connection.

The two couples walked over to a coffee shop nearby, and Jordan gave, in humorous detail, an account of her injury. The three laughed loud and long, as she told of her genuine efforts to ensure that all of her families had the fixings for an appropriate Holiday feast. Yet, at the end of it all, the only thing that she could be sure was actually eaten—was her own kiester! She demonstrated, in painful dramatics, the ride to the hospital, and was now precariously perched on one cheek, as she sat on her chair and spoke. She drew howls from the group, as she used her hand to demonstrate her posture over the hospital exam table! Carolyn looked to Tyler and Marge, and shook her head as she laughed with them. As Jordan spoke, the two seemed more at ease with Carolyn.

Marge filled Jordan in on some of the Group gossip. She talked about Janice's trip to Gaithersburg to spend Thanksgiving weekend with Martin. Janice's parents had taken a cruise with her Uncle Paul Guilford and his family. For the first time, Janice and Martin were able to experiment with a holiday on their own. Janice had even called Karen for a few dessert recipes, and Tyler gave her some pointers on turkey and stuffing. She hoped to finally snare the man she had been chasing for years!

"Do you believe it? She thinks that Martin can be gotten with my award winning, cranberry-walnut dressing! No way! I told her that a guy like that will need at least a sweet potato soufflé, with a chocolate cake chaser! . . . So she's making that too!" Tyler laughed.

"And as for us, we've decided that we'll be starting our own family right off . . . right after the wedding! Nothing cooking now, though, thankfully . . . Thank God for the pill!" Marge added.

They strolled the mall together in search of the perfect Christmas gifts, and talked and laughed as they shopped. They picked up the obvious and the absurd, as they made their way from store to store, glimpsing each kiosk as they passed by. Both couples left the mall with armfuls of holiday wonderment! Marge and Tyler left toward one end of the mall, with Carolyn and Jordan leaving by the other.

"Nice people," Carolyn said, as they walked toward Jordan's car.

"I know what you're thinking . . . Why didn't I just blurt out our relationship, after Marge told us about her and Tyler planning a family . . ." Jordan said.

"Did I say anything? How you choose to handle your friends is your own business! My only concern is that I can fit into that world in time. Besides, I already know how you're going to handle that situation . . . You're not going to tell them! You are just going to let things go on, and let them draw their own conclusions . . . just as you inevitably handle all things that cause you discomfort . . . !" Carolyn snidely replied.

"How is it that you know me so well? Besides, why should I have to tell them that I'm gay? Did they ever tell me that they're straight? . . . And don't you think that by seeing us together, they know how we feel about each other? That's enough for me!"

"Somehow, I knew that would be!" Carolyn responded, as she smiled at Jordan, and entered the car.

The couple went about the remainder of the weekend tending to chores, and to each other. They were acting more as a team, now. They balanced each other's skills and deficits, likes and dislikes. And as if in a blip in time, Carolyn was again heading up the Interstates and back to Vermont, and Jordan was searching for any reminders of her, left behind in their apartment.

\* \* \*

She picked up their rings at Gilbert Jeweler's and headed back to their apartment. It took her longer than that to find a romantic Christmas card that didn't have some male-female thing plastered all over it! Jordan was again anxiously awaiting a visit with Carolyn! But this time, it was much more than that. It was nearly Christmas, and the jeweler had a delay in sizing the rings. Jordan worried that they still wouldn't be ready. The couple picked out the tooled matching wedding bans when Carolyn was down at Thanksgiving. It wasn't a snap decision—they talked about it for months. No public ceremony, no fanfare. It was just a quiet pledge of their love and devotion, sealed with these external reminders of their vowed commitment to each other. Maybe the outside world would hold little value for the verses, and little respect for the trinkets, but in the Gay Community, this gesture was well recognized. And that was the community that most mattered to them. Jordan polished the rings as soon as she got home, and set them in their open boxes on her dresser. The rings shone brightly in the noonday sun. She rewrote her vows for the fourth time, and said them aloud so that she could feel their rhythm. She was amazed at how such things could take on lives of their own. How such simple words could convey a forever promise! Yet, she would happily accept that responsibility, and would eagerly fulfill the meaning of each word written there.

With shopping done, and most items from the toy drive already dispersed to her clients, Jordan was tending to their ceremony. She drove over to the beach, and searched for the appropriate place to exchange their lifelong oaths. She found it, once again, along a secluded stretch of ocean, and just beyond the boardwalk. They had gone there many times together, to run, to swim, to sit holding hands as they watched the nighttime skies—there could be no more perfect place! They would follow this ceremony with the Christmas Eve Midnight Mass. Jordan had already arranged to meet her family at the Church. This time, though, Jordan didn't ask her parents if Carolyn could come—she told them that she was coming! They need not know anything else. Jordan would spend Christmas Day with her own family, and would join Carolyn at her family's home early Christmas evening. The Berringer's insisted on it!

Carolyn came safely back home to Jordan by late afternoon, despite the Vermont snows. The couple purchased their first Christmas tree from a lot near their home, and each shared in carrying it from vendor to apartment. Jordan stabilized the tree in a corner of the living room, and attached the lights. She knew that the tree would be visible through the kitchen window, and to all who passed bayside of the building. Carolyn inhaled the evergreen scent as she wrapped the last few presents. They drank egg nog as they decorated their tree. The ornaments were a gift from Carolyn's parents, a token purchased each year as she grew. There was a continuity there that helped to accent the importance of their ceremony, helped to solidify their commitment. They cuddled together on the couch as they watched TV that night, commented on the 11:00 o'clock news features, and snuggled together in bed. The next afternoon passed quickly amid plans for the Holiday, and for their special ceremony. The gifts were neatly wrapped and placed beneath the Christmas tree, the cards were all written and mailed, the poinsettias were placed in center table, and bits of evergreen were stung along the windows. Even their stockings were in place, tacked into the window sill opposite the tree.

And now the time had come. Carolyn and Jordan held hands as they walked together from the parking lot to the ocean's shore. The beach was deserted, and the sand was half frozen in the cold December winds. The Christmas lights on the Victorian homes near the road added a festive aura to their ceremony. The buildings helped anchor them in time, like ancient relatives standing as silent witness. The winter moon gleamed across the calm ocean tides. Jordan and Carolyn strolled along the shore for a bit, and waited for just the right moment. It was cold that evening, but neither seemed to feel the chill. They were both so nervous. Then suddenly, Carolyn stopped, took hold of both of Jordan's hands, gazed into her eyes, and began to recite her vow from memory.

"Come stay with me, Jordan, here beside me, as we travel this world together. Be there for me, share with me, just as I will be there for you. Wait for me, always, just as I will wait for you. Long for me, Jordan, just as I long for you. Grow with me, please, as I vow to nurture you. Care for me, when I am sick, as I will care for you. Protect me when I am afraid, as I will protect you. Love me wholly and completely, and I will love you forever. Scold me when I need it, but be gentle with me, just as I vow to be gentle with you. Treasure me, Jordan, as I treasure you. I promise that I will place your happiness above all else. I vow that I will place your welfare even above my own. I promise that I will be faithful to you. Jordan, I profess to you my love always. Please stay with me forever."

"I will, now and for always," Jordan replied, looking deeply into Carolyn's eyes, as she placed the ring on Jordan's left ring finger, and sealed it there with a kiss. She kissed Jordan tenderly, and together, they felt the coupling of their souls, each to the other. They held each for a long while, before Jordan took hold of Carolyn's hands, and began her vow.

"I had always felt alone until you came and stood by me. You are my life's companion. You complete me. Let me spend my life caring for you, celebrating your victories, and soothing your hurts. Let me share your life, and let me share mine with you. Let us bond ourselves one to the other, so that no problem will be so great as to hold us apart. Let us blend our lives, so that we can enjoy together the experiences of a lifetime. Let us blend our minds, so that we can enjoy the full being of the other. Let us merge our hearts, so that we can love together. Let us merge our laughter, so that we can enjoy each happiness together. Let us be one with the other, as we were always intended to be. Carolyn, I promise my heart to you today and always. I promise my strength to you, so that you can draw from me whenever you need me. I promise my life to you, so that you will never be alone. And I promise my love to you forever, so that you can wake each morning to the full devotion that I hold for you, and you can rest each night in the full security of that love. I promise you, now and forever, that I will love you, that I will cherish you, that I will respect you, and that I will be faithful to you forever. Please stay with me."

"I will, now and for always," Carolyn whispered, as Jordan placed her ring on Carolyn's left ring finger. She kissed the ring in place, and tenderly kissed her. They held each other in silence, as the waves sauntered slowly and incessantly onto the shore. They stood silently under the night sky, the moon and stars presiding.

They strolled back to the car warm in the glow of their commitment, and secure in the love of their partner. They had each contemplated the meaning of their ceremony, and had discussed it at least a dozen times before they agreed that they were ready. But somehow, hearing the vows now spoken, and spoken by the one person who they loved even more than themselves, brought a deeper meaning to their lives, a permanency to their relationship. As Jordan opened the car door, she could see that Carolyn was teary. And she started crying herself.

"Oh come on, I can't be that bad . . . am I?" Jordan tried to make Carolyn laugh.

"No, you're not that bad . . . really . . . now that I think about it . . . God, I love you!"

"And I love you! You have to know that!" She kissed her tenderly, then smiled at her as their lips again parted.

"Now let's go home, get something to eat, get changed, go to Mass, welcome the baby Jesus . . . AND, see my family! I know you can hardly wait!"

The Mathews' had taken the same pew in the center of the Church that they had occupied each Sunday for two and a half decades. There was standing room only that night, as was usual for Midnight Mass, but the Mathews family had saved two extra seats. Jordan and Carolyn arrived at Church just before the start of the Christmas Concert. They sang with the Choir, enjoyed the Harp and String Instrumentals, and watched the Bell Choir perform. They followed the Mass in their Missals, listened to Luke's Gospel of Christ's birth, gave the Sign of Peace, and took Communion. They prayed to God for His blessing, thanked Him for the birth and sacrifice of His Son, asked Him to bless their families, and, especially, to bless each other. As Jordan watched the candlelight reflect off of their wedding bands during Silent Night, she believed her prayers had truly been answered.

They celebrated the Holiday—and their wedding day—at the homes of their own families, with Jordan later joining Carolyn at the Berringer's. They had chosen not to share the news with anyone, not even with their gay friends, until the time was right for the announcement. They spent the remainder of the Holidays at their apartment, enjoying the familiarity of the other, and charting new territory in the assignment of the household chores. Carolyn's personal items—her toothbrush and make-up, her tooth paste and eye liner—had now bumped Jordan's items to a lower shelf in the bathroom. They had truly begun the process of settling in together! Carolyn would soon complete her fellowship and would be graduating in June. She would then move back home with Jordan. They could decide at that point whether they wanted to purchase a home together, or to find a bigger apartment. Jordan's lease wouldn't be up until the following March. They felt this should give them plenty of time to amass a down payment or a security deposit, depending on the flow of income, and on the various real estate options that might present themselves. They were establishing a homestead.

Jordan was grocery shopping when Carolyn received a call from Betty and Jan. She graciously accepted an invitation for them to attend their New Year's Eve Party. Jan ran off the list of attendees. She and Jordan knew most of the others invited there, although they had not seen many of the people since that dreadful night at the bar. Jordan was excited about the night out. Their only other plan was to stay home, watch the Times Square Dick Clark, sip champagne, and play Monopoly. They were up for a good party.

The party was informal, like all the parties at Jan and Betty's! They lived in an old Victorian still in half a state of refurbishing. The couple had completed the downstairs, but the master bedroom upstairs and the main bathroom were nearly gutted to the studs. But it had a spectacular view of the bay! Once completed, though, the house would be far worth the small fortunes they had each put into it. They often joked that they couldn't leave each other even if they wanted to—they had already invested too much equity to ever separate! They even joked about putting a stitched sampler over their mantle: "It costs too much to leave."

Jordan wore a cranberry knit sweater, a navy blazer, and blue jeans, while Carolyn wore her black lace blouse (with just a hint of cleavage), dark jeans, and a dark green jacket. Although not color coordinated, the two looked great together, as they stood side-by-side and inspected themselves in the full length mirror behind their bedroom door. They were two fitted pieces of the life puzzle, plain as anyone could see!

"Don't you think we look great together? Settled, I mean . . . content . . . permanent . . . a part of each other . . . a complement to each other . . . . We fit, like old shoes, broken in, and sublimely comfortable! We have made that much-sought-after transition to oneness . . . and after only a week's marriage! Who would have thought!" Jordan announced.

"You know . . . you're even starting to look like me . . . especially around the butt!" Carolyn observed.

"Hey, butt jokes are still not funny! . . . Although I am beginning to detect the same bulge here that first attracted me to you . . ." Jordan replied.

"Oh really? I always thought that that bulge was quite a bit higher!" Carolyn teased.

"Probably just one of many bulges that attracted me to you, my Dear!" Jordan teased back. She was still checking her out, even after all this time, dressed or not! And so was Carolyn!

They brought along a box of Godiva Chocolates as a hostess gift, and two bottles of their favorite wines. They were prepared for a nightlong party siege, as they welcomed in the New Year. As they ascended the porch stairs to the home of their friends, they stopped momentarily to catch a side view of the bay. The night was clear and crisp, and they could see the new fallen snow on the shore. The neighbor's porch lights danced across the bay ice, and revealed a large cat crouched under an overturned rowboat. Otherwise, all life appeared to emanate from inside this single home. Clouds of breath rolled from their mouths, as they greeted their hostesses from just outside the door.

"Oh my God, I told you they were going to do it! It told you so! . . ." Jan burst out as she took coats from Carolyn and Jordan. She thrust their overcoats onto a nearby sofa, and held up each of their left hands.

"Look everyone! Look! . . . Sorry Ladies, these two are now goners!" There was a rousing applause, although a few grunts, which, Jordan was convinced, was just to make them feel special.

"So tell us about it! When did you two tie the knot?" All attention was fixed squarely on them.

"Not much left to tell now, I guess . . ." Carolyn said. "You ruined our surprise!"

"Oh No!" Betty answered, "We have been taking bets for the last two months that you would exchange vows at Christmas! Now what time did this occur, and where—we have a pool going . . . Someone here is due for a lot of money . . ."

"Eight o'clock, Christmas Eve, at the ocean . . ." It sounded more like a game of Clue, than a wedding announcement! Carolyn had hardly finished before she was interrupted with riotous chants of "ohhs and humphs."

"Yeah! . . . I win!" Helen screamed from the back of the room, as she threw her arms up in touchdown mode. "I knew they wouldn't hold out till Christmas . . . And I even got the beach right! So fork over that money! As I see it, the forty-five bucks are mine! Come on, now, Money . . . Dance into my pocket! Come on . . . !" Helen held out her hand, as Betty forked over the money in feigned disgust.

"You two are so predictable . . . Have a champagne, and a Toast—To Jordan and Carolyn, a couple as well matched, and as well balanced, as I have ever seen. May they enjoy all the happiness that any two lives together can bring!"

"Here, here! To Carolyn and Jordan!" The room joined them in well wishing.

"And Happy New Year!" Carolyn and Jordan toasted in reply.

And together, with 10 other couples, both male and female, and with at least as many singles, male and female, they played outrageous drinking games, spoof-strip-card games, and dirty-charades! As Dick Clark led the countdown, and a million shivering souls struggled to sing Auld Lang Syne in Times Square, the Gay contingent at Jan and Betty's watched in anticipation. They held their lovers close and kissed them passionately as the ball fell "Three-Two-One!" while the singles blew noise-makers and stole kisses from the unaccompanied nearby . . . And all at the party celebrated the welcoming of the New Year much like everyone else in the world did that night—but with just one difference.

# Chapter 9

It was six months before Jordan felt comfortable in the field, and nearly a year before she actually felt confident there. Her relationships in the office remained friendly but distantly professional. She had learned to avoid most of the pitfalls—she knew not to share matters of her personal life, and not to confide in those around her. She seldom admitted to a lack of knowledge, and rarely looked for professional guidance beyond Tina. She often felt that they stood back-to-back in the office, watching out for each other, monitoring the less careful conversations of co-workers, guarding the space of each other's desk. Not that anyone would want to butt into another worker's cases, but there was a small group of malcontents that might try to expose a less popular social worker, especially, if they thought that the tactic might promote their own goals. Jordan felt sorry for them in a way—too incompetent to make a difference themselves, and too proud to let anyone else make a difference there! She regarded them as the lost souls of the office. Lacking in any real leadership, they would run the mills of rumor and gossip, in an effort to distort information and to wield power. Beyond that, they were clueless! That they wanted more power was obvious—why else would they strive to make mayhem among the staff? But it was equally obvious that, even if they had gained that much-sought-after power, they had no real plan. That fact, more than any other, prevented them from having any real credibility. They were more like office gnats. They buzzed around the heads of their co-workers to sheer annoyance, sucking in conversations and distorting them as they belched them back out! Jordan viewed them as weak minded, and without moral purpose or redeeming merit. They had no compass, no direction. They strove to convert others to their cause, a movement of "misery loves company." Jordan held herself farther and farther from them. She hated their politics, and secretly hoped that they would quit en mass and open a shoe store somewhere, far, far, away from her beloved profession! And they detested her to no end! Although Jordan hadn't realized it yet, they had become an army at Crittenden's disposal.

Jordan's relationships with the Group were changing, too, but they were still pretty much intact. Marge and Tyler had been to Jordan's apartment many times, and had now even met Carolyn on one occasion. Although they seemed uncomfortable when she was around, or even whenever Jordan talked about her, they said nothing that would infer suspicion. They may have realized that Jordan was gay, but they were not ready to confront the issue, nor were they willing to trash their relationship because of it. They were developing a kind of shadow relationship with her now, much as her parents had done. Besides, with their move to Nutley, and their wedding just over, they were less and less available for anyone! Jordan attended their wedding without a date, and was paired with one of the ushers, an old friend of the family. She stayed mostly with the Group, though, throughout the much-too-stuffy and unbelievably formal affair. Martin was the first to express the opinion that the wedding was tailored more to the Jorgensen's friends. The happy couple seemed the after-thought, rather than the focus, of the celebration. Still in all, it was a beautiful affair that would remain the talk of the town for years to come.

Jordan quietly hoped that all of her friends would come to accept her relationship with Carolyn—and to accept her as the real person that she was! Jordan had otherwise only confirmed the relationship to Karen, and only by phone. As usual, Karen remained her staunchest ally, her most formidable support. She had even invited Jordan and Carolyn down to her home whenever they could make the trip. Little Doris was now walking and talking, and Todd was making strides in the polymer business. Karen believed that he might actually realize his dream of heading his family's growing—and potentially international—company! They were getting ready to try for their second child, although Karen was clear that two kids were her limit.

"An heir and a spare like all the great kings!" Todd joked.

Janice and Martin still saw each other about once a month, but Janice confided her belief that Martin would never make a commitment to her.

"So much for the co-mingling of the gene pools," Janice joked, "because that will never happen without a wedding first!"

Besides, she was still living at home and tending to her parents, who were becoming ever more dependent on her. Without expressing this to her, the Group believed that it was this awesome responsibility that really prevented Martin from taking the next step in their relationship. He just seemed content to wait out his time for her.

They talked about Jordan's friends many times, and Carolyn gave her basically the same advice that she had given to her when she worried about her parents.

"You shouldn't have to tread gently around friends you've had for nearly a decade! Don't you think they realize the score by now? If they were going to leave you, they would already have gone!"

"So, would you prefer that from now on I introduce you as my red-hot lesbian lover? Should I announce that this fine woman has bedded me throughout the past year, and that she will likely be there to meet that demand for all the remaining years of my life? I'm sure that would garner a response!" Jordan laughed at Carolyn as she thought about the scene.

"Well, maybe I wouldn't go so heavy on the red-hot lover stuff . . . I wouldn't want to be a disappointment! But I do like the idea of being the 'woman that beds you!' I actually think that would go over pretty well! Yes, I'm sure Janice especially would approve that label . . . Maybe Todd and Martin, too! Marge and Tyler, though, I think they'd probably want a bit more of an explanation! . . . But my bet is, Karen's already told them all! Or rather, she helped to clear questions that they may have subtly posed to her . . ."

"Probably true . . . But she's never let on about it!" Jordan thought about how many times in their relationship Karen had been the communication bridge. Carolyn was always so perceptive. It annoyed her sometimes. And it annoyed her that Carolyn wasn't always available to work these things through. She missed her terribly.

And Jordan was growing impatient as she waited for Carolyn to finish graduate school and to return to their home. She thought that the six month separation was unending, even with the three weekend visits that she shared with Carolyn in that period. But time has a way of marching on at its own pace, regardless of desire, and it passes by far too quickly, regardless of perception. In what later seemed like the blink of an eye, Jordan was seated proudly with the Berringer's, as Carolyn marched up to the podium on the lawn of the University of Vermont, and claimed her Masters Degree! They all celebrated together that night, with Jordan now an accepted member of the family. Mrs. Berringer, in particular, strove to cement Jordan's place there beside Carolyn. She used each conversation as a means to incorporate her manner, her background, her interests, and her love into their family style. Jordan stretched a bit to include Mr. Berringer in all observations, not so difficult a task, really, given his calm and gentle nature. Jordan and Carolyn even shared the room adjacent to the Berringer's at the Champlain Hotel, reservations made by Carolyn's parents. In all ways, the Berringer's demonstrated a respect for the commitment that they had made to each other.

By week's end, Carolyn was unpacked and settled into their apartment. Their relationship soon fell into the familiar patterns of nurturance and survival. Carolyn had accepted a teaching/art therapy position at a regional day school near their town. Her own heightened sense of fulfillment erupted in a creative burst of still life and landscapes, as she worked on an exhibition with her parents for the fall. Yes, she and Jordan had a partnership, a commitment, a marriage, and their relationship was going very well. And all that knew them envied them for it.

And Jordan's relationship with Marsha McMillan was progressing well, too. Although staunchly professional, there were moments, brief moments, when Marsha would occasionally let down her guard, and would give Jordan a glimpse of the woman that she was. This first occurred in the early spring, and in the parking lot of the office. Jordan and Tina had just returned from some home visits, and were walking up to the office doorway when Marsha joined them.

"What is that smell?" Marsha asked as she looked around the lot. "What a horrible odor on such a beautiful spring afternoon!" She then spotted several roofers on a building next door. They were pouring tar on the flat-style roof. "So those are the culprits who have made the air so foul!"

"Why Marsha, that doesn't smell . . . that's a wonderful odor! That's the smell of pot roast and new shoes, and the sounds of laughter at the dinner table. That's the aroma of men working, and families surviving! That's a wonderful smell!" Jordan contradicted that perception before she even realized it. She blushed when she realized how revealing her own statement was. Marsha looked thoughtfully at her, gazing for what seemed like hours, before she nodded to her and entered the building. Tina shook her head at Jordan in puzzlement.

"Always agree with the Boss, never share personal insights, and never contradict them, no matter where you work! Now she has a fix on who you are . . . that can be professionally disastrous! And that can really get in the way of the all-important and time-proven office dodging strategies that I have taught you! I'd be careful with that!" Tina shook her head as she talked. In some ways, she reminded Jordan of Tillie. They certainly seemed to drink from the same fountain of wisdom!

Jordan hadn't been at her desk for very long that afternoon, before Jane Morrison asked her to accompany Barbara Schmidt to a home visit. There was a crisis with an alcoholic mother. Due to the seriousness of the situation, Barbara asked for co-worker assistance. Jordan accepted the assignment, packed her things for the day, and joined Barbara at her desk. Barbara had already gotten a car from Vivian Johnson. Jordan noted that the car had no air conditioning or radio. She wondered what Barbara had done to rate the snubbing of the Head Clerk! As they drove to the home, Barbara discussed the family with Jordan.

"This is one of those hot potato cases . . . you know the kind—a million problems, nobody wants to service them, the mother is non-compliant, the kids are doing OK in school, the DAG can't get the case before a judge . . . so it keeps getting passed around. I inherited it from Jen, the worker who left just before you got here. You heard what happened to her, right? An old D.V. allegation, with the mother and boyfriend reuniting after Jen closed the case. The boyfriend shoots the mother and himself in front of the toddler. Jen had to respond, to place the child in foster care until relatives could be located and approved for her custody . . . Jen said that the kid sat there in total silence, just staring at her, the whole time. She couldn't get that image out of her head. It was more than she could handle . . . plus, she could never forgive herself for not somehow realizing that the couple might reunite. As if THAT was her fault. So she quit . . . Anyway, if I'm lucky, I'll find some way to palm this family off onto somebody else . . ."

"Well don't look at me . . . I've got my hands full as it is!"

"I don't think that Jane would do that to you yet, since you haven't been here for a year . . . That seems to be the magic number. If people stay for a year, they'll likely stay with the agency. And once a supervisor realizes that, you're done! They will show you no mercy!"

"Actually, I've been here for over a year now . . ." Jordan bit her tongue with the disclosure.

"Well then . . . you should pay close attention to this family, because Jane probably staked you out as their next caseworker! That's probably why you got the privilege of joining me today!"

"Anyway, here's the story—we have a disabled, alcoholic mother in her mid forties, living in this dilapidated old house near the woods. That's probably why she gets away with so much—nobody can see her back there, and most of the neighbors don't bother with her. The kids are seven and eight, very sweet, both do well in school, but look like ragamuffins, as you can imagine. They get a lot of help from the neighbors on the next street. Their kids play together. The mother has been through a half dozen programs in her life, but she's in the final stages of the disease. She probably weighs maybe a hundred pounds, if that. She has soup or toast when she's not drinking, bourbon or rye when she is. That's all she can tolerate. She uses a cane due to arthritis, but probably, she's too weak to stand. If she's drinking when we get there today, we'll have to pull the kids. You can't have an active alcoholic, especially a drunken one, providing care and supervision to the children . . . I'll do all the talking, you just watch, listen to what she says, and cover my back."

"Got it," Jordan said.

The children were playing in the yard when the state car pulled into their driveway. Jordan could see about a dozen cats on the property, but there were no dogs. She was thankful for that! The children ran into the house to tell their mother of the visit! Even as they were walking up the stairs to the home, the mother took a swig of the bottle she had hidden under her blanket as she sat at the table. They both could see that she was intoxicated. The mother smiled a pleasantry and slurred a hello. Barbara talked slowly with her about her drinking.

"Yeah, I been drinkin' today, but I wouldn't say that I was drunk . . . Nothing wrong with a woman takin' a drink every now and again, is there?" The mother was loud and challenging toward them.

"Well, yes there is, as you well know . . . because we've been over this about fifty times! Listen, why don't you check yourself back into the hospital for a few days? Give yourself a little time to pull yourself together and . . ."

"Nope . . . ya know that ain't gonna happen, because if I do, what will happen to my kids?"

"Well, we could find a place for them to stay until you're feeling better . . ."

"Like some foster home maybe? You people are always threatenin' me with that . . . NOT A CHANCE!" she shouted. "The kids are fine here, and so am I . . . so please leave . . . LEAVE NOW!"

The mother jumped to her feet, grabbed a bat on the floor near the table, and started swinging it at Barbara and Jordan. Piles of junk fell from table to floor!

"Move!" Barbara shouted, as she pushed Jordan out of her way.

They bumped into each other as they scrambled to make it to the door, with the mother right at their backs! They just made it down the stairs, as a half-empty ketchup bottle sailed inches from Barbara's head and smashed on the rock wall! Red goo splattered across the concrete walk! Jordan could easily see her brains there, strewn out among the mess of weeds and broken stonework. She barely had time to look back!

"Wack!" They heard the crack of the bat as it pounded against the door jamb! The two bolted across the front yard, and as Barbara fumbled with the keys to unlock the car door, Jordan saw that the mother reached the last stair of the porch! She was heading right toward them!

"Hurry up! Come on!" Jordan screamed. They barely dove into the car, before she was at the driveway and calling to them.

"Wait! Wait a minute! Please!" She begged them. She calmed quickly and was now unarmed, and walked slowly toward the passenger side of the car. Barbara could not believe how fast that invalid woman had moved!

"Don't trust her, Jordan!" Barbara cautioned, but Jordan was moved by compassion, as the woman continued to beg them. Jordan partially rolled down the window so that they could talk. She noticed a blank look on the mother's face, and just as suddenly, a rage, as the mother thrust her hands in through the open window, and stretched to scratch Jordan's eyes and face!

"What the fuck!" Jordan screamed, as she forced up her clipboard, and tried using it as a shield, pushing away each clawing hand from her face and neck. Barbara, screamed and threw the car into reverse! As the mother was jerked to the ground, the children ran to her side to comfort her. Jordan saw again, Josie's hand clawing at her through her memory. And she believed again, that there was something in the universe that did not want her in Social Work!

Barbara drove to the police station, where she and Jordan filed assault charges against the mother. She then called Jane Morrison. Jane concurred that the children were at imminent risk, and she authorized their removal from the home under the Dodd Act. This law gave specified persons, like the police or BCS workers, the authority to remove children from their parents, if the kids were believed to be in immediate danger. The matter would then be reviewed by the courts. These kids certainly fit the criteria! Because of the emergency removal of the children, the Police agreed to accompany the BCS workers back to the home. Because of the propensity for violence, two police officers were assigned for the response.

The two cars arrived back at the home within the hour. The mother was still wandering in the front yard, and the children were tugging at her arms trying to coax her back into the house. When the mother saw the cars entering her driveway, she stood motionless, speechless, and waited for the officials to make their move. The Police approached the mother, while Jordan and Barbara waited in their car.

"Ms. Randolph, I am Officer Johnston of the Seacrest Police. I am placing you under arrest for attempted assault of the BCS workers. Your children are being placed in the care of BCS. You have the right to remain silent. Anything you say can and will be used against you in a court of law. If you cannot afford an attorney, one will be appointed to you. Do you understand these rights as I have explained them?"

She did not answer. The mother remained unresponsive and uncooperative. As the police moved to arrest her, Ms. Randolph stiffened her body, then struggled with the officers, but never made a sound—not a question, not a threat, not a curse! She just fought back with the full force of every one of those one hundred pounds her body could muster! The children were screaming at the police, begging them to stop.

"Hey, take it easy!" Jordan pleaded with the officer.

"You're certainly welcome to try this yourself, if you think you can do any better!" he replied, as the mother's fingers raked across his face, while she held firm to the calf of the other officer. Jordan empathized with the police, but she did not want anyone hurt. She never did.

Finally, the officers wrestled the mother into the back seat of the cruiser, arms and legs flailing, as the children stood crying and screaming by the side of the car. The mother was kicking the protective gate that separated front from back seat, as the officers drove her off to booking and to jail. Jordan tried to comfort and soothe the two children, who now believed that the police were going to kill their mother! Barbara explained that their mother was being taken to the hospital, and that they would speak to her by phone in the morning. This seemed to calm the kids, because they knew Barbara. They agreed to go with her to the hospital for a physical, and to stay with one of Barbara's "friends" for a few days. Jordan continued to assist.

Although the pre-placement physical went well, the children became increasingly stressed as they neared time for placement. As the four were about to leave the hospital E.R., Tabitha, the seven year old, decided to make a stand! She lay on the floor and wrapped her arms around the post supporting the public phone in the lobby. Handcuffs would have offered less resistance! She started crying hysterically, and pleaded for assistance from anyone who passed nearby.

"I'm not leavin' here . . . I want my mother! Help me, help me!" Tabitha begged and cried to each and every nurse and patient in the clinic. Even her older brother could not console her. The pediatrician gave her a small dose of benedryl, as Barbara pried the child's hands lose from the phone stand. They waited for her to quiet.

"It's OK., it's going to be OK." Jordan held Tabitha and spoke softly to calm her. She thought briefly about holding Janice when she needed this soothing, and recognized this child's anguish as intense loss. Although no one told her, Tabitha knew that she would likely not return to her home or to her mother's care. Jordan thought about her own strained relationship with her parents, and had a quick fear that that, too, may never resolve. In that sense, they were strangely kindred.

Tabitha was nearly asleep when they left the hospital. They arrived at the foster home at almost 10:30 p.m. Although her own children were asleep, the foster mother warmed dinner for these two newest kids, and drew their baths. The foster mother held and rocked Tabitha to soothe her, while big brother Jack looked on. At eight years old, he would be caring for his sister now. But the children hadn't realized their luck—not only had they been placed together, but they had been placed in the Petruzzi home!

Mrs. Petruzzi had a reputation for holding onto even the toughest foster kids. She had a gift for it really. She just knew what children needed, and she gave it to them in huge quantities. It didn't much matter that they weren't her kids. She didn't care about that. All she cared about was that they were children who needed. She would be their coach, their confidant, their advocate, their friend, and in time, maybe even their mother. She would cherish the cards and gifts made by them in their classrooms and scout meetings, and would post them prominently on the refrigerator, right among the artwork of her own kids. She would accept the irritability and verbal abuse from the children after each visit with their families. She would help them to accept that love doesn't have to be "either/or," but that sometimes, it can be "both." And she could love enough to let go, at those times when families healed enough to live together again. In fact, she would do whatever it took—and she did it time and again, without hesitation or expectation. These two children would ultimately grow up at her home, under her guidance, and in her heart. Their mother would continue to have supervised visits with them, but she was never able to recover, or to regain custody of them. She succumbed eighteen months later to cirrhosis and hepatitis.[76] The children mourned her again, just as they had mourned the loss of childhood and family, all of it lost in alcohol.

---

[76] For discussion on behavioral and psychological issues in children in foster care, please refer to Appendix and Bibliography for Chapter Nine.

Jordan had seen many good gay relationships end the same way. She had seen many good gay people destroyed in the throws of addiction. She thanked God that she had chosen recovery before things really got out of hand. She thanked God that she had chosen Carolyn, who had never once faltered in that way.

Barbara and Jordan sent the responding officers a pizza the day after the children's placement, with a note thanking the two cops for their help. As suspected, the case was reassigned to Jordan the next day. It came with an attached commendation written by Jane Morrison praising Jordan's professionalism and her genuine sensitivity in working with these children. Copies of the commendation were also forwarded to Marsha McMillan and to Jordan's personnel file. Crittenden was beside himself!

"What's the big deal about somebody doing their job? Just look around you and you'll see people doing their job every single day—and without so much as a thank you!"

He made jokes about the commendation to his little army of storm troopers, and the citation was the fodder of gossip for weeks! Jordan ignored them and maintained dedication to her clients, to the agency, and to her profession. She also began advocating for policies that would promote worker safety in the field. Of course, Crittenden opposed these measures, insisting that the police, and not the agency, should be responsible for social worker safety. After some weeks, the safety issue slipped back into the realms of the forgotten, only to re-emerge periodically as one social worker or another was threatened or assaulted.[77]

Jordan had a pretty solid reputation among the office staff and in the community by the end of her second year there, and the casework supervisor delighted in assigning the more difficult cases to her. It wasn't really that she was so much the better social worker than the others. It was more that she was one of the few staff there from a working class background! And most of the

---

[77] For discussion on client assaults against social workers, and an administrative overview, please refer to Appendix and Bibliography for Chapter Nine.

agency clients were either working class, or welfare recipients. The middle class clients either had political contacts or the private attorneys who could repulse a BCS worker from their doors. But the lowest economic levels, the resource-poor and powerless, had no such advantage! Jordan understood these differences far better than most. She understood the clients first hand. Because of this understanding, she seemed to have a knack for getting into people's homes—and into their families—like no one else in the office could! And the worse the case was, the better she seemed to do with it! Crittenden minimized her success, and matter-of-factly suggested that she be referred for remedial training. By the third year, she and Crittenden had developed a genuine animosity. The more he wanted her to fail, the more she succeeded! He really detested her for that, more than anything—except maybe, that she refused to show him the proper deference, the proper respect, as he would often complain. Jane Morrison gently suggested that they ignore each other. She emphasized that she needed both social workers on the job.

If only they had observed this simple folk wisdom! But circumstance and personality, fate and politics, would maneuver them, again and again, in diametric opposition to the other. On one such occasion, Jordan was in the field when the office received word that a teenaged foster child on her caseload died. Nora was walking with some friends, laughing and teasing them, when an old Ford mowed the girls down and sped away. Of the three hit, Nora was the only child that did not survive. Jordan was also supervising her older brother Doug, who had been placed in a different foster home. She knew these kids well, and it made her ache each time she thought about losing Nora. But she had to go on. Jordan visited Doug, told him of the accident, and shared his grief. She also told their natural mother by phone. But Crittenden expressed his wish that the natural family not be notified. He was supervising their toddler sister who was placed with a pre-adoptive family, and he did not want his case plan disrupted. Jane Morrison sided with Jordan, noting that the natural mother's parental rights had not been terminated. The mother still occasionally showed at the office for her scheduled visits with them. Besides, the fact that Jordan had already notified the family made Crittenden's point moot!

Yet, he strove to cover it up, to officially deny the obvious! Crittenden contacted the adoption center, and notified the funeral home, to prevent any services that would welcome the natural mother! Because Jordan did not share this philosophy—and also, because she had already notified the child's family—she contacted the funeral home and scheduled a separate service for them. Although she had arranged for transportation of the mother by cab, Crittenden intercepted the funding voucher, so of course, the cab never arrived! This did not deter the mentally ill mother, who decided to hitchhike to the funeral parlor, but managed to get less than halfway, before she collapsed in the arms of a shopkeeper! On the day of her daughter's funeral, the grieving mother phoned Jordan hysterical from nearly a half hour away, and advised that she could not hitchhike there in time for the service. She begged Jordan for help. Jordan raced to pick up Doug at the foster home, and flew down the Parkway to pick up his mother at a shopping center. She quietly accompanied them to the funeral home. She stayed with mother and son, as they—and she—said goodbye to the teenaged daughter. Although both Doug and his mother cried for Nora, neither made a harsh word against the state who removed Nora from the home; or against the foster parents who cared for her; or against the driver who sped away from the scene, leaving her broken body at the curb. It was as if they had expected no more from life than this.

Jordan drove the mother back to her home after the funeral, and bought some food for her with her own money. She was livid when she returned to the office, and found Crittenden's request that she be disciplined for insubordination! Jordan fired off a memo detailing the full events of the day, and sent copies to Marsha McMillan, as well as to the agency's Regional Administrator. She asked for a full investigation of the incident, requested remedy in the form of new policies and procedures, and suggested disciplinary action against any staff who had contributed to this horrendous breech of agency trust. She made this request on behalf of all client families.

Jordan's memo was so effective that both Marsha McMillan and the Regional Administrator personally addressed her concerns, forwarded apologies to the natural family, and gave Crittenden a reprimand for interfering in clerical functions. Jordan felt vindicated. Crittenden felt violated![78] Tensions between them mounted daily. Jordan made extra efforts to give Crittenden plenty of room. She made her point. Carolyn proudly saved a copy of this memo and placed it in Jordan's scrapbook.

Both Carolyn and Karen helped Jordan with this new approach, coaching her as she tiptoed around her targeted foe. Jane Morrison was careful never to schedule the two on assignment together, never to have them cover for each other, and never to praise or to criticize either of these social workers in the presence of the other. Yet they still found avenue for their hostility! The monthly staff meetings became a battleground! Jordan would raise a suggestion or praise a new policy, and Crittenden, or one of his malcontents, would whine a criticism, cast aspirations on intent, or launch a personality assault at her! Crittenden was that desperate to subjugate her! And Jordan remained all the more adamant that she would never submit! They had irreconcilable political and philosophical differences that frothed at every crack in the structure of civility! Oftentimes, Marsha McMillan would interrupt these meetings and caution both about professionalism and office etiquette. But they were no more successful at keeping these rules and staying apart, than one could succeed at keeping a tongue away from a sore tooth! Jordan sat always with one eye on her back. Tina was careful to maintain a good relationship with Crittenden. She hoped that she could help smooth over the tensions for her friend. But it seemed that nothing would deter him! Crittenden had labeled her as the enemy, and he would not rest until she was defeated or destroyed—he seemed to have no preference, one way or the other. Tina cautioned that Crittenden

---

[78] For a discussion on the clash between classes as it relates to office politics, please see Appendix and Bibliography for Chapter Nine.

might try to set her up, but Jordan dismissed these thoughts as mere healthy paranoia.

* * *

Gradually, the situation between Jordan and Crittenden began to subside, and there was a span of nearly six months without a single incident between them! The office moved back to its semi-conscious mode of investigation, bandage, closing—a numbness brought on by extreme demand! They seemed as a group uninspired, and Jordan strove to build in them a renewed sense of purpose. She had adopted this as her new goal. She tried this subtly, by setting a high example. She tried this quietly, by moving her clients forward without brag or complaint. She tried this purposefully, by advocating for her clients wherever she could. She tried this faithfully, by maintaining the same high energy that she devoted to each of her families. The staff may have resented her for this, but they would never disrespect her for it. Some thought that she was a "hot dog," showing off to gain brownie points for a promotion. Some viewed her as a zealot, on some religious quest to make the place right in the world. Some thought she was an annoyance, putting everyone else on the spot. None recognized that she viewed the agency as the only real opportunity that most of these kids would ever have. None realized that she saw the agency resources—the day care, the counseling, the summer camps, the financial help with rent or utilities—as the only assistance available to keep poor families together. But Jordan understood this perfectly. And it seemed to her, that Marsha McMillan understood this about her. Jordan would be the bridge between the agency and the client base. She viewed herself as the one solid hope for families much like her own—except, of course, for those abuse incidents! But maybe with a little help, and a little hope, these families could rise above the abuse, and live successfully together. Maybe she could help to decrease their stressors so that they could enjoy their children again. She positioned herself as that glimmer of hope, that ray of light, that could help these families move forward! She saw herself as the strength that increased their will to survive. She became the tool that nudged them forward. And these families were having success because of her efforts!

"Think of the impact this office could make, if these beliefs became contagious," Jordan commented to herself as she took her place at her desk. BCS was no longer a job for her—it was now her mission, and she was spreading the word by sheer example.

And most of the time, she enjoyed it. She had become very close to a number of the kids on her caseload as would happen, if she was to nurture them through the many troubles of their young lives. She had worked with some of their families for years. The kids seemed to her, like her own nieces and nephews. She celebrated their triumphs, applauded their A's, and served as their confidants. She became proficient at basketball and pool, so that they could play together as they talked. She watched for signs of abuse, neglect, depression, alcohol or drug use, unprotected sex, criminal activity—she explained things to them, and she served as their interpreter and guide to the universe.

She had one boy in particular that she was really fond of, and who she watched especially closely. She referred Michael's mother to a psych unit for depression, but his mother managed to escape, and hanged herself in the woods nearby. The boy's father was a biker-type, and he was never around. He had drug addictions, heroin and crystal meth mostly, and was doing time in one of the state prisons. Although she knew told herself that his mother's death was not her fault, Jordan felt personally responsible to and for Michael, from that day on. She referred him to counseling, and searched for his extended family. But no matter how hard she shook that family tree, no appropriate caretaker dropped down for him! He was just another kid destined to grow up alone in the system, and Jordan vowed to insure that he would make it out ok.

She piled on the services! She arranged for a Big Brother, and a tutor. She began driving him to and from his counseling sessions. She arranged camp programs and rec. leagues, and enrolled him in sailing classes to help work out his frustrations. He was a likeable kid, really, and kind of a prankster, at that. But Jordan began noticing changes in him, when he realized that his family would not be taking him in. He vowed he would never be adopted! And although Michael never admitted to depression, his behaviors could scream it loud and clear! At other times, his boyhood charm and innocence could hide his real emotional torment. Over time, Jordan learned to pick up the cues.

They were driving back to the foster home once after a therapy session, and were engaged in serious discussion about The Incredible Hulk, as Jordan was approaching a stop sign. Michael suddenly yelled, "Go!" as if he had cleared the traffic on his side of the car. The yell startled Jordan, and as she quickly looked over to him, she saw a tractor trailer about to enter the intersection! Wheels screeched the car to a stop!

"Michael, what are you trying to do, get us both killed?" Jordan scolded him about the dangers of fooling around like that! But as his little face and dark, sad eyes looked up and into her own, she realized that the boy's actions were a death wish—that he really wasn't joking!

Jordan advised his therapist, made an appointment for an evaluation, and made special arrangements with the foster mother to keep a close watch on him. She silently confirmed this as another example of kids not doing well in out-of-home placements, even if there were no other options. She often wondered, as they were driving in the state car together, how far they could get, before the state realized that they were gone. She would have this same thought many times, as she drove her kids through the county and on to counseling sessions, or to visits, or to physicals, or to new foster homes. If only somewhere she could find an island for them all to live on, safely and happily together, far away from the abuse, from the system, and from the caseworkers that ultimately brought them into this new and confusing, chrysalis-like situation!

Jordan asked Carolyn several times about possibly fostering Michael, but she knew well that the state would never approve a BCS caseworker as a foster parent, and certainly, never a couple of gay foster parents! So Jordan watched the boy move from foster home to foster home, powerless to offer more stability. She held on to him emotionally, though, providing agency supports as she could, while Carolyn held on to Jordan, and both held their breath. Michael lucked out at age fifteen, when he was placed with an older chicken farmer and his wife. He accepted the placement as their hired hand, and within a year, he became their son.

Years later, Jordan bumped into Michael at the mall, his wife and four year old son by his side. Michael had grown so, that she hardly recognized him physically, but she knew his heart immediately. He introduced her to his family, as if she had been a long lost aunt he had been searching years for. Then, he took her hands into his own, looked into her eyes, and spoke firmly, gratefully, sincerely.

"I don't know what would've ever happened to me if it hadn't been for you."

It was these brief, sparse moments that kept Jordan glued to a profession that had otherwise not been very kind to her. She often heard his voice play again and again in her mind, on those days when she just wanted to chuck it all, and move on. Carolyn seemed to understand this without any discussion. Jordan thought that she probably heard voices of her own.

In a world that seemed to be pitted against them from birth, depression was the only commodity that her kids could really count on. And it came in huge quantities. It was always there for them, lurking just around the corner at even the best of times. And depression was just as available in the natural home as it was in a foster home! She had a 14 year old girl that she had been monitoring as the result of sexual abuse perpetrated by her mother's boyfriend. Even though her mother made all the right moves when Nancy disclosed the abuse—she terminated the relationship with the boyfriend and demanded his prosecution; she attended counseling sessions with her daughter, and remained a strong ally, a source of emotional support for her—none of these measures could seem to counter-balance Nancy's loss of trust and self-esteem. She quickly hooked up with the wrong kids, got into the drug and alcohol scene, and started carving her arms and legs with a pen knife, a self-mutilative satisfaction to the guilt that she felt about her abuse.

Jordan was trying to locate an inpatient adolescent unit to help stabilize her. But before she could even arrange for the interviews, the girl swallowed a bottle of Tylenol and collapsed at school. Although she survived this near fatal suicide attempt, Nancy found herself even more isolated. Having completed an inpatient psych program, and now pumped up for her return to high school, she was later devastated to learn that school officials now barred her entry. She was told that she would have to complete a month-long suspension. The charge: attempting suicide on school grounds!

Jordan was beside herself with the ridiculousness of the decision. She went into a small conference room, took a few deep breaths to center herself, and phoned that district's superintendent of schools. After the formalities and niceties were completed, Jordan launched into her assault on the school.

"So I have a situation here with a sophomore at the high school that I hope you might be able to help us work out. The girl has never been a behavior problem before, but she's just been suspended for a month. She's had some recent emotional problems, and had a suicide attempt . . ."

"Yes, I'm aware of Nancy's situation. She's been suspended because she tried to commit suicide on school grounds. If we don't take some kind of disciplinary action now, who knows how many other girls will try the same thing here. I stand by the decision of the high school principal."

"I can understand your concern, but I believe that Nancy's actions were more a cry for help. What message is being given, by suspending her?"

"I think the message is quite clear—we will not tolerate suicide attempts on school grounds."

"Wouldn't it better serve the kids, knowing that the school cares enough to help their students work through their difficulties, so that suicide attempts would not be necessary?" Jordan cringed with the sound, the stupidity of her logic. But he bought it.

"So you think that we are being unresponsive by taking such a stance?"

"Well, maybe there could be other measures we could try together. I mean, if she had succeeded in the suicide, would you have expelled her? What lesson would that really teach the other students? Don't you think that they would have already gotten the message?"

"What will keep her safe here? What can you offer us?"

"A fair question—she's completed an inpatient psych program, she's stabilized on medications, she has weekly sessions with a therapist, and a weekly group. I've spoken with her, I think the depression has broken, and she is charged up about going back to school. You already know that her mother is cooperative. Maybe Nancy could connect with the nurse or guidance counselor each day. Or maybe you could come up with another plan at your end."

"Alright, I'll talk to the staff. But she is still suspended. She can start back next week, and we'll commute the suspension to the time she has already missed from school. But if we pick up a single sign that she is in trouble, we will be on the phone with you immediately."

"I wouldn't want anything else. Thanks again. It's been a pleasure working with you on this."

Carolyn laughed loud and long, as Jordan mimicked the school superintendent that evening, and described a half dozen strategies she used not to insult the man! She made bizarre faces as she held the imaginary phone away from her ear. She used her hand like a puppet chattering, and bounced her head back and forth in feigned boredom. She went down on one knee like Romeo and pretended to beg for his cooperation. Finally, she threw herself onto the kitchen table in a self-choke hold, gasping for air, until the superintendent gave in!

"Bravo! Bravo!" Carolyn applauded the dramatics. "But you could have cut to the chase by simply offering him a pay-off, like everyone else!" She then demonstrated the pass and hold, the fine art of the political bribe!

"I wonder why they never covered that in any of my classes?"

Jordan bragged like the proud parent when Nancy graduated high school and went on to Vo-Tech without further incident.

She had another kid that she liked a lot, too. The girl was nearly sixteen when she went into foster care to escape incest by her father. Like most, the mother refused to believe or to separate from him, and she demanded that her "lying" daughter be removed from their home. BCS would have pulled her anyway, with the alleged perp. still there. The kid was pretty together, though, despite her history. Valerie was just an average student, but she loved to write, and she often shared her poetry with Jordan as they drove to counseling sessions. The girl wanted badly to reunite with her family, but her mother would have none of it, unless Valerie recanted her statement. Like most, Val refused to testify against her father, but she would not deny his abuse. Likely, her brother had also been sexually used by him, but he wasn't talking. The father wasn't prosecuted, because without the girl's testimony, legally, there was no victim. So Val chose instead, the goal of reuniting with her aunt.

Aunt Joyce had her own home and was working as a secretary. She lived nearby, and visited Val's family at least several times a week. When the abuse first came to light, she was stunned. She always thought her brother-in-law to be a decent man, but she could recall certain situations she had seen in the past, that now seemed peculiar to her. She never considered Valerie a liar, but she knew how teenaged girls could sometimes misunderstand. But when Joyce learned of the full allegations from Val's mother, she knew that things were well beyond simple misunderstanding. Intercourse and oral sex were pretty outright understood! But her sister would hear none of it, and Joyce felt more and more caught in the middle of this family triangle. So she chose to disengage until the worst had blown over.

Val made several attempts to arrange a visit with her aunt, but she always got excuses. As a last ditch effort, Jordan and Val sent an invitation to Aunt Joyce for a skeeball "Tournament of Chumps." They were both shocked that she took the challenge, and the three played skeeball on the Boardwalk till midnight! They even traded the tickets they won for matching teddy bears, a comfort to the harshness of separation. This simple humor, this creative blend of area resources and family ties helped build a bridge between Val and her family that night. The concept brought the two together, and within two months of graduation, Val was living with her aunt. Perhaps in time, she would reconnect with her mother, too, but that would be much later—when she was strong enough to protect herself from her father's future advances, and when she was strong enough to protect herself from her mother's verbal abuses. Things take time. But it was a start. Sometimes it was just simple folk wisdom that closed the miles between people. Jordan used this same strategy often, and often, she got miraculous results. She toasted these victories in her thoughts.

She sat proudly with Aunt Joyce at Val's high school graduation ceremony, taking up the seat that should have been occupied by her mother. Jordan purchased a charm bracelet for Val that Carolyn helped her pick out, and attached a trophy charm as the first piece. Inside her graduation card, Jordan placed her own agency card, with the following verses written on the back:

> *QUOTES FOR FUTURE HAPPINESS*
> "Live long and prosper."—Spock[79]
> "Laughter is the spark of the soul."—an Irish Proverb
> "I'd love to be intimate. Here's a condom."—Valerie
> "Always remember your pals."—Jordan Mathews.

Jordan arrived at the office the next day charged with the glow of her success! But her enthusiasm quickly waned, when she learned that Jane Morrison had fallen the night before, and this time, had broken her hip. There was no projected date

---

[79] A reference to: Roddenberry, Gene (1966). *Star Trek* [television series]. New York: NBC

for her return. Crittenden would be supervising the unit in her absence! Dust and paperwork left a comet trail as Jordan raced to Linda, the administrative assistant, and asked for a temporary transfer to another unit! Linda was sympathetic, but unmoved. She had a flirtatious nature, and Jordan was never quite sure if she was just being friendly, or if she was looking for something more. Gay people had to be so careful! There never seemed to be a lack of people curiously enthralled with the prospects of a lesbian affair. But gender didn't seem to matter much to Linda—she'd flirt with both the male and female staff. In fact, she'd flirt with anything that moved or took a breath! In that, she was an equal opportunity employer. Rumor had it that she was Marsha McMillan's sex slave, and that she and Crittenden had some bondage thing going. But Jordan was clearly not interested. She indulged these thoughts, though, as she listened to Linda's poor excuses about why the transfer was not possible. She would have to make the best of it, and bide her time until Jane's return. Jordan later learned that Jane Morrison had opted for early retirement. From that point forward, her friend and supervisor would forever be remembered as "Calamity Jane Morrison," and Jordan would be known as the office target. She was as good as gone! As Jordan sat pondering these developments in her favorite stall in the Ladies Room that day, she heard a voice quietly call out to her from the sink area.

"Watch your back!" the voice said. Although ominous and unidentified, she believed that it belonged to Marsha McMillan! Jordan had no idea what was in store for her.

Crittenden assumed his post with the air of a despot, and he dictated over his kingdom with an iron fist. He set out to subjugate the unit, and Jordan bore the brunt of his tactics. He lavished Tina Murdock and Barbara Schmidt with privilege and consideration, while Jordan, Michelle Higgins, and Jennifer Malcolm caught the worst case assignments, were routinely denied time off, and were forced to work extensive overtime. His confrontational manner and his rigidity of thought stymied any possible case discussion. He was blatantly rude and challenging toward Jordan, and he goose-stepped over her with impunity. Gradually, Michelle and Jennifer were able to migrate to Tina and Barbara, leaving Jordan as the unit jerk. Crittenden finally had her where he wanted her! If she didn't like it, she could leave. If she didn't leave, he would destroy her. She never felt more professionally vulnerable in all her career! Jordan searched the eyes of the other supervisors in the office, but they looked away, as if throwing her squarely into Crittenden's pit. The office cadre had risen through the ranks together. They socialized together. They played on the office softball and beach volleyball teams. They were of one mind, one background, one ethnicity. And although she had been there now just over three years, Jordan was still the new guy. And she was a low class new guy at that! And Crittenden defended his actions as necessary, as "a means to quell the renegade," he said. Neither Linda nor Marsha McMillan would intercede. Jordan was on her own.

She again had a strategy meeting with Carolyn, and spoke with Karen by phone. They both suggested that she change assignments completely, that she transfer to a different position in the office, or maybe into another district office. Perhaps she could move to an intake unit, or to one of the north county units. She could pursue the transfer under the guise of increasing her working knowledge and advancing her career goals. Jordan decided to speak in confidence with Linda to determine if such a transfer might be possible.

She met with Linda in her office the next morning, but Linda seemed to have expected the visit. She leaned over her desk toward Jordan as she spoke, and used hand gestures at chest level to punctuate.

"Now Jordan, you know that things can always get a little tense around here. I know that you've been feeling things a little personally . . ." She spoke softly, seductively, using her eyes and her breasts to her full advantage! Jordan found it increasingly difficult not to look at her cleavage as she watched this nonverbal accenting, Linda's fingertips just glancing off of her breasts.

"No, I'm not feeling anything personal," Jordan stuttered, then quickly snapped back into purpose. "Unless you're alluding to Crittenden's harassment of me . . ." Jordan decided to sit down, to be more at eye level with Linda. She thought for a moment that Linda might be trying to assess her sexuality. She wondered whether that rumor was now circulating around the office! It would not surprise her if Crittenden had tried to plant that thought, if he tried to play the "gay" card, in an effort to discredit her. She was not ready to come out at work, and did not want to be "outed" by anyone. That thought horrified her!

"I don't think he's harassing you, but I'll see what I can do for you. Of course, you'll owe me, as always . . ." For a scarce moment, she thought that Linda might come on to her! To her great relief, that thought went no further, but the bargaining continued. Jordan was finally successful in winning a slot in another unit. She would be working exclusively in an urban area of the county, and would again be working with people of color. Her transfer was scheduled in two weeks. Jordan was pleased that she was able to pull off such a deal, and yet, still keep her dignity—and her privacy—intact! But she worried what favors might now be owed.

Crittenden was livid when he learned of the transfer. He challenged that Jordan had undermined his authority by negotiating a transfer behind his back. He tried to make this case with Marsha McMillan, but she had long tired of the issues between them. She welcomed any change that would keep Jordan and Crittenden apart! Jordan was instructed to prepare her cases for transfer. Crittenden was not to be outdone! He developed a priority list of tasks that required her immediate attention. When she objected that such assignment was humanly impossible, he forced her into a time log of her activities. She was working nearly eighteen hours a day, between office and home, to maintain compliance with Crittenden's directives, and still, he continued the harassment! Yet she maintained the regimen gladly, gleefully, as she checked off each day on her calendar. Try as he might, he could not catch her. And she was winning the overall support of the staff who watched the battle from afar!

Finally, as she was about to exit the unit forever, Crittenden called a meeting between himself and Jordan, and insisted that Marsha McMillan attend. During the conference, he presented a series of written directives that he claimed, Jordan had ignored. He attached these to a long memo detailing her alleged insubordination, and he called for her termination. He had not realized that Jordan had collected her own set of "Crittenden" memos, and that she had formulated a grievance regarding his continued harassment of her! Although Marsha refused Crittenden's demands for Jordan's firing, she did acknowledge that Crittenden would be facing a grievance filed by Jordan with the Department of Personnel. Without knowing what he had done, Crittenden had validated Jordan's harassment complaint! As Marsha explained this turn of events, Jordan's mind was awash with a single exclamation—"And against all odds, she had won!" The Crittenden goon squad held a day of mourning, an informal public bitch session in the lunch room. And Carolyn proudly saved a copy of Jordan's memos, and added them to her scrapbook.

. Jordan spent the next year under the supervision of Walter Jamison. He was a mild mannered sort, the kind that kept a low profile, kept a blank stare, and kept a tally sheet on each of his workers neatly tucked in his top desk drawer. Here's how the Jamison System worked: If he asked a worker to respond to an emergency on an uncovered caseload, that worker got a point, like extra credit. If a worker called out without prior notification, that worker got a black mark, like a demerit. If there was controversy over a case plan during a conference, all Walter would have to do was to open the top desk drawer, and immediately, there would be consensus. It reminded Jordan of her mother's approach to child rearing—if a kid was out of control, if a kid ignored her, if a kid was disobedient, all her mom would have to do was to shuffle her feet, as if she was about to pursue the criminal, and the wayward youngster would snap to! Jordan didn't care much for that approach—not at home, and certainly, not in the office! And Walter seemed a bit weaselly to her, as he cowered through the office each day, seemingly waiting for the moment when he, too, might fall prey to the ax! Yet, he was far better than Crittenden, and as long as she kept an equally low profile, she believed there would be no problems.

You could imagine her surprise, when, at Walter's transfer to some low-level administrative position in the Central Office, Jordan learned that he had given her an unsatisfactory personnel rating! She could think of no time when she and Walter had disagreed beyond an initial discussion. She could think of no occasion that caused him to tally a mark against her! Jordan filed a grievance based on the fact that she had no prior notification of any work issues; and based on the fact that she and Walter had not met to discuss the concluding review for the year. Jordan won the grievances on procedural grounds, but the evaluation remained in her personnel file. She was beginning to realize that Tina's theory might be accurate, and that perhaps, she was being set up. She would have shared this view with Tina, if they had still been friends. But once Tina assessed that Jordan was in political dead waters in the office, she bailed out of their relationship like a rat off a sinking ship! Jordan would have to ride this tide of negativity on her own. Still, her memo and grievance were things of beauty—masterfully crafted—even if the efforts did not produce the desired results. Carolyn proudly saved a copy of the memos, and placed them in Jordan's scrapbook.

* * *

As difficult as her life was at the office, Jordan found happiness in a life complete with her Carolyn. Their home was a source of peace, an oasis of tranquility. Jordan retreated to this island paradise each night, and as quickly as she could! She had grown close to the Berringer's and she enjoyed the Sunday afternoons they spent together. She was even learning to paint beside them, although her landscapes could never compare to the exquisite works of her in-laws. Jordan wished that she could share her happiness with her own parents, but they remained cordial but aloof. On rare occasion, they did invite both Jordan and Carolyn to the Mathews home for dinner or a party. But they were always careful to introduce Carolyn as an old friend of Jordan's. Kelly or Jonathan would often drop by their apartment, and they would joke about Pete and Ann Mathews' complete denial of what was so very obvious to everyone else. Even Janice, Marge, and Tyler had begun alluding to them as a couple, although the title itself was unspoken. Jordan and Carolyn held close to their other friends, too. Jan and Betty were regulars at the home, and Bill and Marcus kept up phone contacts and sent the occasional x-rated greeting card at least once or twice a month. So Jordan took solace there in their home, and prayed silently that her career would somehow find a gentle calmness of its own.

And as desolate as Jordan's professional life had become, Carolyn's career was rich with fulfillment and future! She won a teaching award in her third year at the Regional Day School. She had even started working part time as an art therapist at a local children's hospital at the request of their Board. Carolyn cherished her life with Jordan, and she could hardly contain herself whenever Jordan was nearby. And her artwork was especially vibrant! Carolyn's pieces closely rivaled Ben Berringer's work, and oftentimes, they would compete against each other in exhibitions. It seemed that life could offer her no greater satisfaction, and she felt a strange guilt, an unworthiness, that she had been blessed with so much, so soon in her life. She could not fathom the joy that lay ahead! Carolyn could not understand how all this had come so together for her. She did not know why she received such favor, but she thanked both karma and God for Her goodness towards her each day.

And their relationship was a solid thing of beauty! They merged their worldly resources. They joined the land of the joint bank account and the co-ownership of everything. They kept in sight the goal of building their personal empire—accumulating potential financial security to ward off the potential rack and ruin that might confront them in their elder years. They were planning out their lives together! Jordan and Carolyn were a couple in every sense of the word but one.

They stayed connected to the Gay Community through their friends and associations, although they rarely went to the bars much anymore, and usually, only in the summer. They had not kept up with their political alliances, because they no longer felt the need for such things. They had found each other, and that was more than enough to sustain them. They would dodge whatever unpleasantries the outside world might try to heap on them. They were safe in their closet-world, passing and undetected. But they were not totally in the political dark—after all, they had sworn off orange juice as a counterblow to Anita Bryant's Save Our Children Campaign in 1977! And they also knew about the defeats of gay rights laws in California, and in St. Paul, Minnesota. They just didn't want to experience reality on that level. Their own happiness served as an insulation from the prejudice and hatred that surrounded them. They were more concerned about the goings-on of everyday life. So they were taken by surprise, when Marcus made the phone call to them about a murder in San Francisco, on November 27, 1978.

"It was an assassination . . . a gay man, the first out gay public official! He was gunned down yesterday! Haven't you been watching the news? His name is Harvey Milk!" Marcus couldn't believe they hadn't heard about it.

"No, we've been pretty busy here today. And we've been out of the gay loop for a while," Carolyn replied. "It's on the news?"

"Yeah, because there were riots there! Certainly don't think they'd publicize a gay murder do you? No, it's property damage that caused the media pick-up!" Marcus said. "And the political connection, of course. I think it's time for you to get back into the gay loop for your own safety! You never know how these things can impact on your life. You have to know what's going on at all times!"

Marcus shared with them the story of Harvey Milk's murder, just as he alerted them a year later, to the results of Dan White's famous "Twinkie Defense," and his 5 year sentence for manslaughter.

"How could any jury NOT find him guilty of First Degree Murder? He killed Harvey Milk in cold blood!" Carolyn asked incredulously, as she and Marcus discussed Dan White's punishment over the phone.

"Twinkies made him do it!" Marcus sneered. "Good thing he didn't have Devil Dogs, or he may have taken out the whole city! . . . He probably wouldn't have gotten even the 5 years, if he hadn't also shot that mayor there George Moscone.

And Dan White was a City Supervisor there, too! It's a damn shame! Can't even talk to Bill about it. The time has come. I believe what they say. 'Out of the bars and into the streets!' We have to get organized to defend ourselves."

"I hear what you're saying, Marcus, but please . . . be careful! Politics can be a pretty dangerous thing. Every time you put a fist out, there's three times that many fists knocking it down! And you already know that they won't protect gay people. This situation says it all . . . You don't even have to be gay, for that matter, just political. Look what happened to Martin Luther King!"

"So we're just supposed to sit back in fear, while the rest of the world targets us? No! That's not the right answer. We have to mobilize. We have to organize. We have to protect ourselves, because they will not protect us!"

"All I'm saying is, just be careful! Don't be the frontrunner. Don't be the hero. Don't do anything that will jeopardize your individual safety! Let the movement take care of itself." Carolyn knew how easily Marcus could be coaxed into a leadership position, and she was afraid about how he might be used there. He had such charisma! She loved Marcus and Bill and couldn't handle anything happening to them. She, too, wanted an island for all the people that she loved. She wanted to keep them all safe.

Jordan and Carolyn did not attend the Gay Rights March in Washington, DC, in October, 1979, but Marcus and Bill were there to demand their rights for them. But they did contribute cash, and later became part of a lesbian network that pulled strings behind the scenes to promote their friends and the cause of Gay Equality.

\* \* \*

Jordan started the new decade, and her fifth year as a BCS worker, under the supervision of Helen Crawford. Although well liked and well respected, privately Helen had a raucous nature, and she often used her raunchy humor and her truck-driver language to diffuse the stresses of the day. Jordan liked working for

Helen, because she never felt that she was under personal scrutiny. She treated Jordan as she treated all of her staff—as equal partners in the craziness, and equal accessories in accountability! And she let you know straight out, that if she was going down, you were all going with her! Jordan liked her directness. You always knew where you stood—and she let you know what you'd have to do, if ever you found that you did not like the shit that you were standing in! Jordan felt that that was a pretty fair deal.

There was an emergency situation that came about the fourth month of their assignment together. Jordan had been working with a recovering single mother and her five kids, ages six to twelve years old. They had been struggling for a while, even with the help of County Social Services, and with the supports from her mother. Finances were the big issue. Edna never received enough in grants to pay for the costs of the apartment that she needed to house a family that size. So she would supplement the income by subletting to her friends or to her lovers, who would sometimes make the place their home. She used her available funds to pay these expenses, and may have occasionally used any extra dollars for alcohol or weed. Jordan was never sure. Edna was not good at picking men really, and Jordan wondered why she continued in these pursuits. She guessed that like most people, Edna just didn't want to be alone. Besides, every now and then, one of her friends held a job and helped support them. But this family was too big a load for anyone to jump into permanently! Although the grandmother helped care for the children for most of their lives, Edna and the kids were forced to move out, when the grandmother lost the house. The grandmother was staying with a friend in a motel room, and Edna was trying to make it on her own. Jordan was trying to assist, all the while, watching Edna for child neglect, and for signs of alcohol or drug abuse—and Helen Crawford was watching them both! Jordan kept close contact with the grandmother, who hoped to resume care of the family once they found housing again. But Edna would have none of that plan.

Late one afternoon, Jordan received a report that the family's utilities had been shut off. Jordan drove to the home, and found the family using candles for light. They were now crowded into one bedroom of the small house that had otherwise been vacant. There was no running water. Dishes were piled in the sink and kitchen area, and the toilet was now near overflowing with human waste. There was a pervasive stench to the place. The heat was also shut off. A neighbor let Jordan use his phone so that she could speak with the electric and water companies. With Edna by her side, Jordan contacted the customer services rep. at the electric company. She was advised that the family owed $2677.35, and that payment would be required in full. The electric company had traced previous bills listed under the children's names to this same account. Edna did not deny that she had used this tactic in the past, and did not deny that she had never made a payment on her utilities. Jordan got the same information from the water company. She had only been paying rent, and the landlord now wanted them out!

"There's no way that I can help you out of this one," Jordan said to Edna, who stood silent next to her. "And there's no way I can allow the kids to stay here like this. It's not safe for them or for you. Is there someone else who can care for the kids until you get on your feet again?" Jordan already knew the answer.

"No there isn't, and I'll be damned if you're gonna be takin' my kids away! I've had enough of this . . . I'm goin' to see if my friend can help me out." She then walked out the door. Jordan waited with the children for an hour, and when Edna still had not returned, she contacted Helen Crawford from the neighbor's phone. Helen instructed that the children be removed under Dodd Act, and she made arrangements for their placement in a newly approved foster home. Jordan would take the kids to the hospital emergency room for their pre-placement physicals, and then on to their placement.

As Jordan and the children were preparing to leave, Edna and a friend arrived back at the apartment. But Edna was all drama and no plan. The neighbor contacted police when he heard her shouting.

"Oh no you don't—you are not takin' my kids!" Edna was screaming, but her posture was still, and she made no movement toward Jordan or the children. Her friend was coaxing her to stay calm. Although Edna refused to sign the placement agreements, she did not stop the children from going with Jordan. Edna and her friend climbed into the back of the patrol car and were driven off. She seemed relieved that someone else would now be caring for them all, until she could get things together again. Now she had some breathing room, some space to maneuver a real plan for them. Now she might include her mother for the extra help.

The children were quiet during the ride to the hospital. The oldest sisters helped to calm the younger children. They were being placed together as a family that night, but would ultimately require an additional five placements in various sibling configurations over the next seven weeks. The children were frightened, confused, frustrated, and depressed. Jordan was exhausted as she moved them from placement to placement. She worked with the grandmother and Edna to find housing that could again accommodate the family, but with the poor housing stock, and their low incomes, it was an almost impossible task. The children were surviving with their multiple foster placements, but it was the near final foster home that was the worst for them. Luckily, that placement was made for Mariah and the third oldest child, Laneah—the most emotionally solid of the siblings.

Jordan picked the girls up at mid-day and took them out to lunch. They were having daily phone contact with their siblings, and they were prepared for their next foster placement, even if it was in the next county. Jordan liked these kids. They were descent, respectful, religious, and pretty happy. It was obvious that they had known love, and that they loved their family. They sang in their choir, and had a love of music. Maybe that's why Jordan found such connection to them. They watched Jordan as she ate, mimicked her manners, and questioned her as she figured the tip. Jordan hadn't realized the cultural gap until that moment. She gave Mariah her tip card.

The girls had a visit with their mother and grandmother at the office, and then had pre-placement physicals at the hospital. After a quick burger and a jaunt up the Parkway, the three arrived at the foster home just after dusk. The home was in an urban area, and the buildings were closely fitted one to the other. Jordan parked the state car against the curb opposite the address she had been given. Several residents in the house across the street stood up on their porch and watched them as the three got out of the car. One of the women caught Jordan's eye, subtly and negatively shook her head, and looked toward the foster home. Jordan did not immediately understand the meaning of the gesture, and helped the girls carry their garbage-bagged clothing into the home. The house was neat, well maintained, and well organized. The elderly foster mother met them at the door.

"Hello children. I am Miss Ruby. You may come in now, and you may call me Miss Ruby . . . Say that after me now, children." The children repeated her name as she instructed. "Stop! Wipe your feet!" She commanded them as they entered the house. The home was neat as a pin.

"Rigidly so," Jordan thought, but she made no comment.

The children took seats at the dining room table, as Miss Ruby wiped their prints from the storm door window with her apron. She began to question the children about their interests. They talked about TV shows, sports, school, and music. Mariah stood up and walked over to the organ standing against the wall of the living room.

"Don't touch that unless you ask Miss Ruby . . . You may now play the organ," the foster mother gave her consent. Mariah looked to Jordan, and then to Laneah. Jordan could see the stress mounting. She felt knots in her own stomach.

"Maybe you could show us your home," Jordan suggested to Miss Ruby.

"Certainly," she said, as she stood up from the table. "Now see these stairs to the left here? These are the stairs to my room upstairs. Under no circumstances are either of you to enter these stairs without my permission. You are to stay only on this floor. I will be down during the day to meet with you." The girls stood silent and complacent. Jordan was shocked. She began to realize what the neighbor had been trying to tell her.

"This is where you two girls will be staying during the day. You each have your own beds, and this is your sitting room. You may touch anything in these rooms without my permission. You may not touch anything in the kitchen unless you speak with me first. Now come downstairs, children, and I will show you the new room that I just had completed."

They were heading to the basement, and Jordan was relieved, thinking that the old woman had created a game room there. But the basement was unfinished, except for an 8x10 walled area with a lock on the outside of the door. The room held two straight-backed chairs, a small throw rug, and a picture of Christ in the Garden on one wall. The floors were concrete. There was a new toilet installed at the left corner of the room. Jordan suddenly got a chill of fear. She looked to the children, and saw similar reaction.

"Holy Cow!" she thought. "Let's go upstairs and finish the paperwork," Jordan said, as she coaxed Miss Ruby up the stairs, and before her and the children. Jordan looked to the girls, and they seemed to sense her meaning.

As they sat at the table, Jordan pretended to fumble in her briefcase. "I must have left the placement paperwork in the car. I'll be right back. You girls stay right here, and do not get up from this table for any reason. Do you both understand me?" Jordan was deadly intense. The girls shook their heads in agreement.

Once outside, Jordan phoned Helen Crawford at her home from the pay phone at the corner of the block. "Listen Helen, this is Jordan. I'm at this foster home, and I have serious concerns about the mental health of this foster mother. She has a room downstairs that I think she intends to lock the children in!"

"What the fuck? Don't be ridiculous! . . . They would never approve somebody like that . . . You must be fucking kidding, right . . . Or you're fucking exaggerating—tell me that's all this is!"

Jordan could hear Helen fuming over the phone. Her family was yelling at her to hang up! Jordan held her ground. Finally, Helen agreed to contact the foster care unit so that they could seek out another placement for the girls. Jordan went back into the home to speak with Miss Ruby. The girls were still sitting at the table with her, as Jordan had instructed.

"Miss Ruby, I do have some concerns about your arrangements here. As you can see, these are young girls, and I think that they will need quite a bit more care and supervision than you have described. Have you ever had foster children before?"

"Well usually I have college girls, or women placed here by the Church. These are my first foster children." Jordan was thankful that Ms. Ruby hadn't offered to change her regimen for them.

"I'm sorry to have put you through this trouble, but I think we'll find another placement for them. Thank you again for your kind offer." Jordan started leading the girls out of the home.

"Oh, that's no trouble at all. You may come back here at any time." She walked the trio to the door, and again wiped the fingerprints off of the storm door, as Jordan and the girls drove off.

"Oh my God . . . I'm so glad ya didn't leave us there! I thought she was gonna lock ya in 'nat room! I was tryin' to think about how I could stop her, or get ya outta there! . . . And when ya went out to the car, I was afraid that ya weren't comin' back! What took ya so long?" Mariah's mind was racing. Jordan was glad that that the girls had come to trust her.

"I had to call my supervisor." Jordan didn't say more, but she and the children laughed and joked about Miss Ruby's rules all the way back to the office! The three sat in the waiting room. The girls each lay on a couch, and Jordan covered them with used coats from the clothing bank. It was 3:00 a.m., before Jordan received the call from the foster care unit. They had located yet another home, again in the next county!

Jordan decided to let the girls sleep until office opening. They then traveled back up the Parkway, and to their next foster placement. This time, things worked out for them! The Lawson's were an older black family, very active in church and community, very loving, and very attentive to the needs of these two young women. Mrs. Lawson had been a foster child herself, and she could appreciate their odyssey. She handled them with patience and understanding. Within four months, the girls were reunited with their family in a small, but ample old house in their hometown. While Edna would periodically leave the home due to arguments or her dreams of love, the children remained together and with their grandmother, until they were raising families of their own. Mariah and Laneah maintained contact with the Lawson's, who attended their high school graduations. Mrs. Lawson even helped with Mariah's admission to nursing school at the community college. Their families are still friends.

And as for Steve O'Brien, the boy that Tina and Jordan interviewed on Jordan's first field day at BCS? Well, things didn't go so good for him. Tina was right when she said that things were quiet for the moment, but that there were bound to be problems later. She was right by about two years, and just about the time that Steve started dating. He was maybe fifteen then, and really started getting hassled at school. He was beaten up at least three times before the school principal (different school, same intellectual fountain) decided to refer him to an alternate school placement. It didn't matter that in each case, Steve was the victim of the abuse. The principal just thought that this was the best way to handle the situation, the best way to keep him safe. His home was now a battle zone, and the only peace that he could find was in the retreat to the home of his friend. As he bolted out the door each night, his step-father would launch a cascade of insults at him.

"Fuckin' faggot! Don't come back here 'till ya get a set a balls!" Dan O'Brien was always right to the point.

Steve thought about suicide, but with his mother's forever optimism, he always expected that things would get better. He vowed to himself that not his step-father, not the assholes at school, not even the jerks in the neighborhood would beat his spirit or make him bitter. He would shine, no matter what anyone did! He thought that this was his destiny—to overcome the odds that kept stacking up against him. So some days, he would take a rope from the garage, or take a knife from the kitchen, or take a bottle of pills from the bathroom, and sit out in the woods, tempting fate and his own inner strength, daring himself to laugh at the end, as he taunted his own future. His only solace was in the love that he shared with his friend Doug.

He would run secretly to Doug's bedroom at night after the families had settled down to sleep. They would hold each other through the short hours of the middle night, loving each other tenderly, kissing vows of assurance, making plans for the future. It seemed that they would only have to wait for the time that they could break free of the oppression that closed in around them. But one night that paradise was shattered, when Doug's mother heard the stillness broken, and decided to investigate what she most feared. She found the boys making love, an oral expression of mutual desires. And she freaked out!

Steve grabbed his clothes and ran out the door, while Doug tried to calm his mother and explain their relationship to her. But she would have none of it, and was hot on the phone with Steve's parents! Doug packed a small gym bag, and left the house in search of Steve. BCS got the call the next day. They were missing at least several weeks, before they were spotted sleeping under the boardwalk. Police grabbed Steve and Doug and held them for Jordan's interview. She convinced them that she could find a special foster arrangement for them, and they bought into the plan. But when she called back to the office, Helen had gone out on a personal emergency. Jordan had to deal with Crittenden.

"Listen, I have Steve and Doug here at the police station, and they're willing to come in, if we can guarantee that we will not interfere with their relationship. Can you arrange a couple of temporary foster homes until we can work things out with their parents?" Jordan was pleasant and respectful. "Maybe we could start emergency family counseling sessions to help them get though this."

"And where do you suppose we're going to put those two? They're homosexuals! I wouldn't even put them in the shelter! They can't be around other boys! We will not condone this behavior! I will not help them in any way but to send them back home. There are mental health facilities for those kinds of kids. We're not going to expose anyone here to their abominable actions. I will not put that on any foster parent! So you tell them that we will not assist them in any way. Maybe then they'll make the change they need to save their lives." Crittenden sneered the response.

"But you know that Dan O'Brien, Steve's step-father, has threatened and beaten him in the past. He's the reason that Steve ran away in the first place! I don't see that as a viable option. It wouldn't be safe for him. Maybe Doug's mother will be more willing to accept Doug back, but-"

"No! No way! This is how it is! This is how you have to deal with this type of kid! They either learn good moral values, or they fight to survive on the streets. The decision is theirs. I'll call the parents and have them contact you at the police station."

Jordan waited for the phone calls from the families, but only Doug's mother responded. She agreed to take Doug back temporarily, but she had already made plans to send him to an uncle in California. He would teach Doug heavy construction. She believed that he would make a man of him. Steve slipped out of the police station while Jordan was transferring Doug to the care of his mother. But within a day, Doug was also missing. They disappeared into the streets, a no man's land where kids now were nicknames, living a communal-like existence paid for by drugs, and shoplifting, and prostitution. The only thing that Jordan knew for sure, was that Steve and Doug were together out there somewhere. She closed the case when they couldn't be located for over six months, and with the only lead, a rumor that the boys were dancing in a bar somewhere in Greenwich Village.

It was two more years before Jordan got the final news from the New York City Coroner. He had tagged the two boys from the missing persons bulletins she completed some years before. Both boys were dead, apparent heroin overdoses. They were homeless and living in an abandoned building. Doug was recently beaten and raped. The coroner believed that the overdoses were suicides, because the boys were found holding each other, Doug cradled in Steve's arms. There was no note or explanation—just the bodies of two more young gay men.

Jordan left the office and drove to the boardwalk, to the place where she last saw the boys before they disappeared. She sat on a bench overlooking the beach, and she cried. She cried for the boys, for their love, for their lost futures, for their families now devastated, and for the all the kids like them, out there, struggling to survive—and for no other reason than that they were gay. She made a promise to those kids that she would be there for them, that she would advocate for them, that she would protect them even from the agency that was sworn to protect them! And she vowed that she would never again work for John Crittenden!

Jordan and Helen worked together for three more years before Helen was promoted to some admin/support job in the Central Region. Jordan thought it was grossly unfair that the best and brightest supervisors were gleaned from the office, while the D.O. staff and client families were left with the likes of Crittenden! Jordan believed that she had done her best work under Helen Crawford's supervision. They seemed to perceive cases in the same way. They targeted the same issues and formulated similar case plans. They were never at odds with a case goal, and never had difficulty communicating their concerns and beliefs about a client family. And they had worked on some nasty cases together! There was the case of the three month old boy who sustained cerebral hemorrhage due to shaken baby syndrome while in the care of his family. The parents alleged that the babysitter caused the injuries, even though the child had symptoms before the babysitter arrived. The pediatrician's office had confirmed mom's call for an appt. early that day. The agency was unable to prove its case, and the child remained in the care of his parents.

There was rumor that the investigation may have been compromised by the family's business ties, but no basis, as Jordan knew. She and Helen worked exclusively on the case for days! But the prosecutor didn't believe that the medical evidence was conclusive enough to thwart the alibi of the parent suspects. He declined to move the case to trial.

Jordan was furious with the decision. "I can't believe that the prosecutor let them off like that! And to allow that child to remain in the home under those circumstances? Don't you find that infuriating? How can you accept this so calmly, especially with everything we know about the case?"

But Helen saw things more a matter of karma.

"We still can't prove that one of the parents actually caused the injuries, regardless of what we think. But the parents know what happened . . . And they are going to have to face that tragedy every day that they provide care to their son. I don't like the idea of any child being at risk, but I also accept that I can't always stop everything from happening. So I have to be satisfied that some things will have to straighten themselves out karmicly . . . and I hope that I still have the ability to help the other kids placed in my care."

Jordan valued the wisdom of that approach, and held Helen's thoughts as another guide to her professional sense of right and wrong in the universe. She and Carolyn contemplated the peace of that approach as they sipped a merlot in the tub together that evening.

But the cases kept coming at her, landing on her desk, clipped to the case assignment sheets that bore her name! They worried her as she drove home each night. They preyed on her, as she kept dodging the traps laid by Crittenden and his lackeys. They chased her down in her dreams, and cornered her against a wall of demands that yelled obscenities at her. They woke her from sleep in the early hours of the morning. They sapped her of the energy that she should have given to her Carolyn! But she could not back off, she could not give up, she could not let go! Why? Because she knew she could heal! She could make the difference! And that drove her on, unrelenting, from family to family. She saw the sacredness of it, the holiness of the Gift, and that kept her sane. But things began to take their toll.

She caught a case of a sixteen year old girl, whose mother kept her locked in her bedroom except for school. The nurse noted that the girl was withdrawn and underweight, but the mother maintained that the girl had an eating disorder.

Although she said that the girl was in counseling, requests for records proved that she had been to a half dozen therapists, but never beyond an intake session. Jordan managed to make her way into the family, and into the life of the child there. Jordan later discovered that the daughter had been the product of a rape, and that the mother was secretly starving her to atone for the sins of her unknown assailant. This explanation came out through a very carefully directed interview with the girl, and later, with the mother. The interviews were spurred by an empty box of cat food that Jordan had accidentally kicked as she sat on the child's bed to speak with her. The girl had been hoarding cat food and garbage to survive!

Jordan often had such revelations during home visits. While many in the office believed that she had a sixth sense, Jordan believed that these insights occurred at the hand and will of God. She had merely been His instrument. The mother was convicted. The daughter remained in the care of the step-father. He maintained his defense that the girl had an eating disorder, and then, that his wife had lied to him.

Jordan had again fallen behind in her paperwork, and chose another late night stint at the office, in the hopes that she might bulldoze the mountain of files that covered the top of her desk. As usual, she was the last one out, and the parking lot was empty, except for the state cars, and her own car, parked in the back of the lot. She had just walked around the side of the building, when she spotted the red pick-up driving toward her from the far corner of the lot. The truck parked several spaces ahead of her car, and the driver emerged. Jordan realized that it was Arlene's step-father! He came at her slowly, calmly, firmly, and accusingly. She was frightened and quickly glanced around, but saw no one else in the lot or in the area. She had always feared that such a thing might happen, and fought off the denial that that time had now come. She held her briefcase across her chest, in the event that she would need it as a shield. She had flashbacks to her assault by Josie at the Merton Clinic.

"So, ya must think that I'm some kind'a monster, to let my wife do that to her daughter. Well, I'm not. I'm just a man alone in the world. Do you have any idea what it's been like for me? Do you have any idea of what total loneliness will do to a person? Of course not—ya have your fancy job, and your beefed up title . . . ya walk around town and judge everyone around ya! Have ya ever once stopped to think about what the world has been like, what the world has done, to the people that ya judge? You can't possibly know any of that! It doesn't matter now, because your case is closed! Meanwhile, my family is destroyed . . . I have to raise a daughter alone now . . . Did Arlene ever complain to ya about her mother? No! She knew what it was all about, and knows that her mother loves her! But ya couldn't let things go . . . What am I supposed to do now? How am I supposed to live without her? I don't blame Arlene . . . she understands about her mother. But I blame you . . . And I always will. Ya have no idea what ya have done to me. I hope ya think about this talk, before ya step into another family and decide to destroy another person's life . . ."

Jordan could not respond. She was trembling as she watched the man walk slowly back to his truck. Her heart was pounding so hard she could feel it in her head! She jumped with the slam of his door, as she quickly unlocked her own car. She threw her briefcase inside, and plunged down into the front seat. Her hands were shaking. Yet when she looked up, the step-father was gone. She quickly drove out of the parking lot, fearful that he might return. She was afraid to drive home, fearful that he might follow her there! Instead, she drove along the ocean until she was certain he had not tailed her, and she weighed her options. She could not ignore the incident. He might return. She did not want to press charges. It might infuriate him to act further. She decided to file a police report so that the incident would be on record. She would also file an agency report the next morning.

She had a double Scotch rocks that night, as Carolyn listened to the story.

"I'm sorry, Jordan, but I don't want you working late there anymore! The job is too dangerous, even in the daylight! Do you think that the state will really care if something happens to you? Maybe a few friends at the office will, but for the state . . . they'll be meeting with their lawyers right off, and trying to find ways to hold you personally responsible for whatever happens to you! That's just the way of the world . . . It's all business, regardless of any contributions you made there . . . or any sacrifices that you've made in the past, so that they would look good . . . I'm serious, Jordan!"

"I knew it was gonna go like this . . . I even thought about not telling you . . ."

"Not telling me? . . . I'm your partner! I have a right to know! And I have a right to protect what's most important to me. I have a right to set boundaries for the good of our marriage . . . What can you possibly be getting from that job, that's worth destroying what we have here? . . . Don't you realize, that if anything ever happened to you, I could never go on?"

"It was one incident! I was closer to buyin' it at the mental health clinic! . . . When you're working with people, you can never be certain what will happen . . . But I could say the same thing for you! You're working with some emotionally disturbed kids . . . the same thing could happen to you at school . . . Or maybe you piss some parent off at the hospital. The next thing you know, you're at the wrong end of a . . . of a . . . whatever they can grab to use as a weapon! . . . It's like Bill said that time. We're all living with a false sense of security . . . None of us is safe, really . . ."

"I'm serious, Jordan . . . And with all the crap you have to put up with at that place anyway? . . . It's just not worth it! There are plenty of other places that would appreciate a social worker like you . . . I want you to find another job."

For the first time, Carolyn made a demand of Jordan, and she could not refuse it. For the first time, Jordan seriously considered the suggestion.

Carolyn held her close that night as they cuddled together in bed, one spoon tightly fit to the other. She slowly moved her hand across Jordan's back, and let her fingertips run over each curve and muscle there. She touched her as treasure, her mate and life partner—not like the familiar patterns they had fallen into through the years, the daily routines that blind you to the love right before your eyes. Through the years, they had fallen into those patterns, the obligatory steps, the script of the dance, the formula of the night—she sometimes lost sight of the wonder of their love. The demands of the day, the energies diverted to human survival had sapped them both of romance. She stepped back from that now. She let her breasts gently fall against Jordan's back, and let her exhaled breath roll quietly over her neck. She let her palm run the length of her shoulder, and return again along the curve of her hip. She touched her as one would stroke a holy vessel, apprehensive in the awe of it. She tenderly kissed Jordan's back, and let her tongue wander there, as she nudged her knee between Jordan's legs. She pulled Jordan close to her with both arms, rubbed and molded their bodies together, and began whispering to her.

"I love you so very much . . . I can't handle the possibility of anything happening to you."

Jordan turned toward Carolyn, brushed the hair from her face, and pulled her to a deep kiss. She let her tongue slide between her lips, as she pulled Carolyn tightly against her. Her fingertips stretched to touch all of her, as her arms clutched her to her heart. They were inseparable and indistinguishable now, each from the other, as Jordan always wanted.

"Nothing is going to happen to me. Nothing is going to happen to us. We will be as forever, as the universe, as the endless breath. Trust me on this."

She began to move her palms along the length of her lover, and cupped Carolyn over her. Carolyn rubbed her thigh in against her. Jordan began kissing her slowly, gently sucking her lips, rolling her tongue over them, then glancing her tongue along her neckline. But Carolyn stopped her, and laid her back on the bed.

"Let me love you." Jordan said, as she again pulled Carolyn to her.

"Not tonight, Hon. Tonight, I want to love you . . . really love you again."

She began again to massage her shoulders, feeling the firmness of her arms, and the warmth of her body. Jordan let out a sigh as she gently caressed her breasts, and tooled the mounds in her fingers. Her tongue danced across her nipples, circling the boundaries, striding over the centers, and sucking them to erect points. She held Jordan's palms outward from her body, and let her fingertips glide across them, tingling, as the moisture of her tongue descended across her ribs, and played among the ripples there. Her breath sent shivers across her body, as her cheek brushed against flesh and sinew, her palms now massaging the structural form, while her passion sought her soul. And her lips were a wonder as they traveled the full length of the woman she loved, sucking, tasting, nibbling the textures, the saltiness, the slice of life left open to her. Jordan breathed the love deeply, felt the rippling within her, heard her own voice moan out and guide her. She descended into the feeling of tongue and fingers gliding across and within her, the waves of delight now rolling through her, tantalizing delight, a piece of the sublime, and all from the woman that she loved. They were merged now, mind to mind, being to being, soul to soul, as the waves of glorious madness flashed through her, rocketed by each dart of the tongue, fingers spread and molding her, tugging and rolling over her, circling, ever circling the exalted sensations, forming her, stroking her, enthralling her, until she collapsed, whimpering and clinging, to her love. And Carolyn held her close as she returned from heaven to earth.

"I could never live without you in my life."

But cases like this were the exception, and not the rule. Families like this were uncommon. For every case like this, there were a hundred other cases that required only short term intervention—maybe a few home visits for monitoring, and a referral or two for some remedial services. Most parents really loved their kids, and they wanted to do right by them. The trick was convincing them that they were doing wrong! Helen usually stood back, and allowed Jordan the respect to work these cases on her own. She knew well that if she got into trouble, Jordan would seek out her help. But the office had changed so quickly, and now, even that simple respect was gone. But she was still not ready to leave. Jordan often missed Helen, especially as her career sustained the steady blows meted out by the office purveyors of negativity! Although led by Crittenden, these followers now included several supervisors, who believed that Marsha McMillan was far too tolerant of Jordan's "insubordinate ways."

But Marsha believed that one worker's insubordination was another worker's advocacy! She respected Jordan's devotion to her clients, even if her methods and demeanor were a bit unorthodox. Marsha had received maybe ten additional memos from Jordan in that time, most offering suggestions on policy changes that would make the agency more responsive to its clients. Jordan always carefully guarded client confidentiality by citing case scenarios by case number and not by family name. She used these cases to demonstrate opinion and to solidify her position. And these memos were administrative works of art! Carolyn proudly saved a copy of these memos and placed them in Jordan's scrapbook.

With Helen gone, Jordan was again up for grabs. Crittenden asked that she be reassigned to him, but Marsha McMillan denied the request, and placed her under the supervision of Diane Schmaltzborg. Although seemingly innocuous, proper, and polite, Diane had a reputation for some dastardly, underhanded dealings with staff, with clients, and with the community. She was the fist in the velvet glove, a cross between Mary Poppins and the Werewolf, and at a moment's notice, she could shape shift from this one form to the other! Truly, she had earned her nickname "Smellsburg!" She had no respect for the low income community, and only a minimal rapport with its leaders. Because Jordan often advocated for her families, and because her families fell into those demographic characteristics, she and Diane were often at odds. She was convinced that she needed to wrestle control from Jordan. Diane gave her less and less information about the unit functioning. In one case, she even gave Jordan misinformation to prevent her from attending a unit meeting! Jordan was often omitted from unit luncheons ("A mere oversight!" as Diane would claim), and she was never part of their unit social network. Diane, too, let Jordan know clearly where she stood.

At first, Jordan believed this was solely due to her relationship with Crittenden. But she also heard Diane make derogatory comments about gay people. This was not surprising, because she often made nasty jokes about anyone not like herself. But Jordan believed that Diane suspected that she was gay, and this added to

Jordan's uneasiness around her. Jordan made the conscious decision to remain on the periphery of the unit. She also decided not to share information about her families with her supervisor, except in cases of emergency. Besides, Diane seemed to like it better when she didn't know what was happening! They struggled on through this shroud of secrecy for the ninth and tenth years of Jordan's stay with the agency. During that time, at least a dozen more memos—now, regarding the differential treatment of client families based on class, race, sexuality, ethnicity, and politics—made their way onto Marsha McMillan's desk! Jordan was certain that she was making a difference, that she was impacting on agency structure and policy! She used this to convince Carolyn that she had to stay with BCS, at least for a while longer. Jordan believed that she would positively affect client families statewide for years to come! Carolyn reluctantly agreed. She proudly saved copies of these memos and placed them in Jordan's scrapbook.

Jordan Mathews and Diane Smaltzborg had a quiet but permanent separation when staffing was again realigned, and new units were created. Jordan was now transferred to Ted Thomas' unit. Jordan had not realized it yet, but she had become a "hot potato" in her own right.

\* \* \*

But Jordan did not function in a vacuum of office and social service responsibility. The important people in her life were aging, developing, progressing, just as she was. Carolyn continued working as an art therapist and teacher at the regional day school. She loved her job, and loved working with the children there. She had also developed a reputation as an accomplished seascape artist in the area. Kelly completed high school and college, and was now a speech therapist. She recently married a contractor, and they purchased an upscale home bordering an exclusive part of town, quite near Marge's parents. Jonathan also graduated high school, and was attending the Mason Gross School of the Arts. Pete Mathews had long ago accepted the idea that his son would not carry the family business.

Tyler and Marge were expecting their third child. Although she worked part time as a research assistant in a lab, Marge's real love was her volunteer work at the hospital. She began volunteering there when her mother was struggling to beat her breast cancer—a fight that she would ultimately lose. Tyler had now opened his own restaurant in the Montclair area, a bistro that offered an eclectic cuisine, and was featured several times in culinary magazines of some merit. Janice and Martin married after the deaths of Janice's parents. They were now living in the Gaithersburg area. Martin had spun off his own solar energy company, when the corporation he worked for caved to the pressures of the oil elite. They were struggling financially, but they were happy. Karen and Todd were holding firm at two children. Todd was still a mid-level manager supporting his father's executive position in the family business. Although the polymer company had gone global, it would be some time before Todd would assume the mantle of command. Karen was teaching full time and loved it! And she still helped the Group keep in touch through her greeting cards, Holiday letters, and phone calls, as the occasional weekend get-togethers became less and less occasional. Jordan secretly marveled at the unfolding of each life story—the seeds she had witnessed now budding into full flower, until one by one, these flowers would vanish from her life forever. To her, that process was an amazement of its own, cruel though it be.

Jordan and Carolyn clung to their friendships with Betty and Jan, and with Marcus and Bill. They loved their company, but also, they kept them in touch with the Gay Community. They were three solid couples amidst a culture of serial monogamies and one night stands. And they supported each other. They were often invited to Gay political rallies, but they would never speak or actively participate there. Carolyn and Jordan both feared that their careers would end if their relationship became public. And often such meetings were infiltrated by spectators of anti-gay sentiment—people who looked to destroy any sense of peace or belonging that someone might find there. They didn't go to the clubs anymore either. They were older, they were established, they didn't need that kind of support any longer. They had each found permanence and stability in their own relationships. And of course, there was the issue of drinking—their tastes had grown as they matured—from the beer keggers and Mad Dogs of the college years, to the hard liquor mixed drinks of their late twenties, and now, to the wines and cognacs of their thirties. But they enforced "dry spells," when they thought that they had been indulging beyond reasonable good sense.

They did, however, attend several of the Gay Pride Parades in New York City, festivals held each year to mark the Stonewall Uprising. This was a mandatory rite of passage for any gay person of conscience. The crowds were raucous and the costumes a mix of fringe and leather, satins and beads, primp and poor taste! Yet, there was an undeniable sense of freedom and community—a strength in pride, the power of numbers, as the marchers chanted down Christopher Street to Fifth Avenue, under the rainbow flag and balloon archways that led the procession—and the Movement—forward.

Despite the flair of Jan and Betty, Jordan and Carolyn marched inconspicuously—blue jeans, polo blouses, and sunglasses! Although the mood was festive, Carolyn was apprehensive. "Why take unnecessary risks? We're still contributing our number and our voices to the Cause. No need to draw attention to our individual selves . . . It's the sheer numbers that speak our political clout!"

No one could debate that. And no one could debate the rising political overtones of these recent parades! AIDS now congealed a community that previously found cohesion only in a disco beat or an occasional meeting of the Mattachine Society or the Daughters of Bilitis. AIDS was now bringing gay people out of the closet! The crisis was calling for action! The Gay Activist Alliance now had a very real target.

And so they marched on, laughing and cajoling their comrades with each step in the dance, a light-hearted frolic down 5$^{th}$ Avenue, and hopefully, into the living room of John Q Public, as he watched the news that night. With floats and marchers escorted by a blaring beat, the atmosphere was moving to crescendo—the party now morphing to mission, the focus becoming more purposeful, tolerance evolving to demand. The lesbians screamed feminism; the queers, the rising awareness of "Silence Equals Death"—both now streaming into every living room in the country!

Suddenly, the politics of the matter quickly took hold, as the marchers approached St. Patrick's Cathedral and the police barricades blocking entrance to the church. There, riot-geared police officers stood shoulder to shoulder behind the barricades, threatening any gay person who dared tread the stairs to the sacred cathedral! The scene sent chills down Jordan's spine!

"Holy Shit!" Jordan exclaimed before she had even realized that the words were out. She looked toward Betty, who shook her head in disbelief. Carolyn surmised that they expected violence, given the Church's stand on homosexuality, and its hideous response to the AIDS Crisis. But to Jordan, this stood as a stark statement from the Church—she and her gay "kin" were no longer welcome to worship their God, their Savior Jesus Christ, within its confines. The walls and spires shouted out condemnation—as if homosexuality precluded spirituality. This condemnation would surge through the coming St. Patrick's Day Parades that banned gay participants—as if homosexuality precluded ethnicity. Jordan wondered why the establishment was so afraid. "As if homophobia precluded logic!" she thought.

The parades of later years were forced to change their routes, so that a confrontation with the Church would be avoided. But the controversy within the Faith would go on for a seeming eternity! AIDS brought it all to the forefront! And the repercussions were felt throughout all faiths! The churches stood silent, ignoring, unresponsive, unrelenting, as young men and women fell prey to the disease. Gay Catholics prayed at home or attended the Unitarian Churches, united in the invocation that they, too, could be welcomed as children of God. They had come seeking Christ! Yet the churches would deny them this right because of their sexual orientation! The churches would withhold spiritual comfort and material medical supports to the victims of AIDS, condemning them to a lonely death-until finally, ACT UP members taunted religion to action! But that discrimination was not enough! Some churches would even seek out suspected homosexuals in an effort to "convert" them to a straight lifestyle (reparative therapies, they would call this mental torture)—damn the psychological costs that might result, like substance abuse, depression, and other mental health issues, including psychosis and suicide! The churches preached faith, but they taught hate.

But Jordan held close to the Faith, believing that the Catholic Church, a champion of the downtrodden, would also work toward acceptance. She could not immediately accept that the Church would condemn and persecute what God had created. She continued to attend the Church near her home each Sunday as a role model for other Gay Catholics. She stood as an example to those in the Church who doubted Gay devotion to God. She did not believe that the Church would move to exclude any group from worship, and she believed strongly that her spirituality, and her goodness, would be recognized by all who saw her there. She did not understand how straight people of faith could believe that they held exclusive insight into God's plan. She did not understand why they could not see Gay people as part of that plan—even though homosexuality has been a constant in all cultures and throughout the ages! She condemned the arrogance of their beliefs.

"All is vanity!" she thought.

She was appalled when the Catholic Church launched its campaign against gay people as a result of the child molestations by Catholic priests. She thought that the Catholic leadership had scapegoated gay people, another vulnerable group, to divert attention away from their poor administrative response to the child sexual abuse cases. She believed that the highly educated men of the Catholic hierarchy would have known the difference between homosexuality and pedophilia. Yet, they identified homosexual priests—rather than pedophile priests—as the cause of the abuse. She knew from her training and work at BCS that the majority of pedophiles are heterosexual—usually a male relative, or a boyfriend of the mother, and who sexually used a girl in the family. In fact, all of the sexual abuse cases that Jordan had worked had heterosexual perps! She had not met any homosexuals who were pedophiles, but knew, too, that some do exist. That abusive trait is separate and apart from sexual orientation. She thought that by blurring this distinction, the Catholic Church had exploited myth to avoid responsibility. Yet she held on.

Her participation in the Dignity[80] Group at her family's church helped bolster her belief in the goodness of the Catholic Church—at least until 1990, when that group too, was evicted by the Bishop. Another door closed! Yet her group met privately for nearly the rest of the decade! But Jordan lost her connection and her faith in the Church that day. She disavowed her religion, never to return. She remained spiritual, praying to her Jesus daily, and dedicating her work in His honor. BCS had become her temple, and she glorified her God with the good works she did there each day. She and Carolyn shared their faith, as they shared their love, and they believed that their spirituality brought a depth to their marriage that few others had.

\* \* \*

Carolyn and Jordan were content to grow old together. They were building for the future. They loved the sea, and decided that they would someday retire in the area where they spent most of their lives. They loved the familiarity of the place. They could vacation in some foreign and exotic land, but for day-to-day living, there was no place like home! Here, they could drive almost anywhere and tie the scene to a fond memory or a funny anecdote. They had history here. They had roots here. They had friends here. They had story here. So, they pooled their resources and bought a large island cape with a beach front on the bay. It needed a little work, but Jordan thought she could manage it. And they could still walk the several blocks to the ocean when they wished. They were within

---

[80] Dignity is a gay organization within the Catholic Church. For background information on the Dignity Groups, please refer to the Appendix and Bibliography for Chapter Nine.

miles of both Jordan's family and the Berringer's home. And the house was big enough for company! Carolyn's parents often stayed with them on the weekends, so that they could paint on the beach at sunrise and sunset. She would often paint with them, as Jordan read beside her, or took a run along the shore as they worked. But Carolyn's parents were aging quickly now. She and Jordan had already decided to take them in, if Carolyn felt that they could no longer live independently. Their new home could comfortably and safely accommodate them. And Jordan could help arrange any services that they might need. Jordan loved the Berringer's almost as much as she loved her own family. And she loved this additional commitment in her life. And the Berringer's loved her almost as much as they loved Carolyn.

One of Jordan's most prized possessions was a small cedar chest that Carolyn's parents had made together for her birthday. Ben Berringer had accented the chest with hand tooled carvings of swirls and notches that reminded Jordan of the ocean she so loved. The chest had a deep blue velvet lining and a lock at midpoint. Jordan loved the cedar chest, and it became the vessel in which they stored the mementos of their many trips and triumphs together. It held old tickets, and braided twine bracelets, cherished jewelry, and love notes written on napkins from their favorite midnight eateries. It held Playbills from Broadway, and photos of hiking trails, and the scrapbook that Carolyn kept of Jordan's work. The chest had become the treasure trove of their lives together, a monument of their love remembered. Jordan cherished it all.

The Mathews also made small changes of their own. Carolyn was right, when she said that Jordan's parents would accept their relationship in time—but she was wrong on the amount of time that that acceptance would actually take! It was nearly three years before the Mathews actively invited Carolyn to the family home, although she had accompanied Jordan there many times. The Mathews never recognized their relationship as a marriage, but they did accept the closeness of their friendship. And they never again suggested a male pairing for Jordan! Progress was in the eyes of the beholder.

But the Mathews never came to attach a real value to the love that meant life to their daughter. Ann Mathews could not acknowledge that Jordan's relationship had permanence, even after she and Carolyn had shared their lives for nearly a decade. As Ann steered each family heirloom toward Jonathan or Kelly, Jordan felt the sting of rejection. Ann was clear that she wanted certain items passed down to her "children's children's children." Since Jordan was childless, this doctrine put her out of reach of any of the family's most prized possessions—and kept Jordan apart from her birthright! Ann would never understand how insulting that posture was, and she would never realize how hurtful that decision was to Jordan. Yet, Jordan accepted the decision stoically. She really had no choice! And Ann Mathews doled out her love as she doled out her possessions. Jordan would always feel a hesitant, unspoken clarification whenever Ann said that she loved her—always as if the statement had been an afterthought, a sentiment more of social amenity than of genuine feeling. There was always a lurking tension just beneath that superficial welcome. Maybe some of this was a leftover from the teenage tensions that disquieted their relationship so long ago. But even now, Carolyn's warmth could not penetrate those glacial walls of distance, built on disapproval, and painted with a happy face.

Pete Mathews welcomed Carolyn much more quickly than did his wife. He missed his daughter terribly for the years before, but he kept Carolyn's statement close in his mind. He found that Jordan was always there for her family, and that Carolyn was right—all they had to do was reach out to her. And they were doing it now, more than ever.

But that reach was one-directional, and Jordan's stubbornness was a huge deficit, as the weight of their bay front cape lodged squarely on their shoulders. At times, Carolyn suggested that maybe they had bitten off more than they could chew. She even suggested once that Jordan reach out to her father and cousins for help. But Jordan had been disrespected too many times to ever let herself open for another round of subterranean insults. So, they worked both nights and weekends, sometimes till 2:00 a.m., to make the home the masterpiece they had envisioned at the outset. The new kitchen complete, Jordan tore apart the first floor bath, and tackled the plumbing with a book she checked out of the library. She had already seen the process a hundred times in her life, and just needed the book for back-up cues. Besides, she wasn't laying fresh pipe! She was just replacing the sink and toilet! She never anticipated the fountain of water that erupted from under the sink, when the main water valve was turned on, but the sink welding had not held! At 1:00 in the morning, soaked and disgusted, Jordan launched into a tirade, tossing wrenches and plumbing dope, and shattering the newly installed shower doors! Carolyn retreated to the bay front until a calm had again settled over the home! But Jordan had the bathroom remodel complete by 7:30 a.m., the culmination of three solid nights' work. She soaked in the bathtub with a glass of wine, incense and candles ablaze, and called out from work that day. Carolyn joined her in the celebration of their palatial powder room, and they soaked off to imaginary scenes on the words of Pablo Neruda.

It was several weeks before Jordan attempted the next project—building a deck, tearing out part of the back wall, and replacing the back door with sliding glass doors and a view of the bay! Although Carolyn approved the deck and sliding glass door combo, she quietly doubted that they could complete the job on their own. She secretly reached out to Pete Mathews for help. Just by sheer dimension, she already knew that, even together, she and Jordan could not properly install something so heavy! Sworn to secrecy, Pete stopped by the house several times that week, and just talked with Jordan as she built the deck. He helped her set the lag bolts that attached the deck supports to the house, handed her floor joists or a tool, but otherwise, did not offer to intervene.

Finally, the day had come to break out the back wall. Carolyn held her breath as Jordan swung the sledge hammer, bits of sheetrock flying around the dining room.

"You've certainly got a good aim there . . . something I really need to keep in mind in the future . . ." Carolyn joked as Jordan wacked away.

"It's a lot easier than you think. The hard part is raising the damn thing! But once it's airborne, the sledge hammer has a life of its own. It just carries itself right on through the wall. Good follow-through in a tool like this is essential! That's what makes the sledge hammer the hammer that it is! All I have to do is focus my attention on a specific point, lift and swing, and a hole appears on contact!" Jordan gave the statement half teaching, half joking back.

"So true in all obstacles of life! . . . And what are you focusing on, if I might ask?"

"Crittenden, of course!" Jordan shot back. "Who else could give me such incentive! I just visualize his claws holding me back, and I smash them to bits! I see his wall of bullshit blocking my future, and I take it down brick by brick! I see him building a prison of frustration around me, and I beat a path of escape! . . . Or, sometimes, I just see a sheetrock wall keeping us from sharing a sunset in the comfort of our own home, and away it goes!"

"Good answer! I like the therapeutic approach . . . You haven't mentioned him in awhile. I thought that things were getting better for you there."

"Better, if standing still is your life goal . . . but then you have to realize that standing still over time means that you're going backwards . . . No progress, really. It's just something that I have to handle in my life until I can arrange a better position somewhere. Trouble is, I can't find a better position right now . . . and I'm beginning to wonder if I ever will. So, I just keep ducking and hoping that this too shall pass. I can't live my life in the fear that something will happen. I just have to make sure that it doesn't happen! . . ."

"Why haven't you been talking to me about this? We're a team! I'm your partner!" Carolyn held Jordan's arm for a moment to stop the next hit through the wall.

"Because everything is status quo . . . What can I say that I haven't told you before? . . . Besides, if we talked about this, day in and day out, we never would have bought this place, we would never have any laughter in our lives, we would never have anything but Crittenden hanging over the both of us, night and day . . . I'm not about to give him any more power than he already has! My plan is just to buy time, knowing that sooner or later, he's going to go too far with the wrong person, really piss somebody off, and he'll be taken out for me!"

"But how can you work . . ."

"Hey Jordan, Carolyn . . . Wow, you really got a good start on that!" Pete stepped into the house.

"Hey, Dad!" Jordan said as she kissed her father, and took hold of the box of donuts he brought from their favorite shop. "I'll make some fresh coffee. Here, Buddy, enjoy yourself, but remember my famous technique!" Jordan handed the sledge hammer to Carolyn and she began to see targets of her own

"This is a lot more fun than it looks!" Carolyn exclaimed.

By lunchtime, the siding on the outside wall was removed, and the inside wall was demolished. Her father brought over a reciprocating saw, and they removed the studs and outer sheathing. Pete Mathews framed the sliding glass door, while Carolyn went for a pizza, and Jordan took a break. After lunch, they successfully set the door.

"Now this is livin'! . . . Ya set your weber up right over there, ya got your deck benches and your picnic table, your little cooler full a beer, and ya settle down to a view of the bay . . . What more could a homeowner want?" Pete voiced his approval. Jordan felt a special pride in her accomplishments.

"Actually, we need more closet space upstairs!" Carolyn said, not missing a single beat! Pete invited himself upstairs to offer possible ideas.

"Ya got a pretty good sized landing at the top a' these stairs . . . Maybe ya could build a wall out ta here, break through the bedroom wall . . . and extend the wall through here . . . You could have a walk-in closet going the full length of the bedroom! Then, ya put a door in that wall over there, connectin' this room to the upstairs bath, and you and Carolyn have a nice master bedroom suite!" Pete Mathews looked at them both and shook his head. "Probably a day's work together, if ya'd let me help . . ."

"OK, Dad! When can ya be available?"

"Maybe sometime next weekend. Give me a call during the week, OK? . . . Holy Cow! Look at the time! Your mother's gonna kill me! I gotta get goin'!" Pete gave his daughter a kiss on the forehead. Carolyn gave him a hug and a kiss on the cheek.

"We'll see ya next weekend, then! I love ya, Dad."

"I love ya too, Sweetheart!" Pete Mathews was out the new door, into his truck, and off to face the music with Ann.

"So whadeya think a' that, huh?" Carolyn mimicked the Mathews vernacular.

"I think he didn't realize what he said!"

"It's always nice to have the father's permission when one is bedding his daughter!"

"Somehow, I don't think it's wise to put it to him in quite those terms . . . Just be thankful for small miracles!" Jordan said. "Let's stoke up the weber and grill a couple of steaks! I feel like a barbeque . . ."

"You know, I think I'm going take the dinghy out for a row around the bay. Would that be alright . . . I mean, would you mind getting dinner ready?" Carolyn asked.

"Humph . . . No. You're entitled to a little alone time, I guess. I couldn't row with you, even if I wanted to . . . I can hardly lift my arms, I'm so tired. Go ahead, but keep me in sight. I'll call you when dinner is ready, OK?"

"Thanks, Baby!" Carolyn gave Jordan a kiss, pushed out the dinghy and rowed toward the center of the cove. The bay was still quiet, since spring had not yet enticed the revelers of summer. She watched Jordan preparing the grill as the boat darted through the waves. With each stroke, she said a prayer.

"Sweet Jesus, thank you for this wonderful home, and for my partner Jordan." The oars swished through the water.

"Bless us as we enter this next stage of life together." The bow raised with the crest of a wave.

"Keep us safe from all harm and strife." She thrust her body forward for the next stroke.

"Protect the love that you have given us." She pulled on the oars to propel the boat.

"Please God, give Jordan the strength to handle her employment issues." The oars tipped back to the start of the next beat.

"Help our families to grow in love and support of us, and keep them all safe and healthy." She pulled the oars to her chest.

"And thank you, Jesus, for all that you have given me. I know as well as You, that I'm not worthy of it. Yet You love me anyway." She lifted and pushed the oars to the next position. She held the left oar out of the water, as she pulled the other through the current. As the boat finished its circle, she could see Jordan waving to her from the beach. She did a speed row to shore.

They had just finished the last bits of steak and corn and had begun the process of cleaning up, when the phone rang. Carolyn bumped Jordan out of the way to answer the call, and chess pieces went flying. The two were laughing hysterically when Carolyn tried to call out a hello.

"Hey! Marcus! How are things? When are you coming down? You know summer's just around the corner. If you leave now, you might just beat some of the traffic and make it down by the 4$^{th}$ . . . !"

"Very funny, you! We'll try to get down soon. But I have something to tell you . . . Bill was mugged last night, and he's in the hospital . . ."

"What! What happened? Is he alright? . . . Jordan, Bill was mugged!" Carolyn turned away slightly from the receiver to tell Jordan the news.

"Well, he's in the hospital for observation, but he should be home tomorrow sometime, if he's still doing ok. He's got a concussion, a few broken ribs, and his jaw is fractured and wired. Lucky he wasn't killed . . ."

"So what happened? How did he get mugged?" Carolyn couldn't believe the news.

"He's finishing up classes over at the University. You know that adjunct professors get the worst class schedules. So he finished a class at 10:00 pm, and stopped by a local bar for a shot and a beer before he came home. It's the usual stop for him . . . It's a place not far from the farm here, so I don't worry . . . Anyway, he said that as he was walking to his car, he thought someone followed him out of the bar. The next thing he knows, some guy jumps him and knocks him down. Bill gives the guy his watch and his wallet, and he thinks the whole thing is over. Next thing he knows, the guy is kicking him in the head and in the side. As the guy is running away, he calls back 'Fuckin' faggot!' He just left him there on the ground bleeding and ran off. Somebody pulled over in a car and called an ambulance . . ."

"Well, did he see the guy? Did he make a police report?" Carolyn was livid.

"He filed a report, but he didn't tell them what the guy said to him. He didn't think the police would do anything about it anyway, and he didn't want any more trouble . . . He didn't know the guy who did it."

"So how's he handling all of this?"

"He's angry, but he's docile . . . I think he blames himself for not being more careful. But he goes to that bar all the time. And it's a straight bar! I don't know why the guy picked him out as gay . . ."

"Listen, Jordan and I will be right up. We have to pack and get a little sleep, but we should be on the road by 3:00 a.m. That will put us at your place like around 9:00 a.m. Maybe we can help settle him in at home, and maybe give you a break to run errands or whatever you need to do. Is there anything we should bring? Anything you need right off?" Carolyn asked.

"You don't have to do that. You don't have to come. Just knowing that you care will be enough for him."

"Jordan and I are coming, and you can't stop us. If nothing else, at least I can see for myself that he's ok. So let me get going here, so that we can get everything together."

Carolyn and Jordan threw a few outfits into a suitcase, and struggled as best they could to find sleep before the six hour trip up to Vermont. They woke, showered, prepared coffee and snacks for the trip, and were on the road by 3:00 in the morning. They drove in shifts, stopping every hour or so for a break. They saw the sun rise over the familiar landmarks, and were at the farm of Bill and Marcus by 8:30 a.m. Marcus had just showered and was making coffee as they entered the house. He was bleary with a loss of sleep, and worn with stress.

The couple helped Marcus ready for the trip back to the hospital. Jordan drove them as the three talked about the ordeal. Marcus said that he had a problem seeing Bill in the ER the night before, because he wasn't listed as family. The hospital only consented when Bill threatened to leave. Marcus didn't anticipate a problem visiting Bill now that he was on the orthopedic ward. Even friends were allowed there during visiting hours! Neither had tried to clarify their relationship, because some things just weren't worth the trouble. They could hear his bitterness as he spoke.

And he was mad with the hospital chaplain. He said that the chaplain came to the ER for an elderly man who was in a car accident. He just walked passed Bill's bed, though, after he had watched Marcus tending to him. Marcus was certain that the chaplain knew that they were gay men, and that he withheld blessing and prayer as a type of punishment. And he complained that the nursing staff was too slow to respond whenever he asked for help with Bill. He was sure it was all connected. Carolyn thought that Marcus was being overly paranoid because of the attack, but she didn't share that thought with him. Instead, she gave him the warmth, understanding, and support that he needed then.

The girls were taken aback when they walked into Bill's room, and first saw him there. Marcus let out a sigh as he looked over Bill's damaged and bludgeoned face. The swelling and additional bruising made the injuries appear even worse than he had seen last night.

"Oh my Bill, my Bill," Carolyn called softly as she gently touched his arm. He strained to open his eyes, but one was solidly shut, black, and swollen, the result of the beating.

"Carolyn, Jordan, Marcus . . . Are you really here? I can't believe that you two came all the way up here for this!"

"Don't you know that we're always going to be there for you two? You're our family. We're here because we love you . . . Thank God you're ok!" Carolyn said.

"I must look a fright. You know how vain I am! Marcus, how could you let them see me like this?" He was barely audible, his jaw now wired shut.

"We had to see for ourselves that you're ok. I told Marcus that. And we're going to stay with you, until you're feeling better. No objections taken!" Carolyn was firm.

"That could be a very long time . . . I don't think I'll ever feel better. I can't believe this happened . . ." He drifted back off to sleep, as Marcus petted his hair, and the girls sat silent vigil beside him.

Bill was discharged later that day into Carolyn's care, the supposition of the attending physician who had identified her as Bill's girlfriend. Her glance toward Marcus told him not to argue over the misunderstanding. He was coming home, and that was the important piece of information. Marcus would be tending to all follow-up medical care, no matter what the doctor thought. Jordan drove the car back to their farm, with Carolyn in the passenger seat, and Bill stretched across the backseat, his head on Marcus' lap. As they pulled in to the drive leading to the house, Marcus pointed out the barn where their few cows and sheep were housed. He identified the various crops he was growing on their organic vegetable farm, a business made possible by the financial supports of his young, history-professor partner. He shuttered as he thought about how easily, how quickly, their lives could be destroyed. They all thought back to Bill's dissertation that sad night at the M&K, when they all could have lost everything to a hatred unjustified.

Bill lay on the living room couch, as the trio went out on the back porch for some fresh air. The clouds moved over the mountain ridge, casting long shadows over the valley below. A few crows flew past the house enroute to their nightly roost. There was a strained quiet among the three, finally broken by Carolyn.

"You know, maybe it was just a simple mugging. Maybe the creep just said what he said, with no real meaning . . . ." Carolyn tried to help Marcus contain his own hate.

"Doesn't matter what he meant . . . . the result is the same. We haven't had any problems since we moved to the farm 2 years ago. In fact, people here have been pretty decent to us. But now, we'll always wonder . . . . We'll always be afraid that we're being targeted."

"That's the same for any of us, just like Bill said that time. None of us is safe, really . . . But if you begin to think that everything is happening just because you're gay, you won't have normal relationships with anyone . . . . I think it's like that for all minorities. I'm not saying that we should hide our heads in the sand, and make believe that this hatred doesn't exist—because I think that we all know quite well that it does . . . I'm just saying that if we assume that we are always being targeted, than in our minds, we will always be targeted. That fear will become so overwhelming, that we won't be able to survive anywhere. We won't be able to do anything. I'm careful about who knows that I'm gay. I'm selective, because I can acknowledge that hatred exists. But I also see horrible things happening to people who are not gay, and I try to draw a line, a wall, that keeps that paranoia in check . . . Maybe the guy was motivated because he hates gays, maybe he was just an asshole mugger. Maybe the chaplain was motivated because he hates gays, maybe he was just too busy to give a damn. Maybe the nursing staff hates gays, or maybe they just don't care about anyone . . . If I see things in one way, it paralyzes me. If I view things in another, it empowers me. I can think out a clear response . . . See what I mean?" Jordan waited for Marcus to answer.

"I've heard that explanation a hundred times, but it doesn't offer much help when you've just gone through something like this . . . I'm sorry, Jordan. I didn't mean it that the way it sounded. But at this point in time, I can't see things any other way. I know who my friends are in this town, and that won't change. But you can damn well be sure that I won't be so trusting of the whole fucking community any longer, now that I see what CAN happen!" Marcus hit his fist on the rail.

The girls stood in silence.

"Don't you see what happened here yesterday? I could have lost him forever! I can't handle the thought of that ever happening! I always thought that Bill would be the one who'd have problems if anything happened to me. I always thought that I'm stronger than he is . . . better at coping with things, you know? But I realize that I am no good without him . . . and I would never want to go on without him. That scares me more than anything . . . the possibility that I would lose him forever. . . . God, from this point forward, always have everything happen to me, and not to my Bill. It tears me up to see him like this, and I want to lash out at anyone who could have done this . . ."

"Right now, Marcus, Bill needs you here. Totally here, with him. Mind, body, and soul. Maybe you should see a therapist, and work this out a little before you try to help him. Maybe when he's able to attend, he can go, too."

Marcus didn't answer but walked back into the house. He held Bill gently in his lap, and brushed his hair with his palm. He stayed the night in that same position, his hand gently petting Bill's head, a silent guardian over the man that he loved.

Jordan and Carolyn walked quietly to the guest room, settled into bed, and held each other close, each shielding the other from all of the world's evils.

"So why didn't he just call him a fucking Dago, if that's what it was all about?" Jordan said. Carolyn just pulled her closer.

# Chapter 10

"Who said that you could come up here, and who told you to come anyway . . . I did not call for your help, Ms. Mathews!"

The shout was coming from behind a slightly open but chain-bolted front door. Jordan recognized the voice as Ruth Pearson's, but the posture, the greeting, and the mystery were haunting and unfamiliar. This meeting came as part of Jordan's monthly "Dodger Round-Up Days"—unannounced home visits with those clients who had either missed an appointment, or who had refused one. Jordan received several reports from family recently that Ruth was using again. The mother and toddler were still under court-ordered supervision for her drug use of the past! Ruth completed treatment and maintained clean time for nearly eight months before the agency started receiving these newest allegations. And while Ruth completed that rehab. and recovery, her two year old girl stayed with an aunt who still kept watch on them. Ruth maintained her program and had even begun waitressing again before this relapse. But Jordan was certain. She caught the smell of marijuana coming from the apartment, and she thought she saw a "blunt" on the kitchen table as she peered through the opening in the doorway.

"Ruth, let me in. Let's talk about this." Jordan believed that she could convince Ruth to work with her again, to check herself into a rehab., and to place her daughter with her aunt.

"I am done talkin' to you! Whenever you come 'round here, there's nothin' but trouble for me and my kid. I finished my court time, and you have no right to be here. Now I expect you to be outa here!" Ruth closed the door and shut off all communication by blasting her stereo. The neighbor downstairs started yelling at her "to turn that shit down!"

Jordan called back to the office to conference with Ted Thomas, but the call was forwarded to Crittenden. "What're you doing on the line?" Jordan asked, surprised and half-challenging.

"Ted's not in today, and I'm covering his unit. What is it you want now, Jordan?" He was cutting in his response.

"I'm at the Pearson home, and I think that the mother is under the influence of marijuana, and that her two year old child is with her at present. I don't know if anyone else is with them, but I don't think so. The family was previously court-involved, mom went through treatment and regained custody of her child. We started getting new reports of her drug involvement last week. We were unable to substantiate at that time."

"Call the police and ask them to respond with you. If you confirm that she's high, pull the child, take her for a physical, and place her in foster care. I'll have the foster care unit start making calls for a placement for her now."

"Well, Ruth has an aunt that took care and custody of her child when she went into rehab. eight months ago. I'll reach out to her, and have her take the child. I think the mother would consent. The aunt can file for temporary custody in the morning."

"No, we're done with that—she had her chance, and she smoked it up. That child goes into foster care, and we'll refer the case on to the pre-adoption unit..."

"You can't do that, with active family involved!"

"You will do what I tell you to do!" Crittenden then hung up the phone. Jordan was so livid that she was shaking, as she exited the phone booth, and drove to the police station for assistance. While there, she also called Linda, the Administrative Assistant, and asked that she review Crittenden's order. Linda refused to intercede.

"Look, just do what he's telling you to do. We can get this cleared up when Ted is in tomorrow, ok?" Linda hung up the phone.

Ruth knew the drill and was already waiting for them on the balcony of her apartment, when Jordan pulled back into the driveway with police escort. Jordan saw that Ruth's hair was matted, and that she was dressed only in short shorts and a large-mesh tee shirt, without bra or blouse. This was so unusual for the proud woman who was typically clean and neatly dressed. The woman started screaming immediately. Jordan asked her to put on a robe.

"I told you to get outta here, Ms. Mathews. I told you that I don't need nothin' from you. Who do you think you are, anyway? GET OUT OF HERE! LEAVE, NOW! GO FUCK YOURSELF." The police officers interceded, tried to calm Ruth, and advised her to keep her voice down.

"GO FUCK YOURSELF, TOO!" she screamed to the officers, as she flipped them the finger with both hands! Ruth would not be calmed! Her child was standing behind her, dressed only in a diaper. She started crying with all the noise.

"We're going to come up now, Ma'am," the officer replied.

"You are not going to do ANYTHING!" she screamed. She then started shouting at Jordan. "Here, Ms. Mathews, SUCK THIS!" She yelled as she grabbed her right breast, and forced the nipple through one of the holes in the mesh!

"NO, EAT THIS!" she said as she dropped her breast and grabbed her crotch.

"Oh my God!" Jordan exclaimed, mortified, as she covered her open mouth with her hand, her face now a shocking rosette, her legs trembling. She looked quickly to the police officers, who were now mobilizing for an assault!

But Ruth was still not satisfied with the insults! She pulled off her shorts, flashed her butt and said, "NO! PUT YOUR TONGUE RIGHT HERE!" as she pointed to her rectum, and angrily hissed the words, her eyes fully locked onto Jordan's.

Jordan was speechless. The police were furious, and charged up the stairs, into the apartment, and out onto the balcony. Ruth was attempting to climb over the rail to jump at Jordan, as the police grabbed her, cuffed her, and tossed her to the floor. Her child stood in the corner of the balcony and sobbed.

"Mommy, my mommy!" The child could say no more than that.

One of the officers radioed for an ambulance, and advised that the woman was under the influence of crack cocaine. Jordan had never heard of this newest drug until that day. She would never forget the effects it could have on otherwise rational human beings.

As the mother was being wheeled into the ambulance, flailing and screaming obscenities, Jordan completed placement paperwork under Dodd Act. She placed the paperwork on the kitchen table and took photos of the apartment and the child. Jordan gathered up what clothing she could find, gently dressed the sobbing child, and took her to the hospital for her physical. As the girl was being examined, Jordan called the aunt and advised her of the foster placement. She also advised the aunt that BCS would be in court within seventy-two hours to seek custody of the child. The aunt stated that she would apply for the toddler's custody that day! Ruth's daughter was placed in a temporary foster home until the court hearing would determine her fate.

When Crittenden learned that the aunt was seeking custody against his BCS case plan, he flew into a rage! Even after he was reminded by Linda that the case was under Ted's supervision, he pressed for disciplinary action against Jordan. He charged that she acted against his expressed authority. But neither Ted nor Linda would pursue the disciplinary action against her—not because they wanted to protect Jordan, but because they wanted to shield the agency from a possible breech of policy charge! Later that day, Linda called Jordan into her office.

"This thing between you and Crittenden has to stop. It's becoming very disruptive to the office. Don't you realize that he will ultimately win . . . if this thing between you persists? If I were you—and I valued my career—I'd find some meaningful way to put an end to this rivalry immediately. Understand me?" She was again leaning forward in that seductive way she always used to soften the blow of a full scale punch in the head.

"I understand," Jordan responded, but she couldn't see any way to use the advice. She knew that she was on Crittenden's hit list—and that she had been there for quite awhile. She was now aware that this conflict was viewed seriously by the administration. But she would not compromise her principles, and would not sacrifice her clients, to satisfy his ego! She just didn't see any way out of it without resigning—and she would never give him that pleasure! She would consider a promotion or a transfer to some other office, but such things took time. Regardless, she now realized, for the first time, that her relationship with Crittenden had become strictly "kill or be killed." She vowed to herself that the hunter would now be the prey!

Jordan decided to try to push Crittenden a bit, and maybe scare him off of her back. She answered Crittenden's written request for disciplinary action, by calling for such action against him! Jordan quoted agency policy as she defended her inclusion of the client family in all planning for the child. She cited the NASW Code of Ethics in maintaining the client's right to self determination. She concluded by challenging that supervisors did not have the right to establish their own set of policies and procedures. She labeled his actions as a usurping of authority! Jordan called for disciplinary action against Crittenden as a means to re-establish agency boundaries. She demanded discipline against him to reaffirm the agency's integrity and its commitment both to its mission, and to its client population.

Jordan secretly identified this piece as her "Emancipation Proclamation" memo. She read and re-read the lines. She loved the way the words flowed like beautiful music, melding the ideas that exonerated her, and condemned Crittenden. She now believed that she had finally rid herself of the beast with a singular strike of the pen! Carolyn proudly saved a copy of the memo and placed it in Jordan's scrapbook.

Marsha McMillan sent a terse response advising Jordan that no disciplinary action would be considered at that time. Crittenden took a step back from the battle, but he waited to launch his next attack when the opportunity would present itself. Crittenden's storm troopers were running constant reconnaissance on Jordan, who now stood alone against them. She hadn't considered their potential impact. She hadn't considered that they could divide the office against her. In fact, she really hadn't factored them in at all! She realized this as a major miscalculation, a huge mistake.

And Crittenden used his position cunningly—he would lie in wait for those days when Ted Thomas was out, and he would then target Jordan for response on any emergencies that came into the unit. She would cringe as she watched him slither toward her. She soon found herself inundated with difficult investigations, and realized that this pattern was now in force even when Ted was there! Case assignments became public, now made during unit meetings, presumably, so that Jordan would be used as an example. Jennifer, Lisa, and Barbara would pull down the simple custody investigations, while cases like the poor, single, homeless woman with five kids, a serious crack habit, and a boyfriend who beat her, would somehow find its place onto Jordan's rotation. Or, she would get the thoroughly disgusting cases—homes piled high in garbage with only narrow pathways leading from room to room, while she stood ankle deep in one form of human muck or another. Or, she would get the truly dangerous cases—felons without moral or mental limits, who could just as easily lash out in a strangle-hold, as in a handshake. She could manage a few cases at that level of difficulty, but no one could handle a full caseload like that! Still, she tried as she could to meet all the casework demands, and was cited in those instances when she could not. And still, she believed that she would ultimately be victorious.

Jordan believed in herself and in her abilities. She thought that if she kept up her pace, she could outrun the casework demands, because her families would begin to stabilize. She hoped that she could ride out the tide of poor opinion crafted by Crittenden, and that she could again assume a position of some respect in the agency, if not in the office. She viewed each case success as another nail in Crittenden's coffin! She could see that he was becoming impatient, frustrated in his wait to remove her. He started writing her up for issues not against agency policy, and not within his jurisdiction. She would write back suggesting, in patronizing ways, that he address his concerns through the chain of command. Jordan knew that he would make a fatal mistake. She only had to bait him, and to wait him out. His ego gave him no peace in such matters! Carolyn proudly saved a copy of these memos and placed them in Jordan's scrapbook.

As Jordan sat in her favorite stall in the Ladies Room one day, pondering her plight with Crittenden, some sage advice flowed to her from just beyond the sink area.

"No matter how fast, the fox is always caught by the hounds . . ." Jordan believed that the voice belonged to Marsha McMillan! Jordan was unclear as to the intent of the message, though. She believed that Marsha was reaffirming her shield over her, a pledged protection from Crittenden. Jordan still believed that Marsha supported her, and thought that perhaps she was trying to transmit some new strategy against him, some new perspective that would generate the insight for victory! Jordan knew that Crittenden wanted to annihilate her, that he wanted to pulverize her into a million obscure parts. But like a cow in a slaughter house online for the hammer, Jordan did not believe that Marsha would allow that fatal blow!

Ted Thomas' two week vacation would offer both the opportunity for the final throes of battle. This time, Marsha McMillan did not try to avert disaster. She believed in letting things take their natural course. She believed that conflict was inevitable, and that the system would somehow upright itself back into homeostasis. She was a Social Darwinian, and believed that the day would be won by the fittest of the species! She had so tired of the shenanigans between John Crittenden and Jordan Mathews that she secretly hoped that the final cataclysm would take them both out! She could then return to the serenity of an office in quiet apathy. She would support neither of them.

Crittenden struck quickly. In the dark of night, he pulled Jordan's caseload and began reviewing the case goals on each family. He spread case plans across his desk like battle maps, his office now rivaling Patton's headquarters! He studied each log entry until he found the chink in the armor—and the battle strategy suddenly became obvious to him! He targeted cases that Jordan had been especially involved with—cases where she had had a long term involvement; cases where she had an emotional, as well as a professional, stake in the outcome; cases that demonstrated a steady progress toward the goals! Then, through a series of written notes and memos over the next few days, he began to destabilize each family! He contacted a foster mother, and gave her a date for the return of a severely disturbed teen to her manic depressive mother—this, despite the order for long term foster care mandated by the Foster Placement Review Committee! He ordered Jordan to return a sixteen year old from another foster home, even after her own family had threatened to harm the girl—and Jordan—if she ever brought her to their house again. Then, he ordered that a five year old be removed from his own home without court order or precipitating incident, because the mother had been intoxicated once four months prior.

Crittenden reveled in Jordan's anger and indignation. He taunted her whenever they conferenced a case, or even passed in the halls! He loved the sight of her squirming and the sound of her hollow threats of protest. He loved the way she now avoided eye contact, when her eyes had once been so defiant. He loved the contempt he could garner with even a simple hello. He loved to see her muttering to herself for hours after he tormented her for only a second or two. But most of all, he loved that his plan was working, and was working quickly! He felt confident that he would rid the office of the likes of Jordan Mathews, that he would lance a huge boil on the butt of BCS, and that he would thereby re-establish a decent America! Yes, Crittenden felt proud of the accomplishment, and laughed silently to himself whenever the thought of Jordan Mathew's termination came to mind.

Jordan felt the stress of the blitzkrieg! She attempted to lodge complaints in each instance, but Crittenden stifled all communication within the office hierarchy. Without other recourse, Jordan provided the families with the means to seek redress outside of the BCS office. The foster mothers both contacted the Office of the Public Advocate and asked for case reviews. The children were allowed to remain in their respective placements pending these decisions. Jordan contacted the mother of the five year old and gave her the number of the Public Defender. That mother instead hired a private attorney with the help of her sister. Her family assumed care and custody of her child, and threatened suit against BCS! Crittenden soon fell into a screaming match with Marsha McMillan! Half the staff held their breath and listened in seemingly detached silence, while Crittenden lashed out at the boss! Jordan was confident that she had successfully countered his blows! But the silence was momentary, the celebration short-lived!

"Son of a bitch!" Jordan exclaimed, as she read the latest series of memos dropped upon her desk. Crittenden had countered by withholding counseling services from several high risk families in mid-treatment, and before the therapists had slated them for termination! But that wasn't all—he intercepted messages from clients, and withheld information from the office cadre. He refused to conference cases and arbitrarily assigned case goals, or reassigned cases. Jordan had already learned that if she objected, Crittenden would write her up for insubordination. It was the perfect plan! And Jordan received four such disciplinary actions in the ten days that Ted Thomas was gone! She feared for her clients' safety, and felt powerless to stop him.

Jordan was desperate for a counter-blow. She conferenced these issues with Karen by phone, and together, they struck upon a strategy that they believed, would end the harassment and insure the integrity of the case plans. Jordan would write a singular memo detailing the events of the last two weeks, and make connection to similar harassment by Crittenden in the past. She would then conclude that Crittenden was using the clients as pawns, as weapons, against her!

It took her nearly a week to complete, but once finished, the memo was a work of art! Jordan noted that Crittenden stifled communication in the chain of command, by failing to conference key decisions on cases under her supervision. She noted that this caused a distortion of case perception, and negatively impacted on a number of client families. These families threatened suit and later sought recourse from the Public Advocate. She listed several cases as example. She next documented an instance in which Crittenden took a message from Linda's office, and chided Jordan in writing for not using chain of command. Jordan noted that he had not realized that she had merely taken a phone message for Linda. Crittenden had taken the message from Linda's office without her knowledge or consent—an act that would have otherwise denied Linda the important information contained in the message. Jordan then attacked Crittenden's lack of professional respect for her. She cited numerous provocative and accusatory statements made by him, as well as a variety of "catch 22" orders that he issued to her. She even attached memos in his own handwriting to further verify these charges! Jordan assailed Crittenden's failure to address issues in a timely manner, sometimes months after the fact—and identified these as veiled attempts to use such issues later as a basis for possible discipline.

Jordan identified these many tactics as the arsenal in Crittenden's ongoing harassment of her. She was now poised to finish her assault! Jordan concluded with a statement that Crittenden had used the clients as pawns in an effort to fulfill his personal vendetta against her! She called for an investigation into these matters, and asked that Crittenden no longer supervise her, or the cases assigned to her. She suggested disciplinary action wherever appropriate. Jordan read the work one last time. She got chills with the prospects that the memo presented to her! She believed that she had finally taken Crittenden out! Carolyn was amazed with the simple genius of words spoken in truth. She proudly saved a copy of the memo, and again, placed it in Jordan's scrapbook.

Jordan also made copies of the memo, and sent them to Marsha McMillan, to the Regional Administrator, and to the Director of BCS! She waited in the good faith that the Crittenden problem would finally be laid to rest—and perhaps, so would his career! It was appalling to her that such an individual could rise to a level of authority, even a low level authority, and so abuse his power! It disturbed her that anyone could have such little regard for the lives of other human beings—especially, people who so depended on the help and integrity of the system. It disgusted her that such a person as Crittenden existed within her own beloved profession. It was her hope that she, and Social Work, would be rid of him forever!

* * *

Marsha McMillan's hands shook as she pulled the memo from its envelope, and began to read the charges. "I never thought she had it in her . . . I never thought she'd try something like this." She looked at the calendar poised at the corner of her desk, and counted the weeks till her next vacation.

"Vivian, please call Jordan Mathews to my office." After several moments, Jordan appeared at her door. Although she took multiple deep breaths as she neared the office, the look on Marsha's face, the coldness of her stare, still knocked the wind from her.

"Yes Jordan, please have a seat, and close the door." Jordan did as she was instructed. "So, you wish to pursue charges against John Crittenden. I agree with you completely. If these charges are valid as you maintain, I assure you that we will take action. If these charges are valid, I also extend to you my deepest regret. I will be in contact with the Regional Administrator today to determine how he wishes to proceed. I will meet with John and advise him that he is not to have further contact with you regarding these issues. You will report to Diane Schmaltzborg whenever Ted is out of the office. Thank you. That will be all."

Jordan got up to leave. She looked to Marsha and asked, "Shall I leave the door open?" Marsha looked at Jordan and tersely replied, "No, the door is now closed."

Although these simple words did not immediately register, they resounded in her mind, again and again, until she picked up the subtle nuance—Marsha McMillan would no longer support her. Jordan now realized that she had lost the last vestige of power and influence that she held there. She knew that she had no hope of surviving professionally in that office. The best she could hope for was that she would be transferred to some menial position someplace, where she could quietly wait out her years to retirement and pension. How ironic! Although the memo was a success, the strategy backfired! She had inadvertently taken herself out along with Crittenden

"What a loss for the clients," she thought. On some levels, Marsha McMillan thought so, too.

* * *

The weeks following the Crittenden memo were among the loneliest of her life. Jordan hadn't realized how much influence he had actually wielded in the office. She suspected that his goon squad had run roughshod over the more timid workers there. She hadn't realized that the staff had all been watching the conflict between them. They were preparing to dodge any fallout. They liked Jordan well enough, but they didn't want to risk being seen with her. Such actions could easily be misinterpreted as a sign of support. Such support at that point in time would surely place them squarely in the line of fire! They had already seen what Crittenden could dish out, and no one wanted any part of it.

Jordan moved silently to her desk each morning, gathered the messages and mail left in her mail tray, and planned her home visit schedule. She looked forward to her time out of the office and in the field. These breaks really eased the impact, the hostility, she felt growing daily against her. Ted Thomas was strikingly polite and reserved. The other supervisors were cool but professional. Few workers acknowledged her, and none spoke with her. Peer pressure was mounting as the office awaited the decision. They were not necessarily fans of Crittenden, but they viewed Jordan's actions as "snitch-like." The fact that Crittenden drew first blood, that he distorted and even lied against her, and that he blatantly used the clients in such a devious way, was of little consequence. She had breeched trust, by taking the matter out of the office. In that instance, the strategy backfired.

The administration held their review of the issues as an emergent matter, because of the inquiries from the Public Advocate's office. Jordan was not successful in proving the harassment issues against Crittenden. However, the case practice issues were ultimately overturned, and the initial goals in each case were reinstated. But Crittenden only got a day's suspension and some remedial training! Jordan began to feel the crush of peer pressure, as she struggled to rise above the abyss where politics meets ethics.

Her depression was suffocating. She saw few ways out of her predicament. She no longer believed that the tides would change, and that she would recover the respect, or the credibility, that she had once so enjoyed there. She felt like she was a person out of place now—a person bumped into a uniquely separate perspective of meaning and profession; a person bumped onto a different plain of consciousness. For the first time, she tasted her own professional mortality. She could empathize now with the death row inmates, or with the terminal cancer patients. She was experiencing loss of a different kind, but it was still a deep loss. She felt the loss of her friendships, the respect of her colleagues, the prospects of a professional future, even her retirement plans and pension fund. She had now only to wait out the final moments before the ax would fall. Marsha McMillan had made that abundantly clear, with a singular command to close the door! The staff brought the point home with each failure to make eye contact, or with each silence that followed her greeting to them. Only her thoughts of Carolyn got her through the work day. At other moments, she'd think back to her time at college, and to the carefree, easy friendships she had enjoyed there. She held them close now, each time she heard a sneer with her name. And whenever she heard staff whispers about her, she would play again the voices of her youth singing "Rainy Days and Mondays."[81] She would talk herself through the words of the refrain,

---

[81] A reference to: Nichols, Roger S., and Williams, Paul H. (1971). "Rainy Days and Mondays" [recorded by Karen and Richard Carpenter]. On *Carpenters* [audio album]. New York: A&M Records

concentrating on each line. She longed for the solace she had once gotten from that simple song. She allowed the young voices and the laughter of Karen and Todd, Marge and Tyler, and Janice and Martin to sooth her through the pain and insults of the present day. She wished, a thousand times, that she was back with them, and with George, in his car, and headed toward the Appalachian paradise that was her youth.

Carolyn was especially gentle with Jordan during this time. She brought flowers to her weekly, and took her out to dinner three or four times that month. They visited with Marge and Tyler once, and even went out with Jan and Betty a few times, but Jordan could not be consoled. She avoided all talk of her work. Finally, one night at home and just after dinner, Carolyn suggested to Jordan that she look for another job, that she not sit passively waiting for someone else to make that decision for her. Jordan half-heartedly stated that she had been "sort of looking." It was then that Carolyn realized that while she was aware of the truth, Jordan had not yet come to accept the truth. She still hoped that she would somehow miraculously rise above the turmoil in the office, and that she would assume her rightful place there. Carolyn knew that it would be quite a long while before Jordan would recover from that blow.

She decided to take Jordan away for a week on a camping trip to Shenandoah National Park. They camped there many times before, and it was one of Jordan's favorite places on earth. She loved the crisp mountain mornings, and the deer that would freely welcome themselves to campsite and hot dog bun. She could hike off her frustrations along the Appalachian Trail, and regain her peace and perspective. Jordan jumped at the offer, and had little difficulty getting the time off. She believed that the office gave out a collective sigh of relief as she left her desk and trekked off on her vacation. She took her most prized personal possessions with her, and did not look back as she exited the doorway. For the first time, she wanted her mind clear of the place.

The next day was consumed by gear checking and car packing, grocery procurement and map sorting. Their clothing was neatly stored in back packs and duffle bags, their boots stowed on the floor in the back of Carolyn's car. They left at 4:30 a.m. to beat the commuter traffic through Baltimore, and snacked on donuts and coffee, peanuts and oranges as they tooled along the beltways, and finally, into the park. There was little problem getting a campsite in mid-June. Usually the crowds didn't overflow the place much before July 4th. The fog still lay gently over parts of the Blue Ridge, and it reminded Jordan of the hikes she had taken with the Group what seemed like ions ago. But like the ocean, the mountains in the park changed little, and she found comfort in the old familiarity of her Appalachian homeland.

They pitched their tent in one of the sites near the back of the campground and close to a trail entry. They sipped coffee and nibbled on sandwiches as they sat at cliffside and watched the hawks ride the thermals on the afternoon air. Carolyn brought both of her 35 mm cameras, so that she could take black and white and color shots. She loved the way the shadows fell along the mountain slopes, and the way the sun played through the branches of the trees. Jordan loved the sweet aroma of the goats beard and azalea now in full bloom. They took a short jaunt along the ridge, following the trail as they climbed the mountain range. Carolyn thought that this was the first calm that Jordan had enjoyed in over two months. She even joked with Carolyn as they hiked. She hoped that Jordan would find herself again, and that she would move on from this horrendous experience. She did not understand how anyone could cope with such abject hostility, and still maintain their sanity. She respected Jordan all the more for the woman that she was.

They had dinner around the campfire that night—nothing fancy, just hot dogs and beans, but the meal took on a special flavor over the open coals. They saved the steak for the next night, when they would really be hungry. After dinner, they settled by the fire, and tossed small branches and chopped wood into the flames. The embers glowed with reds and oranges, and the occasional pops from the bark sent licks of blue flame dancing along the log. They were quiet for some time before Jordan spoke.

"I am so sorry that this all had to happen. I am so sorry to put this burden on you. I know that it hasn't been easy for you . . . Thank you for standing by me . . . I don't think I could survive this without you." She looked into the flames, but could not bring herself to face Carolyn.

"Hey . . . come on now . . . no one thought this would turn out the way that it did. It's not your fault. It was just an unfortunate thing, that fate brought you and him together like that. Remember . . . even in the beginning, when you first got there, he targeted you . . . I think that you were a threat to him . . . you know, to his masculinity. He never sounded like the kind of man that could handle an assertive woman . . . and you were never the type of woman who could handle a male chauvinist . . . It was inevitable, really, when you look back on it . . . the conflicts, I mean . . . Just too bad that you didn't get the support you needed when this all first started. Maybe the whole thing could have been avoided. You would still have your job, and maybe Crittenden would not have stooped so low to take you out . . . Fate is a funny thing, really . . . What's it they say? We all think we have control over our lives, but in the end, we are merely the vehicles that fate drives . . . it's just dumb luck, like Bill said to us once . . . remember that night? Now that was a scary thing . . . Believe me, I was a lot more concerned about you then, than I am about you now." Carolyn started laughing, in the hopes that the joke might raise Jordan's mood. Jordan continued to stare into the fire. Her silence was accented by the popping and fizzing of the flames.

She suddenly turned onto Carolyn's shoulder and started crying soft low sobs, as her breath jumped with each inhale. "I'm so sorry, so very sorry, to have disappointed you . . ."

"You have never disappointed me! You are the best thing that's ever happened to me, and I spend every day thanking God that I have you. You have never disappointed me. Come on now . . ." She held Jordan against her, and let her cry.

"Honest to God, I don't know what I'm going to do . . . I can't imagine myself doing anything else . . . I can't imagine facing my folks, I can't even face myself in the mirror! I can't believe that this is all over . . . everything I've worked my whole life for, and just like that, it's gone! It's not fair . . . it's not fair!" Carolyn continued to hold Jordan as the embers waned to a dull orange, and then, slowly faded into the dark pile of cool coals that surrounded them. Carolyn gently nudged Jordan, and led her off into the tent. Neither slept that night. They heard an owl calling to them in the distance, in haunting tones that emerged from the stillness. A loneliness overtook them both, yet neither spoke.

\* \* \*

"Come on, Pal, gimme a boost up here. Damn window's stuck . . . Shit! . . . gimme 'dat fuckin' blanket . . . So dark I can't see a fuckin' thing here . . ."

"Quiet! . . . You wanna bring out half the block?"

"See anybody around?"

"Nope, not yet at least! . . ."

"Great!" He took the wrench wrapped in the grease-marked, old brown blanket, and with a single tap, the window pane crumpled inside the kitchen of the large island cape on the beach front. It was the second house they hit that night. They usually didn't come this far down, but they were looking to score big time, and Bingham really didn't have a reputation for affluence. They would have hit Two Harbors, but those million dollar homes all had security. So they picked a couple of houses near the route where their friends were throwing a party. They thought that they should have a little fun before they pulled a job. They were both still buzzed when they picked the house. Tullman wiggled his way through the broken window, then pulled Culp in behind him. They each grabbed a pillow case, as the muffled flashlights shone over each room of the house. They strolled around the layout like two men entitled! They grabbed a camera, a Bose system, and a coin collection, before they started dumping drawers from desks and dressers onto the beds upstairs.

"See anything good there?"

"Ah, just your standard stuff . . . got some nice jewelry here, though. Check out this watch . . ."

"Nice!" Culp looked at the time piece, and tossed it into his sack.

"Hey 'at's mine!" Tullman said. "I was gonna give 'at to Patty!"

"Sorry, it's Maria's now! Pick somethin' else." Culp pointed to the other items on the bed. Tullman started rummaging through the trinkets that lay before him. The curtains fluttered in the night air, a breeze now gently moving from shore through the broken kitchen window and into the living room. Culp startled with the movement and sounds from downstairs.

"Hey, this ain't Penney's! Figure out what ta give Patty later. We gotta get outta here . . . Wrap it up!" The two grabbed all the jewelry they found, and left the other things for the owners. They started moving back toward the window. Tullman was pawing the Llardro statues on the hutch, while Culp ransacked the closets.

"Hey, looky here . . . wonder what's in 'at box . . . Ahh, the fuckin' thing is locked shut!" Culp held the sculpted box in his hands as he examined it.

"Who cares, it's mine now!" Tullman said as he grabbed it from his partner. "We'll break the lock in 'na car. I'm gonna take dis box for my stash . . ." Each then slithered out of the broken window and helped the other with the plunder. They used the blanket to carry the pillow cases and other items to the car, so as not to draw attention to the stuff now claimed as their own. Once in the car, Culp reached under the passenger seat, pulled out a small tin box, and began rolling two stogies.

"Rollin' us a stogie, and rollin' down the road, Ain't got no worries, 'cept dealin' out this load . . ." He started to sing, as he lit the joints and passed one to Tullman. Culp started to pry open the lock on the box with a pocket knife.

"Uhh . . . this is some good shit!" Tullman said, as he took a toke and drove the car up Route 52, and headed for home. The rewards of the night were tucked neatly in the trunk. The two men laughed and joked and sang to the radio as they sped down the two lane highway for home. They got as far as Port Benton, before they attracted the police.

"Fuck! We got company. Quick, open na windas' and get some fresh air in here!"

"Blow 'em off, Tullman! I can't get busted again, or I'm goin' to jail for sure!"

"If I blow 'em off, we'll both be goin' to jail . . . . Let's just be cool, and drive like we don't know anything's goin' down. Then, when we hit the next county, run like hell!"

"We're already in 'na next county, ya stupid Fuck! Run now, or forget about it!" Culp was insistent, and Tullman didn't have a better plan. He cowboyed his way through the next light as he hit the accelerator. The police car flipped on lights and siren, and bolted in pursuit. They had gotten less than a mile, before they were joined by several other patrol cars, now blocking them to one lane of the highway. Without other egress, and with bullhorns threatening them, Tullman pulled over.

"What a fuckin' night . . . I didn't even get laid . . . !" Culp sneered at Tullman.

"Just shut up and don't say anything. Just give 'em your name and tell 'em we were at a party. Right? I'll handle everything." Tullman and Culp put their hands on their heads as they exited the car, with four officers now surrounding them. They accepted their arrests without incident, and were silent as two of the officers searched them. Cloud-like flumes of marijuana smoke followed them out of the car.

One of the officers reached under the seats of the vehicle. "Got a tin full 'a hooch here, and some papers . . . I'll pop the trunk." The officer pulled the trunk release from inside the car, while his partner stood at the trunk. The thieves stood silently, hands held high, as the other two officers stood guard over them.

"Gentlemen, what's all this? Looks like stolen goods to me."

"No officer, we're just helpin' my girlfriend move, is all."

"Interesting that she's only taking her jewelry and a few other items that she could probably fence. Gentlemen, you are under arrest for driving under the influence of a controlled and dangerous substance, for possession of said substance including paraphernalia, and for possession of stolen property. You have the right to remain silent . . ." The two officers carted the men off to booking and to jail, while the other two stayed with the car and arranged for the tow to the impound lot.

As the men were being processed, another officer at Impound confiscated all the items in the car, and posted each individually on a police report and inventory sheet. The officer listed a wide range of jewelry, three cameras, a coin collection, a Bose system, a reel-to-reel tape deck, and an ornate wooden box with a broken lock. He opened the lid of the box and found bits of braided twine, notes on some napkins, some used tickets, old Broadway Playbills, and a binder. He opened the binder, and found what appeared to be intra-office BCS memos. He read the first few, and thought that they were innocuous.

"What the hell? Why would anybody keep office memos under lock and key?" He kept flipping through the binder, and began to see a disturbing pattern. His suspicions were validated when he came upon the Crittenden memos. "Hey Chief, I found something in that car impound earlier tonight that I think you might wanna take a look at." He carried the binder to his Officer of the Watch, who quickly tooled through the memos.

"Ah, it's probably nothing . . . Some malcontent trying to start trouble over there . . ."

"Maybe. But take a look at these . . . And if it's a hoax, why keep them under lock and key?" The Officer of the Watch reviewed the several specific memos that the Sergeant pulled for him. He looked at his Sergeant, and puzzled, shook his head.

"I swear . . . Alright . . . I'll take care of it in the morning . . . My shift's over. Going home to the wife and kids. How's your family? Everybody OK there?"

"Oh yeah," the officer replied. "Life is good . . . for the moment."

The next morning opened with an egg and cheese on a bagel, a car accident at the circle, and a call to the District Attorney. The Officer of the Watch was concerned that the memos detailed some form of malfeasance. He knew the good and the bad in people at every level. He struggled himself from time to time, trying to make the right decisions, trying to make the right moves that would meet his own ethical standards, and still let him keep his job. It was a tough balance, ethics and politics. But in the end, he knew he had to live with himself, he had to be able to sleep at night. That thought became his guiding force. Hell, sometimes he was even lucky enough to move forward, to get a promotion, maybe even rise to become a detective one day. So it sickened him when other people couldn't find that balance. It sickened him when public servants took advantage of the vulnerable and the powerless. That's one of the reasons why he became a cop in the first place. He hated bullies. And he hated corruption. It put the whole system in a bad light, made everyone seem suspect. And if the lives of children were being impacted because of it, he hated that even more! The Chief supported him in the referral.

"What do you think you have there, anyway?" the District Attorney asked.

"I'm not sure, but I thought you should take a look at it . . . Maybe nothing, but maybe something. The whole thing just doesn't seem right to me. There's a ton of memos here . . . most of them reporting some pretty unethical actions about clients over at BCS . . ." He then read the concluding lines of a memo. " . . . Lastly, John Crittenden's behaviors demonstrate a systematic harassment in which he has used clients as pawns to fulfill his own political agendas' . . . She even cites cases as evidence . . . gives some stuff about case plans . . . Did you ever get any reports from BCS like that?"

And before long, Jordan's memos were traveling through channels to the State Attorney General, who requested assistance from the prosecutor in the county of origin, where their investigation would be closely monitored—and where full worlds would begin to collide and to collapse.

\* \* \*

Jordan and Carolyn arrived home just before 10:00 p.m. Carolyn was especially tired, since she drove the last leg of the trip back, while Jordan slept. She could hardly wait for the hot shower and the comfort of their bed. Her muscles ached from too much exercise, and too little REM sleep. Jordan started getting edgy again as they were preparing to leave the campsite. Carolyn knew that she was already thinking about the return to her office, and to all the bullshit issues that waited for her there. She hoped that Jordan would detach from the madness, and that she would think back to their time on the trails whenever the pressures got to her. They would soon be home, among their familiar surroundings, and amidst the combined material wealth of their twelve years together. She believed that they would be together for the rest of their lives.

She woke Jordan gently as she parked the car in the garage. She knew that Jordan had been startling pretty easily lately, probably due to the all the stress. She wanted to handle her gently.

"Hey, Baby, we're home now. Come on, wake up. Let's go in and get some sleep, ok?"

"OK" she replied with a yawn.

"Let's just take in the back packs and duffle bags tonight. We can unpack the rest tomorrow. It's too late now, and I'm too tired. I'm going to take a nice hot shower, and before you know it, we'll be sound asleep. Doesn't that sound good? . . . Come on, wake up now." The two grabbed the bags holding their clothes, and made their way through the garage door and into the kitchen.

"Oh man! Look at this! The window's broken . . . Well, at least it didn't rain . . . Damn kids probably playing ball again . . . We can look for that in the morning. I'll tape up a trash bag tonight, and we'll have to call somebody to fix the thing tomorrow . . . Why don't you get ready for bed. I can handle this."

Jordan wasn't gone for more than a few seconds before Carolyn heard her scream. She ran up the stairs and into the bedroom, and stood shocked, then angry, as she surveyed the damage.

"What happened? Who could have done all this! . . . All of our stuff is dumped all over hell . . ."

"Not all of our stuff," Jordan replied. "Don't touch anything. I'll call the police." They waited, exasperated and outraged, as they sat at the dining room table. They had an overwhelming feeling of filth in their home. "So much for the hot shower and the comfortable bed," she thought.

Within minutes, two officers arrived at the home and took a report about the burglary. A detective used a black, powdery dust to locate any fingerprints. It was almost 2:00 a.m. before they had finished. The officers advised them that another home on the same block had also been robbed. They hoped this would keep the women from thinking that they had been targeted. The cops viewed the burglary as a random act, and probably, because the thieves saw that no one was home. Still trembling, Jordan and Carolyn tried to make an inventory list of all the things that they thought were missing. Jordan was especially upset that her cedar chest had been taken. Carolyn tried to console her by reminding her that at least they still had their wedding rings. They had worn their wedding rings on the trip, the only jewelry that they had taken with them. In fact, the rings never left their fingers from the moment they were placed there on that cold December night so long ago.

The next day was just as unsettling. Glaziers from two different companies gave estimates on repair of the window. By late afternoon, the window was fixed, the kitchen was cleaned, and the bedroom was back in its usual neat arrangement. Still, the girls could not shake the horrible feeling of violation, the creepy feeling that a stranger had pawed through their possessions, and had invaded their personal lives. They slept on the couch. Jordan disinfected everything in the home. She stripped the bed, sprayed Lysol throughout the house, mopped the floors with Mr. Clean, and vacuumed and dusted everything they owned. They kept the windows and doors open to fill the house with fresh air. Carolyn lit candles in each room, hoping to generate a positive aura. One of her paintings now had a large hole punched through it, apparently having fallen and been trampled by the intruder. As she picked up the piece, she started to cry. She felt humiliated, victimized by an unknown entity. She took personally, the callousness of the boot that tread through the beauty and sensitivity of her psyche. Jordan helplessly looked on. She was using all of her emotional strength just to survive herself. She held Carolyn as they cried together. They said few words that evening.

Although she toyed with the idea of calling out, Carolyn convinced Jordan to go into work the next morning. They both knew that it would be no easier for Jordan—that she could not put off the inevitable. Jordan would try to call her on her lunch hour just to get a little moral support. Besides, she needed to feel Carolyn close to her, the break-in had been that unsettling. Maybe they weren't targeted, but they were still violated. They both felt helpless, powerless, as they saw their things taken from them, without care or concern for who they were as people, or what the objects meant to them. They both had visions of their treasured items pawned or desecrated. They carried their mark in their posture, and wore their victimizations as a grim mask. But Carolyn secretly thanked God that they had not been home at the time.

Things for Jordan were worse that week than before she had gone on vacation. Several of her families were in crisis, and the staff resented that they had to cover any of her cases. It didn't matter that Jordan had done her share of case covering while they were on vacation! The thought that her caseload was assigned as a kind of punishment made the staff resent that they "had now been pulled in to bail her out." She could only believe that it was Crittenden who forced that point to the staff. She certainly hadn't unleashed that opinion. No one had talked with her at the office in some time, so who could she have told? She became very uneasy, as she perused the pile of case folders sitting before her on the top of the desk. She noted that many of the files had been rifled through. At first she believed that staff pulled the records to respond to a crisis. But then she realized that several of the more political cases, the cases that were court-involved, or who had a formidable advocate of one sort or another—the Press, a Congressman, maybe a local celebrity—these reports had been unstapled and then re-stapled. She noted that the page numbers were off, that pages were missing! She immediately brought this to the attention of Linda, the Administrative Assistant, who minimized the concern in her usual, sultry manner.

"You know, this place can get pretty hectic sometimes . . . And you were getting ready to go on vacation. Maybe in your push to get things done, you mislabeled, misfiled, mis-stapled, whatever . . . and you're just now realizing it. Check all the files again. I'm sure things will turn up just as you left them." She gave a brief sigh, then leaned slightly forward, again flaunting the cleavage that peeked from just above her bra. She glanced into Jordan's eyes.

"I'll try that again, but I already checked the other cases before I came to you. Don't you think I would have done that? Do you think I would be so careless as to make an unfounded report?" She looked at Linda for a reply, and quietly felt insulted by Linda's provocative behavior. In the deepest recesses of her mind, she was shocked that anyone could think that she would be swayed by the valley between two breasts—especially, by the very breasts that everyone in the office had seen countless times, despite the fact that Linda only popped them out in uncomfortable situations!

"I have a lot of work to do. Is there anything else?" Linda turned away from Jordan and back to the mass of files and To Do Lists piled on her desk.

Jordan returned to her desk and re-examined the files present there. In one case, the whole record was gone, but it later turned up with the DAG. He had taken the file for a court briefing. The other cases stood with their blatant absences, and no concentration, no routing through stuff, no amount of sorting from file to file would make the missing pieces materialize! Jordan was secretly happy that she had copies of these cases at home for just such emergencies. It was a caseworker's code of survival, really—strictly CYA. Everybody had a file of those cases neatly stored somewhere, safe from the eyes of the public, and out of the reach of those who might discredit them. But she was now faced with a perplexing dilemma—should she pull the material from her records at home? If she did, how could she explain their sudden re-appearance? Certainly, whoever pulled the material in the first place would realize what she had done! And she could be fired for such an offence! BCS took a dim view of secondary records lying around some caseworker's house! There were confidentiality issues, and a demonstrated breech of trust in the system. She could pretend to recreate the missing material, and declare the originals misplaced, misfiled, or otherwise lost. But this would give credence to the subtle assertion that she was becoming disorganized or disinterested in her work. Even if she maintained that someone had tampered with the files, the Administrative Staff would only deny the charges and use such allegations to further discredit her! No matter what she might try, she was in a losing situation. Her frustrations mounted, and she could feel the tensions building in her jaws, in her shoulders, and in her clinched fists. She decided to pull the materials from her copies at home.

"There must be some reason why the stuff was taken out of the records . . . Let them take the fall for whatever it is! Likely without it, I'll probably be the one to go down!" She would be as blatant and as brash as they were! She, of course, defined the likely "they" as Crittenden's crew. She defined their motive as an attempt to further discredit her.

She was jotting down the missing page numbers from each case, when she got the call from the Prosecutor's investigator.

"Hi Jordan, this is Bill Corcoran. Wow . . . we haven't worked together in a while. How've you been? How was your vacation?"

"You know how it is here, Bill. Every day's a party! One step in the door, and the vacation is just a memory—a pleasant memory, but a memory none-the-less . . . How about you?" Jordan tried to sound upbeat. She was about a thousand miles from the phone call.

"Same ol', same ol'. Say listen, we got a call on a repeat offender, an old case of yours. Can you get over here today to brief us on it? It's the McCluskey case." Bill would not elaborate on the charges.

"Sure, when do you need me?" Jordan was looking for a dodge out of the office. She was beginning to despise the people around her, all of them! Even if they weren't Crittenden's flunkies, they were silent enough to be. "To quietly accept was to tacitly condone," Jordan thought. She would never have done that to them. Her thoughts were interrupted by Bill's response.

"The sooner, the better. This way we can get out to the school, interview the kids . . . you know the routine. Nothing ever changes." Bill laughed a bit as he waited for her reply.

"OK, let me go talk to Ted, and I'll be right over. I'm sure he won't mind. We'll just take the case as our rotation today. He'll be glad for that . . . at least we got the assignment early." Jordan spoke briefly with Ted, who approved the assignment. She grabbed her briefcase, got a state car from Vivian, this time, without a radio or air conditioning, and headed to the Prosecutor's office. She tried to catch up on some field notes as she waited in the reception area. Bill finally appeared behind the desk and waived her in. He escorted her to a large interview room where they were joined by another investigator, and the Head of the Unit.

"This must be some investigation for the three of you to be here. What did McCluskey do now?" Jordan could not believe the attention to the case. At most, she had had one investigator with Bill before, and never with the Head of the Unit. She couldn't even remember his name.

"Hi Jordan," Bill started. "You remember Sam Smith, and our boss, Dennis Palmer.

"Yes, of course! Good to work with you again." Jordan smiled politely, and played the political game, even though inside, she was still edgy from the office issues that morning, and the robbery the night before.

"Here's the thing. You remember several months ago, when the McCluskey investigation first started. The two girls initially denied the sexual abuse incidents, and there was some disagreement between you and a supervisor over there about whether we should proceed with the case . . . You remember that?"

"Sure, we conferenced with Bill here about whether we should pull the girls, because we thought that the parents might be threatening them to keep them quiet. We realized that we didn't have enough information to warrant a removal, but we did have enough to mandate court-ordered treatment. The girls still didn't talk, the therapist didn't find anything out of the ordinary, the case was closed, and the father wasn't prosecuted." Jordan gave the information matter-of-factly.

"Wasn't there someone else over there that was pressing to have the girls removed anyway? Someone not immediately involved with the case, but who called over here to voice his concern . . . I can't think of who that was . . . You argued with him, and then he wanted the father arrested . . ." Dennis shook his head slightly, as if trying to recall. "Even after we had everything worked out . . . the father was out of the house until the therapist cleared him . . . But still, this guy called us. I can't remember who that was." Jordan did not make any connection, and shrugged in reply.

"That reminds me of the twins case we had, remember that one? The four year old girls, mom was back from rehab. what, six months? And all of a sudden we get an anonymous referral that she's using again. We refer the case over to BCS. Her urine comes up clean, the allegations are unsubstantiated, but the kids end up in foster care. Some supervisor pulled the kids before they finished the investigation, the allegations were not confirmed, but the kids are still in a foster home! Mom's been in Court, but BCS is still holding the kids . . . Strange how things happen sometimes . . . And both of those cases were yours."

"Yeah, I know that case. I wrote a report to the Court recommending return of the kids to the mother, but I had no control over the decisions that were made there . . . I didn't even have any control over the kids being placed. If it was up to me, they would have gone with family until the investigation was completed."

"Wasn't that your case?" Dennis was pressing Jordan for the answer.

"It was assigned to me, but I was out on an emergency on another family. I think that Barbara Schmidt responded to that incident. I didn't agree with the removal when I was told about it . . . I was pressing to close the case. The mother was doing really well with the girls . . . I don't know why the Court would hold it up . . . What's this all about?" Jordan was becoming increasingly suspicious.

"Actually, the Court didn't hold the case. The kids' father did. He filed for custody of the kids, and the Court held them in foster care pending the outcome of the custody investigation." Dennis was searching Jordan's expression for response. He could see that she was becoming uneasy. He wondered what that meant. He tried to minimize the observation, so as not to scare her into a silence.

"Just talking about some of the cases we've had recently. Nothing more than that . . ." Dennis was calm, but persistent. He stood with arms folded and awaited a response.

"I didn't realize that the kids were still in placement. The case was reassigned right after I wrote the report to the Court." Jordan looked from Dennis, to Bill and Sam. She was still puzzled by their interest. The Prosecutor's Office never seemed really interested in any case she sent over before, unless it was some bizarre sex abuse thing, or it involved some political or celebrity figure, or it was likely to end up as some newspaper smear campaign. Not that she didn't like the investigators there—they just never seemed interested in the cases that she brought forward. She usually had the alcoholics or drug abusers, and those cases were a dime a dozen! Jordan wasn't even sure how the Prosecutor would have known that a case was under a custody investigation. Such matters usually fell under the jurisdiction of the Probation Department.

Dennis Palmer continued, "There was another case that we got recently . . . a sixteen year old being starved by her mother who said she was bulimic and under treatment. You substantiated abuse in that case. Yet, when we looked over the file, there was a concluding statement that you wrote. You said that you believed that the girl had an eating disorder . . ."

"No, I made that preliminary assessment after I met with the girl and the family. What you read was the concluding statement for the home visit, and not the concluding statement for the investigation. We still hadn't reviewed the medical reports or the reports from the therapists. There were probably five or six additional visits before we concluded the investigation. Then we substantiated both physical and emotional abuse, and also, medical neglect. Check the whole file. It's all there . . . You even prosecuted in that case . . . I still don't understand. I thought this was about McCluskey . . ."

"It is!" Dennis replied with a laugh. "We were just talking about some of the cases you've sent over to us recently. You really seem to be catching some nasty situations . . ."

"Yeah, sometimes it's like that over there. Luck of the draw . . . and then if there's new caseworker up for rotation, and the supervisor doesn't think they're ready, the case gets assigned to the next experienced caseworker able to handle it. Just my luck . . ." Jordan smiled as she spoke, but the hairs on the back of her neck were now standing as she joked with them. Dennis looked toward Bill Corcoran and Sam Smith.

"Well Jordan, it was nice seeing you again. Stop by when you have the time, and we'll talk some more. Good luck out in the field. Oh, that reminds me . . . we got a call from the Port Benton Police Department. They think they've recovered some of your stuff. Sorry to hear that you were robbed. I hope everything's ok."

"They got my stuff? Thank goodness! I hope they also got the guy who took it! He broke my kitchen window to get in, tossed the place . . . what a mess!" Jordan gave out a sigh as she looked to the investigators. "What do I have to do now to get my stuff back, sign charges? Well, no problem there!" Jordan looked to them for advice. Bill gave her the name and number of the arresting officers, and instructed her to contact the Port Benton Police that day.

"Are you and Carolyn ok? No one was hurt during the break-in?" Dennis asked calmly. Jordan startled slightly with the question. She hadn't realized that they knew that she and Carolyn lived together!

"No, we're fine . . . just upset, as you can imagine. We were on vacation when we were robbed. It can be very unnerving to think that a complete stranger was wandering through your home, touching and sorting through your things, then taking whatever he wants, without any belief that you can do anything to stop him . . . probably why I'm still so jumpy this morning. I'm sorry for that."

"Maybe you should think about a security system, especially in our line of work . . . and you live out where there are a lot of summer homes. You're a prime target for thefts there, even in the summer, but especially, in the winter! It can be pretty isolated out there then." Bill's tone was caring, but his face was expressionless, as if he was reading a script that he had no connection to. Dennis Palmer excused himself from further discussion.

"Funny, we were just talking about getting an alarm system this morning. I'll have to look into that . . . Now what about this McCluskey situation?" Jordan was trying to change the focus back to the investigation, and away from her personal life. She felt very uncomfortable that others in her profession were now aware of her lifestyle. In some ways, they were confronting her about that, too, or so she thought.

Bill led the conference. "The teacher called this morning to report that the younger girl Mellott is drawing stick figures again with what the teacher described as huge penises . . . When I said, "same ol', same ol" I wasn't kidding. How many times have we been through this one . . . How do you think we should proceed?"

"No new allegations have been made . . . We can have the mother bring the girl down here again for questioning . . . and use an art therapist to interpret the drawings. But I doubt that she'll cooperate. With that first call from BCS, she'll be hot on the phone with her lawyer . . . I can go to the school and interview the girl myself. That's probably the better bet. If she gives me any information, I'll call you to follow up. Then we can bring in the art therapist. How's that?"

"That'll work for me . . ." Bill had ten other cases that needed his attention that day. If Jordan could take one case off of his plate, he was all the happier for it. Besides, they already started questioning her about their real concerns.

"Nothing much to do now, but let the natural order of things take their course," Bill said, as he nodded to Jordan. He was confident that those issues would soon rise to the surface—just like the lake-dumped bodies in the mystery novels he read as a child. Old secrets have a way of rising to the surface. The truth would soon come out. He continued to hide his contempt for Jordan, both professionally and personally. He had to play her, if he was going to get what he needed.

Jordan phoned Ted to clear the investigation strategy, and then left the Prosecutor's office en route to the school. Dennis Palmer watched Jordan leave the building, and then called Bill into his office.

"So what do you think of that?" Dennis was referring to the questions about Jordan's cases.

"I don't think that she realizes what's going on. I think she was so upset about the burglary, and so upset about the Carolyn thing, that she didn't even realize what you were actually talking about."

"Maybe . . . maybe . . . Sit on her, Bill, until she does realize. Then let me know what she says. I don't believe that she doesn't know. I don't believe that she's not a part of it. Get an order, and pull her bank statements. Don't let her know that. We don't want her bolting off, or warning the others. Get me the other cases that you spotted." Dennis phoned the State Attorney General with the results of their initial questioning.

\* \* \*

Jordan phoned the Port Benton Police, and made arrangements to claim her things the next morning. She knew that Carolyn would be available to go with her. Carolyn was otherwise enjoying a lazy summer off from teaching. She had devoted her full days to painting and sculpting in preparation for the exhibition with her parents in the fall. Jordan was perturbed by the questioning from Dennis Palmer and the others, but she attributed her suspicion to a kind of stress brought on by the burglary and by the conditions at work. She decided not to tell Carolyn about the questions from the Prosecutor, but would share the comment made about them living together. She planned to talk with Carolyn that night after dinner. Carolyn always had a way of helping her find a peace in the midst of all the chaos.

But the questioning about her other cases continued to nag at her. She never liked anyone criticizing her casework, unless they had direct knowledge of the family and the problems they were facing. There were such differences of perception, when decisions were made solely on a written report. The whole purpose of the conference was to establish better communication between BCS and the Prosecutor's Office. Bill was alright, but he could really be a nudge when he wanted to be. He was more a Barney Fife than a Sam Spade. And she wasn't saying that just because he resembled him. Bill would get an idea from God knows where, extrapolate to hideous proportions, and find felons in every line of a summary, in every turn of a page. Jordan dismissed the questioning as another Corcoran-ist rung in his ladder-climb to the top. She only tolerated him because he was part of the process. Now he would be questioning her lifestyle, evaluating her relationship, and adding that into his assessments of right and wrong. That thought panicked her a bit. It never took much to get his imagination started. She wished the case had been assigned to Freitag or Swaggart instead.

Jordan stopped at a pay phone and called Carolyn to tell her about the recovery of their things by the Port Benton Police. Carolyn was ecstatic and agreed to go with Jordan in the morning. Jordan saved the story about the Prosecutor for their evening dinner discussion. She kissed Carolyn goodbye, hung up the phone, and drove on to the investigation at the Turner Elementary School. The child was enrolled in a YMCA Summer Camp Program there, and was available for an interview.

Although Jordan and the school nurse met with Mellott for nearly an hour, the child gave little information that would lead them to suspect sexual abuse. Jordan kept the questions general in nature, did not use any leading statements, and asked non-specific questions about other family members and their activities. The nurse showed Jordan several pieces of Mellott's work, including an A+ vase she had made from clay, and a potholder she had woven on a loom made from popsicle sticks. The nurse then introduced the artwork in question. Jordan praised the child for the colors she used, and asked her to explain the picture to her. The child coyly stated that she recently visited a farm with the Summer Camp, and that she saw many animals there. When they had art the next day, she painted herself riding a horse. She hoped that one day she could have a horse of her own. She wanted to finish the painting, but was told that they had to get ready to go home. She now asked the nurse if she could finish the painting, but the nurse said that she would have to wait until her next art class. Jordan praised the child again, and encouraged her to "keep up the good work."

After the child left the room, the nurse apologized for bringing BCS out for the interview. The nurse explained that they knew about suspicions regarding the family in the past, and that they intended to watch the child closely. The nurse stated that school staff would continue to report any concerns about the children. Jordan was cautious.

"I appreciate your concern, but we always have to be careful not to over-react. We don't want to mislead any child into making an erroneous statement. She may start to say things, true or not, just to win your support. I think it's best to be vigilant with all children, and not to so closely monitor any one child, just because the family may be known to BCS. The parents could construe that as harassment, and the investigation could be compromised. I'm sure you understand. Thanks for your help here." Jordan left the school mildly annoyed that she might be pulled back into this hornet's nest without just cause. She could hear the family's attorney screaming on her office phone already.

The nurse was furious with the implication! She contacted Bill Corcoran and reported her dismay at Jordan's handling of the case. She even suggested that Jordan was trying to suppress the investigation in effort to protect the children's father! This further raised the suspicions of the Prosecutor's Office. Bill Corcoran chose not to discuss the nurse's complaint with BCS. But Corcoran was concerned that Jordan also hadn't followed through with the art therapist assessment. Jordan advised him that there was not enough evidence to warrant further evaluation. Bill realized that with the investigation completed, the family would not have further contact with BCS. Jordan took the next day off, and Bill reported the finding to his boss, Dennis Palmer.

Carolyn and Jordan were up early the next morning. They had a full breakfast, and, in their usual morning tradition, topped it off with a full glass of apple juice. As gay women, orange juice was still contraband in their home! They used this simple act as their reaffirmation of Gay Power! And that morning, they were feeling very empowered! They were recouping their belongings from men who had no right to them! They were asserting their right to be, to exist. They were reclaiming their identities as women—self-confident, poised, fearless, and strong! Together, they drove up to Port Benton.

The police department was located in the downtown section of this fairly large community, and with the tourist traffic and Jordan's short temper, the ride was a nightmare! Carolyn was perturbed. She attributed Jordan's nervousness to the stress that she was under. Carolyn was just happy that she might get at least some of her possessions back. Most of her jewelry were gifts from her parents or from Jordan. Each piece was special to her. And it was the same for Jordan.

They had no trouble finding the Evidence Section once inside the station. The Sergeant in Charge obtained the items recovered from the car, and brought them into an interview room. Carolyn and Jordan identified each captured piece and claimed them as their own. Jordan was upset when she saw the broken lock and the large scratch across the front of her cedar chest, though. And only some of its contents remained. The girls completed paperwork attesting to their ownership of the stolen items, and were disappointed that they could not retrieve their things until after the trial. But at least they knew where their things were.

As they were driving back home, they discussed the mementos now lost at the hands of the intruders, and reminisced about the many good times no longer saved there. They talked about the Broadway shows, and the late night/early morning jaunts to the diner for coffee and a toasted bagels. They talked about the camping trips that they had gone on, the trails they had hiked, the bracelets they had braided as they sat beside the campfire. They had only their memories now—many of the artifacts were lost forever. As they drove on, an intense, sickening feeling began to overtake Jordan. She now realized that the scrapbook was missing! And suddenly, the questions by the Prosecutor began to make sense!

"Oh my God! The memos, the scrapbook—I think that the Prosecutor has my scrapbook, and that he's gotten the wrong idea! Carolyn, you wouldn't believe the interview I had with Bill Corcoran and his boss yesterday! I didn't tell you, because I didn't want to worry you with everything else going on. But they called me over there to discuss a referral on an old case . . . and then started asking me questions about a few other cases that I had recently—and a lot of the cases were ones that we cited in the Crittenden memos . . ." Jordan's speech was racing as quickly as her thoughts.

"Oh, you're just jumping to conclusions again! Those cases were terrible . . . no wonder the Prosecutor asked you about them when he saw you. Who wouldn't be concerned? . . . Why would he have the scrapbook? . . . He doesn't have it."

Carolyn was speaking comfortably to Jordan, and in fact, she did not believe that the Prosecutor would have any more than a mild interest in anything that Jordan had written. There were always much bigger fish to fry than a renegade supervisor who had already been disciplined! Besides, Carolyn knew that there were two sides to any story. The Prosecutor would never act on the basis of a few memos written by a disgruntled staff member. She did not share this opinion with Jordan, but stated again, her belief that the Prosecutor did not have the scrapbook. She reassured her that no one would have any interest in the memos, outside of BCS.

"I think he does . . . how else would he have known that we live together?" Jordan was challenging Carolyn's conclusions. After all, Jordan had just spent an hour with them! She was convinced that something was up.

"Silly, we completed police reports about the robbery, listed the missing items, and listed our address! The police made the connection between the recovered items and the burglary report. Simple as that." Carolyn was confident that Jordan was wrong, and she was trying to convince and reassure her.

"Yeah? So then why did the Prosecutor notify me about the recovered items, and not our own police department? I'm telling you, he has the scrapbook!" Jordan was equally sure that she was right.

Carolyn was quiet for a moment, and then glanced back to Jordan as she continued to drive. "OK, let's just play with that for a bit . . . What do you think he suspects he has?" In her innocence, she could not imagine an answer.

"I'm not sure . . . I just don't know. With Corcoran, it could be anything! The guy always thinks that everybody's guilty but him! He always thinks he's cracked the case of the century!" She shook her head in disbelief. She thought about all of the memos she had written over the years. "Corcoran could make a case with just about any one of those memos. But why would he want to?" Jordan's voice trailed off . . .

"What do you plan to do now? Is there anything you want me to do?" Carolyn still viewed the whole situation as incomprehensible, but she thought they should develop a contingency plan. Maybe Jordan was right—maybe the Prosecutor was interested in something that he saw there. But what?

"Here's my plan—I intend to live each day from here on out as if I don't know anything. I don't know that he has the scrapbook, and I don't know what he's talking about if he contacts me again. If he persists, I'll swear that we were just messing around, that there's no truth to anything written there. That's how I intend to proceed."

Jordan felt relieved with the simple beauty of the plan. She would deny everything! It would have worked for Nixon, had it not been for those missing eighteen minutes of tape! Besides, Jordan never taped a meeting in her life, and felt reasonably sure that, with the exception of those few clients, no one else had ever taped her. What would be left to discredit her story? The stress and tension now lifted, Carolyn and Jordan drove on home and caught a carefree afternoon on the beach.

If only it was just that simple! But no, the first office call of the following morning was from Bill Corcoran. He oozed charm, but spoke with purpose.

"Hi Jordan . . . Just checking in to see if you have anything new you'd like to discuss . . . you know, about the McCluskey investigation." He used an almost accusatory tone at the end of the statement that led Jordan to believe that he was baiting her.

"No, Bill, things are just as we left them two days ago . . . the girl gave a reasonable explanation of her artwork, the nurse overreacted and will likely do so in the future. We will not be opening the case, although I will have to stop by the house and speak with the parents and sibling. The visit will be low keyed, and if I don't get a sense that something more is at work there, we'll just close the case. I'll let you know." Jordan maintained her upbeat posture despite the stomach now doing flips inside of her. She felt a cold sweat on her palms, and goose bumps running up her arms.

"Sounds good! . . . Is there anything else you'd like to add about some of the other cases we discussed?" He already knew the answer, but wanted to start to press her, to begin to break down her resistance. Ultimately, he would wear her down. He had used this same tactic so many times before, a little something he had picked up from Drag Net, or Columbo, no doubt!

"Don't be ridiculous! If a case is closed, why would I want to look for more work? I've got my hands full as it is!" She laughed, then concluded the conversation. She thought that she had won the contact.

The next few weeks at the BCS office were a jumble of emergencies, confrontations, disciplinary actions, and an increased hostility by the staff. In Jordan's mind, it was just more of the same. Each night she would come home from the office exhausted, and would peruse the classified sections for other jobs. She had already placed requests for transfer within state service, but was growing less hopeful that she could manage to hang on that long. She could cover her desk with the number of rejections she had received so far. Yet still she tried. With the interest of the Prosecutor and his now daily phone calls, she believed that she had no possibility of riding out the storm, of salvaging her position there. Supervisors ignored her, the staff nearly spit on her as they passed by her desk. Whole conversations would fall to a dead silence if she entered within range of hearing—or at least, so she thought. Marsha McMillan kept her office door continuously closed now, and Jordan felt an intense, deep loneliness. She had no allies in the world, save Carolyn and their families. She wondered when it would all end. It could not come quickly enough.

She could only guess that they all knew about the scrapbook, or at least, had heard rumors about it. Her reputation was destroyed, and this destroyed her heart. She had so prided herself on her name. Now she wished she could be called anything but the name she had been given at birth. Jordan could not bring herself to discuss with her father the disgrace she brought to his name. She didn't recognize that in his world, they still hadn't realized that anything was wrong! They lived such worlds apart. The stressors were starting to play on her judgment. She was feeling increasingly paranoid. The abject hostility was unbearable. Her confidence was dwindling, now a shallow facade, a hollow parapet against the world. She could not find peace. She kept the memories of the Group close in her mind, and would detach to that time and place, whenever the viciousness surfaced.

But she did have plenty to feel paranoid about! Bill Corcoran contacted her nearly every day. He always had some harmless excuse for the contact, but would end all conversations in the same manner: "Is there anything you'd like to say about some of the cases we discussed?" Jordan's answer was invariably the same: "Bill, why would I want to discuss closed cases? My hands are full as it is!"

But she was finding it increasingly difficult to maintain her humor. The Prosecutor's Office had occasionally even called her at home! There were moments when she believed that she was being followed, not by an unknown car, but by a squad car! She saw them parked more frequently near her house and in her neighborhood. She found herself constantly glancing into her rear view mirror as she drove, and found herself glancing over her shoulder whenever she walked outside her home. Carolyn tried to calm Jordan, to convince her that she was reacting to the pressures, that the stress was taking its toll, that it was playing games with her mind. But she, too, saw the police presence near the house, and took some of the phone messages left by the Prosecutor. They began receiving advertisements, peculiar junk mail, that could be interpreted as from law enforcement. Carolyn realized that they had stepped up the pace in the last two weeks, and she knew that the harassment would continue. Carolyn privately confided in her own father, who agreed to seek advice from a criminal attorney he knew from college. Within days, she and Jordan were meeting with him.

Charles Ebner had gone to the College of William and Mary with Ben Berringer. He loved Ben as a brother. The two could pick up conversations as if they had just seen each other yesterday, even though they had been separated by years and careers. Charles was a licensed criminal attorney, and was still practicing in the state. Most of his work was non gratis now, usually in landlord/tenant issues in the low income community. He saw this as his redemption for his years of defending the devil! While he believed in the human right to a competent defense, he was haunted by some of the animals he helped return to the world, to torture, to maim, and to prey upon the descent and innocent people trapped in that world with them. He often had nightmares that his cases, both successful and unsuccessful, would one day hunt him down and unleash the savagery of the ages upon him. He was a good man caught in that horrific realm! He tried to be a mediator in it all, but in his elderly wisdom, he realized that some forces could not be reckoned with.

Jordan was so angry that Carolyn had welcomed her father into her pit of misery! She couldn't even make eye contact with the Berringer's anymore, she so felt that she had jeopardized the lives that she and Carolyn shared together. She didn't want to expand that worry to now include Carolyn's elderly parents. Yet once the situation was known, the Berringer's insisted on being a part of it. They had many contacts that they had developed over the years, and thought that they could call upon these friends now—important people who could help remove the grip that the Prosecutor's Office held around the throat of their daughter-in-law. They planned to cash in on a few political favors. They were dumbfounded when their friends seemed powerless to help them! That's when they realized that an investigation of some sort was being conducted by powers far above the county Prosecutor. He was merely dancing to their piper! It was then that they decided to contact Charles Ebner on Jordan's behalf.

The harassment continued for a month before they reached that decision. Jordan's nerves had reached their limit, and she was startling at any sound made around her. The Berringer's physician now prescribed a mild sedative for her. Carolyn's stress was caused by Jordan's distress. She kicked herself each time she thought about saving the memos for all those years. She felt responsible for what was happening now. If she had not amassed them, the memos would have stood individually, a mere quirk in Jordan's personality.

"These memos, taken together . . . that's the issue. The whole is definitely more than its parts. I think there's probably some type of an investigation, maybe malfeasance, within BCS. They're probably trying to turn you to help them, maybe to testify? . . . I doubt that you're the target. Do you think that might be so?" Charles posed the question to Jordan, but she had no ideas.

So Charles drafted a letter to the Prosecutor, identified himself as Jordan's attorney, and demanded an immediate end to the harassment. Jordan approved the letter, and then insisted that Carolyn leave their home until the issues resolved.

"I'm not going anywhere. I'm staying right here with you. We will see this through together!" Carolyn was emphatic.

"No! This is MY problem now, and you're going to listen to me! I can't do what I have to do, if I have to worry about what's happening to you . . . where you are . . . who might be watching you! No! You're going to go far away until this mess is finished! I won't have it any other way!" Jordan screamed back the reply. It startled them all.

This was the first time she had ever even raised her voice to Carolyn! The intensity of the pressure was now quite clear. Jordan was already suspended from her job for a comment she supposedly made to one of the more confrontational storm troopers. She told Carolyn that if the incident had really happened, she would have used far more foul language than what the woman reported! She was awaiting a disciplinary hearing in that matter. And Jordan was drinking again—not daily, and not very much. But for the first time in ten years, she jeopardized her sobriety. Jordan was clear that she could not function as long as she had to worry about Carolyn. She expressed a fear that Carolyn's career, too, would be destroyed, if her part in the scrapbook became known. Although she continued to protest, Jordan was all the more adamant. Carolyn finally agreed to leave when she saw that arguing only pushed Jordan farther into rage and despair. The Berringer's supported Jordan's decision.

Frances Berringer suggested that Carolyn stay with her sister in San Francisco. But Carolyn chose instead, to stay with Marcus and Bill on their small farm in Vermont. Marcus had been ill recently, and she was sure that Bill could use some help with him. They still didn't have a clear diagnosis, but the symptoms were chronic and mysterious. They had been developing over the course of the last year, first, with flu-like symptoms—aches and pains, slight fever mostly—that Marcus just shrugged off, but couldn't seem to beat. But he had gotten much worse by spring. He was losing weight by leaps and bounds. He had been hospitalized three times with pneumonia! On some days, Marcus could hardly rise from his bed, he was so weak. And he now had projectile vomiting, a stream that could shoot almost across the room, and a chronic diarrhea that could sometimes cover the bed. He had a horrendous cough, an often bloody hack that could go on for minutes, but seemed like hours. The doctor had ruled out all manner of cancers, and was targeting infectious diseases. Bill was trying to handle the farm, teach at the University, and care for his partner with the help of only a handful of friends. He was hysterical some nights from the fear and fatigue. Although they both suspected it, they would not say the word. By summer, large purple lesions began to appear on his body, and the hideous proclamation was made: Kaposi's sarcoma. His diagnosis was confirmed—Marcus had AIDS.

Like other gay men so affected, he welcomed the care and comfort provided by the lesbian community, when the medical, social service, and even the religious communities turned their backs on him, and men like him. This fed Bill's anger daily. He struggled to stay at bedside, as he watched his lover disintegrate in body and mind. Some days, Marcus seemed adrift in the lucidless throes of the narcotic. At other times, he was a prisoner of IV tubing and huge doses of pills that, even on his best days, he could hardly hold down. Bill even made a song about "AZT and You and Me" to stifle the protests of his patient. But there were still some periods, rare days now, that Marcus felt better, and his riotous and raucous humor, his booming laughter, would fill the house. Those were the days that kept Bill going. Yet they always seemed to end in the same way—with Bill refusing his pleas for a morphine ending. On other nights, Bill contemplated taking them both out in a quiet, peaceful surrender to the drug. It was only through the support and watchful eye of their friends, that the two men were able to move to a dignified completion of their love story. Carolyn shared these moments with them, careful to watch from the hallway, as Marcus gently touched Bill's cheek or held his hand as Bill tended him. From the depths of her soul, she ached for them, and for herself. But she would never cry in front of them.

Jordan agreed with Carolyn's plan to stay with Bill and Marcus, and believed that she would probably be gone only a few weeks at most. They optimistically hoped for the best. But Carolyn was gone for most of the summer, as Jordan's tribulations continued. Bill Corcoran kept up his daily contacts despite the Ebner letter. And Jordan was finally fired from her job, although BCS maintained that she had quit due to the ongoing stress of a protective services caseload.

Once Carolyn was out of the home, Jordan began to purge the place of any signs of the memos or of the cases that were quoted there. She thought about shredding the copies of the cases she kept, but after only a few passes with the scissors, she realized that it would take years to rid herself of that mound of paper fury! But an idea came to her as she was grilling a burger in the back yard—she would torch everything with a BCS logo on it! And she would do this in the privacy and comfort of her own home! Even driving by, such actions would go unnoticed by the police. No one could see above her fence. Besides, everyone grilled in the summer! She would be just another burger eater, charcoaling herself to culinary paradise! She gathered up all of the paperwork she could find, waited for cover of darkness, pulled out the faithful Weber, drenched the test parcel with lighter fluid, and let it rip! Huge flames flared in the grill, but they went out as quickly as the lighter fluid burned away! A few more squirts, and again the torch was lit. And again, the flames would end when the lighter fluid was gone.

Jordan was amazed at how difficult it was to actually burn something! It always looked so easy on TV! And how did all those homes burn down? Or the libraries? Or the forests? She couldn't even get a ream of paper to ignite, and even using an incendiary! She grabbed the bundle from the smoke and ash, dusted it off, and returned it to its white garbage-bag holder. She would have to think of another way to destroy the evidence! She took the bag inside, and poured herself another cognac. She had no other concerns that evening. Carolyn had gone a month ago, and she could now drink herself into a Napoleonic bliss. There would be no one to stop her. She would find some resolution in that bottle that night.

The next idea was the winner! She was out lounging in the back yard, when her eyes fixed upon the red brick walk that led to Carolyn's flower garden. She eyed the red brick edging that neatly separated the impatiens and the hostas from the weed and gravel, the untended rest of the yard. Carolyn may have seen pathways and borders, but Jordan now saw solution! She would pull up the brick and build it into a fire pit! She would twist the cases into paper logs! She could have a nice fire there for at least several nights. And she could always tear down the pit and restore the walk and garden borders before Carolyn ever returned home! And again, no one on the outside would ever be the wiser!

Jordan got a shovel from the shed, and within two hours, she had the walk and borders dug up, and the bricks neatly stacked as a fire pit that even masons would envy! She spent the remainder of the afternoon, tearing and twisting the case copies into a bundle of paper kindling. Again, she waited for the cloak of darkness before she began her mission of purge and purification. She was ridding herself of the imperfections of her profession and the frivolity of her career. She was torching her idealism, and assuming her place among the drolls that actually ran the show.

With amazing swiftness, the flames began to engulf and to disintegrate the remnants of her career. As she sipped her cognac and watched the flames dance across her folly, she thought about the lives that each of those pages represented. She thought about how her interventions had actually purified them in some ways, separating the abuser from the abused, disarming the drunkard from the drug, freeing the innocent from the violate. With each new thought, she added another group of bundled, twisted paper onto the flames, and they would jump with the new found fuel. Jordan warmed herself beside the fire, and thought about all of the campfires she had shared with Carolyn over the years. How she hoped that such times would never end! She thought back to that one mysterious and wonderful night at college, and then, to the time when the Group had gone camping together. She thought about the struggles she faced as she pushed for her degree. She saw Josie's hand, once again, as she lifted the next bundled group of case notes onto the flames. She thought about Dean, and his counseling sessions with her. She felt sorry that she had not maintained that contact. She watched as the final bundles were strewn upon the embers, and watched the flames dance brightly against the star-filled, summer sky that night. She poured another cognac, and was in mid-sip, when a noise behind her startled her. Someone had opened the fence gate, and had invited himself in!

Jordan quickly looked to see that the last twists of paper were already disappearing into the mass of embers and wood now left behind. Still, the flames danced their last few steps before they, too, would be obliterated. In the dimming light, Jordan saw the figure of Bill Corcoran standing before her.

"I really don't get you . . . I really don't. You've had every chance to talk to me, and you remain as stubborn and as obstinate as a jackass. Tell me what it would take to get through to you . . ."

"Why are you here? I didn't invite you. You don't have the right to walk into my yard, and sit yourself down like you own the place. You got my job. What more could you possibly want?" Jordan's voice was quiet, but her tone was biting. She might have been drunk, but she was still in control.

"Oh, so you blame me for that? You try to take out a fine man like John Crittenden, and you blame me because you lost your fucking job? . . . We know what you've been doing . . . it's all so clear. We were even willing to cut a deal with you, but you were too proud, too self-righteous, to speak with the likes of me. And all the time, you were taking bribes and setting up Crittenden to take the fall! You disgust me!"

"What the hell are you talking about? Nobody's taking bribes, except in your own delusional mind! Leave it to Corcoran to build a federal case out of scraps of sheer nothingness."

Jordan was indignant. She could feel her temper beginning to flair. She took another sip of the cognac, and continued to stare into the fire. She tried to regain her composure. She was acutely aware of the knot now formed in her stomach, of her jaws clenched tightly as she tried to sip, of her arm muscles now tensed, and of the shaking in her hands that betrayed her nervousness. She knew that she had to calm if she was to win him over. She took a breath, and spoke quietly, pleadingly, to the prosecutor's investigator.

"Bill, I'm telling you that you have it all wrong . . . this isn't about bribes, there is no crime that's been committed. You have taken huge leaps in logic, and now, everyone's paying the price—at least I know that I am . . . It was a simple game, a little rivalry among co-workers—nothing more than that! Why can't you admit that you're wrong here? Why are you so insistent . . . why are you making such a big deal about a little stupidity like this? Can getting a promotion really mean that much to you . . . that you would want to destroy anyone that's in your path? Is that really what you want to be? How you want to be thought of?" Jordan spoke to Bill, but shifted her glance from his eyes back toward the fire.

"You can't be so naive as to believe that this is all about a promotion! This is about you and people like you . . . this is about what you have done to innocent people in our community. This is about the corruption and misuse of your power. This is about justice for them now . . ." Bill's tone was biting, but his face remained void of emotion. Jordan thought again that he was more reading a script, then transmitting a thought. His presentation lacked the emotion of firm belief, like he was playing a role that he had no feel for.

"Wait a second, Bill . . . you don't think that I believe a thing that you're sayin' . . . I've worked my whole career to maintain professionalism and integrity. How dare you think that I would stand for anything else! You obviously don't know what you're talking about . . . You think that all you have to do is harass me, and that I will become a pawn in your little quest for power. You have me all wrong!"

Jordan shot Bill a glance, then returned her stare to the fire. She had worked with him for years, yet she knew so little about him. She did know that he wasn't raised here, that he was a "Benny," probably from Newark or Bayonne. No local boy would ever have talked to her that way. They had more respect.

"Oh, I have you all wrong? Let's think about that for a minute. How many people do you think would like to take a swipe at you for the decisions you've made, for the recommendations you've made? Think about all of those clients you've handled over the years . . . How many of them do you think would be above testifying about a bribe to get back at you? Go ahead, take a guess . . ." Bill was smug in his statement.

"What are you saying? That people have actually made accusations to that effect? . . ."

"Surprised? People have actually even given written statements to that effect. In fact, I've been collecting statements from them for over two weeks. BCS workers usually don't head popularity polls. That part was easy. The tough part was getting statements from your co-workers . . . and getting the paper to back up those statements . . . You know, to get the reports in just the right order. That took some doing. Lucky we have a man like Crittenden who can take an assignment like that . . . You know, gather the evidence, separate the wheat from the chaff, so to speak, and then, interpret it in ways that make real sense . . . You should never have fucked with him. I think now that maybe he's fucking back. Of course, I can't make that assessment . . . I have to go with the evidence. And right now, it seems pretty clear to me that he's right! It was you all along . . . all things considered."

"That's a damn lie! This is a fucking frame job! I never did a dishonest thing in my life! How could you believe the word of a scum like Crittenden? You know what he does . . . how he forces his opinion, even when his decisions don't fall in the jurisdiction of the case. How he always presses to remove children, even when the situation is against the BCS policy to do so! Shit, even Dennis Palmer was questioning that! Why don't you talk with him?" Jordan was incredulous at the turn of events.

"Who do you think sent me? Who do you think is pressing for this? Sure, the District Attorney is involved, but you were in the sights of some pretty powerful people before that! Now, we just have to give them all what they've been waiting for . . . simple as that." Bill smiled as he finished, and it took all of Jordan's inner strength not to launch a brick at him.

"What is it that you want from me?" Her voice was raised and her tone was sharp.

"See, this is why people like you should never leave their jobs at the Shop Rite. You can educate them, but you can't take out the background noise! They still cling to their 'moral compass' like they're the guiding light of the civilization, like they've cornered the market on the right and wrong of everything! How can you get so far, and still not get it? . . . There is no right or wrong. There's only what's best! So what's best here? Give us McMillan, and we might be able to cut you a deal . . . She's behind it all, anyway."

"I'm not giving you anybody! And if anything, it's Crittenden that's 'behind it all.' You should be making these allegations against him!" Jordan remained incredulous, doubting, yet in full belief of the seriousness of this visit.

"That's not what he says . . . See, he was smart enough to work with us! He told us how you were sicked on him by McMillan when he refused to join her little circle of power brokers. He told us how you both were doling out case plans, manipulating findings of investigations, and all for just a few bucks! We even found the bank accounts!"

"That's bullshit! If Crittenden really told you all of that, the man is fucking lying to you. How could you believe a story like that? If I were you, I'd start checking things out on his end. He's trying to frame the both of us! Don't you wonder why he would go to so much trouble? What's in it for him? . . . There has to be something, that's how the man works!" Jordan's voice was firm, and her posture imploring. She had to make him understand.

"He's lying? Well, maybe so, but it's your word against his. And he has some pretty convincing evidence . . . So who do you think they're going to believe—a fine married man, a good provider to his family, a good father to his children, a deacon in his church . . . or a lesbian, a dyke, like you? Yeah, we know about that, too. We even know where Carolyn's staying . . . No Jordan, I'd say that it's time for you to do what you have to do to save yourself. Give us Marsha McMillan—Stop trying to protect her." Bill sneered with the statement. Jordan wanted to throw up on him, but instead, she stared and took a breath, still shocked at what he told her.

"I'm not protecting anybody. You can't protect someone from something that hasn't happened. I'm telling you that this is all bullshit!" Jordan nearly screamed the last words, now losing all control. Bill sneered again, pleased that he had gotten her to this point. He hated uppity, low-class, poor folk, and especially, mouthy female ones! And a dyke at that! They really didn't know their place. But he knew that he was breaking her.

"You think you're so fucking smart. But you still don't get it. That's why people like you should stay where they belong. White trash has no place among professionals." His statement snapped like a right hook. Jordan was stunned to silence. She never heard anyone refer to her or her family with such disrespect. She realized then, that there could be no further discussion. His agenda was set well before he arrived there. She still puzzled at his motives, and silently tended her emotional wounds. He knew where to hurt her.

They sat quietly for what seemed like ions in time and space. Jordan watched the embers surge and glow with each breath of air that made its way into the fire pit. Her life shot out before her like the flames bursting along the logs. Like silent, stalking ghosts, the memories seemed to rush out at her from the licks of orange blue flame. She thought about that 17 year old, who secretly snatched a scalpel from the emergency room during a pre-placement physical. Was she ever close to death that night! She wished that that kid would show up now. She saw the face of the young girl she had placed in foster care, after her father had bludgeoned her mother to death in front of her. She thought about the newborn held up by his mother in a filthy motel room, and she remembered the look of his limp limbs, as they raced to the hospital, the child so near death. She saw the sex-perp. arsonist who tried to cut her with a broken beer bottle. And she thought about a home visit she was ordered to make, only to be stopped by a co-worker, who told her that the client had phoned in a bomb threat earlier that morning! She saw the sneers of her co-workers, and the closed door to Marsha's office. She watched her hand signing the UPS receipt as she accepted her personal items packed from her desk, and shipped to her home from the office. She thought of the so many ways that she had been used by a system that viewed her as expendable. Emotionally exhausted, she watched the logs crumble into puffs of smoke and bits of ash, her innocence vanishing with the evidence.

"I'm waiting for an answer, Jordan . . ." Bill was growing impatient.

A wisp of smoke rose from the fire pit, and with it, memories of better times. She smiled about Carolyn and those first few awkward dates. And she thought about Betty and Jan, and Marcus and Bill, her rock solid supports when everything else seemed to shift away beneath her. She wished them to her now.

She thought about Dale and Elaine, and about all of the other friends that she met at the Asbury gay bars. How she longed for that simple sense of belonging! And her twin foster kids who grew up to be respected social workers themselves—she was so proud of them both! She wondered what they would think of her now. She caught glimpses of the faces she had helped during her career. She saw the Costains and the Engleharts, the Wolfs, the DeYoungs, the Clauers, the Parhams, the Krouses, the Moss's, the Cumberbatch's, the Earls, McAllister, and all the families that she had brought to some semblance of normalcy. She tasted the grilled franks she used to enjoy at the Kessler Student Center, and thought about the tons of research she had completed at Briggs Library. She thought about the women of Balmural Hall—Joyce and Judy, and Chris and Mary. And she thought about the Group, not as they were now, after years of life and experience had jaded them; but as they were in the beginning, so full of youthful hope and expectation, so full of the limitless possibilities of life itself. And she thought about her own family, and the shame that she was about to bring upon them. She saw the forest moss, heard the sound of the waters and the cobbles of the river. She was numb with the developments before her. And then a stillness came to her, a warm hand shielding her now from the troubles of her life. And she found a peace with her decision there, sitting by the fire, with the whole of her life's worst possibilities sitting squarely before her. There was a silence there now, a quietness of heart, that brought a strange, fixed calm.

"Jordan, I'm waiting . . ."

She sat motionless, sipping her cognac before the fire that destroyed the case copies she had carted from the office. And still, Bill Corcoran, Prosecutor's Investigator, droned on. She wanted none of it. She wanted none of him. She wanted none of BCS, and nothing to do with Social Work! They had polluted her beloved profession as completely as they had polluted the lands and the air and the oceans. She thought about the times that she ran along the water's edge, and wished that she could be running now, away from here, away from this hideous man, and from the treacherous lies that he represented. She would say no more, but she would ask for her attorney.

"Well Jordan, what's it going to be . . . are you going to help yourself out and cooperate with us, or are you going to make things especially hard for yourself?"

Jordan turned to Bill, made eye contact, and quietly replied, "I love the way that cognac feels as it courses through your veins . . ."

Bill grabbed his walkie talkie, looked into Jordan's eyes, and blurted into the receiver, "Coalter and Fenchel, it's a go. Come in and arrest Jordan Matthews on the charge of bribery. Make sure that you read her her rights. I will witness that you have done so. Make sure that Skar has the paperwork, and have Allely contact Jordan's attorney. Call Copeland and Conti and let them know that it's over now. And make sure that Libby is also aware."

Jordan sat silently, and mentally kissed away the life that she had worked so hard to build. She had made her decision—she would not play his game for him.

# Epilogue

The cuffs fit tightly around the wrists of the suspected felon as she rode in the squad car to the county jail. She sat low in the seat, so that she would not be seen by the community where she had grown up. An anger, then a fear, a shame, a self loathing overtook her, as she was driven through the streets of the town that now seemed so foreign to her. She would become the pariah of her village, the Quasimodo of the Shore area—she could see it all so clearly! Soon people would point and stare, maybe even spit at her, as she walked these streets—if ever she would be allowed on the streets again. She had gone to grade school with the arresting officer's younger brother. She hoped that Coalter had not recognized her. She could not believe how stupid she had been, how naïve and trusting, and more so, how blind she had been to this inevitable outcome! She thought about Linda's warning, and realized that she was light years ahead of the game. It was now so obvious—but Jordan realized that sometimes, you can be so caught up in the throes of battle, that you lose sight of the war. If only Linda had warned her sooner. If only Marsha McMillan had interceded with the first problem. If only Jane Morrison hadn't broken her hip. If only she hadn't taunted Crittenden. If only . . .

As she was processed through booking, through fingerprint and mug shot, she made no comment, and kept her gaze fixed toward the floor. She was not in the mood for small talk. Detective Brendan Staley and Officer Doug Curry both nodded to Jordan as they passed by. They had been out with her on at least a dozen cases, but now, she was the one under arrest! She was too humiliated to even make eye contact with them! Jordan overheard Corcoran advise Dennis Palmer by phone that she would not assist in the investigation. She heard Corcoran confirm that Marsha McMillan was to be arrested in the morning. Jordan suspected that the call was staged as a last ditch effort to gain her cooperation. She would have none of it! She hoped that she would not be there when they brought Marsha in for booking. She did not want another confrontation with anyone. She used her one phone call to contact Carolyn's parents. They agreed to arrange bail and to contact Charles Ebner. They told Jordan to remain calm, and assured her that she would be out in a few hours. They insisted that she stay at their home until the whole mess was sorted out, until she was cleared of all charges. They tried to be upbeat. The Berringer's stood by Jordan's side as if she were their own daughter.

As Jordan sat in the cell waiting for news from the bail bondsman, she thought again about the ridiculousness that brought her to this point. Corcoran used scraps of memos to build a felony case against her! She felt in her heart that Crittenden had actually set her up, and that he had played up to Corcoran's drive for power. It hadn't occurred to her that they might both be part of a larger organism, a political machine, now upsetting the equilibrium of the county.

She sat alone in a corner of the holding cell, and pondered her fate. She thought of the bitter irony of it all—that those same scraps of paper that had been used to advocate for her clients' rights, were now being used to destroy her own. And she thought about the lives that those memos represented. She thought about how she had been able to build an understanding of a client from their own scraps—the bits of their lives that they shared with her. She used those same scraps to help clients build a greater insight; and her clients then used that insight to climb above circumstance. And she thought about herself—how her own bits of cognition, hints of personality traits, her wishes, her desires, her beliefs, her own drives—how she had used her own unique scraps of self to build the woman that she was. To her, these scraps were hints from the Universe—clues about the universal truths that each of us struggles to assemble in some way that makes the most sense. Individual truths that define who we are, and what we believe in.

And she came to realize—in that cold, stark, lonely moment of her life—that all the world and all its beings, all its manifestations, all its religions, and its politics, and its creations, its demands, its happiness, its miseries, its truths, all its realities—were the result of just building it all from scraps. And who knows at the start what the end piece will be?

"Ms. Mathews, you're bail's been posted. You're being released." Jordan sat quietly while the Sergeant reviewed the conditions of her bail. "No leaving the state, no associations or contacts with known felons, no associations or contacts with other parties in the case, no use of alcohol or drugs, no violations of the law of any jurisdiction, maintain a 10:00 p.m. curfew. Any questions?"

Yeah! Jordan wanted to ask if he, too, was "on the take." She bit her lip, quietly responded, "No," and signed the appropriate forms. She admired her own restraint! She picked up her jewelry, including her earrings and wedding band, and got her belt and sandals. Her father was waiting for her in the reception area of the county jail.

"Hi, Princess," Pete Mathews exclaimed, as he hugged his oldest daughter. Although his tone was upbeat, she could see the sadness in his eyes, and could feel the tension in his body as he hugged her. "I'll be takin' you over to the Berringer's for the night, OK?"

"Oh Dad, I'm so sorry . . . I can't believe this is all happening! I . . ."

"Ssshhh, not here! We'll talk outside, alright? Let's go." Pete led the way to the quiet containment of his truck's cab, and was followed by the first member of the Mathews family ever arrested.

"Dad, you've got to know that none of this is true! I've wanted to talk to you about all of this, but I didn't know myself what was goin' on until this evening. And I still don't know really! It's all lies! Nothin' makes sense!" Jordan was pleading with her father for his understanding.

"I know, Jordan." Pete Mathews could only give a half-hearted reply. She didn't feel that he believed her.

"Dad, please take me home. I don't think I can face the Berringer's tonight. I promise I'll go there tomorrow. I just need to be alone right now . . . And to call Carolyn." Pete reluctantly agreed, on condition that he could stay with her for awhile.

Jordan made a pot of coffee as Pete sat in the living room, and tried to mentally formulate the questions he had for his daughter. He knew that she was unhappy, but he had no idea that she might be involved in something illegal! He hadn't raised his kids that way! He thought about some of the things he had seen in the war—squad leaders who didn't like a guy in their unit and did their best to have him busted; the sergeant that harassed the country boys with impunity; the captain that got fragged by his own men. He thought about the sell-outs he had seen in his own business, and among his own friends. And he thought about Jordan, until he arrived at his own conclusions—naïve, yes; criminal, no! From that point forward, he had no doubts about his daughter's character. But he did have strong doubts about how he could help her. He thought about some of the prominent people of the community he had worked for, building their homes or renovating their bathrooms. Maybe he could reach out to one or two of them for help. He thought he might also reach out to Marge's father. He knew him well enough to ask a favor, and he knew that Marge's father knew Jordan well enough to want to help her. He was overwhelmingly grateful that Carolyn's family had taken the lead.

The two sat on the couch, barely drinking their coffee, before Jordan began crying. It was a quiet tear at first that ran down her left cheek. As she moved to brush it away, she felt the rush of emotion that soon forced full sobs from her soul. Pete cradled his daughter against him, until the sobs again became whimper, and she had fallen off to sleep. As he gazed down at her, he saw again, the little girl who used to dance on the tops of his feet, and who cried to him in the morning when her frogs had escaped the bucket. He realized, for the first time, how the world viewed with such insignificance the girl that he so cherished. He, too, was afraid for her.

Charles Ebner met with Jordan only briefly before the arraignment. He planned to discredit the testimony of the clients who reportedly paid the bribes that Jordan allegedly demanded. A key piece in his argument was that there were no glaring breeches of agency policy. There were no glaring errors in any case handling! None of the witnesses had bothered to bring a bribery charge—or any other complaint, for that matter—to the attention of the authorities, until this concerted effort. There was only vague inference and implication that funds were received or paid. Charles Ebner exposed the discrepancies in the statements of the accusers. He had dissected the lies! In one case, Jordan admittedly received funds from a client, but she had also issued a receipt for the money. She thought she had used the money to buy bus tickets for the client family. In another instance, the alleged bribe had been given over eighteen months prior, and weeks before the case had even been assigned to her. Her logs showed that in each suspect instance, decisions were made with supervisory input, and in two of the three cases, supervisor/client conferences occurred to reinforce the case plans. The prosecutor failed to produce enough evidence to even suggest that Jordan had been selling case plans and court recommendations. He could not convincingly establish a pattern of the misuse of power! At no time during the hearing was mention made of the Crittenden interference. The memos were never presented as evidence, but they seemed to form an outline of the prosecutor's case. Only now, Jordan's memos were viewed as more coercive, more diversionary, an attempt to shift blame onto a well respected supervisor, a means to force his cooperation in the selling of influence and power!

Charles Ebner chose to skirt Jordan's private assertion that Crittenden had colluded with Corcoran, the Prosecutor's Investigator, to discredit her and to destroy her reputation. His goal was only to prevent her from being prosecuted. Some of the missing case notes miraculously reappeared at point of the hearing and stood as further vindication. They also demonstrated, at least to Jordan, that she still had a few friends in the office—colleagues who still held close the genuine ethics of her profession. And this miracle reinforced her belief in God. Jordan was not indicted, but she was broken. In some ways, that was worse.

Marsha McMillan would have a much more difficult time clearing herself. The Prosecutor had uncovered several private bank accounts with deposits in thousand dollar increments that McMillan could not explain. These accounts seemed to stream funds for fraudulent services allegedly provided to BCS client families. These monthly deposits coincided with the witness testimony from both clients and vendors of the alleged kickbacks she received. Jordan assumed that she, too, had been framed. With her position in the office, McMillan would not have been in proximity to some of the clients in question. But she did have access to payments for services to them. And she did have access to Crittenden, who determined the case plans. Yet they could not directly tie the accounts to her. The Prosecutor theorized that she had also suggested the same private legal firm as a mediator between the more affluent clients and the agency. These clients later made contributions to a non-profit, charitable organization that masked Marsha's "hidden accounts". One account was even tied to a political organization. The issue was quickly resolved somewhat by independent audit that disclosed only errors in the agency posting of funds. The Prosecutor failed to demonstrate a clear connection between the agency and these political and non-profit organizations. There was no clear or convincing evidence that McMillan had diverted funds to any of the suspect accounts. The Grand Jury did not find sufficient evidence to indict her on those charges. However, with Crittenden's corroborating testimony, she was indicted on charges of malfeasance—using her position to influence the case plans of selected clients. Her defense costs mounted in the thousands of dollars, and her reputation was destroyed. McMillan made a plea deal and was given a probationary sentence of three years. Jordan's memos were used to demonstrate that improper case handling had occurred, and with McMillan's full knowledge and direction. It was as if Jordan's memos formed a shadow structure from which the Prosecutor could build his case, while allowing Crittenden to run free of the mess! Or so he thought!

Although cleared of most charges, the damage was done, the goals were achieved. Both Marsha McMillan and her alleged flunky Jordan Mathews were removed from their jobs. They were replaced by persons more in keeping with the conservative agency hard line. Their careers were over, their lives in shambles. Although they shared in the swiftness of politics being meted out to accommodate need, the connection ended there. They never saw each other again, at least not as anyone knew.

And the memos? They became the fodder of conversation and controversy within BCS for years to come! They were a nuclear cloud over the career of Crittenden and all who shared his company. They helped to establish and clarify agency policy. They spurred the mandatory ethics education requirements for all social workers. They were used as teaching tools in the Human Resources Department. And some even formed the plotlines for local authors! But from that point forward, neither Carolyn nor Jordan ever saved another, single thing!

And Crittenden? He was relegated to some low level administrative post, where he reviewed federal guidelines and stretched the truth to pretend compliance. Finally, they had matched his unique talents to an appropriate job description! He was away from any client contact for the remainder of his career. But at least he still had a career.

\* \* \*

Carolyn came home for the Grand Jury proceedings, and sat with her parents in the courtroom as testimony was heard. The Mathews joined them at the start of the hearing. They were all enormously relieved when Jordan was acquitted. But Jordan was devastated. The experience and the stress sucked the light from her soul, and drained her being of any purpose. Carolyn convinced Jordan to return with her to the home of Marcus and Bill, and to help assist in his care. Marcus was now a confirmed AIDS case, and he was not tolerating the treatments. He had had several major infections that seemed not to resolve. Bill grew pale and weary with his care, but he remained at his side to the end. He stayed on the farm, and continued to grow their organic produce, until he, too, succumbed to the disease. They were never really sure how or when they had contracted AIDS, but they went from this world in the company of thousands of gay men like them, each dying their own scarecrow deaths.[82]

Carolyn and Jordan helped Bill and Marcus whenever they could, and they outreached to friends in the gay and lesbian community when they couldn't be there themselves. They were appalled by the callousness of a society who turned its back on the suffering of a people, simply because they were different. They had never known other terminally ill persons treated in such a degrading way—except maybe the lepers. Jordan often thought of the lesson Bill had given her that night at the diner, and realized what he meant about never really being safe. We are all targets of man and fate. She and Carolyn now actively supported the protests by ACT UP on Wall Street, at Northwest Airlines, at Cosmopolitan magazine, at the FDA's Maryland headquarters, and even at St. Patrick's Cathedral—acts born of desperation that demanded dignity as well as medical treatment; acts that confronted society, the Church, and all churches, with questions of its own morality.[83] Jordan and Carolyn were thankful that they were able to nurse Marcus, then Bill, to a comfortable end. They had shared their lives, as they had shared their loss. Carolyn and Jordan were shocked that the end had come so quickly. That reality was numbing.

Like Jordan, Carolyn's career was over now. But once she stabilized and her resiliency returned, she was again riding a burst of creative genius. Her seascapes became renowned in the area, and several of her paintings were on display in the State Museum. Her sculptures decorated the yard of her parents'

---

[82] For therapeutic interventions regarding AIDS patients, please see Appendix and Bibliography for Epilogue.

[83] For background information on Act Up, please refer to the Appendix and Bibliography for the Epilogue.

home, where she and Jordan moved after her father died of a stroke. Within months, Fran Berringer followed the call of her husband, and passed away peacefully in her sleep. Carolyn and Jordan were able to live modestly but comfortably for several years on the profits of their sale of their home, the island cape on the beachfront. They simply couldn't afford the taxes there after they lost their jobs. And recent memories tainted all pleasantry there. Jordan would sometimes still go with her father on jobs, but he was semi-retired now. She still occasionally made money spackling with a sheet rocking crew led by Pat Jr. She enjoyed most though, the quiet times at home with Carolyn, or the early summer mornings on the beach, where she could play in the surf, or write a chapter or two as they basked in the sun. She occasionally picked up the beach pebbles and marveled at their shapes, and colors, and textures. They were all presented to the shore on the same tide, but they were so different in type and size. Yet they all shared the roundness, though, that comes from being tumbled again and again in the ocean surf. In some ways, Jordan felt a connection to that experience. She would never get that million and two seller she had so often dreamed about as a child, but she would become an author of secondary merit, writing historical novels about the lives of sea-faring families who founded the communities at the shore. She would never return to her beloved Social Work, and would never even consider the thought of doing so. The universe had finally won out.

The Group kept in contact at least yearly, through their Christmas cards and phone calls, but they were never really able to assemble again as the entity that brought them together. Tyler and Marge had divorced after the birth of their third child. They were able to reconcile a few years later, but never remarried. Marge always thought that she bore the brunt of Tyler's unresolved issues with his father. She could see it in his own child rearing practices, and in the distance he would maintain from all family not directly his own—more specifically, with Marge's father! Janice and Martin married after Janice's parents died. They were living exclusively in the Gaithersburg area, but spent much of their time as world travelers. They never had children, but would compensate by caring for the children of foreign lands. Martin used his solar technology to help drive wells and irrigation systems in African villages, and used wind energy to help generate electricity in Bangladesh. Jordan collected the postcards they sent regularly from each city they visited, each culture they impacted. Karen and Todd raised Doris and Paula in the elite southern culture that befitted the Sommers Dynasty. Not only did Todd become president of the family's international corporation, but he had also won a seat in the state assembly, where he remained for nearly 16 years. Karen devoted her life to teaching English and History to sophomores and juniors who would never appreciate the magnificence of the woman, or the wisdom she conveyed in the classes she held each day.

Kelly and her husband David had a very happy, but not quite prosperous marriage, as David followed the career path of the many male members that were in, or surrounded, the Mathews family. Still, he prided himself on the craftsmanship of the homes that he built, and he would often take his kids to show off his jobs. He toted his family around in a brand new pick-up truck with a club cab that could accommodate the children, his family name proudly emblazoned on the driver side door. This was not the life that Kelly had planned, but it was the life that she felt most comfortable with. For the first time, she was truly happy. She stayed with this man, until they too, moved into the memories of the generations beyond them.

Jonathan pursued his love of the arts, but he became a graphic designer for a monthly variety magazine. He would often paint with Carolyn, and they occasionally held joint exhibitions. He spent much of his free time with Jordan and Carolyn, and at various points, he even lived with them. He frequently dated, but never found the one woman who could consistently satisfy all of his needs. Jordan would often counsel him about the improbability of one woman meeting all human needs, but he would reply that he was merely waiting for the right combination. He secretly believed that he had found that combination in Carolyn, but he would never share these thoughts with anyone.

Pete and Ann Mathews grew old together in the same home where they raised their children. They had only a son-in-law to follow in the family business. They had not amassed the wealth or influence that they had dreamed of in their youths. Although each of their children had their own set of problems, the children turned out relatively well—a testament to the fine foundations they had laid together as parents. They never understood, but did finally accept, the relationship between their oldest daughter and her friend Carolyn. They did not have grandchildren from two of their three children. But they did have five grandchildren: David, Laura, Karen, and the twins, Joyce and Gerry. And they had a legacy rich in the memories of their lives together. They had used their own scraps to build a family, a pathway for the genetics of their line. They could see their influence in the houses that he built, and in the smiles of the children's children that he and Ann created together. They could look back now, and grasp the meaning of each daily struggle they had faced together. And they could appreciate the sunset as their lives faded together. All in all, Pete Mathews was happy with the way his life had turned out. And as he looked back, he felt that he had plenty to be thankful for.

# Appendix and Bibliography

## Chapter One

1. Historical context for this chapter was accessed from:

    Braunstein, Peter, M.A.; Carpenter, Philip, M.A.; Edmunds, Anthony O., PhD.; Farber, David, PhD; Foley, Michael S., PhD; Rodriquez, Robert A.; Sanders, Jeffrey C., PhD; Shreve, BradleyG., M.A. (2004). *The Sixties Chronicle*. Lincolnwood, Illinois: Legacy Publications, Publications International Ltd. Used with permission from Publications International, Ltd.

2. **The Erikson Stages of Psychosocial Human Development (a.k.a. Stages of the Life Cycle)** are an extension of the psychoanalytic stages first introduced by Sigmund Freud. Erikson's stages explain the behavioral milestones and thought processes that accompany human physical development. Erikson viewed life as a series of coping choices that result from the struggles, victories, and defeats that we face every day. The Erikson Stages describe the results of the interplay of these life challenges. Certain tasks are presented and mastered at each age level, as we move from infancy to adulthood. These tasks are tied to our biological growth and development. The Erikson stages identify and describe these major tasks, and then describe their probable emotional result, as we face and resolve, or fail to resolve, these challenges. A synopsis of the Erikson stages is given as follows:

a. Trust vs. Mistrust: (coincides with the Oral Sensory Stage)—birth to age 1 year—The child first explores his environment orally, by examining with his mouth. He learns that he cries his wants, and that his wants may be met or unmet by the caretaker. If his needs are met rather consistently, he develops a trust, a sense that all is right with the world. This forms the basis for the trusting relationships and confidence of the future. If his needs are consistently unmet, he develops a mistrust, a despondency, a sense that the world is a hostile place. This forms the basis of tentative relationships of the future, and feelings of being ill at ease with others.

b. Autonomy vs. Shame and Doubt: (coincides with the Muscular-Anal Stage)—ages 2 to 3 years old—The child has begun mastering toileting. He is gaining control of his now better formed stools, and his bladder. He can exert his control in the holding in or the letting go. If mastered, this new ability allows the child to feel good about himself, more in control. The child develops a sense of autonomy. This is especially so if paired with sensible rules. If the child has difficulty mastering this control, though, or if rules are too rigid, the child is plagued by shame and doubt. These new abilities extend to walking, talking, dressing, and feeding by the end of the third year. If the child has mastered these tasks, he will carry himself confidently; if not, he will go through life being unsure and uncertain of himself.

c. Initiative vs. Guilt: (coincides with Locomotor—Genital Stage)—ages 4 to 5 years old—The child is becoming aware of the physical differences and the differing social roles of boys and girls, men and women. He resolves his love for the caretaker, and begins exploring relationships outside of that primary one. Children are now associating together in school and in the neighborhood. Their interests turn away from the home. If the child is successful in mastering these social tasks, he develops a sense of initiative, an ability to start new projects, accept new ideas, etc.

If he fails in these tasks, he develops a sense of guilt, a hesitancy, a feeling of not quite being adequate for the tasks of the future.

d. Industry vs. Inferiority: (coincides with Latency)—ages 5-12 years old—The child continues moving his focus from family to the larger world, and is absorbing information now from the environment around him—from peers, from school, from neighborhood. His serious play interests result in mastery of many new tasks. He is receiving and attempting to meet the demands of the larger world. He is assimilating new rules of behavior, both expressed to him, and subtly transmitted to him. He is beginning to establish a sense of self, a personal identity. If he successfully masters these skills, the child is instilled with a sense of confidence, and he accepts that he is learning skills that prepare him for the future. He feels more industrious with each success. However, if he is unable to master these skills, he may feel increasingly insecure, pensive, and inferior. This may impact on his ability and willingness to invest in his personal plan for the future.

e. Identity vs. Role Confusion: (coincides with Puberty and Adolescence)—ages 12-20 years old—The child recognizes himself as part of a larger ethnic, national, religious, socio-economic group, and derives a satisfaction from being a member of a larger group. Yet, he maintains his unique personality—ego identity is formed. He begins questioning and re-examining what he has learned to this point, often having to face again the dilemmas and tasks of the previous stages. The child chooses ideals as guides for future behavior, and these choices are often heavily influenced by the friendships, by the limitations, and by the privileges the child has encountered. The child is very specific, and can even be cruel, in his acceptance of others. Yet, this posture serves to reinforce a sense of identity. If these tasks are mastered, the child has a strong sense of who he is and where he is going. He becomes goal focused, and holds a belief that his goals will be achieved. However, if these tasks are not mastered, he becomes frustrated, cynical, and unable to rectify the gaps between the ideal and the real. Role confusion results, as goals become obscured.

f. Intimacy vs. Isolation: (coincides with Young Adulthood)—ages 20 to early 30s—The issue of intimacy is the primary theme of this stage. Do we share our life with another, and to what extent do we share it? With whom will we establish these bonds? Do we become so entrenched in our own identity, our own interests, our own strive for success, that we can share ourselves with no one else? How do we arrive at a balance between our own wants and needs, and the wants and needs of our partner? How do we form the bonds of intimacy without losing our sense of self? These are the tasks that must be mastered. If they are mastered, we will find a life rich in the rewards of intimacy. If not mastered, our lives may be experienced as isolating, lonely, and lacking real meaning.

g. Generativity vs. Stagnation: (coincides with Adulthood)—ages 40s to 50s—With the issues of intimacy now mastered, we strive to resolve those tasks that broaden this sense to include a sharing with the larger community. Generativity, the creation, the giving, expands beyond child-bearing and rearing to include charity, the arts, hobbies, a creating of one thing or another. If these tasks are successfully mastered, a sense of new meaning is brought to life. If these tasks are not mastered, a selfishness, a self-centeredness, a shallowness will result, leaving the individual with a pervasive feeling of emptiness and stagnation. Of course, these conclusions are subjective judgments to be evaluated by each person who enters this stage.

h. Ego Integrity vs. Despair: (coincides with Maturity)—old age—The major task of this stage is to come to terms with your life in review. The individual assesses the primary themes of his life and discovers its purpose. He sees the continuity of his life, its driving forces. He can now expand these observations to include all of life. Spirituality is brought to full purpose. If these tasks are mastered, the individual accepts his life as it is, and does not dwell on what might have been, or what will be—ego integrity results. We accept who we are now, and who we have been. But this result is not all exclusive. Old age brings with it despair, as our health diminishes, as our relationships cease, and as we lose independence. But the question here is the prevailing feeling. Has our life been meaningless, and our old age full of self-pity? Or is our life the conclusion of something miraculous, even if not always happy. This is where the true mastery of the tasks at this stage, and of life, are proven.

3. A reference to: A book I've made up, because the author of the book I had originally chosen has refused to allow use of his book's name in a gay novel.

4. A reference to: Another book I've made up because the author of the book I had originally chosen has refused to allow use of his book's name in a gay novel. Yup, we're two for two here!

5. A reference to: Wise, Robert (Producer/Director) (1961). *West Side Story* [musical motion picture]. Hollywood: United Artists.

6. A reference to: Stewart, Roderick David, and Quittendon, M. (1971). "Maggie May" [as recorded by Rod Stewart and the Faces]. On *Every Picture Tells A Story* [audio album].Chicago: Mercury Records

# Chapter Two

**A list of music used in this chapter:**

7. A reference to: Nichols, Roger S., and Williams, Paul H. (1971). "Rainy Days and Mondays" [as recorded by Karen and Richard Carpenter]. On *Carpenters*. [audio album]. New York: A&M Records (1971)

8. A reference to: Russell, Leo, and Bramlett, Bonnie (1969). "Superstar" [as re-recorded by Karen and Richard Carpenter]. On *Carpenters* [audio album]. New York: A&M Records (1971).

9. A reference to: McLean, Don (1971). "American Pie" [as recorded by Don McLean]. On *American Pie* [audio album]. New York: Mediarts/United Artists

10. A reference to: King, Carole (1971). "I Feel The Earth Move". [as recorded by Carole King]. On *Tapestry* [audio album]. New York: Ode/CBS Records.

11. A reference to: "Anticipation".
    Words and Music by Carly Simon.
    Copyright ©1971 by Quakenbush Music Ltd.
    Copyright Renewed.
    All Rights Reserved. Used by Permission.
    Reprinted by permission of Hal Leonard Corporation.

12. **Systems Theory**: " . . . The ecological systems (ecosystems) perspective is a framework for assessment and intervention. It has been a dominant theoretical approach for viewing human behavior in the social environment . . . . based in

the metaphor of biological organisms that live and adapt in a complex network of environmental forces. Von Bertalanffy (1968) believed that living organisms are organized wholes, not just the sum of their separate parts, and that they are essentially open systems, maintaining themselves with continuous inputs from and outputs to their environments . . . . The ecological perspective rests on an evolutionary, adaptive view of human beings in continuous transaction with their environment . . . . This approach makes clear the need to see people and their environments within their historic and cultural contexts, in relationship with one another, and as continually influencing one another, as described by Germain and Gitterman (1995) . . ." This excerpt taken from:

Kilpatrick, Allie C., and Holland, Thomas P. (2003; 1st ed. 1995). *Working With Families: An Integrative Model by Level of Need*. Boston, Ma: Pearson Education, Inc. Pp.14-15

13. **Family Life Cycles**: " . . . the family is a social unit that faces a series of developmental tasks. These tasks vary along the parameters of cultural differences but at the same time have universal roots (Minuchin, 1974). The stages of the life cycle have been defined for "intact nuclear families in contemporary Western Societies" (Tseng and Hsu, 1991, p.8) as the unattached young adult, the formation of the dyadic relationship, the family with young children, the family with adolescents, the family launching children, the family with older members, and the family in later years (Becvar and Becvar, 1996; Goldenburg and Goldenburg, 1980; Rhodes, 1980) . . ." Excerpt taken from:

Kilpatrick, Allie C., and Holland, Thomas P. (2003; 1st ed. 1995). *Working With Families: An Integrative Model by Level of Need*. Boston, Ma: Pearson Education, Inc. p.86

**A list of music used in this chapter:**

14. A reference to: Stevens, Cat (1971). "Peace Train". [as recorded by Cat Stevens]. On *Teaser and The Firecat* [audio album]. Santa Monica, Ca: Uni Records.

15. A reference to: John, Elton, and Taupin, Bernie (1971). "Tiny Dancer" [as recorded by Elton John]. On *Madman Across The Water* [audio album]. Universal City, Ca: Uni Records

16. A reference to: John, Elton, and Taupin, Bernie (1970). "Burn Down The Mission". [as recorded by Elton John]. On *Tumbleweed Connection* [audio album]. Universal City, Ca: Uni Records

17. **Social Policy and Social Work**: " . . . A related function of social workers is to work for changes in social policies that affect people in many informal, formal, and societal resource systems. Thus social workers contribute to the development and modification of social policy made by legislative bodies, elected heads of government, public administrative agencies (Department of Health, Education, and Welfare), voluntary funding institutions (United Fund), and people in positions of authority in societal resource systems . . . . social workers are faced with constraints that limit and otherwise affect the specific objectives they may establish and their ability to achieve their objectives . . ." Excerpt taken from:

Pincus, Allen, and Minahan, Anne (1973; 8th ed. 1977). *Social Work Practice: Model and Method*. Itasca, Illinois: F. E. Peacock Publishers, Inc. p.26

18. **Denial**: An unconscious defense mechanism used to resolve emotional conflict and its anxiety by refusing to acknowledge thoughts, feelings, dreams and wishes, needs, or realities that are consciously intolerable.

19. **Binge Drinking**: Heavy alcohol use that occurs in bouts of a day or more that are set aside for drinking. A pattern is followed that allows this routine intoxication, followed by periods of non-use: ie: the "weekend alcoholic."

## Chapter Three

20. Two books that discuss **the impact of social values on social policy in the United States**:

    Katz, Michael B. (1986). *In the Shadow of the Poorhouse: A Social History of Welfare in America.* New York: Basic Books, Inc.

    Gordon, Linda (1994). *Pitied But Not Entitled: Single Mothers and the History of Welfare, 1890-1935.* New York: The Free Press.

21. The **history of Social Work** can generally be found in the beginning of most Social Work text books, and certainly, in any Introduction to Social Work book. The information contained in this section is a composite of some those readings. However, a great brief history of Social Work can be found on the Internet, as complied by the University of Michigan:

    Taunenbaum, Nili, and Reich, Michael (Fall, 2001). "From Charitable Volunteers to Architects of Social Welfare: A Brief History of Social Work". *Ongoing*. [On-line].

    Accessible at:http://www.ssw.umich.edu/ongoing/fall2001/briefhistory

22. A reference to: Pincus, Alan, and Minahan, Anne (1973; 8th ed. 1977). *Social Work Practice: Model and Method.* Itasca, Illinois: F.E. Peacock Publishers, Inc.

23. The **philosophy, values and beliefs of Social Work** were obtained from:

   Pincus, Allen, and Minahan, Anne (1973; 8th ed. 1977). *Social Work Practice: Model and Method.* Itasca, Illinois: F. E. Peacock Publishers, Inc. Pp. 9-10; 15; 38-39;

24. A reference to: Serling, Rod (1970-1973). *Night Gallery* [television program]. New York: NBC

25. A reference to: Lennon, John, and McCartney, Paul. (1966). "Yellow Submarine". On *Revolver* [audio album]. UK: Capitol Records

26. Romero, George (1968). *Night of the Living Dead* [motion picture]. New York: Walter Read Organization

27. **Differential Diagnosis of Bereavement Issues**, as per the DSM-IV-TR, "Other Conditions That May be the Focus of Clinical Assessment:"

   V62.82 Bereavement
   "This category can be used when the focus of clinical attention is a reaction to the death of a loved one. As part of their reaction to the loss, some grieving individuals present with symptoms characteristic of a Major Depressive Episode (e.g., feelings of sadness and associated symptoms such as insomnia, poor appetite, and weight loss). The bereaved individual typically regards the depressed mood as "normal," although the person may seek professional help for relief of associated symptoms such as insomnia or anorexia. The duration and expression of "normal" bereavement vary considerably among different

cultural groups. The diagnosis of Major Depressive Disorder is generally not given unless the symptoms are present two months after the loss. However, the presence of certain symptoms that are not characteristic of a "normal" grief reaction may be helpful in differentiating Bereavement from a Major Depressive Episode. These include: 1) guilt about things other than actions taken or not taken by the survivor at the time of death; 2) thoughts of death other than the survivor feeling that he or she would be better off dead or should have died with the deceased person; 3) morbid preoccupation with worthlessness; 4) marked psychomotor retardation; 5) prolonged and marked functional impairment; and 6) hallucinatory experiences other than thinking that he or she hears the voice of, or transiently sees the image of, the deceased person."

Excerpt taken from:

American Psychiatric Association (2000). *Diagnostic and Statistical Manual of Mental Disorders, 4th Edition, Text Revised.* Washington, DC: American Psychiatric Association, Pp.740-741.

## Chapter Four

28. **the function of gay bars in the Gay Community**—taken from "Nomenclature of the Community: An Activist's Perspective," by Joshua L. Ferris:

"Stereotypical Lifestyles . . . From the 1950s through the 1970s there were very few places to meet other LGBT people other than bars. Bars provided a safe place for LGBT people to be open about their sexuality and to meet other LGBT people. Bars, though seemingly prominent, play no different role than they do in the heterosexual community. Bars are everywhere, and some people choose to go and some do not. Some LGBT people choose to go to heterosexual bars, and some heterosexual people hang out in LGBT bars.

There are no standards here, and bars by no means stand as a foundation of the LGBT community . . ."

Excerpt taken from:

Ferris, Joshua L. (2006). "The Nomenclature of the Community: An Activist's Perspective". Shankle, Michael D., M.P.H. (ed.). (2006). *The Handbook of Lesbian, Gay, Bisexual, and Transgender Public Health: A Practitioner's Guide to Service*. New York: Harrington Park Press. p.7

29. Information regarding **Gay Bars in Greenwich Village in the 1970s** was obtained from the following:

Ask.com: http://www.disco-disco.com/clubs/identify-clubs.shtml

30. **Resources for information on the Stonewall Riots**:
Duberman, Martin (1993). *Stonewall*. New York: Penguin Group, Penguin Books USA, Inc. Pp.181-212

Carter, David (2004). *Stonewall: The Riots That Sparked the Gay Revolution*. New York: St. Martin's Press. Pp.137-158;

After Stonewall Productions (producer). Scagliotti, John, Baus, Janet, and Hunt, Dan. (1999). *After Stonewall* [motion picture documentary] New York, NY: First Run Features

31. **Resource List on AIDS and Its Impact**:

**"Where Did AIDS Come From?"**. Centers For Disease Control and Prevention. CDC Home Page. *Questions and Answers*. Atlanta: U.S.

Department of Health and Human Services, Centers for Disease Control and Prevention, 2009.[Online]. Accessible at: http://www.cdc.gov/hiv/resources/qa/qa3.html

" . . . the earliest known case of HIV-1 in humans was discovered in a male blood sample taken in Kinshasa, Republic of Congo, in 1959. The virus is believed to have existed in the United States since the mid-to-late 1970's. From 1979-1981, rare types of pneumonia, cancer, and other illnesses were being reported by doctors in both Los Angeles and New York among a number of patients who had sex with other men. These were medical conditions not usually found in people with healthy immune systems. In 1982, public health officials began to use the term "acquired immune deficiency syndrome" or AIDS, to describe the occurrences of opportunistic infections, Kaposi sarcoma (a kind of cancer), and Pneumocystis carinii pneumonia in previously healthy people . . . In 1983, scientists discovered the virus that causes AIDS . . . and the name was later changed to HIV (human immunodeficiency virus) . . . A subspecies of Chimpanzees native to west equatorial Africa had been identified as the source of the virus. The researchers believe that the HIV-1 was introduced into the human population when hunters became exposed to infected blood (of these chimpanzees)."

**"Epidemiology of HIV/AIDS—United States, 1981-2005"**. Centers for Disease Control and Prevention. *MMWR Weekly*, June 2, 2006/55(21);589-592 Atlanta: U.S. Department of Health and Human Services, Centers for Disease Control and Prevention, 2006.[Online]. Accessible at: http://www.cdc.gov/mmwr

"In June 1981, the first cases of what was later called acquired immunodeficiency syndrome (AIDS) in the United States were reported in MMWR. Since 1981, the human immunodeficiency virus (HIV) epidemic has continued to expand in the United States; at the end of 2003, approximately 1,039,000-1,185,000 persons in the United States were living with HIV/AIDS, an estimated 24%-27% of whom were unaware of their infection.... At the end of 2004, an estimated 1,147,697 HIV or AIDS cases have been diagnosed and reported to CDC. AIDS cases increased rapidly in the 1980s and peaked in 1992 (an estimated 78,000 cases diagnosed) before stabilizing in 1998; since then, approximately 40,000 new AIDS cases have been diagnosed annually.... During 1981-2004, a total of 522,723 deaths among persons with AIDS have been reported to CDC. Substantial increases in survival after diagnosis of AIDS have been observed, particularly since 1996. The proportion of persons living at 2 years after AIDS diagnosis was 44% for those diagnosed with AIDS from 1981-1992, 64% for 1993-1995, and 85% for 1996-2000.

**Barton-Knott, Sophie (2007). "Report Fact Sheet: "Key Facts By Region—2007 AIDS Epidemic Update".** *UNAIDS. (Joint United Nations Programme on HIV/AIDS) (Geneva:UNAIDS). [Online].* Accessible at:

http://data.unaids.org/pub/EPISlides/2007/071118_epi

"Global HIV prevalence (the proportion of people living with the virus) appears to have leveled off. However, the number of people living with AIDS has risen to 33.2 million in 2007; from 29 million in 2002 . . . Sub-Saharan Africa remains the most affected region. (there) Some 1.7 million people were newly infected with HIV in 2007 . . . (elsewhere:) Adult HIV prevalence was estimated at 1% in 2007, making the Caribbean the second most affected region in the world . . . Overall, approximately 2.1 million people in North America, and Central and Western Europe were living with HIV in 2007 . . ."

Note: The complete *2007 AIDS Epidemic Update* report is accessible at: http://www.unaids.org

Mail, Patricia D., and Lear, Walter J. (2006). "The Role of Public Health in Lesbian, Gay, Bisexual, and Transgender Health". Shankle, Michael D., M.P.H. (ed.) (2006). *The Handbook of Lesbian, Gay, Bisexual, and Transgender Public Health: A Practitioner's Guide to Service*. New York: Harrington Park Press. Pp.22-23

"The HIV (human immunodeficiency virus) pandemic was first noticed in the United States in 1981 by local clinicians and local health department statisticians (CDC, 1981) . . . . within months it became clear that the common element underlying this phenomenon was impairment of the immune systems of these men. A second common element in these first cases was that these men were all identified as gay. As the number of cases increased, the association with homosexual behavior was reinforced—it became known as "the gay plague". . . . This assumed socio-cultural view bore with it society's homophobia, and so government public health agencies were intimidated from immediately taking those public health measures appropriate for a new life-threatening and rapidly spreading disease. But the LGBT health movement . . . responded promptly . . . . New and relevantly modified LGBT health services sprang up across the country. Thousands of lesbians volunteered in these services. Self help and advocacy reached unprecedented heights, providing volunteer "buddies" for sick gay men . . . . despite the large number needed and the volunteers' frequent burnout. The dramatic street demonstrations of AIDS Coalition To Unleash Power (ACT UP) forced a reluctant society to abandon its homophobic-inspired neglect of its mandated responsibility to protect the health of all. ACT UP held its first demonstration in March, 1987 to protest the profiteering of pharmaceutical companies . . ."

32. **Definitions**: The following information is excerpted from:

Kirk, Sheila, and Kulkarni, Claudette (2006). "The Whole Person: A Paradigm for Integrating the Mental and Physical Health of Trans Clients".

Shankle, Michael D., M.P.H. (ed.) (2006). *The Handbook of Lesbian, Gay, Bisexual, and Transgender Public Health: A Practitioner's Guide to Service*. New York: Harrington Park Press. Pp.150-152:

Transgender—"... an umbrella term that designates someone who does not fit neatly into the societally accepted boxes called "male/man" and "female/woman" and who intentionally rejects the gender assigned to her or him at birth. Thus, it incorporates all persons who consciously transgress or violate gender norms, whether they intend to "pass" or not..."

Transsexual—"... an individual whose internally felt gender identity does not match the biological body he or she was born with and/or the gender he or she was assigned at birth. A phrase previously, and sometimes still, used with reference to transsexualism is gender dysphoria. Transsexuals meet the Diagnostic and Statistical Manual's criteria for the diagnosis of "gender identity disorder" (a term highly disputed since it labels transsexualism as a "disorder.") Transsexuals can be male-to-female (MTFs; also called transwomen) and female-to-male (FTMs; also called transmen). Transsexuals may be "pre-operative" (popularly referred to as "pre-op"), "post-operative" ("post-op"), or may not want surgery at all ("non-op") because they experience no internal conflict between their preferred gender and their genitals..."

Cross-dresser—"... (anyone) dressing in the clothing conventionally worn by the other gender and may be used with reference to both transsexuals and cross-dressers. However, the term cross-dresser (formerly transvestite) is reserved for individuals who like to cross-dress but who do not experience a dissonance between their biologic body and their gender identity and do not wish to permanently change their sex or gender (though some may want to take hormones to enhance their cross-dressing experience). Most cross-dressers are heterosexual men who cross-dress for purposes of amusement, role-playing, stress relief, or sexual gratification. Usually, biologic women are not called cross-dressers when they wear men's clothes because our culture allows females a much greater range of dressing behaviors . . . . Some transsexuals go through periods of time believing or wondering if they are "just" cross-dressers . . ."

33. A reference to: McCartney, Paul (1973). "My Love" [as recorded by Paul McCartney and Wings]. On *Red Rose Speedway* [audio album]. UK: Apple Records

34. **Cross-dressing and treatment implications: Resources**:

Sears, James T. (1997). "Centering Culture: Teaching for Critical Sexual Literacy Using the Sexual Diversity Wheel". *Journal of Moral Education*, September, 1997, Vol.26, Is.3. Pp. 273-284. Taylor and Francis, Ltd, *http://www.informationworld.com* reprinted by permission of the publisher.

" . . . the concept of sexual literacy within the context of four circular models for multicultural sexual education: tolerance, diversity, difference, and differance. The sexual diversity wheel is presented as a pedagogical tool to facilitate student inquiry into the multiple cross-cultural constructions and valuations of gender and sexuality . . ."

Bordan, Terry, and De Ricco, Marc (1997). "Identity Formation and Self Esteem Issues in the Male Transvestite: A Humanistic Perspective". *The Journal of Humanistic Education and Development*, March, 1997, Vol.35, Is.3. Pp. 156-162. The American Counseling Association. Reprinted with permission. No further reproduction authorized without written permission from the American Counseling Association:

" . . . explores identity formation issues associated with low self esteem in the transvestite population . . . . DSM-IV further identifies cross-dressing as typically beginning in childhood or early adolescence . . . . Erikson defines this stage as the fifth in the entire life cycle and specifically deals with the task of Identity vs. Identity Diffusion. A secure sense of self-identity is defined as an integral continuity of one's self-definition which is shared with others and validated in the social context of family and community. Thus, ego synthesis is partly accomplished when a person's inner sense of self and reality is mirrored and confirmed by others . . . . During this phase of identity formation, the transvestite population may be in jeopardy in terms of self esteem, and may experience problematic interference with identity formation. Self esteem is directly related to self-acceptance, which is an essential element of healthy identity formation . . . . His stigmatized, flawed self confronts him at every level . . . . it is a stigma that gives birth to oppression, both internal and external . . . . This lack of mirroring and welcoming are two important variables that hinder the cross-dressing adolescent's psychological health . . . . Greenberg, Siegel, and Leitch . . . . found that a sense of wellbeing was more positively related to parental rather than peer attachment . . . . if the rapport between parents and adolescents is warm and supportive, the adolescent has optimum environment for self-concept and ego identity formation . . . Self-hatred, in contrast to healthy self-esteem, fuels self-rejection and emotional isolation . . . . the development of a more positive cross-dressing identity can be greatly assisted by membership in a cross-dressing support group . . . . Introjected self-hatred fragments one's identity and can retard development . . . . Professional counseling is an accepting and supportive experience through which the cross-dresser's self esteem and functioning may be enhanced by the counselor's humanistic, non-pathological approach . . . The concept of self-acceptance should become primary for the counselor when treating cross-dressers . . ."

35. **Sexuality and Gender:**

Sears, James T. (1997). "Centering Culture: Teaching for Critical Sexual Literacy Using the Sexual Diversity Wheel". *Journal of Moral Education,*

September, 1997, Vol.26, Is.3. Pp. 273-284. Taylor and Francis, Ltd, *http://www.informationworld.com* reprinted by permission of the publisher.

"One method for facilitating a more holistic and critical conversation about sexuality and gender is the Sexual Diversity Wheel. Composed of five concentric circles . . . this teaching tool allows students (and teachers) to visualize the various intersections of biological sex, gender identity, gender role, sexual behavior and sexual identity—and in the process explore the interplay of history and culture as well as class and race . . ."

36. **Integrity as it relates to Gay Identity**—When you think about "integrity" as a quality, your mind's eye pictures someone who is honest, both with himself and with others; someone who is incorruptible, who has a soundness to his character; someone who has a wholeness, a completeness, a spirituality. We are all prompted toward, and aspire to this quality in ourselves and others. But for many, a sense of integrity is being obscured and denied by the very social structures designed to promote it. This is especially true for gay people, who must assert and claim their sense of integrity, yet balance this need against coping strategies required for their survival.

**Some thoughts**:

Ferris, Joshua L. (2006). "The Nomenclature of the Community: An Activist Perspective". Shankle, Michael D., M.P.H. (ed.) (2006). *The Handbook of Lesbian, Gay, Bisexual, and Transgender Public Health: A Practitioner's Guide to Service*. New York: Harrington Park Press. Pp.5-6

"[coming out] For many, it is the first time a person says, "I'm gay." This moment is a very serious one, because for many people it drastically changes their world. This is because most people live in society where heterosexuality is considered the norm . . . . If someone comes out to you, it is because he or she trusts you . . . . Realize that he or she is not a different person, but that you are now privileged to know the same person in more depth . . ."

"Kicked Out Because I was Gay" by Shameek Williamson, from *The Heart Knows Something Different: Teenage Voices from the Foster Care System*, edited by Al Desetta, copyright 1996 by Youth Communication / New York Center, Inc. Reprinted by permission of Persea Books, Inc., New York. p.137

"[regarding her change in foster care placements] Sharon may have had gay friends, but she could not accept a gay person in her family. Sharon may have lived in foster care, but obviously she didn't understand or care how her rejection would affect me. How could Sharon judge me like that if she had once been in foster care herself? Personally, I'd rather be moved than live a lie, but no one should have to live a lie for fear of being moved."

Hernandez, Manuel, and Fultz, Shawn L. (2006). "Barriers to Health Care Access". Shankle, Michael D., M.P.H. (ed.) (2006). *The Handbook of Lesbian, Gay, Bisexual and Transgender Public Health: A Practitioner's Guide to Service*. New York: Harrington Park Press. Pp.188-189

"In all of the studies addressing health care in LGBT community one undisputed fact can be unearthed: homophobic attitudes, whether directed at patients or providers, will ultimately serve to constrict barriers to the delivery of culturally competent care for LBGT patients. Whether it be by limiting the number of out LGBT practitioners in primary care and specialty settings, or by creating an environment that is uncomfortable or inhospitable to LGBT patients and their families . . ."

Sperber, Jodi B. (2006). "As Time Goes By: An Introduction to the Needs of Lesbian, Gay, Bisexual, and Transgender Elders." Shankle, Michael D., M.P.H. (ed.) (2006). *The Handbook of Lesbian, Gay, Bisexual, and Transgender Public Health: A Practitioner's Guide to Service.* New York: Harrington Park Press. p.252.

"Developing resilience in the face of discrimination has helped some gay and lesbian seniors become experts in dealing with adversity, facing change, and learning how to take care of themselves . . ."

37. A reference to: Frank, T.C. (1971). *Billy Jack* [motion picture]. Hollywood: Warner Brothers

38. A reference to: Whales, James (1931). *Frankenstein* [motion picture]. Hollywood: Universal Pictures

39. **Sample Questions: To Assess Suicide and Self-Destructive Behavior (Symptom Questions)** as excerpted from *Clinician's Thesaurus: The Guide for Writing Psychological Reports,"* by Edward Zuckerman, Ph. D

Initial Inquiry:

(a). "You have told me about some very painful experiences. They must have been hard to bear, and perhaps you sometimes thought of quitting the struggle/harming yourself/ending your life . . ."

Death Wish:

(a) "When was the last time you wished you would not wake up/were dead/ thought you/others/the world would be better off if you were dead? Have you ever thought this way before?"

Ideation:

(a) "Have you recently said to yourself or others words like, 'Life is not worth living, I can't take any more of this . . .'
(b) "When was the first time you thought of/considered ending it all/ harming/ killing yourself?"
(c) "When was the last time . . . ?"
(d) "Have you recently/in the last month made any plans to harm or kill yourself?"
(e) "When you have suicidal thoughts, how long do they last?"
(f) "What brings on these thoughts? How do you feel about these thoughts? Do you have any control over these thoughts? What stops/ends these thoughts?"

Affects and Behaviors:

(a) "How often have you felt lonely/fearful/sad/depressed/hopeless?"
(b) "Are there more themes of despair in your writing/reading/art work/ music?"
(c) "Are you now very happy coming out of depression?"
(d) "Have you lost someone close to you?"
(e) "Have you lost interest in work/hobbies/school/activities?"
(f) "Are you more careless/taking more risks?

(g) "Because of bad moods, have you ever: Not eaten? Slept poorly? Gotten drunk or high? Run away? Gotten into a physical fight? Damaged property? Been arrested? Kicked out of school? Been involved in physical or sexual abuse or actions you regretted later? Gotten pregnant/gotten someone pregnant? Increased your use of alcohol or drugs?"

Motivation:

(a) "Why were you thinking of killing yourself?"
(b) "Have you felt, 'My life is a failure' or 'My situation is hopeless'?"
(c) "What would happen to you after you were dead?"
(d) "What effects would your suicide have on your family/ friends/coworkers people who care about you?"
(e) "Has a relative or friend of yours ever tried to/succeeded in killing himself/herself?"
(f) "Under what conditions would you kill yourself?"

Deterrents/Demotivators:

(a) "What reasons do you have to continue to live?"
(b) "What would prevent you from killing yourself?"

Gestures/Attempts:

(a) "When was the first time you tried to harm or kill yourself?"
(b) "Have you tried more than once?"
(c) "Did you intend to die?"
(d) "How did you try to do it?"
(e) "Were you alone?"
(f) "Were you using drugs or alcohol?"

Preparations:

(a) "Have you: Given away any prized possessions? Written a will? Checked on your insurance? Told anyone about your plans? Written a suicide note? Made funeral arrangements?"

Plan/Means/Method:

(a) "Have you thought about how/where/ when you might kill yourself?"
(b) "Have you thought about how easy or difficult it would be to kill yourself?"
(c) "Have you made any plans to harm or kill yourself?"
(d) "How would you do it? Do you have the means? What preparations have you made?"

Excerpts taken from:

*Clinician's Thesaurus: The Guide For Writing Psychological Reports, 5th Edition.* Zuckerman, Edward L., Ph.D. (2000). "Symptom Questions". Copyright Guilford Press. Pp.71-73. Reprinted with permission of the Guilford Press.

### 40. DSM-IV-TR Criteria for Postpartum Onset Specifier (Mood Disorders):

"The specifier with Postpartum Onset can be applied to the current (or, if the full criteria are not currently met for a Major Depressive, Manic or Mixed Episode, to the most recent) Major Depressive, Manic, or Mixed Episode of Major Depressive Disorder, Bipolar I Disorder, Bipolar II Disorder or Brief Psychotic Disorder, if the onset is within four weeks after childbirth . . . Symptoms that are common to postpartum depression-onset episodes, though not specific to postpartum onset, include fluctuations in mood, mood lability, and pre-occupation with infant well-being, the intensity of which may range from overconcern to frank delusions. The presence of severe ruminations or delusional thought about the infant is associated with significantly increased risk of harm to the infant. Postpartum-onset mood episodes can present either with or without psychotic features. Infanticide is most often associated with postpartum psychotic episodes that are characterized by command hallucinations to kill the infant or delusions that the infant is possessed . . ."

Excerpt taken from:

American Psychiatric Association (2000). "Mood Disorders". *Diagnostic and Statistical Manual of Mental Disorders, 4th Edition, Text Revised*. Washington, DC: American Psychiatric Association. p.422

41. **DSM-IV-TR Criteria for Dysthymic Disorder, 300.4 (Mood Disorders):**

"The essential feature of Dysthymic Disorder is a chronically depressed mood that occurs for most of the day more days than not for at least two years (Criterion A). Individuals with Dysthymic Disorder describe their mood as "down in the dumps." In children, the mood may be irritable rather than depressed, and the required minimum duration is only one year. During periods of depression, at least two of the following additional symptoms are present: poor appetite or overeating; insomnia or hypersomnia; low energy or fatigue; low self-esteem; poor concentration or difficulty making decisions; and feelings of hopelessness . . . Early onset: This specifier should be used if the onset of the dysthymic symptoms occurs before age 21 years. Such individuals are more likely to develop subsequent Major Depressive Episodes . . ."

Excerpt taken from:

> American Psychiatric Association (2000). "Mood Disorders". *Diagnostic and Statistical Manual of Mental Disorders, 4th Edition, Text Revised.* Washington, DC: American Psychiatric Association. Pp.376-377

## 42. DSM-IV-TR Criteria for Brief Psychotic Disorder, 298.8 (Schizophrenia and Other Psychotic Disorders):

> "The essential feature of Brief Psychotic Disorder is a disturbance that involves the sudden onset of at least one of the following positive psychotic symptoms: delusions; hallucinations; disorganized speech (e.g., frequent derailment or incoherence), or grossly disorganized or catatonic behavior (Criterion A). An episode of disturbance lasts at least 1 day but less than 1 month, and the individual eventually has a full return to the premorbid level of functioning (Criterion B). The disturbance is not better accounted for by a Mood Disorder with Psychotic Features, by Schizoaffective Disorder, or by Schizophrenia and is not due to the direct psychological effects of a substance . . . . or a general medical condition . . . . [They] typically experience emotional turmoil or overwhelming confusion. They may have rapid shifts from one intense affect to another . . . . the level of impairment may be severe . . . an increased risk of suicide . . . . Pre-existing Personality Disorders may predispose the individual to the development of the disorder . . ."

Excerpt taken from:

> American Psychiatric Association. (2000). "Schizophrenia and Other Psychotic Disorders". *Diagnostic and Statistical Manual of Mental Disorders, 4th Edition, Text Revised.* Washington, DC: American Psychiatric Association. Pp.329-332.

## 43. DSM-IV-TR Differential Diagnosis for the patient "Josie"—

First let us define the purpose of the DSM-IV as it relates to Social Work. The DSM-IV represents a nomenclature or classification of mental disorders. This classification system serves a variety of purposes: " . . . to collect statistical information . . . . to establish a nationally acceptable psychiatric nomenclature. . . . to provide clear descriptions of diagnostic categories in order to enable clinicians and investigators to diagnose, communicate about, study, and treat people with various mental disorders; . . . . for documentation; . . . . as an educational tool; and for limited forensic purposes . . . . Each of the mental disorders is conceptualized as a clinically significant behavioral or psychological syndrome or pattern that occurs in an individual and that is associated with present distress (e.g. a painful symptom) or disability (i.e. impairment in one or more important areas of functioning) or with a significantly increased risk of suffering death, pain, disability, or an important loss of freedom . . . (Pp. xxi-xxxvii)"

Jordan observes a variety of behaviors as she interviews Josie. These include: labile mood; delusions; disorientation to time and place; hallucinations; psychomotor agitation; and homicidal ideations. Dean advises that these symptoms have been recurring throughout Josie's adult life. In assessing the noted behaviors, we consult the DSM-IV-TR to determine a probable diagnosis. However, DSM-IV-TR allows that " . . . clinical judgment may justify giving a certain diagnosis to an individual even though the clinical presentation falls just short of meeting the full criteria for the diagnosis as long as the symptoms that are present are persistent and severe . . . (p. xxxii)"

The initial most glaring presentations are Josie's delusions and her hallucinations. These symptoms indicate psychosis (DSM-IVTR Glossary of Technical Terms, p.827). Immediately, you might consult the Thought

Disorders section of DSM-IV-TR, "Schizophrenia and Other Psychotic Disorders" (Pp.297-344. Wow, that's a lot of stuff!). The introduction to the chapter notes hallucinations and delusions as a prominent aspect of the presentation. But they also note that in Schizophrenia, Schizophreniform Disorder, Schizoaffective Disorder, and Brief Psychotic Disorder, the term 'psychotic' also includes "... disorganized speech, or disorganized or catatonic behavior ...." Josie does present with disorganized behavior (unpredictable agitation). We do not know how long these symptoms had been occurring before she sought help, but she has reportedly been treated throughout her adult life. She certainly has dysfunction in one or more life areas, another criterion. Under schizophrenia subtypes, we find "295.30 Paranoid Type," and note associated features that include anger; and that "persecutory ... delusions with anger may predispose an individual to violence ... (p. 314)" That might fit, but still, the duration is uncertain. Schizophrenia requires symptoms for over six month duration. Until we have more information, we could tentatively classify Josie as an individual with 295.30 Schizophrenia, Paranoid Type, Provisional. That means that there is a strong presumption that the full criteria for the disorder will ultimately be met for a disorder.

However, she could also meet the criteria for 295.40 Schizophreniform Disorder. The essential features are identical to Schizophrenia (Criterion A) except for two differences: the total duration of the illness is at least one month, but less than six months, and impaired social or occupational functioning during some part of the illness is not required (p. 317). Given her presentation and history at the clinic, as well as the latter criteria, this diagnosis would likely be ruled out. Schizophrenia still seems the most correct diagnosis.

But what about something different, like a "296.35 Mood Disorder With Psychotic Features?" Let's look at Major Depressive Disorder, which is characterized by one or more depressive episodes (i.e., at least 2 weeks of depressed mood or loss of interest accompanied by four additional symptoms of depression. Symptoms of depression include: changes in appetite or weight, sleep, and psychomotor activity; decreased energy; feelings of worthlessness or guilt; difficulty thinking, concentrating, or making decisions; or recurrent thought of death or suicidal ideation, plans, or attempts. A symptom must be newly present or have clearly worsened, and must persist for most of the day nearly every day for 2 weeks (p.349). Well, we don't know anything about her sleep patterns, or about some depressed symptoms as noted above. She did have psychomotor changes including agitation and rocking, but these changes would have had to occur nearly every day, as per the criteria. We can note that she has some guilt about the death of her child, because she relates the encounter with Willis. This appears to be a ruminating sense of guilt. Her mood changes are obvious. She admitted some impaired/difficulty thinking, one of the reasons she sought help. But even if we added the specifier "With Psychotic Features," the disturbance still seems better accounted for by either Schizophrenia or Schizophreniform Disorder. Of course, anyone who reads this may have a different interpretation. That's why we have to be careful about how we use the DSM-IV-TR—with such similarities among the diagnoses, we could code patient diagnoses to fit the available treatment programs. In some cases, this can be a real benefit to the client, and we've done good! In other cases, this may deny a client some needed intervention, and we have done badly . . . Maybe it's a "298.8 Brief Psychotic Episode." But it's more likely, "309.81 Posttraumatic Stress Disorder" because her symptoms first arose after a traumatic event . . . See what I mean?

44. **Domestic Violence Treatment and Resources**:

Lerner, Christine Fiore, and Kennedy, Linda Thomas (2000). "Stay-Leave Decision Making in Battered Women: Trauma, Coping, and Self-Efficacy".

*Cognitive Therapy and Research*, Vol.24, No.2. Pp.215-232. Netherlands: Springer Science and Business Media

"Most often, for battered women the decision to stay or leave is not made at a single point in time with finality, but instead, unfolds over time, and represents the most fundamental and difficult decision women may face.... (I)n order to understand the potential differences in women's experiences at different points in time, [the authors] studied four variables .... trauma symptoms; coping; self-efficacy for leaving a violent relationship; and physical violence. Results indicated that dynamic psychological variables such as self-efficacy, trauma symptoms and coping varied depending on whether women were in or out of relationships, and how long it had been since they had left the relationship .... These findings support the importance of understanding and responding to process variables, relevant to battered women's experiences and the potential value in tailoring interventions that are relevant to each woman's needs at a given point in the decision-making process..."

" ... [there is ] a large range in the percentages of women—18% to 74%—who leave violent relationships only to return .... it is estimated that women return an average of 3-4 times .... The barriers of external environment, family and social role expectations, psychological consequences of relationship violence, and childhood abuse and neglect experiences provide a framework for understanding .... The Transtheoretical model of change (TMM) was developed as an integrative model of intentional behavioral change. Central to the model is the construct of stages of change .... there are five dynamic cyclical stages of readiness for change in a wide array of behavioral and behavioral health areas .... relapse to a previous level of readiness can happen at any point in the readiness process ... (T)he stages of the model are: 1) precontemplation .... 2) contemplation .... 3) preparation .... 4) action .... and 5) maintenance .... Given that women's movement is in, out, and back is a dynamic changing experience, working with this movement and better understanding its dynamics may be more empowering . . ."

"Diagnostic rates of Posttraumatic Stress Disorder among women who seek services for violent relationships range from 40% to 80% . . . . complex PTSD [is seen] for those with prolonged exposure to repeated trauma, as in domestic violence . . . . traumatic stress has been shown to effect cognitive appraisals, cognitive schemas, symptom expression, and resolution, as well as behavioral action . . . . Healing the trauma of relationship violence is central to the stay-leave process . . . . perceived self-efficacy is the greatest predictor of behavioral change . . . [and is] viewed as essential to the maintenance of action . . . . Coping is viewed as a psychological resource that helps individuals . . . adapt to stressful periods . . . . women in response to violence tend to generally use passive coping, whereas avoidant strategies have been identified when social and institutional resources are unavailable . . . . Passive and avoidant coping styles may be the most adaptive responses to danger . . ."

"Women most recently out of violent relationships within six months function significantly differently from other groups . . . . a return to the violent relationship is particularly likely at this time . . . . the time period six months after leaving the relationship may be the most psychologically intense and vulnerable time . . . . this group is unique for low confidence about leaving and temptation to return is still high; demand on coping resources is high; and the trauma symptoms such as sleep disturbance, depression, and dissociation are high . . . . Symptoms of depression may be particularly troublesome, whereas post-sexual abuse trauma (PSAT) symptoms such as flashbacks and sexual problems may serve to bolster confidence for leaving . . . . Women recently out of a violent relationship may be in danger or facing many challenges associated with establishing independence . . . . Self-efficacy for leaving appears to be significantly related to symptoms of depression and relationship trauma . . . . Work to remediate domestic violence requires collaborative efforts in legal, medical, social, and psychological arenas addressing prevention, education, and intervention..."

Peterman, Linda M., and Dixon, Charlotte G. (2001). "Assessment and Evaluation of Men Who Batter Women". *Journal of Rehabilitation*, October/November/December, 2001, Vol.67, No4. Pp.38-42. National Rehabilitation Association

"... The National Coalition Against Domestic Violence reports that a woman is beaten by her intimate partner every fifteen seconds. The American Medical Association reports that about 50% of all women will experience some type of domestic violence in their lifetime.... Violence is a behavior that includes any action or words that hurt another person. It involves the misuse of power with the intent of controlling or oppressing another person, and may be defined differently in each state.... A batterer is someone who uses not only physical abuse, but emotional abuse, sexual abuse, economic abuse, and other behaviors that assert control and power.... This control over another person is gained through fear and intimidation.... the male is the abuser in 95% of domestic violence cases... The batterer comes from every social, economic, ethnic, professional, educational, and religious group... Most batterers do not have criminal records and are almost never violent with anyone except their partner.... Batterers frequently have low self-esteem and believe that others are to blame for their problems. The batterer fears abandonment such as divorce, separation, imagined infidelity, or pregnancy, and tends to resort to violence rather than looking for other solutions to the problem..."

"... there are three types of batterers.... (T)he typical batterer usually has no diagnosable mental illness or personality disorder, is no more likely than anyone else to have substance abuse issues, is not violent to people outside the family, and has no criminal record. The sociopathic batterer views violence as an acceptable way of dealing with problems, may have a diagnosable personality disorder, and is likely to have a problem with substance abuse...."

The anti-social batterer usually has diagnosable mental illnesses or personality disorders, substance abuse problems, and a criminal history . . ."

"A detailed assessment of the batterer is essential in order to promote effective treatment . . ." The author recommends these types of assessment tools: 1) Psychosocial Assessment—includes a self-report of the present problem and related history; previous episodes of violence; most recent, and worst violent behaviors in the relationship; violence in family of origin; work history, finances, support system; treatment history; 2) Record Retrieval—past records including police reports, civil and criminal court cases, past arrests, injunction for protection orders, etc.; 3) Role Playing—A quantitative assessment in which the counselor asks the client to role play an argument with his partner; 4) The Assessment Inventory—The Abusive Relationships Inventory is used to "assess the attitudes and beliefs of men who have been physically, mentally or sexually abusive toward their partners. It measures the batterer's tendency to rationalize abusive behaviors and to project blame onto the partner;" 5) Victim reports—"Batterers tend to minimize and underreport their behavior and may attempt to manipulate the counselor. Therefore it is often helpful to assess the batterer's non-physically abusive behaviors such as emotional/mental abuse, social isolation, financial abuse, verbal abuse . . . . Carefully consider the safety of the victim when choosing to involve him in the process . . . ." 6) Substance Abuse Assessment—if the initial intake assessment indicates drug/alcohol abuse; 7) Mental Health Assessment—a comprehensive developmental, social, and medical history can reveal past and present psychiatric disorders; 8) Homicide Assessment—Risk can be assessed: a) one who threatens homicide or suicide; b) if the batterer has fantasies of homicide or suicide and has a plan that includes who, when where, and how; c) Does the batterer have weapons, and has threatened to use them in the past; d) the presence of depression; e) separation is the most dangerous time for the partner of the batterer; f) Attitudes that indicate homicide risk: claiming ownership of his partner, stating she will never be free of him, idolizing his partner, believing he is entitled to her obedience and loyalty; g) when a batterer disobeys court orders such as injunctions, makes public scenes, and exhibits other socially unacceptable behavior in public . . ."

**Note:** The following resource is given due to the race of the characters in the story. There are many articles available that address racial and ethnic sensitivity for many racial and ethnic groups:

Williams, Oliver J. (1994). "Group Work with African American Men Who Batter: Toward More Ethnically Sensitive Practice". *Journal of Comparative Family Studies*, Spring, Vol.25, Is.1. Pp.91-103. University of Calgary

45. **Violence Against Social Workers** :

MacDonald, Grant, and Sirotich, Frank. (2001, April). "Reporting Client Violence". *Social Work,* Vol.46, Is.2. Pp.107-114. Copyright, 2001, National Association of Social Workers, Inc., *Social Work*

"[Abstract by Author] . . . The study discussed in this article documents the prevalence of client violence among a sample of social workers from a broad range of social work settings. It examines respondents' reasons for not reporting or reporting client violence to management . . . . The majority of respondents had experienced some form of violence from clients. Approximately one quarter of respondents indicated that they did not report the incident . . ."

Sarkisian, Gregor V., Ph.D, and Portswood, Sharon G., Ph.D (2003). "Client Violence Against Social Workers: From Increased Worker Responsibility and Administrative Mishmash to Effective Prevention Policy." *Administration in Social Work*, (2003). Vol.27, Is.4. Pp. 41-59. Binghamton NY: The Haworth Press

"Violence has been a common characteristic of most social work agencies, although it is believed that the majority of incidents go unreported due to worker's fears that they will be evaluated as incompetent by colleagues and administrators, [and] that their situations will not be viewed sympathetically .... Physical attacks typically include incidents in which a client comes in direct contact with a social worker with an intent to do harm; verbal threats tend to include verbally abusive language or physical gestures that indicate an intent to harm a worker; and property damage refers to physical damage that has occurred to the worker's private property or agency property .... (T)he new millennium presents challenges for today's workers that did not exist previously, including: increased violence perpetrated by women, violence attributable to the deinstitutionalization movement, psychotropic drug refusal by discharged patients, the right to refuse treatment, social-control issues in both adult and children's protective service delivery, new intervention roles in domestic violence situations, police-social worker teams, custody and divorce settlements . . ."

46. **A brief history of Alcoholics Anonymous**: The following excerpt is taken from "Forward to the Second Edition," contained in *Alcoholics Anonymous, the Fourth Edition of the Big Book*. (2001). New York City: Alcoholics Anonymous World Services, Inc. Pp.XV-XVII:

"The spark that was the flare into the first A.A. group was struck in Akron, Ohio, in June, 1935, during a talk between a new York stockbroker and an Akron physician. Six months earlier, the broker had been relieved of his drink obsession by a sudden spiritual experience, following a meeting with an alcoholic friend who had been in contact with the Oxford Groups of that day. He has also been greatly helped by the late Dr. William D. Silkworth, a New York specialist in alcoholism who is now accounted no less than a medical saint by A.A. members . . . . From this doctor, the broker had learned the grave nature of alcoholism. Though he could not accept the tenets of the Oxford Groups, he was convinced of the need for moral inventory, confession of personality defects, restitution to those harmed, helpfulness to others, and the necessity of belief in and dependence upon God . . . . [The broker] suddenly realized that in order to save himself he must carry his message to another alcoholic. That alcoholic turned out to be the Akron physician . . . . the physician began to pursue the spiritual remedy for his malady . . . . He sobered, never to drink again up to the moment of his death in 1950. This seemed to prove that one alcoholic could affect another as no nonalcoholic could . . . . (T)he two men set to work almost frantically upon alcoholics arriving in a ward of the Akron City Hospital . . . . There were many failures, but there was an occasional heartening success. When the broker returned to New York in the fall of 1935, the first A. A. group had actually been formed, though no one realized it at the time. A second small group promptly formed in New York, to be followed in 1937 with the start of a third in Cleveland . . . . By late 1937, the number of members having substantial sobriety time behind them was sufficient to convince the membership that a new light had entered the dark world of the alcoholic . . ." In the spring of 1939 the first edition of Alcoholics Anonymous was published.

## *The Twelve Steps:*

(1) We admitted we were powerless over alcohol, and that our lives had become unmanageable;

(2) Came to believe that a Power greater than ourselves could restore us to sanity;

(3) Made a decision to turn our will and our lives over to the care of God as we understood Him;

(4) Made a searching and fearless moral inventory of ourselves;

(5) Admitted to God, to ourselves, and to another human being the exact nature of our wrongs;

(6) Were entirely ready to have God remove all these defects of character;

(7) Humbly asked Him to remove our shortcomings;

(8) Made a list of all persons we had harmed, and became willing to make amends to them all;

(9) Made direct amends to such people wherever possible, except when to do so would injure them or others;

(10) Continued to take personal inventory and when we were wrong promptly admitted it;

(11) Sought through prayer and meditation to improve our conscious contract with God as we understood Him, praying only for knowledge of His will for us and the power to carry that out;

(12) Having had a spiritual awakening as the result of these steps, we tried to carry this message to alcoholics, and to practice these principles in all our affairs.

Excerpt taken from: *Alcoholics Anonymous, Fourth Edition of the Big Book* (2001). New York City: Alcoholics Anonymous World Services, Inc. Pp.59-60

"The excerpts from Alcoholics Anonymous are reprinted with permission of Alcoholics Anonymous World Services, Inc. (AAWS). Permission to reprint these excerpts does not mean that AAWS has reviewed or approved the contents of this publication, or that AAWS necessarily agrees with the views expressed herein. A.A. is a program of recovery from alcoholism *only*—use of these excerpts in connection with programs and activities which are patterned after A.A., but which address other problems, or in any other non A.A. context, does not imply otherwise."

47. **DSM-IV-TR Criteria for Differential Diagnosis: Substance Dependence vs. Substance Abuse**:

**Substance Dependence**: "The essential feature of Substance Dependence is a cluster of cognitive, behavioral, and physiological symptoms indicating that the individual continues use of the substance despite significant substance-related problems. There is a pattern or repeated self-administration that can result in tolerance, withdrawal, and compulsive drug-taking behavior. A diagnosis of Substance Dependence can be applied to every class of substances except caffeine (p.192) . . ."

**Substance Abuse**: "The essential feature of Substance Abuse is a maladaptive pattern of substance use manifested by recurrent and significant adverse consequences related to repeated use of substances. In order for an Abuse criterion to be met, the substance-related problem must have occurred repeatedly during the same twelve month period or been persistent. There may be repeated failure to fulfill major role obligations, repeated use in situations in which it is physically hazardous, multiple legal problems, and recurrent social and interpersonal problems (Criterion A). Unlike the criteria for Substance Dependence, the criteria for Substance Abuse does not include tolerance, withdrawal, or a pattern of compulsive use and instead include only the harmful consequences of repeated use. A diagnosis of Substance Abuse is preempted by the diagnosis of Substance Dependence if the individual's pattern of substance use has ever met the Criteria for Dependence for that class of substances (Criterion B, p.198) . . ."

Excerpts taken from:

American Psychiatric Association (2000). "Substance-Related Disorders." *Diagnostic and Statistical Manual of Mental Disorders, 4th Edition, Text Revised.* Washington, DC: The American Psychiatric Association. Pp.192; 198

# Chapter Five

**48. DSM-IV-TR Criteria for 309.81 Posttraumatic Stress Disorder:**

"The essential feature of Posttraumatic Stress Disorder is the development of characteristic symptoms following exposure to an extreme traumatic stressor involving direct personal experience of an event that involves actual or threatened death or serious injury, or other threat to one's physical integrity; or witnessing an event that involves death, injury or threat to the physical integrity of another person; or learning about unexpected or violent death, serious harm, or threat of death or injury experienced by family or a close associate. The person's response to the event must involve intense fear, helplessness or horror (in children . . . disorganized or agitated behavior) . . . . The characteristic symptoms resulting from the exposure to the extreme trauma include persistent re-experiencing of the traumatic event, persistent avoidance of stimuli associated with the trauma and numbing of general responsiveness, and persistent symptoms of increased arousal. The full symptom picture must be present for more than 1 month, and disturbance must cause clinically significant distress or impairment in social, occupational, or to other important areas of functioning . . ."

"The traumatic event can be re-experienced in various ways. Commonly, the person has recurrent and intrusive recollections of the event or recurring distressing dreams during which the event can be replayed or otherwise represented. In rare instances, the person experiences dissociative states . . . during which components of the event are relived, and the person behaves as though experiencing the event at that moment. These episodes, often referred to as "flashbacks," are typically brief but can be associated with prolonged distress and heightened arousal. Intense psychological distress or physiological activity often occurs when the person is exposed to triggering events that resemble or symbolize an aspect of the traumatic event . . ."

"The individual has persistent symptoms of anxiety or increased arousal that were not present before the trauma. These symptoms may include difficulty falling or staying asleep that may be due to recurrent nightmares during which the traumatic event is relived, hypervigilance, and exaggerated startle response. Some individuals report irritability or outbursts of anger, or difficulty concentrating or completing tasks . . . (Pp.463-468)"

Note: 308.3 Acute Stress Disorder has similar etiology and symptom characteristics, but the disturbance lasts " . . . for a minimum of two days and a maximum of four weeks and occurs within four weeks of the traumatic event . . . (Pp.471-472)"

Excerpts taken from:

American Psychiatric Association (2000). *Diagnostic and Statistical Manual of Mental Disorders 4th Edition, Text Revised*. Washington, DC: American Psychiatric Association. Pp.463-472

49. **Exposure and other therapies used in treating Posttraumatic Stress Disorder**:

Marotta, Sylvia (2000, Fall). "Best Practices for Counselors Who Treat Posttraumatic Stress Disorder". *Journal of Counseling and Development*, Vol.78, Is.4. Pp.492-495

This article offers 11 guidelines for best counseling practices when trying to prevent, or to treat PTSD. " . . . the most highly recommended techniques are anxiety management, cognitive therapy, exposure therapy, and psychoeducation . . . exposure therapy for intrusive thoughts, flashbacks, trauma-related fears, and avoidance; cognitive therapy for guilt and shame symptoms; and anxiety management for hyperarousal and sleep disturbances. Play therapy is recommended for children and younger adolescents . . . . [If medication is warranted] the experts prefer the selective serotonin reuptake inhibitors (SSRIs) as the first line of treatment . . ."

50. **A great resource on the struggles of blue collar people in white collar jobs**:

Lubrano, Alfred (2004). *Limbo: Blue Collar Roots, White Collar Dreams*. Hoboken, NJ: John Wiley and Sons, Inc.

"I was a working-class kid from Brooklyn who crossed into the middle class after acquiring a college degree. After a time, it occurred to me that I was becoming a different person from my parents, and I was becoming part of a different class altogether . . . . Straddlers. They were born to blue-collar families and then like me, moved into strange new territory of the middle class . . . As such, they straddled two worlds, many of them not feeling at home in either, living in a kind of American limbo . . . (Pp.1-2)"

# Chapter Six

51. A reference to: Huston, John (Director), and Spiegel, Sam (Producer). 1951. *The African Queen*. [film]. (Horizon Pictures and Romulus Films). Hollywood, Ca: United Artisits.

## 52. Coming Out Issues, the acceptance of one's Gay Identity:

Hellman, Ronald E., M.D., and Drescher, Jack, M.D. (eds.) (2004). *Handbook of LGBT Issues in Community Mental Health*. (simultaneously co-published as *Journal of Gay and Lesbian Psychotherapy*). Vol.8, Numbers 3/4. New York: Haworth Medical Press

"Although 'homosexuality' was removed from the Diagnostic and Statistical Manual of psychiatric disorders [DSM] in 1973, pathologizing of non-heterosexual identities still lingers (p.34) . . . (F)acing LGBT-insensitive environments requires expending tremendous energy to manage one's identity and self-presentation. Significant effort is required to manage fear, anxiety, and the unhelpful reactions of people from whom one might hope to get support: program staff, peers, and family. It is not implausible to assume that such stresses can distract a client's energy and attention from recovering his or her mental health, preclude bringing one's 'whole self' into treatment, and may lead to frustration, anger, isolation, and depression (as found with other experiences of discrimination) . . . (p.39)" Other issues related to a gay identity are discussed as follows: fear of rejection and loss of affection by family (p.32), by peers, employers, etc. (p.33); discrimination as the result of membership in a sexual minority (Pp.13-15); or perhaps the real loss of essential basic needs, including housing, finances, status, etc. (p.33); loss of relationship with a significant other; or relational issues, etc. The list is as boundless as is the human experience. (Note: page numbers coincide with the resource listed above). Discussion of these issues and the need for competent response by mental health professionals can be found in a composite of articles on the subject, as collected in:

Hellman, Ronald E., M.D., and Drescher, Jack, M.D. (eds.) (2004). *Handbook of LGBT Issues in Community Mental Health*. (simultaneously co-published as *Journal of Gay and Lesbian Psychotherapy*). Vol.8, Numbers 3/4. New York: Haworth Medical Press

Morrow, Deana F. (1996). "Coming Out Issues for Adult Lesbians: A Group Intervention". *Social Work*, November, 1996, Vol.41, Is.6, Pp.647-656. Copyright 1996, National Association of Social Workers, Inc., *Social Work*

"The study investigated the effects of a 10 week educational experimental group intervention—The Coming Out Issues Group—designed to address issues pertinent to adult lesbians, including lesbian identity development, homophobia and heterosexism, religious concerns, career concerns, family issues, sexism and racism, and assertiveness skills development. The impact of the intervention was assessed using various instruments in four areas: (1) ego development, (2) lesbian identity development, (3) empowerment, and (4) disclosure. The results indicated modest gains in ego development and lesbian identity development and major gains in empowerment and disclosure . . . Homophobia and heterosexism are oppressive social forces that serve as social silencing mechanisms . . . Those who invest themselves in keeping their sexual orientation a secret expend significant emotional energy to hide a central aspect of their identity. The emotional toll of secrecy can result in internalized shame and self-doubt . . ."

"The group process included both an educative and experimental format . . . The 10 group sessions were: (1) Introduction and Goals and Objectives, (2) Sexual Orientation, (3) Homophobia and Heterosexism and Communication Skills Training, (4) Sexism and Racism and Assertiveness Training, (5) Religion and Spirituality, (6) Workplace Issues, (7) Families and Significant Others—Lesbian Perspective (coming out issues and family), (8) Families and Significant Others—Guest Speakers, (9) Families and Significant Others—Self-determined choices about their degree of outness with their families, and (10) Costs and Benefits of Living Openly, and Closure . . . . Empowerment relates to the development of skills for controlling one's life in reaction to a heretofore socially powerless status . . . (T)he intervention sought to empower participants to determine their own coming-out decisions . . . . The Coming Out Issues Group appears to have had its most compelling impact on lesbian empowerment and disclosure . . . . Using this intervention, social workers have the opportunity to impart knowledge and initiate group discussion and reflection as tools for empowering adult lesbians about making coming out decisions . . ."

Ford, Vanessa E. (2003). "Coming Out as Lesbian or Gay: A Potential Precipitant of Crisis in Adolescence". *Journal of Human Behavior and the Social Environment.* (2003). Vol.8, Is.2/3, Pp.93-110. Binghamton, NY: The Haworth Press

[Abstract from Author] "The homosexual adolescent's decision to come out as gay or lesbian for the first time is a task which requires a certain level of inner and outer resources. Despite the fact that coming out is viewed by the literature as one of many necessary developmental steps in sexual identity formation and self-acceptance, coming out can be viewed as a unique stage in the developmental continuum . . . A whole host of factors, including identity confusion, low self-esteem, depression, alienation, withdrawal, substance abuse, and indulgence in self-destructive behavior, may result if the adolescent has little or no support in this critical developmental stage process. Involvement in the gay community or other types of homosexual peer groups offers a unique sense of support that is especially needed during this coming out period."

53. **Coping Issues and the Coming Out Process**:

Lucksted, Alicia, Ph.D. (2004) "Lesbian, Gay, Bisexual, and Transgender People Receiving Services in the Public Mental Health System: Raising Issues". Hellman, Ronald E., M.D., and Drescher, Jack, M.D. (eds.) (2004). *Handbook of LGBT Issues in Community Mental Health.* Vol.8, Numbers 3/4. New York: Haworth Medical Press. p.33:

**Family Stress and Safety Net**

"People with serious mental illnesses must often rely on family members for help with housing, finances, and emotional support, either as a matter of course or as a back up "last resort" (Schene, van Wijngaarden, and Koeter, 1998). However, information gathered in this study suggests that some LGBT people receiving mental health care may not be able to count on this "safety net" due to familial conflict or rejection regarding their sexual orientation or gender identity . . ."

54. **Substance Abuse and Homosexuality**:

Cabaj, Robert Paul, M.D. (1995). "Sexual Orientation and the Addictions". *Journal of Gay and Lesbian Psychotherapy.* Vol.2(3). Pp.97-117. Binghamton, NY: The Haworth Press.

" . . . as part of the early recovery process of getting clean and sober, sexual orientation must be discussed and ways to accept and live with being gay or lesbian explored. After six months of being clean and sober, a patient may be in a position to effectively utilize psychotherapy to explore and resolve internalized homophobia. Usually the desire to change sexual orientation subsequently disappears, and the patient learns how to fully accept and integrate a gay or lesbian identity into their new found sobriety . . . Gays and lesbians apparently have higher rates of substance abuse than the general population . . . approximately 30% for gay and lesbian populations . . . verses 10-12% for the general population . . . There is continuing and growing evidence that homosexual orientation may have genetic, biological, and biochemical components . . . . (S)uch knowledge . . . may help to relieve both the patients who are having difficulty accepting their homosexuality, and the families of patients who are gay or lesbian . . . . Homophobia itself also contributes to substance abuse in the gay communities . . . . All gay people have internalized homophobia, having been brought up in a homophobic society... The coming out process may be delayed or very difficult depending on the intensity of this internalized homophobia.... Substance use serves as an easy relief to the tensions created in gay men and lesbians in this developmental process (adolescence)... It is well known that alcohol and many other drugs can cause depression which will lead to a worsening of self-esteem—the erosion of spirit..." The author recommends use of a 12 Step Program, with the following points noted: "... (G)iving up or avoiding old friends... may be difficult when the gay person has limited contacts who relate to him as a gay person. Such isolation may lead to relapse... (T)he selection of a sponsor may be difficult... (M)any gays mistakenly link AA and religion. Since religious institutions in general have been hostile and rejecting of gays, even more resistance to trying AA or NA may develop... Once gay people are clean and sober, they will need to reintegrate into a homophobic society. Gay sensitive individual and or group psychotherapy in addition to gay-sensitive recovery work may be necessary for many gay patients in early recovery..."

55. A reference to: Roddenberry, Gene (1966). *Star Trek* [television series]. New York: NBC

## Chapter Seven

**56. Child Abuse Investigation and Issues**:

Pressel, David M. (2000). "Evaluation of Physical Abuse in Children". *American Family Physician,* May 15, 2000, Vol.61, Is.10

"A history that is inconsistent with the patient's injuries is a hallmark of abuse. A pattern of physical findings, including bruises and fractures in areas unlikely to be accidentally injured, patterned bruises from objects, and circumferential burns or bruises in children not yet mobile should be viewed as suspicious for child abuse . . ."

"The location of bruises can sometimes be suggestive of accidental verses nonaccidental trauma. Children commonly fall and scrape or bruise the skin covering anterior parts of the body such as the shins, knees, hands, elbows, nose, periorbital area and forehead. Unexplained injuries to protected parts of the body such as the buttocks, thighs, torso, frenulum, ears, and neck are suggestive of child abuse . . . . Bruises are rare in infants who do not cruise or walk. The shape or pattern of injury may also suggest inflicted trauma. Bruises in the shapes of handprints, belts, buckles, cord loops, or encirclements represent child physical abuse . . . ."

"Cigarette burns leave centimeter-sized circular marks on the skin. Scold marks on the hands, feet, or buttocks that have a glove, sock, or circular appearance and spare the intertriginous areas are caused by deliberate immersion of the child in a sink or bathtub of hot water . . . ."

"Retinal hemorrhages are highly suspicious for abuse resulting from shaken baby syndrome . . . . All fractures must be interpreted in the context of the child's developmental ability and the history of injury . . . A complete skeletal survey is indicated in children younger than two years when physical abuse is suspected . . ."

The article concludes with a **series of photographs of injuries to children**, and includes text explaining the diagnostic factors.

Reproduced with permission from *Evaluation of Physical Abuse in Children*, the May 15, 2000 issue of American Family Physician. Copyright 2000. American Academy of Family Physicians. All rights reserved.

Besharov, Douglas J. (1990). *Recognizing Child Abuse: A Guide for the Concerned*. New York: The Free Press.

This book is a good resource for social workers interested in the investigation and prosecution of child abuse. Along with the history of child protective services, the book offers graphic depictions of indicators of child abuse, as well as charts and checklists on such topics as suspicious situations, children's behaviors used to assess ambiguous situations, and emotional maltreatment. The book concludes with measures used to build a case, including instruction on completion of child abuse reports, and the preservation of evidence. The book also provides supportive information to parents accused of abuse.

57. A Reference to: McLean, Don. (1971). "American Pie". On *American Pie* [audio album]. New York: Mediarts/United Artists

58. A reference to: Ruby, Joe and Spears, Ken (1969). *Scooby-Doo* [CBS animated television series]. Studio City, Ca: Hanna-Barbara

59. **Psychological Impact of Divorce on Children**:

Hetherington, E. Mavis, and Stanley-Hagan, Margaret (1999). "The Adjustment of Children with Divorced Parents: A Risk and Resiliency Perspective." *Journal of Child Psychology and Psychiatry*. (1999). Vol.40, Is.1. Pp.129-140

"Many current researchers take a life course, risk, and resiliency perspective to studying marital transactions . . . They recognize that divorce is just one step in a series of family transitions that affect family relationships and children's adjustment, and that experiences in the family anteceding divorce, and life in a single parent family and possible further marital transitions following divorce, will impact on children's adjustment . . . (A)lthough divorce may be associated with stressful changes and challenges in family members' lives, it also may present a chance for escape from conflict, for more harmonious, fulfilling relationships, and the opportunity for greater personal growth, individuation, and well-being . . . Regardless of circumstances, many children experience problems in the months immediately following parental divorce. As family roles, relationships, and circumstances change, children are often depressed, anxious, angry, demanding, noncompliant, and antisocial and experience a drop in school performance . . . For many children, problems diminish with time as the family restabilizes but, on average, children of divorced parents are less socially, emotionally, and academically well-adjusted than children in nondivorced families . . . . problems can emerge or re-emerge later in life as they confront new challenges and developmental tasks . . . (A)dolescence also may trigger problems in children from divorced families who have previously been functioning reasonably well. The developmental demands in adolescence and early adulthood for self-regulated, autonomous behavior, academic and vocational attainment, and the formation of intimate relationships may be especially difficult and may precipitate or exacerbate problems in adjustment in the offspring of divorced parents . . . However, the effects of divorce are not necessarily adverse. Children who move from a conflictual, abusive, or neglecting family situation to a more harmonious one show diminished problems following divorce . . . ."

" . . . (Y)ounger children may be more affected by divorce than older children and adolescents because they are less able to understand family events, are more likely to blame themselves and fear total abandonment, and have less access to possible support in relationships outside the family . . . [but most studies] find equally negative effects for older children and adolescents . . . . (p.132)"

"In all families, including divorced single-parent families, children's adjustment is associated with the quality of the parenting environment . . . Children need parents who are warm and supportive, communicative, responsive to their needs, exert firm, consistent control and positive discipline, and monitor their activities closely . . . . psychological and health problems compromise the ability of parents to be responsive and sensitive to their children's needs . . . ."

"In contrast to fathers, who suffer only a 10% decline in income following divorce, it is common for custodial mothers to experience a 25% to 45% drop in the family's annual income . . . . (N)ewly divorced mothers are three times as likely to be unemployed and, if employed, are more likely to experience job loss . . ."

60. **National Figures Regarding Annual Foster Placements**:

Temple-Plotz, Lana, M.S., Stricklett, Ted, M.S., Baker, Christena B., M.S.W., Sterba, Michael, M.H.D. (eds.) (2002). *Foster Care Solutions: Practical Tools for Foster Parents*. Boys Town, Nebraska: Boys Town Press. p. 2

"According to studies, the number of children removed from their families by the child welfare system continues to grow. During the 1980s, an estimated 260,000 children were in out-of-home care. By 1997, that figure had increased to more than 500,000. And many of these children had special needs (Annie E. Casey Foundation, 2000) . . . ."

Shirk, Martha, and Stangler, Gary. (2004). *On Their Own: What Happens to Kids When They Age Out of the Foster Care System*. Boulder, Colorado: Basic Books. Pp.4-5.

"Between 1980 and 2001, the number of children in foster care in the United States grew from 302,000 to 542, 000. Ominously, the rate of placement nearly doubled, from 4.7 per 1,000 children to 7.7, which means that a higher proportion of children than before are spending time in foster care . . . Those placed in foster care are most often victims of some form of neglect—failure to provide the basics of life, such as food, clothes, housing or failure to supervise—and in the vast majority of cases (nearly 60.5%), these are failures of parents, with poverty, ignorance, and alcohol and drug abuse being contributing factors. In a minority of cases—35%—the reasons for removal are physical abuse, sexual abuse, or severe emotional abuse.... Only a minority of child abuse reports result in a child being placed in foster care. In 2002, there were more than 3 million reports of suspected maltreatment, of which, more than one-third—896,000—were substantiated. Less than one-fifth of these children—169,000—were removed from their homes.... (N)early one-half are eleven or older. And about one-fifth—100,000—are sixteen or older..."

61. **Adolescent Foster Placement and Aging Out of the System**:

Shirk, Martha, and Stangler, Gary (2004). *On Their Own: What Happens To Kids When They Age Out of the Foster Care System.* Boulder, Colorado: Basic Books. p.5

" . . . Although the rise in overall numbers has made it increasingly difficult to find family settings for all ages of children, this is especially true for teenagers. They are by nature rebellious and difficult to work with, so relatively few foster families are willing to try. As a result, only 60 percent of children fourteen and older live in foster or pre-adoptive homes, compared with more than 90 percent of younger children... Nationwide, the mean stay for children who exited foster care in 2001 was just over twenty-two months, and the median stay was just under a year, though both indicators vary widely among states. Nine percent of children who left in 2001 had been in care five years or more... Each year, between 18,500 and 25,000 teenagers 'age out' of foster care by virtue of reaching the age at which their legal right to foster care ends (19,008 in 2001). Another 5,200 or so run away from foster care before they age out... Generally, the teens who age out of foster care entered care as teenagers, although many have spent their lives in the system... For most of the child welfare system's history, most states did little to prepare the children in their custody for life in the real world... President Clinton signed the bill into law on December 14, 1999. The law is commonly referred to the Chaffee Act, in honor of the late Rhode Island senator, John H. Chafee, a longtime champion of children's issues. Among other provisions, this law requires states to identify teens who are likely to remain in foster care until age eighteen and to help them prepare for self-sufficiency . . . (and provides) career exploration, job placement and retention services, and vocational training. And it permits states to provide assistance with room and board up to 30 percent of their federal allocations . . . (but) neither the funds appropriated nor the state and county systems charged with spending them are adequate to the challenge . . ."

62. **Instability of Foster Placements**:

A good statistical resource for foster placement information can by obtained from: The Adoption and Foster Care Analysis System Reports(AFCARS) found as a part of the Child Welfare Outcomes Reports produced annually by: U.S. Department of Health and Human Services, Administration on Children, Youth, and Families, (Washington, DC: U.S. Government Printing Office) [Online]

Available at: http://www.acf.hhs.gov/programs/cb/pubs/cwo

## 63. Potential Loss of Key Supports Due to a Gay Identity

Lucksted, Alicia, Ph.D. (2004). "Lesbian, Gay, Bisexual, and Transgender People Receiving Services in the Public Mental Health System: Raising Issues". Hellman, Ronald E., M.D., and Drescher, Jack, M.D. (eds.) (2004) *Handbook of LGBT Issues in Community Mental Health*. New York: Haworth Press. Pp.32-33

"It took me a long time to build my life back up again after that (a disastrous phone call to family made at the insistence of her social worker). I believe that the social worker did not really have any idea about the issues of a family totally disowning someone for being gay—how strong homophobia is, and that it (homophobia) is not going to be 'cured' by a phone call (KI Lynn D'Orsay, February, 1998) . . . ."

"For individuals diagnosed with serious mental illness who are LGBT, homophobic attitudes among providers of mental health services, and mental health programs which are heterosexist, create barriers to recovery and detract from the effectiveness of treatment and support services.(Chassman, 1996, p.1-2) . . ."

"Key informants and other data sources said that harassment and belittlement of people known to be lesbian, gay, bisexual, and/or transgender by other clients is common . . . (V)erbal derogation from those who are uncomfortable or hostile towards LGBT people is abundant, threats are not infrequent, and staff often seem to passively excuse both. One person commented, 'Patients in the system also panic; there is lots of homophobia and transphobia, and attacks and harassment. And the staff will usually ignore it, condone it by their inactivity' . . ."

Kennedy, Nancy J. (2004). "National and Public Infrastructure and Policy: Are We Experiencing Scientific McCarthyism?" Shankle, Michael D., M.P.H. (ed.). *The Handbook of Lesbian, Gay, Bisexual, and Transgender Public Health: A Practitioner's Guide to Service*. (2004). New York: Harrington Park Press. Pp.306; 309

"For many sexual minorities working for DHHS, the change in administration meant 'return to the closet'. The Military's 'Don't ask, don't tell' refrain was mimicked within DHHS. Some agencies within the operating divisions of DHHS dismantled their internal workgroups addressing the concerns of not only LGBT employees but also LGBT populations served by the agency . . . (p.306)"

"Given the passage of the Patriot Act that erodes civil liberties, the president's proposed constitutional amendment against same-sex marriage, and the encasement of politics with a fundamentalist Christian framework that uses the literal interpretation of the Bible to rally against the 'immoralities' of homosexuality, the federal government is, once again, not a safe work environment for individuals who are sexual minorities . . . (309)"

64. **Discussion of Behavioral and Psychological Issues of Adolescent Foster Children**:

Temple-Plotz, Lana, M.S., Stricklett, Ted P., M.S., Baker, Christena B., M.S.W., and Sterba, Michael N., M.H.D. (eds.) (2002). *Foster Care Solutions: Practical Tools for Foster Parents*. Boys Town, Nebraska: Boys Town Press. Pp.6; 16

"Many children in foster care have not yet learned how to develop positive relationships. Others misuse what they have learned, and some simply don't understand how it's done. It might not be easy for them to make and keep friends. They might have problems getting along with adults in authority (parents, teachers, employers, and others), and they also might have trouble forming attachments to those that care for them (p.6) . . . . [They] may also have difficulty identifying and setting proper boundaries. They may make poor choices about friends, perhaps trusting people they shouldn't trust or distancing themselves from others who would be good influences . . . (p16)"

# Chapter Eight

65. A reference to: "Born To Run" by Bruce Springsteen. Copyright © 1975, Bruce Springsteen, renewed © 2003 Bruce Springsteen (ASCAP). Reprinted by permission. International copyright secured. All rights reserved.

66. **Philosophy and Controversy About When Foster Placement is Necessary**:

Zuravin, Susan J., and DePanfilis, Diane. (1997). "Factors Affecting Foster Care Placement of Children Receiving Child Protective Services". *Social Work Research*. March, 1997, Vol.21, Is.1. Pp.34-44. Copyright 1997, National Association of Social Workers, Inc., *Social Work Research*

The authors studied the files of 1035 families whose children entered foster care between 1988 and 1989 from a mid-Atlantic city, in effort to find placement predictors, or correlates that are commonly viewed as a need for foster placement by caseworkers. While they provided stipulation as to the probable accuracy of their research, as well as to its limitations, they could draw numerous correlations, quoted as follows. They prefaced their study with observations about the child protective services system:

"The child protective services system (CPS) decision-making process is driven by one objective: the protection of children from further maltreatment. Of the intervention options that can be directed toward this goal, placement of a child in substitute care is the most radical, because of the costs to society and the disruptive life effects for child and family . . . (C)aseworkers and juvenile court judges—the key decision-makers—work without guidelines (Lindsey, 1992b; Pecora, Whittaker, and Maluccio, 1992). Consequently, decisions are unreliable (Lindsey, 1992b) and are subject to individual biases and idiosyncratic factors (Pecora et al., 1992) . . . (p.35)"

"Families with a recurrence of maltreatment as well as families in which the mother had problems stemming from substance abuse, mental health difficulties, developmental limitations, and domestic violence were more likely to experience placement. Families who were substantiated for physical abuse only and for neglect-only were less likely to experience placement than those who had more than one type of maltreatment. Families receiving AFDC as well as mothers who were younger than 18.5 years were more likely to experience placement. Race was not associated with placement.... If recurrence existed (multiple abuse or neglect incidents), the likelihood of placement increased by a factor of 1.3. In addition, neglect-only families were less likely to experience placement by about 25% than families with multiple types of maltreatment; physical abuse-only families were equally as likely as families with multiple types of maltreatment to experience placement... Mothers with drug problems or both drug and alcohol problems were 2.29 times more likely to experience placement than those without such problems, yet mothers with only alcohol problems were equally likely as those without any substance abuse problems to experience placement... (p.40)"

\* \* \*

### And now, some discussion

**Strong opinion is pretty common** when we learn that a child has died from abuse and neglect. "The State should have done more!" we proclaim, as we point a finger, and then turn our attentions elsewhere. But the "State" is really just people—the you's and me's of this world—who come upon a situation and either turn from it, or decide to act on it. No one really knows until the very end, what the best decision would be. That's called hindsight. But some things we do know—each of us comes upon any situation with a set of beliefs that we've formulated over our lives, from the bits and pieces—the scraps of experience—that we've molded into our own reality as we've moved along. These beliefs about the world and how it should function help us through a million different decisions we make each day. These beliefs will determine if we act, or if we ignore; if we become involved, or if we block out the images; if we engage in life, or if we take refuge in the numbness.

**Refer back to the case scenario** of the 19 year old alcoholic mother in partial recovery, and her two year old child (page 317). This was the Jordan Mathews' case that John Crittenden had criticized. Human behavior is not ruled by concrete laws of cause and effect. Although much of the CPS work is then based on judgment call, this has been minimized somewhat by the risk assessment guidelines that have become more standardized over the years. Yet, even the application and interpretation of these tools are subject to one's judgment. Add the complicating factors of race, class, and education—and the difference in perspectives between the clients and the caseworkers who evaluate them become even more pronounced. Next, let's factor in the politics of a bureaucracy often under fire by the public and the media. Now, analyze the scenario according to the Strengths Perspective, an intervention technique that builds on the client's positive aspects to create a case plan that promotes positive change. Jordan's working class background lent many commonalities that she used to bridge understanding with the client. Crittenden was from a middle class background, whose values, experiences, and belief systems were much farther removed from the experience of the client. But does that difference equate to risk, as he perceived? Who would more likely see potential for the client's success? How would these different perspectives impact on the case plan, the goals, and on the outcome? Now the big question—so what would you do?

**The clashes between Jordan and Crittenden** represent the convergence of the old and the new. This struggle represents the differing political, sociological, and societal thoughts as expressed in human services policy today. Jordan's approach is much in line with the Child Welfare Act of 1980. Essentially, this Act mandated that the child welfare system provide reasonable resources to remedy abusive and neglectful situations that might cause a child's harm, or lead to his removal from the home. This act recognized child removal as the course of last resort, because of the devastating effects such removal can have on child and family. The Adoption and Safe Families Act of 1997 represents the Crittenden view that children are entitled to live in a safe environment, and less considers the harmful effects of a child's removal from his natural family and home. This Act was introduced to address the issue of multiple foster care placements, by moving children more quickly to permanency. Among other requirements, the Act stipulates that a permanency hearing be held within 12 months of placement, and that hearings for termination of parental rights occur if a child has been in substitute care for 15 of the prior 22 months.

Given the difficulties and the great losses that most children experience in adjusting to foster care, we must scrutinize closely whether we are sacrificing attachment needs (and causing the potential behavioral, mental health, and aging out issues of the future), for the security of a "risk-free" environment today. This is an especially critical question, when one considers the small number of children seriously harmed or killed from abuse and neglect vs. the great number of children who are referred for child protective services annually. While even one child seriously harmed or killed is intolerable, the fact remains that even under the best of circumstances—and even in the best of families—children can become victims. Harm only takes a momentary loss of control or inattention. And no one can foresee or prevent all incidents from occurring. Should a potential risk be used to justify such extreme interventions as child removal then? Certainly, we should not remove a child from his natural home except under the most serious, and verifiable, circumstances. Given the success of many remedial and preventive interventions (ie: adequate day care for children; substance abuse treatment for addicted parents), we should first exhaust all remedial strategies that can be used to minimize risk. If a child still cannot reside safely in the home of his parents, we should secondarily strive to stabilize that child in the home of a close relative. Under no circumstances should poverty, in itself, be a cause for child removal, and in no good conscience should cost be used as a reason to avoid rehabilitation of these families. What becomes apparent, then, is the need to balance between a child's perceived risk, and his right to be raised in his family of origin. Striking this balance is one of the biggest challenges to human services/child protective services in the 21st Century.

\* \* \*

Alexander, Rudolph, Jr. (1995). "The Impact of Suter v. Artist M. on Foster Care Policy". *Social Work*, July, 1995, Vol.40, Is.4. Pp.543-548. Copyright 1995, National Association of Social Workers, Inc., *Social Work*

"The passage of the Child Welfare Act of 1980 represented the first step in permanency planning for foster children. First, it mandated that each state, by submitting a specific plan, commit to making reasonable efforts to prevent the removal of children from their families and to return them as soon as reasonably possible. Second, beginning October 1, 1983, a judicial determination had to be made that reasonable efforts were used to prevent the removal of each child from his or her family before foster placement was made."

\* \* \*

## Statistical Comparisons: The Child Maltreatment Reports, and the AFCARS Reports

The Child Maltreatment Reports and the Adoption and Foster Care Analysis Reports (AFCARS) are compiled annually from the national child abuse and neglect data system, a mandatory reporting system used by the 50 states, Puerto Rico and Washington, D.C. The Child Maltreatment Reports include demographic and statistical analyses of child abuse and neglect investigation, trends, effectiveness of intervention, etc. The Adoption and Foster Care Analysis Reports (AFCARS) provide demographic and statistical information on children residing in out of home placements.

1999 was the 10th consecutive year of publication of the national child abuse and neglect data (NCANDS). Much of the data included is the result of mandatory reporting by states to the Secretary of Health and Human Services as required by the Child Abuse Prevention and Treatment Act (CAPTA) as amended.

*Child Maltreatment, 1999,* provides the following: "Of the estimated 2,974,000 referrals received (by child protective service agencies nationally), approximately three-fifths (60.4%) were transferred for investigation or assessment, and two-fifths (39.6%) were screened out. Slightly less than one-third of the investigations (29.2%) resulted in a disposition of either substantiated or indicated child maltreatment. More than half (54.7%) resulted in a finding that child maltreatment was not substantiated. There were an estimated 826,000 victims of child maltreatment nationwide. The 1999 rate of victimization, 11.8% per 1,000 children, decreased from the 1998 rate of 12.6%. Almost three-fifths of all victims suffered neglect, while one-fifth (21.3%) suffered physical abuse; 11.3% were sexually abused. More than one-third (35.9%) of all victims were reported to be victims of other or additional types of maltreatment . . . . An estimated 1,100 children died of abuse and neglect (nationally), a rate of approximately 1.62 deaths per 100,000 children in the general population . . . Slightly more than 2% (2.1%) of all fatalities occurred while the victim was in foster care . . ."

U.S. Department of Health and Human Services, Administration on Children, Youth, and Families. *Child Maltreatment, 1999.* (Washington, DC: U.S. Government Printing Office, 2001). [Online] Available at:http://www.acf.hhs.gov/programs/cb/pubs/cm99/pdf (9/19/09)

*The AFCARS Report, 1999* (Adoption and Foster Care Analysis Reporting System) provides the following: "There were 581,000 children in foster care nationally on 9/30/1999. The mean age was 9.9 years old; the median age was 10.1 years old. 4% of the children were under age 1 year. Of the children in alternate care settings, 4% (22,484) were in pre-adoptive homes; 26% (151,864) were in foster care with a relative. 47% (274,100), were in foster care with a non-relative. 8% (46,279) were in group homes. 10% (57,590) were in institutions.

42% (242,571) of children in out of home placements had a case goal of reunification with parent or primary caretaker. 5% (26,368) had a case goal of living with an other relative. 8% (48,828) had long term foster care as a case goal. 19% (107,581) had adoption as a case goal. 18% (105,084) had not yet had a designated case goal."

U.S. Department of Health and Human Services, Administration on Children, Youth, and Families. Statistics and Research. *Child Welfare Outcomes, 1999, Appendix C: The AFCARS Report[Online]*
Available at: http://www.acf.hhs.gov/programs/cb/cwo99/apps/appc.htm (9/19/09)

*Child Maltreatment, 2006* provides the following: "An estimated 3.3 million referrals involving the alleged maltreatment of approximately 6.0 million children were made to child protective services (nationally). An estimated 3.6 million children received an investigation or assessment. Approximately 60% (61.7%) of referrals were screened in for investigation or assessment by Child Protective Service (CPS) agencies . . . 30% of these investigations or assessments determined at least one child was found to be a victim of abuse or neglect . . . 25.2% of the investigations or assessments were substantiated; 30% were indicated. More than 70% of the investigations or assessments determined that the child was not a victim of maltreatment . . . 60.4% were unsubstantiated; 5.9% were alternative response non-victim; 3.2% were other; 1.7% were closed with no finding, and .1% were found intentionally false. . . . 905,000 children were determined to be victims of abuse and neglect. Children birth to age 1 year had the highest rate, at 24.4% per 1,000 children in the same age group nationally."

64.1% of victims suffered neglect. 16.0% of victims suffered physical abuse. 8.8% suffered sexual abuse. 6.6% suffered emotional abuse. During 2006, a total of 150,427 children were removed from their homes (nationally). During

2006, an estimated 1530 children died due to child abuse and neglect. The overall rate was 2.04 deaths per 100,000 children nationally. More than 40% of deaths were attributable to neglect; 22.4% of child fatalities were attributable to physical abuse. 31.4% of child fatalities were attributable to multiple maltreatments. "Nonparental perpetrators (eg: other relative, foster parent, residential facility staff, other, and legal guardian were responsible for 14.7% of fatalities (p.66)." No information was given regarding specific deaths in out of home placements).

Note: This report also states: "The relatively high rates of repeat victimization seen in children with allegations of neglect justify neglect as an important focus for intervention and prevention of subsequent maltreatment. (p.83)." The report also attributes increased numbers and incidence of child abuse and neglect to better data collection.

U.S. Department of Health and Human Services, Administration on Children, Youth, and Families. *Child Maltreatment, 2006.* (Washington, DC: U.S. Government Printing Office) [Online]
Available at: http://www.acf.hhs.gov/programs/cb/pubs/cm06/pdf (9/19/09)

*The AFCARS Report, 2006* (Adoption and Foster Care Analysis and Reporting System) provides the following: "There were 510,000 children in foster care nationally on 9/30/06. The mean age of these children was 9.8 years; the median age was 10.2 years. 3% (17,351) of these children were placed in pre-adoptive homes. 24% (124,571) were in foster homes (relative). 46% (236,911) were in foster homes (non-relative). 7% (33,433) were placed in group homes. 10% (53,042) were placed in institutions.

49% (248,054) of children in out of home placements had a case goal of reunifying with a parent. 4% (20,359) of children had a case goal of living with a relative. 9% (43,773) had a case goal of long term foster care. 23% (117,380) had a case goal of adoption. Of those children exiting foster care in 2006, 53% (154,103) reunified with a parent or primary caregiver. 11% (30,751) were living with an other relative. 17% (50,379) were adopted.

U.S. Department of Health and Human Services, Administration on Children, Youth, and Families, *Adoption and Foster Care Analysis and Reporting System (AFCARS) Data Submitted for FY 2006, 10/1/05 through 9/30/06.* (Washington, DC: U.S. Government Printing Office)[Online]

Available at: http://www.acf.hhs.gov/programs/cb/stats_research/

\* \* \*

**Some other issues to consider:**

Do not think for a moment that foster families cannot make a difference in a child's life. There are thousands of families who unselfishly take children into their homes and into their hearts. They give of themselves, and help develop the foundations that will carry these children into successful adulthood. But be advised that out of home placement is not always the success we would hope it to be. And so, we cannot close our eyes to the dangers that may lurk there, as well.

**Two websites dedicated to children who have died in out of home placements:**

Coalition Against Institutionalized Child Abuse:
http://www.caica.org

Hope 4 Kidz:
http://www.hope4kidz.org

**Songs and Artists used in Chapter Eight.**

67. A reference to: Summer, Donna, Moroder, Giorgio, and Bellotte, Pete. (1975). "Love To Love You, Baby" [recorded by Donna Summer]. On *Love To Love You Baby* [audio album]. New York: Casablanca Records

68. A reference to: "Get Down Tonight".
Words and Music by Harry Wayne Casey and Richard Finch.
Copyright ©1975 (Renewed 2003) EMI LONGITUDINAL MUSIC
All Rights Reserved. International Copyright Secured. Used by Permission.
Reprinted by permission of Hal Leonard Corporation.

69. A reference to: Beck, Billy, et al. (1975). "Love Rollercoaster" [recorded by the Ohio Players]. On *Honey* [audio album]. New York: Mercury Records

70. A reference to: "You Sexy Thing"
Words and Music by E. Brown.
Copyright © 1975 by Finchley Music Corp.
Copyright Renewed.
Administered in the USA and Canada by Music & Media International, Inc.
Administered for the World excluding the USA and Canada by RAK Music Publishing Ltd.
International Copyright Secured. All Rights Reserved.
Reprinted by permission of Hal Leonard Corporation.

71. ibid

72. A reference to: Ashford, Nickolas, and Simpson, Valerie. (1966). "Ain't No Mountain High Enough" [re-recorded by Diana Ross]. On *Diana Ross* [audio album]. Detroit: Motown Records. (1970)

73. A reference to: Masser, Michael, and Miller, Ron. (1973). "Touch Me in the Morning" [recorded by Diana Ross]. Released as a single record. Detroit: Motown Records

74. A reference to: Jabara, Paul. (1978) "Last Dance" [recorded by Donna Summer for the motion picture *Thank God It's Friday*]. Released on *Live and More* [audio album]. New York: Casablanca Records

*NOTE*: Special thanks to: **htpp//www.wikipedia.org** and to **htpp//www.allmusic.com,** major sources for the music information used in this book.

75. A reference to the fictional British spy James Bond, as created by Ian Fleming, whose movie series was first produced by Albert Broccoli and Harry Saltzman in 1962 for EON Productions.

# Chapter Nine

76. **Discussion of Psychological and Behavioral Issues of Children in Foster Care**:

There are approximately 500,000 children in foster care across the country at present. Although many of these children have entered the system with a variety of serious physical, emotional, medical, and/or other developmental issues, they may experience additional psychological and behavioral problems as the result of their foster placement. These issues can include poor self esteem, attachment disorders, and a variety of other mental and physical ailments, and developmental delays. For discussion on treatment planning, foster placement supports, and natural and extended family involvement, please see:

American Academy of Pediatrics: Committee on Early Childhood, Adoption, and Dependent Care (2000). "Developmental Issues for Young Children in

Foster Care". Journal of American Academy of Pediatrics. *Pediatrics,* Vol.106, No.5. November, 2000. Pp. 1145-1150 [online magazine]. Available at: http//www.aappolicy.aapublications.org [8/7/2009]

77. **Discussion of Client Assaults Against Social Workers: Administrative Overview**:

Sarkisian, Gregor V., Ph.D, and Portswood, Sharon G., Ph.D (2003). "Client Violence Against Social Workers: From Increased Worker Responsibility and Administrative Mishmash to Effective Prevention Policy." *Administration in Social Work,* (2003). Vol.27, Is.4. Pp. 41-59. Binghamton, NY: The Haworth Press

"Violence has been a common characteristic of most social work agencies, although it is believed that the majority of incidents go unreported due to worker's fears that they will be evaluated as incompetent by colleagues and administrators, that their situations will not be viewed sympathetically, and/or that nothing can be done after a violent act has been committed against them . . . . Physical attacks typically include incidents in which a client comes in direct contact with a social worker with an intent to do harm; verbal threats tend to include verbally abusive language or physical gestures that indicate an intent to harm a worker; and property damage refers to physical damage that has occurred to the worker's private property or agency property . . . (T)he new millennium presents challenges that did not exist previously, including: increased violence perpetrated by women, violence attributable to the deinstitutionalization movement, psychotropic drug refusal by discharged patients, the right to refuse treatment, social-control issues in both adult and children's protective service delivery, new intervention roles in domestic violence situations, police-social worker teams, custody and divorce settlements . . . (In the cross-sectional study of workplace assault by Driscoll,

Worthington, and Hurrell, 1995:) Among females assaulted, 29% were mental health workers, 8% were clerks, 7% were human service caseworkers, and 4% were nursing personnel. Among males assaulted, 21% were state police personnel, 11% were mental health workers, 8% were guards, and 8% were clerks...."

"Social service clients rarely, if ever, have the option of declining services that are unacceptable to them for any reason . . . In cases of noncompliance with service plans, clients may resort to avoidance behaviors as a means of passive resistance (e.g., refusing to enroll, to participate, or to continue participation in agency or court-referred services), or they may engage in violent behavior as a means of active protest . . . Thus, a client's violent behavior may represent a counterbalancing of self-preservation through aggression . . . (V)iolent reactions are more likely to occur under certain environmental conditions (e.g., high stress and low level of coping skills) . . . (T)he majority of training components under review were related to the characteristics of the worker, including one's ability to assess the potential for client violence and reactions to that violence. Rather than addressing the overarching issue of client empowerment, which can be defined as 'an interpersonal ongoing process . . . involving mutual respect, critical reflection, caring, and group participation through which people lacking an equal share of valued resources gain greater access to and control over resources . . .'

"Therefore it is recommended that social service administrators strive to articulate specific guidelines not only for responding to acts of violence against workers, but also for identifying and addressing those situations that are most likely to give rise to such acts . . . Requiring social service organizations to implement a violence prevention policy comporting with OSHA guidelines would, at the very least, provide social work administrators with a beginning structure for delineating clear policy surrounding agency liability in the case of client violence. Second, the inclusion of clients in the policy development process is essential for true preventive policy and as a precursor to client empowerment . . . including policies that support the development of new training methods and delivery systems that provide opportunities for clients to empower themselves . . ."

78. **A Discussion of the Clash Between Classes in Office Politics:**

Lubrano, Alfred (2004). *Limbo: Blue Collar Roots, White Collar Dreams.* Hoboken, NJ: John Wiley and Sons, Inc. p.129

"Chapter Six: Office Politics: The Blue Collar Way
When I told my folks how much my first paper in Ohio was paying me, my father helpfully suggested I get a part-time job to augment the income. 'Maybe you could drive a cab.' Soon afterward, the city editor chewed me out for something trivial, and I made the mistake of telling my father during a visit home. 'They pay you nothing and they push you around in that business,' he told me, the rage building. 'Next time, you grab the guy by the throat, push him against the wall, and tell him he's a big jerk."

79. A reference to: Roddenberry, Gene (1966). *Star Trek* [television series]. New York: NBC

80. **A Brief History of Dignity groups within the Catholic Church:**

Begun in Canada in 1969, and founded in the U.S. in 1973, Dignity is a group for gay men and women who come together in worship, support, and fellowship under the support of the Catholic Church. While celibacy is advocated, the group has countered that Church teaching allows loving and committed relationships as a matter of personal conscience.

However, on October 30, 1986, the Vatican issued a letter to the Catholic Bishops on the Pastoral Care of Homosexual Persons, and instructed that they withdraw their support. Dignity responded in its letter on the Pastoral Care of Gay and Lesbian Persons that Lesbians and Gay people may indeed engage in loving, life-giving, and life-affirming sex, always in an ethically responsible and unselfish way. Dignity went on to proclaim what Church law does allow, but only in the privacy of conscience.

The Bishops responded by evicting local Dignity Chapters from the Churches for rejection of Church theology.

Above information summarized from: http//www.dignitycanada.org.

## Chapter 10

81. A reference to: Nichols, Roger S. and Williams, Paul H. (1971). "Rainy Days and Mondays" [recorded by Karen and Richard Carpenter]. On *Carpenters* [audio album]. New York: A&M Records

## Epilogue

82. **Resources On Therapeutic Interventions For AIDS Patients:**

Buckingham, Stephan L., and Van Gorp, Wilfred G. (1988). "Essential Knowledge About AIDS Dementia". *Social Work*, March-April, 1988, Vol.33, No.2, Pp. 112-115. Copyright 1988, National Association of Social Workers, Inc., *Social Work*

"It is estimated that more than half of the persons diagnosed with acquired immune deficiency syndrome (AIDS) at some time will present with central nervous system dysfunction resulting from the human immunodeficiency virus (HIV) infiltration of the brain structures . . . . [The patient] may be referred to mental health facilities with initial incorrect diagnoses of depression or some other psychiatric abnormality . . . . [Initial affective changes may include] apathy, psychomotor slowing, mood disturbance, and withdrawal. There may be no signs of aphasia (language disturbance), amnesia (inability to learn or remember information), or other dementia processes . . . .

AIDS patients frequently experience delirium, which is an abrupt change in mental status characterized by striking inattentiveness, confusion, variable level of alertness or arousal, incoherent speech, hallucinations and delusions . . . caused by toxic or metabolic abnormalities . . . . AIDS dementia is a subcortical dementia that can progress to severe global dementia, mutism, paraplegia, and incontinence . . . language functions are usually well preserved . . . rather than presenting with full amnesia, they may present with forgetfulness . . . [and] may have difficulty recalling three words to be remembered, but may recall all three when category cues are given . . . . (S)erious visuospacial deficits are present, as well, so that the person may have difficulty navigating about, or copying complex figures . . . may experience difficulty with tests of abstract thinking . . . and often have difficulty performing tasks involving sequential reasoning. Thus they may have difficulty with a series of instructions, such as 'take this medication with water, this one only when eating' . . . (and) may have problems with a multistep project, such as preparing a meal . . . gait and other abnormalities . . . . (P)atients with subcortical dementia usually will appreciate their predicament and acknowledge their difficulties during an interview . . . (T)he incidence of depression in patients with subcortical dementia is often higher than other patient groups . . . and frequently will respond to conventional treatments such as psychotherapy or pharmacotherapy . . . .

A social worker can mobilize many resources to assist the patient in functioning more adequately . . . (S)ocial workers should work with the patient and his or her partner or close family members in developing memory aids to enhance recall . . . . Patients often are reassured when the therapist is able to listen to their concerns and problem solve a means to deal with them. Specifically, psychotherapy with these patients can assist in: problem solving with everyday concerns and difficulties; guidance in designing adequate structure and limits for activities of daily living; estate planning; decreasing in the level of hypochondriacal preoccupation . . . (by) supportive group psychotherapy, occupational and art therapy, and day treatment programs . . . .

Often, the 'invisible' patients are partners and other family members who may need a great deal of support and attention as their level of responsibility in caring for their loved one increases. The coexistence of AIDS and dementia creates a substantial need for sustained physical, emotional, and financial assistance . . . (F)amilies may be confronted with their member's homosexuality or drug use . . . The use of support groups, family education sessions, supportive psychotherapy, and psychotherapeutic services should be considered . . ."

*Bulletin of the Menninger Clinic.* Kobayashi, Joyce Seiko (1997). "The Evolution of Adjustment Issues in HIV/AIDS". Spring, 1997, Vol. 61, Is. 2. Copyright Guilford Press. Pp. 143-189. Reprinted with permission of the Guilford Press.

"[from the abstract] Discusses the evolution of emotional adjustment and counseling of AIDS patients in relation to medical advances about HIV and potential therapeutics. Need to understand the historical context of rapidly changing therapies for AIDS; Clinical management of persons living with AIDS . . ."

83. *ACT UP* (AIDS Coalition To Unleash Power) was a grassroots movement started in New York by playwright and AIDS activist Larry Kramer in 1987. The group's original goal was to demand the release of experimental AIDS drugs. Although largely gay, the organization identified itself as "a diverse, non-partisan group united in anger and commitment to direct action to end the AIDS crisis." Over the next several years, the group demanded a shortening of the approval times for

AIDS drugs; advocated for a federal needle exchange program; questioned AZT as the only approved AIDS drug; published prices charged and profits garnered by pharmaceutical companies for AIDS drugs; and attacked the 'outrageous lack of government support for addressing AIDS.' ACT UP coined slogans like "Silence = Death" to challenge a nation's perceptions, and to demand meaningful assistance in the fight against AIDS. Some of its actions included: protests on Wall Street (against AIDS pharmaceutical policies and pricing, on 3/24/87); protests against Northwest Airlines (for refusal to seat an AIDS patient); a 1988 take-over of the Cosmopolitan magazine offices (after their published editorial declared that no women were likely to contract AIDS); the 1989 surrounding of the FDA's Maryland building by 1000 ACT UP members; and the protest at Civil Rights Commission's AIDS Hearing, for not responding to AIDS issues. But it was the 'Stop the Church' protest at St. Patrick's Cathedral in 1989 that caused division within ACT UP. During this action, protesters disrupted Cardinal O'Connor's Mass at the cathedral for his opposition to condom distribution. The group thus lost support and momentum. In 1991, members chained themselves to the desk of the McNeil Lehrer Report during a live broadcast and held signs declaring that "the AIDS Crisis is not over." There is no doubt about the contributions made by these courageous people in attacking AIDS in this country, and also, in moving the Gay Rights Movement forward.

The above history was summarized from: Rimmerman, Craig (1998). "ACT UP". Smith, Raymond (ed.). *Encyclopedia of AIDS*. New York: Penguin Group

As located in: Ask.com: *http//www.thebody.com* "The Complete HIV/AIDS Resource."

# For Quick Reference: Article Listings in Appendix and Bibliography

Page 489: HISTORICAL CONTEXT: *The Sixties Chronicle,* Braunstein, Peter, M.A.; Carpenter, Philip, M.A.; Edmunds, Anthony O., PhD.; Farber, David, PhD; Foley, Michael S., PhD; Rodriquez, Robert A.; Sanders, Jeffrey C., PhD; Shreve, Bradley G., M.A. (2004). Lincolnwood, Illinois: Legacy Publications.

Page 489: DISCUSSION: The Erikson Stages of Pyschosocial Human Development

Page 494: (SYSTEMS THEORY) *Working With Families: An Integrative Model by Level of Need.* Kilpatrick, Allie C., and Holland, Thomas P. (2003; 1st ed. 1995). Boston, Ma: Pearson Education, Inc. Pp.14-15

Page 495: (FAMILY LIFE CYCLES): *Working With Families: An Integrative Model by Level of Need.* Kilpatrick, Allie C., and Holland, Thomas P. (2003; 1st ed. 1995). Boston, Ma: Pearson Education, Inc. p.86

Page 496: (SOCIAL POLICY AND SOCIAL WORK) *Social Work Practice: Model and Method.* Pincus, Allen, and Minahan, Anne (1973; 8th ed. 1977). Itasca, Illinois: F. E. Peacock Publishers, Inc. p.26

Page 497: Definition: "Denial"

Page 497: Definition: "Binge Drinking"

Page 497: Reference: "From Charitable Volunteers to Architects of Social Welfare: A Brief History of Social Work". *Ongoing*. [On-line]. Taunenbaum, Nili, and Reich, Michael (Fall, 2001). University of Michigan School of Social Work. Accessible at: http://www.ssw.umich.edu/ongoing/fall2001/briefhistory

Page 498: "Differential Diagnosis of Bereavement Issues, Other Conditions That May be the Focus of Clinical Assessment: V62.82 Bereavement" *Diagnostic and Statistical Manual of Mental Disorders, 4th Edition, Text Revised*. American Psychiatric Association (2000). Washington, DC: American Psychiatric Association, Pp.740-741.

Page 499: Excerpt: "The Nomenclature of the Community: An Activist's Perspective". Ferris, Joshua L. (2006). Shankle, Michael D., M.P.H. (ed.). (2006). *The Handbook of Lesbian, Gay, Bisexual, and Transgender Public Health: A Practitioner's Guide to Service*. New York: Harrington Park Press. p.7

Page 501: Excerpts: "Where Did AIDS Come From?". Centers For Disease Control and Prevention. CDC Home Page. *Questions and Answers*. Atlanta: U.S. Department of Health and Human Services, Centers for Disease Control and Prevention, 2009.[Online]. Accessible at: *http://www.cdc.gov/hiv/resources/qa/qa3.html*

Page 501: Excerpts: "Epidemiology of HIV/AIDS—United States, 1981-2005". Centers for Disease Control and Prevention. *MMWR Weekly*, June 2, 2006/55(21); 589-592 Atlanta: U.S. Department of Health and Human

Services, Centers for Disease Control and Prevention, 2006. [Online]. Accessible at: http://www.cdc.gov/mmwr

Page 502: Excerpts: "Report Fact Sheet: "Key Facts By Region—2007 AIDS Epidemic Update". Barton-Knott, Sophie (2007). *UNAIDS. (Joint United Nations Programme on HIV/AIDS) (Geneva: UNAIDS).* [Online]. Accessible at: http://data.unaids.org/pub/EPISlides/2007/071118_epi

Page 503: Excerpts: "The Role of Public Health in Lesbian, Gay, Bisexual, and Transgender Health". Mail, Patricia D., and Lear, Walter J. (2006). Shankle, Michael D., M.P.HG. (ed.) (2006). The Handbook of Gay, Bisexual, and Transgender Public Health: A Practitioner's Guide to Service. New York: Harrington Park Press. Pp.22-23

Page 504: Excerpt: Definitions: Transgender; Transsexual; Cross-dresser:
"The Whole Person: A Paradigm for Integrating the Mental and Physical Health of Trans Clients". Kirk, Sheila, and Kulkarni, Claudette (2006). Shankle, Michael D., M.P.H. (ed.) (2006). *The Handbook of Lesbian, Gay, Bisexual, and Transgender Public Health: A Practitioner's Guide to Service.* New York: Harrington Park Press. Pp.150-152:

Page 505: Excerpt: "Centering Culture: Teaching for Critical Sexual Literacy Using the Sexual Diversity Wheel". Sears, James T. (1997). *Journal of Moral Education*, September, 1997,Vol.26, Is.3. Pp. 273-284. Taylor and Francis, Ltd, *http://www.informationworld.com* reprinted by permission of the publisher.

Page 506: Excerpt: "Identity Formation and Self Esteem Issues in the Male Transvestite: A Humanistic Perspective". Bordan, Terry, and DeRicco, Marc. Reprinted from *Journal of Humanistic Education And Development,*

Vol.35, Is.3, March, 1997. Pp.156-162 (1997). The American Counseling Association. Reprinted with permission.

Page 507: Excerpt: Centering Culture: Teaching for Critical Sexual Literacy Using the Sexual Diversity Wheel". Sears, James T. (1997). *Journal of Moral Education*, September, 1997, Vol.26, Is.3. Pp. 273-284. Taylor and Francis, Ltd, *http://www.informationworld.com* reprinted by permission of the publisher.

Page 507: Discussion: Integrity as it relates to Gay Identity

Page 508: Excerpt: "The Nomenclature of the Community: An Activist Perspective". Ferris, Joshua L. (2006). Shankle, Michael D., M.P.H. (ed.) (2006). *The Handbook of Lesbian, Gay, Bisexual, and Transgender Public Health: A Practitioner's Guide to Service*. New York: Harrington Park Press. Pp.5-6

Page 508: Excerpt: "Kicked Out Because I was Gay" by Shameek Williamson, from *The Heart Knows Something Different: Teenage Voices from the Foster Care System*, edited by Al Desetta, copyright 1996 by Youth Communication / New York Center, Inc.

Page 508: Excerpt: "Barriers to Health Care Access". Hernandez, Manuel, and Fultz, Shawn L. (2006). Shankle, Michael D., M.P.H. (ed.) (2006). *The Handbook of Lesbian, Gay, Bisexual and Transgender Public Health: A Practitioner's Guide to Service*. New York: Harrington Park Press. Pp.188-189

Page 509: Excerpt: "As Time Goes By: An Introduction to the Needs of Lesbian, Gay, Bisexual, and Transgender Elders." Sperber, Jodi B. (2006). Shankle, Michael D., M.P.H. (ed.) (2006). *The Handbook of Lesbian, Gay, Bisexual, and Transgender Public Health: A Practitioner's Guide to Service*. New York: Harrington Park Press. p.252.

Page 509: Sample Questions To Assess Suicide and Self-Destructive Behavior: (Symptom Questions) *Clinician's Thesaurus: The Guide For Writing Psychological Reports, 5th Edition*. Zuckerman, Edward L., Ph.D. (2000). "Symptom Questions". Copyright Guilford Press. Pp.71-73. Reprinted with permission of the Guilford Press.

Page 512: Excerpt: DSM-IV-TR Criteria for Postpartum Onset Specifier (Mood Disorders): American Psychiatric Association (2000). "Mood Disorders". *Diagnostic and Statistical Manual of Mental Disorders, 4th Edition, Text Revised*. Washington, DC: American Psychiatric Association. p.422

Page 513: Excerpt: DSM-IV-TR Criteria for Dysthymic Disorder, 300.4 (Mood Disorders): American Psychiatric Association (2000). "Mood Disorders". *Diagnostic and Statistical Manual of Mental Disorders, 4th Edition, Text Revised*. Washington, DC: American Psychiatric Association. Pp.376-377

Page 514: Excerpt: DSM-IV-TR Criteria for Brief Psychotic Disorder: 298.8 Schizophrenia and Other Psychotic Disorders: American Psychiatric Association. (2000). "Schizophrenia and Other Psychotic Disorders". *Diagnostic and Statistical Manual of Mental Disorders, 4th Edition, Text Revised*. Washington, DC: American Psychiatric Association. Pp.329-332.

Page 514: Discussion: DSM-IV-TR Differential Diagnosis for the patient "Josie"

Page 518: Excerpts: "Stay-Leave Decision Making in Battered Women: Trauma, Coping, and Self-Efficacy". Lerner, Christine Fiore, and Kennedy, Linda

Thomas (2000). *Cognitive Therapy and Research*, Vol.24, No.2. Pp.215-232. Netherlands: Springer Science and Business Media

Page 520: Excerpts: "Assessment and Evaluation for Men Who Batter Women". Peterman, Linda M., and Dixon, Charlotte G. (2001). *Journal of Rehabilitation.* October/November/December, 2001, Vol.67, No.4. Pp.38-42. National Rehabilitation Association.

Page 522: Reference: "Group Work With African American Men Who Batter: Toward More Ethnically Sensitive Practice". Williams, Oliver J. (1994, Spring). *Journal of Comparative Family Studies*, Vol.25, Is.1. Pp.91-103

Page 522: Reference: "Group Work With African American Men Who Batter: Toward More Ethnically Sensitive Practice". Williams, Oliver J. (1994). *Journal of Comparative Family Studies*, Spring, Vol.25, Is.1 Pp.91-103. University of Calgary

Page 522: Excerpt: "Client Violence Against Social Workers: From Increased Worker Responsibility and Administrative Mishmash to Effective Prevention Policy". Sarkisian, Gregor V., Ph.D, and Portwood, Sharon G., Ph.D (2003). *Administration in Social Work.* (2003). Binghamton, NY: The Haworth Press

Page 523: Excerpt: A brief history of Alcoholics Anonymous: Forward to the Second Edition," contained in *Alcoholics Anonymous, the Fourth Edition of the Big Book*. (2001). New York City: Alcoholics Anonymous World Services, Inc. Pp. XV-XVII:

Page 524: The Twelve Steps. *Alcoholics Anonymous, the Fourth Edition of the Big Book.* (2001). New York City: Alcoholics Anonymous World Services, Inc.

Page 526: Excerpts: DSM-IV-TR Criteria for Differential Diagnosis: Substance Dependence vs. Substance Abuse: Substance-Related Disorders." American Psychiatric Association (2000). *Diagnostic and Statistical Manual of Mental Disorders, 4th Edition, Text Revised.* Washington, DC: The American Psychiatric Association. Pp.192; 198

Page 527: Excerpts: DSM-IV-TR Criteria for 309.81 Posttraumatic Stress Disorder. American Psychiatric Association (2000). *Diagnostic and Statistical Manual of Mental Disorders 4th Edition, Text Revised.* Washington, DC: American Psychiatric Association. Pp.463-472

Page 528: Excerpts: "Best Practices for Counselors Who Treat Posttraumatic Stress Disorder". Marotta, Sylvia (2000, Fall). *Journal of Counseling and Development*, Vol.78, Is.4. Pp.492-495

Page 529: Excerpt: *Limbo: Blue Collar Roots, White Collar Dreams.* Lubrano, Alfred (2004). Hoboken, NJ: John Wiley and Sons, Inc.

Page 530: Coming Out Issues, the Acceptance of One's Gay Identity: Excerpts: *Handbook of LGBT Issues in Community Mental Health.* (simultaneously co-published as *Journal of Gay and Lesbian Psychotherapy*). Hellman, Ronald E., M.D., and Drescher, Jack, M.D. (eds.) (2004). Vol.8, Numbers 3/4. New York: Haworth Medical Press (Pp.13-15; 32-34; 39).

Page 531: Excerpts: "Coming Out Issues for Adult Lesbians". Morrow, Deana F. (1996). *Social Work,* November, 1996, Vol. 41, Is.6, Pp.647-656 Copyright 1996, National Association of Social Workers, Inc., *Social Work*

Page 532: Excerpts: "Coming Out Lesbian or Gay: A Potential Precipitant of Crisis in Adolescence". Ford, Vanessa E. (2003). *Journal of Human Behavior and the Social Environment.* (2003), Vol.8, Is.2/3, Pp.93-110. Binghamton, NY: The Haworth Press

Page: 532: Coping Issues: Excerpt: "Lesbian, Gay, Bisexual, and Transgender People Receiving Services in the Public Mental Health System: Raising Issues". 'Family Stress and Safety Net'. Lucksted, Alicia, Ph.D. (2004). Hellman, Ronald E., M.D., and Drescher, Jack, M.D. (eds.) (2004). *Handbook of LGBT Issues in Community Mental Health.* Vol.8, Numbers 3/4. New York: Haworth Medical Press. p.33

Page 533: Excerpt: "Sexual Orientation and the Addictions". Cabaj, M.D., Robert Paul (1995). *Journal of Gay and Lesbian Psychotherapy.* Vol.2(3). Pp.97-117. Binghamton, NY: The Haworth Press

Page 534: Excerpts: "Evaluation of Physical Abuse in Children". Pressel, David M. (2000). *American Family Physician,* May 15, 2000, Vol.61, Is.10

Page 535: Reference: *Recognizing Child Abuse: A Guide for the Concerned.* Besharov, Douglas J. (1990) New York: The Free Press.

Page 536: Excerpts: "The Adjustment of Children with Divorced Parents: A Risk and Resiliency Perspective." Hetherington, E. Mavis, and Stanley-Hagan, Margaret (1999). *Journal of Child Psychology and Psychiatry.* (1999). Vol.40, Is.1. Pp.129-140

Page 538: Excerpts: *Foster Care Solutions: Practical Tools for Foster Parents.* Temple-Plotz, Lana, M.S., Stricklett, Ted, M.S., Baker, Christena B., M.S.W., Sterba, Michael, M.H.D. (eds.) (2002) Boys Town, Nebraska: Boys Town Press. p. 2

Page 538: Excerpts: *On Their Own: What Happens to Kids When They Age Out of the Foster Care System*. Shirk, Martha, and Stangler, Gary. (2004). Boulder, Colorado: Basic Books. Pp. 4-5.

Page 541: Potential Loss of Key Supports Due to a Gay Identity: Excerpts: "Lesbian, Gay, Bisexual, and Transgender People Receiving Services in the Public Mental Health System: Raising Issues". Lucksted, Alicia, Ph.D. (2004). Hellman, Ronald E., M.D., and Drescher, Jack, M.D. (eds.) (2004) *Handbook of LGBT Issues in Community Mental Health*. NewYork: Haworth Press. Pp.32-33

Page 541: Excerpts: "National and Public Infrastructure and Policy: Are We Experiencing Scientific McCarthyism?" Kennedy, Nancy J. (2004). Shankle, Michael D., M.P.H. (ed.). *The Handbook of Lesbian, Gay, Bisexual, and Transgender Public Health: A Practitioner's Guide to Service*. (2004). New York: Harrington Park Press. Pp.306; 309

Page 542: Behavioral and Psychological Issues of Adolescent Foster Children: Excerpts: *Foster Care Solutions: Practical Tools for Foster Parents*. Temple-Plotz, Lana, M.S., Stricklett, Ted P., M.S., Baker, Christena B., M.S.W., and Sterba, Michael N., M.H.D. (eds.) (2002). Boys Town, Nebraska: Boys Town Press. Pp.6; 16

Page 543: Excerpts: "Factors Affecting Foster Care Placement of Children Receiving Child Protective Services". Zuravin, Susan J., and DePanfilis, Diane (1997). *Social Work Research*. March, 1997, Vol.21, Is.1, Pp. 34-44. Copyright 1997, National Association of Social Workers, Inc., *Social Work Research*

Page 544: Discussion: Child Protective Service Issues

Page 547: Excerpt: "The Impact of Suter v. Artist M. on Foster Care Policy". Alexander, Jr., Rudolph (1995). *Social Work*, July, 1995, Vol.40, Is.4. Pp.543-548. Copyright 1995, National Association of Social Workers, Inc., *Social Work*

Page 547: Statistical Comparisons: The Child Maltreatment Reports and the Adoption and Foster Care Analysis Reports (AFCARS)

Page 551: Website Resources: Children who died in out-of-home placement:

Coalition Against Institutionalized Child Abuse:
*http://www.caica.org*

Hope 4 Kidz:
*http://www.hope4kidz.org*

Page 554: Psychological and Behavioral Issues of Children in Foster Care:

Reference: "Developmental Issues for Young Children in Foster Care". American Academy of Pediatrics: Committee on Early Childhood, Adoption and Dependent Care (2000).*Pediatrics. (November, 2000). Vol106,No.5.Pp.1145-1150 [Online magazine]* Available at: http//www.aappolicy.aappublications.org [8/7/2009]

Page 554: Excerpts: "Client Violence Against Social Workers: From Increased Worker Responsibility and Administrative Mishmash to Effective Prevention Policy". Sarkisian, Gregor V., Ph.D, and Portwood, Sharon G, Ph.D. (2003). *Administration in Social Work* (2003). Vol.27, Is.4. Pp.41-59. Binghamton, NY: Haworth Press

Page 556: Excerpt: *Limbo: Blue Collar Roots, White Collar Dreams*. "Chapter Six: Office Politics: The Blue Collar Way". Lubrano, Alfred (2004). John Wiley and Sons, Inc.: Hoboken, NJ p.129

Page 556: Discussion: A Brief History of Dignity groups within the Catholic Church. Available at: http//www.dignitycanada.org.

Page 557: Excerpts: "Essential Knowledge of AIDS Dementia". Buckingham, Stephan L., and Van Gorp, Wilfred G. (1988). *Social Work*, March-April, 1988, Vol. 33, No2. Pp.112-115. Copyright 1988, National Association of Social Workers, Inc, *Social Work*

Page 559: *Bulletin of the Menninger Clinic*. "The Evolution of Adjustment Issues in HIV/AIDS". Kobayashi, Joyce Seiko (1997). Spring, 1997, Vol. 61, Is. 2. Copyright Guilford Press. Pp. 143-189. Reprinted with permission of the Guilford Press.

Page 559: A Brief History of ACT UP: Summarized from: Rimmerman, Craig (1998). "ACT UP". Smith, Raymond (ed.). *Encyclopedia of AIDS*. "The Complete HIV/AIDS Resource." New York: Penguin Group. Available at: Ask.com: *http//www.thebody.com*

# About the Author

Born and raised in New Jersey, Beverly Ann Kessler is a Licensed Social Worker, who has worked in human services for nearly 30 years. An attendee at Shepherd College, West Virginia, she received her BSW from Kean College, and her MSW from Rutgers University. She has worked in medical, renal and geriatric social work, and in adult and child protective services. She is a member of NASW. Ms. Kessler has dedicated her life to the fight for social justice. She is active in the anti-poverty movement, and has worked as an advocate in energy and environmental issues, and in homeless prevention. Most recently, she has worked with Garden State Equality in the fight for marriage equality in New Jersey. She is active in her Episcopal Church, where she serves as youth mentor, and participates in various social welfare projects. Spirituality and her love of nature have been her combined life force. She has shared this love and commitment with her partner of 25 years.

Made in the USA
Lexington, KY
19 May 2011